DRUID HEIR

BOOKS 1-3

N. Z. NASSER

Druid Heir: Books 1-3
Copyright © N. Z. Nasser 2022
Published by Hanora Sky Press

eBook ISBN 978-1-915151-14-8
Paperback ISBN 978-1-915151-15-5

MIDLIFE DAWN

THE PLAYERS

Alisha Verma - Druid Heir

Rosalie Verma - Alisha's mother

Joshi Verma - Alisha's father

Echo - Alisha's cat

Marina Ambrose - Alisha's best friend

Ezra Neuhoff - Alisha's half-werewolf, half-wizard mentor

Gaia - Mysterious old woman

Sahil Verma - Alisha's brother

Robert Jameson - Detective

Phinnaeous Shine - Shapeshifter, Prime Sorcerer

Orpheus Might - Vampire, Minister for History and the Today

Rayna Willowsun - Druid, Headmistress of Wildwoods School of the
Wondrous

Helio Woodwink - Fairy, the Minister for the Bestiary

Lavinia Drach - Witch, Minister for Defence

Lavinia's coven - Ravynne, Elvira, Agatha, Isadora, Chandra, Morgan

Alisha's night class students - Fei Yen, Faeza, Nita, Marek, Tomás,
Santiago, Farzad, Nagma, Ethan, Hassan

Alex Harrison - Alisha's ex-husband

Melissa Ramsay - Rosalie's colleague and friend

Kraglek - Magical octopus touched by the goddess Ganga
The girls who faced Kraglek - Mirabel, Gaylia, Maura, Nessa, Soleis
Julianne and Milo - Alisha's neighbour and her pet poodle
The electrician
The gravedigger

1

I stood under fluorescent lighting in the hallway of the community centre. I knew better than to take a call in the middle of teaching, but it wasn't every day a detective called to discuss the suspicious circumstances of your mum's death.

She was killed last week, on the eve of her retirement, and my heart had broken into a thousand pieces.

Stifled chatter came from the other side of the classroom door. My students had obviously decided to abandon the comprehension I'd tasked them with and snoop on me instead. You'd think they were of nursery school age, not adults attending a night class.

My phone burned hot against my ear as I processed the detective's words. "What do you mean her car had flowers growing from the metal? Flowers don't grow out of metal, Detective."

"It was as if they'd grown to cushion her. And the flowers aren't the only anomalies we've discovered," said the detective.

I blocked out the sound of the class as my pulse raced. "What kind of anomalies?"

"Your mother was driving at a perfectly respectable speed. There were no other vehicles involved. It could be she saw a fox and made an evasive manoeuvre that went wrong. It wouldn't have been the first time. But the crime scene report showed an electrical fault. It raised question marks, given your mother's car had just been serviced."

They'd found her upside down, still dangling from her seatbelt. What I couldn't work out was how someone who drove at a snail's pace could crash on a quiet, lamp-lit road. "That's odd. I arranged the service myself. I trust the mechanic."

"Nothing to worry about, I'm sure, but I'd rather cover all angles." The sound of shuffling papers reached my ears through the phone line. "Was your mother worried about anything? Did her behaviour change prior to her death?"

I frowned, both at his questions and the ruckus still coming from the classroom. "She'd been working longer hours, I suppose. It's nothing she couldn't handle."

"You know she was reprimanded at work for releasing lab animals?"

"That's impossible." I opened the classroom door.

Four eavesdroppers fell out, righted themselves and gave me sheepish grins.

I shooed them back to their seats before retreating into the corridor again.

"In my line of work, you soon learn that nothing is impossible," said the detective. "Sometimes, we don't know the people we love best."

Wasn't that the truth?

It had only taken me over a decade to accept that my ex, Alex, was a prize jerk.

I didn't intend to end up in a dead-end marriage, but it just happened. Too many meals in front of the television, too few adventures together, too many differing expectations. The last straw was when the loan sharks came knocking. He'd gambled away our life savings, and I hadn't even known. I thought he'd said no to our dream house and travelling abroad because he was being sensible.

Turned out he really liked fruit machines. The arsehole.

"Detective Jameson, was it? Can we pick this up another time, please? I have to get back to my class."

"Not a problem, Mrs Verma. I'm sure we'll be talking again." He hung up.

"It's Ms Verma, actually," I muttered, making my way back into the classroom.

Pages fluttered as the ten students in my night class pretended to pore over the text I'd asked them to read.

I plastered on a smile and sneaked a look at the top drawer of my desk, tempted to grab another painkiller. I'd been swallowing them like sweets all day. After the week I'd had, nothing was going to take the edge off my headache except possibly a rewind button. For now, I pushed aside the discussion with the detective. "Right, you lot. I take it you know the text back to front now. I'll take eavesdropper number one first. You're up, Marek. When was the Great Fire of London?"

"1966?" said Marek with a glimmer of hope, although he was almost always wrong.

"No, afraid not. Scan the text and try again using a full sentence."

I taught English and survival skills to immigrants in godforsaken London, where the streets were mean and job opportunities were scarce. The council paid me a decent wage and didn't pay much attention to the curriculum. I focussed on a mix of English grammar, vocabulary and deciphering texts. I also included cultural norms, like introducing my students to the pub and sweaty gigs and a sprinkling of literature. The balcony scene of Romeo and Juliet could be a great icebreaker.

Mum had been a big reader too.

I didn't want to talk about Mum in the past tense. I wanted to hear her voice and watch her pottering in the garden during her retirement. It wasn't any consolation that she'd lived a full life. I mean, her work as a scientist changed lives, her marriage to Dad was a fairy tale, and her grown children had long flown the nest.

I just wanted her here with us. Were you ever old enough to lose your mother?

Forty-year-old me needed her still, what with my messy divorce and a stagnant career.

Instead, I found myself teaching my third night class of the week at a community centre in South London, pretending everything was okay, just like all the other middle-aged, multitasking women I knew.

Smiling on the outside. Screaming on the inside.

Of course, Mum's death had left me spinning, but I'd been a hot mess long before. Somewhere along the way from radiant fiancée to escapee from a combusting marriage, I'd lost my spark. That's not even including midlife woes like not being able to go braless and needing afternoon naps just to get through the day.

"Miss, Marek has got his hand up," said Tomás, one of my Portuguese students.

I grimaced. "Sorry, Marek, I didn't see you there."

"He's right in front of you," said Nita, my youngest student.

I gave my best encouraging smile and crossed my fingers behind my back. "Go ahead, Marek."

He scrunched up his brow in concentration. "The Great Fire of London is in 1669."

The class groaned. By now, most of them had worked out the answer.

"Not quite. The Great Fire of London *was* in 1666. You'll get there."

Fei Yen and Faeza, two middle-aged Chinese women, put their hands up, eerily in sync with each other as always. They spoke perfect English but enjoyed the social side of the night class.

"Yes, Fei Yen?"

"I think Marek would do better if we were reading about Princess Diana. Everyone likes to read about her."

"Or the Black Death," said Faeza.

"Or Jack the Ripper." Santiago's ruddy face betrayed the beer he'd consumed before class.

I shook my head. "Let's just focus on what we have in front of us. How about you next, Santiago?" I looked down at the page. "Sorry, I've lost my train of thought. Just give me a minute."

"Are you okay, miss?" said Nita.

"Of course, she's not okay. We read it in the cards," Fei Yen and Faeza said in unison. They ran a tea and occult shop called Shanghai Moon around the corner from my flat and were always spouting nonsense about horoscopes and tarot cards and whatnot.

"I'm fine." Except, I wasn't fine. I couldn't tell my class that, obviously. My job was to build them up and send them out into the world, not to burden them with my troubles. I could go home and eat chocolate instead. I'd been working out hard in the gym as an *up-yours* to Alex, but one giant bar of Cadburys wouldn't hurt. Not that my waistline would thank me.

There was no easy way to lose a loved one, but I'd royally messed things up. After forty years of being the *good* child—the one who accompanied my parents to the doctor, arranged for their car to be serviced and always came home for celebration days—I'd lost it with Mum on the day she died. Worse still, our last conversation had been about my ex-husband. Hell, if I could rewind to that day, I'd replace that conversation with anything but him: the time I had worms as a kid, saggy boobs, or the best drain cleaners for unclogging pipes. *Anything* would have been better than wasting our last conversation on him.

I'd already given Alex twelve years of my life. He didn't need to hijack my last conversation with Mum too.

For twelve long years, I was stuck in a rented house with his dirty pants and socks piling up on the floor. Like he'd ever lift a finger. Still, I'd thought he loved me. Why else would he insist we keep trying for a baby? I tried to enjoy Fridays and Sundays, I promise, but some days I had to think of Chris Hemsworth or Chris Pine to get through it. Any Chris would have done, really. I felt bad, of course.

Even after the divorce, he could have just driven off into the sunset and married the next gullible fool. Instead, he stuck around and tried to win custody of my cat—the beautiful Bengal cat, which had been mine since childhood.

What kind of man did that?

Someone who deserved a kick in the jingle bells, that's who.

Still, as soon as I hit forty, I decided to live my life for me and embrace my weirdness. If you're still contorting yourself for other people when you hit middle age, when will you learn to embrace your chin hairs and soar to new heights? I drew a line through my sorry relationship with Alex and moved into a new, smaller flat with my cat. Just your friendly neighbourhood cat lady, that's me. Thank my lucky stars I hadn't taken his name. I could just pretend he never existed.

Only Mum hadn't seen it that way.

Now she was gone, I couldn't tell her that it didn't matter about him. I would take on all the arseholes in the world if it meant one more day with her.

"Earth to Ms Verma," said Nita.

I tuned back into the class. "Right, class, copy down the questions from the board. Reread the text and answer the questions in full sentences. Use a dictionary. You've worked so hard tonight that we're finishing twenty minutes early."

Okay, so it was a lie. We'd not even hit a third of my lesson plan, but a small lie never hurt anyone. It was the whoppers that floored you.

Nita piped up. "But Ms Verma, we thought you could teach us the back kick again."

I shook my head. "Sorry, not tonight."

Adding kickboxing to my curriculum really helped with student motivation. I taught them a few moves if they impressed me with their learning. London was a city of strays. Its inhabitants needed to know how to be quick with their fists and boots to survive the streets.

"We'll practice next time, I promise. Don't forget to do your homework. No excuses." My body sagged with relief when my students scattered into the moonlit night.

I'd taken a big long hard look at myself when I turned forty and wasn't sure I liked what I saw. Sure, my body had weathered the years just fine. My long, dark hair was a little wild but as thick as it had been at university. My mixed-race skin had a glow that offset the incoming crow's feet. I might never have carried a baby in my belly, but I had more flexibility than your average forty-year-old. Still, I'd hardly changed the world. Not even my small corner of it, unless you counted conjugating verbs and teaching cockney rhyming slang to my students.

It was nearing ten o'clock by the time I tucked in the last chairs, switched off the lights and locked up the community centre. I zipped up my coat, pulled my hood up against silver arrows of rain and set off home through the grubby car park, passing high-rise blocks, chimney stacks and asphalt marked with chewing gum and dog mess. Reaching home took a good twenty-minute walk to my flat on the other side of Balham or a ten-minute jog across a couple of grimy estates. The sorts of places that stank of piss in dank corners and A-class drugs swapped hands under cover of darkness.

I kept my eyes open and my keys in my hand as a weapon against any unwanted attention. Every Londoner worth their salt knew to keep their wits about them late at night. It was easy to underestimate a forty-year-old woman, but I could handle myself. Years of yoga and kickboxing had seen to that.

Mum had always insisted I be able to look after myself. London was a jungle compared to her native Brittany. The funny thing was, darting shadows and slinking shapes seemed a breath away since her death.

At the top of my road, something brushed my shoulder. Not a branch but a hand.

Without missing a beat, I held the palm in both hands, twisted under the arm and pushed my attacker into a kneeling position. I raised my leg to kick him in the face, but a gust of wind came from nowhere and knocked him off balance. He flew three feet and landed in a heap on the rain-slicked pavement.

Anger, hot and blazing. "Get lost, arsehole."

I had the upper hand, so I backed away, my fists ready to take him on. I hoped I didn't have to flip him again because my back was sore, but I had no doubt I could handle it. My flat was minutes away, but I didn't want a random knowing where I lived.

Grey eyes, longish hair, low-slung jeans. In any other setting, I'd have given him a second look, but he had no business creeping up on women late at night.

The man gritted his teeth in pain. He opened the palm of his hand. "You dropped your keys."

Embarrassment made my cheeks flush hot. My boss would have skinned me if I'd lost the community centre keys. "Oh, sorry about that. Can't be too careful."

He sprang to his feet, light-footed despite the rain, dusted himself off and tossed me the keys.

I caught them, stuffed them into my pocket and made a show of buttoning it shut.

"Quite the reflexes you have there." The cut of his jaw and the glint in his eyes told me he was dangerous.

I eyed him warily. "Yeah, well, thanks again."

"Don't mention it." He definitely had a wet bum, judging by his stiffness as he walked away.

I waited until he disappeared from sight before pushing on towards my tree-lined road, where headlights flashed over the yellow bricks and mortar of the buildings. I unlocked the door of my building and walked through the Victorian-tiled hallway to my ground-floor flat, half expecting to trip over the cat.

"Echo?" I called once inside, slipping my shoes and coat off.

Still no sign of him.

Usually, he was my shadow. He threaded through my legs when I came in the door and even followed me to bed. He was a mean fighting machine, but he'd been missing since Mum's funeral, and I was starting to get worried. I'd even put out scrambled eggs for him.

If Alex was behind Echo's disappearance, maybe I'd get a chance to kick him in the nuts after all.

I headed for the back bedroom, where I'd left the window open for him. It wasn't like I had anything to steal. The landlord didn't strictly allow pets, but turned a blind eye as long as the other tenants didn't complain.

I checked the living room, hoping to find Echo curled on the sofa. In the kitchen, the scrambled eggs had dried into a rubbery mess in his bowl. I scraped them into the bin and put out some kibble instead, not that the fusspot ate that willingly. My empty fridge hummed in the corner.

"Bed it is then." I downed a glass of water and made myself a hot water bottle. Then I padded to my bedroom and flicked on the light. "What on earth? You've got to be kidding me."

That was *not* how I'd left my flat that morning. An enormous imprint flattened the centre of the bed as if a rhino had lain there.

Patches of dirt marred the white cotton sheets. Even the freshly fluffed pillow had been compressed. I'd only just changed the sheets. The bed should have smelled of lavender, not muck.

Had Echo been back and brought a harem of cats with him? It wouldn't have been the first time.

"It's not my day. Actually, scrap that. I need a reset button for the past week." I dusted off the sheets and then burrowed under the duvet as storms swirled outside, wondering why Mum would release animals from her laboratory and how on earth flowers could grow from the chassis of a crushed car.

2

The next afternoon, I made my way to Balham tube under clouds as dark as iron filaments. I stuck missing cat flyers for Echo on trees, gritting my teeth at the sight of my phone number on display for all to see.

Since the divorce, all sorts of whackos had been calling to ask me out. Meddling Indian grannies at our temple had spread the rumour I was a free agent again. I knew because they texting me hair-raising pictures of their unattached offspring. I might have been flattered, but it was the swan song of my ovaries they were after, not me.

I rode the escalator down towards the platform.

Alex had claimed the car in the divorce, and I let him think he won that round. Car insurance cost an arm and a leg, and London's sprawling public transport system meant I could just as easily get around without one. A few minutes later, I was aboard the rattling northern line tube towards Elephant & Castle in a carriage with open windows, enjoying the gusts of underground breeze. My best friend Marina always said the air down here was grim—moist and full of germs—but I liked it. It blew away the cobwebs in my head.

I needed that today if I was going to be in any fit state at Mum's memorial.

I hopped off the tube and met Dad and my brother outside Mum's former workplace, a grey concrete high-rise with milky windows a stone's throw away from the monstrous roundabout at Elephant & Castle. They were dressed in suits. My brother's gave off distinct Saville Row vibes, which made Dad look even more of a mess in his moth-balled, crumpled offering. A smear of indigo paint sat just beneath Dad's chin like he'd missed the canvas with his paintbrush. When he was in the middle of a piece, no one else existed.

"You scrub up well." I hugged them and wiped the paint off Dad's face.

Dad's haunted eyes stared at me. He'd lost his soulmate, after all. "What would I do without you?"

"You'd be right as rain," I said, though I knew Mum had been the strong one.

"Has Echo turned up yet? I can help look for him."

"Let's just get through this first, shall we?" said my brother, Sahil. At two years my senior, he was a successful businessman with a portfolio of rental houses and a penthouse apartment next to St. Paul's that dripped in luxury.

"It's not a memorial if there are no prayers, is it?" said Dad. "It's not like they'll be praying for Rosalie's soul here. I should have stayed home and prayed at our shrine."

Mum had been Christian, but she hadn't been a churchgoer. She liked Christmas Eve carols and Norwegian Christmas trees, but that was about it. Dad only went to temple for the social side. I couldn't remember the last time he knelt at our Ganesha shrine. Hardly anyone prayed nowadays: Christian, Hindu, Muslim, you name it. These days, most people worshipped mobile phones or Netflix instead.

Sahil looked at his watch, his mouth in a grim line. "I have to hurry, sis. I have a meeting I have to get back for."

"I thought the plan was to go through Mum's things with Dad?"

He raised a well-groomed eyebrow. "News to me."

Fair to say, my brother wasn't my favourite person. He showed up on his terms and rarely softened unless it was for one of his boob tube-wearing or whiskey-drinking friends. Every time I decided to try to like him for the sake of our parents, he pushed my buttons again.

"Let's go." I propelled them towards the revolving door, feeling more like a jailer than a family member.

Inside the lobby, a receptionist in chopstick-thin heels handed out name labels to stick on our chests and ushered us past security. Together, we rode the elevator to the fourth floor and exited past laboratories where centrifuges whirred and employees huddled over microscopes and Petri dishes.

I swallowed the lump in my throat. How many times had Mum and Dad debated whether microscopes or telescopes were better? Whether the greater miracles were cells or stars?

"We've arranged for finger sandwiches, teas and coffees, and of course, the CEO will be here to say a few words." The receptionist led us into a conference room, where rows of chairs had been set out in front of a lectern.

With only a dozen people in attendance, most chairs stood empty.

The receptionist showed us to reserved seats in the front row. "Would you like me to introduce you to everyone?"

Dad and I exchanged looks.

"No, thank you," he said.

We sat down just as the big boss, Michael, entered the room, his bald head gleaming under the spotlights. A hush descended over those gathered as he strode over to us.

A bald head behind a vast desk, Mum had said.

"Joshi," he said to Dad. "How awful to see you in such circumstances. Please accept my condolences."

"Michael, thanks for arranging this." Dad shook his hand. "You really shouldn't have."

He nodded at us all. "What a tragic loss. Shall we get started?" He extricated himself and moved over to the lectern. "Thank you all for coming. We're here to commemorate the life of Dr Rosalie Verma, who was taken from us so suddenly last week. As many of you know, Rosalie may have been French, but she was also a Londoner through and through. She loved her city, and she loved EvolveTech. Why else would she have stayed here for almost two decades?"

The crowd murmured politely.

My mind flashed to the graveyard with the mound of fresh soil.

"Rosalie was a diligent, popular employee. She cared deeply about her work. She was also a wife and mother, and she leaves behind a grieving family and friends. Her work on Parkinson's, MS, dementia and, most recently, on cell regeneration can't be underestimated." The boss's eyes narrowed.

I followed his gaze to the back of the room.

There stood a woman with a cherubic face, though she must have been in her seventies. Her plump frame was wrapped in a green sari. Despite the rainy forecast, she wore flat, gold sandals, and her thick, black hair was plaited over one shoulder. Rosy cheeks, bright eyes and a soft mouth softened her wrinkly face. She was the most interesting person in the room by far—a spark of colour in a sea of black suits and white lab coats—flanked by two disgruntled security guards.

Michael tore his eyes away from the disruption and smiled at a friend of Mum's sitting in the congregation. "Melissa, as Rosalie's closest friend here, perhaps you'd like to say a few words?"

He waited for her to reach him, then strode to the back of the room.

I gave Melissa an encouraging smile as she approached the lectern. Behind me, a scuffle erupted that made my sense of injustice prickle. I'd had just about enough of men pushing women around. Yes, I might have been a little sensitive after Alex and the loan sharks, but I wasn't going to sit back and watch a little old lady be manhandled.

"Where are you going?" whispered Dad as I slipped out of my seat.

"I'll be right back." I grabbed my jacket.

I arrived just as the security guards shoved the old lady back into the elevator, closely followed by Michael.

"We're not sure how she evaded security, sir," the ginger security guard huffed. "We caught her on CCTV in Dr Verma's lab. By the time we got there, she'd snuck into the memorial service."

"I'm quicker than you." The old lady grinned.

"This sounds like a police matter," said Michael. "Unless you want to tell us why you're here?"

"I came here to pay my respects," said the old lady. "It's not often that someone as old as me finds inspiration in mortals."

"She's off her trolley," said the ginger security guard.

I'd heard enough. I reached out, blocking the doors from shuddering shut and plucking the train of the old lady's sari from being swallowed by the doors. "No need for the police or to be so rough." I turned my back on the men. "Are you okay?"

Her eyes glinted. "Quite all right, dear. I'm tougher than I look."

"You knew my mother?"

"Oh, I knew her very well. She had courage and curiosity in spades. When the night nears, those two qualities are more valuable than a hundred offerings."

Maybe she was a little weird, but in my experience, the best kind of people were weird. It was the ones who hid all their flaws that I had to worry about. My blouse had ridden up my arm in the mad dash over to her, exposing my scars.

The old lady's smile widened when she noticed.

I pulled down the sleeve of my blouse, self-conscious. The scars had tingled this past week as if they were fresh and not decades old. Mum had always encouraged me not to be conscious about scars. They told a story, she said. The thing is, these weren't any old scars: a circle of nine dots on the soft flesh of my left inner arm, white and raised as if they were braille. They drew attention. I needed them like I needed a bathtub on my head.

The lift doors pinged open on the ground floor.

I turned to Michael. "I need some air. Could you possibly tell my father I'll see him at his house?"

A cursory nod. "Of course."

I put my arm around the old lady. "Shall we?"

The old lady chuckled. "Fresh air sounds delightful."

She was off her rocker. Smog filled the London air, and clouds threatened rain. No surprise there. I was the third generation to live in South London, and I knew better than anyone how often the skies in London darkened. My paternal ancestors arrived from India back when this city was the crown of civilisation and air travel was cheap. With India booming these days, maybe my father's family should have stayed there. Only then we would have had monsoon to contend with.

"I didn't get your name," I said as we ended up in the same segment of the rotating door and shuffled forward.

Cunning eyes assessed me. "I've been known by many names through the years. The one I like best is Gaia."

"How did you know my mother?"

"Rosalie called me when her eyes opened. We had common interests."

"She called you on the telephone?"

Gaia cackled. "No, dear, I don't need one of those. She did it the old way, with an open heart and an offering."

I searched her cherubic face and saw no malice there. "What were you doing there today?"

"I was hoping to see how far your mother had reached on her project, but those silly sods had cleared everything away." Keen eyes on mine. "I don't suppose she told you anything about it? It was rather marvellous. Of course, it wasn't strictly an EvolveTech project, but I like a woman who bends the rules. Too often, we are constrained by them."

I frowned. It wasn't like Mum to work on personal projects on company time. "Mum and I didn't often talk about her work. I didn't always get the complexities."

Her eyes twinkled. "Never mind. One day your brain might catch up with hers. Genetically, it's not a sure bet, but you might be lucky. Don't worry. We'll find a way through together. Centuries of patience can't easily be undone."

She was weird, but I really liked her. After the week I'd had, a batty old woman with a zest for life was exactly the tonic I needed. "Tell me more. There's a café a few blocks away. Let me buy you a cuppa."

"This isn't my first adventure. I wish I could tell you my stories, but your ears may not be ready."

We'd not even made it halfway up the street. Gaia wasn't exactly racing-horse fit, and I'd slowed my pace to match hers. I stopped to put on my jacket, struggling to hear her over the boom of traffic.

"Ready for what?" I looked up, turning a full circle on the pavement, my brow furrowed.

There was no hint of her green sari among passers-by.

"Charming. She could have at least said goodbye."

I TOOK the bus to Dad's. I'd shown my face at the memorial but preferred to grieve privately. Our family home, a three-storey red-bricked house with pretty sash windows and peeling shutters, overlooked Tooting Bec Common. The walls inside had been lined with books and Dad's paintings. It was miles too big for one person, but I couldn't bear the thought of Dad selling up.

I walked up their driveway and vaulted over the side gate. The ease of movement surprised even me—up and over as if I skated the breeze. I landed easily, feeling pretty cool.

Choosing more kickboxing classes over comfort eating post-divorce had paid off.

I located the back door key underneath the geranium planter, where all the woodlice liked to hide, and let myself into the back door. Inside, I turned on the lights and went straight past Dad's shrine to the living room sofa Mum had always chosen to sit on.

My soft voice pierced the quiet of the empty house. "I wish you were here. I wish you hadn't left us so soon."

How could it have only been a week since we'd been in the back garden, trying to get away from the stink of Dad's acrylic paint in the house? The sudden urge to look at old photos overwhelmed me. I made a beeline for the dining room to find the stash of family albums in the sideboard, scattered them on the floor and knelt beside them for a trip down memory lane. I picked up my parents' wedding album first and turned to the first page.

My heartbeat accelerated. I blinked, in case my eyes deceived me, then looked again, turning the pages of the album quicker and quicker.

Mum had faded from every frame as if the photographs had developed in reverse.

My fingers fumbled as I checked the baby albums, the family holiday albums and the first-day-of-school ones. Mum's image had vanished from every photograph, leaving a void where she had been. As if she'd never existed.

I sobbed, startled as the key turned in the front door.

"Alisha? I'm home," said Dad. Footsteps came my way. He hovered in the doorframe, taking in the mess and my stricken face. "What's all this?"

"Mum's gone."

He sighed. "I know, love."

I shook my head, my voice sharp. "I mean, she's gone from all the photographs."

His eyes clouded over. "Whatever are you talking about, Alisha? Your mother's right there."

A sob threatened to turn into more. What the hell was going on?

I composed myself, not wanting to upset him. "I'll put the kettle on. A cup of tea will see us right."

He put a heavy hand on my shoulder. "Yes, it will, love. I'll just head up to change, and then we can have a natter."

I picked up their wedding album again. The one I'd looked at over and over as a teenager when I'd dreamed of white weddings and a man sweeping me off my feet. The one that made me want to find a relationship like theirs, with their lifetime of secret glances and hand-holding.

Dad was there in all his seventies' glory.

Mum, with her belted A-line dress and Brigitte Bardot eyeliner, had been erased.

3

———————

I invited Marina over to my flat for dinner the next day. I didn't have much in. A perk of the divorce was not having to listen to Alex grumble about an empty fridge. The term hangry had his image next to it in the dictionary. I'd never known a man to be so ruled by his stomach.

Marina and I were like sisters. I didn't have to cook her an impressive meal. My best friend would have been happy with a bag of crisps, which was great because my cooking skills left a lot to be desired. We settled for cheese on toast and opened a bottle of Rioja between us, though I preferred Merlot, being half French. When the microwave pinged, I grabbed our plates. We ignored the small table in my kitchen and slumped on the living room floor to eat with our legs stretched out and cushions to pad our bums.

"I loved Rosalie." Marina's face was puffy, like she'd been crying. "Do you remember how, when I first started getting migraines, my mum would tell me just to get on with it? Your mum would let me come over, tuck us into bed together and nurse me with cocoa and hot water bottles. She was the best."

My throat scratched with unshed tears. "I thought so too, but I didn't tell her enough. We fought about Alex the last time I saw her."

"What happened?"

"It was stupid. She said she missed cooking for Alex. She liked how he always licked his plate clean."

"Gross. Anyway, it's way too soon since the divorce to be saying anything nice about Alex. For the record, he's the absolute worst. You know Rosalie was on your side, right?"

"I know that now, but at that moment, it was like a red rag to a bull. I mean, I wanted her to name his faults to make me feel better, not compliment him. But Mum didn't let emotions get in the way of facts. Then she said it was a shame that money broke us up, and at least he hadn't slept with anyone else."

Marina winced. "Ouch. I'm sorry."

"So I told her Alex could rot in hell. Then I grabbed my bag and left without another word. The crash happened the next day, and we hadn't even patched it up."

"I reckon she just wanted you to have what she had with your dad. It just came out wrong. Do you remember how many times she picked me up when I was heartbroken? She believed in love, and she wanted that for you."

Marina and her parents had fallen out when she'd come out as bisexual as a teen. Her parents thought it was a fad until they caught her smooching both our school's star netball player and a chess club geek at the bottom of the garden. All hell broke loose, and Marina ended up staying at ours for weeks before the uneasy truce with her parents. Marina didn't fall in love with a person. She fell in love with personalities. It didn't matter a jot to her whether the person she loved was male, female or transgender.

She loved without boundaries. It made her formidable as a friend and also as a vet.

"Maybe you're right," I said.

"Alisha, I know I'm right. She loved you. A few cross words won't change that." She hugged me. "I know what you need. A distraction! Before Rosalie died, I'd planned to take you out on the pull. Imagine. All that time in a meh marriage, and now you're free to explore. We could be each other's wing-women. Nothing like some hot stuff to perk up a woman."

I laughed in spite of myself.

"Too soon? I mean, you need to break in that new bed of yours."

"You're trouble, from your gothic nail varnish all the way up to your chemical hair."

"Yes, but you love me anyway. Still no sign of Echo?"

I shook my head mournfully. "Not even scrambled eggs tempted him home."

I was starting to worry in earnest. Usually, I couldn't even go to the toilet without Echo wanting to be with me. He scratched at the door, even if I wanted privacy and refused to sleep anywhere but my bed. His attachment to me meant Mum and Dad had let him come with me when I moved out. He'd been my family cat for as long as I could remember, which was odd because Bengal cats lived for about fifteen years. He had a penchant for salmon, though, and we'd never scrimped on his food and vitamins, so he was in good nick.

Another reason why I feared something had happened to him. Usually, nothing would keep him away from his food.

"Time to up the ante then. Forget about the kibble," said Marina. "Try some really strong canned meat. He'll be able to smell it a mile away. Or put some of his bedding outside the window. Just the thought of another beastie using it will tempt him back."

She was hands down the best vet south of the Thames. Although, it took a while for her clients to see past her cascades of pink, turquoise and purple hair and the plentiful tattoos on her always-bare arms. She was like Jessica Rabbit on acid: an explosion of buxom curves and rainbow colour.

Like I said, Marina Ambrose was a force to be reckoned with.

Almost all my most cherished memories involved her: flour fights in Mum's kitchen when we were small, skating as teens in the deep of winter, phone calls until the early hours, dancing until our feet hurt. We'd been friends since primary school. We'd mopped each other's tears, laughed until our sides ached and held back each other's hair when we vomited. I didn't trust anyone as much as I trusted her.

I filled her in on what the detective had told me and about Mum disappearing from the photo albums.

"There's got to be a sensible explanation. Have you checked the pictures of her in your phone gallery?"

I shook my head. "Why didn't I think of that?"

"Your mum just died, Alisha. I'm not surprised you're not fully functional. Did you know animals such as elephants, chimps and dolphins respond to grief? Give me your phone."

I took a gulp of wine and unlocked my phone. "No, I'll do it. Here goes."

I hadn't taken as many pictures of Mum as I should have. Our moments together had seemed so ordinary I rarely thought to capture them on film. I had to go a way back to find one of her.

But when I did, I sucked in my breath. "Look."

Mum's photos appeared as black squares of nothing.

"Give it here." Marina snatched the phone. Her fingers darted across the keys until she reached the monthly, then yearly overview. "Holy crap."

I flopped on the floor. "I'm losing my mind."

"I'm not surprised. That is some freaky shit."

She lay down too, and we leaned our heads together, just like we did when we stargazed as children.

I breathed out. "I'm glad you're here."

"Where else would I be?"

A thud sounded behind us, followed by a clang of fallen dishes. We clutched each other in fright.

"I think that was the kitchen. Stay here," I whispered, hauling myself up.

"Fat chance," she said. "I'm coming with you, but I'll stay behind you in case you go into warrior mode."

I looked around for a weapon, but pillows weren't going to cut it, and there was no way I would throw the cheesy plates as frisbees or ruin a bottle of good Rioja. I put my fists up, and we advanced slowly, rounding the corner barefoot.

A strange slurping sound met our ears.

"What on earth?" I gripped Marina.

The creature was a metre and a half long, maybe longer, stretched out with its forelegs on my counter and nibbling on the block of Marks and Spencer's mature cheddar I'd left out. It had strong legs, a powerful body, a long tail and a thick, golden coat of fur covered with exquisite rosettes.

I rubbed my eyes and looked again. "That's not… That's a fricking leopard in my kitchen!"

Marina's blue eyes widened. "That's not just any leopard. It's an Indian leopard. Don't move. Stay very still."

"You're the vet," I said. "Got any tranquilliser darts with you?"

She shook her head.

Of all the places Marina and I had been to rescue animals—up trees, in sewer drains, in rundown theatres—it would be in my kitchen that we were mauled to death. Maybe the neighbours would call the police. I thanked my lucky stars we were both dressed at least. Imagine being rescued when you're just in your knickers and bra. Or worse, braless. It's not like we were twenty anymore. At this rate, we'd be lucky to make it to forty-one.

We took an involuntary step back as the leopard swung around, taking in his wide muzzle, foot-long whiskers, jewel-like eyes and teeth that could tear meat from the bone. Even human meat.

Marina sprang to life, shouting, waving her arms and stamping her feet. "Don't run. It'll trigger the chase instinct. Make yourself big. Make noise!"

I followed her lead, clapping and jumping up and down, hoping to scare him off.

"How rude, ladies," the leopard said. "I've been away over a week, and you're acting like buffoons."

Marina and I looked at each other, aghast. We must have had a glass too many. There was no way the leopard was talking.

"What, all those fantasy movies you watch, and you've never seen a talking cat?" He shook his magnificent head and padded towards us, sending my kitchen chairs scattering. "Dear me, you've not figured it out yet, have you? And judging by your expression, Marina, it looks like you can hear me just as well as Alisha." He lifted his lip in mirth. "Which means you're a peculiar too."

Marina cowered behind me.

The leopard was so close now I could feel hot, cheesy breath on my face.

He tilted his head, licked his paw and raised it to his muzzle to bat away the remnants of cheddar. Green eyes rested on my face, and I discerned both gentleness and ferocity there. At the corner of one eye, a three-inch scar marred his striking head. A scar I'd known all my life.

Either I was going mad, or the world I thought existed was something else entirely.

I took a deep breath, my heartbeat a roar in my ears. "Hello, Echo. How about you start at the beginning and tell me exactly who you are and where you've been?"

4

E cho purred in satisfaction, although I wasn't sure how satisfied an Indian leopard squashed into the tiny kitchen of a London flat could be. I ignored the rapid drumbeat of my heart and prayed to Dad's gods and Mum's one God that I wasn't making a mistake. Hopefully, he wouldn't eat us as soon as our backs were turned.

I led the way back into the living room, pushing Marina ahead of me just to be safe, my body a buffer between her and the beast.

"Relax. I already feasted once today," said the leopard, and he didn't mean the cheese. He leapt onto my two-seater sofa, his golden, spotted fur contrasting with the navy fabric. "Although it would serve you right if I devoured you after that photograph of me on the missing poster. It's hard enough having a domestic cat as my face to the world without you publicising such a ridiculous picture."

Marina poked me in the ribs. "Can you hear him too?"

"Yep."

If she could also hear the leopard, then grief hadn't addled my brain. My instincts had taken a hit, but if I concentrated, the leopard sounded like I imagined Echo's personality to be. Having lived with my Echo all my life, I had a habit of talking to him all the time and knew him as well as I knew myself. My Echo was sharp-witted and mocking. I could tell by how he stared at me with disdain if I dropped a vase or said something he disagreed with. He had a thing for the ladies and preened like a peacock. The leopard had vanity in common with him.

Could it be so farfetched to believe what my eyes and ears told me? I'd even smelt the cheese on his breath. My fingers itched to touch his fur, but it was too soon to gauge our safety.

Marina and I took the armchair on the opposite side of the room.

"Maybe this is a new manifestation of migraine symptoms," she said.

"I don't get migraines."

"Was our food drugged?"

"Nope."

"Because that would explain this hallucination."

I leaned into her for reassurance. "Can you explain why we're hallucinating the same thing?"

"Sadly not." She shuddered. "A leopard can leap six metres. We'd be goners if he decides not to play nice."

The leopard grunted. "I'm not deaf. I can hear you. Humans can be so small-minded. Now, if you'll just let me fill you in, I'm sure we'll all feel much better."

"Go ahead," I said, visualising a kitchen knife. It's not that I wanted to stab the leopard if he really was Echo. I wanted to test whether he could read my mind. That would tell me if he was a hallucination after all. A hallucination wouldn't be that clever.

The leopard sat up, his face benign and utterly oblivious to my half-murderous thoughts.

I relaxed. Not a mind reader, then.

His voice was a low rumble in our ears. "I come from a galaxy far, far away."

"Really?" I almost fell off the perch of my armchair.

He gurned, his mouth widening and revealing sharp, jagged teeth, and a honking sound filled the kitchen. He was laughing. "No, not really. I come from the plains of India, and my family has been in service to your family for centuries. Although I don't care much for that idiot father of yours." His gaze softened. "Your grandmother, on the other hand, was magnificent. When she left India, I swam across oceans to follow her here, though she freed me of our ancestral oath. I left the land of my ancestors and followed her to this pigmy island because it is not my fate to be an oath breaker. I will die in service to this bloodline. It is my duty. Luckily, the internet did not exist then, so the evidence of my journey, though unfortunately captured on film, is buried in the BBC news archives."

Marina stared at him open-mouthed.

"Echo, can you possibly skip forward to the bit where you turn from my Bengal cat to an Indian leopard? That's the bit I'm struggling with," I said.

He growled, a gentle admonishment but enough for the hair on my neck to stand on edge. "Pah, have you listened to a word? It was the other way around, Alisha."

"My apologies. Please proceed."

"As I was saying, when I reached these shores, your grandmother Rajika arranged for a glamour so that humdrums would see me as an absurd Bengal cat. Rajika had warned me not to follow her, partly to save me from such humiliation. Having disobeyed her, I had no choice but to agree to the glamour."

"You're quite a showstopper in your cat form, actually," said Marina. "I should know. At least fifty moggies pass through the doors of my surgery each week."

The leopard inclined his head. "I thank you for not mocking me. It is a balm to know that some of my majesty also exists in my smaller form."

He *was* beautiful in both forms, but I was pretty sure Marina was using Animal 101: showing kindness to avoid becoming prey.

"What's a humdrum?" I said.

"A non-magical, of course. A person with ordinary eyes and no magical talents." His eyes glinted, glassy green pools of pleasure. "You two don't have to worry about being ordinary. You've never been that. Surely by now, you've noticed the otherness Rosalie's death unleashed?" He bowed his head, and I thought perhaps he mourned my mother. But when his head rose, all softness had disappeared. His body tensed, and his claws dug into the velvet of the sofa. "Darkness swirls around us."

Icicles of fear encased my heart. "What do you mean, Echo?"

"From the start of their relationship, your parents' heads were filled with humdrum dreams. Buying a house. Setting up home. Raising a family. Establishing their careers. After your grandmother's death, your father shunned his magic completely. He'd always hated the rules and demands of being part of the Otherworld. The artist in him is a free spirit. When the magic flowed between him and your grandmother, he was in his element, but he hated the constraints imposed on them. He didn't understand why his magic had to be supervised. New users of magic have to pass a trial, and his own trial was traumatic. Rajika was always being called away from the family. When she lost her life, it was too high a cost." Echo tilted his magnificent head. "Then came the day that unleashed Joshi's protective instincts and caused him to turn against the Otherworld. You were only four. You found a bird's nest in the garden and kept a careful watch over them. Do you remember that day?"

I nodded, and a shudder ran up my spine. "Three jade eggs with brown freckles all over."

It was my first real memory: the terror of the blackbirds carving my skin, the warm little bodies frantic against my little arm, the nightmarish blood and the bruises.

"You *do* remember. The mother bird tolerated you. When the eggs hatched, everything changed. I was asleep on the lawn, and I heard a screech. The birds flew at your little arm, their beaks drilling in a circle."

"I remember the blood. I remember Dad scooping me up."

"Your father went into a frenzy after that. He knew the baby birds were too young to fly. He knew magic was involved. Your magic had awakened. He decided to bind your magic. Your grandmother must have turned in her grave that day. If she had been alive, she would have persuaded him otherwise, but without her, there was no one to hold your father back."

I traced my scars. They throbbed beneath my finger. "What about my mother?"

"Rosalie wanted to slow down and think it through, but your father was adamant. His grief for Rajika was still so raw, and Rosalie didn't want to add to it. So when your father approached Rajika's old witch ally to bind your magic, she didn't intervene. A drop of blood each from the four of you and a quick spell, and it was done." He sighed. "And since I had vowed to protect your bloodline to the death, I was stuck, pretending to be a Bengal cat."

"Holy shit," said Marina.

The leopard nodded sagely. "Indeed."

I tried to wrap my head around the unfolding family history. "So all this time, Dad's been hiding this from us?" There was not a cat's chance in hell that my brother knew; Sahil would have boasted if he had been the first in the know.

"Your father's a damn fool," said the leopard, "but surprisingly good at giving ear scratches."

"And if I walk down the street with you, my neighbours won't scream?"

"They will not be able to see my majestic form. The glamour is effective against all humdrums, except in the moments directly before death when it is possible that humdrums gain true sight, according to the witch. If I am by your side, your neighbours will simply think I am a brainless cat acting like a dog."

Marina piped up, her voice small. "It's all very hard to take in. You're saying that we're both from magical lines?"

The leopard snorted. "I have no idea what you are, Marina Ambrose, whether stray or purebred, but Alisha is the granddaughter of Rajika Verma. She is most certainly of magical heritage."

"And what does that mean? Do we have hidden talents?"

Echo inclined his head. "Of that, I have no doubt. No peculiar I know of is ungifted, although the extent and form of magical talents vary greatly according to fate, birth, study and experience. It is for you and Alisha to find out what has been dormant in you, and I will stay by your side as you uncover your skills. At least, I will stay by Alisha's side, and if you happen to be here, I will do you the great courtesy of offering you my wisdom."

A question tugged in the recesses of my mind. "And my grandmother Rajika? I assumed she died of old age."

Echo's roar reverberated across the room, a sound wave that made us recoil. "A druid of Rajika's ability? You know not of what you speak. It is nigh on impossible for a woman of Rajika's stature to be felled by mere old age. No. Your grandmother died defending the Celestial Library. It was a battle for the ages. She fought bravely, as did I, but she kept the heathens from the door, loyal to the end." He indicated the deep scar running from the corner of his green eye. "Did you never wonder where I got this laceration? No mortal blade or lowly street moggie could do this to me."

Well, there went my kitchen knife theory.

I leaned forward. "Am I a druid, Echo?"

Emerald eyes glinted. "You are."

5

The city had extinguished its twinkling lights by the time Marina left my flat. I walked her to the door, leaving Echo alone in the living room, his hefty paws kneading the velvet of my sofa.

"Are you sure it's okay to leave you alone with him?" Worry etched her face. "I'm going to cancel my surgery."

"Don't you have a collie going under the knife first thing?"

She nodded. "Followed by a Siamese and a pet rat."

"That settles it. Go and get some sleep. You must be knackered."

"Actually, my head has never felt clearer. Even the residue of my last migraine has cleared. I should stay."

A firm shake of my head. "I've got this. Go."

"I could bring you some sedatives. I'll measure up just enough for his weight." She bit her lip while she calculated. "He must be pushing eighty kilos, maybe more. We should really call this in. What if he escapes and goes on a rampage?"

"Call who? A safari park? London Zoo?"

"Don't be ridiculous. The Royal Veterinary College or the RSPCA, of course. Or Tony, the big cat expert."

"And say what? Excuse me, madam, would you like to extract a talking leopard from my kitchen?"

"You have a point. It's just, he's got nine lives, but you've only got one…"

For an educated woman, Marina believed in a lot of hocus pocus. She refused to walk under ladders or open an umbrella indoors and took great care not to break mirrors. She picked up dropped pennies, hated the sight of crows and avoided leaving her house on Friday the thirteenth.

"Echo, do you have nine lives?" I called down the hallway.

His answer rumbled back. "Do I look like a witch's cat?"

I turned to Marina. "See? I'm safe. I promise I'll give as good as I get if he decides I'm a snack. And I won't let him sleep in my bedroom quite yet."

She hovered on the threshold.

I kissed her cheek and pushed her into the hallway. "I'll be fine."

"Call me at any time, okay?"

I waited until her squeaky trainers exited the building and marvelled at the feelings bubbling up inside me. I should have been questioning my sanity and checking into a psychiatric hospital.

Instead, I sensed a base note of grief, a heart note of curiosity and a top note of excitement. For the first time in forever, my anxiety had melted away.

Despite the early hour, I cleaned the kitchen. Call it middle age, but there was no way I was going to bed with a sink full of dirty dishes. I kept an ear trained for any noises behind me while I worked in case the leopard suddenly approached. I washed up, straightened the furniture, binned the cheese remnants and found a bigger bowl for Echo's water. The dish I'd had for him as a Bengal cat now seemed like a thimble compared to his real needs.

I returned to find him dozing, his long limbs trailing off the sofa and onto the wooden floor. "Echo?"

"Hmm?"

"Have you always been known by that name?"

He raised his head. "My kind have names that honour our ancestors. I have my forefathers' names, names that tell the wonder of war and service. But after the witch cast the glamour, Rajika called me Echo, and the name fit as snugly as a wizard's cloak. London is a city that changes all who come here. Why should I be any different? And so I am Echo, just as I am also my ancestral name, and when I return to India, I will cast off the glamour and the name, and all will be as it was."

His voice had lost its ferocity, and his sleepy state gave me the courage to inch forward and curl my fingers into the soft fur behind his ear. He purred and nudged his head into my hand, encouraging the petting. I responded, taking care not to venture too close to his powerful jaw. If I closed my eyes, I could even convince myself this was my Bengal cat and nothing had changed. His fur had similar markings, but his leopard fur had a thickness and richness that eluded him as a domestic cat. *My* Echo had been an illusion all along.

"Echo, why did you disappear when Mum died?"

"Even the most powerful magic has limits, Alisha. The witch's binding spell, concocted with the four drops of blood, fractured with Rosalie's death. With the spell broken, you regained true sight. I wanted to give you time to adjust before revealing myself."

"I missed you."

The leopard nuzzled against me, his body hot, his limbs wound coils ready to spring. "I was never far."

"What I don't understand is how Marina could see you too."

"Her scientific training dampened her magic. That is why she couldn't see me before. Science and magic coexist unhappily together. I have seen it many times before," said the leopard. "What is more puzzling is why now? What changed to allow Marina Ambrose to see me now? The Otherworld is a fragile place. My best guess is that her empathy for you in your grief, your sisterhood, helped break the shackles of her constrained magic." He growled, suddenly impatient. "Enough questions. The hour is late. You must sleep, and I must hunt. Since you have no salmon in the fridge and kibble is not the correct sustenance for a leopard, I will arrange my own food. I am an opportunistic hunter. And you have been remiss in obtaining my preferred meals of wild boar, deer or fowl."

I raised an eyebrow in question.

"You cannot get these things from Lidl?"

I shook my head.

"How about Waitrose?"

"No, sorry."

He grunted in disgust. "Then I must make do with London street food, such as rats, pigeons, foxes and perhaps the odd stray Golden Retriever. They are juicy, but their hair sticks between my teeth in the most repugnant way. It is hard to be a king in this jungle."

"I'll leave the back window open for you. The sofa's yours tonight. Everything looks different in the light of day."

The leopard clambered up to all fours and leapt from the sofa. "I hope very much that you'll throw away the kibble by the time I return."

He stalked out towards the back bedroom.

I did what I was told. Then I crawled into bed and slept like a stone.

I ROSE WITH THE BIRDS, wondering if there would still be a leopard on my sofa or whether the previous night could be chalked up to a hallucinogenic episode after all.

The dozen missed calls from Marina suggested I hadn't lost my mind.

EvolveTech had left a voicemail asking where I wanted the courier to deliver my mother's belongings. I rang them to say I'd pick them up myself instead. I wanted to prolong my connection to her, and I was running out of ways in which to do it.

I dressed quickly, rolling over my grandmother's name in my head.

Rajika Verma.

Rajika Verma.

Dad rarely spoke of her, and Sahil and I had learned early on not to prod that painful segment of his past. Her name embedded itself into my consciousness as if it had a power all of its own.

I squeezed myself into my jeans, put on a T-shirt and looked for Echo. My breath caught in my throat as I saw him lying on the sofa, emitting a gentle snore. He must have hunted well because he didn't stir when I padded closer and snapped a couple of pictures of him. I tried to send the pictures to Marina with a reassuring text, but the images came up black like Mum's photographs.

Could it be that the defunct photographs weren't just about Mum? I sent Marina the words anyway and snuck out the door.

An hour later, I was at the EvolveTech reception.

The receptionist gave me a smile of recognition. "Alisha, how lovely to see you again."

"I'm here to pick up my mother's things."

"Of course. Please take a seat in the lobby. I won't keep you a minute."

I made my way to an empty sofa and sank into it.

A man opposite put down his newspaper. "Ms Verma."

"Sorry. Do we know each other?"

He had an easy smile and an angular face with a sprinkling of stubble. His slight paunch suggested he was in his late forties. "I'm Detective Jameson. We spoke on the telephone."

"Of course. I remember. Are you here on police business?"

"I have an appointment with the CEO to discuss your mother's case."

"You don't still think my mother's death was suspicious?"

"I take it you don't read the papers."

I pulled a face. "I tend to avoid the news. I've noticed it never puts me in a better mood."

"Well, your mother is not the only scientist to die of late. There have been two more accidental deaths this past week. They were killed using hospital equipment they had used hundreds of times before." He rubbed his hand over his buzz cut. Dark shadows sat underneath clear, brown eyes. "I haven't been assigned to the cases—budget cuts—but my instincts tell me they spell trouble. I'll get to the bottom of it." He rolled up the newspaper and swatted his palm, deep in thought. "You want to know what's really strange? The flower I mentioned growing from your mum's car, the Gallic rose—"

"That was Mum's favourite flower." My pulse sped up.

His eyes snapped to my face. "Now that's interesting. There were enough Gallic roses in there to fill a botanical garden. No shops within a thirty-mile radius stocked as many of that specimen, and your parents' bank accounts show no equivalent purchases. It's a conundrum." He searched my face. "I will find out if your mother had something to hide."

I held his gaze, worried he'd suss out our secrets like a human lie detector. I hadn't processed the fact I had swapped my husband for a talking leopard as a roomie, let alone the alien flowers. There was no way I'd be sharing anything until I figured out what was going on. I wasn't a little girl in pigtails anymore. I had a bellyful of experience that told me that, without a solid explanation for the weird stuff in my life, I'd be laughed at, brushed aside or referred to the doctor for antidepressants.

A click of heels across the lobby floor saved me from having to answer.

The receptionist hurried over, a small cardboard box in her hands. "Here you go, Alisha. I've reinforced the bottom of the box with tape so it stays intact on your way home. Please do come and visit us when Rosalie's memorial bench has been placed."

"Thank you." I got to my feet and tucked the box under my arm, desperate to look inside, to find some remnant of my mother—a strand of hair, her scent, lipstick on her mug.

Detective Jameson pointed to the box. "It'd be very helpful if I could...may I?"

"Afraid not. Family first." I kept my voice breezy. "But I'll let you know if I find anything, shall I?"

6

———————

I held my breath until the revolving door ejected me out on the pavement, half expecting Detective Jameson to grab my shoulder and insist on looking through Mum's belongings. Men didn't always listen when women said no.

When he didn't follow me, I skirted the building to access the EvolveTech gardens. Great oaks, Lombardy poplars and weeping willows dotted the green, interspersed with weathered wooden benches and triangular flowerbeds past their prime. The gardens had become public access some years previously as part of a goodwill gesture to the local community. It was a haven where Mum had spent many lunchtimes, shielded from the heavy traffic just yards away, and where commuters came for respite during the work day.

As I rounded the corner, I caught sight of Melissa, who had spoken at the memorial.

"Yoohoo," she called, setting down a copy of *Riders* and breaking into a warm smile.

"Hi, Melissa." I hadn't expected her to be a Jilly Cooper reader; turned out she was racier than I thought. I joined her on the bench and set the box at my feet.

"Just sneakily finishing a chapter before I get pulled into the fray."

She patted my knee. "How are you getting on? You picked up Rosalie's things?"

"Anything to keep busy. I'm fine, though."

"It's good to see you. You left the memorial so quickly."

"Sorry about that. I'm glad to bump into you. I've been meaning to ask: how did Mum seem to you in those last days?"

"Oh, you know her. Always busy, always working away at knotty problems." Melissa scanned my face. "She mentioned your fight. She said her words came out the wrong way, and she'd make it up to you."

I blinked back tears. "I wish I hadn't stormed off. She was okay at work, then, in those last days?"

The lines around her eyes deepened. "Now you mention it, she was uncommonly secretive about what she was working on. We usually shared our excitement and frustrations about projects, but this time she just gave me some spiel about needing to be ready. As far as I know, she wasn't up against any deadlines." She shook her head, brushing aside the thoughts like cobwebs. "In any case, what does it matter now?"

So Gaia had been right. Mum had been working on a personal project.

"I must get to work. It was so wonderful to see you, Alisha. Don't be a stranger." Melissa walked towards the front entrance, rummaging in her bag as she went.

She didn't see the man on the ladder working a few metres away. There was no danger sign and no high-vis jacket to alert her. He wasn't wearing a helmet or protective gloves. He didn't call out a warning.

Not even when the cable came loose and sparked above her.

Not even when it fell in her direction.

"Move out of the way!" I held up my hands, though I was too far to help.

Melissa spun around in my direction, a quizzical expression on her face.

I darted towards her, pointing.

A sudden gust of wind carried the sparking cable over her, missing her by a hair's breadth. It sliced Melissa's bag and landed at her feet just as a passer-by grabbed her by the wrist and jolted her out of harm's way.

Her bag dropped to the floor as she slammed against the passer-by's chest.

Fear swept across Melissa's face. She swooped down for her bag, chastising the man.

Only then did she notice parts of it had disintegrated. Her singed copy of *Riders* spilt onto the pavement, charred beyond use.

The sparking cable lay just beyond.

Melissa's eyes widened in shock as she absorbed what had happened. "Oh…oh my goodness. Did that cable just drop from the heavens? Did you pull me out of harm's way?"

"You must have the luck of the leprechauns on your side," the man drawled. He looked familiar. Grey eyes, square jaw. Where had I seen him before?

"This man saved your life." I looked around for the electrician. The idiot could have killed her.

His abandoned ladder wobbled in the breeze. He must have scarpered when he realised what had happened. Accidents happen, but he could have at least made it safe for the public. What a tool.

Melissa scooped up her things with jittery fingers.

"Don't touch the cable." I ushered her away from it with gentle hands. "It's probably still live. I'll wait here to make sure no one touches it. Could you tell reception what's happened? They'll have to cordon off this area and get onto the electricity company. Make sure you get a cup of tea and load up on the sugar. That was quite a shock."

"Yes, yes, of course. Thank you." She cast one last look at her saviour and hurried into the building.

I turned to Melissa's rescuer at last. "I know you. You handed me my dropped keys a few nights ago. You seem to have a knack for turning up when the moment requires it. Thank God you whisked her out of the way."

"Don't mention it. I'm glad the lady is safe." His voice was deep and had a slight rasp.

Just perfect for pillow talk.

My stomach fluttered. It seemed like a lifetime since I'd been hyperaware of a man, but my body was definitely saying yes to this one. I hadn't looked at another man that way while I was with Alex, not even while we were dating. I took promises of fidelity seriously, and however relieved I was not to have to deal with Alex anymore, I'd been heartbroken to break my marriage vow.

Till death do us part.

But there were upsides to everything.

"I'm Alisha," I said, pulling my ponytail over my shoulder, a flirting tactic from my university days. What on earth was I doing?

He leaned against the side of the building and lit a cigarette. "I'm Ezra."

I tore my eyes away from his soft lips and the smattering of stubble across his chiselled jaw. He was over a foot taller than me, with a lithe body and broad shoulders. His long brown hair, greying at the temples, flopped into calm, clear eyes. It was tousled and a little grubby, like he'd just spent the day on a building site. He wore low-slung jeans with a thin sweatshirt and a silver chain with charms suspended from it. I read quiet confidence in his grey eyes. This wasn't a man who had to try hard to stand out. Judging from how he'd leapt in to save the day and the energy coiled into even his resting stance against the wall, this man was as capable as he was dangerous.

"Melissa would have been fried chicken without you here," I said, but my tongue tangled, and it came out as, "Melissa would heat fried chicken here."

He raised a puzzled eyebrow and blew out a ring of smoke just as Detective Jameson and EvolveTech staff hurried out to secure the electricity cable.

"Nice to meet you, Alisha," Ezra said. "I'll be seeing you."

I considered giving him my number but decided not to be a hussy until I'd written a list of pros and cons for inviting a man into my life again. He would say no anyway. No way that hot stuff was in my age bracket, let alone my league.

He ambled down the street, and I hurried to retrieve Mum's box from the gardens before I provoked a bomb scare.

I stopped off on Balham High Road on my way home. Balham might not have been central London, but it had everything I needed within a few square miles: leafy parks, the tube, supermarkets, pubs, independent shops, eclectic restaurants, supermarkets, a library and charity shops where I rummaged for pre-loved clothes.

First, I popped into the fishmonger's for salmon, then headed towards the butcher's for rare steaks since Echo had turned his nose up at kibble, and I didn't want dead dogs on my conscience. It was a win-win situation, despite the expense. I figured a well-fed big cat was less likely to turn on me.

The door jangled as I entered the shop and made for the counter. I wrinkled my nose at the overwhelming smell of meat. The butcher took my order and loaded the steaks on his chopping board before slicing them with a sharp blade and deft hands.

"Having a party?" he said.

I took out my wallet. "A party for one. Not for me, actually."

"Lucky fella."

"You could say that."

Back at the flat, I kept a few slabs of meat in the fridge and stuffed the rest into the freezer.

A thud behind me alerted me to Echo's presence. He followed his nose into the kitchen, purring in anticipation. "Where have you been all morning?"

"Just you wait." I avoided him as I put a few choice pieces in his dish, not quite ready to brush up against a leopard yet.

He sniffed the meat and dove right in, swallowing it as easily as a child eating ice cream. "Now I know why they call London a city of food connoisseurs. Never before have I tasted such finery."

I made myself a cup of tea and sat at the kitchen table with Mum's box in front of me. Knife in hand, I sliced the gaffer tap holding the box shut down the middle. Inside, I found Mum's leather-bound appointments diary, a photograph of me and Sahil, a fluffy pencil case with her favourite pens, a cardigan, a book, a chipped mug and a pair of sensible, black heels that she'd sometimes changed into for meetings.

I buried my nose in the cardigan. The scent of her Estée Lauder perfume—white lilies, rain and leaves—made my breath catch in my throat. I reached into the box again and found it empty.

I wanted more. More clues and more of her.

I leafed through Mum's calendar, looking for something to jump out at me that she could no longer tell me herself. Nothing but team meetings, project deadlines, lunch appointments with Melissa and the odd optometrist and doctor's check-ups, together with our family birthdays. I shouldn't have expected anything else. She hadn't been the sort to write her feelings down or to write poetry.

Echo padded over, too close for comfort, his breath hot on my neck.

"Keep your distance, will you?" I said. "I can't concentrate with you so close. This side of you takes a bit of getting used to."

"That's gratitude for you." He swung around, his rump close to my nose, then headed for the living room with his tail swaying in anger.

I was considering whether more steak would soothe Echo's hissy fit when the doorbell buzzed.

Marina's grainy image came up on the intercom. "Only me."

I buzzed her in, left the flat door open and returned to my seat.

She tumbled into the kitchen, still in her work scrubs. "Where's Echo?"

"Sulking in the living room."

Marina took in my face and Mum's belongings in front of me and gave me a hug. Then we caught up on our respective days. Having her as my best friend surpassed having a husband. Alex's concept of conversation had been waiting for his turn to speak. He'd forgotten how to listen within a year of marriage. I might as well have been having pillow talk with a lamp post.

"This knight in shining armour sounds like a worthy notch on your bedpost." For Marina, sex wasn't about relationships. She didn't overthink the act or where it might lead. Enjoyment came first as long as everyone had the same expectations. Anything else was a happy bonus.

"More like a knight in worn denim. I couldn't believe the electrician scarpered. Shame I couldn't put in a complaint at his company."

"Shame you didn't get Ezra's number." She reached for the book. "What's this?"

It was a hardback with the image of a plant on it, with swirly black lettering that read *The Rose of Jericho*. "Oh, I don't know. You know what Mum was like with gardening. It was probably her latest craze."

Marina flicked through it and frowned at the stamp on the internal page. "Hmm. That's odd. It's from somewhere called the Celestial Library. Never heard of it, and I know all the libraries within a stone's throw of here. Let's run an internet search."

Marina spent so much time watching over animals post-surgery that she was a whale reader—she'd been known to tear through the catalogues of all the libraries in a thirty-mile radius of her surgery. She petitioned for new books enough that most local librarians knew her by name. There were fewer brick-and-mortar libraries in London these days, but it was still impressive.

She pulled out her phone and typed into the search box with chewed fingernails. "Now that's strange too. No hits on the ISBN either."

I peered across at her phone. "That's strange. No location or online catalogue? Not even a telephone number to ring?"

"Nope."

"Did you type it in wrong?"

Marina rolled her eyes and continued scrolling. "Hold on. There are a couple of obscure mentions on an online forum for spiritualists."

I grabbed her hand. "What if our reality isn't true? Talking animals. Disappearing photographs. A mysterious library. Do we really want to find out?"

"You mean, like *The Matrix*?"

"I guess. Wouldn't you rather this all goes away?"

"Hell, no." She grinned. "Especially if I can have a nibble of Keanu

Reeves. I don't want to live a lie. The world's never been black or white. If we've uncovered something here, we have a duty to throw ourselves into it. What does *your* gut tell you?"

I bit my lip. "That there's more to Mum's death than meets the eye. That I owe it to her and myself to dig deeper. But I'm scared I'll find out things I don't want to know. We should have everything sussed by now. We're not teenagers anymore."

"Thank goodness for that. I couldn't deal with pimples as well as droopy boobs."

"I don't know if I can take a whole life-aligning event right now."

"Girl, after Alex, I think that's exactly what you need."

I stood up. "Echo?"

He didn't come.

"Echo?"

A growl and a thud, followed by his beautiful head appearing in the kitchen doorway. "You call me like a dog. Next time, I will pay as little heed to you as I would a skunk."

I stroked his neck. "My apologies."

Echo lifted his head proudly. "If you had included me sooner, I would have saved your meandering angst. I tell you, I am a leopard in service to your family line, and you are still treating me like a domestic companion. You will have to learn faster than this if you are to become a druid of any standing, Alisha Verma."

"You heard us?"

"My hearing is five times as good as yours, perhaps ten. I heard it all. I would also like a nibble of Keanu Reeves, Marina Ambrose. You must save me some delicious morsels."

Marina gawped.

"Echo, was my mother's death an accident?"

He growled, displaying his jagged teeth in all their glory. "Of that, I cannot be sure, but if Rosalie has a book from the Celestial Library, it's fair to say she was mixed up in peculiar matters."

"Can you tell me why I couldn't take a photograph of you this morning and why Mum's photographs are disappearing?"

"Did your father teach you nothing? Did you never wonder why there are no photographs of your grandmother?"

I shook my head. I'd just figured that generation didn't have the means or technology to take endless photographs.

Echo sighed. "The vanishing photographs are the work of the Sorcerer's Senate, which governs this country's peculiars. The Founder's Law states that peculiars must hide the existence of the Otherworld from humdrums and re-establish secrecy upon accidental arousal of suspicion. A consequence of the Founder's Law is that photographs of peculiars involved in acts of magic in the humdrum sphere disappear if there is a risk of discovery. In cases of great magic, a whole lifetime of photographs can be destroyed. Call it magical programming. Or magical control. Either way, it's a way peculiars remain hidden from discovery."

A whole lifetime of photographs. I swallowed the lump in my throat. "How can I unravel this all? How can I get her justice?"

He inclined his head. "I may be more than a Bengal cat, but I am only a leopard."

My head spun. I needed to lock myself in my bedroom and unravel this all. "And where can we find this Celestial Library?"

"That, I do not know. The Celestial Library exists between the folds of reality, sometimes there and sometimes not. It houses the most powerful books and artefacts in the Otherworld, and only the Custodian always knows its location. Even those that find their way there cannot retrace their steps. I have been there only once, at your grandmother's command, and that, only because she was the Custodian."

"Well, I guess there's nothing for it but to pop into Shanghai Moon tomorrow and ask Fei Yen and Faeza if they know anything about it. They're bound to know with all that tarot, voodoo stuff they're into."

Marina gave me a sweet smile. "Can you pick me up some Longjing green tea and oolong while you're there?"

7

I'd been avoiding seeing Dad, but I needed answers. The way to get them was to see him alone, face to face, so I could tell if he was lying. I knew where he'd be. He'd been there every morning since her death.

He'd think twice before telling a lie there.

I slipped on a hoodie and jeans, then hopped on a bus towards Streatham Cemetery. The bus lurched over potholes as it chugged along, narrowly missing heavy tree canopies lining its route. I leapt off at my destination and slipped in through the main gates. The cemetery was Victorian era, with two ornate chapels and rich grassland dotted with wildflowers. It was home to graves of fallen soldiers and a war memorial and would have been a sea of tranquillity had my heart not been beating clean out of my chest at the thought of confronting Dad. I used my yoga breath to calm my nerves. Ambushing Dad wouldn't get me anywhere. He'd just clam up.

I followed the path past daffodils that had sprung up in the spring sunshine. On my right, I passed graves buried in ivy and shadowed by six-foot winged angels.

Tears welled in my eyes at the sight of Dad hunched over Mum's fresh grave; a watering can at his side. He held a spade and cuttings I recognised from their garden, a mix of pink roses and orange chrysanthemums. He dug into the topsoil and pushed the cuttings deep before refilling the earth.

I laid a hand on his shoulder and breathed in the scent of him, musky apricot soap and the sharp tang of acrylic paint, and my anger faded a notch. "Dad."

Dishevelled white hair and a twirly, white moustache over still, dark eyes. He turned and smiled. "Hi, Alisha. Perfect timing. Water these, will you?" He handed me the watering can.

I watered the plants as he compressed the soil, then joined him kneeling at the graveside.

His fingers, usually stained with paint, carried no colour. I hoped Mum's death hadn't blocked him—he'd die without his art—but it seemed too cruel to question him now. Instead, we worked together as the sunrays warmed our backs.

We'd chosen a simple, oval headstone in green slate upon a stone base. The inscription read:

In loving memory of
Rosalie Verma
1952-2021
Wife, mother, scientist
She rests where no shadows fall.

I squeezed Dad's arm. "It's beautiful."

"I wanted to give her the world."

"You did."

"She was my world."

"I know," I said. "I picked up some of her things from EvolveTech yesterday."

"You did?"

"I wanted to save you the trouble."

"Did she leave anything for us? A letter, maybe?" The hope in his voice was almost my undoing.

"No, I'm sorry."

His face clouded in disappointment. "We didn't have a goodbye."

I hesitated. "I need to ask you something. About Echo."

He searched my face and stood, trying to edge away.

I grabbed his arm. "No, we do this here. You won't lie here. Not in front of Mum."

"Don't ask me to unlock this Pandora's Box, Alisha. I won't do it. I won't make that decision without your mother."

I shook my head. "How can that be fair? She's gone. And you're saying you'll withhold *our* heritage. Well, it doesn't just belong to you. It belongs to me too, and I want to know. Is what Echo said true?"

"Damn that cat. He had no right. Stubborn creature. He detests this isle. He should have returned to his beloved India."

I exhaled. He wouldn't talk about a domestic cat like that. My pulse thrummed like a hummingbird's wings. "So it's true? You lied all this time. You even lied about the vanishing photographs. How is that okay? You must have known what that meant. What if all the pictures of Mum disappear? What if we can't look at her again?"

Tears rolled down his face. "We can't change the past. We can only try to live with it. Why do you think I did what I did? As long as I had the three of you and my painting, I could live with everything else. Rosalie and I wanted you and Sahil to live a normal life. To have simple joys. We thought when your mother chose science that you would be safe. We filled the house with scientific texts and cut the Otherworld from our lives. It's tricky for magic and science to coexist. They vie for dominance and suppress each other. We thought it'd be enough, but that midsummer's eve when you were four..." He shuddered.

I needed to hear it. "What did you do, Dad?"

"I didn't have a choice."

"Tell me what you did."

"I arranged for someone to bind your magic. Except I can feel the magic returning to our lives now that Rosalie is dead, and I'm terrified. I'm terrified for us all. I can't lose you."

"Dad, you'll never lose me. I'll always be here for you, but I'm angry right now. I can't help it. I want to understand this part of myself. Will you help me?"

His eyes filled with sorrow. "You don't know what you're asking.

This isn't just about you. You know nothing about the Otherworld. You don't know the rules or the factions. You don't know the sacrifices or the demands. And you don't know how to survive. Magic has this habit of spilling over boundaries. Your choices impact us all."

"Then teach me. Please, Dad."

"How can you ask this of me? Magic took your grandmother. It made our choices more difficult. I don't know if I can help you. I don't know if I can."

"Will you think about it at least?"

He nodded, then turned back to Mum's grave.

I left him there, picking stones out of the soil, trying his darnedest to make her resting place beautiful.

A few rows farther, I turned back to check on him, a painful tightness in my throat. I hated hurting him, but I needed the truth. I was my mother's daughter, after all. Secrets set me off like a bloodhound, and facts were too important to bury. They needed to be examined and prodded in the cold light of day. Lives built on lies couldn't ever be rewarding.

"Tough losing someone," said a male voice behind me.

I turned to find an elderly gravedigger leaning on a shovel, skin like worn leather and beads of sweat lining his brow.

"It certainly is."

He rubbed the back of his neck. "Been a fair lot of that recently."

I took in the dozens of graves he'd dug that morning, and the hair on my arms stood on edge. It was definitely time for a wax. "I'm sorry to hear it."

Something skirted the periphery of my vision, a dog or a fox or something.

My imagination went into overdrive, pooling together all the Hans Christian Anderson tales of beasts with claws and teeth and nefarious intentions. While cemeteries were full of stories, they were also creepy.

Watery blue eyes rested on my face. "There's been so many scientists killed this past week. Graves piling up all over London, not just in this neck of the woods, and who knows who's been cremated?"

I gulped and backed away. Maybe I'd be giving Detective Jameson a call after all. Things were looking decidedly too serious for me to handle alone.

ECHO and I spent hours scouring the internet and found multiple reports of scientist deaths. I fell off my chair when I discovered he could read, and he ticked me off *again* for not acknowledging his nobility. Later that night, I headed to my local police station. I could have called, but I wanted to look Detective Jameson in the eyes when I asked him whether the deaths were connected to Mum's.

Echo insisted on accompanying me as far as the entrance, although I wasn't in the mood to test his glamour theory. Sure enough, no one batted an eye when a leopard padded through the streets of London beside me. Turned out all they saw was a Bengal after all. I just hoped no one would try to stroke him.

I couldn't get my head around how the physics of it worked. Echo the leopard was ten times larger than Echo the cat. And Echo the leopard was much less reliable. One false move and this kitty cat would release his inner hunter.

"Stay here," I hissed, shoving his rump into a nearby hedge.

He grunted but did as he was told.

My boots clipped against the dull concrete floor as I walked to the front desk. The policeman there didn't seem very bright or very gentlemanly. He looked me up and down at a leisurely pace, taking in the curves underneath my sweater.

I held his gaze and raised an eyebrow, my fists itching to punch him in the nose.

That wasn't the sort of thing you did at a police station without getting arrested, even if the bloke was a douche. Besides, I'd already hit one police officer that week.

"I'd like to talk to Detective Robert Jameson, please."

He scratched his nose and then scrolled through a database, squinting at his computer screen. A plop of brown sauce marred the front of his jumper like he'd missed his mouth during lunch. "Jameson, you say? Detective Robert Jameson? J-A-M-E-S-O-N."

"He's assigned to my mother's case: Rosalie Verma."

"Well, who do you want me to look up? Jameson or Verma?"

I took a deep breath to stop myself from swatting him. "Jameson, please."

"What's his badge number?"

"How am I supposed to know?"

"No need to get agitated, miss. A little politeness never cost anyone a thing. I'll just locate him on our system." He peered over the top of his computer. "No one by the name of Detective Robert Jameson here. Are you sure that was his name?"

I swallowed the urge to throw something at him and smiled sweetly. "Are you sure you spelt it correctly? Maybe I should type it?"

"Don't be ridiculous. A non-police officer can't use police equipment. That's against the rules." He sighed. "I'm afraid there's no one by the name of Robert Jameson in the Metropolitan Police Force. Why don't you tell me how I can help?"

My annoyance fizzed. "You can help by telling me who's been investigating my mother's death and masquerading as a police officer."

He shrugged as if he didn't have a care in the world. "Impersonating a police officer is a serious offence. I highly doubt that happened. But who knows? It could have been someone having a laugh. Kids these days. I tell you what. You see him again, you call the non-emergency number and file a report."

Then he turned back to the keyboard, humming in a low key while using his forefingers to type.

I made for the exit. "Thanks for nothing."

On the ramp outside the station, I closed my eyes under the night sky and wondered whether to hang around for another officer with more than wool between his ears.

A low whistle sounded by my ear. "You've gone and done it now."

I remembered that voice and swallowed the glee that bubbled in my throat. "Hi, Ezra. Small world."

He raked his hand through dark hair interspersed with copper. "You shouldn't have done that. They're going to be furious. You want the whole of the Metropolitan Police on your arse? Come with me."

My hackles rose. Bloody men, telling me what to do. "Er, no."

"Suit yourself." He rolled his shoulders, and the muscles across his chest rippled under his T-shirt. His strong arms reminded me of a gymnast's. Dammit, he was handsome. "Don't say I didn't warn you."

"I've had enough of warnings. I'll make my own mind up, thank you very much."

The street lamps flickered. Echo emerged from the hedge, his gait slow and exact like he was stalking prey.

"Whoa, tiger," said Ezra, bowing. "Pleased to make your acquaintance."

"Now you've done it," I muttered. "Wait. You see him too?"

"You know full well I'm a leopard," Echo growled. "Ignore this dog, Alisha. He can never be your friend."

Ezra held out his hand to me. "Isn't it time you stop dancing around the truth, Alisha? You've been looking for it, I know, and for someone who has lived forty years as a humdrum, you've impressed me. You have natural talents."

"She knows she's a druid," said Echo. "And she doesn't need you because she has me."

"Not just any druid." Ezra's hand hovered in the air. "The last of an ancient magical druid lineage."

I laughed out loud, but I was intrigued. I couldn't help it. It still sounded so ridiculous, but I could listen to Ezra's voice all day.

Echo bared his teeth. "I know my history, dog."

Ezra ignored him, which was pretty impressive, given a leopard is hard to ignore.

"Just think what you are capable of. You thought I saved that woman yesterday, Alisha, but it was you who used your magic to propel the cable away. I saw it with my own eyes. Trust me." His eyes sparkled with warmth.

I looked from one to the other, ignoring the flickering street lamps and the heartbeat that thudded clean out of my chest.

Didn't I owe it to Mum to take this step? The Otherworld was involved in her death. Hadn't Echo said as much? I wanted to find out how. The only detective on the case wasn't even on the books, so what the hell was going on? I was tired of going in circles. This way, I didn't have to wait for Dad to decide. If I trusted a talking cat, why shouldn't I trust this mysterious man?

Besides, I wanted to believe there was more to life than a messy divorce and a nosediving career. I wanted to believe the secrets in my life could be unravelled.

Echo padded closer. "You're not going to follow this dog to the Otherworld, are you? You aren't ready."

"Ezra, have you heard of the Celestial Library?" I asked.

His eyes lit up. "Of course."

This couldn't be an elaborate hoax. This was real.

I put my hand in his. "Where are you taking me?"

He smiled down at me. His warm fingers folded around it. "To Crystal Palace Park, of course."

I nodded. I'd been there plenty of times in my childhood. It was just another South London park. This wasn't crazy at all.

Shivers of excitement shot up my spine.

It was time for an adventure. To draw a line under the past and find a new me.

"Stop," growled Echo.

"Take a deep breath," said Ezra's deep voice.

"Tell Marina where I am," I said as the ground disappeared from under my feet. "And Echo? There's steak in the fridge."

8

———————

The world spun until it blurred around me in swirls of black and technicolour and patterns that threatened to break my mind. When I could take no more, I closed my eyes and focussed on the sensation of Ezra gripping my hand, holding on for dear life. Then suddenly, it was over, and we were spat out in another corner of South London, on the grassy bank that enclosed Crystal Palace pond.

Ezra released my hand, and I fell onto my hands and knees into the strands of grass while the world stopped spinning.

"You'll be okay," said Ezra, his hand on my back. "Teleporting is hard the first time."

I coughed up phlegm and then wiped my mouth with the back of my hand. That was attractive. "How did you do that?"

He sat down in the grass next to me while I caught my breath. "Long story."

"What are you waiting for?"

"You first," he said. "When did you find out your cat was actually a leopard?"

"A few nights ago."

"That must have been hard."

Leaning against that chest of his would have taken the edge off it.

"Tell me about it. Your turn. Can you teleport to other planets or realms? Like Mars or Middle-earth or Asgard?"

He laughed. "You do know that Middle-earth is fictional and Asgard was destroyed, right? And the answer is no. I can teleport across London easily. I could teleport to Manchester pretty easily. But further afield is tougher. Teleporting to Canada, for example, would wipe me out for a few days."

"Shame."

"Tell me about it."

"Are you going to tell me who you are? Because normal dudes can't teleport. At least, not that I know of."

"You're going to find out soon enough, so I might as well tell it straight," said Ezra. "It'll be like peeling off a plaster. I'll do it quick and let it sink in. Just do me a favour."

"What?"

"Don't scream."

Dammit. I was starting to regret leaving the safety of the police station and coming to a park at night with a strange man without my leopard protection. At least the ground had stopped swaying. I shifted my bum to put a few more inches between us and give myself more reaction space if I had to defend myself. My hand found the keys in my left pocket. If in doubt, I'd shove the Yale into his eye. A makeshift weapon was better than no weapon at all.

"I'm half werewolf, half wizard."

My mouth fell open. "Excuse me?"

He pointed to his chest as if I couldn't keep up. Like Tarzan explaining something to Jane. "Me. Half werewolf. Half wizard. Well, a full werewolf, as it were, and a pretty pathetic wizard, but my charms help."

He jingled his chain to underline his point, just in case I was dim.

I shut my mouth in case any night critters crept inside and then opened it again. "Okay."

"Okay? Okay, you get it, and it doesn't surprise you? Or okay, werewolves and wizards are up there with the Tooth Fairy, Easter Bunny and Santa."

"My man, Santa is real. Do not get me started."

Was I flirting again? I pinched myself hard on the leg, just to make sure I wasn't dreaming.

Nope. All present and awake.

I squinted at his charms in the dark: a moon, a thistle and what looked like a 0-1 hung from the chain, all silver in colour and smaller than the pad of my thumb. "So you're telling me you're a werewolf, and the charms on your necklace allowed us to teleport across South London?"

"Not quite. My ancestors, werewolves in my paternal line, are responsible for my portal magic, not the charms."

"Oh, that's much more sensible." I rolled my eyes. "And what do the charms do?"

"I don't share those secrets unless I must, and much as I like you, I don't know you, Alisha Verma."

"You know my full name. It's more than I know about you."

His laugh reverberated in my ear. "Touché. Ezra Neuhoff, at your service. One more question. Then we have to go. The night is never as innocent as it looks, especially under a full moon."

I looked up and froze in fear at the sight of the full moon in the clear sky. If werewolves were real, didn't they change under a full moon? I gripped the keys in my hand even tighter, weighing how fast a wolf could run and how quickly it could change. My eyes struggled in the dark to assess if the man in front of me was actually a beast of nightmarish proportions.

Ezra glanced at me. "I can smell your fear, but you have nothing to worry about. A werewolf as old as me changes on command. The full moon has no power apart from heightening the call of the pack and the need to run on four legs. You are safer with me than in your own bed, Alisha."

I released my pent-up breath. How old could he be with a body like that? "You said I could ask one more question."

He sighed. "I did."

"How did you find me tonight? It wasn't an accident running into you outside the police station, was it?"

The smile in his voice sent shivers up my spine. "Clever, beautiful and brave. This is turning into a very interesting assignment indeed."

"Assignment?"

"I'm a seeker, Alisha. I seek out new peculiars for the Sorcerer's Senate. I track them, log them, and if the conditions are right, I introduce them to the Otherworld. My wolf form gives me a great tracking advantage. I've been following you since your mother's death. It's been decades since I've tracked a new peculiar who discovered their powers at such an advanced age."

"Charming."

"Are you ready to meet the senate, Alisha?"

I gulped.

He stood up and dusted off his jeans. "Because they are ready to meet you."

"Now?"

He nodded and held out a hand to hoist me up. When he pulled me to my feet, the warmth from his grip transferred to my hand. "This way."

I should have known better than to follow a strange man into a park at night, but I did it anyway. I didn't understand why I felt safe with Ezra or why my curiosity counted for more than my safety at that moment.

Only, I'd always recognised the chasm in myself. Yes, I wanted to find out what had happened to Mum. But it was more than that. Perhaps this was the missing puzzle piece. Perhaps this was how I could be happy. Not by throwing myself into a marriage that showed cracks as soon as Alex slid the ring onto my finger. Not by wondering if I should try to have a child before it was too late. Not by making everything about my students or my dad or my damn leopard cat. Although he was rock-star cool.

Maybe, just maybe, this was me claiming my future.

Maybe forty wasn't old. Maybe it was the beginning—the prime of my life.

If I ignored the first sprinkling of greys, the deeper lines and my need to wee more often.

We walked into the park I knew well from my childhood days, frolicking amongst the dinosaur models with my brother. The night wrapped its thick curtain around us as we passed the maze, the concert bowl, the Italian terraces and the sphinx statues. Just when I thought we might hit the farthest boundary of the park and it had all been a hoax, the scent of mulch and bark and damp lawn deepened, and a vast forest opened up in front of us.

I stopped mid-stride, staring at the ancient trees. "Why have I never seen this before?"

Ezra smiled like sunshine painted onto a blank canvas. "You have true sight now. You'll have to take it easy. Try not to overthink it. It's rare, but sometimes when a peculiar comes late to their gift, their brain can't cope with the realignment of reality."

"Are you telling me this might melt my brain?" I spluttered in disbelief, which turned into a coughing fit.

Ezra thudded my back so hard I feared for my ribcage. "No need to worry about brain-melting if you play it right," he said once I'd caught my breath. "You'll need to approach it like swimming in a fast current. Keep your head above water, but try not to fight it. Trust you will find your rhythm."

We continued in silence until he located a yew tree with a strange symbol carved into its gnarled bark. He placed his hand on the symbol and stepped back.

An eerie glow preceded a vibration in the ground like the rub of tectonic plates.

I grabbed Ezra's forearm to steady myself.

He grinned, and I kicked myself for not choosing a tree to lean on instead.

I blinked rapidly. Instead of an expanse of moonlit sky, a group of buildings stood before us as if they had always been there. "Wow," I said. "That is some reveal. Can you do it again?"

"I never tire of that," said Ezra, his voice as smooth as whiskey. "Welcome to Wildwoods. Come on. They won't wait forever." He put his hand in the small of my back and gave me a firm push in the direction of the buildings.

"Hold on." How was I going to find out what happened to Mum without following her clue? "I thought you were taking me to the Celestial Library."

He shook his head. "I only said I knew of it. Not that I could take you there. No one who wants to live can go to the Celestial Library without the support of the senate. Certainly not an unregistered peculiar. How can you not know that? Wasn't your grandmother a Custodian?"

Why did everyone keep calling my grandmother a Custodian? What did she have in her custody? The skulls of braindead men?

I parked that for another day and pushed back against his attempt to lug me to the strange building. I should have listened to Echo after all. Or at least brought him with me. My self-defence skills were pretty great, but I didn't have the claws and teeth Echo did. I was certain he was stronger and speedier too.

"You're not really suggesting my life might be in danger?" I asked.

"Listen, sweetheart. Magic isn't just for party tricks, not in my world. It's blood and sweat, and sometimes it's dead bodies and running away in the night. It's not too late to turn around. I can arrange another binding spell, and we'll put you right back into your blissful state of ignorance. It's what your dad wants. And that cat of yours would be a lap kitty again. Just say the word." Ezra folded his arms over his chest, giving me a close-up view of his biceps.

Yep, still hot.

I lifted my chin. It was hard staring down a six-foot-something man. I had to make my five-foot-five inches count.

"I'm not your sweetheart. Don't you dare pull the wool over my eyes again. Just stop blindsiding me. I'm a druid of an ancient magical lineage, apparently, and I was born ready." I put up my fists to show I meant it.

He laughed, and I resisted the urge to leap on his back and dunk his face into the puddle. "Fair enough. Come on, hellfire. I'll give you the grand tour."

"Better than sweetheart," I muttered, trailing after him. My ex-husband called me an array of pet names, which I hated, but they were saccharine-sweet. Hellfire, I could just about stomach.

Wildwoods was made up of a series of interconnected treehouses and bridges, built in an ancient woodland I'd mistaken for a dilapidated corner of the park. A gentle light flickered from the buildings, even at this late hour. The only way in or out seemed to be a set of ten cable cars that rose from ground level on a pulley system.

"Wildwoods is many things. It is a school where peculiars learn their art. It's a safe haven for peculiars in need, and it's the seat of the Sorcerer's Senate. Only registered peculiars who have made the blood bond are able to activate the rune on the yew tree. You're with me, though, so you get a free pass."

My stomach fluttered.

"Central to Wildwoods philosophy and, by extension, the Otherworld, is obeying the Magical Constitution. To disobey the constitution is to be an outcast at Wildwoods and to bring the wrath of the senate on your head. I wouldn't advise it." He opened the door to the first cable car, an earthy green that blended in with its environment. "They might feel rickety, but they do the job. Wildwoods has been like this for hundreds of years. The senate likes to keep technology to a minimum here to safeguard the pupils and stop magic from going awry." Ezra winked and pushed his hair out of his eyes. "A pulley system is more reliable than an elevator in an environment like this. After you."

We stepped in, and the cable car shuddered skywards, as if on autopilot, towards a network of buildings nestled in the trees. The air as we rose higher was cleaner than any London air had the right to be, as if the trees formed a barrier to the city smog. I drew in great lungfuls of air filtered by the ancient trees, and calm descended over me. The central oak must have been thousands of years old. It was taller and wider than any tree I'd ever seen.

Ezra pointed to an enormous vaulted cabin with stained-glass windows and a moss-covered roof suspended at the heart of the oak. "That's the seat of the Sorcerer's Senate and doubles as a space for whole school assemblies."

Smaller cabins fanned out around the large vaulted one, connected by rope bridges that swayed in the breeze. Some rested on the boughs of the large oak. Others nestled in their own adjacent trees.

"The pupils learn their magical arts in these stone cabins," said Ezra. "When I was a child here, I didn't have to attend humdrum school, but it's different now. Most peculiars have regular jobs, so most peculiars attend humdrum school and come here in the evenings. The Sorcerer's Senate only gives exceptionally gifted peculiars dispensation to study solely here. Those peculiars are destined for magical jobs."

"Like a seeker? Isn't that what you said you are?"

"Yes, like a seeker. I attended Wildwoods as a child. I never needed a humdrum education. I love it here. The way the outlying cabins sometimes change positions. The way new cabins emerge from the forest for strange purposes. The way the cabins transform with the seasons. We'd come back after the holidays, and they'd be something else entirely—a dungeon, a polar landscape, a summer meadow with scented wildflowers. It never got old. Wildwoods is not just a building. It is a living, breathing organism."

"What's that?" I nodded at a clearing east of the cabins, where an arena reminded me of an old gladiatorial ring, like in history books.

"It's where the pupils train. There are certain skills that can be practised indoors, but for most of them, the safest way to practice is out in the open, testing their skills against each other. Under strict supervision, of course."

I shuddered. "It's magnificent. But you don't expect me to come back to school, do you? I left that behind a long time ago, and to be honest, mean girls and soggy lunches don't really appeal."

He chuckled. "No, afraid there's a different system for late bloomers."

The cable car thudded to a halt, and he shoved it open with his thigh.

"Come," he said, "we're expected at the senate in a few minutes, but I'll show you the library if you like. Where else would I take Rajika Verma's granddaughter?"

My heart skipped a beat. What was it about this man that got under my skin?

I followed him across a rickety rope bridge, thankful for my sensible shoes. Turns out there were endless perks to consigning heels to the back of my wardrobe once I hit my thirties. Keeping up with werewolf wizards was one of them.

The cabin looked ordinary enough from the outside: an arched doorway painted in cobalt blue gave way to a deceptively large internal space packed with cherry-wood shelves that housed endless rows of books. I drank in their scent. Boughs entwined through the walls of the stone structure, and vines wound through the ceiling, forming a skeleton for the room. Desiccated leaves crunched underfoot in hues of deep green and burnt orange.

"I could stay here forever," I said.

His grey eyes lit up. "A girl who reads. I thought they disappeared with the advent of mobile phones."

I wrinkled my nose. "You know all the wrong girls."

A smile played around his lips. "You think?"

Heat pulsed between us. I'd been stuck so long in my loveless marriage that I didn't know this dance anymore. I was pretty sure Marina would have lunged for his lips. All I could think was that suddenly the space seemed too small.

My tongue ran away with itself. "Let's go meet these big, bad sorcerers, shall we? Or senators? I mean, are they wand-wavers or paper-pushers? Do they look like Gandalf? Or Aragorn? Or are they more like Bilbo?"

"Want me to go and fetch you a copy of *Lord of the Rings* you can climb into?" Ezra arched a brow.

"Why would you do that when I've just found out that reality is just as exciting? Don't worry. I know the way. I'm a fast learner. Do try to keep up." I darted past him, ignoring the smile tugging the corners of his mouth, hoping I'd not bitten off more than I could chew.

9

———————

The door to the vaulted cabin—shaped like a railway arch and as heavy as a tombstone—creaked open of its own accord as we approached. Soaring ceilings and limited furnishings gave the room an austere feel. Only the stained-glass windows softened the impact, together with a thousand burning pillar candles. They piled onto window sills and in clusters in the corners of the room, on china plates and candelabras. A ball of light hovered above two semi-circular stone tables, split apart like a pizza missing a slice.

There sat people of varying bearings and fashion choices.

Nine faces turned to inspect us as the doors clunked shut, and I stifled a scream in my throat. It wasn't the Rocky Horror Picture Show, but it was close. I was almost certain I spotted pointy ears, deathly pale skin and fangs. One woman wore a plant twisted around her as an adornment, and a tiny man had a grotesque, overgrown wart on his cheek with a hair poking out of it. It was going to take all my powers of restraint not to take my tweezers to his face.

Ezra tugged me towards him, and his deep raspy tones melted into my ear. "Speak only when you are spoken to. Don't volunteer information. Try to relax. You want to give the impression of being a predator, not prey."

Well, this was going to be easy. This lot looked so creepy I doubted I'd be making it home tonight. That meant more Golden Retrievers on my conscience once Echo worked his way through the meat in my freezer. Unless I could turn this place into a massive fireball using the surplus candles and then dropkick my way through a stained-glass window. My life was worth more than the guilt I'd feel smashing something pretty.

The senate stood. I counted six men and three women, although it was difficult to tell with one glance.

I considered jumping into Ezra's arms and telling him to teleport us the hell out of here. He seemed to be leading me to an imaginary spot closer to the weirdos. I wasn't walking into the gap between the tables and having it squeeze me shut in a pincer movement. No way. I stopped short a few metres away.

Ezra frowned and backtracked to my side.

"It has been a long time since we had a Verma in these hallowed walls," said a tall, bearded man with midnight skin. "I thank you, Ezra Neuhoff, and I bid you welcome, granddaughter of Rajika Verma. Welcome to Wildwoods School of the Wondrous."

I bowed my head and put my hands together in a namaste mudra like in yoga class. The occasion seemed to warrant it. "It's Alisha, thank you. I only figured out Rajika was a big deal a few days ago, and I don't have much of a connection with her yet."

Ezra kicked me. So much for not volunteering information. Oops.

"I'm Phinnaeous Shine, Prime Sorcerer of the Senate." His silver-streaked cloud of hair complemented his robes and gave him the look of someone who had long figured out who he was and didn't need to pretend anymore. "Your grandmother was a great friend of mine."

"I am Orpheus Might, Minister for History and the Today. I, too, welcome you to Wildwoods," said the man with the ghostly white skin and a too-still demeanour. "However, I'd rather you didn't destroy Wildwoods property. I rather like those stained-glass windows."

"Vampires can read minds," Ezra mumbled. "I should have warned you."

I scowled at him.

Phinnaeous sat, and the others followed his lead. "You will learn our names and ways soon enough, granddaughter of Rajika. We are nine, but we each represent many more: shapeshifters, elves, angels, werewolves, vampires, fairies, witches, leprechauns and druids, of course."

"Fuck me." I laughed nervously. My gaze darted across their faces, trying to discern whether this was some elaborate hoax after all and they were making a fool of me with special effects or drugs or something.

Phinnaeous sighed. "Language, please, lest those with tender ears are offended. In the Otherworld, words are more than tools of a sharp tongue or noisy mind. More even than tools of diplomacy and beauty or forgiveness and solace. Here, they are a force of creation and destruction by the spells that leave our mouths."

I bit my lip. I wasn't an English teacher for nothing. I loved the power of them on my tongue and their echo in my head. I knew how their impact lingered and how the right words said at the right time could change the world. I also knew that swearing was a good stress reliever, and hell, I'd just learned that fairy tales were real, so I think he could cut me some slack.

Orpheus, the vampire, was a hunk if you liked your men brooding —longish black hair, a Roman nose, stern lips and heavy brows to match his goatee. He sighed heavily and rolled his hand in the universal sign known to mean the Prime Sorcerer should just get on with it.

"As I was saying," said Phinnaeous, "some of us have held these seats for centuries. Others have taken the place of fallen comrades. All of us remember what it was like to learn our arts for the first time. Let Wildwoods be the safe space for you that it was for us. Let the Otherworld find a faithful servant in you."

Meh. I wasn't sure about the servant stuff. That sounded suspiciously like unpaid work, and I'd done plenty of that as a wife. I was more interested in which of these peculiars could help me figure out what had happened to Mum and whether the short guy with the big nose and boil on his face was a leprechaun. If I had the luck of the leprechauns, I would have magicked that bad boy away or, at the very least, nuked the hair that grew out of it.

Orpheus, the vampire, rolled his eyes in my direction.

Ezra kicked my heel again.

"Stop that," I hissed at him.

"Control your thoughts."

"It is unusual for a peculiar to come into their art at such a late age," continued Phinnaeous. "You have much to learn. For one, it was ill-advised of you to attend a humdrum police station tonight. From now on, you will bring your problems to your assigned mentor and, thereafter, to the senate. Peculiar business cannot be allowed to drift into the humdrum sphere so thoughtlessly. We feel it would be in your best interests to give up your humdrum job while you learn our ways."

I tensed. I might have felt stuck without prospects in my job, but as a newly divorced woman, there was no way I'd give up my independence. How was I supposed to pay my rent or afford Echo's steaks or my kickboxing classes? And there was that expensive skin cream I had my eye on too. And maybe those Kardashian control pants.

Orpheus the vampire spluttered, but I ignored him. He could bloody well stay out of my mind if he didn't like what he found there. I mean, Minister for History and the Today? What was that anyway?

I fixed my eyes on Phinnaeous since he seemed to be the spokesperson here, being Prime Sorcerer and all. "That's not going to happen. I need the income, and I'd miss my students. I refuse to leave them in the lurch. If you want me to learn about all of this…" I waved my hands at the thousand flickering candles and the freakish line-up ahead of me and noticed an older woman in luminous exercise gear from the 1980s. Next to her, a lightly built fellow with translucent skin had a reptile on his shoulder. He didn't even blink when it scuttled into his hair. Urgh. "Then don't get all heavy-handed about my other commitments."

Phinnaeous stroked his beard and exchanged glances with the rest of the senate, then turned back to me. "Highly unusual. Perhaps you might consider reducing your hours at least? As a gesture of goodwill for the resources we are about to invest in you."

I fiddled with my waistband, wishing I was home in my PJs. "Well, I suppose I could ask for compassionate leave. Just for a few weeks." I paused. "Speaking of Mum, I think there might have been some funky business going on with Mum's death. Like, magical funky business. I thought maybe you could help me get to the bottom of that."

Ezra groaned beside me.

Phinnaeous Shine leaned forward, his forehead knotted. "That is impossible. Our Magical Constitution forbids peculiars from harming humdrums. You will soon become familiar with it. What your mother suffered was an unfortunate humdrum accident."

"I'm pretty sure you're wrong."

Orpheus the vampire's eyebrows flew up so fast they almost disappeared into his hairline. "You would do well to learn not to speak to the Prime Sorcerer in that manner. Many have met a messy end for far less."

"Never mind, Orpheus. We, too, were once unrestrained," said the Prime Sorcerer. "Tell me, Ms Verma, did your mother leave you anything else of worth?"

I frowned. My mother's will was none of his business, but I had nothing to hide. "She left enough to cover her funeral costs. Our family home is their only asset, and it belongs to my father, just as it should."

"Your forty years have given you a good sense of what to value in life, granddaughter of Rajika Verma. If only goblins and the majority of humans would learn that lesson as well." He paused and turned to his left with a swish of his robes. "Perhaps now is a good time for you to meet Rayna Willowsun, our Minister for Magical Education. Rayna is Headmistress of Wildwoods and will oversee your progress in mastering your inherent talents."

The woman with the snaking plant adornment smiled and stood up. Long, grey hair flowed over her shoulders, interspersed with plaited strands. To my surprise, she wore a hip belt packed with clanking potions and a dagger. She'd not be wearing that down Streatham High Road without the blues and twos being called out.

Knife crime in London was bad enough without old ladies openly carrying weapons.

Phinnaeous pushed back his chair, and the rest of the senate rose with him. "I'm afraid the senate has other matters to attend to tonight, but you are in good hands with Minister Willowsun and, of course, Mr Neuhoff."

Beside me, Ezra inclined his head.

"There is one last thing." Phinnaeous flicked his hand, and a flash of white emerged as if from an air pocket: a paper bird or butterfly or a winged creature of some sort. The beat of strong wings filled the air. "Learn it, granddaughter of Rajika Verma. Obey it."

The creature spun through the air towards me and fluttered at eye level in front of me.

"Oh. My. God." I eyed it in terror.

Ezra reached up and grabbed it, clasping hands together like in prayer, trapping it inside. For a horrifying moment, I thought he'd killed it.

"Ready?" he said, a gleam in his eye.

My heartbeat was like a wild drummer in my chest. I held out my cupped palms and nodded, not wanting to show myself up as a fool while the spotlight was on me.

He tipped it into my hands.

I winced as it pricked me. "Ouch!"

A pearl-sized drop of blood bloomed in the centre of my left palm. It stung like hell. Only then did the creature settle, warm to the touch, as if it had been alive.

"Happens every time," said Ezra, still and serious at my side. "That's the blood bond taken care of. Unfold it."

My fingers quivered as I unpeeled it. Now inanimate, the parchment was as robust as a rhino's skin. I read it once, then again, my body tingling.

-

Magical Constitution
by order of the Sorcerer's Senate
The Pragmatist's Law:

Never meddle in the affairs of the gods.
The Administrator's Law:
All peculiars and magical artefacts must register
with the Sorcerer's Senate within three lunar cycles.
The Protector's Law:
A sentient peculiar who uses magic to harm a humdrum
will have their magic drained ad infinitum.
The Founder's Law:
Peculiars must hide the existence of the Otherworld from humdrums
and re-establish secrecy upon accidental arousal of suspicion.
The Jailor's Law:
It is forbidden to interfere with the compos mentis of another peculiar.
The Judge's Law:
The delicate power balance between coexisting
peculiar communities must be protected.
The Educator's Law:
New users of magic must be supervised until they pass the trial.
The Monk's Law:
Black magic and necromancy are forbidden.

-

Who were the gods? Did it mean people with god-like powers? Because that paper bird trick had blown my mind. Fair enough if magicians with that amount of skill wanted to be left alone. I wouldn't mess with them. Did vampires drain the magic of disobedient peculiars the same way they sucked out blood in *Dracula*? What trial did I have to overcome before I could fly to Brazil for a beach holiday and see the Christ the Redeemer statue in Rio?

Orpheus, the vampire, turned with a pinched expression to his fellow senate members. "Mark my words; this one is going to be trouble."

"You are one of us now, granddaughter of Rajika Verma." Phinnaeous threw me a satisfied glance and walked away, followed by all but Rayna.

"Gah. It's Alisha." I gritted my teeth.

The candles dimmed in Phinnaeous's wake, leaving the orb

floating above the table as the brightest source of light. It illuminated Rayna as if she were the virgin in a classical painting. She must have been pushing sixty, but her skin was wrinkle-free, and her long dress clung to curves a much younger woman would have been proud of. The lucky cow had obviously won the genetic lottery.

She whispered something under her breath that sounded distinctly like a spell. A soft L, a frothy M and an S rolled on a clicking tongue, and the orb darted in front of her and glided away.

"Come." She followed it at an easy pace. "The night has been long, and I need my sleep before Wildwoods is filled with young minds tomorrow. But there is time yet for a short nightcap in my office while we plan for your schooling."

"God help me." I passed through the tombstone door between Rayna and Ezra as if I were a sandwich filling.

The orb guided us into the night air, across two draw bridges and into Rayna's office, judging by the Headmistress plaque on the door. Her office possessed neither the grand flair of the hall nor the exquisite beauty of the library. It was an intimate space, with wooden furniture sanded smooth with love and silk drapes of muted, earthy colours. This was a woman who knew how to care for plants. Not one was shrivelled or dried up. Her collection included not just succulents but miniature orange trees and flowering fuchsia orchids. A mahogany desk with a green embossed inlay took centre stage, topped with an enormous bronze egg timer, potions in vessels of varying sizes and an inkwell and quill.

Rayna rounded the desk, settled into a high-backed chair and indicated to us to be seated. My ears pricked as she guided the orb to a stand on her desk with more whispered words.

I sat with a bump and felt, rather than heard, Ezra chuckle beside me. The chairs were lower at the visitor's side of the desk.

She pulled a piece of paper from her drawer, dipped her quill into the inkwell and turned her clear gaze to me. "Tell me, Alisha Verma, granddaughter of Rajika, what are you?"

"I am a druid." Unless Echo had been telling fibs. I wouldn't put it past that wily cat. The word still felt strange on my tongue.

Rayna sighed and drew her hair across her shoulder, where it tangled with the weird vine adornment. "Of course, you're a druid. As am I. But what kind?"

I hoped she didn't think she'd be getting brownie points because we were both druids. She was giving me stern mum vibes, and I was no teenager. Besides, I knew nothing of my history. Wasn't Wildwoods supposed to be the fountain of knowledge for all things magical?

Still, I was nothing if not a trier. I decided to pick an answer and say it with great conviction. "I'm a druid of great magical lineage."

Next to me, Ezra barked with laughter.

I gave him a furious stare and tried not to notice his strong thighs straining against the denim of his jeans.

Rayna gave the patient smile of someone used to trying students. "Oh, dear. I see this might take a while. Let me try and explain in a more…humdrum way." She pursed her lips. "There are many types of cereal, yes? Healthy ones, chocolate ones, the one that goes soggy in the microwave."

"Weetabix?" I said helpfully. She wasn't the only one with the answers.

"Indeed," said Rayna. "And well, all druids aren't Weetabix. Some are healthy. Some are chocolate."

I frowned.

Ezra leaned forward. "I think what Minister Willowsun means is that druids have different talents. Some may excel at potions or spells. Others may have control of an element or take energy from natural or urban settings. A few, after decades of study, may be able to change into an animal form." He paused. "I have an inkling of who you may be, Alisha, but it is never wise to presume without clear evidence."

Rayna put down her quill. "Quite right, Mr Neuhoff. We are agreed then. You will become Ms Verma's mentor. You may attend Wildwoods around your other duties and use this safe space and the training arena to uncover and hone Ms Verma's talents. You will provide written reports to me every three days. As someone Ms Verma trusts, you are well suited to the task."

He nodded. "As you wish."

My hackles rose. It was rubbish, not to mention rude, for them to talk about my future like I wasn't even there. I kept my mouth shut, but I wasn't afraid to use it once I worked out what the hell was going on.

"Once Ms Verma's initial training is completed, we will see that she acquires knowledge in the traditional arts as befitting the Wildwoods standards: herbology, healing and ageing; weapons training; spells; magical history; and if she excels herself, wilding." She handed him a form on yellow parchment. "See to it that she is registered and that her knowledge meets the standard required to meet the trial unless, of course, she wishes to forfeit her peculiar nature at that point."

Ezra rubbed the back of his neck and accepted the form. "Time to go, hellfire. Goodnight, Minister."

My mind was like jelly. I needed sleep if I was to process this all. I scrambled after him. "Not sure if I'm up for a trial. I'm definitely up for my bed, though."

10

E zra and I trudged across the rope bridges towards the cable cars to ground level.

"I tried teleporting out of Wildwoods once, but the rune on the yew tree doesn't care to be bypassed," he said. "Wildwoods catapulted me out of there quicker than lightning. I landed in the arms of a willow tree, which kindly shielded me from the worst of the fall. I couldn't sit for days. I now give it a healthy distance before I teleport, just in case."

I let his comment pass. There was only so much my brain could take. Besides, I was far too tired to unpick the Otherworld. The Prime Sorcerer's brush-off about Mum's death still bothered me, though.

"Ezra?" I asked.

Grey eyes turned to me as we glided along in the cable car. "Yeah?"

"Do you think Phinnaeous was right about my mum? That magic had nothing to do with her death?"

"Just because peculiars shouldn't interfere in humdrum lives doesn't mean they don't. They just haven't been caught. The senate's powers aren't all-encompassing, whatever Phinnaeous Shine would like to believe."

"Is it only new peculiars you seek out in your job?"

"No, I seek out criminals too. I seek out whoever the senate demands, and only work with their blessing. It is possible for peculiars to exist beyond the senate's reach, but it's not something I would wish for myself. Your father is a brave man."

We trudged out through the grounds towards the yew tree. The moon hid behind a bank of clouds.

"This should do it." He held out his hand to me. "I promised to take you home."

I shook my head, not keen on inviting back the sickening sensation. "Maybe I'll take the night bus."

"Sorry, hellfire. I can't risk you snoozing on the way home. Who knows who might be lurking." He pulled me towards him and teleported the second I hit his chest.

This time, when the ground disappeared from under my feet, and the swirls of black and technicolour enveloped me, I held on to him like a marooned sailor holds on to a rock at sea.

Only with sharper nails. And sniffing said rock.

He smelt of earth, roll-up cigarettes and mountain air.

"Easy with those nails," he said as we landed on solid ground.

I opened my eyes and found myself in my bedroom with a pile of clean underwear still on my duvet, waiting to be put away. That presumptuous dickhead. I pushed him away, despite the room still spinning around me.

"Whoa," he said. "You said you wanted bed."

"How on earth do you know where my bedroom is?" I shoved the underwear into a drawer.

"I told you I've been tracking you."

"To my bedroom? How does teleporting work anyway? Don't you have to imagine where you want to go?" No way he was playing me for a fool. I might not know all the rules, but I had an imagination.

He had the decency to look ashamed. "I've been in here once to check you were still breathing when the leopard revealed itself, and you let it sleep here uncaged. But I didn't touch anything."

I raised an eyebrow.

Ezra grinned and held up his hands. "As beautiful as you are, a man who touches a woman without consent is lower than a pair of hairy balls."

Echo entered through the bedroom door, his paws padding on the carpet.

His roar made Ezra and I both leap, even though I'd seen him coming.

"Out, dog!" the leopard said, emerald eyes oh so still like he was ready to pounce. "You dare leave me behind when you take a Verma to the Otherworld? You presume you are better placed to protect her when I am hung better than you?"

Ezra shrugged and disappeared in a fizzle of light.

"What excellent timing, Echo. I'm sorry I left you behind." I scratched him behind his ear.

"He didn't take you to the Celestial Library, did he? Wolves are loyal only to their pack. As for you, a clueless druid is a dead druid," said Echo. "I hope you have learned your lesson."

I shoved his tush out of the door. He would have made a wonderful pillow if only I could trust him not to bite my head off. "Goodnight, Echo."

THE NEXT MORNING, I replied soothingly to a bunch of texts from my brother about his powers not manifesting and went for a run with Echo. I pulled on a fresh pair of leggings and a mismatched T-shirt and tied my hair up into a high ponytail to keep it off my neck, ignoring the curls that escaped to frame my face. Whereas once I would have planned my route to avoid dicey neighbourhoods and unkempt alleys, I could now run freely with my leopard protection in tow.

My body loosened, my legs stretched out, and the cobwebs in my head fell away as I ran through Balham past the cinema, the comedy pub and the charity shops where I rummaged for treasure. At the underpass at the corner of the park, small, knobbly, dull grey creatures holding brooms gave me a fright.

I sped up but not before catching the milky eyes of one. It raised a four-fingered hand in greeting.

"What were they?" I said.

"Dark elves cleaning the streets of magical residue, of course," said Echo. "You'll be noticing all sorts now. Best to prepare yourself."

My chest heaved with exertion. "But it's daytime."

"We're not all vampires, Alisha. I'd stay away from them if I were you. It was a dark elf that took your grandmother's life. That chapter might be over, but elves are still trouble."

I stopped short. "Oh, that's terrible."

"Many in the Otherworld struggle to forgive them. It is easy to be suspicious of them. They are small, quick-witted and nimble-fingered. The Sorcerer's Senate employs the majority of elves as clean-up crews, but they are just as likely to spray the buildings in their care with graffiti. When you get lost in London, it's inevitably because an elf has spun the street signs. Why do you think there are so many missing people in this city?"

My lungs were on fire. "The elves?"

"You do listen to what I say. They create dead ends with black holes, and some poor, unsuspecting person is always getting sucked in. If you listen closely enough, you can hear their screams at night."

"I thought that was mating foxes."

"They've even been known to move public telephone boxes to disorientate city-dwellers. Personally, I think it is their mean streak. Who uses public telephone boxes—"

"Doctor Who?" How was he running so effortlessly when I had sweat running into my eyes?

"—unless they are in dire need? In any case, the succubi took up arms over the matter. They petitioned the senate to reprimand the elves for unfairly suppressing the prostitution trade."

"What are succubi?"

"How Rajika Verma could end up with a granddaughter like you, I'll never know," said the leopard. "But still, you're an improvement on the menfolk of this clan. The Y chromosome must be lacking in your kind."

Fifty minutes later, we looped back around to the flat, with me gasping for breath.

"Your fitness could do with some work." He was right, but he didn't need to know it.

My legs felt like jelly. "Huh. Well, it's not like I've had time for the gym recently. And I can run way faster with the right music playing. Although, I was tempted to stick my earphones in with all the moaning you did about the flyers. I only stuck a dozen up. How long could it have taken you?"

Echo grunted. "You try tearing down photos of yourself when humdrums are looking the other way. It was almost as stressful as fighting a leprechaun. Vile things. How the Prime Sorcerer stands for one on the senate is anyone's guess."

Well, that answered my question about the guy with the boil. "Phinnaeous sounded like he knew my grandmother."

"Rajika Verma made it her priority to know those who wielded power, and Phinnaeous Shine has been a man who commands respect for centuries."

"What is his power?" I wished there were an Encyclopaedia of Magical Persons so I didn't have to keep asking. Or a Wikipedia page, at the very least.

"Did the dog teach you nothing? Phinnaeous Shine is a wizard with skin-walking powers, of course, singularly suited to the brief of Prime Sorcerer, which means he leads the senate but is responsible for infiltrating top levels of government, negotiations and planning missions. Most peculiars have humdrum jobs these days, but Phinnaeous Shine is a notable exception. His wealth is rumoured to rival the Queen of England's, and he has just as many charitable interests. Although, unlike the Queen, the Prime Sorcerer has a succubus housekeeper paying penance for her sins."

"Bloody hell." I pushed open the door to my building. "Is slavery still allowed in the Otherworld?"

Echo inclined his head and followed me into my flat. "Of course. Any number of situations wouldn't function without bondage. Peculiars are both hugely advanced and astonishingly retrograde. We are brutish and inspired, sometimes at the same time. It's a good thing you've called a family conference. Your father is right. Now you have stepped into the Otherworld, you will need allies, and you must expect to lose blood, whether it is yours or that of your loved ones." He paused. "Now go, or you will smell like old socks when your family arrives, and I will be too ashamed for you to hold my head up proudly."

"What about you? Surely it is beneath an Indian leopard to be stinky?"

"My tongue is more effective than any loofah."

I laughed and made for the shower.

A quarter of an hour later, I buzzed Dad, Sahil and Marina into the flat. She was family to me, the sister I loved more than my real-life sibling. I kissed them as they walked in, one after the other. Dad had already brought Sahil up to speed but, at my request, omitted to mention Echo's transformation. Call it sisterly love or sibling rivalry, but I wanted to be there when he jumped out of his skin.

"Got to tell you, Alisha, I'm going out of my mind," said Sahil. "I mean, one day you know you're more than ordinary. The next day, you find out you're something else entirely. This is alien-level weird."

"You're telling me."

His eyes widened, lashes longer than mine. "I mean, I wish my talents would hurry up and manifest but just think. What if we can fly? What would I do with all my air miles?"

Marina stifled a laugh.

I ushered them into my living room without giving Sahil a warning about the enormous leopard lounging there. Partly to test whether he had true sight. Mostly for the glee of seeing him jump out of his skin.

He didn't disappoint.

"Holy shit," he said, almost leaping into Dad's arms, all hairy, five-foot-nine of him.

This time, Marina didn't hide her glee. She enjoyed seeing him squirm as much as me. He'd had a thing for her since our school days. I think he was miffed he'd never gotten in her pants.

Sahil gawped. "That can't be real."

Echo gurned like a living nightmare, all teeth and menacing big-cat energy. "Oh, I'm real. More real than the birthmark on the right side of your derrière."

"Nope. I refuse to believe it." Sahil paused. "How did you know about my birthmark?"

"Because I watched you grow up. And I've swatted you more often than I've feasted on Golden Retrievers, a sorry fact I must change."

"You can't be Echo." Sahil shook his head. "How are you so big? How can you talk? I need a beer."

"I'm not a maid, you simpleton," said Echo.

Dad's moustache twitched. Decades ago, it had been fashionable but now gave him a slightly ridiculous air. "I've not missed your sharp tongue, Echo, but your true form is a sight for sore eyes. If only I could convince you to sit for a portrait."

Echo nodded. "It appears we are on the same side again, Joshi Verma, son of Rajika. Perhaps in recognition of our new path together, I will let you paint me."

Sahil turned to Marina. "The cat is a leopard, and the leopard can talk."

She patted his arm as if comforting a toddler.

I raised a hand. "Sit, everyone, please. We aren't here to drink beer, trade insults or paint. I invited you here to tell you I've decided to recover my lost heritage and to ask for your support."

The three of them shared the largest sofa. Echo paced nearby in a deliberate attempt to lord his power over them.

I ignored him. "Yesterday, I went to Wildwoods School of the Wondrous and was allocated a mentor."

Dad's face flushed. "You're going too fast, Alisha. You know nothing of the Otherworld."

"I agree, Alisha," said Sahil. "You can't rush headlong into all of this. It's ridiculous."

"You're ridiculous," said Echo.

Marina raised her voice above the din. "Will you just hear her out?"

I sent her a look of silent thanks and ploughed on. "So you have made your choice, Dad? I don't expect you to make the same choice as me. We're not the musketeers. Even though I'm ready for an adventure, I have no intention of ruining your peace."

"I will stand by your side because I am true of heart," said Echo. "And I will teach and protect you until my dying breath."

"Was that cat always so dramatic?" said Sahil.

"Talk directly to me, you snivelling boy," said Echo.

Sahil ignored him, but the flicker in his eyes revealed his wariness. "Wildwoods, school of the what? You need to slow down, sis. This isn't like you. Is it grief because of Mum, because of your divorce?"

"Sahil's right," said Dad. "The Otherworld has tentacles further than you could ever dream of. Did you ever wonder what my talents were and what it cost me to give them up?"

I gulped. I'd been so caught up in my changes that I'd not given a thought to my dad's peculiar talents or even how genetics might influence my magic.

Dad continued. "Even as a young boy, they made me feel almost god-like. My mother had an inkling of what they could be. She put charcoal in my hands and colour pencils, even putty. It wasn't until I picked up a paintbrush that my talents were unlocked. I could draw a good likeness before I could read, and by the time I was nine, my artwork surpassed my tutors in India." He smiled. "They didn't know what my mother knew. Those very drawings were not merely oils on paper. I painted any creature my heart settled on—dragonflies, monkeys, cows and donkeys—and she could animate them. Those animals came to life before my very eyes. Behind closed doors, of course. This was no party trick to enthral the masses. It came with responsibility, but oh, the joy of creation."

No wonder he'd always seemed a little bitter about the past. To have those skills and to have to give them up must have been gut-wrenching.

"Heaven help us. Alisha and I aren't made from drawings, are we?" said Sahil.

Dad shook his head. "Don't be silly. I can't create humans. Not with my paints. What a ridiculous idea. You were made from a good old tumble between the sheets."

Sahil and I looked at each other in horror. Some things bonded even fractious siblings.

"You created animals?" Marina's mouth hung open. "Without mating and pregnancy and birth? You created real life animals?"

Dad nodded. "*We* did, my mother and I. Not willy-nilly. I practised on insects, and as my talent deepened, the creatures grew larger and more complex."

"Wait, do you think I could do that too?" said Sahil.

I frowned. "What happened to the animals afterwards?"

"Once the animal serves its purpose, it is freed into the natural world," said Dad.

"Just think of all the species you could have saved from extinction this way," said Marina.

"Your partnership with Rajika was written in the stars, Joshi, but you betrayed her when she died," growled Echo. "She didn't devote her life to the Otherworld for you to turn your back on it."

"You don't think I mourned the loss of my mother and the magic she introduced me to?" said Dad. "I had to keep my family safe. We had already lost too much. And after she died, there was no one left to animate my paintings. I was useless, like—"

"A cricket bat without a ball," said Echo.

"A nightclub without the women," said Sahil.

I rolled my eyes.

Dad frowned. "Like a bow without the arrows. And the senate made it worse. The Celestial Library cut itself off from both warring sides. Lives were lost, and artefacts and manuscripts were out of reach. The senate was angry at my choice to cast ourselves adrift, and vengeful as they are, they punished me for it. They forbade me from displaying my art in public spaces in case another animator called forth the creatures. In case with my mother gone, someone else bonded to my gift, someone who didn't follow the Magical Constitution, someone who risked discovery by humdrums. I tried to rebel. Any submissions I made disappeared. If I enquired on the telephone, the line went dead. Eventually, I gave up and turned to greeting cards." He splayed his hands. "What else could I do? I had mouths to feed."

Tears filled my eyes. "Oh, Dad, I always thought you were happy making your living from prints and cards. I thought you were too shy to show it in galleries. What a pity to have our attic stuffed full of your wonderful work because of senate orders. I'm so sorry."

Sahil nodded. "Sorry, old man."

Dad sighed. "What you need to know about the senate is that it didn't have to be that way. The witches' binding spell neutralised my magic. There was scarcely a chance of my original paintings causing trouble. But like all governing bodies, the senate can be as vindictive as it is benevolent, and their goals are often hidden from view."

I bit my lip. "You don't have to trust them, Dad. But can you trust me? I can't turn back now. I need my eyes to stay open."

Dad rocked back and forth like he sometimes did when he prayed. "Why, Alisha? Why is this so important to you?"

I locked my eyes on his. "You know why."

He swallowed hard. "Because of the flowers in her car. She was stolen from us, wasn't she?"

"Yes, I think she was." I turned to look at them all: the dad, who always put his family first; the brother, who had a softer side that only our mum could bring out; the best friend who'd always stood by me; the leopard, who said he'd die for me. "I won't let it go. Will you?"

"You're telling me I could be the next Iron Man or Doctor Strange," said Sahil. "Of course, I'm in."

"I'm in, too," said Marina. "I mean, talking leopards, sexy men and a senate that sounds like it was filled with all sorts of kink? Women with hip daggers and candlelit meetings? Sounds like my sort of scene. Bring it on."

A sad cloud passed over Dad's face like it did now when he was thinking of Mum.

"That's settled then." He pulled the three of us into a bear hug and left Echo out of the mix.

"No turning back," I said. "We owe her that much."

"Not unless we are ambushed by a pack of leprechauns in the dead of night." Echo's lip curled up to show an impressive incisor. "Then we scream like banshees and run. Or call the sneaky wolfman to teleport us out of there. Even dogs have their uses."

11

____

Dad chomped his biscuit. "There comes a time when a father realises he is too old to interfere in his daughter's decisions. I thought Alex might protect you, but instead, it seems you have a wolf and a leopard at your side."

It wasn't enough to be a kickboxing, mini-marathon running, husband-slaying woman. He still wanted a man to look after me.

Marina shot me a sympathetic glance.

Sahil had long since disappeared to his North London penthouse after a flurry of messages from his PA. It seemed the London property market stood still without him. He had left me with Dad in a melancholy mood that I hoped I could snap him out of. To add to the drama, Ezra had crept in through the back window. Lucky Echo had only grazed the leg that had come out of nowhere. We could have been dealing with an amputation.

The three of them sat in different corners of the living room.

"It's your own fault." I dabbed some antiseptic cream on Ezra. "You could have used the doorbell like a normal person."

"I was trying not to invade your space by teleporting in." He gently pushed away my fussing hands.

"Ignore him," said Echo. "I barely gave him a scratch, and wolves heal fast."

"Stop moping, boys. We have work to do." Marina's singsong voice couldn't possibly offend, especially when she used her winning smile. "Anyone would think you need nursemaids."

Echo purred. "You are right, of course, Marina Ambrose." Of all my family, he had thawed the quickest with Marina. He padded over to nestle next to her like he'd done in his Bengal cat form, and she almost didn't flinch. "What would you have us do, Alisha? Your wish is my command."

Ezra's thigh muscles bulged as he stood up. "We have to get on with your magical training. We have three days before I must submit the first written report to Minister Willowsun."

I shook my head. "First, we connect the dots about Mum's death. The training comes next."

"That's a mistake," said Ezra.

"You will regret—" said Echo.

Marina beamed. "So you two agree for once?"

"I'm not moving on this," I said. "I've seen enough CSI Miami to know how quickly the trail goes cold. I've been up all night, and I just can't find the common thread. Who is Detective Jameson?"

Dad shuffled forward, visibly shaky. "Your mother and I argued a few weeks before she died. I never told you kids because what happens in someone's marriage is for them alone. But now, I think my instincts were right. Something was off."

"What is it, Dad?" I said.

"Rosalie did something out of character, and wouldn't explain why. She got in trouble at work for releasing a load of mice and monkeys meant for trials. Dr Williamson docked her pay and gave her a warning, but they watched her closely after that. Rosalie seemed on edge."

I bit my cheek. "Detective Jameson mentioned that. I thought he had his wires crossed." I'd always hated the part of her job that meant she had to experiment on animals. So had Dad. "That's totally unlike her. Why would she do that?"

"I couldn't figure it out either, and she didn't want me poking my nose in it. We didn't have secrets. I couldn't understand why she wouldn't come clean even with me. But when you mentioned that old lady from the memorial…"

I scrunched up my face, thinking back. "Gaia?"

Dad froze. "Her name was Gaia?"

Ezra went from a slouch to a poker-straight back in two seconds flat. "Well, I'll be damned."

I looked from one to another. "What am I missing?"

"I pray I'm wrong. Because if I'm right, we're in deeper than I thought." Dad's words came out slow and ponderous. "I think Rosalie released those animals as an offering. I think Gaia is none other than *that* Gaia, Goddess of the Earth."

"And the Titans and the Cyclopes," said Ezra.

"Don't forget the giants," said Echo.

All air left the room, punctured only by Marina.

"As an atheist, this is a bit farfetched for me," she said.

"The gods are real, Marina," the leopard said. "I have seen them many times over the centuries, though they change their skins to blend in. They can be recognised by the havoc they leave in their wake. You can believe they exist without thinking they deserve power."

"*If* we choose to believe this, let's follow the line of logic," I said. "Why would Mum have made an offering to a god?"

"My gut tells me Rosalie went to the goddess for help," said Dad. "It makes sense, doesn't it? It explains why Gaia was at EvolveTech that day. It shows she's on our side."

"*None* of this makes sense," I said. "Why wouldn't Mum have shared any of this with us? What was she thinking, putting herself in danger like this, all by herself? How could she hide it even from you, Dad?"

Dad hung his head. "All I know is Rosalie was the cleverest, most devoted woman I know. She must have had her reasons. I have to believe that. And if we put our trust in her, we have to follow her lead. We have to speak to Gaia and find out what she knows."

Ezra raised his hands. "Hold on, hold on. You might be an outsider, Joshi, but I work for the senate and abide by the constitution. The first law, the Pragmatist's Law, states that we *never* meddle in the affairs of the gods. That is a non-negotiable. There can be no winning against the gods. Only deep pain comes from walking that road."

"Pah," said Dad. "Those rules never protected anyone from pain. The senate doesn't need to know. And how is it meddling to talk to Gaia when she approached Alisha first?"

"Technically, I'm still an unregistered peculiar until you hand in that form, right, Ezra?" I asked.

Grey eyes narrowed. "Yeah, but the blood bond was taken when you caught the constitution. It must be taken seriously."

"So must Mum's death. If the Prime Sorcerer wanted me to abide by his rules, he shouldn't have shut down my concerns. Echo, how do I summon a god?"

"With an offering that speaks to their interests, of course. Just like Rosalie did before you," said Echo.

Ezra folded his arms across his chest, straining against his sweatshirt. "This sounds like trouble, hellfire."

"Sorry, Ezra. I'm not going to change my mind." I laid a hand on his arm.

A growl from Echo. "You better hold your tongue, dog. Snitches get stitches."

"Alisha's under my care now." Power pulsed from Ezra, causing Echo to whine. "You best focus on the real enemy because, mark my words, they'll be coming for us now, and she's about as ready as a lamb."

WE MADE the offering at dusk, just in case Gaia made a scene. It was easier to hide from humdrums in twilight than under bright skies. I convinced Dad and Marina to let me, Ezra and Echo handle it. Dad couldn't protect me with his paintbrush, and Marina had no idea why she had true sight yet, so she was as useless as me. Echo waited for Ezra and me in a quiet corner of Wandsworth Common while we carried out our mission.

"I can't believe we're doing this," I said. "Will she look the same as she did at the memorial? Like a little old lady in a green sari?"

Ezra frowned. "It's not my area of expertise. The gods are beyond even the remit of the senate. I doubt the Prime Sorcerer himself could answer that question. But my guess is she'll look the same. Rumour has it they are weaker than at any other time in history. In the Otherworld, our talents come from our bloodlines. The power of the gods stems from something else entirely. Their strength gains or weakens in relation to how strongly their believers pray. And in this modern world, churches, mosques, temples and synagogues are not central to our way of life. They are merely a train station people pass through. Money is the real currency, the real god. My bet is that Gaia can't shed her skin as easily as in previous centuries because the lack of prayer will have diminished her."

"What if she doesn't respond? What if this isn't the kind of offering she wants?"

Ezra raised an eyebrow. "Then I'd breathe a sigh of relief. Centuries of toeing the party line, and I break the law within a week of meeting you. Trust me, hellfire, this is not how it usually goes."

I raised my eyes to meet his and then dropped my focus to his lips. I couldn't help it. "How does it usually go?"

"I do my job, tick my boxes and move on to the next job." He tucked a loose strand of hair behind my ear, and it made me feel twenty years old again. "But something about you tells me, even if I bailed out on you and reported you to the senate, you'd still carry on this path, and I'd be left wondering if you made it out in one piece."

My heart danced. I'd learned not to rely on Alex. Even if what I had with Ezra was a cheeky flirtation that never went anywhere, it was nice to feel protected. As long as he didn't get overbearing and didn't mind me calling the shots. There was no way I was ever playing second fiddle again. In this next stage of my life, I wanted to be the queen, not the maidservant.

We were outside a pet shop on Streatham Hill hours after closing time. Inside, beyond the window display full of dog beds, hamster wheels and bags of sawdust, an array of parrots watched from their cages. I'd taken a leaf out of Mum's book and decided that perhaps the Goddess of the Earth would be pleased by us freeing caged animals, and an internet search had brought us here to Dr Doolittle.

"Are you sure they won't have CCTV?" I said.

"Unlikely. The leopard scoped the place out, didn't he?" Ezra grinned. "But don't worry, no one's going to recognise you in that ridiculous getup anyway."

I smacked his arm. I'd worn four jumpers on top of each other to change my body size and borrowed one of the wigs Marina wore in her bedroom antics. It was a Tina Turner-style wig in a golden brown, miles apart from my own dark locks, and it obscured my features to boot. If, at forty, I was going to break into a pet shop, I was sure as hell going to take precautions against getting caught.

I eyed Ezra. "You could have borrowed a dress, you know. Paired with Marina's Little Mermaid wig, you would have been unrecognisable."

"I'll take my chances." He reached for my hand and pulled me closer. "Come on, hellfire."

He wrapped an arm around me and teleported inside.

My stomach roiled, and I opened my eyes to a couple of parakeets in one cage and a pair of African birds of some sort or another. The birds squawked, not in terror, but wide-eyed and yapping, in a kind of greeting.

"How many?" I said. "Will a cage each do?"

"That's fine. It's a gesture." He grabbed the larger cage. "Hold on tight to yours. We're not hanging about."

The gentlest touches on my hand, and we were away again, spinning through the swirls of green and grey. I didn't know what was bird, what was cage, and what was night. We landed more roughly than before, in a bump of bodies, metal and squeaks and whistles. This time, the birds sounded distressed. I opened my eyes to Ezra righting both cages.

"Sorry about that. My hands were too full for a calmer landing," he said. "We lost your wig on the way."

"Marina's going to kill me." I caught my breath and peeled off three layers of jumpers.

"I'll buy her a new one."

"What took you so long?" said Echo. "I hunted three squirrels in the time you've been away, and I turned my attention to a lost Jack Russell. You could have told me they are fearless fellows. His bark almost deafened me. But you are here now. Let us call the goddess and get this over with so I can snooze on the sofa."

I smoothed out my outfit and arranged the cages in an orderly fashion. We stood in a circle of oak trees, our mission lit now only by the stars and a sliver of moon.

"How do I call her, Echo?" I asked.

"By thinking of her, of course, and saying a silent prayer using her name. That should do it, together with those birds. Although, if you don't mind, can I hide in that hedge over there and be your hidden man? I wouldn't like the goddess to think I was part of the offering. A creature of my stature should not be offered up like a piece of fruit. Neither would I like her to slit my throat."

I gaped at him. "Oh my goodness, she won't expect me to kill these parrots, will she?"

The birds squawked in alarm.

Ezra shrugged. His nonchalance at blood on our hands made me wonder about the killer in him and whether he hunted in his wolf form. "The gods are wily. Who knows what she'll expect? But from what I remember of Gaia from mythology, she is more of a creator than a destroyer. At least, I hope so."

"Nevertheless, I bid you adieu." Echo took a running leap into the hedge.

"Guess it's just us." I pulled out my phone.

"What are you doing?" said Ezra.

"Texting my dad and Marina, *I love you*, just in case we don't make it."

I sighed and raked my hair, which was dishevelled from the wig. I wished I'd plucked out the odd grey at my hairline that morning. It wasn't every day you met a goddess.

"Here goes nothing."

I closed my eyes, pictured the old woman in the green sari and said a silent prayer to Gaia.

The trees around us shuddered, and I almost peed my pants.

12

The oaks swayed and shed handfuls of leaves that rained down around us. This continued for a good three minutes until I lost my fear and wondered if anything would ever happen. I looked at Ezra with a questioning frown.

"Any second now, I can feel it." His hands were shoved in his pockets as if summoning a god was just run-of-the-mill Otherworld stuff when I knew for a fact it wasn't, but his eyes were alert for trouble, and a vein throbbed in his neck.

She materialised before us in light so momentarily blinding that we shielded our eyes. The trees seemed to bend in prayer towards her.

Echo emitted a low growl from the hedge.

Gaia turned with laser-sharp eyes to his exact location. "There is many a beast out tonight. Here, kitty, kitty."

Echo padded out, whiskers twitching, and lay at her feet with his belly exposed.

"Traitor," said Ezra.

Gaia bent over to tickle the leopard's tummy, then turned her attention to us. Her face and body were that of the old woman I remembered, but this time her sari was the colour of the deepest ocean and her blouse the silver of a distant planet.

She raised her hand to wave absentmindedly at the trees. "I'm sorry for all the drama. There was a time when I could appear without theatrics. Now it seems it's all foreplay and a little fizzle at the end." She paused. "But back to business. This is not the first time I have been summoned by a Verma. I wondered how long it would be before you came looking for me."

I'd thought of her as a harmless old woman, but now I wasn't so sure. This was no meandering, toothless senior citizen waiting for someone to paint her nails and comb her hair. In hindsight, she had been more than capable of dealing with the security guards.

She frowned. "Speak, child. What are you waiting for? And why have you brought the wolf abomination with you? Is he my offering? He's not the usual calibre, but as this is your first time—"

Ezra cursed next to me and took a step back.

"Gaia, Goddess of the Earth—" I started.

"No need to use my full title," she said generously.

"The wolf and the leopard are with me. We brought the parrots for you."

"Oh." Disappointment clouded her face. "Well, I suppose my love for the earth's creatures knows no bounds."

"They were rescued from a pet shop."

Gaia perked up. "You did well. A plague befall all pet shop owners."

I'd already committed one evil against poor Dr Doolittle. I hoped he didn't wake up in a bed of locusts. "Thank you again for your kind words about Mum when we met at the memorial. I wondered if you could be more specific about your dealings."

Gaia swung her thick, black plait over her shoulder and puffed out her rosy cheeks. "What can I tell you, granddaughter of Rajika? Tell you too much, and I jeopardise your growth. Tell you too little, and I jeopardise your path. What is the barest truth to push you towards what the fates predicted centuries ago?"

Echo whimpered at her feet.

"Sounds like a lot of pressure, hellfire," murmured Ezra in my ear.

"You have learned by now that things are not always as they seem," said Gaia.

I nodded.

"And that sometimes a pawn is a queen."

I had already lost her, but I decided to play along because it didn't seem right to ask a goddess to repeat herself. Reading mythology taught me that gods were big on respect. One look at Echo revealed that he was in a dreamlike state of bliss, but maybe Ezra would catch Gaia's drift if I kept her talking.

"You are an insect that has landed in a spider's web, but all is not lost. Centuries of cunning are on your side. My power is too diminished to stand against the dark, but if, with my help, you live up to the task, all will be well."

My stomach roiled. Dad had been right. It seemed Gaia was on our side, but if she was involved, this was more than a pauper's game. If a goddess was not powerful enough, how could I succeed?

"You see, granddaughter of Rajika, centuries of prayer nourished the heavens and the gods, but when belief dwindled amongst humans, the heavens crumbled." Her dark eyes grew wide with pain, and in them, I saw demons and fire and great cracks tearing through a plain of unbearable beauty. "The father of the gods could not survive. His remaining children flew to Earth on his last breath."

I broke out in a sweat. I had definitely bitten off more than I could chew.

Gaia continued. "The gods languish here in London, like wretched relatives unable to live together or apart, bored of humans and life itself. Boredom corrupts, and an immortal being has no get-out clause. What is there to look forward to when you have seen the pyramids built, civilisations rise and fall, world wars play out, a man on the moon and Concorde fly? What is there when you have kidnapped Marilyn Monroe to sing and pout for you and to stand above an air vent in a barely-there dress? What do you do when all that is left is to watch the rainforests burn? Nothing compares to the scientific revolution, the Renaissance and the Industrial Revolution." She sighed. "Humanity is trifling to the rest of the gods. Especially now, humans are more likely to worship Silicon Valley products than they are the gods."

Right on cue, my iPhone beeped. I grimaced.

"See? Even the book of faces has taken over from the book of God."

"I think that was a text, actually. I'm old school like that."

Gaia nodded pensively. "Time and fate will decide if your innate values and strength are enough to tip the balance, druid."

"But what does this have to do with my mum?"

"The power of the gods is not what it once was, but we are still meddlesome by nature, especially without the Almighty to restrain us." Her eyes flashed fire. "Bored and vengeful gods do not make for good neighbours. How much they desire to be relevant, to be central to mankind again. For temples to rise and casinos and conglomerates to fall."

My heartbeat thundered like the pounding of hooves across a green. "I still don't understand."

"What is happening is a game of bored gods who long to be worshipped like in the olden days. It's inspired, really, targeting scientists. Where is humanity without science? Without healers, humanity would succumb to plagues, like in the dark days of Egypt. You are a race of boils and rats and distorting cells without scientific invention. Of flat-earthers and ape-like tendencies." Gaia was on a roll. "Where would you be without Albert Einstein, Marie Curie, Charles Darwin, Stephen Hawking and my personal favourite, David Attenborough? Kill the scientists, and cause suffering. An increase in suffering means an increase in prayer. It's a great shame about your mother, though. I liked her."

My blood ran cold. "Are you telling me Mum was killed by a god?"

"Yes, dear," said Gaia. "I thought I'd been speaking plain English. Do let me know if I accidentally slip into Hebrew or Aramaic. It has been known to happen. But yes, I believe your mother was on the brink of a discovery, and that's why she was targeted. You know, it's been centuries since a mortal made such an exquisite offering as hers."

So Dad's hunch was true. Mum releasing the lab animals might have been out of character, but she had a logical reason.

Well, logical if you accepted the need to satisfy the desires of a goddess.

"But what led her to summon you, Gaia?" I asked.

"There comes a time in the twilight of a woman's life when she wishes to find out more about her ancestors. Rosalie Verma made a surprising discovery that cast doubt on the decision to shield you and your brother from the Otherworld. A mother's intuition is strong. Like your father, she believed the Otherworld is full of perils, but she realised you would eventually take this path. So she asked for my help to keep you safe."

"Did you give it?"

Gaia raised a hand. "I have already told you enough. It is up to you what you do with this information. I displease the other gods at my peril. While they may not be able to drain my immortality, they can imprison and torture me or hurt the things I love as a proxy for slicing my flesh." She sank her hand into Echo's fur and trailed it along his back while he purred in ecstasy. "They see my nature as weakness, mock me for injecting my immortality into dying pieces of the earth. But I need not worry now. He will find you, and if you prevail, we will talk again."

"Why does this feel like I am David in the lion's den?"

"Because you are." Ezra set his lips in a grim line. He looked like he was fighting the urge to teleport me out of harm's way. "I told you nothing good comes of meddling with the gods."

The goddess toyed with her braid. "The wolfman is right. It will not be easy, but you will not be alone."

"If a god kills, does that even count as murder? Is it even possible to stop an immortal?" My heartbeat exploded in my chest. "And what do you mean he will find me?"

Gaia shrugged. "Gods have an inkling when we fill someone's thoughts. Once, we sensed small and fleeting thoughts. That is no longer the case. We lost that skill as our power dwindled. But if you turn your full attention on him, he will sense you. Just as I knew when you turned your attention on me, he will know, and he will come for you to destroy the threat."

The word *destroy* rang in my head like a bell, over and over again. What had I done?

I turned to Gaia, pressing my palms together in prayer, entreating her to help. "Please. There must be some way to appease him."

"But, child, the gods will always want more. How can you appease that? But do not fear. When you feel small, remember, they are neither the gods of the Bible, nor the Torah, nor the Qur'an, nor the *Bhagavad Gita*. They are not the gods of the *Iliad* or *Odyssey*, or even *Dante's Inferno*. They are small enough to take everyday jobs, and their power is diminished."

"I still feel like I'm bringing a pitchfork to a gunfight," I said.

Gaia's face shone with light. "If in doubt, child, believe. A little belief goes a long way."

"How about you—Gaia, Goddess of the Earth, mother of the Titans and Cyclopes and giants," said Ezra. "Do you have an everyday job too?"

"My landscaping company went out of business some time ago. I am an old lady in the neighbourhood. I look after strays and waifs and live on social welfare." She turned to Echo and sighed. "But now it's time for me to take my leave. It was good to meet you, Chanakya Gunbir Hredhaan of Maharashtra."

My eyebrows shot up.

"You didn't know the leopard's true name?" Gaia's mischievous eyes flashed, and she scratched behind his ear. "You may go, magnificent creature, to fulfil the promise made by your forefathers. But one day, I may call upon you, and you will come with joy in your heart."

Echo nuzzled his head against her hand and then made a deep bow before padding to my side. For the entirety of the summoning, my usually very opinionated, sometimes obnoxious leopard had not uttered a word.

Gaia came towards us in a rustle of silk to inspect the bird cages, prompting us to edge back.

"Goddess," I said. "I'm nothing. I'm not even a fully-fledged peculiar yet. Give me one reason you are trusting me with this."

Her eyes glinted in the moonlight. "Because you're vegetarian. Vegetarians are easy to trust. It's the cannibals I'm wary of."

Ezra sighed heavily. "Says the goddess who has encouraged blood sacrifices since the dawn of time."

"We live, and we learn," said Gaia.

"So you're not going to sacrifice the parrots?" I said.

"What do you think?" She opened the cages, and the birds flew in celebratory loops and landed on her shoulders with a flourish.

"I expect they were already well trained," said Ezra in my ear.

Gaia whistled low and long. A scuttling sounded a few metres away, and the lost Jack Russell appeared from behind us. He pranced over to Gaia with his tail wagging, despite the proximity of Echo. She scooped him up in her arms and kissed his muzzle. Then, she closed her eyes and formed an O with her mouth, emitting a soft hum and sigh rolled into one.

With that, she was gone, leaving only her voice in the wind. "Farewell, druid, and good luck. It is my hope we meet again and that you do not meet an early death."

I released my pent-up breath in a whoosh and flicked Echo, who still seemed bathed in some sort of godly afterglow. "Fat lot of good you were. Now, what was your full name again?"

13

———————

My encounter with Gaia felt like a dream. I sifted through the revelations, analysing each word, but the jigsaw still missed pieces. Ezra refused to let me rest on my laurels. For him, the meeting with Gaia had been evidence of a raised threat level. For me, it showed Mum had blessed this path. It might even help to ease Dad's reservations, knowing Mum's wishes. She might not have succeeded in her efforts to ensure my safety, but she had loved me enough to try, and that healed some of the broken parts of me.

"Two days, hellfire, until your progress report is due with Minister Willowsun. You've learned nothing about your druid nature. But within minutes of embracing your peculiar identity, you have broken the first law by summoning one god and attracting the wrath of another," said Ezra. "I don't know whether to shake you or protect you—"

"Or kiss her?" said Marina. "Has she reached that level of annoying when you just want to kiss her to shut her up?"

"He's my mentor, not my lover." I swung my hair forward so they wouldn't see me blushing. "And we've got bigger things to focus on."

Saying that it'd been an age since I'd been kissed properly, the thought of kissing Ezra was too delicious for words. Alex had been a wham bam thank you ma'am kind of lover. Ezra looked like the type of man who'd take his time, and the gruff wolf side of him would be fun to discover in bed. Plus, I was starting to like how the word hellfire rolled off his tongue.

I made an effort to get my head back in the game and thanked my lucky stars he didn't have vampire mindreading powers.

Ezra's eyes dropped to my lips. "Like I was saying, today, we make a start on your training. I cleared it with Minister Willowsun that you can tag along, Marina. The minister suggested Sahil come too, but I wanted to keep the numbers down. New magic is unpredictable."

"Who will mentor my brother?" I wanted us all to be ready.

If what Gaia had said was true, we'd all need to hone our strengths to stand a chance of survival. I still hadn't managed to get hold of Detective Jameson and had no idea if he could be trusted, what with his disappearing act. With or without his help, there was no way I was giving my mum's murderer a free pass.

Not even if he was a god.

"I suggested your dad would be the safest bet to mentor Sahil. Something tells me if your brother joined our training, it would be less harmonious." He tossed a look in Echo's direction. "As long as the cat plays ball, this should be a fun morning."

Echo descended from a nearby tree head first, his golden fur shimmering in the early morning light. He scowled at Ezra. "Your taunts do not harm me, dog. They merely add fuel to my conviction of your insignificance."

"There, there." Marina patted his head. "He is just jealous of your name, Chanakya Gu…"

"It is Chanakya Gunbir Hredhaan of Maharashtra. Thank you for trying, Marina Ambrose. For the uneducated amongst you, it means 'Bright, Brave One with a Great Heart'."

I still worried the sight of Echo in the city would cause panic, but his glamour held. Indeed, the witch's glamour was so sophisticated it targeted speech as well as his appearance. His words to humdrums came across as a series of miaows. The young mums pushing their little darlings through the park or haring after scooters didn't bat an eyelid at his presence.

I quelled the sadness in my chest. As much as I was relieved at my freedom from Alex, I wondered what it would have been like to nurse a child, read stories and tuck them into bed at night. Still, my breasts were probably perkier than your average mother's, and I liked my lie-ins, especially now that I could roll over in bed with abandon without a great lump fighting me for space and the duvet.

Ezra hadn't been sure about teleporting the four of us to Wildwoods, given Echo's propensity to claw his eyes out. So instead, we'd driven over in Marina's vet van, with Echo complaining the whole way about the stench of inferior animals. I was pretty sure he meant Ezra rather than household pets, which didn't bode well for training.

We walked the stone terrace past a pair of terracotta sphinx statues. A rumble sounded as they turned their heads to look at us, stone lips curving into a grimace as Ezra nodded hello.

"All quiet today, boys?" he asked them.

"Yes, sir," they said in unison. "The arena is all ready and primed for action."

Marina clutched me. "I'm never going to get used to this."

"Tell me about it. Just wait until Wildwoods appears. No prior drug use can prepare you for what you are going to see."

"Not even that weird pipe we smoked in the Amazon?"

"Nope."

We arrived at the gnarled yew tree.

"There is one magical institution in every country, " said Ezra. "Places here are coveted. Today will be a mind-expanding experience, but remember, Wildwoods is a haven. You are safe and amongst allies here." Ezra placed his hand on the small of my back and pushed me ahead of everyone towards the yew tree. "Alisha, press the rune."

Heat sizzled up my spine. "Me?"

"You made the blood bond with the constitution. Only the Prime Sorcerer can revoke your rights to enter Wildwoods now. You must, however, register formally with the senate within three lunar cycles.

This is to allow you enough time to understand our ways. Think of it as a probationary period on both sides."

I pressed my palm against the rune. Warmth shot up my arm, and the ground shuddered beneath us. This time, I turned away from the shifting trees and materialising school and faced Marina instead as realisation dawned and her reality warped. Deep in her irises, I discerned the outline of Wildwoods. Her eyes widened in wonder, and a beaming smile stretched across her pretty face.

"This is wild!" She ran towards it without waiting for us.

Echo bounded behind her in protection mode but soon shed his dutiful side and playfully leapt from ancient tree to tree, rolling in the grass, hiding behind the cable cars, chasing a butterfly that landed on the end of his nose and eventually heading for the arena, which had been prepared with a variety of objects.

"That leopard has more sides than a pentagon," said Ezra. "Centuries old and acting like a cub. Give it a few minutes, and he'll be sharpening his claws and turning murderous eyes on me."

I laughed. "Don't mind him. I just bring out the protective side in him, that's all."

He tugged a hand through his hair. The copper flecks in his eyes mesmerised me. "Funny, you have that effect on me too."

"I do?"

"Isn't it obvious?"

I swallowed hard. "Come on. It's about time I learn what I'm made of."

"The students won't arrive until after humdrum school, so we have a clear morning to do our worst." He took off at a run towards the arena, his jeans riding too low for comfort. "Race you."

I'd dressed in a sports bra, T-shirt, yoga pants and trainers that morning. I was a hundred per cent ready for action but still reached the training arena a full minute after him, my chest heaving.

Ezra cleared his throat. "Wildwoods School of the Wondrous has been in existence since the earliest days of the Sorcerer's Senate. Our peculiar governance structures are the oldest in the world, established not long after the death of Merlin. We are the blueprint which is mirrored in peculiar societies globally. However, there can be no specific structure to a peculiar discovering their powers. It is, I'm afraid, rather hit and miss, even for those of us who found our essence in our youth." He pointed to a triangular structure. "Your first task, Alisha and Marina, is to climb to the top of the obelisk and jump off it."

"This should be good." Echo departed to the edge of the area, lay down and licked his paws without a care in the world.

I guffawed. "You can't be serious. That's got to be twenty metres high. Why would we do that?"

"To test flight, of course," said Ezra. "The height has been carefully calculated to allow enough depth for hidden wings to materialise."

"But what if we can't fly?" said Marina. "Will muscly men appear to scoop us up mid-air?"

"Not quite, but the arena adapts to its students." His eyes were on mine as if everyone else had disappeared. "Trust me. I wouldn't put you in danger."

"I don't know. I want to trust you, but we've only just met," I said. "Aren't there any safety videos we can watch first?"

Ezra grinned. "Technology-free zone, hellfire. I thought you had bigger balls than this."

I gritted my teeth and pulled Marina after me. The frame was cool steel against my sweaty palms, and I was conscious of how big my bottom looked from Ezra's vantage point. We climbed as fast as we could for middle-aged women who were a little wary of heights and a lot worried about falling to our deaths. The only solace I took was that, as the sworn protector of my bloodline, Echo would not allow us to endanger our lives. But he had previous experience of sleeping on the job. At the very least, he'd maul Ezra if we landed in a splat of bones and cells on the sawdust floor.

"You ready?" I took in Marina's terrified eyes.

"Hell, no. But I've done stupider things. One-two-three, jump!"

We jumped—no, plopped—off the side of the obelisk and plummeted to the ground, our hair pointing up like arrows, with no wings in sight. Marina, taller than me, was a pink whirr, a little closer to the ground.

I was going to watch my best friend die.

I opened my mouth to scream and instead found myself in Ezra's arms and then just as quickly deposited on the ground next to Marina, who was coughing up bile.

I held her hair back for her and then spun around and shoved Ezra hard against his chest. "What the hell? I thought you said the arena would catch us?"

"That was more fun." He was obviously enjoying himself. "I guess neither of you has wings. That rules out flight, instant armour and probably reactive adaption too. On to the next round. Leopard, you're up."

Echo sauntered over, a glint in his emerald eyes.

I tensed, sensing trouble, and pulled Marina to her feet. She shook like a leaf. She might have been brave in matters of the heart and would put an arm into a crocodile's throat without a second thought, but this was something else entirely. It had started to feel more like an onslaught than a game of equals, and we hadn't even decided on a safe word. If I called out *stop*, would Ezra and Echo even react?

Pine trees shot out of the sawdust, although they had no business growing there without soil and would never have grown so quickly within natural laws.

This is magic.

I tucked Marina in behind me, limbering up and raising my fists. Behind me, Marina's breaths came in jagged puffs as if she were close to hyperventilating. I didn't blame her. The trees had by now multiplied by the dozen and then again, making up a maze of pathways, blotting out the daylight.

I heard Echo behind me before I saw him. The hair on my nape stood on edge, and I knew he had turned into a malevolent foe by the roar on the wind. "Run!" I said.

We scrambled forward through the pine trees, disoriented, not knowing where we should run and who would help.

She clutched me. "Oh, my god. He's going to eat us."

I gulped, tempted to drag her with me behind the foliage. A chink of silver caught my eye. "Aim for the structure."

A sob caught in her throat. "I can't."

"You can." I grabbed Marina's hand and pulled her after me.

We ran down a passage, both hyperventilating, pine needles crunching underfoot, our access blocked and the trees' branches too slim to hold our body weight. Besides, hadn't I seen Echo climb just that morning?

Marina's ashen face crumpled. "We're going to die. I should have packed those bloody tranquillisers."

I nodded. "We'll be more prepared next time. Who did we think we were? Wonder Woman and Supergirl?"

"What next time? They're *never* going to find our bodies."

"Shh."

"I love you, Alisha," said Marina.

"Save it. We're too young to die."

A pounding of the earth. An eighty-kilo leopard bearing down on us. A roar at our backs.

I stopped and swung around, my movements jerky, pearls of sweat on my upper lip.

Echo snarled, ready to pounce. His emerald eyes shone with fierce intent.

I held up my hands and reached out for him. This was my cat. My beautiful Bengal. He wouldn't hurt me.

"I heard his stomach rumble," said Marina. "Don't, Alisha. Please."

I inched forward and relaxed my body, loosening my shoulders and jaw, trying to exude calm.

Echo roared and jumped, flexing his claws mid-air.

I winced, squeezed my eyes shut and sprang back towards Marina. Her eyes were wide open, and her fingers crossed in a desperate plea for good luck. At least we'd die in each other's arms. My ears zeroed in on a bump, followed by a sliding sound. I opened one eye.

A glass wall separated us from Echo. He lay in a heap on the ground, his limbs tangled, evidently out cold.

I extracted myself from Marina's embrace and knocked on the glass. Nada. My killer leopard was sleeping off his exertions. I had a right mind to send him back to India. Protector, my arse.

The ground hummed as the pine trees dropped into it, and the glass faded away.

"Oh hell," I whispered. "Time to move."

A deep voice behind us made us jump. "It's okay, hellfire. He won't harm you."

I inched closer to Ezra and pulled Marina with me. "He won't?"

"Nope, the training exercise is over."

I turned cold eyes on Ezra and thrust out my chest. "Why you…I have nothing to say to you. Nothing at all." I walked away and then spun back. "Actually, I do. Talk about throwing us in the lion's den. He's my cat, dammit. My leopard. And you turned him on us."

"It was Echo's idea and a pretty good one. We now know you are unlikely to have time manipulation or an unending supply of good luck. You don't have speed or invisibility and cannot tame wild or domesticate creatures. I was hoping that would be your talent, Marina. As a vet, it would have been really cool. Still, the universe doesn't always give us the most useful gifts. Pretty neat idea of yours to aim for the highest ground."

I glanced over my shoulder to make sure Echo hadn't moved. "We didn't make it, though, did we? For heaven's sake, man. There has to be an easier way to discover our talents than this."

Ezra frowned. "Although from the viewing and sound booth, it looked like you precisely identified Echo's motives, Marina."

"The viewing and sound booth?" Marina found her fury at last. "What is this, a production set? I thought you said this was a technology-free zone."

"All magically powered, of course."

"Of course." Marina shot him a dark look. "What do you mean by his motives? As in, he really wanted to eat us?"

Echo padded over to us, the venom gone from his eyes. He rolled his body into a lazy stretch. "I am a man-eating leopard, Marina Ambrose. I thought I had told you as much—"

"No, you hadn't. So much for your great heart. And you can eat the wolf man first, thank you very much," said Marina.

Echo gurned, disgusted by the thought. "I did indeed want to eat you, but only because I reverted to pure instincts for the purpose of that training exercise. I am now myself again."

"Well played, cat," Ezra said.

"Thank you, dog. I am pleased you didn't merely make me your administrative assistant in these matters."

"Hang on a minute, Ezra," I said, undecided whether I preferred the two of them at each other's throats or in cahoots. "I distinctly remember you saying in Minister Willowsun's office that you had an inkling of what my powers could be. And that I was the one who saved Melissa from that rogue electric cable."

"Easy, hellfire. There are no shortcuts to this process. We'll get there in our own sweet time."

I pointed a finger at his chest. "But there is no time. You said as much. What if the god attacks and we can't protect ourselves?"

Ezra folded his arms across his chest. His biceps rippled. The show-off. "Gaia didn't say anything about the threat being immediate."

I snorted. "Did you even listen? The goddess said a god would be dispatched to *destroy* me. What, you think a killer god is just going to play footsie with me?"

He gave Echo a sideways glance as if *they* were natural allies. "You have me. And the leopard."

"Have I? Hell," I retorted. "I feel like Little Red Riding Hood. Unprepared and at the mercy of you all. I don't want you to protect me. I want the tools to protect myself."

He came towards me, and the air thinned despite the vast expanse of arena around us. The scent of him filled my nose—the musky scent of roll-up cigarettes and mountain air—but this time, it didn't turn me on.

I saw red. I held out my hands to ward him off, and my palms tingled. The gust sent him sprawling, his hands windmilling through the air, before he landed five metres away, an enigmatic expression on his handsome face.

"There it is, hellfire. I knew it! A druid with power over the wind. That was some move. Just wait until we really see what you can do." He got to his feet and dusted himself off. "One thing I don't understand. Rajika Verma was an animator. Your father is a painter. The question now is, can you do what they can do, and where the hell did your powers come from if not?"

I studied my hands in astonishment.

"What about me?" said Marina in a small voice.

Ezra lifted a single eyebrow. "You're a problem for another day."

14

O ur four-hour training session in the Wildwoods arena left
Marina and me battered, bruised and sweating like pigs. Ezra
caught my sense of urgency at last, and I almost wished he hadn't. I
preferred a relaxed mentor to a demented one.

"Will you stop chucking objects at me?" I gritted my teeth and sent
a spiky projectile thudding to the floor. "Poor Marina is a sitting duck,
and I could do with a break."

My hands had a mind of their own, as if my magic was instinctual
rather than learned, but my confidence needed work. I didn't want to
take a hit to my face, and I kept squealing and cursing even as I
defended myself. Marina cowered behind me, running when I ran,
entirely at the mercy of whatever Ezra and Echo could dream up next.

"Wildwoods won't let any undue harm come to you," said Ezra.

Marina poked her head around me and recoiled as some sort of
cannon sounded to our left. "*Undue* harm? What does that even mean?
Like you'd be okay if I sliced my knee, but you'd draw the line at
losing an ear?"

Ezra lit a cigarette and took a drag. "The school has an infirmary
for the worst battle wounds, although I'm not sure the nurse is there at
the moment. I could probably rummage in there for a healing potion,

though. How else are you going to learn how to defend and attack? The fact you're a runner and a kickboxer means you're strong, Alisha, and have decent stamina, but in the Otherworld, that's not enough. The talents at your disposal are rudimentary right now. Druids of your kind should be able to manipulate the wind and cause hurricanes, tornadoes and thermal spirals."

"Not even Rajika could do that." Echo's eyes narrowed. "This is very unconventional. If I didn't like you, I would dip a stick in your blood and ask for heritage tests."

"Actually, DNA tests are done with a cotton swab and saliva," said Marina.

Echo inclined his head. "I bow to your knowledge of useless things, Marina Ambrose."

"Gee, thanks."

I scanned the arena to make sure Ezra hadn't lulled us into a false sense of security. My trust had taken a knock after our experience with the menacing Echo. Who knew what this half wizard, half werewolf was capable of or how much kindness and care remained if you were half beast?

Ezra chucked his fag away and ground it into the sawdust, where it glowed for a moment before disintegrating entirely. "Right, that's enough for the day. Next time we'll work on close combat, speed and knowing your enemy."

We retraced our steps out of Wildwoods. The yew tree shimmered as we passed it, and once it was behind us, the air grew thicker again, filled with London smog and the buses that hurtled past the park on the main road. We traipsed through Crystal Palace Park, past two humdrum teenagers flying rainbow kites with trailing ribbons, oblivious to the vast magical world only moments away. I raised my hand and sent their kites skywards, prompting shouts of delight until the kites took on a life of their own, jerking away from their owners, and heading directly for the sun.

"Oops," I said.

Ezra grabbed my hand and pulled me on. "Keep walking, hellfire. That rookie mistake is the sort of thing that could cost you. The fourth law, the Founder's Law, states—"

"Peculiars must hide the existence of the Otherworld from humdrums. Got it. Sorry." I paused, rubbing my shoulder, which had come up black and blue during a tumble in the arena. "What I don't get is why we had to go through the whole palaver this morning. It seems an unreasonable way to learn a skill. Why can't I look up techniques in a druid manual? The Wildwoods library must have something of use."

Echo lifted his head from the puddle he'd been lapping and caught up with us. "Druids are literate, but they are prevented by doctrine from recording their knowledge in written form. Besides, you can't learn everything from books. Somethings you just *do*."

We exited the park towards the side street where Marina had parked her van. She opened the rear doors. Echo sprang in, his hulking weight sinking the vehicle closer to the asphalt, and settled himself on blankets there. She eased the doors shut and then clambered into the front. Ezra and I rode up front with her. I plugged in my seatbelt, noticing Ezra didn't bother. Echo snored in the back, his bulky body causing havoc with the van's suspension as we sped over South London potholes.

"Maybe I could ask another druid to help me," I said, "like Minister Willowsun or my dad."

Ezra shifted in his seat, his thigh parallel to mine. The physical toll of learning magic had been high, and I longed to nestle into him. For comfort only. I still hadn't forgiven him for conspiring with Echo to scare the living daylights out of us. And I had no idea why he had asked Marina for a ride when he could have teleported to Australia and back in the time it took for a traffic light to change. I made a mental note to ask him to take me there if we ever became true friends. I had a thing for kangaroos and koalas.

"The minister is too busy to focus on one student. She has the whole of Wildwoods to oversee. Your father hasn't practised druidry for a long time. You could take your chances with him just like your brother. Druid skills are varied. You wouldn't ask a violinist to teach you how to play the cello just because they both play in an orchestra."

"There must be a common language, surely?"

"I've been doing this a long time, hellfire. It pays to have me in your corner." His deep voice reverberated in my ear, laced with a challenge. "Bottom line is, you muddle along, shooting breeze at unsuspecting strangers, you join a druid tribe—apart from the South London druids, there are some in France and maybe some in Asia—or you suck it up and put all your effort into mastering what I can teach you. What's it going to be?"

I held my tongue, weighing up the options, then shrugged.

"Awkward." Marina switched on the radio. Kings of Leon blasted out of her third-rate speakers, more feedback than crooning rockers.

Echo growled, and the hairs on my arm stood on edge. "When I wake, I will induct you in real music. Lata Mangeshkar, Mohamed Rafi and Jagjit Singh, for starters. For now, will you turn off that racket? Some of us are trying to sleep."

"Gigolo, who?" Marina turned the radio down to a background whisper.

I sighed, having seen enough of my friends' children and my infantile ex-husband to know the signs of hunger and tiredness. "I haven't a clue, but can you put your foot on it? He sounds grumpy."

A FEW HOURS LATER, I rocked up at the community centre to teach my night class. My body ached, and relief flooded me to leave magic behind. I'd left Echo in a steak-induced coma on the sofa, his drool pooling on the fabric. I had no idea whether Ezra lived in a house, a cave or a cottage in the woods, but he seemed keen to hang around my flat until I gave him a push to leave. I didn't want a minder or a protector. The Otherworld could be intense. After the morning I'd had, I just wanted some peace and quiet. Or even better, a drunken girls' night with Marina to wash away my troubles with the help of copious amounts of wine and some chaser shots. My newest favourite was Patrón XO Cafe, but I would settle for Tequila Gold.

With enforced compassionate leave from my teaching job prompted by the Prime Sorcerer, I might even have time for some naps. Joy bubbled up at the thought of starfish naps in my double bed that I didn't have to share with a man. There would be no stinky man smell to mask the scent of my spring daisies fabric softener. A little rest and relaxation before I got to grips with Mum's murderer and my druid heritage was just the ticket to make me feel like a new woman again.

First, I had to tell my night class they'd have a supply teacher for a few weeks. The news would go down like a lead balloon, given the supply teacher didn't offer kickboxing in her repertoire to supplement the language and grammar teaching. More fool him. I knew how to get the best out of my students.

I turned away from the whiteboard where I'd been writing a list of nouns to learn for this week's homework and tucked a lock of jet-black hair behind my ear.

"Nita! How many times have I told you not to play with matches?" I said.

I couldn't help but like Nita, despite repeatedly telling her off for conducting oddball experiments in class. There was no doubt biology was the right degree for her as soon as night class nudged her over the points needed to gain a place. So far this term, I had caught her teaching her students how to use deodorant as a fire canister, how to explode a Coke bottle and how to make invisible ink with baking soda. I'd confiscated ingredients for a hot ice and crystallisation experiment and been livid to discover a foam volcano she'd conducted under her desk to the delight of the rest of my students. I kept a pack of wet wipes in my work bag primarily because of Nita.

And to get rid of grime from riding the tube. London was a cesspool.

The thing is, I didn't mind Nita's messes. Other teachers might have mistaken her behaviour for disruptiveness or an inability to follow the rules. Not me. Here was an immigrant showing up week after week to my class, putting her hand up, doing her homework, making friends and showing she had a passion. That passion was something even adults struggled to find. It would set her in good stead her whole life. It didn't mean she wasn't a pain sometimes, but who said only children who coloured within the lines grew up to be upstanding citizens? I liked students who showed a bit of mettle.

That's how I would have brought up my children had I been lucky enough to have them.

Caught red-handed, Nita bit her lip apologetically. "Sorry, miss."

She pursed her lips to blow out the match, but I lifted a hand, and a breeze got there first, blowing her hair over her shoulders at the same time. Well, technically, like she'd been blasted by a wind turbine.

Puzzled, she looked at the closed window and shrugged.

I hid a smile. I was pretty sure I wasn't allowed to practice magic without Ezra's supervision, but what he didn't know wouldn't hurt him. Besides, I was a grown woman. At forty, you'd think I'd be able to weigh up risk versus reward.

I slotted back into teacher mode. "Copy these nouns into your exercise books, look up definitions in your dictionaries, use the words in full sentences and bring them to our next lesson. No excuses."

Six grown men and four women groaned, united in their disgust of grammar homework.

"Can you show us that kick now?" said Nita. "You promised last time."

I nodded. "Of course. Up you all get. Find some space. Make sure you're not swinging your body parts at anyone."

Chair legs scraped on the floor as they stood up: nineteen-year-old Nita; the middle-aged Chinese women Fei Yen and Faeza, who owned the tea and occult shop; Marek, the Polish builder with the receding hairline and enormous biceps; Tomás and Santiago, the Portuguese couple, who wanted to be able to make friends at Pride; Farzad, the Iranian grandfather, whose goal was to have a conversation with other seniors at the bingo hall; Nagma, the Bangladeshi woman, who assumed I spoke Hindi because I was Indian; and Ethan and Hassan, two high school dropouts who came to my class as a way around a formal English grade at school.

A motley crew, reflective of the city and how it could be a microcosm of the whole world within a few square metres.

Add gods, vampires, werewolves, druids, wizards, fae and talking animals to that list, and my mind was truly blown.

"Before we start, I have something to tell you…I lost my mother recently. She died in an accident, and I need a bit of time to get my head straight. I'm taking a few weeks of compassionate leave. That means there'll be a replacement teacher to take my place."

Ten faces looked at me in sympathy and disappointment.

"We are sorry, Miss Verma." Farzad clasped his hands together. "We will pray for your mother."

"But no one can teach as good as you," said Nita.

"*Good* is an adjective, Nita. You mean the adverb *well*. A good teacher teaches well." I plastered a reassuring smile on my face and crossed my fingers that the killer god took mercy on me. "I'll be back before your exams, I promise."

"We saw Death and the Hanged Man in the cards," said Fei Yen and Faeza as one, giving me vibes of the twins in *The Shining*.

A shiver ran up my spine. Their innate weirdness sometimes marked them out as different, even amongst this group of oddballs, but there was no cure for that. All the best people appreciated weirdness anyway.

"Let's not dwell on it, eh?" I said.

They'd done readings for me in the past, but they really should have asked. I liked my tarot readings to be a bit of fun, not a true reflection of life. It's why I always avoided fortune tellers at fun fairs. Nothing good could come of knowing the future.

Fei Yen shook her head, tousling her silky black elfin cut. "You misunderstand. The card didn't speak of literal death or hanging. They spoke of sweeping transformation and doors opening."

Faeza nodded, her pink rosebud lips turning downwards. "And great pain."

"Well, aren't you two the life and soul of the party? Let's finish on a high note, shall we? Ready for that back kick, class? Check you have enough room behind you, at least two metres. That's it, Marek. You can push that desk back. Yes, you too, Nagma." I bounced up and down on the spot and stretched my limbs. "Copy me. Just a little warm-up so we don't sprain anything."

They wobbled and lunged in front of me, neither the fittest nor youngest group in the world, but mostly willing.

"Give it some welly, Ethan. You'll be back on the sofa soon enough. Nagma, it might be hard getting your leg up in that Punjabi suit. Just take it easy. We're just having a go. It's not going to be perfect, and some of you might not get your leg all the way up." I clapped. "Right, eyes on me. Turn on the spot. Lift your right knee to your chest. A bit higher, Santiago. Well done, Nita. Look over your right shoulder. Extend your leg backwards to your imaginary target, kick and swivel back to your starting position. Good. Excellent work, Farzad."

Ethan and Hassan sent a display flying at the back of the room, and Nagma got caught in the scarf around her neck.

I decided to call it a day before I got sued for negligence.

"That's it for today. Thank you, class." I made a mental note to myself to look at potential sportswear on eBay as a treat when they passed their exams. If Echo's steak money hadn't carved a hole in my finances by then.

They hovered around me to say their goodbyes when I lifted my eyes to find a stranger there.

"Excuse me." I frowned.

The estate had trouble a few months previously, and I had taken to locking the door from the inside while class was in flow to prevent any bother from the local riffraff. I wasn't sure how he'd gotten inside, but he didn't seem all there. Not that I was worried. I was pretty sure any of my students would have been pleased to try out the back kick.

"This is a closed session," I said, "but if you'd like to register for night class, I can give you the details."

"Druid," the stranger whispered.

Now I was hearing things.

I had no idea what was up with the heating or if I was having hot flushes, but my body was burning up.

The class stepped back, their expressions wary, giving me room to take charge.

His eyes were liquid amber, but their overall impact was cold. His short hair stood on end, and he wore a boiler suit in dull tones over a barrel-like flank. He was as strong as an ox, and my instincts told me to run, but that would have been stupid. He was just a man who'd wandered into the wrong hall. I'd probably left the door unlocked. Time off from work would do me a world of good.

"Have we met?" I stepped out from behind the desk, my skin

crawling. I'd seen the suit before, albeit briefly, on the day Melissa narrowly avoided the faulty electricity cable outside EvolveTech.

Amber eyes glinted within a swarthy, leathery face. "There is no hiding from the sun. It stretches across streets and fields and icy plains. It reaches into buildings and creeps under the eyelids."

Farzad approached the man. "Strange man. You drunk. Go home."

He laid a hand on the man's shoulder to usher him out, then snatched it back and staggered away. It sizzled, his skin red and blistering where he had touched the stranger.

Nita screamed.

The stranger turned his unnatural eyes on her.

I put my body between Farzad and the man. I was impressed by Farzad's ability to put together a coherent English sentence on the spot, but he was more cut out for the bingo hall than playing security guard.

"Listen," I said to the man, unsure how he'd burned Farzad. Maybe he had some kind of battery pack under his boiler suit. He really needed to take the safety precautions of his profession seriously. "No need to intimidate me. I didn't dob you into the authorities for your dodgy work that day. You weren't wearing a badge. I'll get the first aid kit and patch up Farzad here, and you can just turn around and walk away. Although, you might need to get more training because I wouldn't want an electrician with your skills wiring a doll's house, let alone a public supply."

He gave a slight shake of his head like he had no idea what I was on about. Maybe I'd pegged him wrongly, and he wasn't an electrician after all. Maybe he was just masquerading as one and had no affiliation whatsoever. Here he was, swanning around when he could have learned his trade—the cheek of it.

He leaned forward.

My students edged back, their faces beaded with perspiration.

"You can call me electrician. I have been many incarnations of myself." A ripple of amusement went through him. "You can call me all the names under the sun, but I will always be me."

"Are you on crack? There's an addiction group here on Wednesday nights. The sign-up info is in the hallway."

He frowned. "The game is underfoot, druid. And you'd do well to stay out of my way."

I froze.

There it was again. I hadn't misheard.

I'd barely stepped into the Otherworld, and here it was, following me to work in the guise of a threatening man. Let's face it; I'd dealt with dozens of threatening men before: outside building sites, inside nightclubs, on the tube and at sweaty gigs when I wanted to dance, not be groped.

But this one was creepier than the rest.

This was an opportune moment for my leopard protector to jump into the fray. I pinched shut my eyes and sent a silent message to Echo.

Come. I need you at the community centre.

We'd not talked about whether our minds could walkie-talkie each other, but I figured it wouldn't hurt.

"For now, I've decided to remind you that insignificant creatures would do well to stay out of the affairs of their superiors." He raised his voice and waved his hands grandly like a preacher at the pulpit. His thick, black nails made me gag. "Let this be a lesson to you all. If you had worshipped us in gratitude, we wouldn't have to cause you pain."

I took up a fight stance.

He didn't look like he was going to turn back meekly into the night. It was going to take some persuasion and maybe a kick to the face.

I stared him out and fought the primal urge to turn away. "Get out of our community centre."

"The guy's on acid," said Marek, like he'd seen it all before.

"Kick his behind, Miss Verma!" Nagma swung her scarf around like a whip, despite her advanced years.

Echo, where are you?

He'd made his point, whatever it was—that he didn't need an invitation, had bigger balls than us and had the right to be a shoddy electrician—but he was still here. I didn't have the faintest clue why.

The man walked towards us, unfazed, as if we were mere flies.

I hesitated and then unleashed a breeze that fanned his hair like he was on the beach.

Without batting an eyelid, he walked through it to Nita.

Nita spun, trying to execute a back kick, but he grabbed her shoe and flung it away. Her rubber sole seemed to melt.

"Get away from her." I went in for a crescent kick, followed by an elbow strike.

"Yes, miss!" shouted Ethan. He and Hassan seemed to be moving in from the side to help me.

"Stay back," I said.

The stranger squeezed Nita's shoulder, leaving her writhing to escape. The arm of her T-shirt disintegrated under the pressure of his fingers. Her eyes widened in horror, and a cry ripped from her throat. She was drenched with sweat.

"Nita, stay calm," I said. "You'll be okay."

"You did this," said the stranger to me. "In fifteen years, she would have been at a Harrow laboratory on the brink of a discovery. I could have let her live. But what is a god without a little vengeance?"

My blood ran cold. It couldn't be.

He had come, just like the goddess had predicted—my mother's killer.

He hadn't come when I'd been on a run with Echo when my magical leopard could have protected me. Or on Wildwoods grounds when the school itself would have channelled its defences, or any number of peculiars could have helped.

This killer god had found me at my most vulnerable.

I kicked myself for being stupid enough to let it happen. I willed the universe to keep Nita safe.

Gaia. Echo. I need you.

A current pulsed between his fingers.

"No, no! Wait." I was defenceless against a god. Gaia had said he'd killed my mother. But how could I fight him with a few kicks and punches and a light breeze? If he wanted prayer, he could have it. I'd pray to him every dawn if that's what it took to keep my class safe.

I pressed my palms together in prayer.

The lights went out. Not switched off, but as if the light had been sucked into a void.

A spark flared, and then a scuffle ensued.

The swirls of black became limbs and tails and muzzles. I fought to decipher the darkness—slick fur and teeth.

A shape leapt at me, passing by a finger's breath away. Panting, an echo in my ears.

I was rooted to the spot, my heartbeat rattling until I couldn't distinguish between the sounds.

Then came a bloodcurdling cry.

15

The light returned to the classroom, though no one had hit the light switch. The god had fled, leaving upturned tables and huddled bodies. I swallowed hard, trying to keep my fear under control, though my instincts told me to get the hell out of there. I hadn't been able to make sense of the sounds in the dark.

My stomach roiled as I surveyed the room.

An enormous wolf lay next to Nita's crumpled body, his tail tucked in, nudging her with his paws. His thick, copper fur clung to his muscular frame, interspersed with silver-white.

When he turned his eyes on me, he howled as if in mourning.

My adrenalin had been racing for so long that I felt lightheaded. I took a deep breath, wiped the sweat from my forehead and risked a look at the class. "Are you all okay?"

Nine scared faces stared back at me. Farzad still nursed his hand.

"Fuck this, miss. I'm out of here," said Ethan, followed by a rush of feet.

Five remained, including Fei Yen and Faeza.

"Go," I said. "The wolf's not a threat. I'll deal with this."

They scurried out, eager to believe my lie.

I gulped. A fox in the classroom wasn't farfetched in a city overrun by them, but a wolf was the stuff of nightmares. They weren't scavengers; they were carnivores.

Nita looked asleep, most likely unconscious. Shock could really take the wind out of your sails. Her creamy skin was flushed, and her singed T-shirt made me wince. There wasn't a mark on her. That didn't mean it would stay that way.

Echo would have scared away or snacked on this wolf for sport, but he was nowhere to be seen, despite my telepathic S.O.S.

Sirens sounded in the distance.

One of the class had probably called the police. Good. I was ready for someone else to take responsibility.

I wasn't going to hang about, though. I needed to get the wolf away from Nita before it hurt her. What was it doing here in inner city London, away from its pack? I couldn't remember what you were supposed to do when confronted by a wolf. Marina would have known whether to back away, stare him out or make noise. Not that it had helped with Echo, but my preferred option—to run away—wasn't an option here. With no saucepans, blowhorn or vuvuzela in my pocket, I grabbed the nearest thing I could find—a stapler—and clicked it like our lives depended on it and added "go away" to the rhythm.

The wolf cocked its head like I had lost my marbles. If he were in a zoo enclosure, I would have called him beautiful. He yapped and pawed at Nita's chest, his claws retracted, and then dipped his head.

Outside, Marek and Hassan banged the window, trying to help out, and Ethan thudded some wheelie bin lids. Only Fei Yen and Faeza seemed morose and calm.

The wolf must have been deaf because the noise didn't faze him at all. I put down the stapler and edged closer, signalling my students to go away. I owed it to them not to add 'mauled teacher' to their list of traumas.

The sirens grew nearer.

Huge balls told me it was probably a male. "It's okay, boy. You can go now. Go on, shoo, before the police sling you in the dog pound."

He whimpered again.

For a moment, I thought he was trying to communicate. I must have been more under strain than I thought. I crouched down on the opposite side of Nita's body to the wolf, moving millimetre by millimetre.

All it would have to do was spring across her body to take me out.

I put my hands up and channelled my focus. My breeze had always worked for me in moments of terror. One false move and the wolf would think he was in a tumble dryer.

The wolf put his wet nose on my palm.

I almost emptied my bladder there and then. That would teach me to increase my water intake. His glossy fur smelt familiar, evoking a buried memory, but it was only when he turned his grey eyes on me that I noticed the silver necklace tight around its neck, threaded with charms: a moon, a thistle and binary code.

No bloody way.

"Ezra?" I breathed out in wonder.

He whimpered as cars skidded to a halt in the car park outside and blue lights flicked across the classroom.

Taking my courage in my hands, I reached for the soft fur on his neck and pushed him gently towards the door. "You need to get out of here before the police come. Find me later. Go, now."

I turned my full attention to Nita, although every cell told me to check Ezra made it out safely. "Hang in there, Nita. Help is on the way."

I put her into the recovery position, rolling her over onto her side, rearranging her knee, tilting her head back a fraction and checking her airways. I stopped short. Her body was hot to the touch, feverish even, as if she'd spent the day baking on an exotic beach. London was a cool five degrees Celsius tonight.

My hands trembled as I checked her skin again. My own heartbeat became sluggish with dread as I checked for a pulse.

"Nita?"

I felt her neck, then her wrist, hoping my rusty first-aid skills were to blame for my panic. I stared at her chest, determined to see it rise and fall, and then listened for breath at her lightly parted mouth.

No. No. No. "Someone call an ambulance!"

I started compressions, worried about breaking her ribs but determined not to lose her.

Fei Yen approached from my peripheral vision and laid her hand on my shoulder.

I shrugged it off and continued the compressions. The seconds seemed like hours. What was taking the police so long?

Fei Yen squeezed my shoulder and then pulled me back. Her eyes filled with sorrow. "Why deny what you know to be true?"

"I have to help her."

"She's dead," said Fei Yen. "She has already crossed to the other side."

I knew she was right, even though Nita was unnaturally hot to the touch and not cold like dead bodies were supposed to be. I picked up Nita's slight body and rocked her.

Fei Yen waited a moment. Then she took Nita from my arms and laid her carefully on the floor, straightening her limbs and running a hand over her eyelids. Mascara crumbled from Nita's thick lashes.

"I did this," I said.

A heavy sigh. "No, you didn't. The god did."

A shiver ran up my spine. What did Fei Yen know about all of this?

There was nothing godly about murder. That so-called god had killed my mother. He had killed my student. He was responsible for the other deaths Detective Jameson and the gravedigger had talked of.

Weren't gods supposed to be benign and merciful? He had killed for no other reason than to create chaos for attention. So what if he wanted to be loved? I wanted to be loved. Everyone did. That didn't mean we went around killing people.

Rage unfurled inside me. Nita had been loved. She'd been loved by me, her fellow students and her family. She'd already been through so much leaving Turkey. It had been my job to protect her, and I'd failed. There would be no more mess in my classroom because of her. No more baking soda experiments or future glory. All her promise, all her passion and determination amounted to nothing now that her body lay lifeless on the classroom floor.

I needed air. I stumbled to my feet, and rushed outside into the black night.

Nagma made a beeline for me. "Miss Verma, is Nita okay? What happened to the wolf?"

Ethan's face loomed large. "Tomás and Santiago took Farzad to Accident and Emergency for his hand."

"Miss Verma, what's a druid?" Hassan asked.

Faeza gave me a sad smile, wrapped her arms around Hassan and ushered him away. "Did you hear druid? I heard druggie. Makes sense. That guy must have been on something."

I vomited onto the grass.

In the distance, under a crescent moon, a wolf howled.

It was close to midnight when two police officers gave me a ride home. I slumped in the back of the car and leaned my head against the window. Shadows lurked all around me, flitting in and out of my peripheral vision.

An officer leapt out to open my door. "Please get in touch if you remember any further details, Miss Verma. Don't worry; we'll catch the creep."

I nodded my thanks, although I doubted these humdrum police could catch the god, let alone hold him. They had even less information than me. They had no idea what he was, if he could change faces, who he'd target next or what Nita had died from. The police promises were as reassuring as a gerbil squaring up to a bear. They were completely outmatched and outgunned, just like me.

They did a U-turn while I walked to my building. I looked hard into the void of night, my heartbeat rattling. Nothing came for me, though I feared it would. The door opened before I put my key in the lock, and Marina tumbled out in a blur of pink.

"I'm glad you're here." I fell into her arms, ready for someone to look after me for a change. Whoever said grown women couldn't both be strong *and* need comfort obviously had no idea about women.

"I've been worried senseless since I got your text. I'm so sorry, Alisha." She pulled back to reassure herself I wasn't hurt. "Echo let me in through the back window."

One of my ex-husband's complaints was how often Marina came over. He was right. I should have given her a key

"Ezra's here too, even though Echo threatened to gnaw his leg. He said you told him to come by."

I raised a weak smile. "Something like that. Just let me have a quick wash and change into my PJs."

She gave me an encouraging nod. "I'll make you some tea and toast."

I ignored the voices in the living room, shut the door to my bedroom and took a ragged breath before kicking off my shoes and peeling off my clothes. Then I headed for my en suite bathroom, turned on the shower and let hot soapy suds wash away the day's grime and soothe my soul.

Three faces floated in the nebulous pink of my closed eyelids: Nita, crumpled on the floor; the swarthy amber-eyed god; and Ezra in his copper-silver wolf form.

I sighed, washed my hair and stepped out of the shower before dressing in my PJs and yanking a comb through my hair in front of my steamy mirror. Not a scrap of makeup remained on my face, but I didn't care. I wanted my tea and toast. While makeup could make me feel ready to take on the world, sometimes I just wanted to be myself.

I padded barefoot to the living room, the remnants of coral nail polish on my toes and wet hair making my T-shirt stick to my back. The lamp lit the room, which suited my mood just fine. That was, apart from the slight whiff of a zoo, but a leopard and a wolf couldn't be expected to smell like a spa.

Echo purred in greeting. He dwarfed Marina on one sofa, taking up two-thirds of the space. A steaming mug of tea and a plate of thickly buttered toast waited for me on the coffee table a few inches from Ezra.

"Hey, hellfire." His gaze softened as it drifted over me.

"Thanks for tonight, Ezra. You put yourself in danger for my class."

"I did it for you."

My mouth felt dry. I must have been gagging for my tea.

He wore chequered boxers and a thin button-up shirt, only it wasn't done up to the top. There wasn't a goosebump on him. I figured wolves were warmer-blooded than humans and druids. The charm necklace that had been tight around his wolf neck now hung just above his pecks. A closer look told me he'd lost the top three shirt buttons. Had he ripped it off when he changed into his wolf form? The shirt sleeves were rolled up, and one arm had a nasty run of blisters.

"Don't let your tea get cold." Marina waggled her eyebrows.

Flushing, I gave her my best WTF look.

She grinned and gave me the peace sign.

I sat next to Ezra, averting my eyes from his bulging thighs. Then I reached for my tea, wishing belatedly that I'd put on a bra. Like most women, my breasts preferred to be wild and free, but hell, I wasn't twenty anymore.

My eyes flicked to the blisters. "What happened to your arm? Shall I get some antiseptic cream?"

"The dog heals more quickly than any of us," said Echo. "He has no need for humdrum lotions."

I missed the days when Echo would slink around my feet to show his affection. This Echo was tough as old boots.

"Echo's right. It's just a scratch." Grey eyes turned sombre. "Sorry I couldn't save the kid. That cuts deep."

Tears welled, but I pushed back my despair. There would be time for grief later. I wanted the killer god to pay.

"It could have been much worse, dog, if you hadn't been able to slip from the god's grasp," Echo said. "Who knows what the outcome would have been without your presence? I owe you my thanks for protecting Alisha when I was otherwise occupied. I admit the deer I caught in the royal park was the highlight of my year, but I would never have forgiven myself had Alisha been harmed."

I glared at him. "You were hunting when I sent my S.O.S., Echo? I could have done with your help."

Echo growled. "Did you use my full name? Usually, the magical post is more reliable, Alisha. I am sorry it failed you. I will have a word with the cloud master."

I blinked rapidly. "The cloud master?"

"Yes." He talked to me as if I were a distracted toddler. "You throw your message into clouds, where they are transformed into raindrops to be caught and held to the ear to decipher. Isn't that what you did? A system that works much better in London than in the Sahara, I might add."

"Er…no. I just asked you to come with my mind."

He threw up his magnificent head and emitted a strange honking noise I realised was laughing. "The granddaughter of Rajika Verma thinks I'm a *telepathic* leopard?" The honks continued. "Rajika's spirit is rolling her eyes; I just know it. You have a lot to learn."

"So everyone keeps telling me." I turned to look at Ezra because Echo liked being centre stage too much to stop the honking of his own accord. "How did you know to be there, Ezra? And what happened to the light? Did you hit the switch on the way in? Neat trick."

He rolled the moon charm between long, lean fingers. The silver threads amongst his chestnut brown hair made him more handsome. "See this? I told you my father was a werewolf. That's where my beast comes from."

"I remember." I took a bite of my toast and pulled my sopping hair over one shoulder. The wet patch spread too close to my chest for comfort. I grimaced. "I should have brought out a towel."

Ezra's eyes dropped to my chest. He looked away. "Shall I get you one?"

My stomach fluttered. It must have been my new single status. My hormones were obviously in overdrive. Hardly surprising, really. I had years of monogamy to make up for. I only had a decade or so before menopause and I wanted to enjoy myself before my libido took a hit. I pushed the thoughts out of my head. "Sorry, I interrupted."

"My wizard side is from the maternal line. My parents are dead, but when my mother died, her three sisters couldn't take me in. The pack wouldn't have it. They'd tolerated my mother, but to trust her witch sisters was a step too far. I was never going to be one of the great wizards. Pack law wouldn't tolerate it. It was more trouble than it was worth to go up against an alpha. My aunts knew that, but they loved my mother and wanted to give me a fighting chance. Werewolves tend to die young, especially werewolves with portal magic. We're rarer than an equinox. So my three aunts each gifted me a charm. I used the moon charm tonight. It allows me to suck away artificial light for a minute to allow escape. It gave me the edge of surprise." His eyes gleamed. "But if any of you betray this secret, I will kill you."

Marina smiled, showing even white teeth that had never needed braces—the lucky cow.

"What the hell, Marina? He just threatened to"—I pulled my finger across my neck—"and you *smiled*?"

"Easy tiger," said Marina. "I discovered something tonight."

"I'd prefer it if you didn't bring up other big cats in my presence, Marina Ambrose." Echo's head was too close to hers for comfort.

We all rolled our eyes at him.

He lifted his head in the haughty manner of a king who could not be lowered by mere subjects.

"What did you discover?" I said.

"You turfed Ezra out, and he teleported into my van just as I was doing a three-point turn. I got spooked, mounted the kerb and crashed into a post box. Long story short, I invited him back to mine to knock around some ideas about how to encourage you to embrace training more—you know, given you're in the shit with the gods more than I am—and something clicked in me. I just *knew* you were in trouble. I felt it. Like here." She patted her heart. "I shoved Ezra out of the door, trying to explain, completely forgetting he could teleport. Next thing I knew, his clothes were on my floor, and his naked butt had teleported out of there."

I quashed a pang of jealousy.

It's not like I had a claim to Ezra. If Marina wanted him, I wouldn't fight her for him. Sisters before misters. It's not even as if I really wanted him. It would be really bad juju to get into another entanglement without exorcising Alex from my head.

"Point is, I smiled because I *know* Ezra wouldn't hurt you. I feel it in my bones. Just as I felt in my bones that Echo wasn't himself in the arena."

"Turns out your best friend is an empath, hellfire," Ezra said. "She saved you tonight as much as I did. I wouldn't have known you were in distress without her."

I frowned, not liking the suggestion I was a damsel needing to be rescued. I had no idea how I'd manage it, but I was not putting myself in that vulnerable position again. I was not going to fail someone who needed my protection. Even if that meant I armed myself with kitchen knives and had to booby-trap my whole flat.

"So what does an empath do? Read thoughts and stuff?" I tried to keep my voice upbeat.

Echo groaned. "I don't know why I expect so much of you, granddaughter of Rajika Verma. I really must ask the Minister for History and the Today if I can look into your ancestral records to see if there are any unexpected blips there." He huffed. "Telepathy is reading thoughts. Empathy is sensing feelings. Even a troll would know that."

Marina squealed in glee. "I'm so excited to find out what I can do. And just think, if I know what you are feeling, I might be able to sense when animals are in pain too. Veterinary Awards, here I come!"

I was happy for her. She'd wanted so badly to find out what her peculiar nature would be and had cheered me on, despite her own pangs of disappointment. I'd even wondered whether it had all been a mistake and she was a humdrum after all. Logically, given she could see Echo's true form, I knew that couldn't be true, but the Otherworld was so new to us that we needed proof to believe each step. Marina would never have been a lesser person as a humdrum. She was extraordinary in every incarnation, but I was relieved to have her as my peculiar sister. I just wished I'd been there to find out first.

"It is not the done thing to profit from your magic, Marina Ambrose, but in this instance, I suspect only good will come of it," purred Echo.

Ezra shrugged. The skin on his arm had almost completely healed. "Technically, there's no rule against it, although the Sorcerer's Senate has discussed it according to the minutes of their meetings. It is *very* hard to profit from magic while obeying the other rules, so they didn't think an additional one was worth the effort."

A knock sounded at the door. At 1 a.m.. Who turned up at that hour?

Echo leapt off the sofa, energy rolling from his magnificent body, claws no longer retracted but ready to do damage.

"Holy shit, you think that's the god?" Marina was paler and stiffer than I'd ever seen her, as if she had soaked up all our fear.

"An *invited* guest would use the buzzer. Hit the lights," I said in a whisper. "That gave us an advantage last time."

Ezra shook his head. "My charm only lasts a minute or two. Best to just switch off the lamp the humdrum way."

Marina dove for the lamp in a poorly executed forward roll and yanked out the plug at the socket. I'm not sure it made covering the distance any faster, but I dug that she was getting into the spirit of things.

"Don't touch that!" I shouted, worried the electrician god would have sent a powerful current through the walls.

She stood up tentatively, right as rain.

A second knock on the door, this time more urgent.

I sucked in a shaky breath. "Maybe the electrician god is more polite than we thought."

"More likely he can't teleport like Gaia can or is saving his energy for bigger fights. Be great right now to be able to get guidance from the senate on his history. We're flying blind here," said Ezra.

"Stupid laws." I gritted my teeth and ventured into the dark corridor to open it. The rules of hospitality left me no choice. My house, my job.

Ezra followed on my heel.

"Get back here, granddaughter of Rajika Verma, or I will raise hell in this neighbourhood," roared Echo.

"You might need to," I said.

I nodded at Ezra, counted to three and unhooked the latch.

16

———

I opened the door a crack at a time, letting in a sliver of light from the hallway. Ezra's breath fanned the back of my neck. Echo and Marina stood alert and ready a few paces behind us. My fingers tingled, ready to unleash whatever I could at the murderous god—at least this time, I had back up.

A foot wedged the door open.

I saw red and used the door as a battering ram.

The squealing voice on the other side gave me pause, but I didn't care. I slammed the foot over and over again until I reckoned it was a pulpy mess.

For Mum. For Nita. For the scientists that could have done good in the world.

The god deserved everything that was coming to him.

"Yes, Alisha. Get him!" said Marina.

The foot stopped struggling.

The battle had been easier than I thought, so I opened the door a fraction more and frowned when the pool of light revealed a familiar trainer and sock. The ball of anxiety in my belly transformed into fury. I'd washed those stinky socks a million times before and bought those trainers for his last birthday before the divorce.

I wrenched open the door. "Alex? It's one in the morning. What the hell are you doing here?"

My ex-husband groaned, and happiness bloomed like a rose inside me.

Not only had we lucked out and avoided doing battle with the god, but I had dealt with Alex as easily as an exterminator deals with a rat. It felt good after all our angry emails and telephone calls to go to bat. He couldn't even blame me for thinking he was an intruder. I bent down to check on him.

I was an angry ex-wife, not an arsehole.

He gazed up at me like he was seeing stars. Blond hair and blue eyes with more wrinkles than in his prime, but we all had those. I'd still look twice at him if we didn't have our history.

"What did you do that for? I didn't even have a chance to tell you I love you." He reached for my cheek, and a cloud of beer breath hit me, possibly plus salt-and-vinegar crisps. "But I do."

Marina stormed over to us, flicked his hand away and stuck a pointy finger at his chest. "Don't you *dare* say that after everything you put her through."

Alex slid out from under her finger and staggered to his feet. "Still sticking your nose in where it doesn't belong, Marina? You girls been partying tonight?"

I cringed. When I started challenging him about his gambling, he took to using belittling nicknames for me: baby cakes, sweet cheeks, muffin, you name it. They made me want to hit him with a saucepan. "You reek of booze, Alex. It's late opening at The Rose and Crown tonight, isn't it?"

He held up his hands like I'd pointed a gun at him. "I only had a few."

He hadn't always been an idiot. There was a time when we could talk until the sun came up, laugh until our sides hurt, and we couldn't keep our hands off each other. Twelve years we'd stayed together, and not all of them had been bad, but there came a time when I gave up hoping that the old Alex would come back.

His eyes narrowed as he looked past me. "You've got another man in your bed already? That's low, pumpkin."

Ezra leaned against the door frame, completely at ease in his half-buttoned shirt. His muscular thighs burst out of the chequered boxers that rode dangerously low on his slim hips. His folded arms accentuated his toned body. He grinned, not bothering to correct Alex's assumption.

"You don't love me then, baby cakes?" Alex said.

"Afraid that ship has long sailed."

"Hallelujah," said Marina.

Alex curled a lip at her. "Then you won't lend me any money?"

"Jesus, Alex." I rolled my eyes. The man had become a worm.

His face turned green like he was going to vomit. Then he perked up. "Echo, my boy. Here, kitty, kitty."

Echo jostled Ezra aside and padded out. "Imbecile." He gave Alex a casual swipe. "Like I ever would have chosen to live with a gambling fool. You are worth less than the shit on a Verma's shoe."

Alex recoiled. "Why did he do that?"

"Blind as a bat and deaf as a doorpost, this one," purred Echo. "He wouldn't know the truth if it bit him on the rear end. Shall I?"

"No!" said Marina and I in unison.

"No, what?" said Alex.

"No, I won't lend you any money," I said.

He flushed. "Listen, sweet pea—"

"Go inside, the lot of you. I'll deal with this," I said. We'd probably woken the neighbours up already. I was bound to get an earful from Dotty, who lived a few doors down.

They turned to go inside when Ezra tensed.

"You catch that scent, Echo?" Ezra said.

Both leopard and barely dressed wolfman—with his perfect tush—stared down the length of the hallway. Echo growled and inched past me, his pupils dilating. His sense of smell was inferior to a wolf shifter's, but his eyesight was pretty darn good. Their sightline was obscured by Dotty's bicycle and boxes of recycling waiting to be taken out. The lobby lay around the corner. It always gave me the shivers when I went out, a perfect hiding place to get the jump on someone.

Echo roared, picking up speed.

My mouth went dry, and I considered using Alex as cannon fodder to slow down the god while we made a getaway. Maybe he'd do it to prove his love.

A man in a puffer jacket rounded the corner, his hands in the air.

"Call off the leopard," said the man as Echo bared his teeth. Ezra swooped in to twist the man's arm behind his back and pin him against the wall. "Call the wolf off too. I'm the police, you dimwits."

I squinted down the hallway. "Detective Jameson?"

"Duh," he said, in pretty spirited form, given his cheek was pressed against the grimy magnolia wall.

"Let him go." My heart raced. He'd recognised Echo's true form. And Ezra's. "I've been looking for you, Detective."

"I should rip this stranger's spinal cord out. That goes for your lowly ex-lover too." Echo backed off with a jaunty spring in his step, like he enjoyed hunting humans as much as he liked deer and Labradors.

"No need for that," said Detective Jameson. "I contemplated charging that one for drunk and disorderly behaviour. But seeing as he took the early heat of this encounter, perhaps we should give him a free pass and get on with our discussions. We have a lot to talk about, Ms Verma. It's about time we put our cards on the table, don't you think? Given how I could just as easily charge you with perverting the course of justice."

The lights in neighbouring flats started to go on.

I gulped. My immediate future wasn't looking that rosy, but there could be fewer things worse than letting my shame play out in front of nosy neighbours.

"You'd better come in." I swung towards Alex, who was already being frog-marched towards the exit by Marina. "As for you, don't come back in a hurry." I wrinkled my nose. "And for heaven's sake, sober up."

We crammed back into my flat, and I switched on the lights before rounding on Detective Jameson.

"Can I see your badge, Detective?" I said.

He rummaged in his puffer jacket while I waggled my eyebrows like a demon-possessed at Marina and Ezra, hoping they'd get the hint. Detective Jameson might look human and act like a police officer, but given he hadn't appeared in the Metropolitan Police database, nothing was certain. We needed to be on high alert for fangs, hairy arms or worse.

"There you go." He shoved his badge under my nose.

I'd given it a cursory glance on the night we met, but this time I took care to memorise his warrant card number and check the photo. His hair had thinned since the photograph had been taken, but it was the same man. No obvious funny business stood out to me, but I still wasn't sold. The detective might think he had the upper hand, but this wasn't a one-way street. I had plenty of niggling questions of my own to ask.

I grabbed my dressing gown and pointed down the hallway. "After you. We can talk in the living room."

Detective Jameson edged towards the living room, his eyes trained on Echo. Judging by the nerve pulsing in his jaw, he not only had true sight but a healthy fear of Echo. I could use that to my advantage.

He wrinkled his nose. "What is that smell?"

"Just my leopard marking his territory." I'd noticed it much more recently. Although Marina's nose seemed immune to putrid animal smells and Ezra was half animal, so he seemed to have a high threshold too. I murmured in Echo's ear. "Keep moving around the room. It will destabilise the detective until we know what he is."

Echo nodded. "With pleasure. This is a battle tactic your grandmother would have approved of."

My tiny living room couldn't accommodate us all easily, so I didn't invite Detective Jameson to sit. Instead, we stood in an uncomfortable face-off. Rainbow-haired Marina and barely dressed Ezra flanked me on one side of the room. Detective Jameson stood a few paces away. Echo prowled the outskirts, making everyone nervous except me.

My heartbeat had settled into a calmer rhythm than when I thought the electrician god had come for us, but I was still on alert. Even with the weirdness of the situation, never in a million years would I have swapped back to a life of sitting on the sofa with Alex while he watched reruns of *Top Gear*.

"A bit late to call around, isn't it, Detective?" I said.

"Some things can't wait." His face was all shadows and angles like he hadn't slept in a week.

Marina held out a hand. "I'm Marina Ambrose, Alisha's best friend. Your aura's really pretty."

"It is? Thanks." He shook her hand. "A pleasure to meet you. Although, it turns out you and your friends know far more than you let on. You've not been straight with me."

"This is between you and me. Don't bring Marina into it," I said. If he really was a copper, I didn't want to risk her landing in the slammer. This whole escapade had started with my family's secrets. Marina was guilty of nothing except being a great friend.

"Ah, but your friends are in as deeply as you, Ms Verma. They can't play the game and expect not to get burned."

Next to me, Ezra bristled like he was going to lose it.

I refocussed on Detective Jameson. "I went down to the station a few nights ago. Turns out you're not on their books. Why is that *exactly?*"

Bleary brown eyes held my gaze. "I could have been more upfront with you. But then again, you're no ordinary woman, are you, Alisha? Ordinary women don't know about the Otherworld."

My heartbeat raced. Any minute now, he was going to transform into some hellish creature.

I didn't let him see my fear, though. "Ordinary men can't see magical leopards."

His eyes widened in surprise. "I thought he was a tiger."

"Dude, even five-year-olds can tell the difference," said Marina. "I'll give you a crash course if you like."

Detective Jameson nodded as if a tête-à-tête with my bestie was a real possibility.

"So go on, Detective. Who the hell are you, and what have you been hiding?" I said.

"I'll lay out my role in all this on the proviso you keep your mouths shut. You know how it is. If you spill, I'll have to kill you." No smile played on his lips. The man was deadly serious.

That expression told me he'd put us in a ditch and then go and buy doughnuts.

"Sounds a bit harsh." I looked at the others. Marina nodded, Ezra shrugged, and Echo looked distracted by a fly. "Okay, deal."

He drew in a deep breath. "I'm in the Shadow Squad. I apologise for the charade, but it's protocol. There's a reason why the Shadow Squad isn't on the Met database. All personnel files, in addition to past and ongoing investigations, are secret. There's a handful of us. We work alone."

Echo grunted. "This is a lie, granddaughter of Rajika Verma. Police officers do not work alone. Even I know the old joke—how many policemen does it take to screw in a lightbulb?"

I shook my head. "Not the time, Echo. Please continue, Detective."

My teaching career and gambling husband had given me plenty of experience sniffing out lies. The detective's story sounded dubious, but the boundaries of reality had shifted since becoming a druid. This week taught me anything was possible. My gut told me to hear him out.

"As I was saying, we are answerable straight to the Prime Minister. All interactions with the public are on a need-to-know basis."

I frowned. "What is the Shadow Squad responsible for?"

Shaky fingers pinched the bridge of his nose. "We investigate infractions committed by magical and otherworldly folk against humans."

"Well, smother me in cream and eat me up." Marina smiled at Detective Jameson as if he'd gone from run-of-the-mill copper to a light-sabre-wielding knight of the realm.

I knew that admiring, coquettish look well. It was the look she gave someone before she jumped their bones. I made a mental note to run an intervention when we were alone.

"I've never heard of a Shadow Squad," said Ezra. "And I wasn't born yesterday. If everything is hush-hush, how do we know you are telling the truth?"

"It's a conundrum, isn't it?" He paused. "Listen, mate, get some trousers and button up, will you? No need to flash your pecks in polite company. Some of us haven't had that body in twenty years. I've yet to meet a shifter who isn't an exhibitionist."

Ezra scowled. "That's how we roll, *mate.* Comes with the territory."

I pushed on, ignoring the prickles between them. If there was something I was good at, it was picking my battles. "Why did you come here tonight and not last week when it became clear Mum wasn't the only one who had been targeted?"

"What happened at the community centre tonight forced my hand. Things are hotting up. We know now beyond a shadow of a doubt the perpetrator is a serial killer. Not only that, he's enjoying the spectacle. That makes him even more dangerous than we thought."

"Who is *we*?" purred Echo. "Have you got any Labradors on your team? German Shepherds are too bristly, but how about Dobermans? I've never tried one of those."

The detective scratched his jaw. "Is he joking?"

I shook my head. "Afraid not. So what you are saying, Detective, is that you made me question my mother's competency at work and the foundations of my parents' marriage, *and* you didn't alert me to the known dangers of the situation. My student died tonight. She was a good kid. A great one. Now you're at a dead end, you come to civilians for help."

"But you're not civilians, are you, Ms Verma? At least, not in the powerless sense."

"Touché," I said. "But how do we know you're not something *other* too?

"You'll have to take my word for it." Detective Jameson patted his slight beer belly. "To my great regret, I'm as normal as they come. Can you imagine investigating the Otherworld day in and day out and being utterly depressingly human? To make matters worse, I can't even tell my own father what I do for a living. He thinks I'm a traffic officer."

"Well, that sucks," I said. "Is there a magical x-ray machine we can use to be certain?"

Echo stopped mid-prowl and honked with laughter. "I must start to record these ridiculous things you say."

I gawped. "You can write, Echo? I didn't know that."

He held his magnificent head high. "That was a turn of phrase. Of course, I can't use a pen with *paws*. I'm not a primate. I don't have opposable thumbs. But if I could write, I would be the next Ursula K. Le Guin. Our paths crossed in Paris in 1953. Where else do you think all her ideas came from? As for an x-ray machine to scan for magical powers, there are no shortcuts in nature, granddaughter of Rajika Verma. This man will show his true colours, and we will be waiting to see if he has tried to pull the wool over our eyes."

Detective Jameson sensed Echo's implicit threat and swallowed hard.

I furrowed my brow. "How is it that you have true sight without being a peculiar, Detective? My understanding is that for humans, the veil is only lifted in the few moments before death."

"The Shadow Squad goes through training to both toughen and open up our minds. Hypnosis is part of the training. A hypnotist uses suggestions to achieve cognitive realignment. Not every mind survives exposure to the pierced veil. Some become trapped in a nightmarish twilight zone. But the success rate amongst recruits has improved over the years. Once you see the Otherworld, you can't unsee it. At least, not without magical intervention." He sighed. "The thing is, we're mostly an intelligence-only unit. We monitor. We clear up the debris. At most, my superiors reach out through diplomatic channels to have a word when the Otherworld gets out of hand. Our government doesn't have super soldiers knocking about. Captain America and Iron Man aren't waiting in the wings to suit up."

Ezra snorted. "It seems your Shadow Squad are toothless chihuahuas. It's best we work alone, Alisha."

"Maybe we should give Detective Jameson a chance." Marina sank into the sofa and tucked her bare feet up under her. She'd obviously missed my cues to stay alert at all costs. "His heart is in the right place. I can tell from his bright aura. Auras can't be faked, you know."

"Marina Ambrose," said Echo. "In Otherworld terms, you are an infant. Less than an infant. You are an embryo. As much as your empathetic skills might seem en pointe to you, this muscle is as undeveloped as a sumo wrestler's waist. You should not act as a guarantor for strange men, especially if they flash badges to compensate for shortcomings in other areas." Green eyes dropped pointedly to the Detective's nether regions.

"Well, that was unnecessary," said Detective Jameson.

"The cat is right." Ezra cleared the detective's height by three inches. "We don't know yet that our goals align."

"I can't sit back and do nothing while people die," said Detective Jameson. "What use is information if I just sit on it?"

My stomach knotted. He really believed we could tip the odds in his favour. "Tell us what you know."

He hesitated, then spoke rapidly as if divulging the information went against his nature. "The preliminary post-mortem report for Nita Dogan shows she died from cardiac arrest as a result of electrocution. There have now been twenty-four other suspicious deaths across London, all of them scientists. All of them with oddities that show these aren't average murders. Your mother was the first. It was the roses growing from metal that first put her on the Shadow Squad's radar. She was assigned to me, but my efforts to close her case satisfactorily or predict the next target have come to nothing. Our government is impotent. Only the mounting bodies persuaded my bosses to engage with the Otherworld. When they reached out to their Otherworld counterpart, they met with a brick wall."

Ezra's grey eyes smouldered. "They spoke with the Prime Sorcerer?"

Detective Jameson gave a curt nod. "He didn't dispute the evidence we presented, but the senate refused to get involved. Their priority is not humans."

"Indeed," said Ezra. "They wouldn't want to bring the wrath of the gods on the Otherworld. The Pragmatist's Law states—"

I groaned. "Never to meddle in the affairs of the gods."

Detective Jameson chewed the inside of his cheek. "The gods are closer to men these days than to all-powerful gods of mythology. The Shadow Squad doesn't have the resources or the reach of something like Interpol, but I was still able to piece together a sketchy history. Our unit was formed a little over a decade ago. Since then, the god we're after appears in our records sporadically. He's been a baker, a blacksmith and the owner of a tanning studio. Would you believe it?

He's now a freelance electrician. He takes cash in hand and doesn't pay his taxes. He knows how to live off grid because he doesn't need the grid."

My heart raced. I put my fingers to my lips. "You know who he is. Don't say his name. He'll know. I'm his target. No need to give him another one." Hadn't Gaia said as much? I darted to the kitchen for a notepad and pencil. "Write it down."

Detective Jameson accepted the paper and knelt by the coffee table. He wrote two letters, then drew a symbol and handed me the paper. "If I were a betting man, I'd say this is our perpetrator. All roads lead here."

I looked down, suddenly lightheaded.

You can call me all the names under the sun, the electrician god had said.

Here, in smudged lead, was the detective's best guess. The electrician god was so confident he hadn't bothered to cover his tracks or hide his identity. His murderous image flashed before me: swarthy skin, amber eyes and black-singed fingernails. He had taken Mum, Nita and countless others. He had snuffed out lives like he was blowing out candles.

He was Ra, the sun god.

"Holy shit," said Marina. "I knew there was a reason why I wasn't religious."

Ezra read the word, only his stillness revealing his rage.

Echo came to rest by my side at last, and he, too, deciphered the page. "I do not believe it. If the sun god were here, he would have brought sunshine to this wretched rain-soaked isle."

I tried to keep my voice calm. "If the sun god is behind this, then why not kill us all? He can just decide to burn us all to a crisp or cover the world in darkness out of spite."

Marina's forehead knotted with worry. "Even if he went easy on us, a change in the light would be catastrophic. Crops wouldn't grow. There would be famines. Our bodies need vitamin D to function and melatonin to sleep. The sun even has an impact on testosterone levels."

"The power of the gods has been castrated. It took me a lot of legwork to piece it together. That's why he's an electrician. He might be less powerful than he was, but he's still lethal," said Detective Jameson. "His historic activities showed boredom and a disregard for human life but never such bloodlust. I'm still looking for a motive, but my instincts tell me his killing spree has only just begun."

Echo's emerald eyes glinted. "Did no one listen to the goddess? She told us his motive. The gods want us to offer more prayers."

"Fat chance," said Marina.

"Echo is right," I said. "He doesn't want to kill us all because there would be no one left to pray. He just wants to add to the weight of human suffering to make us pray."

"It's days like this I wonder whether I'd prefer being a community copper chasing down bike thieves." Detective Jameson sighed. "There's nothing for it, now. We need to neutralise him, and I'm going to need your help to do it. The ball's in your court. At some point, you have to decide whether to take a leap of faith. Can you trust me, Alisha?"

Ezra's breath fanned my ear. "He has given us more information than the senate would be willing to share. There's no turning back now the god has marked you out. You're under my protection. Seems to me we have no choice but to join forces."

Marina trusted the detective, Ezra had given his reluctant backing, and Echo could be swayed by the offer of a good meal, so his opinion was flighty at best. More allies could only be a good thing. This was the right call.

"You win, Detective," I said. "We can play on one team. Let's call it a time-limited partnership."

"I can get on with that." He pulled a business card from his jeans and handed it to me. "Here's my mobile number to save you from going down to the nick again."

I took the thick, cream card. There was no insignia, organisation, job title or email address, just his name and mobile phone number printed in block capitals.

"And one for you, Marina," he said.

Marina beamed and slipped the card into her bra.

I hoped Marina's instincts about him were right, but I had kept some wildcards in my pocket all the same. The detective knew nothing about Gaia, the Celestial Library or about my suspicions that Fei Yen and Faeza were peculiars.

Time would tell if he came through for us.

If not, Echo could chase him screaming into the night.

17

I should have heeded Echo's warnings about Ezra. It turned out he was like a dog with a bone. Barely six hours after he left my flat, he popped his head around my bedroom door, startling me awake.

"Rise and shine, hellfire," he said.

I groaned, emerged from the folds of my duvet and wiped the spittle from the corner of my mouth. The clock on my bedside table read 9.50 a.m. "Go away, Ezra."

He scanned my sleep-smudged face. "You can't rest on your laurels. Do the work. Get stronger, get quicker, and hone your skills. Or not only will this amber-eyed god hunt you down with the ease of a phoenix besting a pigeon, but the wrath of Minister Willowsun will rain down on me."

"Huh?" Complicated conversations before my morning cup of tea weren't a good idea. Ezra should have realised that already. We'd been spending more time together than I had with Alex in the heady heights of our marriage.

"Your progress report is due today. Minister Willowsun's office has already chased for it once. I am already known for my somewhat novel ways of fulfilling my missions. I could do without another black mark against my name, so will you *please* change into some active wear and come closer so we can be on our way? I've booked us some sparring time in the Wildwoods arena."

I ached, and my head was all over the place. "Sorry, no can do. Marina has to work, and judging by the snoring coming down the corridor, Echo needs his beauty sleep."

I did too. My wet hair had dried in loose waves that resembled a scarecrow more than a mermaid.

"An empath doesn't need to get into the thick of battles. The cat has plenty of experience using his teeth. You, on the other hand…"

I decided he was more bulldog than wolf, gave him my most unimpressed look and went to get changed.

Four hours later, I wiped the sweat from my forehead and put down the staff that Ezra had insisted I practice with. My kickboxing training meant I preferred to punch and kick during fights, but he wanted to push me out of my comfort zone. He armed us each with a bō, a Japanese staff. In Ezra's hands, the bō was a graceful, effective weapon he used to swing at and strike his opponent. In my hands, it was a crude instrument with which I slashed the air and attempted to poke his eye out.

Ezra's breathing was even, in contrast to mine. "No time in the ring is wasted. Every practice session results in quicker feet, better hand-eye coordination, and new sequences learned."

I panted like I'd just given birth. Or at least, how I imagined that would be from romcom movies. "Why do you even need to be combat-ready? As a wolf, you have teeth and claws. And as a wizard, you can teleport. Plus, you have the moon charm, so you can pull your light-switch trick."

He inched closer, and a slow grin spread across his face. "I can do much more than that, Alisha." Then he handed me my bō. "Let's go again."

I grew light-headed as the arena changed yet again around us, an assault on my mind and senses. Objects emerged from the sawdust: not only trees but monoliths, great columns that belonged in Roman times and hideous statues of gargoyles. The air thickened around us or swarmed with bees. An eerie child's voice sang a nursery rhyme, and unfamiliar creatures chattered and squawked.

I tried not to overthink every moment, fearing my mind would melt. That I'd end up in some London crack den railing about my experiences, and no one would ever believe me.

Better to breathe, be present and take each moment at a time, one footstep at a time.

It was how Mum approached science and how Dad approached art. Hell, it was how I approached teaching languages. I just needed to hold on to the threads of my sanity and believe in myself.

"Wildwoods is in simulation mode. It tests your powers of concentration and your strategy skills. Use the arena to your advantage to block my advances or camouflage yourself. Your job is to overpower me. Let the arena become part of your toolkit rather than a distraction."

I ducked and dove around the structures. Ezra might have been faster, but I was lighter on my feet. I swung my bō in an arc and almost landed a blow, but he was too quick.

Monoliths fenced us in, and we went hand-to-hand, blow after blow. He was going easy on me; I could tell. He didn't teleport or put his entire weight behind his blows, but I didn't go easy on him.

I'd missed the gym and my punching bag. I let out all my anger on him—about Mum, Nita, and all the secrets that had been hidden from me.

I adapted my footwork from kickboxing to surprise him and landed the odd kick to his shins before following up with a strike with the bō and interspersing my moves with wind.

It felt good going on the attack.

The bō was mostly in both hands, so I could put as much force behind it as possible. The weapon suited me, so light and smooth it was almost an extension of my limbs. I released my left hand only to call the winds. The winds came more easily to me the more I practised, like breathing. My left hand was almost as consistent as my right, and I no longer knotted my brow in concentration.

My job was to come out as the winner and show him I was fearless. To prove I didn't need a protector and I could take him.

I closed in on him, ignoring the crackle of fire and the scent of smoke the arena had conjured. Ezra set his jaw and upped the ante. He didn't want to lose any more than I did.

I lunged towards him, got in close and jabbed his throat with my left fist. I landed my punch and didn't hold back. He'd said there was a nurse with a cabinet of healing potions in the main building.

Ezra swore and darted back. I swung the bō at his head.

He swivelled out of reach, stuck his bō in the ground and pole-vaulted over me like a gymnast.

Next thing I knew, I'd taken a kick to the small of my back and sprawled face-first in the sawdust.

My ego was more wounded than my body.

Strong hands grabbed me by the waist and lingered there a moment before setting me back on my feet.

Around us, the Wildwoods arena reverted to a blank canvas.

"You almost had me there." Ezra touched his throat, where a pink cauliflower bruise marred his skin.

"Sorry about that. That was some move you pulled at the end. What are you? Some kind of circus acrobat?"

"A wolf isn't a circus animal, hellfire. We aren't the performing type." He collected the staffs, and they vanished from his fingers like they'd been stored in a pocket of air. "Come on," he said, nodding towards the cable cars. "The school is alive with students today. It's a good day to show you around."

My knees were muddy from a swampland the arena had thrown at us. My ponytail of raven waves had so much sawdust in it that I could have been mistaken for a blonde. I smelt like a farmhand. Ezra, however, looked like he had stepped out of a Diet Coke commercial.

"I didn't bring a change of clothes," I said.

In this light, his eyes were molten steel. "We could skip the tour, and I could teleport you home."

I shook my head and made for the cable cars, determined to beat him there after the thrashing I'd taken in the arena. "No, just show me where the loos are. Five minutes in there, and I'll be sparkling new."

149

EZRA LEANED against a wall outside the toilets. His eyes brightened when he saw me. "Looking good, hellfire. Are you ready to meet the big wigs?"

I tossed my still dirty hair and grimaced. "A little bit of spit and polish, and I'm good to go."

We'd ridden the cable cars up to the great oak, and I'd spent ten minutes in the less-than-sparkly pupil toilets, shaking the sawdust out of my hair, spot-cleaning my trousers, and blasting toilet roll around like confetti while I tried to dry the wet patches.

"We make our report about your progress. We keep things tight and necessary," said Ezra in my ear. "No spilling about Ra. Not yet. I don't want you falling foul of the senate just yet. First, you impress them. Later, we can talk to them about how you're digging your own grave, and maybe, just maybe, if they like you enough, someone will put themselves out for you."

"Sounds a bit like getting my mother-in-law on my side."

He grinned. "Did it work?"

"I guess. She wanted to feed me up like a prize pig. It would have been better if she'd hated me."

"Come on; they'll be on a tight schedule. It's a stand-out day in the Wildwoods calendar. With any luck, the Prime Sorcerer won't mind if you stay on and witness it."

"Phinnaeous Shine is here? Doesn't he have better things to do than hang around at a school?"

"The Prime Sorcerer always attends the ceremony. He has many duties, amongst them leading the senate and negotiating with humdrum agencies, but his office is here for a reason. Wildwoods is the centre of the Otherworld. Every now and then, he likes to teach a class. It's a good way of earning the admiration and loyalty of new students. His teaching is legendary at Wildwoods, as well as his habit of pop quizzes to catch out anyone who doesn't listen. On his best days, he could inspire the Mona Lisa to come to life."

"So he taught you?"

Ezra tugged at his charm necklace, visible tension in his neck and shoulders. "He's a shifter. Not my kind. Phinnaeous Shine isn't a mere wolf. He can shift into any two-legged form he touches. It gives him an affinity for those of us with similar talents. He knows what it means to shed one identity and inhabit another. What a toll it takes physically and psychologically. How you're never fully satisfied in either form, never whole."

"Sounds tough."

"Nothing's perfect."

I scuttled after him like a crab as he strode across the rope bridges, my legs still heavy from the training session. I could have sworn Minister Willowsun's office lay in the opposite direction. New cabins had sprouted up, literally by magic. We approached the cabin with the Headmistress plaque on the door. A curtainless window revealed two grey heads bowed together over files on the desk: the tall, reedy headmistress with long hair and a shorter woman with a full head of sassy, silver curls in luminous exercise gear.

"Who's the silver-haired lady in the exercise getup?" I asked. "I remember her from the senate."

"My aunt, Lavinia Drach."

"A witch?"

He lowered his voice to a gruff whisper. "Be careful around her. She might be family, but she's not always on my side. She heads up the coven, and her allegiance is to the witches, but she'll help me out if it suits her. You ready?"

Ezra gave a clipped knock on the door.

"Come in."

We stepped inside, leaving the bright light behind us and entering Minister Willowsun's boudoir of drapes, smooth wood and plants. The scent of vanilla and chocolate wafted over from a group of flowering orchids, in addition to the pong of hairspray holding Lavinia's curls in place, which smelled like it'd been concocted in chemistry class.

"Just like clockwork, Mr Neuhoff. How nice not to have to send a wraith to chase you," said Minister Willowsun.

Ezra gave a slight bow. "Ministers. I hope we're not intruding?"

Minister Willowsun shook her head. "Quite the contrary. We'd just finished. I'm looking forward to Ms Verma's progress."

Ezra's aunt approached and reached up to kiss him on both

cheeks. "Let me feast my eyes on you. Why such a stranger? The coven misses you. That dirty old wolf Gunnolf must be keeping you busy."

"Actually, aunty, it's Alisha that's taking up most of my time these days. I'll be sure to pop into the gym when time allows."

Lavinia clapped in delight. "Oh yes, you could lead a weightlifting class for me. You know you're always a hit with our clients. Ravynne also quite likes a sweaty wolf. But how rude of me to get carried away with my nephew." Her sallow, lined face broke into a warm smile. "How lovely to see you again, Ms Verma."

"Please, call me Alisha." I curtsied and then felt stupid when Ezra chuckled.

His aunt swatted him. "Leave the poor woman alone. Alisha, you must call me Lavinia in private and save the minister malarkey for formal occasions only."

"Done."

"Come, let's go for a walk and leave these two to their boring business." She took my arm and grabbed her umbrella, a sturdy full-sized one with a dull brown canopy and shimmering brass handle.

"Oh, the weather is peachy. Not a cloud in the sky," I said. "No need for an umbrella."

"I'm going to have to turn you into an umbrella aficionado, dear. Don't you know, an umbrella is a shield against the sun and the rain. It's both a weapon and defence and much more besides. Queen Victoria herself had her parasols lined with chain mail after an assassination attempt. I always liked her—a lot of chutzpah for a queen. My umbrella is from the company used by the royal family. Their brollies keep royal hairstyles intact, even in the worst London downpour. Mine's been upgraded, of course. I'd be more likely to leave home without my dentures than without it."

What a strange old lady, waxing lyrical about an umbrella. "I'm more of a rain jacket girl, myself."

Lavinia winked. "Then you haven't lived."

Ezra gave me a wry smile over his shoulder as she ushered me out of the office and closed the door behind us. We walked the rope bridges in a circuit, surrounded by luscious tree canopies and twittering robins and blackbirds.

Lavinia hooked her arm in mine and swung her umbrella like a baton. "Tell me, are you interested in Zumba? We have a new class at the gym. If that's not your thing, maybe a spin class? My motto is eat and drink to your heart's delight. Just squeeze in some endurance, strength and flexibility training if you want to be swinging from the chandeliers in your old age."

I'd pretty much try anything if I could wear pink Lycra leggings in my sixties.

"You run a gym?" I said, a little overwhelmed by her friendliness. The woman could thaw an igloo with her presence.

She cackled, revealing a mouthful of pearlescent teeth that didn't look like dentures at all. "Yes, dear. Witches aren't all cauldron-loving, cave-dwelling hermits, you know. Or would you rather we were the Women's Institute? How quaint." She chuckled. "My coven aren't the sort for church bake sales and knitting needles. You must come by. We're in the heart of Wimbledon, next to an orthodontist's surgery." She let go of my arm and waved her hand in front of her face as if she could see the name in lights. "Baba Yaga's Gymnasium on Dundonald Road. White script on a green sign. You can't miss it. Plenty of tennis players for clients if you're into hot totty."

"But you serve on the Sorcerer's Senate too?"

"I'm Minister for Defence, dear. I keep my small witch army at full strength and train the reserves a few times a year. The last time we were at war was the day your grandmother died, but the threat never quite recedes, regardless of what the lily-livered think. My coven and I conduct security missions. We're always ready for escalation."

I had my doubts. A gym-loving granny wouldn't have been my first choice for Minister for Defence. Orpheus, the vampire, had been much more threatening. Even Rayna Willowsun, with her hip dagger, might have suited a defence role. Lavinia Drach's bubble-gum pink, effervescent cloud of hairspray vibe didn't scream danger.

But then, a chihuahua had bitten my ankle once. It had clung on for so long that I thought it had lockjaw. I'd needed stitches and antibiotics. So I wasn't one to knock the deadly impact of small packages.

"My humdrum gym is a lot of fun. We have a giggle and keep fit, so when the time comes, we can break bones. Of course, there is no point in breaking bones without having a sideline in healing and protection spells. It's very lucrative generating both supply and demand."

We'd come to the end of a bridge. She ducked underneath a rope and stepped neatly into a snug seat for two that had been carved into the bark of a tree.

"Come along, dear. Any longer, and I'll be on my deathbed." She patted the space beside her. "I discovered this nook many moons ago. To think, it's still here providing solace and joy. You know, I'm very glad to have run into you."

I gritted my teeth and took the leap over to the nook, finding it too snug a fit for two grown women's bottoms. From this close, I could almost taste her hairspray.

Her hazel eyes gleamed. "My nephew seems to have taken a shine to you. It's been a long time since I've seen him protect anyone other than the pack."

"You gave him the moon charm?"

"No, dear. The moon was my sister Chandra's gift. The thistle is from me." A sad smile tugged the corners of her pink-frosted lips. "As much as my nephew doubts my intentions towards him, he is the last living piece left of my eldest sister." She brightened. "Now, tell me. I'm an old woman now, and to be honest, I've not needed men for a long time. But I recognise attraction when I see it. Have you bedded Ezra yet?"

I spluttered with surprise. "Er…no."

She frowned. "Shame. But he has teleported with you?"

A frisson of wariness crawled up my spine. "Yes."

"Silly boy. He won't give his dear aunty a little drop of blood, but he'll sweep a stranger off her feet."

"Hardly a boy."

"Forty-four is nothing these days, Alisha. And repdigits—11, 22, 33, 44, et cetera—give a year real pizazz. It's scientifically proven.

Then there's the devil, of course. Another case in point. Best not to say his number, though."

I grinned. Ezra had been decidedly cagey about his age. About his life, really. But his aunt was like an encyclopaedia.

Lavinia sighed. "Teleporting is such a nifty trick."

"Rather vomit-inducing, I'm afraid."

She raised a pencil-thin eyebrow. "Really? Oh well, I suppose vomit can always be mopped up. A bit like sea sickness, I suppose. Not a deal breaker by any means. He has that from his father's side, you know. I've always envied it. The places that his father Levi took my sister Morena. To Paris in autumn, Jerusalem in spring, Tokyo in summer and New York in winter. Just think of the adventures. And no jet lag! Teleporting in Levi's arms must have been worth all the downsides of being a wife. Of course, Morena would have married him even without the teleporting bonus. She was sickeningly in love."

"What happened to them?"

"Ah, that's a long story, dear, and we have a ceremony to attend." She pointed to pupils making their way to the yew tree rune, so far in the distance they looked like an army of ants. "It's not a day to be missed. You are staying? It's all rather brutal but necessary, much like childbirth."

The old ache throbbed, the one that groaned into being when I imagined children of my own. "I don't have children. I wouldn't know."

"Oh? Well, never mind, dear. A vagina has multiple uses, you know." She rolled her eyes. "All these mother duck types who go *on* and *on* and *on*, like a womb is the answer to their life's calling, are rather tedious, aren't they? The brain's a far sexier organ. Especially at my age when all the moisture's gone."

My toes curled. "Jesus."

"More like the Virgin Mary. You shouldn't take the Lord's name in vain, you know. He was a good egg, or so I've heard."

I pasted on a smile that likely resembled that of a constipated child's. "Ezra must be wondering where I am."

"Ezra is wise to make allies. His pack won't be enough in the coming fight. He's always been a good boy. I just hope his loyalty isn't his undoing. The senate has been preoccupied with pressing business these past few days. Darker times are coming."

My heart skipped a beat. Lavinia had to be talking about Ra. What else could she be referring to?

Maybe Phinnaeous Shine cared more about humdrums than Detective Jameson thought. He'd need a lot of firepower and cunning, but perhaps he planned to break the Founder's Law to protect them after all.

Relief flooded me. I preferred to be left out of the fight, being a new druid and all. The Prime Sorcerer was much more capable of taking on this fight than a virgin peculiar.

"The Prime Sorcerer is usually more philosopher than warrior," she said, "but this time, he's in a tizzy."

I wanted to trust Lavinia and tell her my secrets, but Ezra had warned me not to give anything away. "If you don't mind me saying, the Prime Sorcerer's household set-up seems rather combative. I don't know many who keep a succubus slave as a housekeeper."

Lavinia's laugh tinkled in my ear. "Oh, well, you've been missing out, Alisha. Having other people scrub your floors and fold your knickers is freeing."

"You're not wrong there."

"My intuition tells me there is a lot riding on the ceremony today. As you know, a witch's intuition is not to be taken lightly. Phinnaeous is hellbent on finding the eternal girl. Without her, we don't stand a chance."

I gave her a blank look. "The eternal girl?"

"Why, yes, dear. Your parents must have told you a version of the Chameleon Tale when you were a child as a bedtime story perhaps, or on special days as a treat."

"My parents read me Mr Men stories."

"How humdrum. Well, dear, it's all up to me then. The Chameleon Tale speaks of an eternal girl who blends in even though her talents are brighter than the sun. When Death opens the door, only the eternal girl may stop the coming Dusk, together with a disintegrating tome lost to the world."

"Sounds heavy," I said. "I prefer Mr Tickles."

"You have no idea." Lavinia glanced at her watch with a gasp. She picked up her umbrella. "That's enough nattering for today. My nephew will never forgive me for filling your head with my nonsense. I'm due at a senate meeting, but I hope to see you soon."

She pushed off the nook and dropped like a stone in a well.

I stifled a scream as Ezra's aunt descended to her death and summoned wind to cushion her fall. My attempt failed, and my fumbling hands managed only a slight flurry of leaves. I peeked over the ledge, anxious to find her splatted in the arena, being magically cleaned up like she was some gunk simulation.

Lavinia twisted in the air. She flung a Lycra-clad leg over her umbrella, then straightened her posture like she was on horseback. The umbrella jolted like it had come alive and carried her up towards me.

She hooted with laughter at my expression. "I told you it was handy! Oh, how marvellous. I've not surprised someone like that in decades. Toodle-oo!"

Off she went, gliding like a swallow to the other side of Wildwoods, where she disembarked with the finesse of a gymnast.

Giddy excitement bubbled up in my belly at what I had seen. I couldn't imagine how anyone would choose to live like a humdrum when they could experience sights like this. When Lavinia faded from view, I dug out my phone and searched the internet for Baba Yaga's Gymnasium. They certainly knew how to keep old ladies fit.

18

———————

Ezra and I stood mercifully alone in the vaulted cabin where I had first encountered the Sorcerer's Senate. Without the candles and soft furnishings, the cabin had an austere feel. Instead of the split stone table, a newly erected stage with nine high-backed wooden chairs commanded attention. Rows of trestle tables and benches in cherry wood filled the bulk of the room, arranged around a central clearing. The afternoon sun streamed through the stained-glass windows.

"The senate meeting might run over a few minutes," said Ezra. "We've been asked to keep an eye on the children until more responsible adults arrive."

"You could have warned me about your aunt. She's like a firework in a small room. You never know who's going to be hit."

He picked a twig out of my hair with careful fingers, despite it being greasy enough to fry an egg in. "I *did* warn you, but she's the kind of woman words can't explain. You have to meet her in the flesh. I was hedging my bets you could take care of yourself."

"Wait until Marina hears about her flying umbrella."

"If you let my aunt surprise her, you'll earn extra brownie points.

Especially when the coven take to the skies en masse. It's better than the Red Arrows."

"How effective is she as Minister for Defence?

"She's the best one ever to hold the post. Her skills are legendary. They say you can judge how effective she is by the wars that *haven't* happened on her watch. Lavinia might look like Barbie Senior, but she's as sharp as a tack. The sort of foe that would stab you between the shoulder blades for the greater good. My parents wouldn't have died if she'd been there the night they died."

"I'm sorry."

"So am I."

"How good are her protection spells?"

"Good enough for the coven to make a killing out of their protection racket. Expensive though. And Lavinia doesn't take mere money as payment. She only takes what interests and amuses her."

I brushed aside his hair and checked his neck. "Not like you need her protection, though. Being a werewolf has obvious perks. The bruise I gave you has already disappeared."

His grey eyes sparked with copper at my feather-light touch.

I rambled on to distract myself from the electricity between us. "She seemed very taken with your teleporting powers."

He stiffened. "That'd be right."

"I liked her. She's more Dolly Parton than Machiavelli. She's sunny, clever and in cracking shape."

"I've been landed with an incurable optimist." He shook his head.

"How did it go with Rayna?"

"Fine, I think. She was underwhelmed by your talents. I think she expected more from the granddaughter of Rajika Verma."

"Charming."

"Like a sparrow trying to live up to the legacy of a phoenix."

"You're not helping."

"You're too easy to wind up. It's one of the things I like most about you."

In came three girls and a boy carrying instrument cases. They wore slim, grey trousers with a crisp, white shirt that was more Burberry than Asda multipack. Instead of a jumper, the uniforms were topped with short, hooded robes in navy velvet.

Ezra nodded hello. "Don't mind us. We're just here to make sure you don't get into mischief."

The pupils gathered to the left of the stage, pulled out and set out four chairs in a circle and then tuned their instruments. A few moments later, they launched into a Bach piece, entirely in sync despite the absence of a conductor.

The quartet mesmerised me.

"They're incredible," I said. "I'm pretty sure they don't need supervision. If my new skills are anything like that, I'll be a happy bunny."

He laughed. "It's not the geeks I'm worried about. Today marks a special day in the Wildwoods calendar. It's a good day to experience the heartbeat of the school. We'll just lurk here at the back of the room so you can get a sense of the place and its culture."

I turned my attention to the stained-glass windows decorated with scenes from Grimm's fairy tales. I spotted Hansel and Gretel pushing the witch into the oven, the Pied Piper leading away children with his tune and Rumpelstiltskin tearing himself in two.

"The vaulted cabin is the biggest indoor space at Wildwoods," said Ezra. "Pupils take courses in the smaller cabins according to specialised schedules and hone their skills in the arena. There's no boarding here. It's strictly a part-time offer. They'll be home before their parents finish work. The vaulted cabin is for senate meetings, school meals and assemblies."

"Impressive, but aren't the stained-glass windows a bit gruesome for this age group?"

"Are you kidding me? Teens in this day and age play gory computer games far worse than anything depicted up there. What's the point in wrapping them up in cotton wool when the world has teeth?"

"If you say so." I'd long decided any future children of mine would be raised on a diet of Mr Rogers and Sesame Street, supplemented by Peter Rabbit and Winnie the Pooh books.

Wildwoods had an old-world feel. This wasn't your bog standard comprehensive with sticky lunch trays, the clank of lockers, the squeak of trainers and stinky toilets.

The string quartet launched into Brahms, filling the room to the rafters with their sound. In came a column of children, aged from about eleven to seventeen years old, in their grey trousers, shirts and hooded, knee-length, navy robes. Each robe bore the school crest—a golden W—crowned with posies of plants. The children took their seats on the trestle tables. Some girls clutched each other, their eyes trained on the clearing.

London was a melting pot of cultures, but Wildwoods took difference to a whole new level. I absorbed every detail: pointy ears, diaphanous wings, teeth of varying sizes that no braces would ever help, far more hair than a pubescent teen should have and great big feet.

I smiled at a passing girl I pegged as a druid—she wore her uniform with matted locks and goth boots—and received a stony stare in response.

"Just your average day in South London," I muttered. "Where are the gorgons and goblins, the centaurs and trolls?"

"As much as Wildwoods likes to see itself as a bastion of equality, some peculiars would rather gnaw their own foot than come here. Representation on the Sorcerer's Senate is a big clue as to the movers and shakers in the Otherworld and who must skulk in the shadows. Nine groups represented on the senate and nine house colours."

A wolf boy at the table just ahead set his sights on a luminescent girl fluttering past with auburn hair that fell in ringlets about her shoulders. She wore a long, white gown underneath a navy robe that rippled behind her like the sea. The wolf boy launched a projectile at her, his aim strong and true. As the music crescendoed, the ball arced through the air and plummeted towards the girl.

I held up my hand, shifting the path of the ball slightly. Instead of hitting her square in the forehead, it ricocheted off her arm.

She jerked to a halt and identified the culprit by his raucous laughter. She blinked hard, her face a storm, muttering under her breath all the while. Wolf boy's trousers crept higher, over his belly button and higher still. He wriggled in horror, reddening with pain as they gave him an almighty wedgie. The material thinned, threatening to tear.

I poked Ezra. "Do something. The Prime Sorcerer told us to keep watch."

He moved closer, then stepped back. "She doesn't need any help."

"Are you serious? Men don't let women get away with that."

The girl blinked again, freeing the wolf boy. Wolf boy and his four friends stood as one, twice her size in both height and girth. They closed in, eyes flashing with malice. Within seconds, she was cornered, skittish like a deer, attempting to fly beyond their grasp as they pulled her down by her gown and bounced her between them as if she were a ping-pong ball.

"No magic without supervision, Mirabel," said the wolf boy who'd suffered the wedgie and started it all.

"Told you so," I said over my shoulder as I waded into the thick of it and shoved the bullies aside to stand back to back with Mirabel. I lifted my hands and skewered the ringleader with a fiery glare. "Back off."

He smiled with malice. "Make me, girlie."

It might have been my height, maybe the greasy workout hair or the hazy afternoon sun, but he seemed to think I was close to his age. Unlucky for him, I was old enough to have learned how to deal with bullies. I took a deep breath, narrowed my gaze in focus and flicked my wrists, sending all five bullies onto their bums.

Then I took Mirabel's hand and pulled her with me over their sprawled bodies.

"I thought I could handle it," she said. "Thank you."

Behind us, the wolves gathered again, but Ezra, his lips twitching with mirth, strode towards them. He laid a hand on the wolf boy, power rolling lazily off him in waves like he'd flicked a switch.

His gravelly voice brooked no argument. "That's enough. You had it coming. Go take a seat before bigger beasts decide to make an example of you."

The wolves whimpered and did as they were told, skittish and wary as they passed us to return to their seats.

I sent Mirabel on her way and leaned into Ezra when he returned to my side. "I could have done with that kind of authority when I taught at an inner London comprehensive school."

He laughed, low and easy. "You were pretty impressive yourself. I counted five foes."

"Of school age."

His voice was warm as honey around the edges. "Maybe. But you're a virgin druid, aren't you?"

I blushed. "I learn quickly."

"That you do. It's easy to subdue wolves of a lower rank. It would've been different if I'd tried that with a group of vampires. As a seeker, I have no authority with Wildwoods pupils. I'm not a member of staff. More like an uncle supervising naughty kids."

"High school life is hard enough without adding fangs and claws into the mix. Although Mirabel has guts. It must be therapeutic to thump a bully. Will they get in trouble?"

"I won't tell if you don't. Pupils are still learning to control their impulses at this age. Unsupervised children tend to get away with what they can. Bullying is rife for the more unsightly and unusual creatures and even worse for the mixed breeds. I love Wildwoods, but let's just say that Minister Willowsun has more of an affinity for potions and academic progress than pastoral care. It's not a deliberate oversight. She merely notices the emotions of plants more than that of the children."

By now, the trestle tables had filled with pupils, and a palpable sense of anxiety filled the room amongst the girls in particular, judging by the darting eyes and heads cowed together.

I gripped Ezra's arm. "What's going on?"

Ezra sighed. "A tradition as old as time. Cruel to boot. Whatever happens, try not to draw attention to yourself and keep your cards close to your chest. You'll soon find out—at Wildwoods, the walls have ears. Here we go. Wait for it."

The string quartet shuddered to a halt, and two hundred odd heads turned to face the stage, like a hall full of demented dolls programmed to exterminate. Nine ministers filed onto the stage, an oddball crew of imposing, misshapen and luminous figures.

Unlearning my humdrum ways wasn't an overnight exercise. My

pulse quickened. My eyes drank in every detail, and my mind worked hard to accept them.

Phinnaeous Shine took the central chair, flanked by Rayna Willowsun and Orpheus the vampire, whose heavy brows shot up when he looked in our direction. Lavinia, farther down the line, gave us a cheery wave. Ezra nodded to Gunnolf, the werewolf minister.

The Prime Sorcerer raised his hands like a preacher. "Welcome, all of you, to this remarkable day. There is a story, repeated so many times over the centuries, that it transforms every time it is spoken aloud. You have heard it many times from the lips of your parents, your friends and your teachers. You have heard it around campfires and whispered in the shadows. You've heard it when a girl-child is born into the Otherworld. The Chameleon Tale tells of our destruction and our salvation. Never has our need for the eternal girl been so great."

The room darkened, even though the sun had not faded from the sky and no curtains covered the windows, as if the vaulted cabin had a weather system all of its own. Lavinia appeared to be muttering a spell.

"Today is a chance to find the eternal girl. Only she may stop the coming Dusk. Only she may find the book," said the Prime Sorcerer. "The ceremony marks a rite of passage that all peculiar girls endure. Today, the youngest girls amongst you will stand in hope against the dark. Today, you will shine brightly, lighting the way for the eternal girl, even if you are not her."

He swirled each of his hands in the pattern of an eternity sign.

There was a collective intake of breath as freshwater crashed through the vaulted cabin, streaming from the stage down the aisles between awestruck and trembling students. The water pooled in the clearing, the droplets and rivulets clumping together, leaving the body of water suspended in a cube.

I squinted at the water as dark particles writhed at its centre. An enormous, bulbous head with large, intelligent eyes and eight limbs swam in the water. Hundreds of suckers protruded from its arms, trailing blue ink.

The air in my lungs constricted.

Five girls lined up, Mirabel amongst them, their faces painted with terror. They couldn't have been more than twelve. They cast their robes aside, exposing long, white gowns like Victorian nightdresses but without frills. The girls clutched hands, knuckles white.

"Is that an octopus?" I ask.

"Not just any octopus," said Ezra. "Kraglek is the most important creature in the Wildwoods bestiary. Centuries ago, he was touched by Ganga, the goddess of the Ganges. It made him immortal and gave him the ability to sense the eternal girl. At the beginning of her first term, every Wildwoods girl must spend a minute in the tank with him and will be rendered unconscious by his venom unless she is the girl in the prophecy."

"Are you insane? This is a school, not the London Dungeons, dammit." My stomach churned. Even the creature's name made me want to run a mile. "How can their parents allow that?"

"Think of it as a bar mitzvah or christening. This is integral to the Otherworld way of life. I've seen this year's list. The auburn-haired girl is Mirabel, a fairy. We met her earlier. The plump elf is Gaylia. Poor thing looks like she's going to pass out. The girl with the plaits is Maura, a witch. She has already made a name for herself in the first term for potion making. Then there's Nessa, a vampire girl, newly turned. She's still ravenous with hunger, and that will stand her in good stead to recover from Kraglek. If I were a betting man, I'd say of this year's cohort she has the best chance of being the eternal girl. The blue-eyed doe there is a druid. Soleis, I think her name is. Druids take the longest to regain consciousness, possibly because they are inherently pacifist by nature."

I thumped him. "Well, I'm not a pacifist. You think this is okay? I don't see you jumping into the tank with that thing."

"No, hellfire, I don't think it's okay, but I don't make the rules."

"Aren't they carnivores?"

"Yes, but Helio Woodwink, the Minister for the Bestiary, won't let that happen. Kraglek will have been well fed before the ceremony, and Helio has not once across the decades allowed a girl to be permanently dismembered. He'll be on standby for extraction." Ezra winced. "Although, there was an issue with the minister in the post before him."

I broke out in a sweat as the girls approached Kraglek, holding hands as if they were a chain of fragile daisies.

They took a deep breath and stepped into the wall of water.

"Do something." My voice was low and urgent.

Grey eyes full of sorrow. "I can't. We don't play by the same rules as humdrums here."

Kraglek shrank his gigantic form, compressing his arms as the girls entered his space, but his clever eyes were wide open, waiting to strike. The cube of water measured roughly six metres squared, and he lurked near the top surface. The girls trod the water towards the bottom of the cube, holding their breath. Their cheeks were puffed out, silken tresses floating underwater, dresses swaying in the current. They held fast to each other, moon eyes jerking and wide as they tracked the creature above them.

The Prime Sorcerer looked on with interest as if watching a horse race. A small man, who I assumed to be Helio, the bestiary minister, had left his chair on the stage and hovered next to the body of water, bright eyes following the beast's every move.

Inky fluid shot out from Kraglek, darkening the water further still and blackening the girls' dresses. They shrank from him in terror as his lumpy purplish arms stretched out, reaching for them in the confined space. There was a movement as quick as the strike of a cobra, water gushing as the octopus surged downwards, all nodules and prehistoric brain, even more terrifying in his squelchy bonelessness.

A scream built in my throat.

Kraglek reached for the elf Gaylia and the druid Soleis first, dragging them up and breaking the daisy chain.

I closed my eyes and buried my head in Ezra's side.

When I opened them, the two girls were limp, discarded by the octopus. Kraglek's purple tones had become the colour of the inky water, so I barely discerned him. Seconds became hours. The three remaining girls cowered, with only Nessa, the vampire girl, defiant in her gaze.

I held my breath, and those in the vaulted cabin breathed as one as Kraglek revealed his pink innards. A sharp, parrot-like beak emerged from his centre, where his arms converged. Kraglek dropped on them from above, his mouth open, venomous saliva at the ready.

The girls lost consciousness.

I couldn't hold back. I rushed at the cube of water, my mind a blur, my footsteps ringing across the floor.

Somewhere behind me, Ezra shouted, but I didn't break my run. I lifted my hands and sent a whirlwind through the cube. It spun diagonally, wrenching the cube of water apart and splitting it in two.

In one segment, Kraglek swam, enraged by my interference. His eyes bulged, his tentacles thrashed, and the disgusting beak-like centre snapped in vain.

In the lower segments, the girls floated, mercifully free of the beast but unconscious.

Ezra grabbed my shoulder as a rush of feet entered the clearing. "What have you done now?"

Helio, the bestiary minister, frowned at me and shocked the creature into submission with some kind of Taser.

Five small men hauled out the girls, leaving only limp Kraglek in the water.

A smattering of applause broke out from the students. They might have clapped for the girls or the spectacle, but all eyes were on me.

Not that I cared what they thought. Traditions like that belonged in the dustbin of history.

On the stage, the Prime Sorcerer sent me an icy look, flanked by Orpheus, whose eyebrows had disappeared into his hairline. The string quartet picked up their instruments and sprang into a rendition of Mozart's "Eine Kleine Nachtmusik."

Ezra leaned down to whisper in my ear. "It's my fault. I should have prepared you better for that. You've ruffled some feathers today, but at least the ceremony has concluded."

"That's what you're worried about?" I hissed.

"Alisha, it's okay. The girls are safe now. The leprechauns have them. A bit of luck, a night in the infirmary, and they'll be right as rain. In the morning, the girls will be heroes. Even the wolves will congratulate Mirabel. And hopefully, the senate will forgive you."

I breathed through the thickness in my throat.

My maternal instincts blazed. It didn't matter that I wasn't a mother. If the Sorcerer's Senate were willing to put small girls through this ordeal with a monstrous octopus, their constitutional laws could go to hell.

19

———————

Baba Yaga's Gymnasium in Wimbledon didn't smell, look or feel like other gyms I'd trained at. Instead of masculine decor in monochrome shades, Baba Yaga's had a Barbie's Dreamhouse vibe, a sort of bubble-gum pop scheme that matched Marina's hair. A faint aroma of jasmine masked the stench of sweat. Judging by the turnout on a Friday morning, the gym had more female than male members, and all abided by an unspoken jazzy dress code. There were no black sweats and baggy T-shirts in sight. Here, sculpted bodies shimmered in Lycra and baby oil.

I shuddered, feeling like a rhino in a room full of gazelles.

Marina, of course, felt right at home.

I'd roped her into signing up for an aerobics class with me for moral support and her empath antennae. I needed to know if Lavinia could be trusted. The head of the London coven looked like butter wouldn't melt in her mouth. She was all smiles leading the class in a series of step touches, grapevines and bicep curls.

"Lucky I chose my best sports bra. This is wild." Marina whooped as "Love Shack" drifted seamlessly into "Video Killed the Radio Star." She took a swig of her water bottle and then picked up the beat again.

I clenched my teeth. The music made me want to run for the hills,

169

let alone the moves. All this prancing about was a far cry from the kickboxing training I was used to. I'd take a punchbag over shaking my booty any day. Lavinia had put us in a triangular formation opposite a floor-to-ceiling mirror.

Judging by our reflection, she had moves, but the rest of us most certainly didn't.

"And once more through the routine. That's right. Keep pushing. One…and two…and twist…that's it. Lunge left, lunge right, box step, and big finish—shimmy!" Lavinia beamed. "That's enough for today. Well done, everyone, especially you, Marina. What a natural. Good effort, Alisha. It gets easier. See you all next week."

I plastered on a smile and wished for the ground to open and swallow me up.

Marina mopped her brow. "I'm going to need another shower."

"I thought it would never end. Good thing you drove us. Otherwise, we'd be a sweaty mess on the tube."

She grinned. "Your aura is a muddy green. Shake off that insecurity. It doesn't matter if I wipe the floor with you at aerobics."

"Shut up. You're giving me flashbacks to you overtaking during athletics at school with that arsehole P.E. teacher."

"Miss Andrews?"

"That's the one. Enough to scar a girl for life."

Lavinia bustled over. Her hair hadn't moved an inch, and her skin glowed with a ladylike sheen of perspiration. "My dears, how lovely to see you. And in much better circumstances than last time when you embarrassed yourself at the Kraglek ceremony, Alisha. Still, I suppose in my youth I got up to worse. Like the time I commandeered a woolly mammoth from the bestiary to impress a lover. The yew tree still bears the scars from its tusks." She hooted with laughter. "How did you enjoy the class?"

"We had a blast," said Marina. "Didn't we, Alisha?"

I nodded.

Lavinia beamed. "How lovely, dear. The first one's free, you know."

"I would happily have paid, Minister Drach," said Marina. "And what a playlist. I especially enjoyed 'Wake Me Up Before You Go Go.'"

"Oh yes, wasn't George marvellous? We were great friends, you know. I advised him on the dance moves for 'Outside.' We had such a hoot." A shadow passed over her face. "But you mustn't use Otherworld terms here. Lavinia is just fine. Now come along. I have just about enough time for a smoothie break."

"If you're sure it won't put you out?" I said.

"Not at all. You must meet the other girls." She led the way out of the bright studio, nodding to clients as she went. "It can't have been easy witnessing the ceremony the other day, Alisha. I trust my nephew held your hand throughout—metaphorically, of course. These traditions we have can be quite disembowelling."

I raised an eyebrow at her choice of adjective. Lavinia had a bleak vocabulary, despite her bubble-gum facade. Perhaps she was more suited to the role of Minister for Defence than I first thought.

"We have a reception, the main gym floor, three studios, unisex changing rooms, state-of-the-art massage jet showers and a chill-out lounge with drinks and healthy snacks. Upstairs are living quarters for the team. Men are allowed by invitation only." She cackled. "We send naughty ones to the rats in the basement."

"You have a problem with rats?" I said.

"No, dear, our rats are more beloved than most men." She checked the coast was clear of humdrums. "We each have a rat as our familiar. What else would we choose in London? They are clever little things, easy to sneak into a pocket and make the best spies. Not to mention their ability to land a ferocious bite and to capitalise on the fear reaction they provoke. And do you know what the best thing is?"

We shook our heads.

Lavinia preened like a peacock. "Our rat familiars train secondary rats to run on power-generating wheels in the basement. That means we are utterly self-reliant. It was my idea to migrate to a more ecological model in the late seventies when I started worrying about the ozone layer. I've always been well ahead of my time."

"You're kidding," said Marina, slack-jawed.

Lavinia chuckled. "Would you like to see them?"

Aerobics followed by a basement of rats? What fresh hell was this? I shook my head. "Maybe next time."

"Just say the word, dear. They really are quite marvellous." She darted up the carpeted steps to the first floor like a woman half her age, not stopping for us to keep up. A palm against the handleless door at the top of the stairs, and it swung open. Lavinia disappeared inside.

"Into the lion's den," whispered Marina behind me. "Lavinia's a riddle. I like her, but there's something bubbling just beneath the surface."

"Stay close."

"Aye, aye, captain."

Curls of smoke from pungent incense sticks drifted through the inner sanctum of the London coven. Sumptuous wallpaper in ornate motifs lined the walls and begged to be touched. Here, pinks and reds bloomed alongside purples and blues. These were women who weren't afraid to make their mark on the world.

"Hurry along," called Lavinia's voice from farther along the warren of rooms.

We scampered after her voice, taking in tasselled lamps and scurrying rats, spell books and golden chandeliers dripping in jewels that couldn't have been real. In every corner, umbrellas lurked: travel ones and golf ones, frilly ones and plain ones.

"So many umbrellas," said Marina.

I nodded. "Wait until you see their party trick."

"Fingers crossed they don't open those indoors. Think of all the bad luck they'd have in one fell swoop."

We continued in the direction of Lavinia's disappearing back. A woman with long, raven hair emerged from a steamy bathroom in a barely-there towel and smiled a hello, beckoning us to follow her.

In the kitchen, a tray of green smoothies and a plate of oatmeal biscuits waited on a marble island. The raven-haired woman pressed two smoothies into our hands and took her place in a circle of women sitting cross-legged on a rug.

"Come sit." Lavinia patted the industrial-style concrete floor. "We bury bodies here, don't you know."

We joined them in the circle, nursing smoothies that smelled of the sea and had the thickness of oil.

"Sisters, please wish a warm welcome to the druid, Alisha, who has captured our dear Ezra's attention, and her empath friend, Marina. Alisha, Marina, please meet my biological sisters, Isadora and Chandra. No less loved are my chosen sisters, Ravynne, Morgan, Elvira and Agatha."

A chorus of murmurs welcomed us.

All three Drach sisters had hazel eyes flecked with the same copper that Ezra, too, possessed, a trait handed down the maternal line. Whereas Lavinia had a head full of silver curls, her equally petite sister Isadora had a short red elfin cut. Chandra, the tallest of the three, had blond locks and a gentle manner.

"It's an honour to meet you all," I said.

"Drink up, and it'll give you the strength of a horse," said Ravynne, who had handed us the smoothies.

Marina raised her glass and tipped back her head, but I put a hand on her wrist.

"Please, you first." I smiled at the circle.

"The druid does not trust us, sisters." Isadora tilted her head like a bird.

Lavinia smiled. "A woman can be formed in many ways. Through adventure or misadventure, through battle in the home or workplace, through childbirth or a call to arms. This world offers so much wisdom but so much pain. I'd be more worried if forty-year-old women had the innocence of newborn babes. That would be toe-curling."

Marina raised her hand. "Actually, I'm not yet forty."

"Bottoms up, ladies!" said Lavinia.

I expected them to go into downward dog, but they downed their smoothies instead and slammed the glasses down in the centre of the circle.

I murmured to Marina. "Can we trust them?"

She turned her palms skywards like a set of scales, subtlety entirely lost on her. "I am getting a curious mix of readings. Their auras are aligned to each other, and there's a dark current running through I can't put my finger on."

"Fat lot of good, that is. We're going to have to hedge our bets." I held my nose and gulped down the ghastly concoction. Marina followed suit.

"That's it," said Lavinia. "Drink it all up."

The room swam. The glass fell from my hands.

"Oh shit." Marina clawed at my arm before collapsing onto my lap.

The witches' faces blurred before me. I lifted a hand and heard glass shatter.

"She's strong, that one," said a familiar male voice.

I cradled my best friend before I, too, lost consciousness.

A GENTLE HAND stroked my hair back from my face. A sofa beneath me. The hum of unfamiliar voices.

I struggled to remember where I was. When it flooded back to me, icicles of fear gripped me. I froze, playing dead lest the witches try to finish me off.

The hand at my forehead paused. "She is rousing."

"Let it be so," said Lavinia.

A glass at my lips. I clamped my lips shut and opened my eyes. I wasn't restrained.

"Shh," said a member of the coven. "It's water."

"You can trust her, Alisha," said a man's voice from the other side of the room.

I sat bolt upright, discarding all pretence and ignored the gentle witch that tended to me. "You! You're in cahoots with the witches? You bloody swine! Where's Marina?"

"Easy," said Detective Jameson. "You don't know all the plays on the board."

I whirled around, ignoring the coven and the traitor in their midst. If I had to turn the coven's headquarters into a whirlwind, so be it. I'd do it if they'd hurt Marina. I'd do it with a smile on my face if one rainbow hair of hers had been harmed. I'd send umbrellas and treadmills and yoga mats flying out over Wimbledon's Lawn Tennis Club if that's what it took, and I'd have no regrets.

"Tell me where my friend is," I said.

"I'm here, Alisha. I needed the loo when I came round. That smoothie really didn't agree with me."

I ran to hug her on unsteady feet.

"I'm okay. I'm okay," she said.

I turned my fire on them all. My breath came in short bursts, and my tongue was sandpaper. "What did you do to us?"

"Calm down, dear. It's just a truth tonic," said Lavinia. "No harmful effects, apart from the need to empty your bladder. Just honesty on tap."

"You haven't told them anything, have you?" I said to Marina.

She shook her head.

"We're not telling you anything. I will go to my grave with my secrets."

"No need to be dramatic, dear," said Lavinia. "We have everything we need. Ravynne, here, is a dab hand at extracting thoughts. We temper the truth tonic to allow her access. Not an easy thing to do in public, given she has to be washed and naked, but here in our own home, it's a synch—centuries of practice, you know. You shouldn't be disheartened. You really are quite young in Otherworld terms but show tremendous promise. We really are very glad you came by."

Ravynne, she of the long black hair and tiny towel, gave a friendly wave.

I bristled with anger. "Jameson, you double-crossing son of a—"

Marina gripped my hand. "I didn't get him wrong, I'm sure of it."

"Oh, the empath is quite right," said Lavinia. "Don't mind poor Robert here for coming to see me. He's a regular, after all."

"Your spin classes are something else," said Detective Jameson. "I wouldn't go anywhere else."

Lavinia giggled like a schoolgirl. "Oh, stop it, Robert. You're too much."

I scowled at Detective Jameson.

"I'm a police officer," he said. "We're not married, for goodness sake. I told you I am a member of the Shadow Squad. You think you were my only Otherworld contact?"

"Of course not. But you could have told us about where your tentacles reached. You're as bad as that octopus Kraglek."

My needling made no impact.

He exuded calm and focus. "Says the woman who hid that she had dealings with the earth goddess."

Lavinia patted her helmet of silver curls. "Kraglek is a pussy cat, really. You just have to get to know him."

I felt a stress headache coming on.

"What did you expect me to do when I suspected you were holding back information? Haul you down to the station and use a lie detector? I told you. The Shadow Squad doesn't work like that. We use our wits and our contacts. It's good old-fashioned policing, except the chips are against us because we can't rely on peculiar talents."

I turned to Lavinia. "Why did you drug us, Minister?"

She shrugged her bony shoulders. "I'm responsible for the defence of the Otherworld. I needed to know if you were a friend or foe. When Robert came to me because he suspected you were hiding information, we decided to act."

My heartbeat was a hummingbird in my throat. "What did you find?"

She stared me out while I tried not to flinch. I realised Lavinia's bubbly persona hid a steel core, just as Ezra had suggested.

But she didn't realise I could give as good as I got. I met her stare and added a curled lip.

"Tell her," said the dumpy, soft-spoken witch who had stroked my hair so gently.

Lavinia shook her head. "You know our code, Elvira. We only share the information we must."

"You mistake her for prey when she is a predator," said Elvira, her brown eyes wide like a doe's. "If we mean to act against the gods, we need to act as one."

"Very well. We found that the empath and you have a bond worthy of your own coven. She is governed by her loyal heart and has a peculiar love of unicorns, although this is a childhood fantasy and not worthy of a grown woman. We found that you are governed by logic and are attached to Bengal cats." She frowned. "This is not optimal, given cats eat rats. However, more interesting still was that you met with Gaia and have therefore cavorted with the gods behind the senate's back. That in itself is a reason to expel you from the Otherworld."

Fear snaked through me. "Lavinia—"

She held up a hand. "But I am a practical woman and a protector of secrets. You see, this coven has seen plenty of humdrums and peculiars die in our time. We've been the cause of it. But we only condone killing when there is no other choice. Phinnaeous Shine might be prepared to turn a blind eye to humdrum deaths, but I am not." She smiled. "Of course, I have a price."

Detective Jameson regarded us with sombre eyes. "If you want to stop your mother's killer, you'll hear her out."

20

"I know how we're going to do it," I said to Marina on the telephone. "I know how we're going to defeat the electrician."

We were reluctant to say his name out loud, in case it had the effect of summoning him when we weren't ready, like some sort of Candyman.

"Of course, you know how to defeat him," said Marina. "I wouldn't expect anything less. Are we going to send him to one of Her Majesty's prisons or maybe resurrect the purpose of the Tower of London?"

"Er, no."

Excitement bubbled down the telephone line. "Ooh, ooh. Don't tell me. Let me guess. We could put on a WWE match between him and Gaia. Maybe at the O2 Arena or the Millenium Stadium so they have enough room and can be contained. Or better yet, in the gardens of Buckingham Palace so the Queen can have the winner over for high tea."

"I think the Queen might worry about her prize roses being felled. You do know that wrestling is playacted, don't you?"

"Killjoy. I know, we could set Echo on him."

"Actually, that's not a bad idea," I said. "Now listen up."

If I had learned anything from my time as a wife, it was how to use my feminine cunning and wiles for short-term gain. Sure, my marriage had combusted like a dump truck hit by a flame thrower, but there had been moments when things had gone my way, and those victories were sweet.

Chief among my tactics was throwing a party. I much preferred that to putting on doe eyes and batting my eyelashes or slipping into lingerie.

Who didn't like vol au vents served with chilled white wine and wiling away the evening under a starry sky with friends? How utterly perfect, too, that vol au vent was French for *windblown*. Light and airy puff pastry vessels whose name spoke to my druid talents and Mum's birthplace.

As if the gods were on my side tonight.

Except they clearly weren't.

Still, there were many benefits to this not being my first rodeo. Twenty-year-old me would have found it hard to think with a man like Ezra in spitting distance. Forty-year-old me could savour his handsomeness without seeing stars. That gave me a fighting chance of pulling tonight off.

To defeat Ra, I needed Ezra to trust me enough to give me his bodily fluids, and I had roped in my best wing-woman and cat to help.

I gave myself one last look in the mirror. The nude lipstick had a nice plumping effect, and the glossy black eyeliner brought out a sultry side. My hair tumbled around my shoulders.

I wasn't classically beautiful, but I was proud of my body. The lines and bumps and stray grey hairs I'd accumulated over the years were signs it had served me well. I hadn't hidden the circle of dots on my inner arm. My skin glowed, and my waist was trimmer from the training we'd been doing, especially with the added help of my control pants. For once, I'd picked a balcony bra instead of a comfortable one. My curves looked amazing in the little dress I had squeezed into—black was so forgiving—and I'd decided to swap my trainers for heels. My toes protested a little, but heels made me feel sexier as long as I didn't have to walk anywhere.

A smile tugged at my lips. I'd missed this feeling of being a woman who knew her own power. The divorce had taken the wind out of my sails, but that was behind me. I felt more like myself than ever before.

Still, I couldn't host the party at my flat, not if I wanted a good ambience. Since Echo had shed his Bengal form, there'd been an uptick in marking his territory, and my poor flat had suffered. He'd been spraying urine upwards in the corner of the living room to get his scent as high as possible, and I'd noticed it happening more since Ezra had been coming round.

Thankfully, he hadn't marked his territory with droppings yet. There was a limit to what I could stomach.

The resident's roof terrace was usually used for drying racks of my neighbour Dotty's enormous, greying underwear.

Tonight, I'd reserved it and decked it out with candlelit lanterns and cushions. An ice bucket with bottles of prosecco and sauvignon blanc waited for us, together with a bottle of tequila. I figured Ezra was more of a whiskey man, but that wasn't as fun as shots. At the last minute, I prepared a plate of cubed salmon for Echo. A glass dome I'd inherited from Mum covered vol au vents filled with garlic mushrooms and brie and cranberry. I wanted her to be a part of tonight. And to protect the vol au vents from London's wretched pigeons.

Echo slinked up behind me, his fur caressing my bare legs. "Va va voom." His emerald eyes shone. "You didn't dress up like this for the other one."

"I'm not a car, Echo."

"Not vroom vroom. Va va voom. From a Nicki Minaj song. I decided if I have to live in this century, I should make an effort to learn the lingo."

"I'm impressed."

"You can count on me to elevate the conversation tonight," purred Echo. "I have learned lyrics from the Bee Gees and the Spice Girls. I thought 'Stayin' Alive' and 'Viva Forever' were particularly apt, given we've incurred a god's wrath. Although 'You Win Again' and 'Goodbye' could work equally well."

"Actually, Echo, you're here tonight in more of a bodyguard role."

A growl, far too loud to be overlooked by neighbours. There were only so many times I could use the noisy dishwasher excuse. "The granddaughter of Rajika Verma mistakes me for a bodyguard. A bodyguard is traditionally a corpulent male of human origin with gold teeth who hopes his fists will meet a jaw, only to fall asleep on the job, stinking of nicotine and body odour. That is most certainly not me."

I leaned my forehead against his head, mimicking the affectionate nuzzling he did when he was my Bengal cat. "I need you tonight, Echo. If the electrician shows his face, I need my family around me. We'll need to work as a team."

He relaxed, allowing himself to enjoy my caresses. "It is good to know that you view me as family. This part of you is akin to your grandmother. Your father, however, saw me as a mere appendage, like a wart on an otherwise pleasant face. Or a—" Echo raised his nose into the air. "I smell wolf. And the fresh citrus notes of Marina's favourite perfume."

The intercom buzzed.

"It is time, granddaughter of Rajika Verma, to put your plan into action. I wish you fruitful hunting."

WE SAT on the rooftop of my building under a medley of stars, picking out the constellations we recognised: The Plough, Orion's Belt, Castor and Pollux. I'd been filling Ezra's glass, but he showed no signs of intoxication.

Although the sun shone brightly over Balham during the day, the evening cooled quickly. Goosebumps chased up my bare limbs, and my teeth chattered. I could have fetched some blankets from downstairs, but as a true London stalwart, I decided instead to down alcohol to warm my cockles. Copious amounts of booze needed a solid base, ideally a burger or a kebab with a good dollop of garlic sauce. Vol au vents, with their airy, fragile nature, were about as much use as a set of dentures on a vampire. I ate them anyway, one after the other, matched mouthful for mouthful by Marina.

I'd missed our time together. She knew how to make me chuckle and when to call out my bullshit. So we drank. We drank with abandon and glee. With each clink of our glasses, Marina's habit of staring directly into my eyes to avoid seven years of bad sex became more and more comical. Before I knew it, we'd polished off two bottles of prosecco and most of the food between us.

"You know, this empath thing has been working out brilliantly," said Marina. "I've not had a migraine in weeks. I mean, can you imagine if I never have to deal with one again?"

"That's brilliant. I'm so happy for you." I thought about how I couldn't share this with Mum. How she would have kept Marina's secret but investigated the science behind it.

"*And* I've been able to make some uncanny diagnoses about the animals in my care. The colours of the auras are so pretty, and they're a guiding light, even without x-rays. I've saved my own skin a few times too. I got a flash of anger from a pet snake the other day and warded off a volatile hamster before it stuck its teeth in. The nurses just can't work out how I'm doing it."

Echo propped his paws on the guard rail to gaze longingly at a passing poodle.

"Come down from there, Echo," I said.

Ezra's T-shirt had ridden up to reveal the bronzed skin of his abs. He lounged against a pile of cushions and looked at me from under hooded eyes.

Like, *really* looked at me.

Marina waggled her eyebrows at me teasingly. She was about as subtle as a ten-tonne truck.

I flushed and offered him some vol au vents. "Have some more."

My control pants were starting to cut off my circulation.

"Mushrooms aren't my thing," said Ezra. "But the brie and cranberry were delicious."

"How about *mushrooms*?" Marina left no doubt about why she had been suspended twice from school.

Ezra grinned. "Also, not my thing."

"Shall I top you up?" I said.

"Sure. You know your wines. This one is excellent." He knocked back the rest of his glass. The stem looked fragile in his hands.

"My Mum was French. No one understands wine better than the French." I swallowed a burp, masked only by a Cafe del Mar playlist I had on in the background, and poured more wine into his glass.

"The Germans would beg to differ," said Ezra. "You should come by my place sometime and try a bottle of Riesling. I have one that is aged to perfection."

I blushed. It was probably the prosecco wreaking havoc with me because that definitely hadn't been a come-on.

Echo bounced off the guard rail, knocking over a trough of yellow crocuses. He stalked over to us, the rosettes on his golden coat breathtaking in the evening light. "Where do you live, dog? I have been unable to picture your kennel. With your teleporting skills, it occurred to me you could live anywhere. It must be nice not to be subjected to border controls like other humanoid creatures. Luckily, I, too, possess the wit and skill not to be subjected to a pet passport."

Ezra chuckled. "I live in a farmhouse near Windsor, as per pack law. Although our alpha Gunnolf turns a blind eye when I disappear for a while. He understands it's part of the nature of being a seeker. The farmhouse backs onto woods ideal for running when the moon calls. Those woods are more home to me than the house itself."

Marina tumbled into the ice bucket, sending the bottles crashing.

A whoosh and Ezra was at her side, righting the bucket and steadying her.

I frowned. Either werewolves had a higher tolerance to booze than us, or Ezra's tall, muscular frame meant he needed more to hit a high. My plan didn't work without him being happy-clappy drunk.

A frisson of anxiety spread in my belly.

Maybe he was a mean drunk or a hopeless one like Alex. Or one of those people who kept drinking until sunrise and then dropped out cold.

I needed him lucid. Pliable, not comatose.

"Tequila! We need tequila." Slurring my words wasn't intentional.

I stumbled to my feet, resisted the urge to kick off my heels and swayed over to the booze, sensing Ezra's eyes on my arse. My control pants rolled down like they wanted to escape me.

He was at my side in a flash, his hand cupping my elbow. "Are you sure tequila is a good idea?"

"Hell yeah, cowboy." I poured out three shots.

"I live on a farm, not a ranch."

The world spun around me. "Why aren't you drunk?"

"Why do you want me drunk?"

I raised an eyebrow in challenge. "I like living dangerously."

His eyes smouldered. "I'd choose tedium over danger every time. Time for wild runs and skinny dipping. Time for deckchairs in the sun and rereading favourite books. Time for watching the changing expressions on a loved one's face. Time for sunsets and breakfasts in bed."

"All right, grandpa. Tonight, we live on the wild side. I propose a drinking game." I put the plate of cubed meat in front of Echo and handed out shot glasses to Marina and Ezra, together with a wedge of lime and the salt shaker. "Go ahead, load up. A shot to get us in the mood. Ready? 1-2-3, tequila!"

We took the shots, grimacing after sucking on the lime, and I refilled our glasses and put the plate of lime wedges and salt between us. "The game is called Fabled Creatures. It's a twist on a game we used to play as kids around the dinner table. Marina and I will call out names of mythological creatures. If we hit the jackpot with a creature that exists in the Otherworld, Ezra must drink. If we are wrong, Marina and I will drink. Got it?"

Echo huffed, his tail swishing. "This is what you people call fun?"

"Echo, you may eat a cube of salmon with each wrong or right answer," I said.

He purred with pleasure. "This is an honourable game, granddaughter of Rajika Verma."

"My turn first." Marina screwed her eyes up in concentration.

We'd been mythology geeks in high school. I knew she could reel off as many as me.

"Unicorn." She tossed her freshly dyed rainbow hair and pointed to the tattoo on her arm.

I shook my head in rue at her lousy guess.

"They don't exist," said Ezra.

We drank.

"Manticore," I said.

"Nope." He shook his head.

We drank.

"Centaur," said Marina.

"Nope," said Ezra.

"No centaurs? I don't believe you," I said. "Is he lying, Echo?"

Echo lifted his head from the plate, strings of fish hanging from his teeth. "The dog is correct."

"Why, thank you, cat," Ezra said. "It appears our protégées are basing their guesses on Narnia."

"The pleasure is mine, dog. C.S. Lewis had nothing on Ursula K. Le Guin," said Echo. "Drink, ladies."

We drank. The plan was well and truly off the rails now.

I crossed my fingers. "Dragons?"

"All dead."

I punched the air. Dad used to make up tales of dragons. Forty-year-old me was still attached to them. "Ha! So they lived once?"

He nodded.

"So we all drink."

He shrugged and knocked back a shot with us. "Continue."

Marina chewed her lip. "Lizard folk?"

"Nope."

"Whose side are you on, anyway?" I threw a cushion at her.

We drank, and I reconciled myself to having the most brutal hangover in the morning.

"My turn." I tried hard to stay upright. "Let's double the stakes."

"You sure you can handle that, ladies?" drawled Ezra.

"Bring. It. On." Marina went cross-eyed.

"I got this." I cast back my mind to the stories Dad read me as a child. "Basilisk."

He drank a double.

"Oh wow," breathed Marina.

"Satyr," I said.

Another double. He recoiled from the taste.

"Selkies."

"Of course. The Minister for Information is a selkie." He downed another two shots, shaking his head at the nearly empty bottle. "Enough, enough, or I will be useless."

Four storeys beneath us, a dog barked.

Echo lifted his head from his bowl and crooned the melody from 'Bohemian Rhapsody'.

"Did the leopard just hum Queen?" said Ezra.

"He has been swotting up on popular culture. Nicki Minaj, Taylor Swift and now Queen, apparently," I said.

"Blimey," said Marina.

"I have something to ask you, Ezra," I said.

He smiled. "Go ahead."

"We need to give Lavinia a drop of your blood in exchange for a protection spell against the electrician."

He frowned, processing my request. Then his face turned cold, like a trapdoor had closed, and we were on opposite sides. "No. Absolutely not."

I reached for him. "Just think about it for a second."

His whole body tensed. "There's nothing to think about. Is that what tonight was about, an elaborate ruse to manipulate me?"

"Alisha's not capable of that." Marina rode on a wave of tequila endorphins. "She would never harm you. She *adores* you."

"I would harm you," said Echo, eagerness brimming. "But I like you enough to do it quickly."

The dog at street level gave a plaintive yowl.

Echo hesitated, gave a guttural moan and then raced to the guard rail to take stock. "The poodle is taunting me. I will only eat a third of him. That will leave enough for his burial."

"Echo, don't you dare!" I said.

He leapt off the rooftop, landing cleanly in a nearby oak.

"It's nature. You can't stop him," Marina said with the detached passion of a wildlife commentator. "He'll get as close as he can, then dispatch it with a bite to the neck."

I rushed to the guard rail. He was no longer my pet but a beast driven by instinct. And his timing couldn't have been worse, judging by the storm on Ezra's face.

"Echo, get back here, right now!" I called.

"I will pull my kill into the tree. No humdrum will know what has happened here."

"There's a little old lady attached to the lead." I prayed she was deaf and couldn't hear my pleading.

Echo clambered down the tree headfirst. He stalked his prey, belly inches from the tarmac, keeping close to the shadows. I found my Dutch courage, kicked off my shoes and climbed up past the crocus boxes on the roof rail in my bare feet.

"What are you doing?" Ezra grabbed my wrist.

I twisted away from him and jumped, holding my hands out at my sides and channelling my power. The wind eased my descent, and I jerked downwards in spurts, my dress thankfully moulded enough to my body to stay in place. I landed just as Ezra materialised beside me.

His pinched expression said it all. This was duty, not friendship. "I was ready to rescue you."

"I don't need rescuing, but thanks for being by my side."

"What's the plan?"

I took a deep breath. "Distract the old lady. I'll deal with Echo. He's less likely to turn on me than you."

We ran, side by side, to the street corner where the old lady tried to tug her unwieldy poodle onward. Echo waited in a bush to pounce. His body simmered with tension, eyes on his target.

I crept up behind him and took my chance, grabbing his tail and holding on.

He swung around, growling. "You dare to come between a leopard and his prey?"

Betting that his duty to protect my family would outweigh his anger, I leapt onto his back like I was riding in a rodeo competition. He shook me off like a fly and refocused on the poodle. I thudded into a bush. Its prickles sank into my feet and scratched my limbs.

Next, I directed a blast of wind at him, but Echo's four legs and hunting posture low to the ground meant he barely noticed my efforts.

I risked a look at Ezra. He'd engaged the old lady in conversation. My foot squelched into pigeon poo as I ran over to them. To be fair, I'd stepped in worse in London. I did my best to ignore the gunk on my foot and prayed Echo hadn't decided all four of us were fair game.

I channelled calm, even though my heart hammered. "What a beautiful dog."

It was clearly a lie. A severe underbite meant it was no show dog. It needed a good dunk in the bath to loosen the filth in its coat. I ignored the yapping and scooped it up in my arms. It struggled for a second and then let me feel the full force of its dog breath.

Or periodontal disease.

Ezra unleashed a dazzling smile that didn't reach his eyes. "Darling, how many times have I told you to wear shoes when you are out walking? This is Julianne. She lives around the corner in the same house she moved into when she and her husband were young sweethearts. Milo here is a nuisance if he doesn't get his nightly walk. I was telling Julianne about the robbery the other night and offered to walk her home."

The man could charm a statue to life.

"Nice to meet you, Julianne," I said as dog slobber dripped onto my shoulder.

Julianne beamed, her snowy perm a halo in the street light. "What a lucky girl you are to have a man like this. A gentleman and a looker to boot. You would have had a fight on your hands had I been in my prime. There's no need for you to walk me home. I can see my flat from here. But next time I need some muscle to take out the bins or replace a lightbulb, I'll know where to come."

Ezra winked, his playful nature in stark contrast to his true dark mood with me.

I returned the poodle to Julianne, and she hobbled towards her flat.

"Thank you for your help," I said to Ezra when she had gone.

"I could hardly let you blast your way through a humdrum neighbourhood. You're under my supervision, remember?" He paused. "I thought we were friends, but I guess not. All this time, I've avoided giving the coven what they wanted. You know nothing about this life and what people will stoop to. How can you presume to do a deal behind my back?"

I balled up my fists. "I haven't promised Lavinia anything. I just wanted you in a good mood before I asked you. But in case you hadn't noticed, my mum was *killed*. Nita was *killed*. Countless others too. How can you just sit there and do nothing if we have a chance to stop it?"

"The first law—"

"The first law is obsolete. You heard Detective Jameson. The senate knows what's brewing, and still, they do nothing. But your aunt is willing to step up. She just wants a small drop of your blood. That's all."

Copper glinted in Ezra's eyes. "Have you listened to a word I said? You're like a newborn babe picking up a weapon. You have no idea what is at stake here. It's not our call."

"Then whose? *Nothing* happens in this world unless we stand up and fight."

Ezra gritted his teeth. "In the Otherworld, a drop of blood is not just something to be mopped up. A drop of blood is needed for the most potent spells. It can be used to steal powers or harness them. It can be used to control, sacrifice or even kill. To boil a foe's blood, track their movements or corrupt their souls. Blood magic is something to run from, not towards. And my aunt can't be trusted. Who are you to decide otherwise?"

"Come back to the rooftop. Let's talk about this."

All gentleness had fled, leaving stony eyes in a chiselled face. "No, I don't think I will."

"I'm sorry."

In his voice, I heard the wolf. "Find another way."

My disappointment stung.

He vanished, leaving the night empty without him.

I could have asked Marina to bring a syringe from work and stolen his blood, but I couldn't bring myself to stoop that low. Ezra was my friend. I wouldn't go behind his back, even though every cell of my body screamed it was the right thing to do.

Without him, there was no deal with Lavinia's coven. Without him, we were just two girls in control pants plus a poodle-mad leopard trying to defeat a god.

I bit my lip and drew blood. I wanted to stop Ra so badly. I wanted him to pay for Mum's death. It hurt to give up, but I didn't have another choice.

Without Ezra and the witches, I didn't stand a chance.

21

It wasn't often that I regretted not owning a car in London. The city's Victorian streets were often gridlocked, and owning a car was expensive. Public transport made sense unless a magical leopard decided to accompany you.

Even in his Bengal cat form, Echo would have raised eyebrows hopping onto the bus with me. It was okay for a spaniel to follow its master onto a bus, but cats had no master. A free-range cat on the 219 would have prompted too much attention, so I dug out a cat carrier from the back of the wardrobe.

I had no idea how Echo's glamour worked metaphysically—it would be a nifty trick to squeeze my forty-year-old self into my twenty-year-old clothes—but there you go. He fitted into the cat carrier, and I carried him onto the bus, ignoring his plaintive miaowing.

"You are wise beyond your years, granddaughter of Rajika Verma, to trust your own instincts over the wolf," said Echo. "He should have agreed to your plan. It was a good one."

"You're just sore he stopped you from devouring the poodle," I said in a whisper, testing his excellent leopard hearing. The bus passengers could only hear miaows, but I had no such glamour and had to be careful.

"This may be true, but alas, my anger propelled me to seek thrills further afield. The royal deer herds of Richmond won't forget last night in a hurry."

I groaned. "I'm glad the poodle escaped, at least."

Echo grunted. "How the mighty fall. One day, I taste a deer's fleshy behind. The next, I, Chanakya Gunbir Hredhaan of Maharashtra, have been stuffed into a handbag."

"Well, you didn't have to come." We were heading towards Tooting Bec to see Dad.

"As much as I tolerate your minuscule flat, I have a fondness for the Verma family home. It was my first abode here with Rajika Verma, and I will not pass up the opportunity to relive my grander days on this measly isle."

"It's a cat carrier, not a handbag, by the way."

"It is beneath me. And it stinks of urine."

I sighed. He wasn't going to let me forget this. "Well, you shouldn't have released your bladder at your last vaccination appointment. It would need an industrial cleaner to get the stench out."

"A magical leopard doesn't need to be vaccinated against feline diseases. At least this year, I won't have to suffer the indignity."

"Actually, Echo, I signed up for a three-year vet plan, and I'd much rather we kept up appearances."

He emitted a roar that frightened the beautifully coiffed lady on the opposite aisle of the bus.

I gave her a sympathetic smile and made a show of poking Echo through the netting of the bag. "Be quiet, you silly thing."

He bit my index finger and drew blood.

"Ouch!" I sucked the puncture wound.

The beautifully coiffed lady threw us a disturbed look and changed seats.

I had a right mind to leave Echo on the bus. To teach him a lesson, I stood to ping the bell and let him sweat it out without me while the driver propelled the bus through the last mile towards Dad's house.

When the doors opened, I grabbed the carrier at the last second and jumped off the bus.

"You are walking a dangerous line, granddaughter of Rajika Verma, by treating me like a housecat," hissed Echo from the carrier. The scar across his eye gave him a savage air, especially when his tail swished like a python in attack mode.

I turfed him out of the carrier onto the street before he decided to maul me. "You'll all be relieved I've dropped the thought of challenging a killer god. We'll be much safer if I just have you to deal with."

Echo prowled along next to me. "So you have reconciled yourself to being a lily-livered spectator, have you? Where is your oomph, druid?"

"What else can I do? Ezra barely trusts me. The deal is off with Lavinia, and Jameson seems not even to have a truncheon to take to this fight. I should stop trying to be more than I am and take small steps. Plus, Dad needs me. I need to concentrate on him."

It had been the series of texts last night that had given it away. For the first few weeks, he'd busied himself prettying Mum's grave. Gaia's revelations that Mum had been killed by Ra had hit him like a tonne of bricks. He'd distracted himself from grief by mentoring Sahil. It meant a great deal to him that the senate had entrusted him with the task, although he would never have admitted it to them. It had been a way to bridge the cracks with the Otherworld that had formed when he had abandoned it.

Only he and Sahil had come up against a brick wall.

They were no closer to discovering whether Sahil had any Otherworld talents. So Sahil had decided to clear out Dad's attic and ignore any further attempts at training. Dad consoled himself by eating Mum's freezer food.

Two grown men, not speaking to each other and acting like schoolchildren.

While Sahil grunted in the attic, hauling boxes back and forth, Dad had eaten every last morsel of the meals Mum had batch cooked for the days she'd worked late. The last taste of her lovingly made meals had sent him over the edge.

His texts had come into my phone like an S.O.S.

Your brother and I aren't talking.

I miss your mum like a hole at the centre of my life.

Her ratatouille tasted of love, and I've eaten the last bite.

Oh wait, I have found her Roquefort and caramelised onion tart in the freezer. I think I will be okay until morning.

Truth be told, I'd not given Dad the time he'd deserved since Mum had died. I'd been too caught up in my own wild goose chase to uncover my powers and bring her killer to justice. I'd decided to swing by today to offer him a shoulder to cry on and a stack of takeaway menus. Plus, I could try to bridge the gap between him and Sahil.

I walked up the driveway with Echo at my side and rang the doorbell.

Dad opened the door. His white hair hadn't seen a comb in days, and remnants of tomato sauce marred his collar. There was not a paint blotch in sight on his person or his fingers.

Things were bad.

"Oh, Dad." I held out my arms to him.

He was taller than me but came to me like a child and laid his head on my shoulder. He smelled anything but fresh.

"Where's Sahil?" I asked.

"In the attic. It can't still need tidying."

I tucked my arm through his. "Don't worry. He'll come around."

"You brought the leopard."

"You have seen better days, Joshi Verma," said Echo. "Luckily, you still have family because friends would desert a person whose odour resembles a toilet."

I shushed Echo with a pointed look and ushered Dad into the belly of the house, past the shrine where he prayed for Mum and spent tealights showed the fervour of his prayers. I peeked into his studio facing the garden and gasped.

"Your father seems to be teetering at the abyss," the leopard said as quietly as possible.

He was right. Dad had cleared out all his joyful paintings of the animal world.

Instead, my mother's features stared back at me from the easel. Monochrome had replaced his colourful palette. In one study, he'd painted her eyes. In another, her mouth. In yet another, her profile replete with the fall of her hair when she woke in the morning.

As if in homage to each part of her. A jigsaw of love. A way to cheat the senate's erasure of Mum from pictures.

I sprinted up the stairs and called out for my brother. "Sahil, are you up there? Fancy a cuppa?"

He poked his dusty head out of the attic hatch. "Hi, sis. I'll be down in a minute."

"He needs us."

A raised eyebrow. "I've been here. Where have you been?"

I sighed and returned to the kitchen, where Dad opened the window to release some of the noxious gases from fermenting food remnants and dirty dishes. Mugs with dregs of breakfast tea littered the granite worktop.

I picked up a pair of washing-up gloves and gave Dad a grim smile. "Sahil's just finishing up. Why don't you have a hot shower while I get to grips with this lot?"

He shook his head. "I've turned into a pig. What would your mother say?"

"That you obviously miss her." I kissed his cheek. "Go on. You'll feel better in a fresh set of clothes."

"You'll be here when I get downstairs?"

How frail he'd become. "Yes, Dad."

He left with a sigh and a meandering step, stopping to look at the family photographs as he went, where Mum had faded to nothing.

My chest hurt for him.

"I will leave you now, druid, to make my mark on the once-beloved home of Rajika Verma and relive my glory days," purred Echo.

"Don't dig up the flower beds. They were Mum's pride and joy."

Echo lifted his nose into the air, his pride unmistakable. "I'm not a heathen, as you well know."

"And stay out of the pond."

"The koi will have missed me."

"Echo…"

"I will not eat them, but my frolicking and snarl may cause them to leap in fright. It is quite a show I used to perform for you in your childhood. You used to clap in delight. Especially when I nudged the stupid creatures into the pond and scared them out again."

I raised an eyebrow. "I expect I wiped it from my memory."

He pawed open the back door as if he'd done it a thousand times before and bounded into the garden, pure joy in every fibre of his body. As promised, he leapt into the pond, rolling in it as the koi leapt in fright. He pranced playfully, knocking them back in with his paw, catching them wriggling between his teeth, spitting them out into the water and repeating his antics.

Poor fish. Thankfully Dad didn't have a clue.

I got to work cleaning the kitchen. Mum had been like Mary Poppins in the kitchen, cheerfully cracking on with her tasks. I was more like King Kong, crashing about, grumpy at the enforced domesticity. But Dad needed me, and Sahil was hopeless at this sort of thing, so I pushed on until the kitchen sparkled. Then I made three portions of eggs and toast, setting Sahil's in the oven to keep warm.

Creaking wood behind me signalled someone's arrival.

"Dad," I said, turning. "You look so much better." He'd put on PJs instead of day clothes, but at least he was clean. He smelled of lemon-fresh shower gel, and that was a huge improvement.

His eyes swept the kitchen, and a red flush crept up his neck. "I would have cleaned up."

"I know, but you don't have to now." I set the plates on the table and gave thanks that he'd not yet noticed Echo taunting his prize koi. "Go ahead and eat. Sahil will come down when he's ready."

He sat at the table. "Rosalie's eggs were so fluffy."

I nodded. I couldn't compete with Mum's culinary skills, but I could make sure Dad felt loved and had a full belly. One of the perks of being middle-aged was knowing your own strengths and not taking everything personally.

"If only Rosalie's years hadn't been stolen from her. Can you imagine how the world would have changed if your mother had succeeded in yet another discovery?" He turned wounded eyes on me.

"What news of bringing her killer to justice? Has the senate found its moral centre yet? All those deaths, and they dilly dally until it is too late as usual."

I bit my lip. All this time I'd hidden my real intentions from him. It would only have worried him. He didn't need to know I'd wanted to lead the charge against Ra. Especially now that my plans were dead in the water. I filled him in about Nita's death, Detective Jameson and the Shadow Squad, and the witches keen to protect humdrum lives even though the Magical Constitution prevented peculiars from meddling with the gods.

"You know, darling, you have your mother's eyes. And I still have part of her to cherish because she lives on in you and Sahil. I'm as impatient as you for that weasel god to get his due, but we have to leave it to the big shots. We are tiny players in this game, and I wouldn't forgive myself if anything happened to you."

I blew out my breath. "I've been hearing that rather a lot."

"I worry so much about you that I forget you are old enough to make your own decisions. It comforts me that Rosalie realised before her death that you would take a magical path. I can hear her voice in my ear telling me to trust everything will be okay." He sighed. "Why do you think she didn't tell me when we fell out about her releasing the lab animals at work?"

"I don't know. You know what she was like. She was so precise at managing every part of her life. Like how she made freezer meals or pruned her rose bushes or conducted her experiments. Maybe she knew you'd be upset about our family embracing the Otherworld after all these years. Maybe that's why she was so wrapped up in her project at work. My guess is she wanted to ensure our safety before telling you. To make it easier for you to accept."

He chewed his lip, deep in thought, then put down his fork. "Look at me, so caught up in myself. What is done is done. What matters is she loved us. Go on, distract an old man. I'd love to see what Ezra has been teaching you. So my daughter has power over wind currents, eh? Show me what you can do."

I smiled and cast an eye around the kitchen. Ezra had told me it would be easier for me to manipulate the breeze than indoor air currents, but I needn't have worried. The window was still open, which helped.

The pile of takeaway menus I'd brought Dad sat on the worktop.

I pursed my lips and raised a hand. The familiar tingle spread through my fingers, and the menus took flight, looped in a circle above our heads and then swooped down into a pile next to his plate.

Dad's eyes lit up. He lunged across the table to grab my face and kissed my forehead. "That is magnificent! What ease, what control! You have power over the currents. I am so proud. Prouder than when you got full marks in your Shakespeare exam in high school."

I grinned. "I'm glad you approve."

"You'll get stronger with every passing day, with every bit of practice. If only your brother would take heed. Mentoring him has been a disaster. I don't know why I expected any different. Sahil's ego is wounded, but magic can't be rushed. But you, my girl, you persevered."

I'd learned to persevere during my dead-end marriage, and it had brought nothing. It was nice when it paid off. "We should go up and speak to Sahil. I can help smooth things over."

Dad slumped. "It's no use. He's a good boy, but he's stubborn."

"He just needs time to get his head around this all. God knows, I still do. Come on." I tugged him to his feet.

We traipsed up the stairs.

He started muttering to himself. "It is rather strange for a Verma to have wind powers. I knew you weren't a painter. Anyone who saw your art attempts would know that, but I wonder whether... It didn't work with Sahil, but maybe, just maybe... I mean, the binding spell did neutralise my magic too, but if Rosalie's death broke the spell and the dormant powers of my children have been unleashed, maybe my paintings have life again."

We reached the upper landing and climbed at the wobbly ladder, Dad taking tentative steps in his bare feet and chequered pyjamas, his hair damp against his neck.

It had been years since I'd been up in the loft. A dusty bulb flickered light across the boarded space. A sun ray crept in through a damaged roof tile.

Sahil had made good progress. In one corner, he had stacked up empty suitcases and plastic boxes full of childhood mementos. The rest of the space was an explosion of Dad's art: line drawings, canvases full of oil paint and watercolours in simple frames.

My brother, kneeling over a plastic box of trinkets, looked up. "Ah, sorry, Alisha. I got caught up."

I bent down to kiss his cheek. "More like you were avoiding confrontation."

"What do you think, Dad? It looks better, doesn't it?" said Sahil.

"It looks great, son."

Sahil chewed his lip sheepishly. "Sorry for blowing off at you yesterday. I need to get back to work, and this fishing for Otherworld talents seems to have hit the bottom of the rock pool with me."

"I didn't learn overnight either, son."

I looked from one to the other. "See, that wasn't so hard, was it?"

"Son, I want Alisha to try to animate the paintings. Like we tried with you. You wouldn't mind?"

"Why would I mind?" But his eyes carried a different message. He picked up a bear I knew from one of Dad's greeting cards and offered it to me.

Dad shook his head. "No, not that one. You don't animate a bear in a loft. You animate a bear in a field. Or in the woods. Or, if you must, in a garden. A bear in a loft causes carnage." He picked up a watercolour of a mouse nibbling on cheese and then discarded that too. "Too easy to lose up here. I don't want to introduce a mouse problem into the house."

Sahil reached for a canvas of a sloth on a tree. "How about this?"

Dad shook his head. "No, no, not for a novice animateur in suburban South London. Sloths may be sleepy, but they can be very noisy." He reached instead for a tiny canvas on a shelf. "Yes, yes...I think this is it." He handed me a painting of a frog on a lily pad. "If you manage it, we can release him into our pond."

All well and good if Echo was finished with the pond.

I held the painting, my heart thumping. The loft suffocated me, and I longed to blast my way out to clean air. I wasn't sure if I wanted this talent, but Dad's face shone with hope. "What do I do?"

His voice jittered with excitement. "Your grandmother always started by closing her eyes and thinking of a purpose for the animal. Then take a deep breath and reach for the threads of my drawing as if you're a puppet master. Then pull out the creature from the page."

"I can't—"

"But what if you can?"

A nerve throbbed in Sahil's cheek. If I succeeded, it would be hard on him.

I sighed and squeezed my eyes shut, feeling like a fool. A forty-year-old woman playing make-believe. No wonder I'd taken compassionate leave from work with all this madness around me. I silently assigned the frog a name and a purpose.

Dad hadn't mentioned a name, but I didn't want the poor thing to be born with some sort of existential crisis, and I thought a name might help. Gerry the frog's purpose would be to make friends with the traumatised koi in Dad's pond.

I opened my eyes, took and deep breath and twiddled my fingers above the drawing, resisting the urge to laugh.

I'd never felt so ridiculous in my life.

"No, not like that. Like this." Dad moved his fingers like a harpist.

I tried again, mimicking his movement.

Nothing. Nada.

"You're not putting enough belief behind it," said Dad.

"Give her a second, Dad," said Sahil.

I grimaced. "Maybe this just isn't my talent. I already have one. The universe probably doesn't want to give me two."

Dad's face crumpled. "But how can your grandmother's talent have disappeared with her? It's not fair."

"It doesn't matter." I put the painting aside and took his arm, ignoring my own pang at the evaporated link to my grandmother. "I'm so glad you showed me your work. They shouldn't be hidden away up here."

"Alisha is right," said Sahil. "We should hang them in the house."

"Maybe the senate will reconsider you exhibiting in galleries," I said.

The three of us clambered down the ladder and returned to the kitchen, where I handed Sahil his food. Through the open window, I noted Echo's sleeping form on the lawn. The dishwasher had completed its cycle, and I picked out some new cups and popped the kettle on just as my phone trilled in my pocket.

Detective Jameson's name flashed up on the screen. "Sorry, guys, I have to take this," I said. "Hello, Detective."

"I hope I'm not interrupting anything," he said. "Do you have a minute?"

I leaned against the worktop. "Yes, of course. I was going to give you a ring today. I'm afraid our deal with Lavinia won't work."

"The wolf said no."

"He did, yes."

"Actually, I was calling about something else. Are you sitting down?"

Anxiety flared inside my stomach. I pulled out a chair and sat opposite Dad and Sahil. "I am now."

"I'm sorry to tell you that at roughly seven this morning, Melissa Ramsay, your mother's colleague at EvolveTech, was killed on her way to work."

A vice clamped around my heart. "She what? What happened?"

"She flew into the third rail at Elephant and Castle. A few dozen other commuters were further down the train, but they had their head in their phones or had headphones in. No one got to her in time. She was dead by the time paramedics arrived."

"Oh, that's terrible." I squeezed my eyes shut, picturing Melissa the last time I'd seen her. She was just a woman who liked baking and racy novels.

"If it's any consolation, my best guess is that she died quickly." Detective Jameson's voice cracked. "The CCTV was shorted, but Alisha, I have to tell you, my gut says it's him."

The noise in my head drowned him out.

Dad took the phone from my numb hands and said goodbye to the detective. There was fire in his eyes. "I heard everything."

"The woman from the memorial?" said Sahil.

I nodded. "She didn't do anything to deserve this. It's my fault she died. It's my fault for not making her a priority. If I'd acted sooner, she'd still be alive. Instead, I convinced myself that I could just walk away from you know who's killing spree. What kind of person does that make me?"

"Call me a coward, but I think you made the right call not going up against a god," said Sahil. "Some people would say that's the only call."

I clenched my fists. A grown woman didn't shy away from her problems. I had to make this right, whatever it took. I would not sit on my sorry arse while even more families were torn apart.

Even if I had to headlock Ra or turn into a banshee to make him pay.

"I know that look. It's the look of a woman about to run headfirst into enemy fire." Dad patted my arm. "You must make your own decisions. You need wit and courage to survive. You have those. But you also need allies."

He looked at my brother.

"Don't look at me," said Sahil. "I don't even have wind powers."

Dad sighed. "Don't make your grandmother's mistake, Alisha. She fell because she didn't have enough allies when it counted. Choose carefully who you trust. Betrayal is rife when power is at stake."

"Take care, Alisha," said Sahil. "And thanks for the eggs."

I hugged them both and then darted over to the open window. "Echo!"

He lumbered over, stretching out his lithe body as he came. "You called, druid? I was minded to ignore this summons, but I am in a good mood after my koi games."

"How would you like to go hunting?"

Emerald eyes sparkled with interest. "Who am I hunting?"

"A god."

22

I'd suffered from insomnia during the dark days of my divorce. The sleeplessness returned with Mum's death. Nita and Melissa's deaths only made it worse. I tossed and turned, starfished across my sheets, got up for a wee, downed water and downloaded meditation apps.

Nothing changed except my determination to act against Ra.

In the morning, I woke, put on my favourite knickers—comfy but supportive—and tried in vain to cover my dark circles with concealer. I then invited Marina over to join me on the rooftop to summon Gaia. Between my steak-eating, flat-marking, sofa-slobbering leopard and being distracted by more pressing matters, my neglected flat was in no fit state to host a goddess.

It turned out it was marginally easier to summon a magical leopard than a goddess.

There was no doubt we needed Gaia's help. An uninitiated peculiar like me was no threat to Ra. I was like an insect on his sandals. He'd crush me and not even bother disposing of my body. But with allies, I'd stand a chance.

Detective Jameson had understood that all along.

Even Lavinia, powerful as she was, needed a coven.

Marina and I had been making offerings to Gaia on the rooftop of my building for three hours straight before we realised Gaia wasn't coming. How could we hope to beat Ra without an equally weighty force on our side?

"Well, that's a bit shite," said Marina. "I was hoping to meet her. You and Ezra got all the fun last time."

"I was there too," said Echo. "She loved me best."

"That she did," I said. "Which is why I'd rather you weren't here, Echo. If she decides she wants you, we'll never see you again."

Echo put his nose in the air. "If the goddess wants me, she can have me. Who am I to stand in the way of the divine?"

"You're happy enough to stand in the way of you know who."

"That is true, but only because he is a cretinous villain and hardly worthy of god-like status."

I nodded. "Gotcha. Any further luck tracking him?"

"No, I wasn't there when Melissa was first attacked and when Nita was killed, so I don't yet have his scent. Even with a scent, it is next to impossible to track a god. I tried to track the goddess after tasting heaven at her feet. I couldn't find her either."

I chewed my lip. It would have been easier to plan our attack if we could track Ra's movements and get ahead of his next target. "In that case, we'll have to lure him to us by focusing all our attention on him, as Gaia suggested, or by making him angry enough to come and find us."

Echo inclined his magnificent head. "We need the witches, whatever the wolf says. Without them, we have no hope of gaining the upper hand, especially without Gaia beside us."

Marina grimaced. "Well, after releasing a colony of rats, a cloud of bats and a swarm of bees on this rooftop, I think we can safely say that Gaia isn't coming."

"There is someone else with information that might help," said Echo. "I crossed paths with the wolf on my travels. He had another lead to follow up, but he means to come here to speak with us."

My heart leapt a beat. I'd missed Ezra.

More importantly, I knew how to get what I wanted from Lavinia and to make it up to Ezra.

"But first, we must step up your training," said Echo. "We cannot wait for Wildwoods to sanction the next stage of your education. They may have assigned the wolf as your mentor, but they forget that I, Chanakya Gunbir Hredhaan of Maharashtra, have deep knowledge of my own. It was for good reason that I stood beside Rajika Verma. My beauty may turn heads, but I am powerful in my own right."

"Lighten up, dude," said Marina. "You're starting to sound like a 1990s supermodel. No need to prove how big your rod is to us. We know you're awesome."

He swished his tail. "Everyone likes others to be aware of their value, Marina Ambrose. It doesn't hurt to state it out loud sometimes. It's a good thing you brought me some rump steak this morning because otherwise, I'd think your mockery was fighting talk."

"Oh, I meant nothing of the kind, Echo. A little teasing between friends solidifies the relationship." Marina caressed him behind the ear. She was no longer nervous around him. She could sense his moods and no longer carried tranquilliser darts with her.

Her charming nature and ability to bond with all kinds of people and animals all made sense now we'd discovered she was an empath. All these years of friendship, I had pegged myself as the moon to her sun, the shade to her warmth. She had innate strengths, just like I did.

I looked around the rooftop to ensure we were still alone and rolled up the sleeves of my blouse to show I meant business. "You say I need more training. This is as good a place as any." I raised my hands and called the familiar tingling sensation to the forefront of my mind.

Echo shook his head. "No need for that, druid. I want to teach you to cast spells."

I exchanged glances with Marina. We might have been middle-aged, but something about this new life made us feel like kids in a sweet shop.

"Are you sure?" I said. "The Educator's Law states that new users of magic must be supervised until they pass the trial."

"Am I not supervising you?"

I didn't dare say that he technically didn't count as much as a person. To be honest, I preferred him to most people anyway.

"Minister Willowsun said that learning spells would happen once my initial training was completed."

Echo narrowed his eyes. "Always the paper-pushers thinking they know what's best. Let me tell you, druid, there will be no completion of the initial training if you don't survive the next encounter. What will it be?"

I took a step forward. "Teach me."

"And me," said Marina. "Can I cast spells too?"

"Any peculiar can cast spells, given enough instruction and practice, so long as they have a source of power to draw on. For druids, this power is nature. For empaths, it is depth of emotion. You, Marina, must harness the strongest emotion you can muster and hold it there while you perform the spell. Alisha, you must learn to feel the currents around you. It might manifest as a vibration or a hum. Or you might learn to see them, even though they are invisible to the naked eye. Ground yourself in nature, draw on it, and your spells will rise to the occasion."

"Why have I never seen you cast a spell?" I said.

"How do you think I make the carcasses of all the animals I eat disappear? It's not like I can leave them scattered around London, leading back to me like breadcrumbs."

I gasped. "But when you stalked Milo the poodle the other night, you said you'd leave enough for burial."

"That was just a lie to make you feel better," he purred.

Marina tucked a lock of pink hair behind her ear. "I'm impressed. Let's do this. What's our first trick?"

"I'll begin by teaching you a handful of spells I think will be useful. Later, with deeper study, you may be able to create your own spells and your own manner of performing them."

Marina shuddered. "Next, he'll have us playing with voodoo dolls."

"No voodoo dolls required," said Echo. "I knew this moment would come. I have been meditating on the very choice of spells during my nightly jaunts. The taste of blood always brings me my best ideas. The first spell we will practice is Būmarēnga."

"Būmarēnga," said Marina.

"Wait, what does Būmarēnga do?" I said.

Shrewd emerald eyes shone. "That's why it's so perfect. It returns a spell to its owner. For example, if Ra turns his heat on you, act quickly, and this spell will turn his own powers against him."

Marina's eyes widened. "Will that work on a god?"

"That, I do not know," said Echo. "But it is a magnificent defence spell, and without it in this fight, you are dung beetles on your back. Now, listen closely. It is important to make the first B soft, to roll the R and to end with a soft G. Gather your emotions or ground yourself to nature, focus on the subject of the spell and say the word exactly as taught. Any discrepancy and the spell won't work, and your death will likely be swift."

"Do we need a wand?" said Marina cheerfully, completely at odds with my sombre mood.

I was starting to realise we were preparing for a battlefield.

"Do I look like I need a wand?" Echo said with the disdain of a bored king. "There are any number of tools that are used in spell casting. Some use wands. For others, a word plus a gesture suffices. Some spells call for feathers or bells. Others yet use airborne seeds or knotted ribbons. Sometimes spells use frankincense or clover or the heads of decapitated flowers. Some dark souls use blood or body parts. Spells require imagination and skill and are only as small as your ambition. I, too, take my energy from the ground I have soaked with the blood of beloved pets, roaming livestock and decorative beasts."

Marina raised an eyebrow in question.

"Don't ask," I said. "It's better not to know. So Būmarēnga then. Shall we give it a go?"

"For a language teacher, your pronunciation leaves much to be desired, druid," said Echo. "Send me a strong breeze, and I will use the spell and show you how it is done. Remember to brace yourself for the reverse blast."

"Okay." I raised my hands and braced my feet. My hands tingled, and I directed the current at him with more force than I intended.

Echo's green eyes skewered me with an intense gaze. There was a slight rocking of his head and then, "Būmarēnga," spoken with gentle determination.

The breeze reversed, hitting me full in the chest, with a force I hadn't expected. I flew backwards across the rooftop, past the drying rack with Dotty's greying underwear, past the motley assortment of chairs, past Marina, her eyes wide in shock, and towards the guard rail.

My heartbeat in my ears, I reached out to grab something, anything, but my fingers flailed.

I thudded against a hard chest. Strong arms helped me regain my balance.

"Looks like I got here just in time," said a familiar voice.

He was a sight for sore eyes in rumpled clothing, bringing with him a rueful smile and the musky scent of mountain earth.

I disentangled myself from Ezra and scrambled over to Marina's side for safety. My legs were jelly, probably from my near-death experience, but I couldn't rule out Ezra as the cause of the butterflies in my tummy.

"Now, now, cat, what's going on here?" said Ezra.

"Just a spot of spell-casting, dog. You know, to build up the home team's arsenal. I told Alisha you were coming."

"I am indebted." Ezra bowed to him as if there had been a shift in their relationship, and respect had taken root. Brown hair flopped into grey eyes.

Marina piped up, "Hi, Ezra. Want to join us in practising Būmarēnga?"

He let out a low whistle. "So that's what you've been teaching them, cat. It's a bold move."

"Do you cast spells, wolf? You are half wizard, after all," said Echo.

"You have the upper hand there, cat. I have only a rudimentary understanding. I was brought up by the wolves, after all. I rely on my wolf side, my teleporting and my charms."

"Then I can teach you a trick or two."

"I am perfectly happy with my lot. Wolves have enough to cope with during the change without inviting more unpredictability into our lives." Just as I was starting to feel forgotten, he turned to me.

"Before you continue, I have something to say to Alisha. I heard about your mother's friend, hellfire. I'm truly sorry. She seemed like a nice woman."

"She was." I held his gaze. "Where have you been?"

"I've only been gone two days. You miss me?"

"Urgh, get a room already," said Marina.

I ignored her. "You didn't answer my question, Ezra."

He shrugged. "I'm not good at conflict. I get angry. For some wolves, that means changing to work out their anger; damn the consequences. Others run wild to iron out the rage. For me, teleporting means I get the hell out of there. I'm sorry I walked out on you."

"I'm sorry I wasn't up front."

"When I stopped smarting about our disagreement, I decided to make good on that promise I made you when we first met." He jerked his hand through his brown hair. "You did want to find the Celestial Library?"

A warm glow spread through me. He'd put me first despite being angry at me. Not even my husband had done that. "Did you find it?"

Ezra shook his head. "It should be a cinch for me to hold on to the threads of it, but it's been moving around. I can't get a grip. I teleport, and there is only residue in the slipstream like the library has moved seconds before."

Echo growled. "That only happens for one reason. The Custodian has activated the library's defences. She thinks it is under threat."

"Exactly," said Ezra. "But that's just it. Why would the Custodian feel that she is under threat? There has been no word from Aunt Lavinia that the Celestial Library is in danger, no noise in ministerial communications or mobilising of the Otherworld armies. It got me thinking we're being blindsided, and I was stupid to doubt you. That's why I came back. The right thing to do is rarely the easiest. You might be new to all of this, Alisha, but I trust your instincts. If I have to surrender a vial of my blood to my aunt, so be it."

Electricity pulsed between us.

"I won't let it come to that." I frowned, putting the pieces together. "Gaia said the gods had been weakened without prayer. At night class, the electrician said that if humans had worshipped the gods in gratitude, he wouldn't have to cause you pain."

"He hopes to trigger an outpouring of grief," said Marina.

Ezra sighed. "Grief is a more reliable basis for prayer than gratitude."

"We need to call the detective," said Marina. "And not just because I fancy him."

"We need to call Lavinia, too," I said to Ezra. "I have a plan. The question is, do you trust me?"

A frisson of static electricity sparked between us.

He nodded. "I trust you, Alisha."

"If we fail, it's possible he'll come after us."

"Let him come," said Echo. "We will be ready."

"I'm going to load up on horseshoes and four-leaf clovers and wear my grandmother's cross," said Marina. "I reckon we'll come out okay."

"We're all on the same page, then," said Ezra.

I took a deep breath and dialled Baba Yaga's Gym.

23

———————

Lavinia Drach's singsong voice swam down the phone line into my ear. "Baba Yaga's Gymnasium. How can I help?"

I prayed I was doing the right thing. "Lavinia? It's Alisha Verma."

A pause during which I sensed her glee. "Why, hello, dear. The detective crushed my hopes of you calling."

Ezra, Marina and Echo leaned in to listen. A vein throbbed in Ezra's neck.

I blocked out their anxious faces. "I changed my mind."

"My nephew is on board?" said Lavinia.

"Yes."

A shriek of delight. "How wonderful."

"You are prepared to go against the senate to help in this matter?"

"The coven is agreed. We shall proceed to protect humdrums. It won't be the first time the Magical Constitution can be interpreted this way," said Lavinia.

"And the witches will fulfil their role steadfastly, despite the difficulties of facing this opponent? He is very powerful."

"So are my sisters and me," said Lavinia. "These meagre gods are nothing like they once were. Our protection spells guard us well. What's the worst the electrician can do? I suppose he could pull the plug on the studio, but as I said, my little rat darlings have long seen to it that Baba Yaga's Gymnasium is self-sustaining. I take it you have a plan?"

I outlined it for her. It was a long shot, but I'd found a way for her to protect scientists. We just had to figure out how to ensure Ra didn't try this stunt again.

She listened, um-ing and aah-ing. "What an unusual approach, but yes, I think it might work. Of course, it will need a lot of focus, a pound of flesh from the electrician and maybe the third eyelids of a thousand lizards, but I can give my supplier a call."

"We will need to make sure he is neutralised and can't do harm again."

"You are asking for miracles that aren't possible, druid. We are a motley crew of peculiars facing a god. He may be diminished, but he is still a god. I cannot bind his powers. If I did, what would happen to the dawn? We can only clip his wings and make sure he is sufficiently subdued. Imprisonment may be a possibility, but I think the best we can hope for is thwarting him and escaping with our lives. Is that enough for you?"

I wanted more, but the witch was right. Without the sun, the earth would wither. "It is enough."

"After this, you will always have to look over your shoulder. I have the coven at my side. Who do you have?"

I looked from Marina to Ezra to Echo. "My friends."

"That leaves only one thing."

My throat was parched from the stress of this conversation. "What's that?"

Her laugh tinkled down the phone line. "It's time to talk terms, of course."

"I thought we could discuss that side of things at the gym. Bring the detective on board."

"The detective has nothing to trade, dear. At least, nothing of value to me. Whereas you have my nephew in the palm of your pretty hand."

I clipped my words, a tactic adopted from managing unruly kids in the classroom. "State your terms, Lavinia."

"A vial of forty millilitres of Ezra's blood then, not a drop less, to be taken by one of the coven at the conclusion of our business. No refunds, no hanky-panky. If you fall foul of these terms, the coven will forcibly take what we are owed. Do you agree to these terms, Alisha?"

How neatly she had stepped from the role of aunty to businesswoman. Ezra was right to fear her. "You promise that the threat we face will be neutralised?"

"I do."

I pressed my lips together. "Then we have a deal."

"Marvellous, dear. Heads up."

"Excuse me?" A whistling came down the line like the nearing of an aeroplane, culminating in a rush of sound and a prick on my neck. I touched my neck, bewildered.

Marina rushed over to inspect it. "There's a black dot on your neck, like a mole. It's really weird."

"Hello, empath. It's just a reminder to Alisha to honour our deal. The mole will fade when I am satisfied I have received my lot. Otherwise, it'll be a stain on her body to mirror the stain on her conscience. I was feeling kind. She's lucky it's not a nasty wart. I save those for the dodgier characters I deal with."

"Bloody brilliant." I frowned at Ezra. He could have warned me about his aunt's weird rituals. I made a mental note to zap it with my cupboard full of face creams. Time was enough of a meddler in a person's appearance without witches getting involved too.

"Shall we meet at the gym tomorrow evening to have a run-through, say six p.m. after closing?" said Lavinia. "We can strike at midnight when the humdrums are sleeping. It's Tuesday, so with any luck, they won't be out drinking, although you never know with the Brits. Any excuse for a booze up."

"That is wise," said Ezra. "The sun god will be weakest when the night is darkest."

My heartbeat sped up. "You want to attack tomorrow?"

"Why yes, dear. We'll strike while the iron is hot. No use risking even more lives being lost to that debauched soul. I'll invite the detective to the warm-up, but he best stays away from the real fight. He's a humdrum, too, after all."

I gulped.

"Be sure to get some good rest. And maybe do some stretches in case you have to dodge any projectiles. Too late to get you to lose the extra inches, I suppose, but limbering up will help."

Charming. "Until tomorrow then, Minister."

"Until tomorrow, druid."

I hung up the phone and turned to my friends. "It's all set."

Echo broke into a rendition of Kelly Clarkson's 'Stronger (What Doesn't kill You)'.

Ezra sighed. "We have come to our moment of reckoning, and the cat is quoting song lyrics again."

"Even in the face of death, I am continuing my attempts to integrate into this culture," said Echo.

"Just for the record," said Ezra, "there's not an extra inch on you. My aunt's a little militant about fitness, that's all."

Marina nodded. "Too right. Now shall we practice Būmarēnga? I have a feeling we're going to need it."

———

THE LAST OF Baba Yaga's buff, Lycra-clad clientele left as my friends and I, Echo in tow, entered the gym on the dot of six p.m. I kept glancing at my watch as the minutes ticked away to when we'd face Ra. If we could lure him to the fight, that was. We sat on pink tub chairs in reception while the coven and their rat familiars cleared the gym, our mouths gaping.

Only Ezra kept his calm. He had visited his aunt's gym often enough to know what to expect.

"They look tasty," said Echo. "A rat before a hunt is like a humdrum eating olives as a starter. It's a very civilised thing to do."

"I wouldn't kid yourself," said Ezra. "They'll transform you into a bug before you have the chance."

"The witches?" said Echo, still considering it.

"The rats."

"Did you bring what I asked?" I whispered to Marina.

"Yeah. With any luck, they won't search me." She knocked on the wooden coffee table in front of us, then raised her voice a notch. "Poor Ezra was a bit of a wally about the extraction, but he'll live."

"I heard that," said Ezra.

She ignored him, fascinated by the rats at work. "Rats really are much more intelligent than I gave them credit for. Look at that one using antibacterial spray on the CrossFit. And that one over there, levitating while his teeny tiny rat hands get the smears off the mirror. Oh, and that one over there. He's my favourite. Who knew rats were strong enough to lift weights?"

"Magical rats," said Ezra. "There's a big difference."

"I'd guess magical rats are much like their humdrum counterparts. They are incontinent, of course, but with a little effort, they can be litter-trained."

"Yuck." All this talk of incontinent rodents was making me want to vomit in my mouth.

"I think they're rather magnificent. Not as magnificent as you, Echo, but much less expensive to keep. They're easy on the eye too. Look at that sweetheart over there, all snowy white with a pink nose and a flourish of whiskers. I'd quite like one of my own. Think what a help it would be after surgery. Or if I could use one to help with procedures I hate. Like squeezing anal glands," said Marina as Detective Jameson tumbled through the door.

He caught the tail end of her sentence and pulled a disgusted face. "Hello, folks. Did I miss anything? There's never a good time to talk about anal glands in public, Marina. Nice to see you've fully recovered from Ravynne's truth serum, though. I did feel guilty playing along with that."

Marina gave him a warm smile. "Nice of you to say. You must have to make tough choices as a detective."

"You have no idea." He settled into a chair and eyed the coven at work. "First time I saw this, I passed out. When I came round, I was laid out on the floor with Elvira holding smelling salts under my nose, and Lavinia had taken off my shoes to make me comfortable. That's when I knew they were a good lot. A criminal would have taken the chance to stick the boot into a vulnerable officer."

Echo honked with laughter. "The detective doesn't seem to realise the witches probably pickled parts of him while he was unconscious."

Lavinia strode over, wiping her hands on a towel.

"I'll have you know we did no such thing. Robert is one of the few men we tolerate very well. Not as well as you, of course, dear nephew." She reached up to kiss Ezra's cheek.

"Aunty, you look well," he said.

She pulled back to look at him. "You could do with a shave."

"There'll be time for that later."

"Indeed." She turned to Echo. "And you must be Rajika Verma's famed leopard."

Echo growled. "You speak as though I am a belonging, witch. Although it is true my purpose is to be of service to the Verma family line."

"Lucky them," said Lavinia. "I am honoured to meet you, Chanakya Gunbir Hredhaan of Maharashtra. I have been looking forward to our paths crossing since Rajika Verma registered you at the Wildwoods data bank."

He purred in delight. "You took time to learn my name."

"Of course, Chanakya. It is not often that one lives in the same city as a magical leopard of historical note. Your name is hard to forget."

"I like this witch," said Echo.

Lavinia swung around to the coven and the familiars, still bustling around the gym and clapped above her head like a flamenco dancer. "Right, my dears. That's enough for today. The gym is positively sparkling."

Her coven and the rats lined up, waiting for her next command.

I waved goodbye to Elvira, the soft-spoken witch who had tended to me so kindly. She struck me as the coven member I'd most like to go for a drink with. She seemed to lack the fire and the manipulative agenda of the rest of the coven, and I liked her all the better for it.

"We'll use studio one for our planning session," said Lavinia. "Any hungry souls can make requests of the rats. Ravynne's little one is especially talented in the kitchen."

I cringed inside but kept my expression polite, just as Mum had taught me as a child. "I've eaten, thanks. Anyone else hungry?"

"Nope," said Detective Jameson.

"Nah, all good." Marina wrinkled her nose.

"I think we're all set, Aunt Lavinia," said Ezra.

Lavinia nodded. "As you wish. Let's get on with business, then. Six hours until midnight, and our success lies in how well we prepare. Come along, now. Studio one is this way."

We followed her into the studio and lined up against the walls: seven witches and their rats, a werewolf, a druid, an empath, a leopard and a humdrum. I'd hoped Lavinia would take command, but when she beckoned me into the centre of the room, I swallowed my nerves and stood by her side.

"Over to you, Alisha," she said. "You're in the driving seat."

Eighteen sets of eyes turned on me.

I'm pretty sure a trickle of wee escaped me.

My voice wavered, growing stronger as I hit my flow. "Tonight, we face the sun god. He's not going to be an easy foe. While Gaia had a hand in guiding us here today, she had not responded to my calls for aid. The electrician is one diminished being who has lost his path. A fallen god. A murderer. We are many, and we stand on the side of right. On the side of the innocent. On the side of the healers. In the next few hours, though we are strangers, we will become a team, and we will prevail."

"She's good at pep talks," said Ezra.

"You should have seen her debate at school. I'd follow her anywhere," said Marina. "She's an exceptional teacher."

I gave them a stern look. "Pay attention, you two."

Marina grinned. "See?"

"Step forward, Detective. You brought your Taser?" I said.

He nodded. "I did."

"As a humdrum, the detective will not be on the battlefield. But he will be available on the phone to coordinate the operation should anything go wrong. For now, he will play the sun god as we practice our roles. Pick a partner and make sure you have each other's backs. As soon as the electrician appears, we will surround and subdue him. It may take force, and you must be willing to use it."

Lavinia gestured to a roll of thick rubber material in the corner.

"Morgan, Agatha, Ravynne, bring that here. Our goal is to wrap him in it until the deed is done. An immobilisation spell may slow him down. Maybe a lasso spell to bind him. We'll be practising on the detective shortly."

I nodded. "While the sun god is subdued, Lavinia, Chandra and Isadora will cast the protection spell over the world's scientists. We have no hope of subduing the god after the deed is done, but the witches can fly, and Ezra can teleport the rest out of there to take stock. Objective one is to save the scientists. Objective two is to escape with our lives."

Lavinia spoke up at my side. "A nice practical approach, druid. I'd much rather be a realist than an idealist. I have gathered most of the ingredients for the spell. The third eyelids of a thousand lizards, one kilogram of rosemary, 308 grams of eucalyptus, 268 grams of Egyptian sand, eighty-one tablespoons of Himalayan salt, a dozen stethoscopes, an amethyst, an inch-wide chunk of obsidian. It is a difficult spell, given the vast coverage required, but I have checked and double-checked my calculations. The memory stick? A quite brilliant idea, Alisha, if I might say."

"Detective, do you have it?" I asked.

Detective Jameson pulled a slim silver-and-red memory stick from the pocket of his jeans. "They are all here. NHS numbers for every scientist known to the British government, together with a list of private health insurance policy numbers for international scientists. This should do the job."

Sorrow filled my voice, but I had wracked my brains and hadn't had a further lightbulb moment. "Those without health cover will fall through the cracks, but most will be protected. Unless anyone else has a better idea?"

Lavinia shrugged her bony shoulders. "All spells have their caveats. We are not gods. Beyond pulling a hair, fingernail or tooth from every living or decomposing scientist, I can't see a better way of casting such a large protection spell. Of course, protection spells don't impact natural causes and have been trialled before."

"A blanket protection spell is also used as a safety net for pupils at Wildwoods," said Elvira.

"And for much-loved rat familiars who are on missions without the protection of the coven," said Ravynne.

Lavinia steepled her fingers together. "There's just one more ingredient the spell requires. The pound of flesh we will need to take from the sun god tonight."

"You ridicule us, sister, by insisting on this folly. Taking flesh from a god is nigh on impossible," said Isadora, Ezra's red-haired aunty with the elfin cut.

Lavinia's voice was icy. "Quiet, sister. Always the dissenting voice. Always the one to rain on our parade. The diminished god is no match for a united coven nor our fleet of umbrellas." She turned her eyes to Ezra. "What we win is more than worth the risk."

"Your hubris will be the death of us, sister," said Isadora.

Lavinia stepped towards her, full of intent. "Calm yourself, Isadora. Or leave the room."

Isadora lowered her head.

Lavinia pressed on. "Aim to take a toe. That should suffice and will be far less risky than leaving his hands exposed."

"Echo, that will be your job. Your teeth will be quicker than any knife. Just ensure you don't swallow it. Ezra will be your partner. If you are in danger, he will teleport you to safety."

"You have experience summoning the gods. How will we lure the electrician to the battleground?" said Lavinia.

"Experience would be an exaggeration. I succeeded once with Gaia, but I had help."

"You sell yourself short," said Lavinia. "You are the only one in this room who has seen the gods four times in the past fortnight. I understand Gaia attended your mother's memorial, you summoned her to Wandsworth Common, you crossed paths with the electrician while saving Melissa Ramsay's life, and he killed Nita Mubarak at your night glass."

I gulped. "You are remarkably well informed."

"I told you, our rats are formidable spies."

A large rat, the size of my forearm, saluted and bowed as if claiming credit for the missions involving me.

I gave him a thumbs-up in appreciation of his skill, then addressed the room. "I have no tried-and-tested means to summon the electrician, but if I were to guess, it would mean that we acquire an offering of value to him and then clasp our hands together and focus all our attention on his name. It worked once for Gaia."

Lavinia nodded. "Then that is what we will do."

"But what is of value to the sun god?" said Marina.

"Remember, the sun god is now an electrician. How about a new set of tools?" said Detective Jameson.

"That would be fine if we wanted to bore him to death," said Lavinia.

I nodded. "An offering must inspire. We can't risk him ignoring us."

The large rat emitted a series of squeaks.

Echo honked with laughter. "The rat cannot speak."

"We understood perfectly what he said." Elvira smiled. "Those are very clever ideas, Ignacio. He suggested shares in a solar panel company or a swanky Tesla."

A smile spread across Lavinia's face, making her wrinkles seem less harsh. "That is it! Chandra, you know Elon. Call in that favour. I'm sure he can spare something from the London showroom. Maybe one of the ones with doors that open like wings."

"Consider it done," said Chandra.

"In ancient Egypt, the sun god was known to be partial to pomegranate wine. Fei Yen and Faeza sell it by the bucketload at Shanghai Moon," I said.

"I'll head down in the van to pick some up," said Marina.

I nodded. "A swanky Tesla and a bucketful of pomegranate wine. I hope this works."

"Hunting hour is almost upon us," purred Echo. "May we be victorious."

Lavinia's copper-flecked eyes glinted. "May we shed the blood of our enemies."

"Detective, are you ready for role-play? Let's have a run-through, shall we?"

He clenched his jaw, eyeing us all, and readied his Taser.

I raised my hands.

The witches picked up their umbrellas. The rats, who had been standing on two legs, braced themselves on all fours. Ezra's hand hovered above his charm necklace. Marina mouthed Būmarēnga under her breath.

Echo grinned, sensing blood. "Watch out for your toes, Detective."

"Go!" I said.

The wooden floor sprang as we launched ourselves towards him.

24

———————

The night was cold and dreary. I'd dressed in yoga leggings and a hoodie and popped some paracetamol in advance in the hope of warding off any forthcoming pain. My courage flickered on and off like a faulty lightbulb. I hadn't told Dad the plan because his anxiety, on top of my own, would be my undoing.

The thought of burying myself under my duvet with only Netflix for company was all too tempting. Hell, I even preferred the thought of a raging argument with my ex-husband across the kitchen table.

But Mum had died at Ra's hands. What kind of daughter would turn a blind eye?

I wouldn't close my eyes. I wouldn't wish myself back into my hellish marriage. I chose to live my best life, and this was it.

For the summoning and subsequent battle, Lavinia and I settled on a dilapidated carpet warehouse in Tooting. On a road full of storage depots, sofa shops and building merchants, the area was deserted at night.

We arrived separately.

Ezra teleported, Detective Jameson had his own car, and Chandra roared up the street in the Tesla. Echo and I rode with Marina in her work van, together with the case of pomegranate wine from Shanghai Moon.

Outside the warehouse, the moon illuminated our sombre faces and the sparkling red Tesla.

Ezra reached for his moon charm. The street lamps reflected on the rain-slicked road, then flared and petered out. A hum met my ears as the coven flew through the sky in formation. The witches were dressed in matching neon gym gear, more cheerleading squad than coven.

"That is awesome," Marina whispered.

"The time is nigh." Lavinia dismounted with ease.

"Fast forward a few hours, and this will all be behind us," said Detective Jameson.

I nodded. "Time for you to take your position, Detective."

The bumps and bruises he nursed from our practice run showed the Otherworld was no place for humdrums.

"Good luck." He sprinted across the street to his car, where a vast array of laptops and mysterious phones waited. His role was to keep local police away and to be our safety net in case we messed things up.

At least someone would be able to tell Dad our fate.

"Does everyone have their heatproof gloves on? Have you applied sunscreen?" These seemed logical precautions to take against the sun god.

"Yup." Marina played nervously with her grandmother's cross. She'd gone overboard in a thick layer of Soltan and dark glasses, despite the late hour. She wore skateboarding gear with elbow and shin pads, plus a bandana pulled over her rainbow locks.

I'd been tempted to bench her like Detective Jameson. Her empath powers meant she had fewer offensive moves than the rest of us, but the truth was, I always felt safer with Marina at my back, and I needed her here with me to help pull this heist off.

"We should limber up." Lavinia jogged on the spot, along with the rest of the coven, rats included. "At our age, it makes all the difference. Many a battle has been won or lost on the flexibility of the fighters."

"This is quite unlike Rajika Verma's battle preparations. And quite ridiculous." Echo had almost gone on strike when he'd realised the freezer steaks were all finished. A hunt was his bread and butter, and he didn't seem fazed by tonight.

Lavinia tutted. "Nevertheless, Chanakya, you should not discourage us. A leopard may not need a warm-up to progress from a sedentary position to battle mode, but the rest of us do."

"Ezra, can you get the Tesla inside?" I transferred the crate of wine to the passenger seat.

He wore his usual low-slung jeans and a T-shirt, but a stiffness radiated from his body like he was keenly aware of the stakes.

"Give me a minute to check the internal layout," he said.

Ezra vanished and reappeared seconds later next to the car. Then that, too, disappeared with him into the innards of the building.

We followed him inside and surveyed the layout. High ceilings, solid walls and the odd abandoned roll of carpet littered the concrete floor. The roof had seen better days, but holes in it allowed the airborne ones amongst us to swoop in and out. The fire-engine red Tesla stood in the middle of the space.

Behind me, Lavinia, Chandra and Isadora pulled in a wheelie bin and extracted ingredients from their satchels. I'd expected a more traditional cauldron, but by now, I'd learned the vast differences between what I had read in fairy tales and the reality of Otherworld customs.

The ingredients in the wheelie bin caldron fizzed along with my nerves.

Ezra had the roll of rubber tucked under his arm. My skin tingled as he leaned into my ear.

"Be careful," he said. "I have my own role tonight and won't be able to jump to your rescue. Make sure Elvira has your back. I'm the one who coaxed you into your first steps as a peculiar. I won't forgive myself if you get hurt."

The gentle witch Elvira and I had been paired, while Marina had inexplicably been paired with Ignacio, the fat rat. Marina didn't seem to mind, and Ignacio himself had entered a state of bliss as soon as Marina had invited him into the crook of her arm. He might have had a reputation as a master spy, but the gooey eyes he was making at Marina left me in severe doubt that he could protect her. So I'd relegated her to the outer circle of the warehouse.

I read the worry in Ezra's eyes. "You're not responsible for anything that happens tonight. I'm a grown woman. I make my own decisions. Besides, I'm as tough as old boots. I'll be fine. Just make sure you are too."

He'd be responsible for teleporting the rubber roll next to Ra before we subdued him. It took either stupidity or supreme courage to take on that role. I couldn't figure out why he'd take the risk, but I was grateful he was part of the team.

My watch showed it had gone midnight. The sun was set to rise at 5.40 a.m. Ra would be stronger then. We needed to use the window of darkness to our advantage.

"It's time, Lavinia," I said.

I sent up a prayer to the universe that we would come out of this unscathed and victorious.

Lavinia looked up from the wheelie bin. "Very well, druid."

"We work together. We stay clear of Ra's hands. We do the job cleanly. We get the hell out of there and regroup," I said.

We stood in a circle and raised our gloved hands in prayer.

It didn't matter that Dad was Hindu, Mum was Christian or that I was ambivalent about religion. Or that we had a Jew, pagans, agnostics and atheists within our number. We pressed our palms together in prayer because that was what the god wanted. His vanity would be how we lured him here.

"Ra." I rolled his name off my tongue. "We pray to you. We entreat you to appear to us."

"Ra," chanted the team. "We pray to you."

We repeated our pleas three times over. Just when we had begun to lose heart, the air stilled, and we fell silent. The goosebumps on my skin from the cold night receded.

Elvira grabbed my hand, her face white as a sheet. "He comes."

Warmth filled the room and deepened into heat. I closed my eyes to the blinding light, and my body broke out in a sweat.

The god's voice boomed. "You dare summon me, druid? What odd ensemble of worshippers have you brought me? What novel offering is this?"

I peeked through my fingers. A surreal, golden glow filled the warehouse, despite the moonlit sky.

Ra stood before us, naked from the waist up, with eyes of liquid fire in his tanned face. He had the build of a manual labourer. He was a brawler, not a talker. His black-tipped fingers sparked with heat.

Fierce pride bubbled up inside me. It had worked.

This was our chance.

I ignored the beads of perspiration that threaded down my back. I needed to keep him busy. "Mighty Ra, this electric car is for you. It will be self-sustaining with your talents."

He surveyed it with a bored expression. "The London underground quite suffices for my needs."

Gaia was right: there could be no pleasing eternal beings.

Echo bowed, showing immediate deference as he had to Gaia. "Perhaps a Tesla is not to your taste. Indian rickshaws are excellent, your godliness, if you want to feel the wind in your fur."

Amber eyes swept across us like a predator searching out his prey.

My voice jittered as I gestured to the passenger seat. "We present you also with a case of pomegranate wine."

He peered inside, his strong biceps and barrel body sending spikes of fear through me. "The wine is a welcome gesture, druid. It evokes memories of a bygone age."

With the god distracted, the witches stepped out of the circle to the wheelie bin.

The rest of us edged closer to him in pairs, bracing ourselves against the heat: Elvira and I, Ezra and Echo, plus the witches Ravynne, Agatha and Morgan clutching their umbrellas, accompanied by their rat familiars.

"Now, Ezra," I muttered under my breath.

Quick as a flash, he teleported closer and appeared behind Ra with the roll of rubber.

The god spun around, his eyes blazing gold.

We surrounded him, struggling to get the material around him. I raised my hands to call forth my powers and encircled Ra in a channel of wind, a buffer, to keep him from our vulnerable bodies. I fought instinctively to keep our team safe, pushing myself further than I had before, crying out as we held him in position.

His sparks flew at us, seeping into our skin and causing tiny welts.

Ezra teleported back and forth, evading Ra's rage, attempting to trap him as planned. We pressed Ra against the red wing door of the Tesla, and it sizzled, melting out of form. Agatha, Ravynne and Morgan chanted their immobilisation spell, but Ra broke free. His arm sent Agatha spiralling to the floor and singed her familiar, who lay belly up on the floor.

I sent a gust of wind to edge the unconscious rat out of harm's way.

"You'll pay for this!" bellowed Ra, turning up the heat.

Grunts of exertion met my ears. As the temperatures reached sauna level, I wasn't sure how long we'd last.

Agatha dragged herself to her feet, cast a look at her familiar and returned to the fold, her face a storm, her umbrella held aloft like a wand. Sparks and smoke flew from its end, but they bounced off the god.

I watched in horror as the friendly fire came my way.

"Būmarēnga," I said, but it didn't work.

Elvira shouted another unfamiliar word, and the sparks evaporated between our eyes.

There wasn't time for thank yous.

Ravynne and Morgan chanted their spell, their faces pained with concentration as they slowed him down. Their rats scuttled over the thick rubber, hot-stepping across the surface with nimble hands, but they didn't dare bite the god for fear of being burned.

Any moment, Ra would break free of the spell and tip the balance in his favour.

"We need the final ingredient, druid. Hurry," shouted Lavinia over the ruckus.

"He's too close to the car," I said, struggling to breathe. "We'll never manage it."

I leapt onto the car, followed by Elvira and then Ezra.

"No skin contact. Now!" I called.

We leapt. Elvira and Ezra shoved him with their gloved hands. My blow came a fraction of a second later: a foot jab from kickboxing class, as if all my classes had led to this moment. As if my forty years of trundling along at average speed suddenly caused me to blow a gasket, lending extra oomph to my kick and sending Ra toppling to the floor.

"Yeah!" whooped mild-mannered Elvira as I skidded across the roof of the Tesla like a scene from *The Fast and the Furious*, feeling more badass than ever before.

The rubber of my shoes melted, and sore skin poked out.

But it was worth it. The move took the wind from his sails.

We had a brief moment to shore up our advantage and rolled him like a sausage in a blanket across the concrete until he was tightly wrapped. Ravynne turned her belt into a lasso that snaked around him to keep the rubber in place.

My heart hammered in my throat. "Echo, now!"

He hadn't played a part so far, but his paws were a disadvantage. Now was his time to shine, except he didn't look in a hurry to move. His head had dipped, and the fur on his neck lay smooth. Usually, his tail flicked in excitement in anticipation of a hunt. Right now, it lay between his legs. He neither snarled nor snapped to show his aggression.

Panic flared inside me. He was submitting to the god.

"Echo, you have to move. Just like we discussed."

He turned emerald eyes on me.

"You are in service to the Vermas. To me."

Behind me, Ra stirred. "He is in service to me now. Make her pay, leopard."

Echo growled, baring his teeth. He leapt, and his fur shimmered like I had never seen before as if he had the metallic sheen of armour.

I tensed, a rush of blood in my ears.

There was no good way to die. I would be with Mum. Dad would be okay. Ezra would get Marina out of here. At least I'd tried.

Echo leapt, and when he landed, I heard a roar and realised the roar was not his.

My leopard held the god's toe between his teeth like a trophy and ambled over to the wheelie bin, where he dropped the last ingredient into the spell.

My heart bloomed.

"There can be no good fortune for those who defy the gods." Ra dripped with gore. Rage filled every syllable. "Humans forget how short their lives are and how expendable."

I nodded. "Perhaps, but Rosalie Verma was my mother." I needed to say her name. "And this is for her."

25

Lavinia, Chandra and Isadora rocked on the balls of their feet over the wheelie bin, their brows covered in sweat. The stench of molten plastic and garden herbs filled the room. Particles dispersed into the air, and the witches' perfectly composed demeanour evaporated. Their hair grew frizzy. Their eyes rolled back in their heads. Their bodies made jerking movements.

This was unlike the spell at the Kraglek ceremony at Wildwoods. This spell wasn't effortless. It seemed to cost them.

It cost Ra, too, judging by the milky pallor of his skin.

Finally, Lavinia came back to herself. She looked older than when she had started. "It is done. The scientists are safe. Who knows how many lives we have saved tonight? But the rubber and lasso have already begun to weaken. They will not hold him long. Hand the vial of Ezra's blood to Elvira, and we can leave."

Ra had closed his eyes.

A duo of witches, Ravynne and Morgan, watched him while their coven sister tended to the fallen familiar. I wasn't fooled. There was no way Ra would give up this easily. And I was pretty certain I didn't want to be around when he broke loose or another toe grew. That would be gross.

"We'll make the exchange elsewhere," I said.

Lavinia held my gaze, ignoring the weakened god at my feet. "No, we'll make it here."

The mole on my neck throbbed like I'd been stung by a mosquito.

Ezra bristled. "Aunty, have you no trust?"

Her tight smile did not reach her eyes. "A deal's a deal, nephew dearest."

This was all wrong. Our plan to protect Ezra hinged on us handing over the vial of his blood in a celebratory atmosphere where the witches would be distracted. But what choice did I have with the minister being so insistent?

I beckoned Marina. "Fine. Go ahead."

Marina closed the gap between us, accompanied by Ignacio. I understood now why he had been paired with her. His keen eyes followed her every move. They gave Ra a wide berth and approached Elvira at my side. Marina fished out the vial from the pocket of her skater shorts and handed the vial to Elvira.

"Thank you," said the gentle witch, uncorking the vial.

Ravynne momentarily left her post by Ra to smell the blood and clasp Ezra's wrist. "It is his."

"Then the deal is done," said Lavinia. "And the night's business is concluded. I thank you, Ezra and Alisha. It was a fair trade. Elvira, get the vial to the gym. Guard it well, child. The rest of us will destroy the evidence of this spell. Hurry, child."

I swallowed hard. Ezra hadn't wanted this. I'd failed him.

"Don't worry, druid. All will be well." Elvira walked a few steps but hesitated at a sound behind us.

A cry came from Ravynne's lips as first Morgan and then she were flung aside.

I spun around, aghast.

Ra stood tall, freed from his binding, electricity arcing from his fingertips, finding his enemies one by one.

This time, there was no element of surprise to aid us.

I turned to Marina, my chest tight with fear, and sent her and Ignacio soaring as far as I could. In the other direction, where Ezra and Echo fought side by side, a crack of bones met my ears. I swung around, fearful of whether a friend or ally had been injured, and found that Ezra had shifted. The leopard and the beautiful copper-grey wolf fought side by side, circling the god, trying to contain him.

But it was no good. As fast as they dodged his strikes, they couldn't get close enough to do enough damage. Their whimpers cut me to the core.

"Move out of the way," I said.

Echo and Ezra leapt clear.

I raised my hands, felt the familiar tingle and focused hard. A tornado unleashed from my palms and spiralled towards the roof. Great chunks of the rafters, roof tiles and chimney fell on Ra, slowing him down.

We needed a better plan.

Ra shook off the pieces of tile and wood that had fallen like rain, his eyes gleaming as if he enjoyed vengeance. As if the sun god had tired of stimulating growth. As if killing suited him better, and he could gorge himself on it.

Elvira raised her umbrella at last, a pretty travel-sized one with white polka dots on a candy-pink background.

Before she could unleash a word, she took a deep hit to her stomach.

She looked down at her wound, disbelief written on her face, and sank to the ground.

"No!" Marina rushed towards the witch, paying no heed to the vengeful god or my attempts to keep her safe.

She sank to her knees in front of Elvira just as the Drach sisters took to the air.

"Save my coven sister," called out Lavinia, swooping by.

The Drach sisters circled above Ra's head. The rest of the coven worked at ground level, sending projectiles towards the god, seeking to bury him, bringing down the building around us. Round and round went the air-bound Drach sisters, despite the heat, despite the futility of it, buying time for us to tend to Elvira.

Ra's light flooded the warehouse, but when my eyes acclimated, I saw the threads the witches had cast out, like a spider's web that trapped the god as long as they were moving.

I dropped to my knees next to Elvira.

Marina appeared to be in a trance. Her jaw was slack, and her eyes brimmed with tears. She'd removed her bandana and applied it to Elvira's wound, but the fabric was drenched in blood. Her hands rested gently on Elvira's chest.

Ignacio nuzzled the witch's hair, his eyes mournful.

I tore off my gloves and took Elvira's hand. "I didn't protect you."

Her hand was a tight fist, and her voice was barely audible. "You did what you could, druid. This isn't your fault."

I shook Marina. "Why aren't you doing something? If you can't help her, we should be calling an ambulance."

"She's taking away the pain," said Elvira, a ghost of a smile on her lips.

"I didn't know you could do that," I said.

"Neither did I," said Marina.

"Hold on, Elvira," I said as her colour drained. "Ignacio, get Lavinia. She'll know what to do."

A mere whisper from Elvira. "Stay, Ignacio, please."

The rat leaned his head against her cheek and then scurried off.

"It's too late to save me, druid." Her chest shuddered with the exertion of breathing, but there was no pain in her eyes. "I have no fear, thanks to your friend."

I glanced at the Drach sisters. They tired, circling the god.

Ignacio leapt on the floor, trying to get Lavinia's attention. Echo and Ezra fought valiantly, but they, too, were nursing wounds.

I pressed my hands together in prayer, closed my eyes and pictured the goddess. I didn't have an offering. I didn't have pretty words. But she owed me. She had set me on this path. She was the earth goddess. She could save Elvira if she wanted to; I just knew it.

"Gaia, I need you," I prayed.

The ground shuddered. "I am here, druid."

I opened my eyes, and there she was, resplendent in a sari the colour of moss, her thick, black hair loose, her cherubic face lined with worry.

"Can you save her?"

"No, but I can see to it that her essence is not lost. Life continues to flow long after mortals shed their coil." She turned to Elvira with the gentleness of a mother. "What's your favourite tree, child?"

Elvira's eyes glistened with tears. "A cherry blossom."

"It will be done," said Gaia.

Elvira's hand flopped open to reveal the vial of Ezra's blood. "Alisha, take what is yours."

My gaze darted to Lavinia, still battling to hold the god with their web. "I can't."

"You must. I have seen your path. This is the only way."

"Elvira…"

Her eyelids fluttered shut. "Tell my sisters and Ignacio I love them."

When the vial rolled off her fingers, I caught it.

A sob escaped Marina. She took Elvira's pulse and shook her head.

"She was a dear girl," said Gaia. "Like other witches, a little misguided perhaps, to use animals in servitude or as ingredients in spells. But she had a beautiful bond with her rat, so she shall have her cherry blossom."

Her graceful fingers twirled like a dancer's and coaxed a bough from a crack in the cold, grey concrete. The bough thickened as it reached up, and from its arms, cherry blossoms bloomed.

In the hiss of its growth, I heard Elvira's voice once more.

"Give me the other vial, Marina," I said.

Marina cradled Elvira's body at the foot of the cherry blossom tree. "Are you sure?"

Now was as good a time as any to make a switch. The witches were satisfied the original vial passed muster. They'd never realise this vial of wolf's blood had been prepared by Marina through her veterinary contacts. If they did, it was Ravynne who'd be in the firing line for approving the original vial.

"You heard Elvira." I prayed we'd get away with it. Lavinia wasn't one to be crossed.

I closed the dead witch's fingers around the new vial.

"Well played, druid," said Gaia. "You have the wits of Odysseus. Your grandmother would be proud. But now I must deal with Ra."

A glance at the battleground revealed that the Drach sisters had lost their grip on Ra. They retreated, along with their coven.

Morgan had sustained an arm injury, and Isadora's dress hung in threads around a wound that snaked around her torso. Echo and Ezra fought Ra still, a combination of herding and dodging that exhausted them, and they had no hope of winning the battle.

Gaia glided onto the battlefield, her hair flowing behind her.

Ra turned his blazing eyes on her, spitting the words from his bleached teeth. "Can a century pass without one god betraying another?"

Lavinia rushed over with the coven on her heels. "We need to see to our injured Elvira, and then we must all leave. When the immortals battle, mere mortals must flee."

I bowed my head. "Elvira is gone, Lavinia. I'm so sorry. Marina ensured she had no pain."

Lavinia's face crumpled.

Isadora rushed forward and knelt at Elvira's side. "I told you we'd regret this, sister. Why do you never listen?"

The coven surrounded Elvira. Their cries tore at me.

Ignacio scuttled up the fallen witch's dress and lay his body above her now still heart.

Behind us, the battle raged.

"Her last words were of her love for you all," I said.

Lavinia bent down and stroked Elvira's hair. Then she picked up Elvira's candy pink-and-white umbrella and dusted it off like a mother might tend to her daughter's things. She fought to regain her composure and addressed Marina. "Thank you, empath, for helping my fallen sister in her time of need."

Then she and the witches lifted Elvira from Marina's embrace, with Ignacio riding still on her heart.

She turned to me. "I will send a rat clean-up crew to clear the site at dawn."

The five remaining witches and rats took to the skies, holding their tender haul. They evaded the warring gods and flew up through the wrecked roof as sombre and slowly as a funeral procession.

Ra tossed out a whip of electricity, sending Echo whimpering into a corner.

I had to help.

"The leopard is under my protection. Leave him," said Gaia as vines wound around Ra.

Ra spat his words as the vines disintegrated. "You would stand here and tell me that you value these insects more than me?"

I shook Marina. "I have to get Echo and Ezra out of here before we become cannon fodder."

Marina's eyes were empty with exhaustion.

I shoved her in the direction of the door. "I'll watch your back. Get to Jameson. Meet us at the flat. We'll be right behind you."

She didn't move.

"Now!"

Marina ran out of the door, past the half-melted cauldron and abandoned gloves, into the night, where Jameson waited. The gods paid us no heed, embroiled in a war of words, energy sparking between them.

I ran to Echo and Ezra, my heart in my mouth. Both had suffered blackened flesh. Would they even be here without my insistence?

I skidded to a halt beside them. My melted rubber soles were useless. "We have to get out of here."

Echo lifted his head.

"I can't abandon the goddess," he said, bloody-minded as ever. His forelegs and neck bore Ra's impact. His beautiful coat of rosettes and white belly had been replaced by matted, bloodied fur.

The wolf nuzzled my hand. His tail had been singed, and his side charred. He, at least, seemed to agree about leaving.

I stood and raised my hands, ready to use a whirlwind to propel Echo out of the building if I had to.

Behind us, Gaia lost patience. The ground trembled. "You think this is what our father would want?"

"Our father sleeps while the world burns, Gaia. Perhaps this will wake him. Or perhaps we are on our own. Still, you simper along according to his commandments as if you have no will of your own." Ra paused. "Look at me, druid."

Heat scorched my back.

Ezra whimpered and pushed his nose against my leg, shoving me in the direction of the door.

"Look at me!" boomed Ra.

I turned in spite of myself.

His eyes held nothing but hate. "You think I'm the villain and Gaia is the heroine. How little you see. Yes, I killed your mother. But Gaia could have saved her."

Light flared from his black fingertips and rocketed in my direction.

My hands were already raised. My clever hands, which had learned to defend me in such a small, thrilling space of time.

The air moved around us as I called forth a whirlwind to surround us. Within seconds, my hair whipped around me, and both wolf and leopard struggled to remain on their feet. Their front paws lifted off the ground, and whimpers met my ears.

My heart pounded. This was the greatest show of power I had managed.

But I didn't know how long I could keep it up, and my tingling fingers were deadening.

Ra's great sparking whips of electricity wound around us, but the whirlwind acted like a shield. Gaia's vines and roots snaked up from the ground and wound around Ra, but he burned great sections away, determined to reach us. Determined to have his vengeance.

He smiled when his current sliced through and hit me.

I cried out in pain and sent one last gust from both palms at Ezra and Echo before my magic fizzled out. My efforts sent them clear of the sun god, giving them a chance to escape.

The atmosphere changed around us like the earth goddess had gone nuclear.

Or maybe it was Ra. I could barely see.

Another agonising blow tore through my body. The noise that left my mouth was alien to me. I crashed into the remnants of the Tesla. The cracking of bones filled my ears, and fire burned through me. Pain seared through every cell of my body. My legs gave way, but my fall was cushioned by something soft.

As I floated into unconsciousness, I heard Ezra's voice.

He pressed something small and cool into my palm.

"You'll be all right, I promise," he murmured into my ear. He lifted me into his arms as if I weighed nothing. "Get to the detective, cat. Tell him to arrange for the defences to be lowered at Wildwoods. I need to teleport her into the infirmary."

I leaned my head against his chest and relinquished control as the world spun.

26

Dawn rose as a pale shadow of itself. I woke tangled in bedsheets far inferior to the thread count a forty-year-old woman was used to. A stifled snore next to me frightened me into thinking I was back in bed with Alex. I jerked myself into a sitting position in an unfamiliar room, surrounded by my father, Marina, Ezra and Echo.

Ezra's snores sounded like a pig eating from a trough. He seemed to be wrapped in a bed sheet from the waist down.

Dad closed his artist's pad and came to kiss my brow. "She's awake. Thank the gods, you're okay. The shrine will be laden with offerings tonight. Why didn't you tell me your plan?"

My throat was parched. "I didn't want to worry you."

"Beta, what is a father for if not to pray for his child?"

"I hate to break it to you, Joshi," said Marina. "But the gods were responsible for this."

"The gods can be both good and bad. Surely you realise this by now, Marina?" said Dad. "I might have lost you without your friends' quick thinking. Marina sensed your distress and made the detective do a U-turn. Echo caught up with them. It was his idea to ask the

Prime Sorcerer to lower the defences to allow Ezra to teleport straight here."

Echo padded over to the bed. "The dog loaned you his healing charm. If he had got you here any later, you might not have made it. He carried you in here butt naked without a thought for his own injuries."

"Is everyone else okay?" I remembered charred flesh on the battlefield and Elvira's limp body.

Marina squeezed my hand. "We're all fine."

My insides ached. I looked under the sheets, astonished to find I had nothing on except some wafer-thin hospital knickers and a barely-there gown. What had happened to my control pants?

A cursory check of my body revealed no obvious areas of concern. A map of mottled blue veins had appeared on the sorest parts of my body, but I figured I'd had a lucky escape. My skin was intact, and no bones were out of place.

I ran my hand over my head and down my neck. My hair had been combed, and the weird mole had disappeared.

Thank God. Or thank the Otherworld.

Ezra stirred. "Hi, hellfire. How are you feeling?"

"Okay, thanks to you." My face warmed as he shifted in his chair, and the sheet dipped.

Marina grinned and brought me a glass of water.

"So this is the Wildwoods infirmary?" I took a sip of the water and cast my eyes around the long dormitory-style room with eight beds.

Unlike a hospital, there was no bleeping machinery to be seen. An assortment of leaves and potions stood on a trolley nearby. Luscious tree canopies swayed outside the window. A vase of my favourite purple tulips sat on my bedside.

We'd done the unimaginable, but Ra's words ran through me like a jolt. *I killed your mother. But Gaia could have saved her.*

I didn't want to think of Gaia as anything but my ally, but I'd made so many mistakes these past weeks. I couldn't be sure if she'd been one of them. "What happened to Gaia?"

"I don't know." Ezra glanced at the dull dawn sky. "I whisked you out of there, and we didn't look back. But the coven's rats should report back soon."

Dad left my side to tear the first page of the paper out of his artist's pad with care and handed me a watercolour. "We've been here for hours, and I've been trying to distract myself. Do you remember the childhood stories I used to make up about Tielbu the dragon?"

I nodded. "Tielbu the Magnificent."

He beamed and handed me the paper. "That's right. I painted him for you while you slept. It always helped to tell you a Tielbu story when you were scared as a child."

In my father's stories, Tielbu had always been the protector. The protector of children or villages or magical castles. Whatever the foe, there was always a happy ending.

The long-tailed blue dragon stared at me from the page. Calm, amber eyes sat within a rounded skull, just as I'd imagined him as a child. Iridescent scales covered its body. He had four slim limbs and curved talons that could do monstrous damage, along with his fiery breath and colossal wingspan.

Tears filled my eyes. "I love it, Dad."

A cough sounded and in came Phinnaeous Shine, replete in his robes despite the early hour, stepping out of the shadows along with Rayna Williamson. "How lucky you are, Miss Verma, to find yourself within these hallowed walls rather than in a grave. It seems you disobeyed the first rule: never meddle in the affairs of the gods. What makes you think you are above the law? I should have guessed as much after your shenanigans at the Kraglek ceremony. The senate would be justified in banishing you from the Otherworld before you have even attempted the trial."

I held my breath. There was so much I still wanted to learn. I was only getting started.

"Now, hold on a minute, Prime Sorcerer. Surely you can make an exception," said Dad.

"Blame me," said Ezra. "I should have controlled her better. I'm her mentor, after all."

"You would dare blame the granddaughter of Rajika Verma for last night?" growled Echo.

I arched my eyebrow. "I knew exactly what law I was breaking, and I'd do it again."

Rayna considered me. "Maybe we shouldn't be hasty, Phinnaeous. After all, Minister Drach participated in this scheme. Would we also banish her and the coven? I would think the loss they suffered would be punishment enough. And Miss Verma managed to enlist the help of the earth goddess. By extension, Gaia is also an ally of Wildwoods. Ra poses no immediate threat after the goddess's intervention. On the contrary, Miss Verma and her merry crew appeared to have saved a great number of humdrum lives."

"At this rate, we'll be giving her the Wildwoods Medal of Honour," said the Prime Sorcerer. "And what of the destroyed warehouse in Tooting with the cherry blossom emerging from its centre? Journalists from the local paper are already sniffing around."

"Phinnaeous, you know very well it's Lavinia who must answer for disobeying the rules. Mr Neuhoff has always been her weak spot," said Rayna.

Marina nodded sagely. "The warehouse was already in a sorry state. No one will remember it tomorrow. Besides, if Alisha is banished from the Otherworld, I go too."

"And me," said Dad, who probably would have preferred that anyway.

"Not me," said Echo, "but I object all the same."

The Prime Sorcerer sighed. "You were lucky this time, but mark my words: this is a dangerous game you are playing. While I'm inclined to leave it at a warning this time, you have won a reprieve only because of your exceptional bravery. I'll be watching you *very* closely."

Rayna approached with a wooden spatula. Her potions and hip dagger clanked on her belt. Her long, silver hair brushed my arm as she leaned over me. "Stick out your tongue."

I did as I was told and made an *aah* noise on reflex like Mum had taught me to do.

Marina stepped forward, all ears.

"The pickled beetroot, together with the bee's sting, the juice of a honeydew melon and the tears of a pony born in a southwest-facing stable seem to have done the trick. Take it easy over the next few days, Miss Verma. And be sure to pass the trial when the time comes, won't you?" She skewered Marina and me with a pointed look. "We are expecting great things from you both."

"We will train with renewed focus as soon as Alisha recovers, Minister," said Ezra.

Rayna looked down her nose at him. "You would do well to get your priorities in order, Mr Neuhoff. We have any number of peculiars willing to take up the role of seeker. Consider this a black mark on your record."

Ezra dipped his head in acknowledgement.

"Er, Minister, I don't suppose you could teach me how you healed Alisha's wounds? And Echo's and Ezra's, for that matter?" said Marina.

"The wolf and the leopard have some healing powers, although I did help things along. Alisha has no such natural defence system, but Ezra's thistle charm gave her a temporary boost. Still, it is inappropriate to ask me to share my secrets with you, empath. I am surprised you asked. A couple of training sessions in the arena and some lucky escapes from vengeful beings do not make a successful peculiar."

Marina winced. "Easy. I was doing okay until you crushed my ego."

Cool blue eyes twinkled. "No need for that, Miss Ambrose. You're quite the enigma yourself. No obvious history of magical genealogy, according to our scholars. My best guess is that you had a predisposition to empathy, and your talents were triggered by your open nature and the depth of your sisterhood with Miss Verma. Such a leap has only happened in a handful of circumstances across history. New magical lineages born overnight. It's quite exciting."

Marina beamed.

"Then we will proceed as agreed." The Prime Sorcerer sprinkled dust on me. "The dawn is weak today. It will not trouble us. Now rest, granddaughter of Rajika Verma. Your body needs to heal. Your loved ones will be here when you wake."

I fought his spell. But my eyelids didn't respond to my command, and I drifted on clouds into a deep sleep.

THE INFIRMARY WAS dark when I woke, and my loved ones had gone. I listened for other possible patients, but no breathing met my ears.

Creeping out of bed, I switched on a light and checked the other bays. Not a soul in sight, but I did spot my clothes folded on the neighbouring bed. They stank of molten rubber and burnt flesh, but they spared my modesty. The leggings had a tear just below the bottom, and the hoodie was missing an arm, but I whooped when I found my control pants and sports bra.

A few minutes later, I had dressed, picked up my father's drawing of Tielbu the dragon and plotted my escape. Walking through Crystal Palace Park and onto the tube barefoot would probably raise some eyebrows. I didn't care.

I missed home.

I missed Marina and Echo.

I missed Ezra.

I wanted a proper reunion without the big shots from Wildwoods cramping our style.

Outside the window, the tree canopies shuddered with such magnitude that I thought a storm had erupted just in time to prevent my getaway. I pressed my forehead to the window, exhausted from the past twenty-four hours. My reflection showed huge eyebags and a pasty complexion, but it was nothing a powder puff and a slick of lipstick wouldn't fix. I let the cool glass take the edge off my fuzzy head.

A movement in the window reflection sent a shiver of panic up my spine.

"I am pleased to see you survived, Alisha, granddaughter of Rajika Verma."

The storm outside petered out.

The tulips in the vase on the nightstand bowed their heads in her presence.

"Gaia." I swung around, and my father's drawing slipped from my fingers.

She wore a sequinned, burnt orange sari, chosen perhaps to taunt Ra. Her hair no longer flew wild about her shoulders. A benign smile shone from her cherubic face. She looked harmless. In the humdrum world, this Gaia was simply an old woman. But my eyes had been opened.

I remembered Ra's words, and my anger swelled at her betrayal. But I swallowed it. I had learned to choose wisely before spitting in the face of the gods, and I didn't want Rayna Willowsun to find me in a puddle on the Wildwoods floor.

Gaia smiled. "It takes years for a druid to master their talents. I know this because I have known many druids across the ages. I have found them natural allies. Their talents have been varied: potions, plants, communicating with god's creatures, and transformation abilities. As such, we have much in common. I'm relieved I don't need to lower myself to fraternising with vampires or goblins." She shuddered. "It is my job to love all creatures, but there, I draw the line. A druid, however, is a worthy ally and a sweet-smelling one."

To be honest, I had smelled better. I took a step back and tried to slow my breathing.

"You have no need to fear me, druid. We are on the same side."

In her eyes, I saw the turning of the Earth. I blinked, wondering if Rayna's medicines had hallucinatory properties. I quite fancied asking for more.

"Are we on the same side, though?" I said, my heart thumping. "Ra said you could have saved my mother. You chose not to."

"There was a breath's instant to make the decision." Gaia paused. "A daughter is always a child until her mother dies. You wouldn't have taken the steps you did without the impetus of your mother's death. You wouldn't have discovered your place in the Otherworld."

I couldn't imagine going back to my old life.

But I would give it all up to have Mum back.

"It was you who filled the car with her favourite flowers, wasn't it?" The penny had dropped when I'd seen the cherry blossom push through the concrete. It all made sense now how the detective had found flowers growing out of metal.

Who else but Gaia had that power?

Gaia nodded. "She didn't smell death or the burnt electrics in the car. She didn't see the twisted metal or her broken body. The garden of Gallic roses grew around her. Their scent filled her nose, and her pride for her family filled her heart."

"For that, I thank you."

Her wrinkles deepened with a frown. "It occurred to me that I may not have been entirely fair to you. You are lucky not to have lost an eye or your life. I have a gift for you."

I bit my lip. Gifts rarely came without expectations. Hell, Alex had expected a lifetime of bondage in return for my wedding ring. How else could I explain the amount of time I'd spent at the kitchen sink, the stove or the washing machine?

"There is no need for a gift, goddess," I said. "I managed just as well without one."

She eyed my torn clothes and wan face. "The evidence says otherwise. Would you refuse me, druid? Am I not the giver of gifts? Would you risk failing at your task because of pride or mistrust?"

I searched her face. That sounded scarily like my task wasn't over. I definitely hadn't signed up for a rematch. "Will Ra return?"

Gaia shrugged. "Perhaps, one day. For now, he has skulked off with his tail between his legs. May his retreat be long-lived. Yesterday took its toll on both of us. Still, immortal beings can never be entirely vanquished. Mortals, on the other hand…" She pulled out a sword from the folds of her sari. "You will accept this gift if you hope to survive. Next time won't be so easy."

I stared open-mouthed at the sword. It looked like something that belonged in a museum. It had a slender, black blade. The hilt was ivory, smooth and unadorned, except for a small, deep-set blue jasper.

"The sword was given to me by Death when we were lovers. Its blade, once translucent, was made from a heavenly cloud. When Death blessed it, the blade became obsidian black. In mortal hands, it is only as strong as the bearer's magical lineage, and you can channel your ancestors through it. If the strike is true, an ancestral thrust can add power and disrupt the mind of the attacker. Its name is Transcender."

"Goddess, I can't accept it." My voice quivered.

Her eyes flashed. "You would say no to me? Would you refuse an abundant supply of food or the gift of children or a place in paradise?"

"When you put it that way... It's just I'm afraid of not meeting your expectations."

"Mortals rarely meet my expectations, druid, but once in a while, they surpass them. Would you take that chance?"

I gulped.

"Besides, it is a meagre weapon in my hands. It is lightweight and double-edged, perfect for an untested swordswoman. I never cared for it. Death never paid attention to my likes, even when we were lovers. She was utterly inattentive and more interested in corpses than pillow talk. The sword's hilt is made from mammoth tusk. What kind of fool offers the earth goddess a gift made from a creature? Still, in the right hands, Transcender is capable of doing much good. Beware of listening too carefully to the voices when you hold it. They are often more of a distraction than a help."

She handed me the sword.

"Thank you." A rush of sounds filled my head like the wind-laden voices on a carousel. I dropped the sword like a hot potato.

Gaia sighed. "Be careful with that, druid. Perhaps put it down until you have regained your strength."

I laid the sword on the bed.

The voices disappeared like someone had lifted the stylus from a record player. Pretty freaky gift, if you asked me. I much preferred Dad's painting.

Gaia pointed to the floor, where I had dropped the painting of Tielbu. "That is one of your father's inkings?"

I nodded. "A dragon."

She smiled. "One of the earth's most magnificent creatures. Have you such disdain for art? Pick it up, druid."

"I dropped it in fright when you arrived."

"No doubt a sneezing ant would also frighten you. Centre your mind, druid. Match my breathing." She inhaled to a count of three and then exhaled. "That's it. Match the breath of the universe, and when you are ready, rest your fingers gently on the inking of the dragon and draw them back. Not so hesitant now. With belief."

I focussed on the image of Tielbu. It was easy. I knew his stories. I loved his face.

My breathing came steadily, at one with the earth goddess's. My fingers caressed the painting, and when I drew them back, I sensed the dimensions in the paper. Not two or three but many more. I sensed blood and veins and cells. I sensed danger and friendship and hot, burning flames as if the painting wasn't a page but an ocean, and I could coax the dragon from deep inside.

The blue lines of the Tielbu swam before me, lifting off the page. Smoke filled my nose, and reptilian skin danced beneath my fingertips.

I jerked my hand away from the page and let the watercolour plummet to the cold floor, breaking the connection. The dragon became cold and lifeless on the page once more.

This was madness. I wasn't ready.

I stumbled, dizzy, and blackness crept in from the corners of my eyes.

Gaia laughed. "You didn't think that wind was all you could do?"

Soft hands coaxed my trembling body into bed—a feather-light kiss on my brow, like the ones Mum used to give.

"Rest now, druid." The goddess's voice was a lullaby. "Your body tells you to sleep. All will be well. Be sure to give the leopard my regards when you wake."

27

———

After my run-in with Gaia, I slept like a stone. When I eventually made it out of the infirmary the next day and over the Wildwoods rope bridges, I half expected Ezra to appear, toss me over his shoulder in a fireman's lift and whisk me home. That would have been hot, but it turned out he wasn't that protective of me.

I missed him, but he didn't owe me anything.

Besides, I was an independent woman. I didn't need him to rescue me. I hailed a cab home, squelchy bare feet and all.

Over the next week, Dad and Marina did their best to nurse me back to full health. They even managed to restock the freezer with premium salmon and steak for Echo. Surf 'n' turf, just like he liked it. I breathed a sigh of relief at not having to worry about any poodles, Labradors or deer he might get his claws into.

Processing what had happened was harder than my physical recovery. I didn't regret putting myself in the fight. I was proud of myself, and I was proud of my friends. We had avenged Mum. We'd faced a fearsome enemy and won, despite only just getting our training wheels in the Otherworld. Turned out an old pony could learn new tricks. What was more, not blowing my own trumpet or anything, but the earth goddess seemed to like me. She didn't have to give me the sword. She didn't have to show me that my druidry extended to more than the wind.

I was an animator too. That was if I ever got the hang of it.

On the morning of Nita's funeral, I woke with an aching heart. I knew I had to go, despite my pangs of guilt for putting her in danger and not saving her. Her family didn't blame me for her death. Detective Jameson had informed them that the intruder at night class had compressed Nita's windpipe.

"It's easier that way. They don't need to know the truth," he said on the telephone. "A loss is hard enough without distorting their view of reality. Some things are on a need-to-know basis. Otherwise, the world would descend into chaos."

Who was I to argue? The Founder's Law, too, stated that peculiars must hide the existence of the Otherworld from humdrums.

I arrived at Streatham Cemetery early to pay my respects at Mum's grave and Melissa's.

Then I joined the mourners at Nita's funeral under a cloud-heavy sky. Her parents stood bowed at the graveside as the priest spoke his words. Ashes to ashes. Dust to dust.

My night class students had turned up in full—Tomás and Santiago in matching suits; Farzad handing out spare hankies; Nagma dabbing her eyes with the scarf of her salwar kameez; Ethan, Hassan and Marek, whispering hello and their regrets. All readily accepted the detective's explanation, with the exception of Fei Yen and Faeza.

"We won't say a word," said Fei Yen under her breath.

"Not a word." Faeza gave me a thumbs-up.

I still hadn't unravelled their place in the Otherworld. This wasn't the place.

Afterwards, when the service had concluded and we had thrown handfuls of dirt onto Nita's coffin, I hugged her parents, murmured my condolences, and then walked away past mounds of fresh earth, weeping angel statues and weathered gravestones.

Suddenly, Ezra materialised next to me. Like the universe had told him I was in need.

I jumped three feet high.

His damp hair and skin had the tang of the sea like he'd taste of sun and salt. "Hey, Alisha."

I ignored the butterflies dancing in my belly and swatted him. "Hey, yourself. Are you *ever* going to make a normal entrance?"

"Surprises are the spice of life. Haven't you learned that by now?" Grey eyes locked on mine as he turned serious. "I'm glad you're safe."

"Thanks to you."

"Thank you for not forgetting your promise about the vial. It takes a gutsy druid to cross a witch. I won't forget it."

"How did you find me?"

He smiled. "I'm a seeker. It's what I do. But this time, a leopard told me you might need me."

I swallowed hard. "I don't need you."

"You don't? Are you sure?" He cupped the small of my back and leaned down to kiss me.

Heat travelled all the way to my toes. I leaned into him, closed my eyes and returned the gentle pressure of his lips.

Energy pulsed between us like static electricity.

The ground moved, and I travelled through time and space in his arms.

He pulled away, and we were back on the path leading out of the cemetery.

"There's something about you that makes me want more," he said. "Do you feel it too?"

My heart raced. I let my lashes shield my desire. There was no doubt I wanted him. I looked up at him and smiled.

"Tease." He cupped my cheek and pulled me closer again, this time with more force. "I have some werewolf business to tie up. It shouldn't take more than a few days. It's about time we go on a date, don't you think?"

Then he was gone, leaving just the hint of his presence on my skin.

I ARRANGED an afternoon picnic in the park with Dad, Sahil, Marina and Echo. The fresh air with family and friends was exactly what I needed to clear my head after a week of being cooped up in the flat.

I poured out some lemonade. "I visited Mum's and Melissa's graves before the funeral this morning."

"How thoughtful of you," said Dad. "The flowers I planted seem to like it there."

I nodded. "Melissa's grave was empty, but I brought along a racy Jilly Cooper novel I found in a charity shop and left it there for someone to discover. She would have liked that."

"The book will turn into sludge in the London rain," purred Echo. "It would have been better to leave a deer carcass. That would have made a real statement and would have had the dual purpose of making wandering creatures happy."

Dad laughed, and it did my heart good to see him smile. "You may be centuries old, but you still have much to learn, Echo."

"That might be true, Joshi, but did you hear? The goddess sent me her regards," the leopard said.

"Hooray for you, Echo." Dad rolled his eyes. "My wife dies, my daughter allows herself to be a pawn of the gods, and I've not had so much as a hello. She could have at least let me witness Alisha bringing Tielbu to life."

"No need to be sour about it," purred Echo. "You may be past your prime, but your time may yet come. Especially now that Alisha has inherited Rajika's talents. Animator and painter pairings are blessed by the heavens."

"Actually, you two, I barely lifted him off the page. What I don't understand is why it didn't work for the frog in Dad's attic."

"Well, darling, you probably weren't giving it any oomph," said Dad.

Sahil rolled his eyes. "See how he blames a lack of magical talent on us instead of our genes?" He swallowed a chocolate-covered strawberry and offered me one. "You're lucky, sis. I'd be happy with one, but the peculiar gene seems to have skipped me. Even Marina ended up with empath gifts. It's not fair I'm the odd one out. Who can a man speak to about getting an upgrade on peculiar talents?"

Echo paused from chasing butterflies. "The man-child is jealous."

"Do you blame me? I mean, the goddess even gave Alisha a sword." He eyed me warily like I'd snuck it out underneath my vest top. "Where is it anyway?"

"In my knicker drawer. I figured any thieves brave enough to put their hand in there would be welcome to it." It called to me in the dead of the night when all I wanted was sleep. Part of me wished Gaia had never given it to me.

"Seriously?" laughed Marina. "I reckon that's the best place for it. You know, Sahil, I could help you unblock your talents."

Sahil waggled his eyebrows. "You just want to get me flat on my back."

Marina groaned. "Unlikely. Afraid these days I'm sharing pillow talk with Robert Jameson."

Dad coughed to hide his embarrassment. Indian Dads weren't great with this level of sexual honesty.

Marina took pity on him. "I'm so glad Rosalie's pictures are back, Joshi. That must be a relief."

"My heart sang when I saw them," said Dad. "She had such a beautiful face. I was afraid I would forget it. Now I don't have to paint her features individually. It had rather a frightening effect when I walked into my studio. We've been through so much. Your mum would be proud of us all."

I believed it. It had taken forty years to understand my own worth.

I cleared up the remnants of our jam sandwiches and lemonade, then stood up. "How about a game of humdrum Frisbee? Four players, two teams. Echo doubles as referee and ball boy. Dad, you're with me. Sahil, you're with Marina."

"Game on." Sahil sprang to his feet. He put his arm around me. "You look trim. Are you on the stinky cabbage diet again?"

Marina guffawed. "More like she's pining for Ezra. Not that my radar says she should worry."

The mottled blue veins on my skin were receding, and although I wasn't quite bikini-ready, bumps and bruises aside, I was slimmer than I'd been in my life. I almost didn't need my control pants. I put my weight loss down to grief and running hell for leather from crazy gods. I'd accidentally found a new exercise fad. Some women would kill for that knowledge.

I chucked my flip-flop at Marina. "Actually, I saw him this morning."

She grinned and nibbled on a sandwich. "You sly fox! Tell us all the details."

"Later, I promise." I couldn't wait to fill her in on all the details when we were alone, but they weren't for Dad's ears. "But first, I'm going to whoop your arse at Frisbee."

Sahil grinned at Marina. "We're going to make a great team, Ambrose."

Echo picked up the Frisbee between his teeth and tossed it at my feet. "Everyone feeling good? That's a Nina Simone lyric." He honked with laughter. "No peculiar powers allowed. Take your places. Begin!"

I felt a tingle in my fingers, the druid gift that was becoming as familiar to me as my own skin.

What else were rules for, if not to be broken?

ACKNOWLEDGMENTS

This pandemic year has been the perfect time to write Alisha's story. Escaping into fantasy is a way to soothe spirits and right wrongs when the world is troubling.

My deep thanks to the thirteen authors who founded this genre for magic-wielding heroines over forty. It's a joy to write about wise women with life experience who kick arse.

I'm so grateful to my beta readers, Debbie, Sherry and Jen, for your book instincts and wisdom. To Bianca, your support and keen eye mean so much. Thank you to my editors Jeni and Toni, and my cover artist Maria for making this story shine.

Thanks to our daughter Hana for dropping what you were doing every time I asked you to read and for not pulling your punches when giving critiques. To our son Raiyan, you keep me on track with your word count demands, and your interest in my workday makes me melt. To our little one, Noah, your cuddles lift me, and yes, you can have a snack.

The biggest thanks goes to my husband, Jan, for always being in my corner, being my first reader and letting me warm my cold feet on you.

And thank you, dear reader, for taking a chance on this story. I hope you stay for the ride.

A FIRST DATE IN PARIS

SHORT STORY 1.5

DRUID HEIR
SHORT STORY 1.5
A FIRST DATE
IN PARIS
N. Z. NASSER

A FIRST DATE IN PARIS

SHORT STORY 1.5 - EZRA'S PERSPECTIVE

My heartbeat raced as I pulled on a clean pair of jeans in my room at our farmhouse on the outskirts of Windsor. It took me a fraction longer than usual to button up my crisp, white shirt because anticipation made my fingers clumsy. It was not like me to be nervous. I swore off women after my last relationship ended, but everything changed when I met Alisha.

Earlier this week, I teleported to her side at the cemetery and kissed her. I knew what I was doing. A man doesn't kiss a woman like that without meaning it. I wanted to make her ache for me. I think I succeeded.

I've wanted to kiss Alisha since the night on the lawn at Crystal Palace Park, but my job was to ease her into the Otherworld. She didn't need me to make a move then. She needed a friend and a mentor.

Tonight, I didn't have to hold back. There would be no family, friends, leopards or gods to come between us.

A knock on my door, and Seth came in with his bulging torso on display. He was the strongest of us in both human and wolf form. "We're off for a run in the woods to catch the last of the light. Are you in?"

I shook my head. "I have a date with the druid."

"About that. Gunnolf wants a word. He's not happy."

Banging and clanging in the kitchen next door put my nerves on edge. My nose told me my alpha Gunnolf, the senate's Minister for Justice, was in there. "I gathered."

"You're going to dig your heels in." Seth grinned. "Well, have fun, old boy."

Pack law said that wolves should mate with wolves. The truth was many peculiars preferred magical communities not to intermingle. For Gunnolf, it was bad enough when my werewolf father married my witch mother. It caused anomalies.

In my case: a teleporting werewolf with some witching ability.

After my parents' death, Gunnolf claimed me from the witches. I knew the score. He wanted me to forget my witch ancestry and pledge full allegiance to the wolves. But I'm my own man. I might not be an alpha, but no one told me who to love or who to fight for.

I never thought I'd fall for a druid.

When I ran with the pack, thoughts of her filled my mind. Wild, brunette curls that begged to be touched, rosebud lips that she chewed when anxious and curves that made me rethink my vow to stay alone. She was a bright light threaded with darkness. A woman who knew her own mind and power but was soft where it counted.

New peculiars tended to shake like leaves. Not Alisha. She had grit. She drove the fight back against the god.

Werewolves were used to bravery. I'd seen plenty of it, but she impressed even me. She played havoc with my concentration on the mission I had just completed. She intruded on my dreams last night. When I was away from her, I wanted to teleport right back to her side to check she was okay. To see her smile or catch the fierce look in her eyes when she was up to no good.

I could teleport to my date with Alisha—the other wolves didn't have this skill—but I'd pay for it when I returned. Ignoring Gunnolf's summons never ended well.

My dress shoes clicked across the stone floor as I entered the kitchen to the scent of spilt beer and burnt roast. Through the window, I caught sight of the rest of the pack running into the woods. Rashida, my ex-lover, a fiery red wolf with a snow-tipped tail, was with them too. We'd dabbled in the past, but I'd been burned once too many.

Gunnolf took in my attire and grunted. "So you're going to see the druid then, despite what I said?"

I kept my voice light. Challenging my alpha's authority was not my intention. That would be a death wish. "It's a date, not a wedding."

A growl laced his voice. "You choose a woman over your pack."

I bowed my head to take the sting out of my retort. "You've done worse."

Gunnolf's eyes flashed amber. I was a hair taller than him, but he had broader shoulders. He was of Ghanaian heritage with pent-up terseness that suggested power lurked beneath the surface. In wolf form, he never hesitated to use his teeth or claws. "It won't end well, cavorting with another kind."

"Perhaps, but sometimes a wolf has to scratch the itch."

Gunnolf cuffed my ear. "I can't have my most able wolf compromising missions."

"Have I ever let you down?"

"No, but there's always a first time, and it's inevitably always when there's a woman involved."

"I won't let you down."

"Too right. I didn't bring you up to have you betray me now. Make sure you're at the Court of Wolves during the full moon tonight." He dropped his trousers and peeled off his T-shirt.

"As you wish."

The cracking of bones met my ears as he shifted into his wolf, coal black with silken fur and over six feet long. An earthy scent filled my nostrils. He growled, and I tried not to flinch.

Then he was gone. Deep in the woods, the pack howled, and I knew again what it was like to be an outsider.

The deck creaked as I stepped onto the porch and picked a single orange dahlia from a border. I closed my eyes, and in the nebulous pink of my eyelids, I envisioned the bright yellow front door of Alisha's Balham flat. My body compressed with the pressure I'd long grown accustomed to, and the world faded to a monochrome point before expanding again and spitting me out in the communal hallway outside her flat.

My pulse jumped at the thought of seeing her as I rapped my knuckles against her door.

She stepped out with a smile and reached up to kiss my cheek. "You scrub up well."

Brown eyes in a sweetheart face, her dark hair tumbling around her shoulders. She wore a black dress with spaghetti straps that hugged her curves, and she had painted her lips cherry red.

I smiled and gave her the dahlia. "You're ravishing."

She placed it behind her ear. "Why don't you come in? You can say hello to Echo."

The air crackled between us. "I've made plans. Are you ready?"

She clicked the door shut, and I caught the scent of apricot. "Always. Where are we going?"

"It's a surprise."

"Okay then." She stepped closer and leaned her hands on my chest.

The world swirled around us. The distance was further than usual, and the effort winded me. I held her close, and when we opened our eyes, she gasped.

We stood on the deserted terrace of a friend's café. The balmy night air and cloudless sky made it the perfect evening for an outdoor rendezvous. A table for two awaited our attention, laden with two sparkling glasses and a bottle of prosecco, but it was the skyline that caught her attention.

An iron tower made of a lattice framework pierced the night sky. A golden light illuminated it, and as the clock struck nine, the lights began to sparkle.

Her eyes widened with wonder. "Ezra, you brought me to Paris? This is incredible. I haven't seen the Eiffel Tower since I was a child!" She hugged me. "Don't we need passports?"

I laughed. Her joy was infectious.

"Teleporting werewolves don't need to go through passport control." I poured out the prosecco. "Let's sit a while and take in the view."

She shook her head. "Uh uh, mister. Let's explore. Mum was born here, you know."

I handed her a glass. "I know."

"Thank you for bringing me here."

We clinked glasses. She poured the drink down her throat, and I followed suit. When she grabbed my hand, I let myself be tugged along. She was a whirlwind, and I understood now that her powers were a perfect match for her and she was still evolving. Her grandmother's magic flowed through her veins too.

I, on the other hand, had been escaping situations my whole life. In her, I had finally met someone I didn't want to run from. At least, not yet.

Alisha shook her head. "How is it possible that I reach forty years old before realising what the world is really about?"

"In the Otherworld, age is really just a number. We can defy the laws of physics and biology."

"Lavinia told me you were forty-four."

He smiled. "More experienced than you."

"For a while, I thought you might be a hundred. With witch ancestry, you never know what is real and what is an anti-ageing potion. That would have been really weird."

"Not up for grandpa sex?"

She laughed. "I'm having such a magical evening, but I don't want to rush this. You're still my mentor. I don't want to ruin that."

I took her hand. "We can take things slow."

We walked through the Parisian streets, past an opera house, gossiping friends drinking coffee, impossibly chic old lovers, grand hotels, the Champs-Elysées, and boulevards lined with florists, boutiques and old-world restaurants. When her feet tired in her heels, we sat on a bench under willow trees on Pont Neuf, watching disco barges floating along the night-time river Seine. Our conversation was easy. Easier than it was with the pack or with my aunts. Easier than it had been with Rashida.

My sides ached with laughter. "Gaia gave you a sword gifted to her by Death, and you hid it in your knicker drawer?"

Alisha grinned. "I don't have a safe."

A frisson of fear ran down my spine. The gift was a clear sign that danger lurked around the corner.

She grew sombre. "Can you feel it coming?"

I frowned. "Feel what coming?"

She sighed. "The dark."

"I can, hellfire, but it's not snapping at our heels."

"I don't know if I can face a threat like Ra again."

"Maybe you won't have to. But if you do, I'll be at your side."

"I've been burned before. I don't trust easily."

"I'll just have to earn it."

She chewed her cherry red lip. "Kiss me."

I leaned in and took my time, there in the city of light. The world stilled around us. The scent of her soft, apricot skin washed over me. My hand slipped to the small of her back, and she knotted her fists in my shirt.

When we drew apart, her lipstick had smudged. I used the pad of my thumb to fix it for her, tipping back her head to see her clearly under the streetlight with the scent of the Seine filling our noses.

I didn't want to look at my watch, but I had no choice. I had my orders from Gunnolf. I pulled her to her feet and murmured in her ear. "One last sight. Hold on."

She clasped her arms around my waist. A man teetered along the path beside the Seine and tipped his hat to us. His eyes were bleary with alcohol, his cheeks ruddy with veins. I gave him a cheery wave and then teleported, floating through time and space, giddy from being with Alisha. My heart thawed.

I took her to the top platform of the Eiffel Tower, and she squealed as she found her footing. She didn't flinch from the gusts of wind and turned her face into it, her hair wild. She revelled in the sensation of freedom, unleashing her own power to mix with the earth's.

She fizzed with excitement. "There's the Louvre and Montmartre. Look! The loops of the Seine. And Notre Dame and over there, is that Arc de Triomphe?"

I caught her hand. "We have to go. Security is on its way up."

One last look at Paris, and she ran into my arms just as two puffing men ran into sight. My heart drummed as we whirled through the shadow world, away from Paris, across the English Channel, over land masses and through brick, water, dense air and thick clouds, to her bedroom in Balham. Her cornflour blue bedsheets lay rumpled.

The roar of her troublesome, lovable leopard filled my ears—his instinct to protect her rivalled mine.

Alisha kicked off her shoes and looked at me from under her lashes. "Do you want to stay?"

I wanted nothing more than to take her to bed. "Not this time, hellfire. It's a full moon tonight, and the pack calls."

She threw a heel at me. "I wasn't offering up my body."

"You weren't?" I drawled.

"Paris was nice, but you have to work harder than that, wolf."

The leopard threw his body at her bedroom door. "You whisk a Verma away without my permission?"

I gave thanks he didn't have opposable thumbs, flung a rueful smile in his direction and ignored him. Then I picked the dahlia from Alisha's hair and laid it on her bedside table before tucking an errant strand of hair behind her ear. "I'll work as hard as I have to. I can promise you that. Good night, Alisha."

"Good night, Ezra."

Her voice echoed in my ears as I teleported into the moonlit night, where the Court of Wolves awaited.

DRUID HEIR
BOOK 2

MIDLIFE TREMORS

N. Z. NASSER

THE PLAYERS

Alisha Verma - Druid Heir
Marina Ambrose - Alisha's best friend
Echo - Alisha's leopard sidekick
Ezra Neuhoff - Alisha's half-werewolf, half-wizard mentor
Fei Yen, Faeza, Marek, Tomás, Santiago, Farzad, Nagma, Ethan, Hassan -
Alisha's night class students
Flinar - a dark elf
Mirabel - Wildwoods student
Joshi Verma - Alisha's father
Sahil Verma - Alisha's brother
Gaia - Goddess of the Earth
Robert Jameson - Detective, Shadow Squad
Phinnaeous Shine - Shapeshifter, Prime Sorcerer
Orpheus Might - Vampire, Minister for History and the Today
Rayna Willowsun - Druid, Minister for Education, Headmistress of
Wildwoods School of the Wondrous
Lavinia Drach - Witch, Minister for Defence
Gunnolf Zev - Werewolf, Minister for Justice
Helio Woodwink - Fairy, Bestiary Minister
Cillian O'Meara - Leprechaun, Minister for Finance

Margola Silver - Selkie, Minister for Information
Erelim - Angel, Minister for Diplomacy
Mr Costello - executor of Rosalie's will
Calypso Archer - the Custodian
Nightfall - a horse in the Celestial Library
Tielbu - a dragon
The royal gamekeeper

1

I stood in front of the desk in the community centre and lifted my fists in a fighting stance. Two rows of faces smiled back at me, eager to learn. Kickboxing was their favourite part of this night class, after all. After the sun god killed a student in my class, it seemed only fitting to take my students' training up a notch.

Only three weeks ago, my friends and I had defeated the murderous sun god after he'd killed my mum and a host of other scientists, including Nita. We had run towards danger and won. After a lifetime of living in the slow lane, I had avenged Mum's death and stacked up new experiences at a tantalising rate. A whole new world had opened to me, and I had magical talents and a toned butt to show for it. Plus, a hot new romance with Ezra, my werewolf-wizard mentor.

Not bad for a forty-year-old divorcée.

But a woman needed money, and I liked my job, so I'd spent the evening teaching holiday vocabulary, followed by a bout of kickboxing drills.

"Keep those feet moving," I said. "Fists up. Turn those wrists. Punch, punch. No, Tomás and Santiago, play punching each other is not what I called for."

"Forgive me, miss," said Tomás, turning all the charm of his Portuguese heritage on me.

I smiled. "Four deep squats next. Let's get those thighs and glutes working."

"I don't know what a glute is, Miss Verma, but if I do the squat, can I eat more cake?" said sixty-five-year-old Nagma, who didn't let her traditional dress hold her back from achieving as deep a squat as any of the younger students in the class.

I grinned. "They are muscles in your bottom. And more squats definitely mean more cake. Next one, lunge back and kick up. Repeat." I did the move myself, modelling the breath work, trying not to think about the empty seat where Nita had once sat. "Well done, Hassan. Try the kick a little higher, Marek. Remember, class, if you can't do the move for whatever reason, then adapt it. Take it down a level. Don't stretch your body all at once. With each practice, you'll get better."

I turned to the two Chinese women in my class, Fei Yen and Faeza, and my heart skipped a beat.

There they were again, showing unbelievable flexibility for two women of advanced age. They had to have a decade or two on me. Not that I could tell by their wrinkle-free skin. But here they were in traditional Chinese dress, lifting each other to execute the most perfect high kicks as if age wasn't a barrier at all. As if they had an innate strength and fluidity of movement that scoffed in the face of mere ageing.

I kept my voice upbeat even as I plotted how to get to the bottom of their secret. "Excellent work, Fei Yen and Faeza. You've improved. Did you have martial arts training in China?"

"No, Miss Verma," said Fei Yen.

"Definitely not," said Faeza, as they reverted to performing the moves like decrepit old women.

As if I'd not seen. As if they hadn't given me a dozen other reasons to believe they were from the Otherworld.

Well, tonight, I would get to the bottom of it.

It wasn't like I wanted to go home to the dragon nightmares that plagued me no matter how much lavender-scented mist I sprayed on my pillows—reptilian skin. Amber eyes. Fierce wings slashing through the pink sky. Lofty monuments smashed into rubble. The dreams left my heart pounding.

So, I would do what any grown woman with worries did. Distract myself. And my two sneaky students had given me just the way to do it.

I ducked behind buildings on the rain-slicked London street after locking up the community centre. Around me, high-rises loomed with glowing television screens visible through windows. Londoners sprawled on their sofas, stuffing fistfuls of crisps into their mouths, and a restless baby's cry rang out into the night. Up ahead, two of my students meandered under the streetlamps and heavy clouds, oblivious to my presence. I'd grown convinced there was more to my students Fei Yen and Faeza than met the eye. Come hell or high water, I was going to get to the bottom of it tonight.

Their clothes made them easy to track, despite the dark night. Tonight's night class had celebrated cultures from around the world. Fei Yen and Faeza had come in traditional Chinese dress. Their silk qipaos were ankle length, with high necks and simple knotted buttons with loop fasteners. The dresses stood out against the black starless night: Fei Yen in red with intricate phoenix embroidery and Faeza in blue, with dragon and floral embroidery.

I felt plain in comparison, but then I had channelled my chic French side rather than Indian extravagance for the lesson. That meant faded jeans, a camisole with a silk scarf tied around my neck, a jaunty beret and a black blazer to hide the sword Gaia had given me.

I darted after Fei Yen and Faeza, pleased that my flat shoes muffled the sound of my progress and that I'd tied my unruly hair in a ponytail.

Approximately fifteen metres separated us. At first, nothing out of the ordinary happened.

But as we left the main road and all other pedestrians slipped away into the night, Fei Yen and Faeza transformed. A shiver ran up my spine. Gone was the slow heaviness brought on by age. They bounded along the pavement arm in arm, like gossiping teens. I strained my ears, but they weren't speaking English, although they were the strongest students in my night class. Wisps of Chinese floated my way.

My phone trilled in my blazer pocket. I took my eyes off my targets and hissed into it. "Not now, Marina. I'm on a mission."

My best friend's laughter bubbled down the line. "One success, and you think you're Jane Bond."

"I'll call you later." I flattened myself against a tree trunk.

"I'm just wrapping up at the surgery," said Marina. "Fancy coming over for a quick gin?"

A movement flashed in the corner of my eye. A street bin arced through the air and bounced onto the road, spilling its contents across the asphalt.

"Alisha? Your heartbeat just spiked." Her empath skills grew with each passing day.

"I have to go," I ended the call and spun around.

There was no sight of Fei Yen and Faeza.

The street bin lay on its side in the dim light of a dilapidated bus stop shelter. No drunken louts or wayward schoolchildren out long past bedtime filled the South London streets. So who had shunted the bin across the road?

I stepped closer.

A dozen fat rats scurried around the bin, pulling, pinching and kicking a bony, dull-grey body trapped by the bin. Judging by the pallor of the man's skin, he was seriously ill, and the rats were trying to finish him off.

My skin crawled. It wasn't the first swarm of rats I had seen in London, but the thought of the poor man being cannibalised churned my stomach. London rats were absolute stinkers, opportunists and always ravenous.

I sprang into action. "Hey!" I shouted, running towards them. "Leave him alone."

A rat the size of my forearm turned beady eyes on me. "Stay out of this, druid."

My jaw hit the floor.

The loathsome thing reminded me of the Banksy artwork, where a medallion-wearing rat held up a Welcome to Hell sign.

I composed myself before I swallowed any flies or the rodents got the better of me. "I said, step away from him."

I'd met talking rats before. Some had formed part of the team that had helped me defeat the sun god. I'd seen them at the witch Lavinia's gym too. As Minister for Defence, she had trained her coven's familiars to be formidable spies. They were the ears of her operation, cleaned her gym, and by all accounts, could cook up a storm.

I had no idea they were bullies too.

"Make us stop if you dare." His toothy rat grin sent shivers up my spine. "Come on, lads. Let's teach the druid not to mess with witches' work."

The rats gave the man a last flurry of kicks. Then they lined up in a semi-circle formation on their hind legs, showing their muddied bellies and yellowed claws. I counted seven in all, with some right hefty beasts amongst them. No doubt they could do some damage in those numbers.

And I didn't fancy a battle on the streets of London with no backup and the chance of falling foul of the Magical Constitution. Severe punishments awaited those who compromised the secrecy of the Otherworld. No doubt, the rats had Lavinia to vouch for them, but I had no one. And I was on a short leash with the Sorcerer's Senate after breaking the first law: never meddle in the affairs of the gods.

The man groaned and freed himself from the bin trapping his body. He shook off greasy wrappers from the nearby kebab shop, retching as he heaved himself up. He was short for a man and wore a Roman tunic and knickerbockers as if he didn't give two hoots about fashion. No wonder the rats had taken a dislike to him. Bullies always picked on those who stood out.

He turned, and the light from the bus shelter illuminated his face at last.

I gasped.

This wasn't a human. He had knobbly legs and arms attached to a small, muscular body. One of his arms hung limp. His large, milky eyes were suspended within a dull grey, triangular head with wisps of grey hair. A deep cut above his eyebrow marred his smooth face. He had a small nose and full lips, but it was his ears that stood out. They sat high up on his skull, shaped like the sails of a ship, angular and billowing, and twitched with emotion.

"What, you've never seen a dark elf before?" the chief of the stinky rats said.

My leopard companion Echo had warned me about elves once before. They were employed by the Sorcerer's Senate to clean up magical residue but were also mischief makers. They were more likely to graffiti buildings and tamper with street signs than to sweep the roads.

I addressed the elf. "Are you okay?"

Milky eyes searched my face. "Go on your way, druid, or they will harm you. Elves are used to being the lowest in the pecking order."

The rat sighed. "For good reason. You're new around here, so you probably don't know he's not worth your trouble. His kind was responsible for the Battle of the Celestial Library. The scoundrels almost toppled the Otherworld and outed us all. So we give them a kicking every few weeks or so, just to show them who's boss. Witches' orders."

I frowned. "Listen up. This gentleman doesn't seem to deserve a kicking for something his kind did. Do I give you a kicking just because one of your lot once left its droppings in my kitchen?"

"I'll have you know that Otherworld rats are far superior to humdrum rats. We're house-trained, for one."

I pretended to be awed. I hadn't been best friends with a vet all my life without learning a few tricks of the trade. It was far better to persuade an animal to do my bidding than to get into a fight I might not win. "How clever of you. You're far too clever to make the mistake of picking on this elf when I've asked you not to."

"We do, druid," the rat said.

"I think you'll find that Lavinia and I are friends."

"I'm afraid that is old news. Our mistress is displeased with you. She suspects you might be more foe than friend."

I winced. "Charming."

If Lavinia had found out we had cheated her of Ezra's blood, then a storm was brewing.

"So you see, druid, we have no reason to spare you." His front teeth gleamed in the moonlight like two knives. "Attack!"

They sprang in my direction, bouncing off surfaces, somersaulting through the air. The stench of wet fur and putrid breath made me gag. These rats weren't like the coven's familiars. They were coarser in appearance and nature. They were Lavinia's fixers rather than her favourites. Any second now, they would land at my feet, chew my ankles and drag me to my death like the poor elf.

"Wait!" I held up my hands, and my palms tingled with power.

They froze in the midst of their advance as if they were far more accustomed to taking orders than using their own initiative. The lead rat glared at me, all bulging black eyes and twitching whiskers, a few inches from my calf. "You wish to share your last words, druid?"

"No, actually. I wanted you to double-check you're not making a mistake. I am dating Lavinia's nephew, you know. You wouldn't want to come to blows with his new lady love, would you?" I gave him my most charming smile.

Okay, love was pushing the nature of my relationship with Ezra. What we had was a friendship with more than a hint of frisson, plus one sexy-as-hell date in bonne Paris, but framing it as love might save a whole heap of trouble.

"Just leave the elf alone," I said, "and we can all go home safe and sound."

Behind him, the elf, to his credit, awaited his fate. His knobbly body curved over as if we had already been defeated, but there was a fragile courage in the set of his lips. If it had been me, I would have scarpered while no one was looking.

The rat's eyes turned cold. "We take orders from the coven, not you. And you ruined a simple evening's pleasure."

I shrugged. Backing down wasn't an option. I couldn't stand bullies. "Don't say I didn't warn you."

The rats came at me en masse, their gnawing teeth and claws threatening mortal damage.

I bit my lip to swallow the scream that built in my throat. My fear was instinctive, but I had a chance of coming out on top if I held my nerve like Ezra had trained me to do.

The tingling in my hands signalled I was ready. My beret flew off as I kicked and punched, my routines from kickboxing classes triggering my muscle memory, interspersing the moves with gusts of winds that sent the rats flying. The elf helped, too, making projectiles of the rubbish, infuriating but not slowing down the rats.

But they were too many.

With each rat I cast away, another returned. I wanted to subdue them. To kill them would earn Lavinia's wrath, and I had already risked making her my enemy.

I breathed hard and fast, cursing as a rat crawled up my trouser leg and sank its teeth into my calf. If it were a case of the rats or me, I'd have to kill them, but it went completely against my vegetarian, peace-loving nature. I shook my leg, and the rat spun through the air and thudded against the side of the bus shelter.

The chief rat led a charge up a lamppost. "Grab her ponytail."

Rage swept through me.

I pulled out the sword Gaia had given me. I'd mostly carried it around like an ornament, but this was as good a time to practice using it as any. A weapon blessed by Death promised to be devastating. At the very least, it would scare them off.

A woman could hope.

I gripped Transcender in both hands. Its ivory hilt felt cool to the touch, a huge relief, given how I was slick with sweat. I swung round, slashing the obsidian blade through the air.

The rats scattered.

Voices surged in my head, and I dropped the sword like I had been burned.

Seven pairs of black beady eyes turned in my direction, and my last thought before the rats rushed at me was how the poor elf would be next.

2

The elf gave a blood-curdling scream that signalled our end, there on a dimly-lit, rain-soaked London street fouled by rubbish. No doubt the noise would alert nearby humdrums in their homes. Even in death, the Sorcerer's Senate would insult me for outing the magical community in the most ignominious circumstances. The chief rat would take Transcender to be his own, and armed with my sword, he'd rule over London.

My headstone would read: *Here lies a druid, outsmarted by rats.*

What an end.

They knocked me off my feet by targeting the backs of my knees. I fell and let loose another two gusts of wind before the seven rats colluded to bind my hands with a vine. Then they dragged me into an alley, uttering a spell to make light of their load.

I spat the words. "You won't get away with this."

I meant it. That's the thing about endings: they depend on the life you lived and the love you gave. My friends and family would avenge me. I was sure of it.

The chief rat preened over his swarm's work, his pot belly puffing up with pride as he approached, twitching in anticipation of his bite. "The time for talk is over."

I cursed. Being told to shut up reminded me of my ex-husband. I closed my eyes, not wanting his wretched face to be my last.

Where was a teleporting werewolf-wizard when you needed one?

I hadn't even managed to bed him yet. What a waste.

Suddenly, a woman's cry of distress met my ears. I opened one eye.

There, at the end of the alley, stood two vivid red foxes with fur more silken than I had seen on any London fox. They were medium-sized and well-fed, with intelligent, inquisitive eyes.

I couldn't believe my luck. Hopefully, we had stumbled into their territory. I was pretty certain rodents were a dietary staple for foxes. That meant I had a chance to turn the tables.

The rats, too, recognised the stakes had changed. Their whiskers twitched, and their beady eyes bulged.

The foxes glanced at one another, their bushy, white-tipped tails swishing, before baring their teeth and running into the fray. The leaner one was quicker. It arrived first, snarling and snapping at the rats, picking one up by the tail and hurling it with ease. The second one was more of a brawler. It reared up on its hind legs, seeking to crush the slower rats, its mouth gaping open, the vocalisations ear-splitting with intensity.

I wanted in on the action. With my hands tied, I used my non-existent stomach muscles to manoeuvre into a sitting position and my teeth to tear off the vine. Fuelled by anger, the tingling in my hands reached a crescendo—better late than never— and I released a whirlwind that sent the rats scurrying up buildings and into the sewers.

The trembling elf cowered a few metres away, and the foxes' posture relaxed. Their tails no longer swung wildly, and their closed mouths hid their teeth. So they probably didn't want to eat me.

"Thank you." I gave them a wide berth before inching out of the alley, where two piles of clothing caught my eye.

A scream built in my throat as I took a closer look. Two pairs of lacy knickers, an A-cup and a B-cup bra from Marks and Spencer, two pairs of ballet pumps, a red silk dress with phoenix embroidery and a blue one with dragon embroidery.

Fei Yen's voice behind me made me jump. "So now you know our secret as well as our bra sizes."

I whipped round, my heart hammering. "Holy moly."

There stood my two students, half-smiling in the moonlight, in all their naked glory. They had dishevelled hair and muck under their nails. A deep gash marred Faeza's thigh, blood red against her olive-toned skin.

I stared open-mouthed. "I *knew* you were different."

Faeza covered her bits. "Do you mind passing us our clothes?"

"It's the least you can do after stalking us," said Fei Yen. "Then we can talk."

Heat rushed to my face as I handed them the two piles. "Er, sorry about that. I'll be right over there with the elf."

I spotted him across the road at the dilapidated bus stop. I retrieved the bin rolling in the street, set it aside and joined the elf on the bench at the bus shelter, his eyes moving skittishly across my face as if he still didn't know whether I could be trusted, despite all the trouble I had gone to in order to protect him and the bruises and stinging cuts I had to show for it.

Not to mention the rabies injection I probably needed.

I laid a gentle hand on his knobbly grey arm. "I'm Alisha."

"Thank you for seeing me, Alisha," he said, his voice brittle from shock. "Not everyone does. Most other peculiars would have gone along their way. Elves are not beloved."

I frowned. "I'm sorry to hear that."

Dirt and blood smeared his face. "Why did you help me?"

"All creatures should have self-determination, and the rats were trying to control you. It wasn't right." I paused, searching the street. My heart dropped like a stone in a well. "Oh no."

"What is it?" said the elf.

"They took it. They took my sword."

The elf lifted his hand of four fingers and reached into the darkness. When he drew his hand back, it held Transcender as if he had plucked it from a pocket of night. He handed it to me with a slight bow of his triangular head. He picked something else out of the void. "And here's your beret."

I gasped, put the beret on my head and accepted the sword, stashing it in my blazer before any harm came to it. "How did you do that? Why couldn't you hide yourself from the rats with a trick like that?"

"Elven magic isn't what it used to be. Everything changed after the Battle of the Celestial Library. We aren't welcome at Wildwoods School of the Wondrous. We aren't allowed to gather for long. We are harassed and harried. Our magic is depleted and untrained, and while I can create pockets, it takes time. The rats raging at you bought me time to hide the sword. It is much easier to hide a small object than a large one."

I kissed his cheek. "Thank you."

His ashen skin creased into folds as he smiled. Then he eased himself off the bench and turned into the night. "I must go, Alisha, and you should too, lest the rats return. The streets of the city are not safe at night. Thank the foxes for me."

"Wait," I said. "I don't know your name."

"I am Flinar," said the elf.

"Will we meet again?" I asked.

"Perhaps one day." Flinar cast a worried look over my shoulder. "But I don't like crowds." He limped away in his torn tunic and ridiculous knickerbockers, and I quelled my instinct to mother him.

"Charming." Fei Yen dressed once more in her red phoenix qipao. She plonked herself down next to me in the bus shelter, exhausted. "He could have stayed to say hello. It's not every day you meet a dark elf."

Faeza joined us more slowly, her face pale in the moonlight. They must have been in their fifties. Despite their slim dancers' bodies, the fracas with the rats had taken its toll. Her wound bled through the blue silk of her qipao.

The odd car sped past, but the drivers paid us no attention. We were just three women waiting for the bus.

"You really should find a safer place for your sword," said Fei Yen. "It's been flapping about inside your jacket for weeks. You're lucky Neighbourhood Watch haven't noticed it, let alone the police."

I frowned. "Surely I wasn't that obvious?"

"You jerked in fright every time it poked you," said Fei Yen. "It's been rather hair-raising watching you. It's a wonder you're still whole."

"How's your leg, Faeza?" I asked.

She sighed. "I'll survive. At least until we work out why our night class teacher was following us. Were we mistaken to save you, Alisha? I'm not sure it was your best professional decision to stalk us, and I'd hate to have to give up your class. We enjoy it so much."

Fei Yen nodded. "It is a wonderful group of people, and the kickboxing moves help keep us fit."

"Ha! I knew you weren't attending primarily for the language side," I said.

"Why would we need a class to practice English?" said Fei Yen. "We even dream in English."

"We have lived in London for over seventy years," said Faeza, "But it is in our nature to be able to speak all languages common to the area we inhabit, as well as the language of animals."

"Bloody hell."

They looked so toned in the nude for women of their age. Between them and Lavinia, it was enough to give me a complex.

"I had it all wrong, didn't I?" I asked.

If they were over seventy, their boobs were doing marvellously well. They were positively springy, the lucky cows—or rather foxes.

Faeza's eyes narrowed. "So tell us, Alisha, why on earth were you following us?"

They were right, of course. I had violated my duty of care. Technically, it would have been more sensible to ask Detective Jameson to investigate. That was what the Shadow Squad was for. Except, I wasn't the most patient woman.

I stood up to look them both in the eye and give myself more room in case they attacked. I had seen them in action. These two definitely had teeth.

A bus pulled in, crushing remnants of rubbish.

I waved the driver on and then focussed on my students. "I agree. You deserve an explanation. You see, I clocked the clues that there was more to you than you told me. Demanding answers was a big no-no in front of humdrums and would have led to me falling foul of the Magical Constitution, so I decided to follow you home. I'm sorry. I really am. In my defence, I did try waggling my eyebrows at you during night class, but it didn't provoke the confession I hoped."

"We just thought you had developed a nervous tic," said Fei Yen.

Faeza swatted her and gave me a sympathetic look. "It's been a hard year for you."

"You know, the Magical Constitution isn't worth the parchment it's written on," said Fei Yen. "Neither is belonging to the Otherworld. We don't need to register as peculiars to feel valued, and we certainly don't need to follow their rules. Foxes are natural outsiders. Our cunning tells us to live on the outskirts and not to risk our skin."

Faeza nodded. "Except we consider you a friend, and when we saw that bin arc through the air and the scuttling, devilish witches' rats, we knew you were outnumbered. We couldn't look away, even though our instincts told us to avoid confrontation."

"Thank you for risking your skins for me," I said. "Faeza, you need to stop that bleeding."

"I'll be fine. You think we haven't been in scrapes before? Finish explaining." Her look brooked no nonsense.

I took a deep breath. "Okay. You saw transformation and great pain in the cards the night the sun god killed Nita. As if you knew of my druidry and what the night held in store."

Fei Yen smiled. "This is true. How else do you think we fund all the Chinese take-aways Faeza likes to order? Card reading is the largest source of revenue at our shop."

They ran a tea and occult shop called Shanghai Moon around the corner from my flat, and the card reading table was always full. I had always thought it to be hocus pocus, but Marina was a real convert.

I nodded. "Then there was how you weren't fazed by Ezra appearing in wolf form in the classroom."

"Of course not. A wolf is part of the Canidae family. Like foxes," said Fei Yen.

I spluttered. "Are you telling me that Ezra has candida? Isn't that a fungal infection?"

Fei Yen laughed. "No, silly. Canidae is the Latin name for the biological family tree from which foxes, wolves and dogs branch."

A wave of relief flooded me. "Phew."

Faeza gave a watery smile. "Are you two up to hanky-panky then?"

I blushed. "Let's get back to the subject at hand. Neither of you fell for Detective Jameson's explanation that Nita had been killed in a rogue attack. As if you knew the killer was a god all along. So those were my reasons. There's nothing else to it. Except maybe your spooky thing of finishing each other's thoughts. If that doesn't scream Otherworld, I don't know what does."

"That's not spooky. That's love." Fei Yen turned to Faeza with concern. "Are you sure you are okay, my darling?"

Her wispy voice wasn't her own. "I was just thinking that Alisha should have a baldric to keep her sword safe."

Then she slumped and slid off the bench, transforming into her true self as she did.

I gasped. There was no cracking of bones, just a shifting of skin, a shrinking, a reframing, that all happened in a blink of an eye. Like Faeza was both woman and vixen, and both identities were as fluid as water.

Quick as a flash, Fei Yen caught the limp vixen in her arms. Her eyes were closed. Her clothes pooled at our feet.

Fei Yen looked at me aghast, her eyes filling with tears. "How could I be so stupid? She always takes the brunt of it when we have to fight. I didn't think it was that bad."

I gripped her shoulder. "There's no time for emotions right now, Fei Yen. We must get her some help."

"We can't take her to the hospital. We'll have to take her back to Shanghai Moon."

"No, I have a better idea," I said. "Do you trust me?"

Fei Yen nodded. "I do."

"Then we have no time to lose."

I thanked my lucky stars for friends like Marina, who raced across moonlit London in her van to pick up a wounded fox. Twenty minutes later, Fei Yen scooped up Faeza and followed Marina into her surgery. I trailed behind with the discarded clothes.

My job had been done. This was Marina's domain, and I could rest easy knowing Faeza was in safe hands.

The smell of disinfectant filled my nose. I hovered in the treatment room as my best friend worked on her patient with a whirr of rainbow hair and deft fingers. Within minutes, she hooked up Fei Yen to fluids and cleaned and bandaged the wound. Finally, she placed gentle hands on the vixen's head and closed her eyes, synchronising her breathing with the animal.

Within seconds, the vixen stirred. Her bushy, red tail sparked to life, and then she rolled over, startled at the strange, sterile environment.

My best friend, the empath, the animal whisperer.

"It's okay, sweet thing," said Marina.

"I'm here," said Fei Yen. "It's okay. You can shift here. You are safe."

Only when she heard Fei Yen's voice did the vixen's stress ease.

She sighed and curled up in a ball, and her silken red fur became a woman's skin. Her vixen's ears became human ones, and her snout receded to become a petite nose.

Marina trembled as Fei Yen embraced Faeza and covered her in a blanket.

I rushed to Marina's side. Her fingernails had been chewed down to the quick. "Are you okay? You're quivering like a leaf."

I didn't need her to tell me the truth. I knew her well enough to recognise the signs of anxiety—the signs that heralded another fight with her mum or an exam at school she was worried about. I didn't need a therapist to fill me in. Marina's quivering showed she hadn't managed to control her empath powers yet. Just like my dragon dreams were a sign of my fears that I'd never measure up to my long-dead grandmother, the legendary animator Rajika Verma.

Marina's blue eyes clouded over. "Just ignore me. The important thing is that Fei Yen is going to be okay. We got her here just in time. That wound might not have looked terrifying, but rats can be terrible carriers of disease. She'll need a course of antibiotics."

I grimaced. "Yeah, I might too. I'm covered in bites from the bloody things."

Marina looked at me in horror. "What on earth happened tonight?"

"We'll need a huge gin while I fill you in. And maybe a lasagne from Tito's," I said. Marina just happened to have one of London's best Italian restaurants next door. "But first, can you tell me why you're trembling? I'm worried."

"I'm finding it hard to switch off the empath thing after helping patients. Like their residual pain and fear seep into me."

I squeezed her. "We're a right trio, aren't we? Less than a month to our magical trial, and there's you with no off switch. There's me with unreliable wind druidry, a flat zero on animation powers and a deadly sword that, in my hands, might as well be a toothpick. And Sahil, who has failed to find any powers at all."

The door to the treatment room swung open, and in padded a familiar creature. His thick, golden coat of rosettes gleamed in the fluorescent light. His scarred face, with its emerald eyes, provoked gasps from my students.

"No one said being a peculiar was easy," purred Echo, leaving us with no doubt about his superior hearing. "You went out looking all chic, Alisha, and now you look like you've been dragged through a bush backwards."

I wasn't surprised to see him here. Since her entry into the Otherworld, Marina had been receiving more and more peculiars as patients. Echo acted as a consultant for her. It wasn't like the Royal College of Veterinary Surgeons would have been any help. Marina's approach to Otherworld patients was a combination of veterinary knowledge, winging it, and Echo filling in the gaps.

God help us all.

"Hello, Echo." I scratched his ear. "I thought you were hunting tonight."

He inclined his magnificent head. "I was, but I rushed over when Marina paged me about an Otherworld fox."

I raised an eyebrow. "She paged you?"

Echo honked with laughter. "Of course not. I have neither opposable thumbs nor a pager belt. But since I'm now employed here, I like to use professional lingo."

Fei Yen and Faeza gawped.

I turned to them. "Ladies, I'd like you to meet my magical leopard, Echo, who started life as my Bengal cat."

"The pleasure is all mine." Echo grinned as Faeza's blanket dropped, and she scrambled to cover up again. "You need not worry. I prefer to eat animals who aren't scavengers. Deer are my current favourite. Herd animals are an easy kill. You can always pick one off. Sometimes I even sing the Bee Gees's *Stayin' Alive* at them. The chorus, not the mumbling bit. You know, to give them a bit of a boost before I go in for the kill."

He paused and yawned, showing pristine rows of jagged teeth. I had brushed those teeth when he'd been a Bengal cat.

"But truth be told," he continued, "I am turning over a new leaf. I promised not to eat the animals in this surgery, and so far, I have upheld the bargain. Although outside of this surgery, you could be fair game, dependent on how terrible my hunger pangs are. And I always leave enough of the carcass to allow for burial. I'm not a

Neanderthal."

"I'm injured. He'll eat me first." Faeza clutched Fei Yen. "Save yourself."

"Don't mind him," I said. "He talks a good game, but he doesn't actually kill that often. One kill can sustain him many months, and I keep the freezer well stocked with salmon and steak."

"She's very generous," said Echo. "And since you are her students and, therefore, indirectly pay for my sustenance, I shall give you a free pass from a mauling."

"How kind," said Marina. "We'll hold you to that. Now, will you please zip it and let these poor women tell us what exactly they are since we missed all the fun on the streets of London."

Echo turned steely emerald eyes on her. "Marina Ambrose, you do not need—"

Marina straightened her spine, all hint of trembling gone, and imbued her voice with quiet authority. "My surgery, my rules." She smiled at the foxes. "Tell me who you are."

Faeza stood supported by Fei Yen, but they spoke as one. "We are *hu hsien* from China."

"We didn't hide that from you, Alisha," said Fei Yen. "*Hu hsien* are foxes who can shapeshift into maidens of renowned grace and beauty with a fox's tail. They heal quickly, can speak many languages and become an ephemeral spirit. A man who falls in love with a *hu hsien* is in great danger, for the *hu hsien* can devour the souls of such men and leave them as mindless zombies."

"But that was a long time ago," said Faeza. "When we left China, we evolved past *hu hsien*. We can no longer become spirits and no longer have tails in our human form."

Fei Yen laughed. "Thank the gods."

Faeza smiled. "It took me a long time to walk as a maiden without my tail for balance."

"It did," said Fei Yen. "But we have adapted well these past decades. "London was the perfect place to blend in once we left China. Do you know how many foxes are in this city?"

"I do," said Marina. "Approximately ten thousand."

"But why did you leave China?" I frowned. All this time as their teacher, and I had no idea why they had left their home.

Marina smiled at me. "Because they are in love with each other. And some men would rather crush beautiful women than let them love freely. I didn't need to be an empath to know that."

Faeza nodded. "So we were forced to kill. Over and over again."

"One day, we just couldn't do it anymore. So we saw the pictures of China Town in London and decided to come here," said Fei Yen. "Except it was too expensive to live there."

Faeza kissed Fei Yen's cheek. "So we opened Shanghai Moon in Balham."

"The rest is history," said Fei Yen. "Thank you for recognising our love, Marina. And for helping my love to heal. We don't know how to thank you."

"Some longjing green tea and oolong would be just perfect." Marina poked me in the side. "My best friend promised to get me some but kept forgetting."

"What in the heavens? You have the same surname. I thought you were sisters," I said.

"Oh my goodness, Alisha. You're terrible at love," said Marina. "They're married, doofus."

Fei Yen and Faeza held up their rings.

"Since 2014," they said as one.

I furrowed my brow. "What I don't understand is why you choose to live amongst the foxes and humans of this city yet reject closer contact with the Otherworld."

"Because, while we trust you, we don't trust the Sorcerer's Senate. As long as the senate is in charge, we will continue to live in the shadows, where it is safe," said Fei Yen.

Faeza nodded. "We are your friends, Alisha, and as your friends, please think wisely about whether you want to take the Wildwoods magical trial."

"You are surprised that we can hear as well as the leopard," said Fei Yen with a twinkle in her eye. "Your rainbow-haired friend is not surprised. Even as we stand here now, I can hear the burrowing of rodents underground."

"And I can hear a wall clock ticking in the surgery reception area right now," said Faeza. "Your footsteps behind us were like the stomping of an elephant."

I made a mental note to get tips from Echo.

"Mark our words, Alisha," said Fei Yen. "Once you are a registered peculiar, the senate will have a claim to you. And what the senate wants, the senate gets."

4

———————

W ildwoods School of the Wondrous had become a second home to me since the revelation that I was a druid. Sometimes it seemed as though I spent more time there than at my own flat. Up in the cluster of treehouses surrounding the great oak, I felt safe to explore my druidry. Little wonder generations of peculiars had gravitated here to learn and push the boundaries of their magical side. How sad that Fei Yen and Faeza didn't trust the Sorcerer's Senate enough to take advantage of all Wildwoods had to offer: the community of peculiars, the library with its cherry-wood shelves and carpet of desiccated leaves, the arena that adapted to the training needs of students and the guiding hand of headmistress Rayna Willowsun, the Minister for Education.

When the Prime Sorcerer had wanted to banish me from the Otherworld before my magical trial due to my disobedience, it was Rayna who had vouched for me.

Like a grown woman's priority should be obedience. My top values were loyalty, authenticity and hope. Obedience came at the bottom of the list. I had spent my whole life unlearning that crap.

What mattered was being true to myself.

Still, acquiring new knowledge and skills took effort, and part of me would have been relieved if Phinneous Shine had kicked me out and I'd returned to sitting on my sofa dipping fistfuls of Doritos into guacamole. It had been so long since I'd really rested. Since my head had been empty of questions. There was much to be loved about the contentment of not striving for answers.

And this morning, in a cabin suspended like a bauble from a sycamore tree, I was faced with a teacher who demanded nothing more than my best.

"I must tell you, Alisha, these history lessons with the three of you really are the bane of my life," said Orpheus, the scariest and only mind-reading vampire I had ever met.

"Well, Minister, if you could just tell me how you would like me to behave, I will do my best," I said. "It must be a relief not to have to teach me, Marina and Sahil all at once."

Orpheus sighed. "Yes, it's just wonderful to prolong the pain threefold."

I chewed my lip. "Perhaps you can outsource this particular responsibility."

The fact that he could read every thought made me twitch with anxiety. Ezra had tried to teach me how to shield my thoughts, but as a new druid, my skills lagged aeons behind a hundred-year-old vampire.

Orpheus gave me a steely look. For a miserable vampire, he was pretty smoking hot—something about those dark eyes against skin as white as the cliffs of Dover.

"What?" he said. "And miss all this fun? No, druid. As Minister for History and the Today, this duty is mine alone. And for all that is unholy, can you please stop thinking about the werewolf?"

I couldn't keep Ezra out of my thoughts since he whisked me to Paris on our first date. He teleported us to the top of the Eiffel Tower and showed me the Louvre, Montmartre and Notre Dame. I should have jumped his bones there and then before his pack summoned him.

Let's face it, he'd earned it.

Orpheus turned beetroot red. He'd obviously read every carnal thought.

It served him right. If I couldn't keep him out of my mind, maybe I could gross him out enough that he chose to stay out.

I wrenched my attention away from Ezra's come-to-bed eyes and low-slung jeans. "You know, from an English teacher's perspective, placing 'the' before 'today' in your title is grammatically odd. Would you consider changing it?"

His eyebrows shot up into his hairline. "You want me to change a title that has been passed down through the centuries and denotes the importance of the present over dusty history books? Hmm. Let me give it some thought." He scratched his beard so theatrically that I regretted showing any initiative. "No. I don't think I will. Do you know your problem, Alisha Verma?"

I sighed. "I'm sure you'll enlighten me."

"You have no hope of passing the magical trial."

I had to give it to him. Marina and I had come to the same conclusion. She could just about manage to keep her focus when the emotions of others became too overwhelming, but I was as unpredictable as Russian roulette. What's more, there had been such a buzz amongst Wildwoods students about our impending trial that my stress levels had skyrocketed. By all accounts, the trial took place in front of an audience, like some sort of gladiatorial show.

There was every chance we would be humiliated.

Since Fei Yen and Faeza had raised doubts about the Otherworld, my terrifying dragon nightmares had morphed into scenes of humiliation: my trouser seam splitting to reveal my control pants in the middle of the trial; Ezra lustily grabbing my hips and pulling me closer, only to change his mind when he saw me naked and just last night; my sword deciding I wasn't worthy and stabbing me in the eye.

"Alisha, if those winds don't die down, this cabin will become a projectile."

I slammed my tingling palms against my thighs. "That isn't me."

Only a desk separated us. He reached for me with long fingers, his dark eyes unfathomable, and laid his hand on my shoulder. "There, there. Calm yourself, druid."

The clouds in my mind cleared. It wasn't that my worries lifted, more that they no longer seemed insurmountable. Outside, the winds quietened. "How did you do that?"

"I can do more than read minds, move fast and bite necks, you know." He wasn't joking. "I also have the ability to wipe minds. Sometimes an emotion, sometimes a singular event, sometimes completely."

A shiver ran down my spine.

"These traits are passed down in a minor way to the vampires I have sired. You see, I have experience teaching new peculiars to master themselves and others." He peered down his Roman nose at me, making me feel small in comparison. It would have been sexy if he hadn't been such an arsehole. "I want you to take your studies seriously, Alisha. Can you do that? Passing the trial isn't just about raw talent or luck. You have proven you have that. There has never been an initiate who has a goddess on her side. I thought you were an imbecile when we first met, but you faced up to a god. You have proven yourself not to be the fool I took you for. However, you still show foolishness in spades."

"Well, aren't you a delight?"

"Nothing wastes time more than being delightful just to save feelings. Or are you too fragile for the truth?" The sleeves of his gown flapped angrily as he wagged his finger at me, and I wanted to bite it off. "Then listen, druid. Being a peculiar is about grit and the choices you make on a daily basis. Take your grandmother. She changed the course of the world by standing firm when it most counted. All her learning, all her magic and experience, led to that moment when she fought against dark forces at the Battle of the Celestial Library." He bent to open a drawer of his desk and placed a thick history book in front of me. "Read aloud from the top of page 581."

On the front was the Wildwoods crest: an embossed W, crowned with posies of plants.

I flicked through featherlight pages edged with gold. "The Battle of the Celestial Library. On 9 March 1982, when Uranus entered retrograde motion, a fifty-strong group of dark elves led by Meriel Naehorn breached the defences of the Celestial Library in an attempted to seize the magical artefacts stored there. The Custodian

Rajika Verma, a druid who had warned for many years of the nefarious intentions of Naehorn, together with her leopard Chanakya Gunbir Hredhaan of Maharashtra, fought valiantly to defend the library…"

I shivered with anticipation. I'd known Echo had fought at my grandmother's side—that was how he'd received his scar, after all—but reading it in a history book filled my heart with pride for my loved ones.

"Continue," said Orpheus.

"With the stolen magical items, the dark elves planned to shred the Magical Constitution and turn the egalitarian council and Otherworld into an elf dominion. When Meriel Naehorn's forces disabled the Celestial Library's defences, Rajika Verma and her leopard stood singlehandedly against them until Defence Minister Lavinia Drach's army heeded the distress call. The Custodian then retreated to guard the inner sanctum. The battle raged for thirty-six hours. While Rajika Verma ultimately lost her life, her actions prevented the dark elves from gaining possession of a single artefact."

I exhaled loudly. My grandmother had only ever been a ghost to me, but I could sense her spirit now. I understood why she'd been held up as such an example.

A half-smile played on Orpheus' lips. "You are beginning to understand. Finish the paragraph, Alisha."

"Defence Minister Drach apprehended the dark elf leader Meriel Naehorn and her followers, who were subsequently stripped of their magic. On 11 March 1982, with the conjunction of the Moon and Mars at hand, after all-night deliberations with the Sorcerer's Senate, the Prime Sorcerer Phinnaeous Shine cast out the dark elves from the senate and expelled elven children from Wildwoods School of the Wondrous. Their return to the school would be permitted only on condition of a generous donation to the Wildwoods coffers." I gasped. "But that's not fair. How can all elves be blamed for the actions of a few?"

"The senate took decisive action. Thank the stars they did, or you would be living in a dark elf dominion right now."

"It was nearly forty years ago."

He frowned. "They murdered your grandmother."

"And would the senate's decree have been any different had she lived?"

"Bad behaviour has consequences. The attempted destruction of our society is a grave crime."

I thought of Flinar, my new elf friend, and the sadness in his eyes. "Are you so sure that the senate is above reproach?"

His conviction chilled me to the bone. "I am. And your grandmother would have been too."

Something told me Ezra wouldn't have been as quick to write off a whole section of the magical community. He'd put himself in harm's way to help me avenge Mum's death. A man who went to such lengths for a stranger had more compassion than the senate had when they had cast out the elves.

"You do realise that the werewolf was thinking with his carrot and veg rather than his brain when he helped you? You could have lost your life against the sun god. A true mentor would never have acted so recklessly." He paused and leaned forward, and I was struck again by how his handsome, chiselled face was wasted with his heartless personality. "The werewolf is not fit to be your mentor. It would be in your best interests to switch to me."

I gawped. "You want to be my mentor? Why? You don't even like me."

Orpheus shrugged. "An immortal vampire runs out of challenges. You are a challenge."

I pictured the vampire and the werewolf fighting over me like in *Twilight*. It wasn't my favourite fantasy, but I could get used to it.

His sculpted lips curved into a smile. "My intentions are anything but romantic, druid."

I laughed uncomfortably. "That's a relief. What *are* your intentions?"

"To take you to the next level. It's particularly disappointing you haven't managed to access your grandmother's powers yet. What is the werewolf's strategy? Surely he has one?"

I sighed. I had been a little disappointed at how often pack business took Ezra away from my training needs and my side. How was I ever supposed to gain my confidence if he kept disappearing? Not to mention the lack of opportunities to seduce him.

"The pleasures of the flesh are all well and good, Alisha, but sometimes you have to think with your mind."

"Rather than my lady parts?" I said helpfully.

He spluttered, and I gave myself a point for ruining his composure. But Orpheus wasn't the kind of man who'd let me get the upper hand for long. My adrenalin spiked as he moved in a sudden blur and came to sit on the desk. He towered over me, dark eyes holding mine, and I caught a whiff of dark chocolate and sweet cherry.

My hand slipped under my jacket to grasp Transcender's hilt.

"Whoa, you're a fast mover. Is that beard oil I can smell?" I blurted out to mask my nerves.

"Vampires have dry skin. So what if my goatee needs a helping hand?" he said in exasperation. "And don't think I haven't noticed your sword. Stop posturing. You wouldn't have a chance to get in a strike if I wanted to kill you."

I gulped. I had a feeling that duty of care meant far less at Wildwoods than it did in humdrum society.

"I'll only make this offer once, Alisha. You are too enamoured with the werewolf to take proper instruction. The results of your magical trial depend on your decision. What do you say, druid?"

My mind whirled. I had already made enough enemies in the Otherworld to fill a granny annexe. I didn't need another one.

The cabin rocked as if we were caught in a storm.

A note of warning. "Alisha—"

I gave him a blank look. "I promise that isn't me."

Then we fell.

5

Orpheus and I clung together. I cried out as we hit the rafters before plummeting in a mass of flesh, books and classroom furniture. Screams filled our ears. Any second now, we'd hit the ground and be smashed to a pulp in our wooden casket. Not that Orpheus should have minded. I was pretty sure he couldn't be killed by falling, and vampires liked caskets.

Still, he seemed hellbent on getting us out of this one. He gripped me tightly against his chest as we fell, his eyes narrowed in concentration.

Little did he know, I didn't need to wait for a knight to rescue me.

My palms tingled as I formed a cushion of wind around us.

"What are you doing?" he grunted, his feet floundering in the air, the current giving him oscillating fish lips.

I panted with exertion. Sustaining the wind took all my focus. "Saving us with a cushion of wind, so we don't break our necks."

"Let me do my job, you cretin." He pinned my hands to my sides. When the cushion of air dissipated, he propelled off the falling debris and launched us into the woods.

My scream stuck in my throat as we ripped through the air. We tumbled to safety by a grove of trees, rolling over and over before coming to a stop in a tangle of legs and arms and hair and dirt.

A couple of hundred yards away, the cabin broke into a hundred pieces.

I groaned in the vampire's arms. My body would be bruised black and blue by our fall. What's more, the jutting edges of my sword hilt had imprinted themselves onto my skin during our tumble.

Orpheus shoved me aside without ceremony, stood up and dusted himself off. His eyes flashed in surprise as the ground shook with tremors. "What is going on? Has there been a mishap in the arena? Whatever it is, someone is going to pay for that lesson interruption. My history classroom has been all but destroyed. What are you still doing sprawled on the floor, druid?"

The tremors subsided at last, and I sat up.

My heartbeat jumped as a familiar face loomed into sight behind Orpheus.

Ezra's eyes, full of concern, drank in the sight of me before he tore them away to speak to Orpheus. "I take it you haven't seen the news, Minister."

Orpheus snorted. "Humdrum news has been taken over by a clan of Murdochs and is little more than fiction. Better to trust my own eyes."

He disappeared in a flash towards the arena.

Ezra crouched by my side. "Thank the stars you're okay. I came as soon as I realised what was going on."

"My knight in denim jeans." I stared up at him, dazed by the fall. He hadn't had a shave in days, and his rumpled clothes indicated he'd slept in them, but butterflies still darted in my stomach.

He pulled me to my feet and kissed the top of my head.

I melted into him, then pulled away to check how much damage Wildwoods had sustained. My jaw slackened. "Oh my goodness, we have to see if anyone is hurt."

I ran full pelt towards the school.

"Stay here. It might not be safe." Ezra cursed and followed, hot on my heels.

My lungs burned as I ran. Only when we stood in the middle of the site did we stop, aghast.

Two cabins that had fanned out from the great oak had fallen in addition to ours, leaving huge craters and debris on the ground. Torn books, discarded school bags and shattered glass crunched underfoot. Some rope bridges had been twisted or torn, and many others had become dislodged altogether. Felled beech trees had crushed apparatus in the training arena. The cable car track had been mangled.

"The luck of the leprechauns was on our side today," said Ezra. "If this had happened in the evening, Wildwoods would have been full to the rafters."

Orpheus's vampire speed had propelled him ahead of us. By the time we arrived in the thick of it, he loomed over the clusters of distraught pupils, taking names. Rayna Willowsun tended to three pupils on stretchers with capable hands, uncorking clinking healing potions from her belt, her expression solemn.

"There were fewer than fifty people on site, but the children need calming. Rayna is already tending to the injured, but their injuries are mild, especially in the hands of a druid with healing powers," said Orpheus to us. "You can help calm the children. What are you waiting for?"

Ezra and I rounded up the children away from the rubble.

"This way, children," I said, putting on my brightest voice. "It was just a little mishap. Your parents will be here soon, and you'll get a day at home. It's just like a snow day. And everyone knows how fun snow days are."

They gazed at me in awe.

The Wildwoods rumour mill had gone into overdrive after my intervention during the Kraglek ceremony. Once word had got around about my antics with the sun god, I'd been turned into a heroine overnight.

Not that I was complaining.

I spotted a familiar face amongst the assortment of shapeshifters, druids, vampires and witches. Mirabel, the gutsy fairy who'd refused to back down from a pack of werewolves and had faced Kraglek, sobbed a few feet away.

I wrapped my arms around her slight shoulders and pushed her auburn ringlets out of her tear-stained face. "It's going to be okay, Mirabel, I promise."

"But that's just it, Alisha. It's not going to be okay. Everyone is saying it's the dark elves." Mirabel gulped back her tears.

I frowned. This didn't look like an enemy attack. I spotted neither assailants nor weapons. How could the dark elves have pulled something like this off unseen, with all the magic and defences that dwelt in this place?

Ezra knelt next to us to tie Mirabel's trailing shoelace. "That's highly unlikely, Mirabel. People say all sorts of things when they are scared. That doesn't make them true."

I nodded. "You're safe now, Mirabel. Just hang in there until your parents arrive. A duvet day always makes me feel better. Tomorrow this will all seem like a bad dream."

She brightened. "Do you think I can get out of doing my history homework?"

"I'll have a word with Orpheus," I said.

"You're the best." She floated back to her friends.

I turned to Ezra with a frown. "Dark elves? Sounds a bit farfetched to me."

His grey eyes smouldered. "I agree. I haven't caught their scent, and my nose never lies. If it were the elves, Lavinia would have called in her army already. Orpheus may scoff, but the BBC is reporting an earthquake measuring magnitude 6 on the Richter scale. A chunk of Westminster Bridge even fell into the Thames."

"Bloody hell. An earthquake in London is impossible. There aren't any major fault lines here."

He rubbed the back of his neck as if he'd been working long nights and needed a little kneading of his muscles to set him to rights. "I thought you knew by now, Alisha? Nothing is impossible."

Orpheus came up behind us. "You don't belief that codswallop, do you, Mr Neuhoff? An earthquake of this magnitude in London? It beggars belief. The dark elves are a far likelier explanation. Your aunt has been warning of an impending attack for quite some time."

Ezra raised a dismissive eyebrow. "My aunt has been a sworn

enemy of the dark elves since the Battle of the Celestial Library. Unless she provides actual proof, I hope you'll take her declarations with a pinch of salt."

"The yew tree rune has been compromised. Would an earthquake disable the school's defences?" said Orpheus coldly.

My mind flashed to my loved ones. I needed to know they were safe. "So Ezra can teleport in and out of Wildwoods?"

Orpheus looked down at me. "Indeed. And the dark elves can use their black hole magic to wreak havoc. Now do you see the stakes?"

My heart hammered in my throat. I clutched Ezra's arm and got a whole load of bicep. "Ezra, will you check on my family for me? I can't breathe if they might be in danger."

He locked eyes with mine. "I won't be a second."

Then, he disappeared.

Orpheus's jaw hardened. "What a loyal sheepdog you have there. It's plain to see who is in charge. No wonder he is failing as your mentor."

I chewed my cheek to still my sharp tongue. Now was the time to pull together.

Just because Ezra had agreed to check on my family, it didn't make him a sheepdog. It made him someone who had recognised my anxiety and done the human thing. I bet Orpheus was a caveman—the type of man who expected women to launder his Y-fronts and be happy about it.

He stalked off as the rest of the cavalry arrived: the Prime Sorcerer, flanked by Defence Minister Lavinia and her two sisters, the Bestiary Minister Helio Woodwink and his assistant, the Justice Minister, the alpha Gunnolf and two burly werewolves. A vice tightened around my heart as they huddled together like a war committee on a battlefield.

Inside my jacket, Transcender pulsed against my skin like it was trying to tell me something.

Like it knew that danger approached.

My anxiety grew like a tidal wave. When Ezra reappeared with Echo at his side, I breathed a sigh of relief.

"Joshi, Sahil and Marina are all well and accounted for. The leopard insisted on coming, but he doesn't travel well." Ezra wiped the drool from his trouser legs.

A dizzy Echo padded over to nuzzle my leg with the gait of a drunken sailor. "I am relieved to know the dark elves have not torn you apart, Alisha Verma. Although you are no longer completely incapable of protecting yourself, I would be breaking my ancestral oath if I had allowed the wolf to return alone."

I scratched him behind his ear. "How is Dad?"

"Glued to the humdrum news with your idiotic brother," said Echo. "Marina is soothing her animals at the surgery."

Ezra ushered us forward, his warm hand on the small of my back, lingering there. "Come, you two. The Prime Sorcerer calls."

Phinnaeous Shine had reigned over the Otherworld as Prime Sorcerer longer than any other peculiar. As Echo had explained, a wizard with skinwalking powers was singularly suited to the brief of Prime Sorcerer. He could infiltrate top levels of government as easily as a woman slipping on a new dress. His transformations were not limited to his own gender. He could walk in anyone's shoes, and his skinwalking extended to voice and mannerisms, although his target's memories were, of course, alien to him. Still, with a little research, he could emulate just about anybody on earth and wear his new skin for as long as it took for the sun to rise and fall.

However, his skinwalking didn't impress me that day; his sheer resourcefulness and strength did.

"Children, stay out of the way." His black skin shone with perspiration as he bellowed.

Phinnaeous Shine stood, legs in a wide stance, his gown billowing behind him as he raised his arms left and right, like a conductor of an orchestra. The debris around him rose: the splintered cabins, torn rope bridges, the derailed cable cars and broken crockery. He hoisted them into the air, and they knitted back together in front of our eyes in such a spectacle of power that even the most troubled students cheered.

Helio sprinted away to check on the bestiary and round up any errant creatures. Up amongst the tree canopies, silver-haired Lavinia flew on her dull brown umbrella with its shimmering brass handle alongside her sisters Chandra and Isadora on their umbrellas. They looped through the sky, lassoing Wildwoods back together, their lips synchronised in their spells. Gunnolf, Ezra and the two burly werewolves heaved the fallen beech trees out of the arena while druid Rayna used her knowledge of plants to repair the yew tree that served as Wildwoods's primary defence.

Lucky old me and Echo had been assigned to Orpheus to patrol the ground for dark elves.

"I will rip out the throats of any elf I see." Echo's emerald eyes gleamed.

"It would be better to check with me first, Chanakya Gunbir Hredhaan of Maharashtra. There are still some elves who are pupils here, whose parents managed to raise the tuition fees," said Orpheus. "Although I have my suspicions that the money comes from dark dealings."

"Your instincts are as finely tuned as Ravi Shankar's guitar," Echo purred.

"I'm more of a Jimi Hendrix fan myself," said Orpheus. "It is an honour to have a warrior from the Battle of the Celestial Library here on the day the dark elves have returned."

"Steady on." I pushed through thick foliage. "We've not found a shred of proof."

Echo growled. "They are a tricky race, Alisha. Do you think it was just anyone who killed the great Rajika Verma? It was these treacherous elves that conspired to kill your grandmother. They do not deserve your compassion."

I sighed, grateful Echo hadn't been at my side the night I had met Flinar. He might have sided with the rats.

How quick these two were to judge. While geography had never been my strong point, I agreed that earthquakes in London were a ridiculous thought. But I would not cast blame on an entire group of magical individuals without more evidence, and for that, we needed Detective Jameson. That was after we had finished patrolling the Wildwoods boundary for non-existent boogeymen.

"Tell me, leopard, have you yet written a memoir of your life? You are talented in that respect, I seem to remember, and as the Minister for History and the Today, I would like to remind you how valuable eyewitness accounts are."

Echo lifted his chest with pride. "You heard where Ursula K. Le Guin got her ideas from?"

Orpheus nodded. "I did. But writing fiction is entirely different to non-fiction. I would be happy to read samples once you have a manuscript for your memoirs."

"I would be indebted, Minister. First, we have dark elves to hunt." Echo prowled close to the ground like he had caught a scent. He pounced on a bush, flushing out a red squirrel who scampered up a nearby sycamore.

I rolled my eyes.

A deep gong sounded, rippling like a wave across Wildwoods.

"Come, the Prime Sorcerer summons us," said Orpheus.

We hurried to the now spotlessly clean arena, where Phinnaeous Shine clapped for the attention of those gathered. Lavinia stood at his side, dressed as usual in bubble gum pink, her shoulders pushed back and her posture as straight as a military general.

By now, the numbers had swollen. We gathered in a throng of not only pupils, teachers and ministers but parents who had hurried to the school to check on their offspring and individuals from the magical community who had felt the pull of Wildwoods in their hour of need.

The Prime Sorcerer raised his voice above the sound of the breeze and the rustling leaves, and the crowd fell silent.

"Wildwoods is many things. It is a school. It is a safe haven. It is the seat of the Sorcerer's Senate. It is our most treasured resource. And yet, today, our treasure has been plundered by forces who, as yet, hide in the shadows. And we will be ready when they show their sorry faces. The dark elves will be punished."

The women laid protective arms around their children. The men in the crowd cheered and stamped the ground.

A shiver ran down my spine as Echo, too, threw back his head and roared his approval.

The most experienced faces, the ones lined with age, who had seen battles before, stayed quiet.

This is ridiculous, I thought, though I didn't say it out loud. Who was I to speak up against Phinnaeous Shine?

Orpheus, next to me, leaned down to murmur in my ear. "You see, you're learning to trust others with more wisdom."

I pledged to find a way to keep him out of my head.

An enigmatic smile danced around Orpheus's lips. "I haven't yet earned your trust, Alisha. But I will. I'm right about the dark elves and being the superior mentor."

"That remains to be seen, Orpheus," I said.

The Prime Sorcerer led the way back into the reconstructed building with the air of a triumphant king at his homecoming.

Dread bubbled up inside me.

Phinnaeous Shine stood out even amongst the deeply impressive and jaw-dropping peculiars I had met on my Otherworld journey. But what were resourcefulness and strength if they made you rush headlong into mistakes? The senate had a duty to act responsibly, but instead of pausing to gather evidence, it had doubled down on a decades-old grudge. Had Fei Yen and Faeza been right to warn me about where I placed my trust?

6

———————

Twilight had fallen by the time we reached my family home overlooking Tooting Bec Common. At this hour, the streets would usually have been filled with the sound of spluttering engines, drivetime radio and hooting as stony-faced drivers sat in traffic jams.

Not today. A quiet fear gripped the city.

Families sat glued to their television sets, where regular broadcasting had been interrupted by footage of the tremors and their aftermath.

It wasn't only Westminster Bridge that had been damaged. A deep crack had desecrated memorial stones in Westminster Abbey, and the foundations of the London Eye had become unstable. The city's emergency services had been working themselves ragged all day. News agencies reported hospitals full of patients suffering minor injuries and countless insurance claims from civilian homes and businesses.

Echo padded alongside Ezra and me, his tail swishing in disappointment. "I was rather hoping to terrorise hapless dogs having their walkies on the way to Joshi's house, but the streets are empty. Trust the elves to ruin everything."

"Not you too, Echo." Ezra stopped short on Dad's driveway. "You can't believe all that guff from the senate."

"I can, and I do," said Echo. "I fear there are troubling times ahead. This has elvish fingerprints all over it."

Ezra shook his head. "All I see are pieces of a puzzle and a lot of folks eager to jump the gun."

"Well, if I had opposable thumbs, I would point a whole armoury of guns at them," Echo growled. "Since I am lacking in that department, my claws and teeth will have to do."

I clenched my jaw in frustration. "And what if you are wrong?"

Echo yawned as if he didn't care either way. "It doesn't matter. I feel nothing but disdain for the dark elves since the night we lost your grandmother. If the dark elves receive boots up their backsides because of this morning, it reminds them to stay in their place. Look what happened to your fox students when they intervened in elvish troubles. Nothing good comes of siding with them."

I massaged my temples, tired of explaining the obvious. "But it was the coven's rats who hurt Fei Yen and Faeza, not Flinar."

"More like the rats knew the dark elves were up to something. Flinar could very well be a dark elf general."

My tone was sharp. "He was nothing of the sort. You didn't see him, or you would think the same."

"I have been a peculiar for centuries longer than you, Alisha. What you see with your newly unveiled eyes is not always accurate. Now, if you'll excuse me, I can hear the gentle flapping of koi in Joshi's pond that require my attention." He bounded up and over the side gate, and within seconds, splashing indicated he was toying with Dad's koi.

Ezra and I headed across the block-paved driveway to Dad's front door.

"You didn't have to come, you know." I rang the doorbell. "As far as we know, this morning was a geological anomaly."

Ezra leaned against the pillar of Dad's porch with his thumbs hooked in his jeans pockets. "Can't a guy miss his girl?"

My heart leapt a beat. "Is that what we are to each other?"

The lines around his grey eyes deepened as he smiled. "What do you want us to be?"

"I want us to have enough time to find that out."

"I wish I could whisk you away again, but my gut says things are hotting up. You have the trial to concentrate on. And then there's this ridiculous thing with the elves. I've never seen the senate so gung-ho. I would have stayed away today, but I needed to know you were safe."

"It's sweet, but it seems like all the men around me are rushing in to protect me—even Echo. Take right now. I'm perfectly capable of breaking bad news to Dad myself."

Ezra's grey eyes glimmered with amusement. "I know by now that you're an independent woman, Alisha. Just because I rush in to stand by your side doesn't mean I don't respect you. I just thought it was fairer that Joshi heard Rayna's decision from me. If your dad's unhappy with me usurping him as Sahil's mentor, I'd rather take the brunt of it. Besides, it's about time your brother and I bonded if I'm going to mentor him too."

I gave a throaty laugh. "So that's why you're here? For Sahil? I thought it was for me."

Ezra pulled me closer, and the scent of sweat from the morning's exertions and the tang of soap travelled up my nose. "If I'm honest, Orpheus sniffing around you made me a little possessive."

I grinned. "Vampires don't sniff. That's more of a werewolf thing. And you didn't look too bothered when you and the pack were playing at being lumberjacks in the arena."

His eyes dropped to my lips.

My heartbeat raced, but there was no way I'd let Dad catch us smooching. Mum would have given me a cheeky wink and offered to take me corset shopping. Her French heritage meant romance and sex were no big deal. Indian dads were more uptight. Even when their daughters were forty. Mine would rather have eaten his own toenail than see me locking lips with Ezra.

I pulled away and murmured in Ezra's ear. "Much as I love your hands on me, I don't want to make Dad's day any harder than it is already. No need for him to see his daughter in a compromising situation."

His eyes twinkled. "My apologies. I had no idea you were so…proper."

I fidgeted to hide my flushed cheeks. I thought my divorce had turned off my need for romance, but it turned out the right man could switch it right back on. "Oh, no, Mr. Neuhoff. I'm not proper. Just a daughter sensitive to her father's needs."

The air smouldered between us.

"In that case, a rain check," he said.

The door opened, and my brother Sahil emerged with a look of surprise. "Hey, Alisha, good thing you're here. Dad's been wound up like a spring since the quake." He nodded warily at Ezra. "Thanks for checking on us before, Ezra. Glad the tremors didn't flatten you."

"So you felt them here too?" I said.

"A shudder. Nothing more. Like a train had passed by. Weird, though, isn't it? It's not like we're in Tokyo or San Francisco. It was worse for some of my tenants. I was just about to nip down to Peckham to look at a crack. You can babysit Dad while I'm gone."

I grimaced. "That bad, is it?"

"Uh-huh. And you know what we're like. We exist in the same space like passing ships because we have no idea what to say to each other. Anyway, top timing." He grabbed his keys and stepped out over the threshold.

"Actually, Sahil, I wanted to have a word. Alisha's going to tell your dad, but between the two of us, Rayna wants me to take over mentoring you for the trial in a few weeks."

A look of horror crossed Sahil's face. "You know, about that, I reckon I'm not a peculiar. I have no magical talents. Me taking the trial is a waste of time."

Ezra put a hand on his shoulder. "Once the trial date is set, it must be taken, or you forfeit your chance. Let me see what I can coax out of you. What have you got to lose?"

Sahil heard the challenge and squared up to Ezra, all bristly, thin-lipped five-foot-nine of him. Ezra cleared him by a few inches and exuded calm. Which meant nothing because if there was one thing ingrained in me from the days my brother would pin me down when my parents weren't looking, it was that he was a live wire and knew how to play dirty.

I cringed, staying out of it only because Ezra held up a hand to say he could handle it.

"I could lose my pride," said Sahil.

Ezra raised an eyebrow. "Perhaps. But I can't see how it's any different if you chicken out."

Sahil often brought the child out in me. I was tempted to do a chicken dance there and then, but Echo came bounding around the side of the house, stinking of pond life and trailing water with him.

Sahil visibly shrank as the leopard approached. "You."

"Yes, who else?" said Echo. "Were you expecting The Lion King?"

Sahil wrinkled his nose. "You smell like a marsh."

His fur was bedraggled, and algae clung to his ear. "You speak the truth. I, too, cannot stand my own smell. Unfortunately, there is such an infestation of algae in the pond that I can't locate the koi. Assuming they still live and haven't succumbed to the poor water quality."

I sighed. "Dad has no idea how to maintain the pond without Mum. You promised you were going to call an expert in."

Sahil's eyes flashed. "How much more do you all want to ask of me? See to Dad, will you? With me, Echo. You need a hose down."

Echo's tail swished, and he bared his teeth. "I am a majestic leopard from India. Not a toddler from kindergarten."

"How about I help with the cleanup?" Ezra ushered the grumbling leopard back around the side of the house. "And we can talk over your options about the trial? Between your sister, Marina and me, I'm sure we can get you up to scratch. That is if you want to be a part of this world."

Sahil followed, keeping his distance from Echo's swinging rump. "Marina has agreed to help me? Why didn't you say?"

Ezra caught my eye. "Yes, I thought I had mentioned that already."

I shut the front door and walked past the shrine with Mum's garlanded photograph. In the kitchen, I found Dad looking worse for wear with mad professor hair and his shirt buttoned up wonky. An old school television stood on the counter—Mum would have hated that—blaring out news of the tremors. I turned down the volume.

Dad swung around, his face brightening at the sight of me. "Alisha, thank the gods you are here. I can't seem to find my comb." He closed the spice drawer. "I could have sworn it was in there."

I turned my full attention to him and picked up his comb from next to the kettle. "Your comb is right here. Sit down; let me help."

He sank into a chair while I fixed his buttons and tugged a comb through his errant hair.

"Why are you dressed in a shirt?"

"Oh, I don't know. When Rosalie was here, it was easy to take pride in myself. She was such a beautiful woman. I didn't want to let her down. But now, I walk about all day in my pyjamas."

"Well, that doesn't sound so bad."

He slumped. "It is if the pyjamas have three-day-old chilli stains on them. So today I thought I'd wear a shirt. And the first thing that happens is the city experiences an earthquake. If that isn't a sign, I don't know what is."

I put the comb down. "Don't be ridiculous. That was nothing to do with you."

"Well, of course not. It's all over the BBC. It just *feels* that way." His brow furrowed. "Unless there's something else. What's going on, Alisha?"

"Oh, nothing much," I lied, wanting to shield him from more worry. "Phinnaeous Shine was very impressive. The building took some knocks, but everything is now as it was."

"He pursued my mother romantically once, long before I came along." He squinted at me. "Hang on a minute. I know that face. I have known it your whole life. You're hiding something. Like when you missed the potty and covered the poo on the carpet with a doll's blanket."

"Dad!" I thanked the heavens Ezra hadn't heard. Through the window, I could see him and Sahil grappling with Echo and the garden hose. I gave a heavy sigh. "The senate think the dark elves are behind the tremors."

Dad let out a wail and covered his face with his hands. I'd never heard him make that sound before, not even when Mum had died. It was as if a dam had burst within him, and he didn't know how to stop.

I held him tightly, bent down so he'd hear me and be comforted by my presence. "Dad, what's wrong?"

He lifted his stricken face, his breath coming in gulps. "The dark elves are here again, just as my children have stepped into the Otherworld. They killed my mother. How can life be so cruel?"

His wails recommenced, rising in pitch until they became hysteria.

Ezra, Sahil and Echo gathered at the kitchen window to peer at us, the garden hose forgotten.

Do something, mouthed Sahil.

It felt wrong, but I slapped Dad's face.

He sighed and then collapsed into my arms. "I'm sorry. I needed that. Sometimes it's hard being the adult."

I gestured at our onlookers to give us some privacy and pulled back to make eye contact with Dad. "I know it is. For what it's worth, there's no evidence the dark elves are behind this. I'm sure there's a simple explanation."

"This is why. This is why I never wanted the two of you involved."

"Dad, I have something to tell you. Rayna has decided you are too distracted to train Sahil properly for his trial."

He let go of me, and his ageing hands, which had once painted so joyously, curled around his middle. "She wants him to drop out? Maybe that's for the best. Maybe you should step back too."

I shook my head. "No, she wants Ezra to train him too."

His chin trembled. "So be it. But the trial is two weeks away, and none of you is ready. You will fail, and it will be for the best. And then we won't have to think about the dark elves ever again. I will ask for the same fate."

I frowned. "Whatever do you mean?"

"Alisha, if you fail, this will seem like a dream to you. You won't even remember the Otherworld exists."

"I don't believe you. Surely we'd just learn for the trial again and retake it?"

Dad fidgeted. "There are no do-overs for the magical trial. Once you enter Wildwoods grounds, the decision is out of your hands. If you don't take the trial or if you fail it, you lose your memories of the Otherworld. The senate's vote is binding. Anything magic has touched—your mother's death, our talents, Echo. After a visit from the magical clean-up crew, it would be as if those memories warp into something humdrum. Not entirely different, but with the magic sucked out of them. You would wake in the morning and believe that your Bengal cat had simply gone missing."

My heart pounded. How cruel to find our true potential, only to have it snatched away should we fail. "You're just saying that because you don't want us to succeed."

"No, my darling. I'm saying it because it's the truth, however painful."

"Your painting would revert to humdrum level."

"Like most of my married life. I wasn't unhappy. There is much more to being above than being a peculiar."

My stomach clenched. "Dad, it might not be the elves."

"It will always be something."

I bristled with anger. Not at Dad so much as at Ezra. Why had he left me in the dark about the trial and all that was at stake? It was his job to fill me in. Orpheus flashed into my mind. At least he told it how it was. At least he didn't try to protect my feelings.

Ezra had a lot of explaining to do.

And then there was Dad. How was I supposed to concentrate on getting through the trial with him in such a state? If the dark elves were out of the picture, he could rest easy that the immediate threat had diminished. Then maybe he would get behind us. Maybe his fear would seep away, and he would find joy in his life again. He had always been the more cautious parent. That was nothing new. But right now, he was in danger of crawling into his shell and never coming out—more mollusc than man.

Dad stood up shakily. "I'm sorry, Alisha. I know you didn't want to hear that. Please stay for dinner. Shall I set up the dining room?"

Mum had made all the hosting decisions.

"Sure, Dad. The dining room will be just fine. I'll come through in a minute, okay? I have to make a call." I dialled Detective Robert Jameson, Marina's current fling.

Robert was my contact at the Shadow Squad, a small team of

humdrums working off the books from the Metropolitan Police, whose remit was supernatural. He picked up on the third ring, sounding harried. "Alisha, it's not a good time."

"Robert, I need a favour."

"The city is in freefall. Can it wait?"

"Dude, I'm your only druid friend. And you're dating my best friend."

He sighed. "Be quick."

"The senate seems to think this morning's tremors were the work of the dark elves. Are they on the money?"

"I'm not a hundred per cent. Not yet. My sort of grunt work takes time. I've been out all morning, checking in with my Otherworld contacts, taking in the damage with my own eyes. If you want a definitive answer, you're not going to get one today."

"I just need your best guess, Robert."

"Okay, well then, I'd say the senate is talking bollocks. The dark elves no longer have the resources to pull off something like that. Their networks were shredded back in the eighties, and we've heard no whispers of plans. Nada. Tell the senate it's barking up the wrong tree. The last thing we need is them stirring up tensions in the Otherworld while the city is reeling from a natural disaster."

I breathed a sigh of relief. An earthquake was bad but not half as bad as an old enemy rearing its head. "So you think it was an earthquake?"

"I think it could be. The scientists are saying London's not as geologically stable as was once thought. What makes it worse is our overloaded infrastructure. Nine million people, diminishing green space, more and more high-rises, jammed roads and densely populated areas, even in the richest parts. It was pretty hairy this morning. Anything further up the Richter scale could cause loss of life."

"Yikes," I said. "Well, let's hope it was a one-off."

"I've got to go, Alisha. Give that rainbow-haired best friend of yours a kiss from me. I'll get over to her as soon as the clear-up's over today."

"Kiss her yourself. And Robert? Thanks." I hung up and turned around.

Ezra leaned against the door frame, his T-shirt drenched. He'd be right at home in a hot-stuff car wash or a Magic Mike show.

A shiver of pleasure ran through me. "How long have you been standing there?"

He crossed his arms with no self-awareness about how damn attractive he was. "Long enough to wonder why you're getting involved with this when you have the trial to focus on."

I cursed my traitorous body and adopted a cool tone. "Are you serious? After all you've been keeping from me?"

"What do you mean?" He stepped forward.

"When were you going to tell me that if I fail the trial, there are no second chances? That I'll be back in my humdrum life faster than I can blink?"

A shadow passed over his face. "Shit, you can't think that of me. I was protecting you. You've already had so much more pressure than a normal initiate. I didn't want to add to it by laying that on you. It was a tactic to keep your mind focused."

My restraint snapped. "Well, I'm not focused, Ezra. And do you know why that is?"

His voice was flat. "I'm sure you're going to tell me."

"I'm not focused because you've been prioritising pack business over me for weeks."

His eyes pleaded. "You have no idea about the rules of the pack. About what a fine line I walk. You don't know everything yet, but I really want to share it with you."

"Well then, tell me."

"I really want to, but we need to get through the next few weeks. Get through the trial. Then we can get to know each other slowly, I promise."

I clenched my fists. "I barely even know what the trial entails. How on earth are we supposed to prepare when the requirements are so nebulous? It's two weeks away, and I still have no idea what to expect. Without you being present, our chances of success are nil. And yet you have the cheek to tell me I'm distracted?"

His jaw clenched. "No, Alisha, I'm trying to tell you that the senate is a law unto itself. Whatever you find out about the tremors, you're not going to change the senate's path. You're not even a fully-fledged peculiar yet. And you're not doing yourself any favours by not falling in line."

I arched an eyebrow. "Do wolves always fall in line?"

A vein throbbed in his neck. "That's not fair."

"Isn't it? Maybe I just don't like turning a blind eye to the things that are wrong in the world. Maybe I'm focused on more than myself. You know what I think? I think you've run out of ideas, and you're staying away because then it's on me when I fail the trial."

He sighed. "It's okay to be scared about the trial, hellfire. Most peculiars take it far earlier."

"You're saying teenagers are more capable of this than me?"

"Stop putting words in my mouth. I'm saying it's different taking it at a young age with the rest of your contemporaries, compared to at your age."

I seethed. Had Orpheus been right after all? "You actually went there. Age has nothing to do with how well I'll perform. Yes, age has drawbacks. Maybe I'm not as fit as I was. Maybe my boobs are less bouncy. But dammit, my experience and intuition more than make up for it. I know my flaws, I know my strengths, and I know who to trust. Except maybe I made a mistake with you."

His voice was a low note of warning. "That's ridiculous."

"Is it? How do I even know I can trust you? How do I know you're not some shady geezer who will never put me first?"

He shrugged. "Because actions speak louder than words. I'll always be there when it counts."

"Yeah, well, I won't hold my breath." I gave him a look that might have sent a lesser man running for the woods.

"Careful, you might say something you can't take back. Look, I'm soaking wet. You're right that you need more of me in the run-up to the trial. Let's meet at the Wildwoods arena tomorrow evening. Sahil and Marina can come too. And the leopard, if I ask nicely."

I chewed my lip. "I'm teaching night class."

"In the morning then, with Sahil and Marina. We'll go through the trial and get some practice in." He paused. "Look, I'm sorry. I've been neglecting you. It's a wolf thing. My duty to serve the pack clashed with my desire to be with you. It won't happen again."

"I want to believe you. I really do." I sucked in a shaky breath. "If we fail, all this falls away. I saw past the veil, Ezra. I learned new things about myself. I can't lose that. I can't lose Echo. And I don't want to lose you."

He pulled me into his arms. "You can do this."

I went to him reluctantly and laid my head against his hard chest. "I don't want to go backwards. I can't give it up."

"You have to promise to leave the matter of the dark elves to the senate. Phinnaeous, Gunnolf and Lavinia won't rest until justice has been served. You can't stop a rocket in motion."

I stiffened and mumbled into his chest. "I can't promise that, Ezra."

"I thought you might say that."

8

———————

Sleep was not my friend that night. I fell from great heights, grasped by a teleporting werewolf, a cold vampire and an amber-eyed reptile. They fought over me like meat. The pieces of me scattered in the wind for vultures to find, so there was nothing left for Dad to bury.

In the morning, I pulled on some workout clothes and piled on the concealer before heading out the door with Dad's picture of Tielbu in my pocket—I was apparently an animator, after all—and Echo at my side.

A half-hour later, the early morning sun glinted through the trees as Ezra, Marina, Sahil, Echo and I trudged towards the Wildwoods arena. Marina and I let the men and leopard walk ahead. They had somehow found common ground in Dad's garden. Ezra and Sahil had bonded over the struggle to wash Echo, and Echo was delighted his tormentors had ended up as wet as him.

"Oh love, you look like shit. That sounds like a rotten fight," said Marina. Her rainbow hair was tied into space buns, and she wore workout gear bought from Baba Yaga's Gym: a bubblegum-coloured sports bra and leggings get-up that would have looked at home on

Lavinia's own clothing rail had she been as buxom. "Joshi's just scared, that's all. You're still his baby girl."

"The only thing I have in common with a baby girl is my need for naps."

"Last week, my biggest desire was to watch *Grace and Frankie* and stuff my face with ice cream. But I've had itchy feet since the tremors. The city is pulsing with worry. I can feel it. Robert said it was all hands on deck, and here I am, twiddling my thumbs. I should be doing something. You know, comforting those in need. Or at least comforting him. My newest push-up bra hasn't even had an outing yet. I'm gagging to give him an eyeful."

I grinned. "It'll be worth the wait, I'm sure. But there's no bloody way you're going out helping humdrums using your empath skills. What happens when people start asking questions about you? The Magical Constitution rules that out for a good reason."

"Just imagine, though, Alisha. I helped Elvira. I could help the sick ease their pain. Like a shot of morphine, you know? Only natural. There'd be no side effects."

I tucked my arm into hers. "Except on you. Your skills aren't ready for that yet. I know your instinct is to help, but I saw what toll your talents took on you when you comforted Faeza. Besides, at this rate, we'll be back to being our bog-standard selves before we can say abracadabra."

Marina gave a weighted sigh. "Quick, before we get started. Tell me how it's going with lover boy. I get you're angry at him and why, but are you still hot for him? You know, you've got eyebags from hell, but your dewy skin tells me another story."

"He hasn't paid me the slightest bit of attention in weeks."

"That's not what I heard. Echo told me he hasn't been able to keep his eyes or hands off you. He said you have Ezra by the short and curlies."

Echo bounded over, his hearing too acute for his own good. "This much is true. He rushed to Wildwoods when the tremors occurred to be her knight in shining armour, and the vampire had saved her first. The wolf is as hot for Alisha as I am for a harem of newly groomed and fluffed Persian cats."

His glamour made him a beacon for household cats. He had grown to like frolicking with the local feline population. He revelled in the attention. Although I most certainly did not like coming home to sheets soiled by excessive rubbing and rolling that he got up to with his little friends.

I folded my arms. "For the millionth time, will my closest friends realise I don't need saving?"

Marina waggled her eyebrows. "There is a world of difference between being strong-armed by a man and being able to rely on him. I wouldn't be so quick to complain if I were you, my love. It might have gone tits up with Alex, but Ezra's cut from a different cloth. Speaking of which, looks like it's time to roll up our sleeves."

We scurried to catch up with Ezra, handsome in blue jeans and a vest.

Ezra led us to a stone table with cube seats at the edge of the arena. He had his work cut out with the three of us, and the clock was ticking. "What's with the glum faces? This could be the day you unlock your potential. Half of being a peculiar is about belief. That's what we're going to work on. Take a seat."

"What I want to know is why every other test I've taken in my life has a list of content I'm required to know." I chose a cube and crossed my arms.

Marina nodded. "Preach, sister."

"Because every trial is different," Echo purred. "It resembles neither a driving test nor a school exam. It's not even like a lawyer taking the bar or an athlete at the Olympics."

"Well, that's about as helpful as a chocolate teapot," I said.

"What made you think the trial should be easy?" Echo prowled up and down. "It is because it is difficult that it is worthwhile. But we are here to make sure you are ready. I am here to be the cat to Ezra's dog. The head to his tail. The Diana to his Supremes."

Sahil grinned. "Was that supposed to be a pep talk?"

"I don't suppose you brought a sedative for the cat, Marina?"

She grinned. "Not this time, but I'll be sure to remember next time."

Echo sat and curled his tail around his body. "No need to be tetchy. I was just trying to lighten the atmosphere."

Ezra slid onto a seat around the stone table. "The magical trial isn't based on humdrum boundaries. The Otherworld has no boundaries. Therefore, the test is naturally more ambiguous. Magical trials test courage, quick thinking, creativity and loyalty. The purpose of the trial is for the senate to ascertain your chances of surviving or destabilising the Otherworld. Rayna will devise one she feels adequately tests the newest initiates. The rest is up to us."

Us. The word reverberated in my head, and I fell in love with him just a little bit.

Marina bit her lip. "Okay then, hotshot, how do the foxes survive without being sanctioned by the senate? Why do they get to keep their magic?"

Echo growled. "Because once you walk through the doors of Wildwoods into the bosom of the magical world, once you've taken the blood bond with the Magical Constitution and broken bread with the senate, only one of two paths are available to you. Why do you think I didn't want you following the wolf to Wildwoods? The foxes are cunning. They knew the reach of Wildwoods, and they knew to avoid it. You jumped in headfirst without even understanding the ground rules. And if you fail, the curtain falls. Just like that. This is the way it has always been. Do you understand now what is at stake?"

My pulse raced. "Is that true, Ezra?"

"It's always been true that there are rules for belonging to organisations and penalties for disappointing them. It's also true that being an outsider is not easy. You know that from your work at night class. I was doing my job the night I first brought you to Wildwoods. I'm trying to do it now."

"Well, this is awkward," said Sahil.

Ezra rubbed the back of his neck. His biceps flexed as he did, and I tried not to notice. "It's not the only thing that's awkward. Let's lay it all out on the table. Why do you want to live your life as a peculiar? You first, Sahil. You have the longest way to go here."

"This feels less like a training arena and more like a psychologist's office," Echo purred.

"No freaking way," said Sahil. "I'm a forty-two-year-old man. This is all blooming weird. I'm practically constipated with fear. Let the others go first."

I swallowed down my anger. "It's okay. I'll go first. I want to be a peculiar because, for the first time in my life, I understand who I am, and I don't feel trapped or that a part of me is missing. And when I summon the wind, I feel free."

Ezra nodded. "How about you, Marina?"

She looked down at her hands with her gothic-black nail varnish. "I want to help. My hands are magic. I can sense how people feel. It's the key to unlocking everything. I can't lose that."

"Now, your turn, Sahil. Go on. There is no shame in the arena," said Ezra. "We are all learning, but we can only learn if we are honest with ourselves."

"I'm here for Alisha."

Ezra shook his head. "No, that's not it. Shall we get a helping hand? Marina, will you do the honours?"

Marina took Sahil's hand. "He's lying."

Sahil snatched his hand back.

"Why are you here, Sahil?" said Ezra.

Sahil's brow furrowed. "If you have to know, I'm here because I don't want Alisha to have all the glory. She was always the golden girl. Always sunny. Always willing to help others. Then she goes and makes friends with a goddess and solves the mystery of Mum's death. She even got the better of the sun god. I know I should be grateful, but it makes me sick."

"You make it sound like I did that all alone. It was blind luck." I frowned. "What makes you sick?"

Sahil shrugged. "The thought that you get all the power. I want a piece of that pie."

Marina winced. "I guess being the only child isn't that bad. At least you're telling the truth now."

"This is the reason I will always prefer Verma women," said Echo. "The men are pansies or have no honour."

"Do you feel lighter now, Sahil?" said Ezra.

"A bit. Still constipated. But lighter."

"So, now we all know why we're here—finding our true selves. Helping others. Power. I've worked with worse." His grey eyes met mine. "The question is, do you want to work with me?"

I lifted my chin. "I don't see what choice we have."

His eyes dropped to my lips. "Then let's begin. We'll get you over the line. Anything else will have to wait."

Echo edged forward. "The trials always take place away from Wildwoods. This is for a good reason. Your magic will be tested in the real world, not here, where the school adapts to your every need. Out there, there are no safety nets."

"I can tell you that your trial will take place in the London Underground after the tube lines have closed."

I breathed a sigh of relief. I felt at home on the tube. I knew the London Underground as well as the lines on my palm. It didn't seem daunting to be tested down there. "Will there be an audience?"

Ezra nodded. "The Prime Sorcerer will send orbs to follow you, which will show your progress to the senate and school community back at Wildwoods. A small staff from the infirmary will be present at the site of the trial in case any medical assistance is required."

"How long will it last?" asked Marina.

"As long as is required to determine the outcome," said Ezra.

"You will have to prove you can get by alone and as a team—and without breaking the Magical Constitution. Do you remember the laws?" said Echo.

Marina waved her hand in the air like the class swot. "Ask me!"

Echo inclined his head. "Go ahead, Marina Ambrose. Speak slowly and clearly. We will only go over this ground once."

Marina turned her blue eyes to the sky like she was taking an oath. "1. Never meddle in the affairs of the gods. 2. All peculiars and magical artefacts must register with the Sorcerer's Senate within three lunar cycles. 3. A sentient peculiar who uses magic to harm a humdrum will have their magic drained ad infinitum. 4. Peculiars must hide the existence of the Otherworld from humdrums and re-establish secrecy upon accidental arousal of suspicion. 5. It is forbidden to interfere with the compos mentis of another peculiar. 6. The delicate power balance between co-existing peculiar communities must be protected. 7. New users of magic must be supervised until they pass the trial. 8. Black magic and necromancy are forbidden."

Sahil's eyes bulged with incredulity. "That necromancy thing is wild."

"Can anyone tell me which law, in particular, is going to be the hardest to follow on the night of your trial?" said Ezra.

I gave a curt nod. "Number 4. The Founder's Law. Peculiars must hide the existence of the Otherworld from humdrums and re-establish secrecy upon accidental arousal of suspicion."

"Exactly. With the trial taking place out in the open, away from Wildwoods, this is the biggest pitfall. It is this law that leads to the biggest proportion of initiates failing. If our existence becomes common knowledge, the whole survival of the Otherworld is compromised. Secrecy is the one thing all magical races agree on. Which means when it comes to a vote, if you break that rule, each and every senate member will vote against you."

"Point taken. We'll guard our secrecy," said Marina.

"Then it's time for the next lesson. Teamwork." The copper flecks in Ezra's eyes glinted. He pointed to the triangular frame that pierced the clouds. "Sahil, I'd like you to climb that."

Sahil squinted at the dizzyingly high structure. "Then what?"

Marina and I exchanged glances. We knew what was coming next.

A glint in Ezra's eyes. "Then you jump."

"You're out of your mind. Why would I do that?"

Echo toothy grin showed his mirth. "Joshi's style as a mentor was to wrap you in cotton wool, and it brought nothing. Our way is much better. We fling you off a building to rule out flight, instant armour and reactive adaption."

Sahil jerked his head in fright. "Over my dead body."

"I told you he was a pansy," purred Echo.

"Don't worry, Sahil. The arena will catch you," I said. He might be a lousy brother, but he was *my* brother. "You can do it."

Ezra cleared his throat. "Actually, Alisha, this time, it will be your job to catch him. Let's stretch those wind powers of yours. See how you do under duress."

I gulped.

"And Marina, you're going up to see if you can use your magic to soothe Sahil's fears. I have no doubt you can. Hell, you managed to assuage a dying woman's fears." He lit a roll-up cigarette and took a drag like this was a walk in the park and not life and death. "The test for you is to keep your own emotions in check. Being an effective peculiar is all about balance. As a werewolf, I balance my duty with my desires. My anger with my passion. You have to learn to balance negative emotions with positive ones. Focus on good memories to anchor you. A past success. A loved pet. A joyful experience. Think of it less as a gushing river and more as a canal lock. You are not at the mercy of the tides. You control the levels."

Marina pressed her palms to her cheeks. "I got it. A canal lock." She took a deep breath and stood up. "I'm ready."

"I'm bloody not." Sahil dragged his feet in the sand of the arena as we tugged him up.

Glee bubbled up inside me. I relished the chance of unleashing my power on Sahil. All the times he'd wrestled me to the ground as a child. I planned to bring him to the ground like a ricocheting rollercoaster. "You want power? This is your chance, big bro. I'll be waiting at the bottom. I won't let you fall."

He followed us with a pinched expression, fingernails digging into his palms. "If I don't make it, I don't want this getting out. You hear me?"

Marina put an arm around him, her forehead knotted in concentration. "It's going to be okay. I'm here, aren't I?"

He relaxed enough to climb up the structure alongside her, pausing every few minutes to look down, his eyes wide.

Ezra and Echo joined me in the arena. From the ground, I could make out Marina murmuring in Sahil's ear. Around us, the trees rustled, and the birds chirped. Every now and then, the cable car juddered to life, taking pupils to Wildwoods.

Just when I thought Sahil was going to chicken out, he jumped.

Falling like a brick, faster than my eyes could track. Screaming, high-pitched like a woman, as if he'd shed his coat of manliness.

Echo's roar filled the arena.

"Now, Alisha," said Ezra with urgency.

My palms tingled. I held them towards my brother, and the breeze became something I could mould and direct. I focussed, narrowing my gaze, so I saw only him, ready to cocoon him.

Just a bit closer.

Then poof.

His clothes tumbled through the air and landed strewn across the arena. His Calvin Klein boxers dropped inches from my feet.

The bottom dropped out of my stomach as though I was the one who was falling.

"The Verma boy has revealed his true self," said Echo.

My tall, handsome brother, with his designer stubble and Saville Row clothes, had transformed.

In his place was a feathery creature common in London.

A grey breast, pink clawed toes, orange beak and green-tinged head with fiery eyes.

Echo rolled around on the floor, cackling. "Karma is good. He wanted power, and the universe made him a pigeon."

Sahil swooped closer. When he came to a standstill at our feet, he stood more upright than a pigeon, as if he were half man, half bird, albeit only as big as a Wellington boot. His chest was more muscly than a pigeon's, his feathers ruffled, not smooth.

He looked as mad as hell, and when he opened his mouth, he had teeth. "I don't feel right. Will someone tell me what's going on?"

I recoiled in horror. "Er, Echo, I don't think he's a pigeon."

Marina ran towards us, heavily panting in her haste. "Where's Sahil? What did I miss?"

"He's right here, Marina," Ezra scratched his jaw. "That's progress for you. Always a surprise."

I stared at my brother. "But what is he?"

Ezra knelt in the sand to Sahil's level. "I'm not a hundred per cent sure, but I think he's a werepigeon."

Sahil made a mournful, throaty coo and passed out.

9

————————

"It's not that bad, Sahil," I said. "Remember when you were little, and you wanted to fly?"

It had taken him a while to come around, but smelling salts from the infirmary had helped. Only that had also brought a stampede of pupils from Wildwoods into the arena to gawk at him. They pooled around us like Sahil was a circus curiosity and not a peculiar in need of some privacy at an unsettling time. It only took one to break into giggles, and the domino effect rippled through the rest, a belly-clutching hilarity at his weird muscly bird body, his pointy teeth, his cooing and strutting.

My brother usually loved attention, but their laughter struck a nerve. He stamped his pigeon toes. "Will you tell this lot to piss off?"

The Prime Sorcerer sighed and turned to the pupils gawking with a swish of his gown. "Ignore his bad language, children, and come along. Perhaps Mr Verma can come and speak to us about his transformation once he has got to grips with this new side of him."

"Not bloody likely." Sahil ran at the children with flapping wings.

"I must get Orpheus to take a look at your genealogy again. This is most unusual." Phinnaeous Shine gave me a stern look. "You know, I think back to Rajika Verma, and I wonder, where it all went wrong?

She had such vitality and strength. To think, her descendants may be too lacking in focus to even pass the magical trial. Is it true you have been unable to animate the dragon yet? You do realise the resources that have been invested in you and your merry little crew?"

I gulped. The man made me feel five years old, not forty.

Gaia's voice chided me in my head. "You didn't think that wind was all you could do?"

Ezra's hackles rose. "You have my word she will pass the trial, Prime Sorcerer."

"I'll hold you to that, Mr Neuhoff. I seem to remember you spoke up for Ms Verma after her last disaster. I hope I wasn't wrong to give her a second chance. Talent is not everything. It's character that is the real game changer." He glared at me, nostrils flaring. "You have neither your grandmother's talents, druid, nor her beauty, but you can make something of yourself yet. Maybe try a little more sleep, a little less booze and a whole heap more moisturiser. Hers was honey-scented. Her yoga regimen gave her great flexibility and focus and kept the love handles at bay. Perhaps you should try taking a leaf out of her book." Phinnaeous Shine stormed off.

I stared after him. "I should give him a piece of my mind once I've planned a stinging retort."

Marina stared after him. "Mansplain much? What a wanker." She hugged me. "Don't worry; we'll get there."

"Ignore him, hellfire. He's got a lot on his plate. The senate has been war-gaming through the night. Gunnolf didn't get back to the farmhouse until the early hours."

"Right, I'm off, you two," said Marina. "Echo's taking me to work my magic on some creatures in the bestiary to practice some of Ezra's balancing techniques. Unless you want some help with him?" She grimaced at Sahil, who was pecking the sand of the arena like he wanted to tunnel out of Wildwoods. "I don't think he realises he has wings."

Sahil flapped in our direction. "I heard that. You can laugh all you like. You still have your body. I can't leave looking like a bloody werepigeon. If they catch me on Trafalgar Square, they'll take one look and think I have rabies."

"There is no rabies in the United Kingdom." Marina edged away.

"Fat lot of good you were," said Sahil. "This bloody well wouldn't have happened if I hadn't listened to you."

"Go, Marina," I said. "It's not her fault. And I think you are pretty powerful. Think about it. Not only can you fly, but pigeons have awesome camouflage. This city is so grey. Think of all the concrete and rain, not to mention the other pigeons. You blend right in."

"I don't want to blend in. I want to stand out. This isn't what I imagined. I'm a laughingstock." Sahil plopped down in the sand, rocking his green-grey head back and forth like a lunatic. Or a bird.

Ezra gave him a hard look and sat down in the sand next to him. "Sahil, I'm a *were*-something."

Sahil tilted his head and pinned one fiery eye on him. "A werewolf. That's a massive difference."

"Not how I see it. The *were*- prefix is a corruption of the Latin *vir*, which means man. It means virility and strength. Like me, you'll be strongest at the full moon. You will learn to shift between man and bird. You have teeth and claws that can do extensive damage. You can soar. That's more than I can do."

"Also, pigeons can produce loads of poo, so that's your secret weapon," I said. "You can destroy an entire area in seconds if you put your bowels to it."

"Not helping, Alisha," Sahil cooed.

"You don't even need your posh flat anymore. You can make as many nests as you want to."

"Jesus," said Sahil. His werepigeon voice was more nasally than his human one, possibly because all his components had to fit into a smaller form. Although a pigeon's brain was much smaller than a human one, so there might have been some shrinkage. I decided it was best not to bring that up.

I petted his head. "I'm proud of you."

He pecked my foot. "Too soon, Alisha. And stop pretending you're not enjoying this."

"Okay, Tweetie. Sorry, I meant sweetie."

"Now, can someone find my clothes and teach me how to shift into human form? Being this small is giving me an inferiority complex and making me feel quite murderous."

I backed away. "Ezra, teach the man what he wants. Or failing that, does Wildwoods have a therapist?"

Ezra grinned. "All part of being in the were-family. I've got a better idea. Ready to whip up a breeze, Alisha? Let's watch him soar."

The morning became afternoon, and with the arena being used by Lavinia to drill Wildwoods students in defence skills should the dark elves attack, Ezra and I retreated to the shade of a sycamore tree.

I lay on my back, looking up at a bank of cumulus clouds. "Thank goodness Sahil went home. What an exhausting morning. I can't believe that a few hours with you unlocked his magic. I'm just not sure how Dad will feel about it."

Ezra cocked an eyebrow. "So you're done doubting me then?"

"You put us first for a morning. You're just getting started."

A laugh rumbled through him. "You're sexy when you speak your mind."

"I am?" I said. Alex had hated me pressing a different point than him. It was always the start of an argument.

"I love a woman who can challenge me." He held up a hand. "But I wasn't the key to Sahil's breakthrough. It was a team effort. Sibling rivalry is a potent thing, and Marina's empath skills played a role too. Rayna knew what she was doing when she suggested group sessions for us. She's not Minister for Education and Wildwoods Headmistress for nothing."

I squirmed. "It's weird, though, isn't it? Him being a werepigeon?"

Ezra snorted. "I can't say I've met many. They don't fly around in a flock. We'll have to keep an eye on him. It's not like he has a pack. He's going to be lonely."

"I can pretty much guarantee he's in the pub right now, drinking away his sorrows."

"Yeah, well, right now, we have something else to worry about. Did you bring what I asked you to?"

I nodded. Out came Death's sword, Dad's drawing of Tielbu the dragon and a leaf from the park.

"That sword is a thing of beauty." He lifted Transcender and turned it over in his hands in awe.

"And yet when I hold it," I said, "I hear voices that overcome me. It happened when I tried to protect Flinar. I dropped it like a hot stone, and only then did the voices still. Maybe it's more of a burden than a benefit."

He shook his head. "I don't believe that for a second. Gaia is a friend to you. If she gave you this, it is with good reason. Maybe what you need is to relax and not overthink. It doesn't matter that your grandmother was Rajika Verma. It doesn't matter that she was a huge figure in the Otherworld. Right now, all that matters is that you are on your own path. As imperfect as you feel you are, your journey is not yet over. Your path is just beginning. So take a deep breath, lie back and close your eyes."

I sank back against the ground, feeling every twig in my back, aware of the rise and fall of his breath and mine. The soil was cool against my back, and my eyelids fluttered as the light changed above me, and the nebulous pink was shadowed by Ezra coming closer. I stiffened as he trailed the leaf over the bridge of my nose and down one cheek, across the curve of my chin and onto the other cheek.

"What are you doing?" I asked.

"Relaxing you."

"You didn't try this with Sahil."

"Different strokes for different folks."

"I'm starting to get that." I held onto his hand and opened my eyes. "I'm still angry at you."

"I'm trying to make it up to you." He lay down next to me and kissed me, soft and sweetly, as if in apology, before nibbling my bottom lip and deepening the kiss until I was hot and needed him more than I had ever needed my ex-husband.

In fact, it took me a minute to remember Alex's name.

Ezra pulled away and grinned. "So, are you relaxed?"

I was pretty sure I saw stars, and we weren't even in Paris this time.

"Pick up your dad's drawing."

"Huh?"

"Pick it up." He uncurled my hand from his shirt and pushed the drawing of Tielbu into my hand. "You have no need to be scared. You are on your own path. And it's just me and you here. No Joshi, no Sahil, no Gaia. Reach into the picture and find Tielbu there. Not an inanimate dragon but the real, breathing, fiery one you know from your stories. Who won't hurt you, who is bonded to you and is just waiting for you to awaken him."

I pressed my lips together and felt the calm of the leaf across my skin, the comfort of being in Ezra's arms and the quiet of the woods. I touched the page and trailed my fingers over the strokes of Dad's paintbrush. Tielbu was turquoise blue like he'd risen from the Pacific Ocean, not Dad's imagination. I filled my lungs with the smog-free Wildwoods air and imagined Tielbu's own lungs inflating, the beating of his colossal wings, the life in his amber eyes, the dry iridescent scales of his skin.

The page deepened, and I was no longer sure what was in my head and what was under my fingers. Heat travelled into my body from Tielbu's fiery breath, and his veins throbbed beneath my fingertips as if he and I were one.

I reached into the page.

"Well," said Lavinia's plummy voice. "About time you worked on that, Alisha."

I dropped the page as if I'd been scalded and opened my eyes.

Ezra was on his feet. "Now's not a good time, auntie. We were in the middle of something."

"I could see that," said Lavinia. "I thought I could offer some words of encouragement. Impress upon you just how important this is."

"How important what is?" I asked. Dejection washed over me. I'd been so close.

"My dear girl." Lavinia strode over to press her powdered cheek against mine before kissing her nephew.

I'd not seen her at close hand since our battle with the sun god. The spell to stop him had aged her. She'd been far too busy rebuilding Wildwoods after the tremors to find me, and I had avoided her like the plague after my run-in with the rats. After all, they'd said she had suspicions about whether I was friend or foe. Far better to leave sleeping dogs lie.

"You don't look yourself, Aunt Lavinia," said Ezra. "You should take it easy."

She waved a dismissive hand. "Hogwash, Ezra. I am Minister for Defence, after all, and we are under threat." She primped her helmet of silver curls and sighed. "Although, I suppose you could say the spell against the sun god took its toll. Not only did we lose poor Elvira, but my skin lost at least a decade's elasticity. It really is a shame. Especially since that vial of your blood didn't bring us closer to the secret of your teleporting." Her eyes narrowed as she searched our faces. "Some might say we were hoodwinked." Her voice brightened. "Still, we live and learn. And there is another battle on our plates right now. We're going to crush those brutish dark elves once and for all. How dare they trample sacred ground?"

"Auntie, about that. Aren't you barking up the wrong tree?" Ezra said.

She cackled. "I'm not a wolf, Ezra. I have known this was coming for a long time. The coven is ready. Wildwoods is ready." She swung round to me. "But there is something that would make it easier."

I darted a look at Ezra. "What do you need, Lavinia?"

"You know how much I'm a fan of efficient transport. Especially after the terrible disappointment of transferring the teleporting skills to the coven. Efficient transport has the capacity to lighten the load during wartime. You can't underestimate its impact. Particularly when the transport has military potential." She bent down to pick up the drawing of Tielbu.

I clenched my fists and bit down hard on my lip to stop myself from taking what was mine.

Lavinia's shrewd, hard eyes assessed me. "I want to trust you, but something just doesn't sit right. It's an easy fix, though. Raise the dragon, Alisha. We could do with a dragon in the fight against the elves. The war would be over before it had even begun. Just think how pleased the senate would be. How pleased I would be."

My skin grew clammy, but I held her gaze and turned the corners of my lips into a tight smile. "I'm afraid, Minister, that I have failed at this task every time I've attempted it. But if I succeed, you'll be the first to know."

She pushed her shoulders back. "Well, that's all I ask. We must spend some time in the reading nook again at some point. Toodaloo, lovebirds."

She shimmied away.

My breath came in rasps, my gaze unfocused.

In an instant, Ezra was at my side, his hand on the small of my back. "Breathe, Alisha."

Lavinia turned around. "It just occurred to me. Why don't the two of you join us for dinner at the coven flat? All the movers and shakers will be there. In fact, you should all come. Bring your dad and the empath. Heavens, bring the werepigeon. Not the leopard, however. The rats wouldn't like it. It'll be such a giggle. Friday night, 8 p.m. Don't forget. And make sure you dress the part. The ladies like to put on some sequins and heels every now and then."

I waited for her to leave, then covered my face. "What are we going to do?"

Ezra tipped my chin up with a gentle hand. "We take this one step at a time. What Lavinia says and what the senate decrees are two entirely different things."

"Maybe I should leave Tielbu on the page. Maybe this is the reason I'm struggling to bring him to life. Like the universe is telling me not to put a weapon in the senate's hands."

He gave a firm shake of his head. "It's the wrong decision to give up a major win just because the consequences are difficult."

I chewed my lip. All my biggest turning points had required blind courage: my university degree, my freedom after the divorce, and my right to know this side of me.

"You were on the verge of a breakthrough, Alisha. The colour on the page began to oscillate just before my aunt arrived. I've never seen anything so spectacular. You can't give that up."

He was right. I had felt Tielbu taking shape beneath my fingers. My senses tingled with the knowledge. The thought of never meeting him made me despair, but I couldn't let him fall into Lavinia's hands.

I took a deep breath. "Putting Tielbu in a drawer doesn't mean I can't animate another creature. I can ask Dad for another drawing."

Ezra's face tightened. "That would be a mistake. I've been thinking for a while. You failed at your attempts to animate in your father's attic, right?"

"Don't remind me."

"That's just it. When Joshi gave you the picture of Tielbu in the infirmary, he inadvertently gave you your best chance of success. Your connection with Tielbu is why you were almost there. We only have ten days until the trial, Alisha. This is your best shot. Animate Tielbu, and it will unlock everything else."

"There has to be another way." I put space between us, thinking hard, staring through a clearing in the tree canopies towards the clouds. "I've got it. Maybe I can animate him where Lavinia won't know."

"That's brilliant." A slow smile spread across his face. "It couldn't be here. Or even in another city. Her rats and their network of snitches are too good. She always finds out eventually. No, it can't be here. There is only one place that is hidden from Lavinia."

"Where, Ezra? I would say the sewers. No CCTV and no self-respecting humdrum would hang out down there. Only that would be a natural habitat for the rats. How about the royal palaces? Security has to be pretty tight in there. Or maybe the end of the Northern Line? That's pretty much No Man's Land."

His grey eyes glinted. "The place we need keeps itself hidden within the seams of the world. Even Lavinia's moles can't find their way there. It'll buy you some space to bond with the dragon without my aunt staking a claim. You're going to animate Tielbu in the Celestial Library, and she will never find out."

10

———————

The day of Mum's will reading arrived. So much had changed since her death. She had known the minutiae of my life from the moment of my birth: my tottering first steps, my favourite books, the women I admired, and the lay-back-and-think-of-England state of my marital sex life. It seemed cruel that she didn't get to be there for the next stage of our lives.

Dad, Sahil, Echo and I waited for the solicitor in my parent's mahogany dining room. I'd hoped to find Dad in a better state, perhaps painting, but there were no tell-tale stains on his person. No paint splotches to show that he was getting back to his happy place. Only a stale house in need of airing, dirty dishes piling in the sink and dirty laundry spilling out of the utility room.

"I'm not ready to hear Rosalie's final wishes." Dad sniffed. "She doesn't even know you're a werepigeon, Sahil. She'd be so proud."

Sahil looked up in surprise. "She would?"

Dad grimaced. "Maybe not, but she'd definitely find it amusing, and her scientific brain would be in love. It's rather impressive that Ezra managed to unlock your peculiar nature so quickly. We got nowhere together. It's enough to make a man feel useless."

"Yeah, well, I'm glad you didn't witness it," said Sahil, downcast.

"It wasn't pretty. There were all these kids pointing at me, and my clothes went AWOL."

Ezra had managed to teach him to shift back into his human form, but there was still something feathery about him in the fall of his hair. It had always sat smoothly against his head, but now he had more of a ruffled look. It suited him and made him look less uptight.

"Take a page out of Eric Idle's songbook. 'Always Look on the Bright Side of Life'," said Echo.

Ruffling Sahil's feathers was no way to be supportive. I shot Echo a look of warning and turned to Dad. "Mum must have told you what's in the will?"

Dad shook his head. "I thought I knew, but the solicitor said Rosalie went to see him the week before she died."

"Well," I said. "We'll just have to face it together. Like we do everything else."

"I don't know. I feel quite alone in this pigeon saga," said Sahil.

"I can count the number of leopards in this city on one paw. You are certainly not alone amongst pigeons in London, Sahil Verma," purred Echo. "As Michael Jackson would say, 'You Are Not Alone'."

"Mock me all you want," said Sahil. "Mum is gone, and I am a werepigeon, and life couldn't be any worse."

"Echo, stop it," I said. "Otherwise, I'll cut back on your freezer goodies. The butcher's bill this week was astronomical."

The doorbell rang.

"Saved by the bell." Dad heaved himself up to get the door. "You kids and your fighting. Some things never change."

We listened as Dad greeted the solicitor and ushered him past Mum's shrine into the dining room.

"My condolences once again," said the solicitor as they entered the room. He was a bald man in his fifties with a tummy that bulged over his suit trousers.

"Thank you, Mr Costello. Please take a seat," said Dad. "This is Sahil, my son, and Alisha, my daughter."

"I'm sorry for your loss. What a beautiful Bengal cat." The solicitor bowed as deeply as a Japanese businessman.

"He bowed to me, did you see?" Echo purred.

"Bengals are so rare." Mr Costello sat down. "I had no idea how vocal they are."

"You don't know the half of it." I stared at his briefcase, a glossy red leather decorated with diamanté studs.

Mr Costello snapped it open and pulled out some papers. "Oh, the sparkles were my granddaughter's doing. In fact, she insists I wear sparkly underwear too. I'd do anything for her. Being in my line of work, you realise how short life is."

Sahil cocked his head in a distinctly bird-like matter.

I hoped Ezra had taught him some self-control, or this would get messy. "Shall we get started?"

Mr Costello put on his glasses and picked up a single-sided page. "As executor of the will, I'll now read Rosalie Verma's Letter of Wishes and disclose the beneficiaries of her estate. All three beneficiaries of the will are here and present."

"I take it he doesn't mean me," said Echo. "I will presently retreat to the other side of the house to croon Celine Dion's 'All By Myself'."

Mr Costello cleared his throat. "Let us begin.

"I, Rosalie Verma, hereby appoint Mr Bernard Costello of Davidson, Costello & Son the executor of my estate. In the event of my death, this Letter of Wishes should be shared with the beneficiaries of my estate. My dear family, if my death comes to pass, know that I would not have spent my life any other way. Joshi, our life together was so much more than I could have envisaged that day you held a rose between your teeth on the university grounds and went down on one knee to ask me to be your wife. Before I met you, I had science, but I did not have love. And while science had been a driving force in my life, it is love which has truly changed me."

Mr Costello paused to wipe a tear from his eye.

"Your wife was a poet, Mr Verma. And a true beauty with her raven hair and full hips," he said. "I like to think if I'd met her as a young man before I lost my hair, I might have stood a chance."

"Steady on." Sahil flapped his arms. "That's my mother you're talking about."

"No need to worry," said Mr Costello. "She can't very well change her mind now, can she?"

Dad smiled weakly. "Rosalie liked gallows humour. How wonderful to hear her voice though she is gone."

"Then you'll love our latest innovation, Mr Verma. From next year, the soon-to-be-deceased will read their own Letter of Wishes in a pre-recording expertly made at our firm," said Mr Costello.

Dad recoiled. "Well, I am rather hoping not to lose any more family members."

"Where did Mum find your services again?" said Sahil.

Mr Costello lacked any self-awareness. "On page three of the Google search, I believe. She worked her way down when she required a solicitor immediately, and we were happy to help."

He pushed the plastic wallet across the table and snapped his briefcase shut.

I leaned forward. "Mr Costello, would you mind continuing to read the letter?"

"How silly of me. Of course.

"To mon amour, Joshi Verma, I bequeath my share of our family home on Tooting Bec Common, where we raised our family. Please never lose your love of painting, and when the time is right, find a new love of your own. Though I am no longer by your side, I trust you will use all your skills to help our children and never clip their wings, however painful you may find it. For what is life if we cannot soar?

"To my eldest child Sahil Verma, who has built such an extensive property portfolio. I am proud of you. Your interests lie in the tangible world, not the ephemeral. You chiselled your way forward in the world, but remember, your heart is equally important. To you, I bequeath my car and a cutting from my favourite rose bush to show you how far you have come and how far you can still go.

"To my youngest child Alisha, the dreamer, you are capable of so much more than you know. I'm sorry for all the times we stood in your way. I'm sorry for holding you back from what is rightfully yours. To you, I bequeath my books, the rights to my scientific research and a choker with an amber stone. You will find it between the seams of the world.

"Whatever sum remains in my accounts following the settling of my funeral expenses and related costs should be divided between STEMNET and Benoit's Patisserie in Kensington.

"In closing, I entreat you. Tend to each other faithfully so that you may find the answers that came to me too late in life.

"Your loving Rosalie.

"That concludes the letter," said Mr Costello. "Phew, that was heavy. I mean, searching Ancestry.com is one thing, but she went a little far with 'between the seams of the worlds', didn't she? Still, never fear. At Davidson, Costello & Son, we stand ready to hold your hand." He reached out a chunky fist across the table and wiggled his fingers.

We ignored him.

"In this folder, you'll find copies of Rosalie's testament and Letter of Wishes. We'll see to administering the estate, and you'll hear from us in due course." He shook each of our hands. "I wish you well and bid you adieu."

Dad rose to shake Mr Costello's hand.

"I will see this imbecile to the door," said Echo.

Mr Costello beamed. "The cat is miaowing at me to follow him. How delightful."

The door clicked shut behind him.

Sahil thumped the table. "She left money to a bakery instead of us?"

"We shouldn't think badly of her. She did like her cake," said Dad. "What I heard in that letter was love for us all."

"She left me the banger she died in, and a cutting of a rose bush. How is that love?" Sahil's flapping had become more and more erratic.

I shrugged. "The car was touched by a goddess."

Dad slumped and rubbed his hand over his face. "How could she ask me to love again? It just doesn't bear thinking about. Maybe she wasn't in her right mind. Take the mention of a choker with an amber stone. I've been doing mental gymnastics thinking about it. I never saw her wear anything like that."

The penny fell, but he wouldn't like it. "What stood out to me is the phrase 'between the seams of the world.' Ezra said that when referring to the Celestial Library. We know she'd been there, Dad. Remember? She had a book from there called *The Rose of Jericho*. I have to go there. I have to see what it is all about. I have to try and animate Tielbu there. It all leads there, don't you see? I've been too stupid to see it."

Dad stood up. "Did you not hear me last time, Alisha? I forbid it."

"You heard Mum's words. She said explicitly that you shouldn't stand in my way. For heaven's sake. I'm a grown woman."

The dishes in the sideboard began to shake, but he didn't notice.

"I don't care what it says in your mother's will. She's not here. I want you to grow, to find out more about your new identity, but it's too much of a risk going to the Celestial Library. Your grandmother died there. I can't lose you too. Will you just get that into your head?" He stopped, his arms spread wide for balance, his legs akimbo, like a drunk on the deck of a rocky cruise ship.

The house shook. Not just a little, but enough to make my heartbeat race.

"Oh my god," I said, "is that…"

A vase on the sideboard shattered on the floor.

We looked at each other in horror.

The house juddered to its very foundations, a rippling of brick, mortar and glass. A treasured picture of the Algarve fell off the wall, its frame shattering. The sound of smashing dishes came from the kitchen. A bookshelf full of encyclopaedias tipped forward, narrowly missing Sahil.

Dad shouted, "Get under the table. Now!"

He ran for the door, adrenalin making him quicker than his years.

I reached out to him. "Where are you going? Wait until the tremors stop. Echo will be fine. He's probably up a tree."

"My paintings." Dad charged out of the door past the rocking chandelier. "The portrait of your mother!"

Sahil cowered under the table. "Has he lost his marbles?"

I cursed long and hard enough to make my ancestors turn in their graves. "He's going to get hurt."

The sound of cracking lightbulbs and then popping filled my ears.

"Not if I can help it," said a nasal voice. A whirr of grey feathers flew past.

My brother's clothes lay in a heap on the floor. His trajectory was ragged, as if he didn't quite know how to fly in a straight line yet. He narrowly missed being sliced by the door.

"Whatever next?" I tore after him, a rush of blood in my ears.

The house rocked like a ship. Picture frames and books became projectiles. Screams in my ears from the street outside. The sound of falling objects became indiscernible. I was aware only of the hammering of my heart in my chest as time slowed.

I reached the studio after my dad and brother, and as I turned the corner, there Dad was, surrounded by canvases knocked from their easels.

He lay there, oh so quiet, beneath a fallen shelf heavy with art books.

His eyes were closed, and Sahil flapped on his chest.

My brother's green-tinged pigeon head moved side to side in panic. "Get help," he said. "Get help now."

11

———————

I kept vigil at Dad's side while he waited his turn to be seen in a packed Accident & Emergency Department at St. George's Hospital. Three hours later, I crept out into the night under twinkling stars. Sirens blared across the city. A prayer group chanted in the middle of the car park. A young mother pleaded with her two young children to hurry up before they missed visiting hours.

A sadness settled on me. I dug out my phone and called Marina.

Her frantic voice came down the line. "How is Joshi?"

She'd known I was in pain across the miles. She'd texted me when the ambulance came for Dad. I wasn't sure if it was Marina being an empath or just Marina being a bloody good friend.

"He'll live," I said. "He has fractured ribs, a concussion and a gash on his abdomen, but nothing he can't recover from, thankfully. The doctors patched him and are sending him home. Echo's with him now. They're just waiting for his discharge papers."

She gave a sigh of relief. "That's good news. And what about you? How are you feeling? Your mum's will reading and then your dad ending up in the hospital is one tough day."

I kneaded my neck to ease the tension stored up there. "I'm utterly stressed."

"I'm not surprised. Let me treat you to a spa day when this is all over. How's Sahil bearing up?"

"He's gone AWOL. He's probably stuck in werepigeon form somewhere."

"I'll keep an eye out in case he turns up at the surgery." She giggled. "Although it was a lark seeing him flapping about like that when he's usually so sure of himself."

"You say that, but he's a liability. If I were you, I'd keep an eye out at your bedroom window. Now he's small, dark and can fly. Who knows what kind of voyeurism he'll get up to once he gets a grip mentally? You know what a thing he has for you. I'd keep your blinds shut if I were you."

Marina made a gagging sound. "Yuck. I'm happy to say I have my hands full with Robert. Literally. That man puts on quite a display of bedroom acrobatics. You know, maybe you and Ezra need to get your Moulin Rouge on. Who needs a spa day? That would relax you in twenty minutes flat."

The thought of being in bed with Ezra made my pulse race, but I kept my voice cool. "Err. We've kissed twice and had a bit of flirting. And a lot of aggro with his aunt. I think it'll be quite a while before I'm jumping into bed with him."

"Your loss. A wing woman has to try. A bit of attention from Robert has me beaming ear to ear. I finally got to put that new push-up bra to good use. Although I got to say, the underwire was so painful I whipped it straight off."

"I don't suppose the detective minded?"

She chuckled. "No, he didn't. It's just the thing to take his mind off his work. Speaking of which, he wants a word."

"Put him on then. Love you."

"Love you. I'll hand the phone over."

The line fumbled. "Alisha, remind me never to eavesdrop on you two again. I'm glad your father's okay."

"Thanks, Robert. What can I do for you? I should get back. I only came out for some air."

"It's a professional call, actually. The situation is worse than I thought."

I rubbed my temples. "You mean, the scientists are worried? Is there going to be another one?"

"At first, they thought the sensors were out. That there'd been a technical failure, you know? The state hasn't been investing as much as it should against natural disasters. You know how it is. Roads, schools and hospitals get the most investment. Governments should have a long-term vision, but there's no electoral benefit. The punters want to see the results there and then. So, politicians get blindsided until something like this happens."

"So, they need more earthquake protection in the future. Fortify our structures. Get some sirens or something."

"That's just it. It wasn't a technical failure. The machinery has been checked. They couldn't figure it out. The scientific community started backpedalling. Word is, the Prime Minister was raving mad. He's answerable to the people, after all. He stepped up to the podium outside number ten and told them it was an earthquake. He's been broadcast all over international media. But the scientists want the truth out. They won't be gagged if it happens again."

My stomach churned. "You're not going to tell me that it's the dark elves?"

"No, I told you before. There's no indication of the elves being that organised. But that didn't stop Phinnaeous Shine from walking into the Prime Minister's Office and telling him what he wanted to hear: a reason for the tremors."

"But that's crazy. The Prime Minister couldn't have bought it?"

"When a man is on the ropes, he'll buy anything."

"Phinnaeous Shine promised to solve the problem and sweetened the deal by providing a substantial donation to the Prime Minister's personal expenses in exchange for a free rein."

My tone was incredulous. "And the Prime Minister agreed?"

Robert's voice dripped with sarcasm. "What can I say? He's a class act. The way the Prime Minister sees it, if the earthquakes stop, he's home free. He gets the scientists in question to sign The Official Secrets Act, and then the country can move on. The wheels are turning fast on this one. It's shadowy stuff. No paper trails. Just nods and winks. Brown envelopes and secret handshakes. Phinnaeous Shine has already made a start."

"Whatever do you mean?"

"I mean that the elves are persecuted by the senate and Lavinia's forces. Elvish homes searched. Disappearances. An elf washed up on the banks of the Thames the other morning, just before the first run of the Thames Clipper. Luckily, the Shadow Squad got there first to pick up the body."

I sank heavily on a bench on the hospital grounds. Flinar flashed into my mind. "That's awful."

"Listen, I'm already crossing a line laying all this out for you."

"Then why are you?"

"Because it's my job to protect the peace."

"But there's not going to be any peace. The earthquakes aren't a natural phenomenon, and they aren't caused by the elves. So, both the Prime Minister and Phinnaeous Shine are chasing their own tails."

"Precisely, Alisha. It's a conundrum." Robert paused. "But it got me thinking. London is a secular city. Here, banks, restaurants and theatres are worshipped. Not gods. But there's been an unprecedented uptick in religiousness. People are spooked. The churches, mosques and synagogues of the city are overflowing. And our run-in with the sun god taught us that when there's more prayer, the gods of this city become stronger."

The world around me stilled. "You think the gods are behind this?"

"It's the only logical explanation. And you were key to stopping them the last time around. You might be featherweight, but you can definitely land a punch or two. Fancy another round?"

My pulse raced. "My dad just got hurt in an earthquake. I have an elvish friend. And I bloody hate bullies. You betcha I'm in. Where do I sign?"

"Er, mate, it's all off the books," said Robert. "Like, on the real down low. Shadow Squad style."

"I know, Detective. I'll be seeing you." I hung up but wasn't ready to go into the hospital yet.

My shoulders ached, and I felt all of my forty years. On a whim, I opened my camera app to check my face. My head said I was in my twenties, but the camera image made me wince. Having a scare did that. It aged you, or rather, it made you feel your age. I straightened my posture and sucked in my gut. A halo of frizz sat around my head, framing my bloodshot eyes and dry lips. I needed to hydrate and sleep and get to a kickboxing class or two to get my mojo back.

A huge furry thing loomed in the corner of my eye. I yelped and recoiled.

"It's only me," said Echo. "Or is it your reflection you object to?"

I slapped his rump, none too gently. "I thought you were a spider or one of Lavinia's bloody rats."

Echo grunted. "If that is so, the appropriate response would have been to pull out Transcender and slice a leg off. Not to scream like a girl."

"Girlie screaming can be very powerful, I'll have you know, Echo. It can propel babies down birth canals and scare off attackers. Think of it as a gathering of energy before we kick arse."

"Maybe if you're a banshee. Yours was a little lacklustre. Next time, I'd go for the sword instead."

"Noted. Dad all right?"

He inclined his head. "He's had enough painkillers to take the edge off and is sleeping soundly. Since I've never been to this hospital before, I spent my time scoping it out and marking my territory by leaving droppings in my favourite places."

I screwed up my nose. "That doesn't sound very hygienic. Next time, please remember a hospital needs to have sanitary conditions."

"In India, it is said pellets from a magical leopard are as lucky as a four-leaf clover. Some even suck them like boiled sweets," said Echo. "However, the hospital will no longer benefit from my bowels. I had to hightail out of there to avoid excessive fondling from the matron. She did a kind of pulsating movement on my belly that I think she learned from a vibrator." He jumped up on the bench next to me, and it creaked under his weight. "I was in half a mind to bite off her fingers, but I didn't want to ruin my appetite for tonight's hunt. It's not often we venture down to Tooting. The wind is carrying the scent of fresh meat." His whiskers twitched. "And something more divine."

I leaned my head against him and listened to the slow rumble of his chest. His fur was pillow soft and warm, despite the cool night. "I just talked to Robert Jameson."

Echo nodded. "I heard, druid. He might be a police offer, but he is an honourable man, and the argument he presented rings true. We are living in strange times when the Prime Sorcerer is in cahoots with a humdrum politician for nefarious reasons."

I was no longer shocked by the leopard's hearing. "You bought their story then? I thought you hated the elves."

"I do, druid. But my ancestors have always sided with the forces of good. I won't let my experiences sway me to back someone who does not deserve it. And then I remembered. Rajika Verma turned down Phinnaeous Shine's romantic advances. She was in her twenties then and had been struggling to animate the creatures her brother drew. This was before your father was born. Phinnaeous Shine promised her loyalty and more power than she could imagine."

"Dad told me she said no."

"She did. She didn't trust him." Echo growled. "And of all the people I have met during my long life, Rajika Verma was my guiding light. So, when you ask me if I believe the detective, I can tell you it reminded me I can't go wrong if I am led by what Rajika would have done. I am sorry for not standing by your side before, druid. I let an old enmity colour my judgement. But I'm ready to stand by your side now."

"Thank you, Echo."

"What do you want to do?"

"I want to sleep for a hundred years." I closed my eyes and nestled deeper into his fur. It was almost meditative, matching my breathing to his. I gave thanks to the gods that Dad had the care he needed. That the house hadn't crumbled. That I had my leopard. That the world was still beautiful despite all things wrong with it.

A purr rolled through Echo.

I straightened my spine and opened my eyes to find Gaia, Goddess of the Earth, standing before us on the sticky pavement, her cherubic face beaming. Her chiffon sari rustled in the night-time breeze. "I was wondering when you'd call me, druid."

I stood up and bowed my head, stuttering. "You have had a wasted journey, Goddess. I didn't call you."

Echo leapt from his perch and rolled over at her feet.

She tickled his snowy belly. Her voice was like mellow honey or bread and butter pudding, and everything was honest and good in the world. "Oh, I didn't come far. London is my city, after all. But you did call me, druid. You prayed, did you not, and gave thanks for your blessings on this bountiful earth."

"I did."

"Whose bell did you think rang in response?" She smiled with the patience of a mother talking to a child who hadn't quite caught the drift. "Mine, of course. It helps that I was listening. If I'm not, an offering comes in very handy."

I frowned. "You hear a bell when believers pray?"

Gaia swung her thick, black plait like a whip. Playful but somehow deadly. "It's more like a tug. As if someone is knocking me on the shoulder. Not all gods experience it that way, obviously. I believe Cupid experiences the twang of a bow on his heartstrings. And Apollo used to speak of the sense a white flag had been raised. And who knows what Loki of Asgard felt. He'd never give me a straight answer." She grabbed the folds of her sari and crouched down to Echo. "You are a sight for sore eyes, Chanakya Gunbir Hredhaan of Maharashtra."

Echo's adoring eyes had not moved from her face. He let out a pitiful mewling. "Goddess, I searched high and low for you. I yearned for your presence. I will abandon this druid forthwith and attend to your every need."

I did a double-take. "Hang on a minute. You just said you'd never leave my side, Echo."

He didn't take his eyes off Gaia. "That was before the goddess returned. If she desired it, I would throw you into a well and never look back."

"Traitor," I muttered.

Gaia gave us an amused look. "Now, now, I'm not here to steal away your leopard, druid. I am here to make amends after what happened with your mother."

My chest tightened with sadness and lingering resentment.

"I would like to invite you for a cup of masala chai in my favourite café. It is my daily ritual. Chai is always better when someone else makes it for you." She pushed a papery hand into her sari blouse and pulled out a clinking money bag. "My social security check just came through, and I thought I would spend a little on you."

I blinked. "I'm not—"

She held up a hand. "Wait. I know you are a little upset that I chose not to save your mother, but it is not every day a goddess invites you to a cup of masala chai. From all my travels and all my centuries, it is this tiny, unpretentious place across the road from Tooting Broadway tube station, squeezed between a fast food restaurant and a betting shop, that makes the perfect brew. Their masala chai is a milky, golden brown with cardamom, cloves, fresh ginger and a pinch of cinnamon. The leopard can join us if he promises not to leave his scent all over."

Echo purred in ecstasy.

I bit my lip. "I don't know, goddess. Maybe another time. My father needs me."

Her eyes flashed like the last throes of a falling star. "You refuse me, druid? After all I have done for you? Your father is in the hands of god's own NHS, and you have no need to worry. Mark my words, you will not survive the coming days without heeding my counsel."

Echo growled as if he was Gaia's protector and not mine.

My breath caught in my throat. "It's the sun god, isn't it? You're here to break it to me that he is back."

She sighed and sat on the bench. Then she placed her money pouch back in her blouse, pulling out a mint and offering me one. "He is still licking his wounds, but yes, child, he is back. Does the sun not rise? As much as I despair of his choices, the earth needs the sun. I didn't want to get involved. My place is in the shadows, but when your life was in danger, I rose against my kin at great risk to myself." She picked a dead leaf from a bush and rolled it between her fingers. It disintegrated, and the remnants floated away in the breeze. "The truth is that Ra's efforts to bring about suffering had the impact he desired. Prayer houses are full. Shrines are being set up by believers." She cast a warm glance at the prayer circle singing a familiar hymn in the car park. Her ears pricked at the chants from a mosque. "I feel my own strength increasing. The gods have been emboldened. They have yearned for this increase in power. They will keep on coming. We won the battle but not the war."

I wanted to trust her, but something niggled at me. "You speak like we're a team, but I've seen your power. You could crush me like an ant. You have power over the earth. How do I know the tremors aren't your doing?"

She swivelled to face me, and her anger hit me with the force of a tsunami. "Have you no faith, Alisha?"

"Sometimes faith isn't enough."

The rustling of the trees became thunderous, as if they had woken from sleep. "What a bitter disappointment. After all the miracles you have seen…Well, every soul has free will. I won't try to convince you. It is beneath me."

"I don't understand why you are leaving this up to me."

"God has always had his apostles, reluctant or not. Who says you're the only one?" She stood and patted my shoulder. "My masala chai awaits. I have three pieces of wisdom to impart to you, Alisha Verma. Not every battle is solved by escalating into war. Everything will unfold as it is meant to." She tugged Echo's ear with affection. Her eyes gleamed. "Goodbye, Chanakya. Stay away from the royal parks if you know what's good for you." She walked away in the direction of the main road. "Just one more thing, druid. Don't let your guard down with the vampire. I've warned you before about the undead. There is nothing the living should learn from them. Their corpses belong in the ashes, not walking the earth."

12

The next morning, after checking with Dad that he had slept well and was recovering, I made my way to Fei Yen and Faeza's tea and occult shop, Shanghai Moon. It only took me down my street, across the zebra crossing and past an old Edwardian building called The Vicarage that I suspected was a swinger's club, given the glimpses of scantily clad couples in the windows and the sense of seediness that seeped out from it.

Shanghai Moon was tucked away on a side street, between a penny shop and a laundrette. A bell tinkled as I pushed the door open, and my two students looked up from the wooden counter. They were dressed in short, white lab coats, with their hair tied neatly in chignons at their nape. Fei Yen, the more ostentatious of the couple, wore bright pink lipstick. Rows and rows of transparent jars lined the shelves behind them, filled with all sorts of exotic leaves, pods and seeds, each marked with yellowing parchment of Chinese calligraphy.

"Alisha, there you are," said Fei Yen. "We spent the morning clearing up after the earthquake. We've just finished preparing the order for your dad."

I'd called them in the morning to ask for some Chinese herbal medicine to help him back on his feet. It felt odd for them to use my first name rather than Ms Verma, but only fair, given how much they'd opened up to me the night they rescued Flinar. Formality after that vulnerability wasn't right. Especially given I needed their help.

I hugged them. They were more than students to me now. They were friends. "I hope the damage wasn't extensive. What a shock that was last night."

Fei Yen sighed. "The city is reeling, Alisha. We can't complain about a few broken jars."

"And how about you, Faeza? It's good to see you back on your feet. I trust you are back to full health after our run-in with the rats?"

Faeza smiled. "Quick healing is one of the perks of being *hu hsien*."

"It's a shame we couldn't see your dad in person to assess him. It would've been much better to take his pulse and examine his eyes, ears and tongue before prescribing a remedy," said Fei Yen.

"I sent you a photograph of his tongue last night. Didn't you get it?"

"A photograph can't compensate for an in-person examination. Balancing the *yin*, *yang* and *qi* is a delicate process. You know that." Fei Yen wrinkled her nose. "What the photograph did tell us is that your dad has let his mouth hygiene go downhill since your mother's death."

"I'll get his dentist to look at that," said Alisha. "How much do I owe you?"

Faeza handed me a brown paper bag. "Don't be silly. It's on the house, especially after what Marina did for me. The instructions are in the bag. Make sure he continues with the prescribed treatment until his symptoms ease. There are no shortcuts when it comes to health." She grinned. "Unless you're *hu hsien*."

"I appreciate it." I looked around the shop. To the right, adjacent to a display of teas, crystals and what looked like voodoo dolls, was a painting of a landscape I'd never seen before. "Actually, there was something else."

As much as I missed Ezra and how his presence made my nether regions tingle in response, I hated being beholden to him. Hadn't he been the one who had suggested the Celestial Library as a solution to my Lavinia problem? Where was he then? My last attempt to animate Tielbu had been scary, but I'd made progress and was eager to try again. And if our hunch was right, once I had animated Tielbu, animating other creatures would be easier, and passing the trial would be a cinch.

Except I had no way of getting in touch with him. He seemed just to turn up when it suited him. Like I was Miss Available, and he was Mr Popular.

Or maybe it was that werewolves didn't seem to like mobile phones. They had their own way of calling each other. I'd asked, and apparently, Gunnolf preferred them to communicate the old-fashioned way and was averse to mobile phone contracts. They had biology on their side. According to Google, a wolf's howl could be heard six miles away, and werewolves were even more powerful. Ezra had promised to put me first, at least until the trial, but his disappearing act seemed hard to break.

Or maybe he didn't want to be answerable to me.

I got it. I wasn't his wife. My ex-husband had hated being answerable to me. He hadn't said it out loud, but I was pretty sure he regretted putting a ring on it. I could see it in his eyes.

Men were weird like that. They didn't mind being answerable to their bosses. But when it came to women, they kicked up a stink. Like a teenager sulking because their mum told them to clean their room. Even though their mum was right and their bedroom smelled of nuclear farts and old socks, and the stains on the bedding were embarrassing.

But Ezra wasn't the only person who could help me get to the Celestial Library. That was where Fei Yen and Faeza came in.

"What do you need? Some green tea perhaps or some lotus-scented tea lights or maybe a plush panda toy to cheer up your dad?" said Fei Yen.

I shook my head. "Oh no, that's not really his thing. It was really for me. You see, Ezra was going to help me, but he keeps disappearing on me."

Faeza's tone was gentle. "I'm sorry, Alisha. Wolves are devoted to their family. Perhaps you're not quite his family yet. How long has it been since you've seen him?"

I frowned. "A day or two."

"A lot changes in a day or two," said Fei Yen. "We know this city like the back of our hands. But the streets are whispering to us. They say the seekers have been mobilised against the elves."

I gripped the paper bag more tightly. "Ezra wouldn't do that. He's a good man. He saved my life not so long ago."

Fei Yen sighed. "He did. But orders are orders, especially for wolves, and maybe he doesn't have the courage to say no. This feels like a witch hunt, like in Shanghai. The elves are at the mercy of the senate. There's panic on the streets. Lavinia's forces show no mercy. Flinar almost came to a sticky end last night. It was blind luck he could harness his black hole magic to come here."

I held my breath. "You saw him? Is he okay?"

Fei Yen nodded. "He's rattling with fear. We let him hide in our store cupboard. But then the rats started to sniff around. Flinar didn't want to put us in danger again, so he escaped through the back window. We've not seen him since."

I crossed my fingers. "No news is good news. He's probably holed up somewhere."

"Or maybe he's lying in a ditch. We warned you, Alisha," said Faeza. "The senate cannot be trusted. If the British state harmed civilians, there would be an uproar. The police, judges and journalists would step up to defend humdrums. Within minutes, people on Twitter would raise banners and hashtags in support."

"Do you know what happens when peculiars are harmed by the senate?" said Fei Yen. "Absolutely nothing. There is silence. Because the senate is the judge, jury and executioner. It is the treasurer, the education, and the holder of the keys to the palace. It can wipe our magic and minds if it chooses, and nobody would stand against them."

I bit down on my lip. "So you won't help me?"

Fei Yen and Faeza spoke as one. "We didn't say that."

"You must decide your own path," said Fei Yen.

"Do you choose, like us, to stand outside the remit of the senate? Unsanctioned but free of their control?" said Faeza.

I shook my head. "I don't. I choose to pass my trial. But I choose to help the elves and stand against the senate, where they have fallen foul of their own laws. The Judge's Law. The delicate power balance between co-existing peculiar communities must be protected."

Fei Yen sighed. "Then I suppose I should give you this." She reached under the counter to bring out a brown leather strap with a slim holder at one end. "It's a baldric to hold your sword. Can't have it getting into the wrong hands."

I turned it over in my hands, then reached inside my jacket for Transcender. I slipped the sword into the pouch. "It's perfect. I can't thank you enough." I looked up. "But I'm afraid I need one more thing. I need you to tell me how to get access to the Celestial Library."

"Well, that is easy," said Fei Yen. "We haven't lived for centuries as *hu hsien* and increased our knowledge of Chinese herbal medicine without access to ancient texts. There is not only one way of reaching between the seams of the world, but our way is the easiest. What you must do is choose an auspicious day and step through our gate."

I frowned. "You have a gate?"

"Oh, it's not a normal gate. You can teach us about the English language, British culture and kickboxing, but we can tell you still have a lot to learn about the Otherworld," said Faeza. "The library is an evolved being made of more than bricks and mortar."

Fei Yen ruffled through a calendar on the wall. "Mmm, that will do the job quite nicely. Come back tonight. Luckily for you, it's May Day today, known to the druids, of course, as Beltane, one of the eight Sabbats, marking the halfway point between the spring equinox and the coming summer solstice."

"Of course." I had no idea what was going on. A druid with no idea about my culture's calendar: the minute I was out of there, I would pull up my Google search box.

Fei Yen came back to the counter. "The festival of Beltane will make your passage easier. The library will be more amenable to druids tonight. Added to that is the fact that you are a descendant of a Custodian. I'd wager you'll slip right through the gate."

"It will be as easy as sliding on a pair of gossamer stockings," said Faeza.

I had no idea that anyone wore stockings anymore apart from in S&M role play, but I nodded along. "Hang on a minute. I'm invited to a coven dinner tonight. I didn't want to go, but I can't get out of it."

Faeza swallowed hard. "Well, you'll have to come along afterwards, then. Just make sure those rats don't follow you."

13

———————

My heartbeat was a hummingbird in my throat as I walked into the history cabin at Wildwoods. It was crucial I got the better of Orpheus today. His ability to mindread jeopardised my plan to animate Tielbu at the Celestial Library. If he found out, it was only a matter of time before Lavinia came knocking. I had an idea of how I could pull the wool over his eyes, but it wouldn't be easy, especially since I was the kind of girl who wore my heart on my sleeve.

Orpheus strode in, impressive in his Wildwoods robes. His chiselled face was like granite, with no sign of warmth. He pulled out a chair and lowered himself into it without taking his eyes from my face. "And so we meet again, Alisha. Let us hope that today's history lesson will be less dramatic. Tell me, what strides have you made in your training since the last time we saw each other? Your brother tells me he has discovered his werepigeon side. Although, judging by his internal monologue, his ego is a little fragile. And Helio tells me that Marina did good work in the bestiary."

I nodded. "She is getting better at controlling the flow of emotions."

"How about you, Alisha? Your emotions are raging today."

"Get out of my head, Orpheus."

361

"Only very few people can shield their thoughts from me, Alisha. It takes years of practice, and many just don't bother." His eyes darkened. "I, on the other hand, have years of practice in delving into the thoughts of others. It's as easy for me as—"

"Peeling a banana?"

He jerked. "Your mind is a gutter, Alisha. Will you stop referencing phallic objects?"

"I was doing nothing of the sort." I grinned. What I had learned was that throwing in the odd curveball for Orpheus could throw him off track. Today was as good a day as any to practice. I jumped to all the phallic objects I could think of: cucumbers, carrots, bratwurst, ice lollies, cacti, willy straws, the sell-out rabbit vibrator from my local corner shop…

"Can you stop that?"

"Oh, I can go all day," I said. "The question is, can you?"

He grimaced. "Your immaturity is toe-curling. I've never known anything like it."

"Then you haven't lived." I switched tactics and thought of iced buns, melons, lemons, Alex's favourite blow-up doll and Robert DeNiro's strap-on bra from *Meet the Fockers*.

Orpheus flung back his chair and stood up. "What is wrong with you, woman? You are a demon."

I smiled sweetly. "I am a druid, and I am eager to learn. How about we call a truce, Minister? You stay out of my head, and I'll stop polluting your fragile sensibilities."

He sighed. "I imagine it's the only way to get any work done with you in this mood. The purpose of today's history lesson is to talk about ancestry. Ancestry plays a large role in the Otherworld. That is to say, ancestry and genealogy can make the difference between being a slug or a lion."

"Well, that sounds a bit harsh."

"Or being a werepigeon or a shapeshifting sorcerer."

"My goodness, I hope you didn't give my brother this speech. You would've crushed his already fragile soul."

"I don't tell my pupils what they want to hear. I tell them what they need to hear," said Orpheus. "I am the Minister for History and the Today, not the minister for holding hands."

I looked at his white, paper-thin skin. The man needed some Vitamin D. "I imagine your hands are quite cold."

"You can mock me, druid, or you can pay attention. That is if you do want to pass your trial."

"All right, grumpy pants. Teach me."

"As I was saying, ancestry has an impact on what kind of peculiar you will be." Orpheus continued smoothly, with no need to inhale or exhale and a voice that was sharp all around the edges. All business and no humanity. "The most, dare I say, desirable peculiars are the result of the same kind of peculiars mating."

I spluttered. "Bloody hell, does that mean my brother has to find a werepigeon?"

His stillness creeped me out. He was either still or moving faster than light. The man had no middle gear. "The conclusions are not mine to draw. It is my duty only to share the wisdom of the senate, especially when pupils of marriage age are being initiated into the Otherworld."

"I've got to say, Orpheus. I don't think you need to worry about that. I got marriage out of my system a long time ago. And I'm not looking to do it any time soon."

"Then you will remain childless?"

My shoulders drooped, but I kept my voice steady. "My ex-husband and I tried for a baby, but it wasn't meant to be. It's probably a good thing. I couldn't imagine sharing custody with a tool like him. The doctor said I have a minuscule chance of carrying an embryo to term, even if I were to get pregnant. I have this condition, you see. Amenorrhea. It means I don't get my period."

He winced. "I don't need all the details, druid."

"What? I thought vampires liked blood?"

Orpheus flushed with embarrassment, and I chalked that up as a win for me. "Blood from the veins, not from the nether regions."

"You're the one who asked me to share."

He nodded slowly. "Alisha, I trace the genealogy of all the students in my class. It is often a way to make breakthroughs in their understanding of themselves and their talents. Your case is no exception. If your parents had not shunned Wildwoods, you might have come to this realisation sooner. As it is, your parents were too focused on their mundane lives. Imagine spending all that time in a humdrum laboratory, slaving over a stove or worrying about what your next car purchase should be when all this power coursed through your fingertips."

I frowned. "You are wrong, Orpheus. My father might have been wrong, but my mother lived the life that had always been intended for her. She was born to be a scientist. No magic ran through her veins."

His thin lips curved upwards. "Do you really think a virgin peculiar such as you could befriend a goddess and go up against the sun god if you were ordinary?"

I lifted my chin. "I'm not ordinary. I'm Rajika Verma's granddaughter."

"My research proves you are more than that, druid. Your grandmother didn't know it, of course. I remember her. She was powerful, yes. But she was also romantic. She believed love surpassed all. It was why she wouldn't bed Phinnaeous Shine. He wouldn't have wed her. They were the same kind of peculiar. But as his mistress, she would've known power beyond all her dreams. But a loveless union was something she couldn't envisage. Years later, when your father met Rosalie, it's why she didn't stand in their way. She recognised true love, despite Rosalie's shortcomings as a humdrum. Despite her knowing that, if Joshi married a humdrum, his allegiance to the Otherworld would be weakened."

"She was right."

His lips twisted. "Oh, the twists and turns of history. If Rajika had lived, I am certain she would've found out what I uncovered, and we would not be sitting here today. I would not be teaching you about the bones of the Otherworld. Your family would be one of the most powerful families the Otherworld has known."

My pulse raced. "Spit it out, Orpheus."

"It took me hours to piece it together. It's when I found out your mother was born in Brittany that the penny dropped. When I found your maternal grandmother's name in the journals of Jules Renard, it finally clicked."

"What did?"

"Why did your mother leave France?"

I thought back to the threads of conversations I'd had with Mum over the years. "She came to the UK as a student. Her village was too small for her to pursue her passion for science. She got a scholarship from a London university, and that's where she met my father. She didn't look back."

"Do you ever see your mother's family?"

"She barely had anyone left. She didn't have fond memories of the place, so she made her life with my father. The rest is history."

His heavy brows furrowed. "The ghost of history always surprises us in the present. Today is one of those days. You don't have amenorrhea. I would bet my favourite coffin on it."

"How could you know that? Have you been snooping around my doctor's records?"

"Your mother wasn't a humdrum at all. I think your mother's side stems from a community of virgin priestesses. Not all were virgins, and not all were priestesses, but legend says it was a powerful place."

"Surely my mother would have known that?"

"Not if the druid practices had died out. According to Renard's journals, the few holding onto their heritage were simply thought of as lunatics. They lost their homes and, after a time, were simply known as the village idiots."

My spine tingled. I didn't believe it for a second, but it was a cool origin story.

"Do you know what this means, Alisha?"

"I'm sure you're going to tell me, Orpheus."

He leaned forward. The dark-chocolate and sweet-cherry scent of his beard oil assaulted my senses. "It means that you and your brother are the culmination of two druid lines, one French, one Hindu. That's a potent mix. It's a mix that the senate approves of. And it explains why you are so intriguing."

I fidgeted, tempted to bring out my shopping cart of phallic objects. This was getting way too intense. "Well, hooray for that. Hasn't changed whether I can have children, though, has it?"

He paused. "Who knew we would have something in common? I, too, am childless."

I patted his hand. "I'm sorry to hear that."

"I'm a vampire, Alisha. We can't create life."

"I forgot. It's been a while since I watched *Twilight*."

He rolled his eyes. "The vampire in *Twilight* has a child. I quite enjoyed the movie, especially its depiction of sleeplessness. The concept of vampire baseball was quite a revelation and is something I'd be keen to establish at Wildwoods if the leprechauns didn't ruin everything with their stubby legs. However, when the child was born, I gave up my commitment to the saga."

I gave him a thumbs up. "Orpheus, who knew you were a movie buff? I'd pegged you for an opera-only kind of bloke."

His eyes glinted. "*La Bohème* is rather marvellous. I think we have more in common than we both thought, Alisha."

I screwed up my face. "Like what?"

"We are both childless. We have both seen *Twilight*."

"I hate to break it to you, Orpheus, but that's a grand total of two things. One tiny and one huge. I reckon, given the Law of Probability, I'd have as much in common with any old Joe off the street."

He pretended to stake himself in the heart, and I warmed to him a little more.

"You know, you're not so bad. I thought you couldn't stand me, and here you are, trying to spend time with me. What's the deal, stiff?"

"Please don't call me that again. Perhaps it's just as well I'm not your mentor." He sighed. "Let's just say that your potential intrigues me. Particularly the possibility that a childless woman can animate lifeless objects. Are you any closer?"

I thought of Tielbu's reptile skin quivering under my fingertips.

Orpheus smiled.

I clenched my fists. "Hey, I thought we had a deal for you to stay out of my head."

"Oh, I've been in your head all this time, druid. I warned you; it is not easy to outsmart me." His eyes flashed. "My contemporaries will be very excited to hear of your plan."

I looked at my cuticles, trying to feign disinterest, but thoughts rattled through my brain like a runaway train: my annoyance with Ezra, my fear of Lavinia, my rage at the senate for targeting the elves, my longing for Tielbu and my hopes of reaching the Celestial Library.

He smirked. "Both your thoughts and your racing heartbeat give you away, druid."

I took a deep breath. "What do you want, Orpheus?"

"I want you to sit next to me at tonight's dinner."

"That is all?"

"That is a start."

14

I rang Dad. "Are you sure you don't want to come to the dinner party tonight? We can swing by and pick you up."

"No, no, I'm fine. You go and have a good time. I need my rest, and Alma next door has offered to bring me some lasagne. My appetite is better. In fact, my mouth's watering just thinking about it. Bay leaves are her secret ingredient, you know. She's as talented in the kitchen as your mother was."

"You sound so upbeat." I didn't tell him about Mum's ancestry. No need to burden him or anyone else with Orpheus's ridiculousness. The man had probably been sniffing the glue of all those ancient book bindings. Next, he'd be telling me he had access to Marcel Proust's or Anais Nin's journals, too.

"I am upbeat. A brush with death will do that to you. I'm lucky you and Sahil were there to call the ambulance. Sure, the house took some knocks, but nothing that some tender loving care won't fix. The way I see it, the tremors were a reminder not to lose my faith. A man can lose his way if he drifts from his faith."

"So you're okay with my choices?"

"I wouldn't go that far, but I'm trying not to get worked up about it. Just in case my old ticker can't take it."

"Enjoy Alma's lasagne, Dad."

"Thanks, love."

I put the phone down and went to my wardrobe, tossing clothes onto my bed until I finally found something I could feel powerful and comfortable in at Lavinia's party. A niggling sense of dread permeated my stomach at the thought of the evening ahead. Getting ready tonight felt like putting on armour, especially my control pants. Those things gave me a peachy shape, but damn, they were like a medieval chastity belt. I was determined to scrub up well. No doubt, the witches tonight would dress to kill. Hell, I wouldn't put it beyond them *to* kill. I hadn't forgotten the knockout punch Ravynne's truth serum had delivered the last time I was at the coven flat. Wily Lavinia would be on the lookout for any hint I was untrustworthy, and this time Elvira wasn't around to soften her coven sisters' more ruthless instincts.

"Echo, will you just stop crooning and leave me to get dressed in peace? You're worse than a toddler."

"Party pooper. I was just trying to be helpful. Don't you appreciate the party soundtrack I'm providing? 'The Love Shack' is an excellent mood maker. In my experience, it is impossible to listen to without shaking a rump."

I picked up a cotton bud to fix my eye makeup. "That rump-shaking made me ruin my eyeliner, but it wasn't as bad as you doing Jay-Z's rap in 'It's a Hard Knock Life.' I shudder to think what the neighbours made of that. They probably think I'm on acid because no normal person makes that noise."

While he wandered off, I fussed with my hair, pulled my long hair over one shoulder and put a leafy, vintage silver hair clip on the other side to add some glamour.

The sound of gushing water came from the bathroom.

I popped my head around the door. Claw marks marred my new shower curtain, and wee trickled down it.

"Echo!" I rushed forward to shoo him out. "For the millionth time, you don't need to mark territory here. There are no other leopards to compete with."

"But there are wolves." He gave me an appraising look. "You have never looked so beautiful. Except perhaps on your wedding day to that imbecile. Still, I can hear your heartbeat from here. Erratic, like that of a gazelle being chased across the savannah before I tear its throat out. You could give tonight a miss, you know."

I sighed. I could have called with an excuse. Dad's injuries were common knowledge, and it would not have been farfetched to say I needed to play nurse. But the dinner at Lavinia's was an opportunity for unprecedented access to the Sorcerer's Senate, and I wasn't missing the chance to flush out some intel about the tremors and whether Phinnaeous Shine was as sordid as the detective and the foxes believed. Plus, this was the perfect foil for the plan I had hatched with Echo.

"No, we're not backing down," I said. "How about we just go through the plan again?"

"As you wish, druid. The plan is for me to roam the wilds of London using my superior nose, ears and speed to work out whether the gods are indeed behind the tremors. All while you are dining with the senate. I am not to engage the gods or give away my presence without consulting you." He huffed. "Thereby allowing you to swoop in and take all the glory."

"Echo," I said. "It's not about the glory. I want us to work as a team. I don't like sending you out without backup, but Fei Yen and Faeza are too worried about you devouring them to go on a mission with you alone."

He turned his nose up in the air. "Well, this is going to cost you a freezer full of premium steaks. Plus some caviar if I don't make an acceptable wild kill tonight."

"I wouldn't expect anything less." I gave myself one last look in the mirror and slipped on some silver sandals.

Echo gave an appreciative growl. "You look more and more like your grandmother every day."

"I wish you could come with me tonight."

With Dad recuperating at home, I counted on having four allies at the party: Marina, the detective, Sahil and Ezra, if he bothered to show up at all. And then there was Orpheus: handsome but cold-blooded and stiff as a board, with dead, emotionless eyes. But underneath it all, I suspected he just needed a hug. If it floated his boat to sit next to me, I wouldn't refuse. Of course, it was an extra bonus if keeping him busy meant he would keep my plan from Lavinia.

I looked at the clock on my bedside table. Marina and Sahil were early.

"Are you going to get that, druid, or would you like me to be your butler?" said Echo.

I threw a pillow at him, tucked the picture of Tielbu into my bra and went to open the door. My mouth went dry.

There stood Ezra. His usual tousled, chin-length hair had been slicked back. An uneven tan clung to his skin, deepening his warm moon glow to a golden sand. His snugly fitting tuxedo accentuated his taut chest, slim hips and rock-hard thighs. The moonlit runs with his pack apparently kept him in shape. He held a bouquet of flowers in his hands.

I wanted to sound authoritative, but my words came out in a stutter. "What are you doing here? I'm capable of getting to Lavinia's by myself."

"I thought it would be a nice gesture to pick you up. I brought you these." He handed me the sunflowers.

I raised an eyebrow. "This isn't a prom date. We're going to your sneaky aunt's house for dinner with a nest of vipers."

"You've had a hard week. I thought this would lift your spirits. If you don't like them, we can give them to Dotty a few doors down. Judging by the state of her grey knickers on the drying rack she always displays, I reckon she doesn't get much company. *She* might like some flowers." His eyes roamed over me, taking in the slinky, azure blue dress and the strappy, silver sandals I'd chosen. "You look amazing, by the way."

My stomach somersaulted. "Where've you been?"

Grey eyes implored me. "I can't tell you, Alisha. It would put you in danger. Are you going to let me in?"

I walked ahead of him into the flat, hoping that his wolf's nose didn't catch the scent of Echo's liberal marking of the new shower curtain. "It's the elves, isn't it? Were you tracking them down as part of your seeker role? What have Lavinia and Gunnolf got you doing?"

He took my hands. "Nothing. I told you I'd focus on you, and I've kept my promise. When are you going to realise I'm on your side?"

"How can I? You're never there when I need you. Maybe it's because of your parents dying so young or you never trusting anyone wholly. Or maybe it's the teleporting thing. You can just disappear. In fact, disappearing comes to you as easily as breathing."

Ezra held up his hands defensively. "Easy. What's going on with you?"

Echo slinked into the room. "Perhaps she needs a poo. I have noticed her habits aren't as regular as mine."

We both swung around in unison. "Shut up, Echo."

I turned back to Ezra. "When are you going to be open with me?"

"When I know you won't fly off the handle." His thumbs caressed my palms. "I found it, you know. I found the Celestial Library."

"You did?"

He nodded. "It was tricky, but I made it to the door. I finally managed to hold onto the threads of it. The Custodian wouldn't let me in, though. I don't blame her for being cautious. There's a tonne of concentrated power in the library, and she doesn't let any old peculiar in. I would have come sooner, but I've been trying to puzzle it out."

"Actually, I found my own way in."

"You did?"

"I did. I'm going there tonight after the dinner at Lavinia's."

Ezra whistled. "I didn't think the student would surpass the mentor so soon. Impressive, hellfire. The question is, are you going to let an old man hang onto your coattails?"

"You can't come. It works for me tonight because it's Beltane."

His brow furrowed. "Bell, what?"

Google was my friend.

"May Day. A Gaellic festival important to druids. Think maypoles, bonfires, dancing and fertility rituals." I grimaced. I guess that last bit wasn't meant for me.

A mischievous look danced in his eyes. "Now you're really making me want to go."

"Well, you can't."

He sighed. "It makes sense, now you mention it. Gunnolf once told me that his only entry to the Celestial Library was on the full moon, and when he passed the threshold, his wolf became submerged, even when he tried to call it forth."

"Passage for me will be easier because I'm Rajika Verma's granddaughter."

Echo purred. "Finally, you appreciate her majesty."

We turned on him. "Shut up, Echo."

"No need to be so tetchy. Rajika Verma never raised her voice at me, and she let me eat all the pet dogs I wished," said Echo.

I rolled my eyes. "She was obviously a better woman than I."

"So we agree," said Echo.

I bent down to scratch his ears. "It's time for you to go forth and do wondrous things tonight. Be clever, but more than that, be subtle. No singing and no eating pets."

He puffed out his chest. "I'm honoured to be of service."

I headed for the open back window.

"When the mice are out, the cat will play."

"What was that about?" said Ezra.

"I'll fill you in on the way." I picked up my phone to send Marina a text. "Dad's too tired to come. I was going to hitch a ride with Marina and Sahil."

"And now? Can I escort you to Baba Yaga's? A belle like you shouldn't turn up to the ball in a vet's van. It's much more appropriate for you to arrive in a werewolf's arms."

My traitorous body told me to go with him. I stepped into his arms, and the scent of spice and nuts filled my nose. "Was I ever going to say no?"

He smiled and murmured into my ear. "Those sandals make me want to take you straight to the bedroom."

"Soon. If you're a good boy."

Ezra grinned and hooked his arms around the small of my back.

I clung to him. The world slipped away in swirls of monochrome as we shot into our future.

15

———————

The sensation of teleporting wasn't quite like flying. It was more like being suspended in a vortex, clinging on, waiting to be ejected at your destination point. No wind whipped through my hair —I would have welcomed that. It was just me in Ezra's arms, holding my breath. I kept my eyes shut and tried not to think too hard about the physics of it. About how teleporting wasn't like a plane. There hadn't been engineers poring over plans down to the smallest calculation. There hadn't been test flights and scrutiny and government backers. I put my life into Ezra's hands simply because I fancied the pants off him. I'd made life-changing decisions on far less information, but they hadn't resulted in me being flung about the atmosphere like a projectile in a pinball machine.

When we arrived outside Baba Yaga's Gym in Wimbledon, the sunset was an orange glow on the distant horizon.

I stepped out of Ezra's arms, releasing my grasp on the silken lapels of the dinner jacket.

His eyes drifted to my chest. "Er, you may want to…"

He turned away to spare my blushes.

My breasts had sprung out of their optimal position in my dress. Oh, the shame. I jiggled them back into place and adopted a falsely bright tone to hide my humiliation. "We might be in for a bit of drama tonight, but at least it's not a spin class. They are the very definition of sadomasochism."

Lavinia's gym, with its white script on a green sign and its window front displaying dumbbells of various sizes, was couched in darkness.

I peered inside. "Are you sure we got the day right? It's awfully quiet in there."

"The coven guards its secrecy fiercely. It might seem quiet out here, but inside, it'll be a completely different scenario." He knocked lightly on the glass door.

"They're never going to hear that." Dread pulsed through me. "Maybe we should just go."

He gripped my bare arms. "Listen here, Alisha. The rats are going to be here any second. Since Orpheus knows your plan, we're in the shit. But it's salvageable. We just have to get through tonight. Sit next to the vampire to keep him sweet, but don't trust him. Don't trust my aunt. In fact, don't trust anyone who isn't me or you haven't known all your life. I'll be watching. If your tap your chin, I'll come and rescue you."

"My chin?" I thought my last wax job had fixed the errant hairs, but maybe not if Ezra had honed in on it. He was a wolf. Did that make me a pig? *Not by the hairs on my chinny, chin, chin,* sang my head.

Orpheus was in for a treat tonight if he delved into my mind.

The door opened, and we looked down to find an upright rat wearing a bowtie and a tiny waistcoat.

Ezra gave a gentle smile. "Good evening, Maurice."

The rat bowed. "Good evening, Ezra. Good evening, druid. Please follow me."

We walked in darkness past the glossy reception desk, bubble gum walls, pink tub chairs and the mirrored studios. Floor lanterns holding jasmine-scented tea lights glowed at the bottom of the stairwell that led to the coven flat. My sandals sank into the carpet as I followed the rat springing from stair to stair in front of me, with Ezra close behind me. The rat leapt up to the top step and placed his left forefoot on the handleless door at the top of the stairs.

As the door swung open, a wave of noise—classical music, raucous chatter and clinking glasses—crashed over us, so much so that I took a step backwards. Ezra's warm hand on my back seeped through the material of my dress, compelling me to keep going. We followed the rat into the opulent inner sanctum of the coven, with its embossed wallpaper, clashing colours and imposing chandeliers that would have looked at home at The Ritz. The coven's umbrellas lurked in every corner, a reminder of their power. Rats skittered between the guests, bearing trays of grapes and cheese and wine and champagne. From a distance, it was clear that the senate had turned out in full force.

Ezra bent down to accept a flute of champagne from Maurice, the rat, but I refused. I'd learned my lesson last time.

"Heads up, incoming," said Ezra.

His aunties approached, sashaying over in a rustle of taffeta and silk and chiffon, looking more like sirens than family.

"Nephew." Red-haired Isadora wore a black evening gown and gloves that set off her hair to perfection. She took his hands. "If only your mother were still with us. She'd be so proud. And Alisha, I do hope your father is recovering well. How good of you to tear yourself away from nurse duties to grace us with your presence."

Ezra gave a tight smile, his skin tan against his crisp white collar. "Aunties, aren't you magnificent? The centuries have no impact on your beauty."

Lavinia tossed her head of silver curls and cackled. "Oh, stop it, Ezra, or I'll send you to the rats in the basement for a spanking."

"Just like old times," drawled Ezra.

"Whyever are you emptyhanded, Alisha? Did the rats not offer you a drink?" said Lavinia.

I grimaced. "I refused it. It's hard to forget the green smoothie last time I was here. The truth serum's a little hard to forget."

Lavinia gave me a hard smile. "Don't be silly, dear. This is a party. Besides, it's not like you have anything to hide. Besides, Ravynne had no time for potions today. She spent all day buffing and polishing and curling to look like that. She's no catfish."

Ravynne waved at Ezra from across the room, and he grinned at her.

I bit down hard on my lip, tempted to kick her to kingdom come.

Lavinia patted my arm. "No shortcuts or falsies for her. Beauty takes work, you know."

She knew I was wearing control pants. There was no other explanation for her tone.

"Druid," said Chandra. "The last time we spoke was the night we lost Elvira. Let's hope this time you're more of a good luck charm."

Elvira's loss still stung me too, but the witch didn't have to rub my nose in it. I decided to play it saccharine sweet rather than spoil the mood so early in the evening. Sometimes a velvet glove was better than a sledgehammer.

"Speaking of good luck, your skin looks wonderful," I said. "What a glow. You must tell me your secret. I'd kill for it."

Lavinia thrust her conical, pneumatically impressive chest out. "Oh, we did kill for it. Pilates can only do so much good. We needed a dozen collagen potions and the blood of a goat to bounce back from that spell on the sun god. But let's not ruin a perfectly pleasant evening. I can't wait to hear about your progress in animating the dragon. I've barely been able to think of anything else."

Her sisters exchanged glances.

I rambled on like a train threatening to come off the rails. "It's quite a crowd."

Lavinia sighed. "I was rather hoping Roger, Raphael and Andy would come, but alas, they are too busy preparing for Wimbledon. Although I did cast Roger a little spell to help speed up his serve. I have a soft spot for the way that man wears a suit. He could ask me anything, and I'd be putty in his hands."

Isadora leaned in conspiratorially. "My sisters have bedded at least one tennis player in every generation. It's one of the perks of living in this neck of the woods. And you know the most surprising thing?"

I shook my head.

She tittered. "Not all of them wear tighty-whities."

Lavinia looked over our heads. "The last of our guests have arrived at last. The empath is going to give the Prime Sorcerer a heart attack in that get-up. She looks as scrumptious as his succubus house slave."

Off they went, in a cloud of hairspray and sweet perfume, to greet Marina, Robert and Sahil.

Marina had missed the memo and dressed like she would for a rock festival, with a PVC skirt and bustier, together with a spiked collar. Judging by the look of disquiet at the bowtie-clad rat, Sahil was having problems leaving his humdrum side at the door. Only the detective looked as cool as a cucumber in his threadbare tux.

"Relax," said Ezra. "Your heartbeat sounds like the drummer from Rage Against the Machine."

"I'm trying." I glowered, trying to avoid Orpheus's glare from across the room. By the looks of it, he'd opted to leave his robes at home. Instead, he wore a sleek suit and white shirt. "Any chance you can wrangle it so Marina is sat next to me? Since you're on first-name terms with the rats. I'm going to vomit with anxiety otherwise."

He gave a curt nod and strode away, leaving me alone like a fly in a spider's web.

With the scene clear, Orpheus approached and bowed with stiff civility. "This is an unfortunate place to have your friends desert you, druid. May I escort you to dinner?"

I gulped and looked longingly at my friends. Then I tucked my arm into his. "I'd be honoured."

His eyes narrowed. "Then let the evening unfold just as each of us wishes."

16

———————

I had to give it to them. The Drach sisters and their rat familiars knew how to stage a party. We followed them into the dining room, where a magnificent oak table and burgundy upholstered chairs had been prepared for dinner. The centre of the table had been decorated with an arrangement of orchids and dahlias, church candles, gleaming cutlery and napkins. In the corner, a harp played of its own accord, the strings plucked as if by a ghost.

I nodded at senate members as Orpheus guided me to our seats. He didn't bother with niceties. True to his word, Ezra had arranged the table so I was wedged between Marina and Orpheus. He sat between his Aunt Chandra and her coven sister, Ravynne, who had done such a devious job with the truth serum.

Thank you, I mouthed at him.

My best friend's arms closed around me, and I swung around to hug her.

She whistled like a yob on a building site. "You look like a warrior princess."

"And you look like a rock chick from the seedy part of town."

Marina's eyes twinkled. "Mission accomplished. I may be an empath, but I'm more goth girl than Mary Jane."

I patted the seat next to me. "You're here, next to me."

"Perfect. I was hoping to play footsies with Robert all night, but since he is sandwiched between man-eating coven sisters, you'll have to do."

Diagonally opposite me, wedged between Lavinia and one of her coven sisters, Sahil jittered with nerves.

I gave him a thumbs up.

"Your brother's in bad shape tonight," said Marina. "His aura is off. I tried to get him to open up on the way, but he wasn't having any of it. Closed up like a clam."

There was a scraping of chairs against the concrete floor as we all took out seats.

Orpheus raised an eyebrow and leaned closer to me. "This sort of thing makes me want to stake myself in the eye. But the rats can cook, and it is usually easier to bend Lavinia's will than to say no. I've always found it illuminating where Lavinia chooses to seat me at the dinner table. There was a time I would be in the centre. But now, like you, I find myself next to the kitchen."

"I quite like this view, actually." An army of rats could be seen dressed in tiny white coats and chef hats, stirring, chopping and plating up exquisite wares for our consumption. It was like Ratatouille on acid, an assembly line of skilled rodents. "A good thing the worktop in there isn't porous. Rats are incontinent, apparently."

"Yes, they are," said Marina cheerfully. "They use urine to mark routes and territory. I'm pretty sure we'll be ingesting some tonight unless the witches have gone to the effort of house-training them."

Orpheus sighed. "I am very picky about what and who I eat. There will be no bodily fluids in our dinner tonight. The coven rats are better trained than a dog at Crufts."

"Good to know," said Marina.

"It's all part of Lavinia's show of power. And she does like to revel in it. When you're as old as us, you realise that love, talent, beauty and happiness are all fleeting. Humdrum power, too, is fleeting. There are too many variables. Stock markets, housing values, divorce settlements." He raised a sardonic brow. "But for peculiars, power is easier to hold onto than other desires. An army of rat spies and chefs.

Cauldrons and spells. Aerial acrobatics on umbrellas. That woman is drunk on her sense of importance. Her very own aphrodisiac."

I stared at him open-mouthed. "Why, Orpheus, who knew you could talk in more than monosyllables about anything other than history?"

"Perhaps I'm not the person you think I am, druid." His eyes gleamed. "Of course, I know exactly who you are. For example, I know that you have no desire to be powerful. I'm not sure if that's to be pitied or lauded."

Marina leaned in. "Interesting how the non-coven women have been pushed to the sidelines. Who's the woman with the cat-like glasses next to Rayna Willowsun?"

"That's Margola Silver, the Minister for Information," said Robert.

"Men are allowed here by invitation only," said Orpheus. "When we enter the inner sanctum, it's all eyes on us. At least the ones currently in vogue. We're the prize, the toy, the entertainment. Female guests are the add-ons, not the main meal."

"Charming," said Marina. "So much for the sisterhood."

Phinnaeous Shine sat at the head of the table in a top hat. To his right was the werewolf alpha Gunnolf in a shirt that had been ironed for once. Just along was Helio, the Bestiary Minister, whose translucent wings fluttered in tandem with his expressive hands. There was Cillian O'Meara, the leprechaun Finance Minister, rubbernecking at the jewels and artefacts decorating the room, which I had assumed were fake until I saw the gleam in his eyes. I sucked in my breath at the sight of what could only be an angel with dirty wings and long, stringy blond hair. He reminded me of Kurt Cobain, and judging by the looks on the faces of the coven witches, he had exactly the same effect on them. I pulled my eyes away.

Orpheus rolled his eyes. "That's Erelim. Minister for Diplomacy."

"He's an angel."

"Erelim is an angel in physical form only. He's a tricky scoundrel, but then what would you expect from a diplomat?"

"Why are his wings so sooty and tattered? I imagined his wings would be more cloud-like, you know?"

Orpheus cocked an eyebrow. "Everyone's fallen nowadays, druid."

Lavinia occupied the central seat at the table. She stood, tapping a spoon against her champagne flute for attention.

The room quietened.

"Welcome, dear guests. Although dark times are upon us, I am grateful you've taken the time out of your busy schedules to break bread with us tonight. The rats have been toiling all day to cook us a feast that will delight our senses and sate our bellies. There is one who is not here tonight. Our darling Elvira was taken from us too soon and in the most heinous circumstances. But she, too, would want us to drink and be merry." Lavinia took her seat, smiling benignly at her guests.

As if on cue, the rats filed out to stand behind us, one for every guest, each balancing an aperitif and a starter of what looked like baked goat cheese with roasted pears and rocket salad.

Sahil physically recoiled.

"My darling werepigeon," said Lavinia. "Once you get used to the rats, you'll find they are as good as any concierge, chef or street fighter you'd find anywhere in the world. And their salaries are so cheap. A chunk or three of Appleby's Cheshire cheese or Red Leicester keeps them happy to follow orders."

The rats leapt onto the table with our starters, like gymnasts—aware of every body part from their tails to their whiskers. I looked on in awe as Marina gasped in delight.

"They are not so adept at serving soup," said Orpheus. "I should know."

I took a bite of my salad. "You know, it's actually quite nice sitting next to you when you're not delving into my thoughts."

He pushed his food around his plate, waiting for the rats to return to the kitchen. "I'm playing nice. It occurred to me after your revelation at our lesson that I need to ask something of you, Alisha. Do you think you can give it to me? Just a small favour."

"A favour? So can I refuse?"

Orpheus dropped his voice. "It wouldn't be wise, druid. There are plenty of those here eager to get their hands on your dragon. This request would be the cost of my silence. It would be so easy for me to open my mouth in this company. There are so many here waiting for you to slip up." He paused. "But I am also a useful ally."

My voice was cold. "What do you want, Orpheus?"

Beside me, Marina stilled. She squeezed my leg under the table.

"I'm a proud man. I don't ask a lot of anyone. If you find the Celestial Library, I need you to get something for me."

"Why can't you go yourself?"

Dark eyes that I couldn't read. "I have tried many times, but vampires are an embodiment of death. And death doesn't belong in something heavenly. Sometimes, death occurs inside the library, as with Rajika Verma. But death can never enter from the outside. The library's defences don't allow it."

"What is it you want?"

"In 1564, the theologian John Calvin died. At the time of his death, he had a chest in his home that contained all his worldly treasures. During Calvin's lifetime, many men had hunted for pieces of the cross of Christ. The cross had been found by St. Helena during her pilgrimage to the Holy Land in 326."

I frowned. "This isn't a history lesson, Orpheus."

His heavy brows snapped together. "Patience, druid. The cross was lost in the folds of time. Some theologians claimed the blood of Christ made the cross indestructible. So over the years, fragments of wood started to be sold as relics, and the relics multiplied until nobody knew what was real and what wasn't."

"But you started talking about Calvin's treasure chest."

"That I did. He had said that if all the supposed pieces of the cross were gathered, they would fill the cargo hold of an entire ship. When he died, a piece of the cross was found."

I gasped. "He had been hiding it all along?"

Orpheus nodded. "He had. That remnant, druid, is stored in the Celestial Library. And I would very much like you to obtain it for me."

"Why me?" I bit my lip, drawing blood.

His eyes followed the motion of my tongue. "Because I know you have a way to get inside. And I know you don't want me to spill your secrets."

Marina scooted under the table to retrieve a napkin and leaned across to give it to Orpheus, her hand lingering on his. "Would you look at that? You dropped your napkin, Minister."

He accepted the napkin with a curt nod. "So, do you have an answer, Alisha?"

I didn't want to make an enemy of him. I had already slighted him by choosing Ezra as my mentor over him. I lowered my voice to a whisper. "I don't like being threatened, Orpheus. And we're not friends, so I'm not doing you a favour for free, regardless of your threat to tell Lavinia of my dragon plans. What will you do for me in exchange?"

"I won't rig the magical trial in your favour or influence the vote," said Orpheus.

I flung up my hands in protest. "I wasn't going to ask you that."

A smirk. "Weren't you?"

I sighed. "Okay, maybe it crossed my mind. But a thought isn't a crime."

"I like you, druid, against my better instincts. That's why I'm going to tell you this as compensation for services about to be rendered. Your werepigeon brother has set something stupid in motion. I'm surprised it didn't happen sooner, given the state of his internal monologue. I had hoped he'd come to terms with his new self, but his jealousy of you riles him into poor decisions."

My blood cooled. "What has he done?"

"He is a changed man. If you value your relationship, you need to act now. Otherwise, it bodes ill for the future."

I stole a look at Sahil. "He what? What's he done?"

Orpheus rolled his eyes. "I might be a mind reader, but I don't know everything. Your brother's brain is a swamp. You don't want to know what he thinks about the empath. Especially in her outfit tonight."

Marina leaned forward. "I heard that."

"I suppose I have to give you something else in return for this titbit of information?" I said.

"No, that one is for free, as a sign of our friendship. Watch your back. He is not the man you think he is." He paused. "So, are we agreed?"

Ezra's eyes bored into me.

Talk about abandoning me in the viper's nest. "If I agree, there is no guarantee I will succeed."

"How right you are, Alisha. Nothing leaves the Celestial Library without the Custodian's permission. You will have to persuade her. But I will know if you failed or are deliberately thwarting me. Your thoughts will tell me. This will be our secret, druid." He pulled a card from his suit and pressed it into my palm. "Bring it to my den, not to Wildwoods."

"Watch out," said Marina. "My ears are burning. Someone's talking about us."

Lavinia raised her voice from across the table. "Would you look at that? Look at Orpheus and the druid in their cosy tête-à-tête. It's enough to make the rest of us feel left out. How selfish, Orpheus. You must share her with us. Tell us, druid, what do you think of our endeavours against the dark elves?"

I could feel Ezra's hackles rise from across the table, and I'd not even touched my chin yet.

The words came out before I could stop them, despite Marina's goth-girl boots kicking me under the table. "I think you've turned your might on the wrong people. You've already crushed the elves once before. They are not responsible for the tremors. You're as bad as bullies in a school playground. Or drunken louts in a pub who target someone just because they look different."

I could hear a pin drop. The rats stopped scuttling in the kitchen. The harp paused. Mouths stopped chewing, and cutlery was laid gently on plates. Blood rushed to my ears as all eyes turned to the Prime Sorcerer for the inevitable explosion. What I wouldn't have given to have Echo crooning a pop song to break the ice.

I scratched my chin.

Grey eyes held mine.

Phinnaeous Shine finished his mouthful, and when he turned to me, his eyes burned with passion. "Your accusation reeks of ignorance, druid. The Sorcerer's Senate embraces difference. Just look around you. You would do well to stay out of matters which don't concern you. The big guns are at the table. You're nothing more than a mewling lamb. Your grandmother would be turning in her grave."

I shrivelled with embarrassment. Would no one jump to my defence? My friends and even my brother remained quiet.

Orpheus coughed. "The dark elves are indeed a blight, Phinnaeous. But we cannot discount the theory of another reason for the tremors. My vampires have been trawling the city in the dead of night, as is their habit, and they have seen unnatural things. Herds of cows and deer moving in great swells across the city. Great wails coming from the caged beasts at London Zoo and in small holdings. One reported seeing a two-legged goat in Richmond Park who raised a top hat at him. Could it be that our intelligence has led us astray? Facts are more important than fiction."

The Prime Sorcerer slammed down his cutlery. "Hogwash, Orpheus. Besides, you know as well as I do that history is as much about the stories we tell ourselves, not about facts. I'm surprised to see you spout this nonsense. The Otherworld is only strong because we use all the advantages we have. In a few weeks, the elvish networks will be so destroyed they will struggle to even host a tea party, let alone launch an attack on an institution like Wildwoods." He turned to Robert. "The outcome of this war is practically signed, sealed and delivered. Isn't that right, Detective Jameson?"

Robert coloured. "Quite right, Prime Sorcerer. The Prime Minister is counting on it."

I smarted at the detective's cowardice and glowered at him. "You are destroying elvish lives, Prime Sorcerer. And for what?"

Lavinia banged the table.

"Enough! I won't have this insolence. I'm disappointed, Alisha." Her eyes glinted.

I wondered if this was what she'd wanted all along. To see me fail the trial because she had lost so much more than she had gained when we made our deal to defeat the sun god.

"You are one of our brightest initiates, Alisha," said Rayna. "I suggest you consider your next moves very carefully."

"Hear, hear," said Helio, the bestiary master. "You have so much to contribute to this fight. Not since Kraglek have we had the prospect of such a magnificent creature in our sights. A dragon would be my crowning glory."

Anger coursed through my veins. Tielbu wouldn't be theirs.

"You'd be wise to keep your mouth shut, druid," murmured Orpheus.

Ezra raised a glass. "I propose a toast to our new initiates. May they cover us in glory."

"May only the worthy pass the trial," said Phinnaeous.

"May they obey our rules," said Gunnolf.

"May they be the allies we deserve," said Lavinia.

I held Ezra's gaze, and we drank.

When Lavinia came around to murmur in my ear, her voice was hard. "I was wrong to trust you, druid."

I stuttered. "You weren't wrong, Lavinia. Together, we saved lives."

Cold fingers gripped my shoulder blades, but judging by her eyes, it was my throat she wanted. "I gained nothing. The vial of my nephew's blood didn't work."

I bit my lip. "You could ask for another. He is family, after all."

"You fooled me once. I won't fall for it again. No one denies me what I covet. You will pay for your deceit. I lost Elvira and the respect of my coven sisters. I won't be so quick to get into bed with you again. Bring me the dragon, or you will be sorry."

17

A main meal of stacked roasted aubergine, sautéed potatoes, tiramisu for dessert and a cheese board worthy of Buckingham Palace followed my outburst. I kept my mouth shut. Marina's hand on my knee, Ezra's tight smile and Orpheus' stony expression made sure of that. Once the ordeal of the coven dinner was over, Robert, Marina, Ezra and I slipped out into the night. Only Sahil stayed behind, buoyed by my public flogging and having far too much fun with the minor coven members to leave the party once the alcohol had eased his anxiety. Judging by the tentpole in his trousers as we left, he was feeling much more of a frisson than fear.

Ezra kept his silence until we piled into the front bench of Marina's van, which she'd parked on a side street. He was too clever to speak out beforehand. London had many rats, but the rats in Wimbledon were the most prolific of all, and the majority were loyal to the coven. What was more, I had just shown the head of the London coven that I was not on her side. The Minister for Defence knew only one mode of thinking. If I wasn't with her, I was against her.

"Well, at least we got out of there in one piece. Holy moly, the emotions were high in there." Marina turned the key in the ignition. The engine spluttered to life. "Rob?"

"Yes, sweet cheeks?" said the detective.

"Thank you for not assuming you'd drive."

"No problem. This beauty is your baby."

Marina grinned. "Don't you forget it."

Ezra swivelled to face me, his thigh pressed against mine. "Sorry to break the harmonious vibe in here, but I am so angry I could murder you, Alisha. What part of 'don't rock the boat' do you not understand?"

I winced. "Well, a good thing you didn't teleport me out of there. Judging by the look on your face, I would have ended up at the London Dungeons."

"A blessing, if you ask me," said Marina. "She would have puked all over you with all that goat cheese, burnt aubergine, cream and potentially rat piss floating around her stomach."

Ezra tore off his bowtie and opened his top button to reveal his charm necklace. "I'm not joking, Alisha. That was not good in there. You need votes to pass the trial. That means you need allies. The problem is, every time you open your mouth, you end up making enemies."

"Huh," I said, skewering Robert with a scathing look. "At least I had the balls to speak my mind."

"That's not fair. What was he supposed to do?" said Marina.

"It's called playing the long game, sunshine," said Robert.

Ezra bristled. "What did the vampire want? He was whispering in your ear all night."

I stiffened.

"Are you going to tell him, or should I?" said Marina.

I shrugged. "He wants me to convince the Custodian to let me take him a stake from the cross of Christ from the Celestial Library. If I don't, he'll tell them my plan to animate Tielbu away from the grasp of the senate."

Ezra cursed long and hard. "You've got to be kidding me. It's one thing, you going to the library tonight and animating the dragon, but two things can't happen. Orpheus can't get his hands on the stake, and your dragon can't fall into senate hands. You make sure when you animate that thing that you tell it to fly far away from here."

Warmth spread through me. "So you think I can do it?"

He gave me a black look. "You can do anything you set your mind to. If Phinnaeous Shine thinks you're a mewling lamb, he's mistaken, and it will cost him."

Robert rubbed his hand over his face. "Why would Orpheus want a piece from the cross? It's not my area of expertise, but an old sod knows that vampires fear holy relics."

"Actually, that's not true. They wouldn't be thrilled, but they can take a splash of holy water or a cross being shoved in their face," said Ezra. "But this is different. A piece of wood from the true cross, on which the son of God bled, would do real damage. So the question is, really, unless Orpheus is a hoarder of historical artefacts in his own right, why does he need such a deadly weapon?"

I held onto my seat as Marina flew over a pothole. "Maybe that's it. History *is* his jam."

Marina drew in a shaky breath and kept her eyes fixed on the road. "I know why. I felt it when I handed him his fallen napkin at dinner. Orpheus wants a piece of the cross because he wants to end his life."

I frowned. "That's ridiculous. An arrogant, self-serving beast of a man like that is having too much fun making other people miserable to take his own life."

"You're wrong, Alisha. It wasn't just tonight. I've sensed his sadness in my history lessons too. He's always droll, often obnoxious and sometimes downright scary," said Marina. "He is never happy or even content. He's in pain. I sensed it when I touched him tonight. That fragment is his exit out of the world."

"Holy shit," said the detective. "I'm pretty sure I don't have a duty of care to a suicidal vampire, but it's still enough to break your heart. Not mine, obviously. I'm as tough as nails, but like, your general observer would find this a sorry state of affairs. He needs to buddy up with someone, you know, so he can spill his thoughts and find peace."

Ezra gave a mirthless laugh. "That is the most ridiculous thing I've ever heard. Firstly, a centuries-old vampire finds peace by kicking the bucket. Secondly, if he opens his mouth to the senate, the ancient laws don't mess about. There's no workplace protection. He'll be kicked off for being unfit for duty. And if what Marina says is true, I'm pretty sure being a senate member is what's keeping him going."

"Well, then maybe he should talk to the other vampires in his den," I said.

"Those arseholes? The tiniest show of weakness, and they'll stick him in a coffin at the bottom of the ocean," said Ezra. "No, we stick to the plan. Find the library and claim your identity as an animator by bringing the dragon to life. Make sure you assign him a purpose when you do. Remember, his will is tied to yours at the moment of birth. The vampire can take care of himself. We're not going to make his problem better or worse. We're going to preserve the status quo."

I took a deep breath. I didn't like being told what to do. He had a point, but he wouldn't be in the field making those decisions. "Okay, so I have my orders. So it's time to give you *my* orders."

The copper flecks in his grey eyes danced. "I knew you were trouble."

An object flashed in the corner of my eye, coming at us like a bat out of hell.

I gripped the seat tightly as we chugged along. "What on earth? Stop Marina, that's…that's…"

I squinted into the darkness. It was in the middle of the road, straddling the dividing marker. It raced towards us, smaller than a car but bigger than a motorcycle.

Marina held her course, not slowing down, putting us on a collision course.

"Slow down, you lunatic," I said. "Pull over!"

Maybe it wasn't mechanical. It had a golden glow. A gracefulness of form that was familiar.

Marina pulled over to the kerb and rolled down her window. "It's Echo. Hey, Echo, over here."

Echo slowed his pace, and his glow subsided, revealing the rosettes on his coat so familiar to me. He padded over to the window. "Open the back of your van, Marina Ambrose. I came this way, hoping to find you all. I have much to tell you, but the ears out here are many."

The van groaned with his weight as Marina settled him into the back, cushioning him with blankets. She closed the doors and returned to the driver's seat while the rest of us swivelled to face Echo.

"What did you find?" I said.

He sank his head onto his paws. "I roamed the streets of the city. It was a night of respite from Lavinia's forces. Nothing was untoward, so I accepted the invitation of an old man, who gave me a tin of sardines. In thanks, I didn't eat his sausage dog. I talked my way into an elvish drinking hole and listened to their tales of woe. A group of pussies invited me to join them on the banks of the Thames for an evening of revelry, but I rejected them because I am a protector of the Vermas first and foremost, and the tremors had wounded Rajika's son."

"Are we any nearer to the point?" said Ezra.

"Nope," said the detective.

"Ignore them, Echo," soothed Marina, keeping her eyes on the road.

Emerald eyes glistened. "It was in the Royal Park of Richmond I found him. Disheartened that I hadn't been able to find any clues, despite my superior assets compared to a lowly detective—"

"Watch yourself," said Robert.

"I decided to buoy my spirits by hunting the deer in Richmond Park on my way here to meet you."

I jutted out my chin. "Gaia told you not to go there."

"But did she, Alisha? The goddess knows how to play me like a violin. I think she meant to nudge me in that direction without becoming embroiled in matters herself." He gave a throaty purr. "It feels good to be used by her."

Robert smirked. "The leopard sounds like a teenage boy."

Echo's growl reverberated in the van. "I was doing your job, Detective. You see, as well as over six hundred roaming deer in Richmond across a thousand hectares, I stumbled across the epicentre of the tremors—a being whose music called to me. Who would not be drawn to a rendition of *We Will Rock You* on the flute? It's very impressive, given his missing thumb."

I gave him a blank look. "The flute?"

Marina slammed on the brakes. "Pan, as in god of the shepherds and flocks, chaser of nymphs and lover of musical instruments?"

I flew forward.

Ezra pinned me back against the seat.

"Pan, the horny dude who also goes by the name of Faunus?" said Robert. "He's no threat. He settled down. He used to be a porn site owner. He has a thing for mating animals. But now he's a royal gamekeeper and a board member at Battersea Dogs Home."

Echo nodded. "He's quite a strange fellow when you meet him. His clothes reminded me of an English gentleman's, all cord and buttoned-up tweed. Except he had a forward-leaning body, with skinny calves and strong thighs that gave him a ridiculous air. He had pale green eyes and a mop of thick, brown hair. Worst of all were the horns that protruded from his head, covered only by a tatty top hat, which fell off when he saw to the fire. Not forgetting his missing thumb, of course."

My pulse accelerated. "I remember Pan from my parents' stories. He's half divine, half animal. That dualism runs through his personality. He's cheerful and playful one minute and devious and terrifying the next. He likes both disorder and harmony, depending on his mood. He's a trickster god. A god of panic. Which Pan did you meet tonight, Echo?"

"It was a delightful half-hour in his company. Luckily, I hadn't harmed his flock yet, although I had been eyeing some juicy rumps. He was tickled that I shared my given name with a beautiful nymph he used to know. He played his pipe and confided in me that Ra's exploits led to him regaining some of his old strength."

I grimaced. "Pan's strength is legendary. Him getting stronger is not a good development."

Echo growled. "I met a god who is tired of blending in. A god who has reclaimed the thrill he gets from causing panic. A god who agrees with Ra that human suffering causes panic."

Marina frowned. "But how is he making the tremors occur, Echo?"

"By moving the flocks as one, of course. Pan controls them all: the deer, the sheep, the geese, and the goats. It is effortless for him. A simple run of notes on his flute, and they do his bidding, sending tremors through the earth. He revels in the chaos and the panic. The ensuing loud noise of crashing buildings and urgent sirens excites him. He doesn't mean to kill or maim, but this destructive side of him is as much a part of him as the caring side of his flocks. He grows stronger from the prayers of the fearful and grieving. He is enjoying himself for the first time in centuries. He told me himself, from his own lips, just before I came here. He's not going to stop without reason."

Marina sighed and started up the van again. "But why isn't Gaia doing anything about it?"

I folded my arms in anger. "Why does Gaia do anything? She's a law unto herself. And here we are, stuck in the middle of this again."

A wolfish growl met my ears. "I've given up scolding you for flouting the Magical Constitution. There will come a time when you will reap the consequences, but it is not for me to police you. But one thing is set in stone. You promised me that you'd put the trial first, Alisha."

"He's right," said Marina.

"No," said Robert. "He isn't. You lot may not be police officers, but you can't stand back and do nothing about this. It's us, or it's a whole lot of innocents harmed. Will you have that on your conscience?"

Ezra glowered, and nobody said a word. The silence was punctuated only by the splutter of the engine.

"I'm not backing down on this, Ezra. We just can't. I won't," I said. "But tonight, I'm going to meet my dragon, and nobody is holding me back from that."

The tension in his jaw eased, and he sighed. "Okay, hellfire. We'll do it your way. Get your dragon, secure your destiny as an animator, and then we'll find a way to appeal to the trickster god's gentler side."

"Be careful, Alisha," said Echo. "The Celestial Library can be a dangerous place."

Marina drew to a halt outside Shanghai Moon. "It's decided then. Go kick some butt, Alisha. Echo can stay at mine tonight."

I nodded and kicked off my strappy sandals. Then I pulled out my hair clip and left it on Marina's dashboard before tying my hair in a ponytail with a hairband knocking about the van.

Marina gave me a knowing smile. "Uh oh. She means business."

Ezra and I climbed out.

My bare feet hit the asphalt.

Marina's rainbow head leaned out of the window. "Call me."

They drove away, bumping along the uneven street.

Ezra sighed. "Since I can't come with you, do you want me to walk you inside?"

I leaned into his chest for a brief moment. I almost spilt the beans about Orpheus's concerns that Sahil had done something stupid, but I held back. We already had so much on our plates. My brother would have to wait. "Nah, I got this."

"Okay. Good luck, Alisha." He kissed the top of my head and teleported away, leaving me standing in the deserted street, wondering if I had bitten off more than I could chew.

18

Pungent smoke from an incense burner curled through the air as I walked into Shanghai Moon at half past eleven. Fei Yen and Faeza, in matching chequered pyjamas, rushed over in a fluster.

Faeza ushered me towards a small round table. "You're cutting it fine. In half an hour, Beltane will be over, and your passage to the Celestial Library will not be so certain."

"I'm sorry," I said, pressing a kiss on both of their cheeks. "I got here as soon as I could."

Fei Yen frowned. "Why are you barefoot? Have you had trouble with the rats?"

"No, actually, they were delightful tonight if I block their incontinence out of my mind. The bare feet are more because I can't run in high heels." I looked at their tiny feet. "And I'm pretty sure you don't have trainers in size 6 for me to borrow."

Fei Yen shook her head. "I'm afraid we wear children's shoes. A consequence of foot binding. You have your father's picture?"

I nodded and craned my neck to look around the shop. "Are you hiding the gate in plain sight?"

"Something like that." Faeza cleared away a stack of gloopy Chinese takeaway boxes from the table. "Take a seat."

We sat, three women around the table, one in an evening dress, the other two in pyjamas. On the table were a simple lamp and a stack of tarot cards. A midnight blue curtain hung from a circular rail on the ceiling. Fei Yen pulled it over the rail, enclosing us in the soft velvet folds, which glittered with silver sequins that looked like stars.

"Take some deep breaths, Alisha, and remove the frown from your face," said Fei Yen. "While you look quite the picture in that dress with your dirty feet and the scowl, you do not come to the cards with a fighting disposition. You come with a softness."

I filled my cheeks with air and blew out what I could of my stress, although, to be honest, it would take a day with a masseur to really get anywhere. "This isn't what I was expecting."

Fei Yen snorted. "If you are going to succeed in the Otherworld, perhaps it's time for you to clear your mind of expectations. They will only hold you back. Now take some deep breaths."

I resisted the urge to roll my eyes.

Faeza picked up a deck of cards bordered in gold. She shuffled it with the ease of a casino croupier. "In my hands are twenty-two Major Arcana cards and fifty-six Minor Arcana cards across four suits: Cups, Pentacles, Swords, and Wands. I'd like you to tap the deck to spread your energy through them."

I tapped them, and a frisson of anticipation made me shiver.

"Now I need you to ask an open question that will get you closer to the library," said Faeza.

"Sounds easy enough," I said. "Will I make it inside?"

Fei Yen rolled her eyes. "That's just about as closed as it gets."

"Way to put me at ease."

"It's okay, Alisha. Just try again," said Faeza.

"How about…how can I get into the Celestial Library?"

Faeza chewed her lip. "Better but not quite there. It's a little self-serving. The library likes its visitors to be pure of heart."

"Gah, hang on." I slowed down my breathing and closed my eyes. Then it came to me. "Where is the hidden opportunity in a druid visiting the Celestial Library?"

"Yes, I think that might be it." Fei Yen's eyes shone. "And just in time. Hurry, Faeza, Beltane is almost over. We have mere minutes. You'll have to go with a three-card spread, not the Celtic Cross."

Faeza nodded. She cut the deck by dividing it into several piles and then folded them into one again. Then she spread the cards across the table with an artful swish of her hand. "Choose three cards, Alisha. Quickly."

I scanned the cards, my heartbeat hammering. Their backs were satin black with rounded edges. Three floated towards me. I reached out and touched them. "Those ones."

We all leaned forward as Faeza turned over the cards.

"The Two of Cups," she said. On the card, a barely clad man and woman exchanged cups in a ceremony. "This card implies balance, respect and honour. You have the opportunity for new partnerships if you are aware of your talents and strengths as a couple and trust one another to do what you are good at."

"Hurry, my love," said Fei Yen.

Faeza turned over the next two cards in quick succession. "The Ten of Pentacles and the Wheel of Fortune. Oh, Alisha, Alisha. Only your intuition will tell you if these are auspicious cards or not."

On the second card, an old man sat beneath an archway leading to bounteous vineyards. At his feet sat his family. The final card depicted an enormous wheel covered in symbols of the zodiac. A sphinx that reminded me of Wildwoods sat on the top of the wheel. A devil on the bottom.

"My intuition is currently as useful as a lump of rock," I said.

She patted my hand. "The Ten of Pentacles speaks to your ancestry and your future. Your family roots have set you in good stead, and you should have no fear. The wheel symbolises that greater forces than us are at work here. The same forces that govern the changing of the seasons. But the wheel is no cause for fear. It symbolises the relentless forward motion of time but also renewal and growth." They gathered the remaining deck and put it to one side, leaving the three cards I had chosen facing upright. "These are your cards, Alisha, but only one is the gateway. This is your journey now. Choose the door."

I gulped.

"Quickly, Alisha," came Fei Yen's frantic voice. "The window of opportunity is almost gone. Thirty seconds until the clock strikes midnight."

I lunged forward and touched the Ten of Pentacles, thinking of the mum I had lost and the grandmother I had never truly known. I gasped as icy cold travelled up my arm and spread to my whole body, giving me nipples as hard as bullets and stiffness to my very bones. I clamped my eyes shut as fear clouded my mind.

"Breathe," came Fei Yen's soothing voice from far away. "Trust in the universe."

The cold was everywhere. My eyelids, my bum cheeks, my ears and my nose. Everything was so cold it hurt.

Then, somehow, just as Alice went through the looking glass, I went through the tarot card. In that fleeting second, I sensed the turning of the Earth, the heat of the sun, and the death of distant stars. But it was Neptune that called to me, the windiest planet in the solar system.

Part of me wanted to let go, to be lost in the folds of the world without the need to think or strive or do the laundry. Still, even as I considered it, I knew my loved ones needed me, and I needed them. I was as likely to let them down as I was to eat a whole bag of doughnuts without regrets.

I drew on the strings in my mind and pulled my question close to me. *Where is the hidden opportunity in a druid visiting the Celestial Library?*

Something snapped, and I catapulted forward, too cold to even tremble.

A sudden stop. A warming of the temperature.

I opened my eyes. I was in a great hall bathed in golden light, with white marble pillars threaded with pink veins. A fireplace had been lit in the corner next to two armchairs. It crackled and spat and beckoned me with its glow. I approached it, shaking like a leaf, and sank into an armchair. The blue tinge to my extremities struck me with horror, as if my fingers and toes had been frozen deeply. I was too afraid to check that my bra still held the picture of Tielbu, in case my fingers snapped off before they thawed.

As I considered my options, a strange scratching sounded across the stone floors. A woman wearing a three-quarter-length trouser suit approached. She had a grace about her, from the silver threads in her shoulder-length dreadlocks to the calm in her brown eyes and the sheen of her tawny skin. She wore lashings of mascara and metallic eyeshadow the same shade as the blade runners strapped to her thighs.

A calm descended over me. My intuition told me she wasn't an immediate threat. Well, my intuition and the fact she was carrying gifts which could only be meant for me.

"Welcome, druid," she said with a sad smile. She handed me a hot water bottle, a fluffy dressing gown, slippers for my feet and a cup of sweet, milky tea.

I relaxed into the dressing gown, realising with a start that it was warm, then eased my toes into the slippers. Then I hugged the hot water bottle to me for a moment, placed it on my lap and took a slurp of the tea. Warmth spread through me, and I started to feel more like myself.

"Thank you," I said. "How did you know how I like it?"

"I know lots of things, Alisha Verma. I am the Custodian, after all. I even know that you prefer your tea without sugar unless you are overly tired or have been through an ordeal, in which case you like two heaped spoons of brown sugar."

"How wonderful. Can I stay here forever?" I frowned. "I didn't mean that. Although it is nice here." I blinked, and endless rows of books appeared: leather-bound, pocket-sized, gilded, hardbacked and spiral-bound. "I mean, really nice."

"Oh, this is just the pre-chamber." She sat in the other armchair and crossed one leg over the other so her trouser leg rode up to reveal scarred skin underneath. "First, we must deal with formalities. You came through the tarot?"

I nodded and took another slurp of tea. "I did."

"It was made easier because it is Beltane. The first of May."

The colour had returned to my fingers. "That's right."

She leaned forward, and though the fire spat embers her way, she did not flinch. "And because your grandmother has been here and your mother before that. That is why you came in so easily. Third generation rights. Although that hasn't always worked out so well in the past."

I punched the air, and my tea slopped dangerously against the edges of my cup. "I knew it. I knew Mum had been here."

The Custodian regarded me with narrowed eyes. "Regardless of your gene pool, your visit will end abruptly unless you pass the test."

"Did my mum pass the test?"

A grunt. "Well, of course, she did. She had the wherewithal to bring me a signed first edition. A marvellous addition to my collection, I might add, and a gutsy ploy. She was an impressive woman. I am sorry for your loss, by the way. But for those who fail the test, there is no guarantee that you will be able to return from whence you came."

I sat bolt upright. Now that I was warm, I really didn't want to risk the journey again. Not yet. "My friends didn't tell me that."

"Why would they? Fear would only have made the pull of the dark greater." The Custodian paused. "Regardless of your natural advantages, it's not easy to find your way here. Many have failed before you. Tell me, druid, how did you hold on?"

"My leopard's supply of steak needs replenishing, and I am the woman to do it."

"It is an unusual reason but a valid one." She tapped her knees. "We will begin."

The flames of the fire leapt higher. It blazed, casting shadows deep into the room.

I put my cup aside.

"First, we test your druidness. The library itself is a living organism with likes and dislikes. Just as humans are picky about who is allowed into their inner circle, the library, too, has requirements. For example, it won't lend to people who bend the corners of pages or break the bindings of books. It has a particular dislike for people who leave bogies on pages, which is why a certain Bestiary Minister is never allowed through these doors again."

I wrinkled my nose. "Eww. That's disgusting."

"Since you have entered on Beltane, we will ascertain how druid you are." She raised an eyebrow. "Nobody likes cultural appropriation."

I thought of Orpheus's insistence that I was the product of two druid lines. "I have it on good authority that I am quite druid."

"Then you won't mind answering these questions. Are you a Bard?"

I shook my head. "I am not."

"Can you play any folk instruments?"

"Er, no."

"Not even the banjo?"

"No."

"How about a mandolin?"

"Nope."

"Not even a kazoo?"

I hung my head.

"A sitar?"

She frowned. "Well, that's a disappointment. The sitar is my favourite."

I looked up. "My parents have one gathering dust at their house."

"That's hardly something to boast about. I was hopeful when I saw the tone of your skin that you might be a sitar virtuoso, with you being Indian."

"I have both French and Indian heritage, actually. And I haven't asked you if you can rap just because you are black."

She laughed. "I like straight-talkers. Not many of them left these days." She stood up, and her blade runners tapped against the floor as she strode to the mantlepiece. "Hang on, just let me get the implement."

I didn't like the sound of that. It sounded like some sort of sixteenth-century torture device. "What implement?"

"The one that tells me if I can take a chance on you." She picked up a small oblong object from the mantlepiece and came to my side. "Say ahh."

"Is that hygienic?" I said, just to register some sort of protest. I opened my mouth anyway.

She held it under my tongue, and the clouds cleared from her face.

"Just as I thought. One hundred per cent druid. Which means no elvish or vampire blood."

I baulked and drew my head back. "That didn't seem very hygienic. Why are you against elves and vampires?"

"For two very different reasons. This is the Celestial Library. Death doesn't belong in something heavenly. And the elves are a difficult people. All people have both good and bad in them, except the elves too often have let their good side be submerged underneath the darker side of their natures. Whether that is their fault is another matter entirely." She sighed. "Still, it is time for the final obstacle. We must ascertain the purity of your heart."

"How can we possibly do that? Do I pinkie swear? Or do the Scouts' Promise?" I shuddered. "Or must I take a truth serum?"

"Are you always this melodramatic? There is only one way for us to test your heart, and that is by introducing you to Nightfall."

"Nightfall?"

A clacking of hooves echoed through the great hall. My heart clamoured when I saw an enormous black stallion approaching. He whinnied and snorted as he trotted over to the armchairs, and when he reached the Custodian, he tossed his mane and bowed before her. She laid her forehead against his. He nuzzled her, and she laid a gentle hand on his muzzle.

"To pass the test, all you need to do is ride Nightfall from here back to the end of the hall."

"But he's not even wearing a saddle."

Nightfall turned his head towards me. When his demeanour changed, I almost wet myself. I would have preferred to do endless pelvic floor exercises than to ride him. God knew my bladder could have done with a bit more control. He bared his teeth. His ears were forward like he was some sort of Soviet spy actively monitoring me. He surged forward and nudged me.

I recoiled. "He looks a bit demonic if you ask me."

"Alisha, he's in the Celestial Library. Trust me, he's not demonic."

I grimaced. "Oh, I don't know. He looks pretty villainous to me. Is frothing at the mouth normal for him?"

The Custodian sighed. "This is your test, not Nightfall's. Unless you are giving up?"

I shrugged off the dressing gown and my slippers. I'd only ridden a few times before—on family holidays when the horse had been trained to follow a course regardless of who was on its back. This was going to be a whole different ballgame. I took a deep breath and approached Nightfall.

He whinnied, his tail swishing.

"Do you have any carrots? I think I can get him to follow me."

"It's ride or die," said the Custodian.

"Like literally?"

"Your guess is as good as mine."

"That's comforting." I held my hand up to calm Nightfall, whose tail had now reached a frenzy.

He towered over me, his coat so glossy that, without a saddle, I feared falling off. That was if I even made it up there.

"In your own time." The Custodian's voice dripped with sarcasm.

I looked behind me at the armchair.

The horse followed my every move.

I leapt on the armchair, hitched up my dress and sprang onto Nightfall's back, using my strong kickboxing legs to hold on for dear life as he bucked, leaning forward to keep my centre of gravity low.

"Easy, Nightfall." I patted his flank and murmured against his skin. "I'm not going to hurt you."

His ears turned sideways, and the bucking stopped. But I still had no idea how to get him to move in the right direction. I couldn't cling on in a stationary position forever. Not to mention the large expanses of skin I was exposing in an outfit utterly unsuited to this task.

I clamped my legs tighter and windmilled backwards so one arm could reach Nightfall's rump. I was an animal lover. I wouldn't have used a whip even if I'd had one.

Instead, I lifted a hand, my heart racing, and sent a gentle breeze up his arse.

I shrieked and catapulted forwards, slipping and sliding and cursing. The sound of thunderous hooves filled my head: twenty metres, ten metres, five metres from the end of the hall. The books were a blur beside me, and I wondered what would happen if my life ended here, in this limbo place my loved ones couldn't reach.

Nightfall jerked, his hooves now sliding against the floor, his motion slowing.

I took my chance and slipped from his back, twisting as I fell. Horror filled me as I took in the void beyond the hall. The fear in the whites of Nightfall's rolled eyes cut me to the core. I hit the deck and ignored the blunt pain in my forty-year-old back. I raised my hands, called the wind to me, and created a buffer between horse and void. I held it until he regained his footing and then released it. Only then did I collapse onto the floor, utterly spent.

The horse trotted over to me and nuzzled my hair.

I'd need a salt bath after that knock, a whole load of paracetamol and a chiropractor, but at least I'd made a friend.

The Custodian loomed over me. "Bravo, druid."

"I passed?"

A serene smile flitted across the Custodian's lips. "You chose Nightfall's welfare over your own. I'd say that proves your purity of heart, and the library agrees."

"Well, that's a relief." I tugged my dress to preserve my modesty.

"Did you really doubt yourself? Isn't it odd? Women can be as glorious as the night stars but waste time navel-gazing. And yet, flawed, crusty, self-congratulatory men never once consider that someone else might be better placed to pick up the sword."

I looked at her feet. "Is that how you got those? By picking up the sword?"

The Custodian tutted. "That's not something you ask a person on the first encounter."

I flushed. "I'm sorry. I don't even know your name."

"Most people call me by my title. But before that, I was called Calypso Archer."

Now the test was over, I searched her, looking for pointy ears, wings, fangs or hairy body parts. Anything to give me a clue as to where she fitted in the Otherworld. "May I ask what kind of peculiar you are?"

"My dear druid. My talents are many, but they are not peculiar.

Come. Time passes quickly between the seams of the world, and you will want some sleep before the day dawns. We find ourselves poised at the threshold. Soon, you will tell me why you have come, but first, your reward for passing the test. You do wish to see the library? All you have to do is open your eyes."

I sat up and groaned. "They are open."

"No, I mean *really* open them."

19

I blinked, and the great hall transformed. The walls vanished, and the pillars sank into the ground. The floor surged until it reached farther than the eye could see. I sucked in my breath.

Paintings of angels and cherubs danced on the ceiling in the flickering light of stars and planets. The bookshelves existed still, but they multiplied in number and rose higher still, endless reams of wisdom and love and entertainment between those bindings. Behind us, the fire roared still, primitive and true. The armchairs, however, had become iron thrones with high backs and gilded ridges, and I frowned, thinking how plush the seat had seemed underneath my bottom. Feathers lay under my feet. I wondered if this was a room of tricks or true desires.

Nightfall gave a neigh of goodbye and cantered off into the distance.

Calypso smiled. "You didn't think the library would reveal its true image without you passing the test, did you? Even in the throes of battle with the dark elves, it kept most of its secrets."

I stood, groaning at my aching muscles, then looked around in wonder.

She strode ahead like an impatient guide at a museum. "Do follow.

The Celestial Library is not the only moving library in the world. There are physical libraries that are passed down through households, of course. Then there are libraries in the minds of passionate readers, who are just as likely to offer a quote as they are to kiss their mothers. There are libraries on e-readers, entire worlds that fit into a jacket pocket. That's a special kind of magic. There are libraries on rickety wheels that offer a lifeline to poor communities. I especially like those. Oh, and libraries in little boxes at the end of driveways. Not the most glamorous sort but an exemplar of generosity. And finally, rather ridiculously, there's the main library at Indiana University, which sinks an inch into the ground each year because engineers failed to account for the weight of all the books it would eventually hold." She paused. "All those libraries are worthy places, but they are not quite like this one."

I didn't know whether to look up at the angels and planets or sideways at the bookshelves, where I spotted Gaiman, Angelou, Hawking, Austen, Hemingway, L'Engle, Nin and a curious tiny book from 1913 called *Don'ts for Wives* by Blanche Ebbutt.

Calypso grimaced. "Sadly, I'm a custodian, not a curator."

"It's a wonderful collection. I did English Lit at university, you know." For some reason, I craved her approval.

She raised an eyebrow. "There are many other languages with valuable literature apart from English, Alisha."

"Oh, yes, I completely agree." I flushed and stared at the shelves. "There's no particular order. It's not alphabetic or based on genre or even on colour. How are you supposed to find what you want here? Is there a catalogue?"

"Don't be silly. The best reads are discovered by accidental browsing," said Calypso.

"But what if I wanted to read something in particular?"

"Well, then you close your eyes, of course, picture what you want and walk the way the universe pulls you."

A shiver ran up my spine. "That sounds dangerous."

"No worse than crossing the street in London." She gave me the eye. "Now tell me, druid. You are allowed to take one item away from the library. What is your request? Perhaps the first draft of *The*

Handmaid's Tale or *Jekyll & Hyde*? Maybe Frida Kahlo's journal interests you more. Or John Travolta's script from *Pulp Fiction*?" She rubbed her hands in glee. "No, I don't think that's quite it. How about an interactive set of *Harry Potter* books? No? Then maybe a copy of *Faustus* once read by the devil himself?"

I took a deep breath. "Actually, it's not books I am after today."

Calypso's brow furrowed. "An English Lit graduate who does not wish to borrow a book?"

"I'd like to read everything in these walls, but sometimes need has to come before desires." Anxiety exploded in my stomach. "I thought after coming all this way, I'd be able to take as much as I wanted."

Calypso grunted. "Like a spoiled child in a sweet shop? I'm sorry, druid. It doesn't work that way. What you take from the library, the library will require back in some form, whether now or at a later date. In a more beautiful world, of course, dealings with the Celestial Library would be less transactional. But this is not a beautiful world. It is a world of monsters."

I gulped. "That's a bit bleak."

"I like to think it's truthful. How can we stand in a place of knowledge and not speak the truth?" She pressed her lips together. "Make your request pure, druid, or the library will exact a price from you greater than you wish to give."

My mind raced through my options. Ezra had encouraged me to focus all my energy on animating Tielbu here. But he was unfamiliar with the Celestial Library.

How could I turn down the opportunity to return with something wondrous?

Orpheus wanted the remnant of the cross for himself, but he was possibly suicidal. While I didn't want to be responsible for his death, I didn't take his threat to reveal my plans to the senate lightly. Except if I animated Tielbu in the library, the senate wouldn't be able to get their hands on him anyway. Even if Lavinia heard about it, it's not like I had anything to lose. Her trust in me was already broken. So Orpheus was shit out of luck.

I frowned. I could ask for the choker necklace from the will, the one Mum had said I'd find in the seams of the world. The Custodian had confirmed Mum had been here, so it only followed that my hunch had been right. Although maybe it was selfish to come all this way and ask for something of value only to me. Hadn't my very own grandmother laid down her own life in this place for the good of others?

"You seem to be torn," said Calypso.

Something niggled at me. Echo had confirmed that Pan was behind the tremors.

I jumped, sending feathers wafting up. That was it. "I need an artefact, not a book."

Her eyebrows shot up. "And what makes you think we hold artefacts here, druid?"

"I may be new to all this, but I've been listening in my history lessons. I have gone unheard when teaching so many of my own lessons that I always listen when the tables are turned." I paused. "I need something to convince a powerful being to lay down his weapons."

Calypso sighed. "That is never an easy task. You have two options. You can overpower them or convince them of the error of their ways. Neither is easy. Follow me."

She strode on, faster on her blade runners than I could keep up with.

I scampered after her, dirty and tired but with growing certainty that I was right to ignore Orpheus's needs and my own.

The run of bookshelves ended, and Calypso turned into an arched doorway made of oak. She whispered three short words in an unfamiliar tongue, Welsh or Gaelic or something altogether unknown. The door creaked open, and she stepped over the threshold. "Are you coming or not?"

I followed her in with a darting gaze.

The room was small, with low light and a cool temperature. On the floor was a thick rug that muffled the sound of our feet. I inched forward to get a closer look. Brass tables lined the walls, topped with red velvet pillows which displayed wares as if this were a high-end jeweller.

Calypso turned to face me. "There are a small number of vaults like this dotted around the Celestial Library. They are never in the same place. They move like blood cells around a body in a never-ending but random cycle. It's a system put in place by the very first Custodian."

"My grandmother?"

She folded her arms. "I've lost count of the number of times I've been asked that very question. Rajika Verma was the seventy-eighth Custodian. She was an impressive person, but it's tiresome when everything is attributed to her."

I winced. I'd obviously touched a nerve.

Calypso waved a neatly manicured hand. "Each vault contains a number of objects stored separately from the main collection. They are varied in nature, donated by or stolen from heroes and heroines across history. Here is a Girl Scout sash that imbues the wearer with an extraordinary sense of practicality. How do you think Mary Poppins was able to get those Banks children in line? Over there is a telephone that can call anyone, dead or alive."

My heart hammered in my throat. I definitely would be back for that one.

"And over there," said Calypso, "is a key that will fit any type of lock of any type of door or window. We're very careful about who we lend that one out to. There's Shakespeare's quill that makes any struggling author a master playwright, Hemingway's typewriter, of particular value to those who struggle with brevity, and a lens once belonging to Galileo, for those poor at directions."

I frowned. "Isn't that what sat navs are for?"

"Yes, druid, but they always need updating." Calypso walked over to the far corner of the room, where a tightly woven straw bag rested on a cushion. "This is what I think you are looking for: the bag of storm winds gifted to Odysseus. It is a bag of cunning as well as great power because your opponent will not know you are carrying a weapon when they look at it. And as a wind druid, you are well suited to wield this power. It will only be yours momentarily, but it will allow you to carry your opponent far away so that he may never cause harm again." Her tone sharpened. "However, I must warn you,

Alisha, that a weapon like this should not be used lightly to solve an argument between men."

"And what if the person in question isn't a man?"

Calypso frowned. "Is he an animal?"

"Half animal, half god, I think."

Her head jerked in surprise. "Do not bite off more than you can chew, druid. The laws of the universe are many. Some are written. Others are convention. Many more are unspoken. It seems to me that you like to bend the rules. Just don't break them, or even your allies won't be able to come to your aid."

The dim lights in the vault turned up a notch and then faded once more as if they had a faulty connection.

"Well, isn't that something?" said Calypso. "It turns out that the library would like me to bend the rules this time in honour of your grandmother, who once served here." She turned on her heel, crossing to the brass table on the far side, from where she picked up a small piece of wood.

I recoiled, thinking it was the remnant of the true cross and that the universe was telling me to fulfil Orpheus's request after all.

Calypso turned the wood over in her hands, taking great care not to damage it. "I should really wear gloves when handling this. It's cypress wood, found amongst the plains of Mount Ararat where the borders of Turkey, Armenia and Iran intersect."

I peered closer. "Am I supposed to know what it is?"

She huffed. "It's a piece of the bow from Noah's Ark."

"*The* Noah?" There was a nursery around the corner from my flat called Noah's Ark. She was probably talking about that one.

Calypso rubbed her temples like I was giving her a headache. "Of course that Noah. Which other Noah goes by one name only? This artefact might not seem like much, but it has a gentle power. It reminds the holder of their better natures. And believe me, druid, lasting success comes only when you appeal to a person's humanity. Generosity is always more effective than barbarity. Whether you choose to heed my advice is your choice."

I'd heard that advice three times now. From Dad, who had said, *a man can lose his way if he drifts from his faith.* From Gaia, who questioned my own faith and had told me that *not every battle is solved by escalating into war.* And now from the Custodian. *Generosity is always more effective than barbarity.*

"I don't know how to thank you."

She handed me the artefacts.

The bag weighed nothing at all. The wood, too, was so light it was easy to think I was coming away with some fancy dress knockoffs.

"You may take both items, druid, although you may use only one. Borrowers may use artefacts for seven days unless they have a special exemption. On the seventh day, I will collect the items from wherever they are in the universe."

This woman couldn't be cooler.

I wanted her job. The view. The books. The secrets. I wanted to be her.

"If that is all, druid, I will ask Nightfall to take you to the void. You are not the only visitor here tonight."

I swallowed hard. Now didn't seem the right time to ask her for a favour. "Actually, there is the small question of a dragon."

20

Calypso led me out of the vault and locked the door shut behind us. She frowned. "A dragon? There has not been a dragon on earth for many moons, Alisha. Unless you are talking about a fictional one? Smaug from *The Hobbit* perhaps, or Viserion from *A Song of Ice and Fire*, now rather commonly known as *Thrones*?"

I set down the artefacts on a shelf. The picture of Tielbu poked me. "I have something in my bra."

"I'm not the sort of person who responds to being propositioned, druid. I prefer to do the propositioning myself."

My cheeks flushed. "Oh no, you misunderstand. I'm seeing a werewolf, and before that, I had a humdrum husband, who is now an ex-husband, and to be honest, I really should have given myself more time to be alone. So, you see, I really wasn't propositioning you."

She shoved her hands in her pockets, taking her coolness level up to a whole new level. I was pretty sure Marina would find her irresistible.

Calypso pursed her lips. "I don't know whether to be offended or relieved, but we move on."

"Is it true that what happens within this library cannot be seen by anybody on Earth, even gifted peculiars?"

"Not only is that true, but not even those from other planets can see what occurs here. Why do you ask, druid?"

I reached for the picture of Tielbu.

Realisation dawned across her face. "So you have even more in common with your grandmother than I thought. What is it you need from me, granddaughter of Rajika?"

"I need a safe space to animate my dragon. I've been close a few times before. I can feel him underneath my fingertips, but I've never quite had the courage to see it through." I looked around the central space, where the ceilings had opened up again and the planets shone above in the vast void of space. "My gut says that my dragon would quite like to be born here, amongst the stars. What is more, he will be born free, not a slave to those on earth who want to use him. I don't have a child, so I have no idea what it is to be maternal. Maybe the dragon is the closest I'll come to that emotion. All I know is I feel a great sense of responsibility to him. He wouldn't have to stay here, but if this could be the place of his birth, I would be very grateful."

"This is no place for a dragon. Just imagine what his fiery breath would do to my books." Calypso scrutinised me far longer than comfortable. "But I, too, value freedom. I will grant you your request if you grant one for me."

"What do you want?"

"I wish for a day where you swap places with me, and I can roam the world without care or responsibilities."

A day to roam this library without someone looking over my shoulder. Hell, yes. I almost bit her hand off. "Done."

"Then pick up your artefacts, druid, and be quick about it."

She raised her hands like a conductor, and the Celestial Library responded. A shuttering sound occurred, a twisting, a closing, and suddenly the bookshelves vanished, and only bare shelves remained. Calypso whistled low and long and in cantered Nightfall, satin black against the feathery floor. She leapt as he approached, bouncing high off her blade runners and landing cleanly on his back. He whinnied in greeting.

"What are you waiting for?" She leaned down for the artefacts, then again to haul me up behind her, my pelvis tucked in close against her bottom. She rode hard towards the fireplace as the library closed behind us, and a series of locks and bolts echoed in our ears.

This was exactly the kind of dramatic but gentle erotica that made Marina horny. It just made me terrified.

"Phew. That was close," said Calypso as we reached the fireplace. "I hope my other visitor holds his nerve until I get back."

I unpeeled myself from her back, jumped off Nightfall and reached for the artefacts. "Sorry to break it to you, but I'm pretty sure they've pissed on the floor."

"Well, never mind. Clean-up is not part of my job," she said. I was really starting to covet her job. She rode Nightfall to the farthest corner of the room. "It's time to find your courage, druid."

My stomach churned. I laid aside the bag of Odysseus's winds and the piece of Noah's Ark. The air was still and quiet, apart from sighs coming from Nightfall. I blocked out both horse and mistress and unfolded the crumpled picture of Tielbu. I knew him, even though I hadn't yet met him. He'd been with me all my life, so this wasn't like conjuring a stranger. It was conjuring a friend.

A few cleansing breaths later, I was ready to begin.

I trailed my fingers over the page. The flames from the fireplace cast shadows over Tielbu, making him more fearsome than in my childhood stories.

I looked into his gentle, amber eyes. I didn't know if it was the otherworldly strangeness of the Celestial Library, the knowledge that nobody could find us here or the lingering presence of my grandmother, but I formed an instant connection. What I wouldn't have given to have her lead me through this process, but she was long gone. I willed myself to carry on, despite my sweaty palms and quivering limbs.

The lines of the painting danced underneath my fingertips. They shimmered in the half-light, stretching and pulsing like veins. The dragon's thoughts were my thoughts. Or perhaps my thoughts were his thoughts. He was confused and excited, just as I was.

Rings of smoke floated into the air from the page. No, from his nostrils.

It shouldn't have been possible, but it was.

I pushed aside all rules of reality from my brain, concentrating on making the dragon's flesh real, coaxing him off the page with fingers that instinctively knew what to do. His wings stretched off the page, and I couldn't believe my eyes.

The Custodian gasped behind me.

I held my breath.

The dragon's wings solidified before my eyes, bat-like, with the bone structure visible through thin skin. The iridescent blue of the painting oscillated like it was a body of water: blood and cells and fire and heat.

I reached into the page and pulled like I was a midwife delivering a baby. Like this was the deepest meditation of my life.

Tielbu emerged.

He had a round, scaly head with large nostrils and sunken, amber eyes that meant me no harm. Four horns protruded from his head. They were white and tiered, with the two smaller ones at the front near his angular ears. His breath was hot and rancid, with teeth that reminded me of tombstones. He had a long neck, scaly and turquoise like the rest of his body, and a long tail that ended in a sword-like edge. Four slender limbs carried his muscular body, each one ending in sharp, black talons. He was as large as a two-storey house.

My heartbeat thundered as the page disintegrated between my fingers and fell to the ground in embers.

The dragon landed with a thump on the floor under the starry, planet-filled sky of the Celestial Library, and he was the most beautiful, awe-inspiring creature I had ever seen. He retracted his wings and lay in a dazed heap.

Nightfall screamed and galloped away into the dark, shuttered library.

"Tielbu," I breathed.

The dragon tilted his head.

"Mummy?" His voice broke my trance. It was raspy. And needy.

I almost lost all bladder control then and there.

"Well done, druid," said Calypso. "New things always take bravery, and you have excelled yourself many times over tonight. That is not a sight I will ever forget, and for that, I thank you. But now, you must leave."

"What? How?" I said, breaking my eye contact with the dragon at last. She could have let us hole up there for the night. I mean, I felt like I'd just given birth. A cup of tea and toast to recover my energy would have been nice.

Calypso grimaced. "You leave by riding him, of course. That should up your chances of reaching home, and at least you won't be cold this time. Although, a newborn dragon could be pretty erratic. Oh well. Just think of the gateway from which you came. Don't lose focus. I'd hate to have to collect your body, too, when I come for the items you are borrowing."

I gulped. It'd been hard enough riding Nightfall. How on earth was I supposed to ride Tielbu?

"Ride him, druid. Leave it too long, and the bond will wear thin."

I frowned, realising I hadn't thought this through. I'd been so focussed on animating Tielbu and hiding his birth from the senate that I hadn't considered where he would go next to remain under the radar. "But where is he supposed to go?"

The dragon made a rumbling sound in his throat.

I looked at him in alarm.

"That isn't my problem, druid. Did you think you could bring a creature to life just to oil the wheels of your talents and then walk away from him? He is part of you now. It's not like you can release him into space."

"No, of course not." My eyes darted from her to the dragon and back again. I was going to need Marina's help. Hell, I was going to need all my friends. "I'll think of something. I will. Could I have a backpack, at least?"

She kept her distance but pointed to the iron throne. A luminous MC Hammer rucksack hung off its arm, emblazoned with the slogan 'Hammertime'.

I cringed.

"You didn't think a hot water bottle, dressing gown and slippers were all this room was capable of providing, did you? I had front-row tickets to that concert, I'll have you know. MC Hammer headlined, supported by TLC, Boyz II Men and Jodeci." Her eyes had a faraway look. "What a night."

I took small, tentative steps to the iron throne so I didn't unnerve Tielbu. I retrieved the rucksack, placed the artefacts inside, put it on, adjusted the arm straps and clipped on the waistband. "I guess I'm as ready as I'll ever be."

She gave me a wry smile. "I wish you luck, Alisha Verma."

My shoulders were tight as I approached the dragon. Beads of sweat broke out on my upper lip and underneath my breasts as I neared him. Usually, sweaty underboobs were a sign of forty-year-old buxom me weathering a hot summer's day, not the need to mount a flipping dragon.

I steeled myself, remembering how Tielbu from Dad's stories would never harm an innocent. And he had called me Mummy, so that indicated he probably liked me.

The dragon gave a gentle roar as I approached.

I gritted my teeth and drew closer.

His amber eyes narrowed, and his head turned to face me, nostrils snorting smoke.

"We're going home, Tielbu," I said brightly. "You're going to take me, and then Marina is going to know what to do. You're going to love her as much as you love me."

He lifted his head as if he understood.

I hoped it wasn't to turn those sharp canines on me. I took my chance and clambered onto his scaly back, slipping and sliding across the great expanse of reptilian skin that felt like worn leather, only bumpier, like the scaly underside of a rhododendron leaf.

Tielbu stood up in surprise, turning in a circle and extending his wings.

I shrieked, trying desperately to hold on. My dress had bunched around my waist, and my legs were splayed outwards in a wide-legged straddle, except this was no horse.

Calypso raised her voice above the rush of blood in my ears. "You'll need a better grip than that."

I rolled my eyes. "That's helpful. Thanks."

I shimmied higher up his body, towards his neck. Between his wings was a little dip. I settled myself in it in a jockey position, bum up in the air, centre of gravity low.

"What now?" I asked.

"Think of the gateway," she said.

The floor fell away, and we plummeted like stones in a well.

21

———————

"Oh, my god." Fear clouded my vision as I hung on for dear life. "We're going to die."

How tragic for Tielbu to come to life and then die with me here without fully realising his potential. Forty-year-old me had at least done some cool shit these past few months, and before that, my life had been pretty decent, if you didn't count my gambling ex. Even in the dying throes of my marriage, at least I hadn't been in freefall.

Unlike now.

We fell through the night sky with no chance of survival. Tielbu's hulking body gave me some protection from the cold, but the iciness penetrated my body all the same. Maybe that was why he didn't flap his wings, though each was expanded to a span of five metres. We plummeted, getting closer to death with every passing moment. I had no idea how dragon mummies coached their offspring to fly. My legs seized up in their jockey position, and it was all I could do to hold on.

All coherent thought threatened to leave my brain as hysteria set in.

I'd only managed to animate a flightless dragon—clever me.

Yet, even in the depths of that darkness, against the reptilian skin of the dragon and the deathly beauty of the night, it was my loved ones' faces I saw. Dad, pale against the sheets in his hospital bed with his wiry, unkempt moustache. Rainbow-haired Marina in her rock-chick party outfit. Echo crooning one of his favourite songs. And travelling through the cosmos safe in Ezra's arms. I had to get back to them.

I was done with the freeze response.

My options were fight or flight.

I lifted my hands, numb with cold, moaning as I channelled wind to the dragon's wings. I didn't know if this was all in my head or if I could control my fate and the dragon's, but I tried all the same. I gave it my all.

The dragon roared.

His wings began beating at last.

I collapsed against him, all spent, and pictured Shanghai Moon. There, against my closed eyelids, I conjured curls of incense smoke and rows of teas and, within it, the round table and the tarot card from my reading: the Ten of Pentacles, with its archway, vineyard and elder surrounded by family.

My consciousness slipped away, and I laid my fate in the hands of the universe.

***

A TUMBLING. A crash.

Some viciously spoken Chinese words that could only have been cursing.

A wail. "She brought the dragon with her. Was that her intention?"

"Who knows? She is like a toddler learning its first steps. A bringer of carnage but lovable."

I lay sprawled and shivering on a hard surface.

Hot breath on my legs warmed me. The heat spread up my limbs and to my flank.

Someone wrapped a blanket around me. "Did she have to land on the table? It's not like we can ask her to pay for the damage on her teacher's salary. Why would a young woman wear such huge knickers?"

The dragon growled with such intensity that my blanket oscillated. He shifted his bulk, and glass shattered.

"We have bigger problems than Alisha's knickers. We should call the vet. She will know how to control it."

"Perhaps his arrival is auspicious."

"Dragons are destroyers."

"They herald great change."

"Perhaps we should tie it up before it fully recovers. If we can get close enough. We might stand a chance as foxes."

The dragon grumbled, but he sounded as dazed as I felt. Thank the stars.

"Maybe we should run for it. A dragon doesn't just sit pretty. They are apex predators."

"We can't leave Alisha here. They eat humans, you know. Night class is nothing without her."

I opened one eye and then shut it again. I wasn't ready to face reality.

"She is pretending to be unconscious. See, just like a toddler. Next, she'll want us to play peekaboo."

A shadow fell over me. "Wakey, wakey, Alisha. It's time to clean up your mess."

I sighed and sat up. "Hi Fei Yen and Faeza. Surprise. I made it."

The dragon turned his head my way. Wounded amber eyes that needed me.

Fei Yen slapped her forehead. It was the biggest break of politeness I'd ever witnessed from her. "Not a good surprise, considering the chaos you have brought with you."

"You can scold her later, Fei Yen. She must close the gate." Faeza fumbled in the pocket of her pyjamas for the Ten of Pentacles. The card, which had been in pristine condition, was now curled and blackened at the edges.

I stared at it. "What must I do?"

"Burn it, of course," said Fei Yen.

My eyes widened. "With dragon breath?"

Faeza snorted. "No. We are in a populous city of millions of people. We are also standing in the home that Fei Yen and I care very much for. No dragon breath in here. Use matches."

She handed me some from her other pyjama pocket, impressing me with her organisational skills. But in her mood, I decided not to compliment her in case she bit my head off.

The dragon tried to get up, but I was certain he'd take down the ceiling if he did.

I put up my hands. "No, no, Tielbu. You must stay with your belly to the ground, or you'll destroy their home. No getting up and no opening your wings."

He grumbled and collapsed his weight onto his slim forelimbs. Then he crept forward in a belly shuffle.

Immediate danger over, I turned back to the tarot card. I didn't need eyes at the back of my head to track Tielbu's progress through the shop. The sounds of chaos gave it away. I held the card up and set light to it, letting it smoulder in my fingers before using my power to suppress the flame. A pang of sadness flared in my stomach. Who knew when I would see the Custodian and the Celestial Library again?

Fei Yen swung in my direction. "Now that the ritual is complete, it's time for some home-truths."

I smiled. "That is an excellent word, Fei Yen. Well done."

Her delicate eyebrows knitted together. "You're not a teacher at this moment. You are a very naughty student. You brought a dragon to our shop. This is our home, not a playpen for dangerous exotic creatures."

The dragon upended a crystal display with a resounding clatter.

I winced. "I'm sorry. I was out of my depth up there. I was winging it."

"We were afraid he was going to breathe his fire on us and turn us into charred husks," said Fei Yen. "But we are in one piece. For now. Dragons are volatile creatures."

Truth be told, he didn't look volatile, judging by his body language: relaxed muscles, retracted wings and slightly forward-leaning ears. He was clumsy but content. His long tail swung as he snorted and sniffed the shop with all its exotic wares. He had taken a particular fancy to a bucketful of what appeared to be magic mushrooms.

Faeza took the mushrooms away, careful not to turn her back on the dragon, and disappeared into the back of the shop, returning with a hot mug with a lid and what looked like a portion of duck pancakes in a metal dish. She gave Tielbu the duck pancakes and pressed the mug into my hands. "Drink up. Hot tea without milk will give you energy and lower your stress hormones. The snack will keep the dragon busy while we decide what to do."

I accepted the tea gratefully. The sweet scent of pumpkin and aniseed washed over me as I flicked open the lid of the mug. I slurped it down in one go like I'd gone days without water, then set it aside. "I'll pay for the table and the broken items, you know. I wouldn't leave you with this mess."

Fei Yen nodded. "We'll send the bill to your flat."

"How long was I gone?"

"Forty minutes, tops," said Faeza.

I looked at the clock in amazement. "That's impossible."

A rumbling purr came deep from within the dragon. Apparently, the duck was going down well.

"Time passes differently in the Celestial Library." Faeza tore her gaze away from Tielbu, who picked at the duck pancakes and seemed to take up at least half of the shop, even sprawled on his belly. "What happened to you, Alisha? It looks like you've been through the wars. Your dress is ripped to shreds. And what is the rucksack on your back? You didn't travel with that. What is hammertime?"

"You can't touch this," I said.

Faeza frowned.

We didn't have time to explain pop culture references. I decided to leave that for the next night class. "Never mind. Before we get to the rucksack, we need to call Marina because I'm pretty sure the dragon isn't going to sit prettily for much longer. I should let Dad know too. Tielbu is his creation as much as mine."

"Fair enough, but you should change into a spare set of our pyjamas because your father has had too many scares recently to be frightened out of his wits by you looking like that," said Faeza. "A daughter should always care for her father's feelings. Unless he is an arsehole."

"Faeza," I said. "I had no idea you had a potty mouth in English."

Fei Yen smiled at her wife. "She has a potty mouth in many languages. Let's call your people, Alisha. Just promise that when this is all over, you will get back to being the night class teacher we love so much."

22

We squeezed into Shanghai Moon: six adults and a dragon.

"I never thought the day would come when I'd see a dragon in Shanghai Moon," said Marina.

Faeza grinned. "Then you underestimated the power of our humble little shop. Everything is possible here."

Luckily, Marina had the foresight to leave Robert at her flat baby-sitting Echo. Not that I would have minded the detective joining our meeting. It was more that Echo's presence always added to the unpredictability of a situation, and we currently had much more unpredictability than I could possibly stomach. The quick wash in Fei Yen and Faeza's bathroom hadn't been enough to rejuvenate me.

My heart craved a pen, a crossword book and an empty room.

My mind knew we had to solve the problem of Tielbu and quickly.

My body wanted Ezra there and then, with cream on top.

"Let me get this straight," said Ezra. "In less than an hour, you found your way to the Celestial Library, gained both the library and the Custodian's trust and borrowed two magical artefacts?"

"Uh-huh. But the question is, what were you doing at Marina's place? The last I knew, she was racing off with Robert and Echo, and you had teleported away."

Grey eyes shone. "You wanted the world to stop for you just because you weren't in it? Or are you jealous of Marina and me spending time together?" He glanced at Fei Yen and Faeza. "What is it with the three of you wearing matching pyjamas?" He grinned. "I dig it."

I made a Herculean effort to focus, despite my tongue tangling. "No flirting right now. Can't you see what's in the room?"

Tielbu lumbered towards us, his tail swinging like an axe, hacking down a display of aromatherapy posters.

Ezra didn't miss a beat. "I'm trying *not* to see him. I'm torn between exasperation and awe. You've done something amazing, but I hoped you'd keep the dragon hidden away a bit longer. You've made it a thousand times harder to pull the wool over my aunt's eyes by bringing him to the city so soon. She's still in the throes of her madness against the elves."

My heartbeat accelerated. I needed my friends right now. I couldn't pull off a dragon heist across London without them. "You will help me, though, Ezra? And if Lavinia asks you outright about the dragon, will you lie for me?"

His voice lost its hard edge. "Look, you've put me between a rock and a hard place. I don't want to declare outright war on my aunts if I can help it. And as Justice Minister, Gunnolf is gunning for the elves too. I'll help you, Alisha, but I'm not sure I can lie for you. The pack bond is so strong that my alpha would know anyway. And opposing my aunts never ends well."

It hurt that he wasn't putting me first, but maybe that was asking too much, too soon.

But I had to protect Tielbu.

"Will you two stop bickering and look at this magnificent creature?" Dad teared up. "I thought I saw my mother do astonishing things, but this is right up there with her greatest feats."

Marina's jaw had slackened with wonder. "I don't think I've ever seen a creature so magnificent. Not even the tortoises on the Galapagos Islands or the penguins at Boulders Bay. I can die happy now I've seen him."

Ezra sighed. "After all your doubts, Alisha, you managed to

animate a dragon in a strange place without any of us holding your hand. I've never trained an initiate quite like you. You'll pass the trial with flying colours. That is if you don't turn the whole senate against you by waving a much-coveted dragon under their noses and then denying it to them."

"Then we have to hide him quickly, before anyone notices and before Lavinia or Gunnolf puts you on the spot."

The dragon half-heartedly clawed a display of calligraphy with his black talons.

Ezra stared at him. "He's not very driven, is he? I mean, in the stories of old, a dragon would be rearing up against its enemies, burning them alive, plucking villagers from their dwellings and dropping them from a great height. This one is almost aimless. More sloth than dragon."

"He's concussed," said Marina. "I expect he took quite a knock falling into the shop. But look at his eyes. It feels like he's following our conversation."

I winced. "Yeah, about that. I might have forgotten to give him a purpose as I was animating him. In all the stress, it kind of slipped my mind. But I think his lacklustre scouting in this shop is because I told him to be careful."

Ezra turned on me. "Dammit, Alisha. You can't be serious. A purpose might have prevented him from being manipulated by the senate, and you even failed to do that. We went over this. It's how it's been done for centuries. Animators assign purposes at the moment of birth. Now we have a deadly weapon that is a blank slate. I could kill you."

Tielbu lunged at Ezra with a roar.

Ezra flinched and teleported a safe distance away.

"It's okay, Tielbu." I laid a trembling hand on his dry, reptilian skin. It couldn't have been more different to stroking Echo.

"I'd say right now the dragon's instincts are to protect Alisha," said Marina. "As for you two, you might be in love, but you sure know how to be at loggerheads."

I frowned. "We are not in love."

"You can't pull the wool over an empath's eyes," said Marina. "So unless you want this city to fall to pieces, zip it. No one says a word unless you put dragon care at the top of the agenda. Do you want my professional help or not?"

Fei Yen and Faeza grinned.

"She is awesome," said Fei Yen.

"We should invite her for takeout," said Faeza.

Marina gave them a quizzical look.

"We don't cook," said Faeza. "But we'd learn for you."

Ezra snorted. "That sounds like a booty call if I ever heard one."

I rolled my eyes at him. "Marina's right. We need to focus on the dragon."

Marina neared the dragon, taking her sweet time, and when she was a few inches away, she picked up a piece of duck that had been a victim of Tielbu's poor table manners and placed it in front of his talons.

Tielbu surged forward on his belly and retrieved it. His tail swung around.

I gasped. "Watch out!"

Marina jumped back, narrowly avoiding being slashed. "I'd quite like to keep my body intact, thank you very much, Tielbu. My Merck Veterinary Manual isn't exactly going to help work out his needs, and we don't have time to go through folklore or Grimm's Fairy Tales for inspiration. Despite his full-grown size, he's like a newborn. He doesn't know how to exist in this world, and he doesn't have a mother to teach him."

Tielbu swung his horned head towards me. The word came out as clear as day. "Mummy."

Marina's eyes widened. "He can communicate with words?"

"This isn't the grandchild I expected," said Dad drily.

Ezra gave a heavy sigh. "What I see is a weapon that just became even more valuable."

"Fictional dragons eat humans, but let's hope it doesn't come to that," said Marina. "I think since he's a newborn, he'll take his cue from us about eating. I'm a bit reluctant to feed him live sheep, and I really like lambs." She pressed her lips together. "He definitely needs more space. I don't know what to suggest, apart from maybe letting him loose in Richmond Park and letting him eat Pan. That would kill two birds with one stone."

I raised my eyebrows. "Er, Pan's immortal, Marina."

"Oh yeah, I forgot. My bad."

"I watched a documentary on bearded dragons recently," I said. "They eat live food. Crickets, mealworms and ringworms, that sort of thing. They also eat veg and leafy greens. A hipster menu. You know, sweet potato, lettuce, kale, parsley."

"That's like comparing a tadpole to an alligator," said Ezra. "Look at those canines. He needs meat."

Marina brightened up. "I know. I have this friend who is into picking up roadkill. He gives saving them a go, but more often than not, it's too late. Like, these deer and squirrels and pigeons are properly squished. It's really sad. I'll get him to hook us up for Tielbu. Plenty of fresh water also, please. And be prepared for the amount of waste he's going to excrete. It's not going to be pretty."

Fei Yen and Faeza groaned.

"You have an hour to move him," they said in unison.

I turned pleading eyes on Dad. "How about your house, Dad? You've got plenty of space."

Dad shook his head. "Uh-uh. What would the neighbours think? We can't get a glamour from the witches because they can't know he exists. Even if he did have a glamour, word would spread amongst peculiars within seconds. My house isn't becoming some sort of magical peep show."

"I wish we could be more generous. As foxes, we have a few hiding places around the city, but none is big enough to house a dragon," said Fei Yen. "We work hard at keeping our boundaries. You know how it is. Everyone wants to take an inch."

Faeza winced as the dragon lumbered forward to sniff a sticky patch on the floor. "We're truly sorry. We know what it is like to be outsiders, but we need to think about our well-being. We don't bear the dragon any ill will. But there is only so long our neighbours will chalk his roaring up as the sound of a passing freight train, and we have a shop to run. If we can help to move him safely, we stand ready."

Dad peered at Ezra's charm necklace. "Are any of those trinkets you wear around your neck of any use?"

"Afraid not, Joshi," said Ezra with a hard smile. "Dragon-charmer isn't really something that comes up often. But there are some woods I know. They could work as a hiding place just until the dust settles. The woods are off the beaten track and border the motorway, so any noise the dragon makes will be masked by the sound of the cars. There are no houses for miles."

"The woods where the wolves run? Next to your farmhouse?" I asked.

Ezra frowned. "Hell, no. That would be serving him up to Gunnolf on a platter. There's no way I want to reignite a war between the witches and werewolves. It was bad enough when they were warring over me."

"Okay. Other woods then," I said. "Only, how on earth are we going to get him there?"

Marina frowned. "I could tranquillise him, but I'd be taking a wild guess on how much I'd need and how long he'd stay down. It's not like he can fit in the back of my van anyway."

"There's no way I'm teleporting him," said Ezra. "That was hairy enough with the leopard. And we can't go to the bestiary master for help, or the dragon will end up in captivity like Kraglek. Whatever else, he is bonded to you, Alisha. You could ride him to the woods, couldn't you?"

Marina perked up. "That would be awesome."

"With all the CCTV in this country? Or do you think I could just ride up until we have cloud cover and hope not to show up on flight radar? Look at the size of him. You haven't even seen him fully stretched out. It's not like he'd be mistaken for a seagull or eagle. There'd be geeks with binoculars talking about UFO sightings within minutes." I cringed. "Riding a dragon isn't like taking up horse reins. I have no idea how to guide him. It's not like he'll follow sat nav directions. It's a shot in the dark."

Dad nodded. "I don't know about the rest of you, but I'd rather my daughter didn't fall to her death."

"As far as I can see, we have two choices," I said. The dragon's unblinking amber eyes followed my every move. "We call Gaia or Orpheus."

Ezra groaned. "Neither vampire nor goddess can be fully trusted."

"Orpheus might be demanding, but I think he's on my side, and his abilities could come in handy," I said. "If the dragon is seen, he has the ability to wipe the episode from the minds of witnesses. But he is quick to anger. It must be a vampire thing. And he's going to be livid that I didn't bring him the stake." I sighed. "If we can't have a glamour from the witches and we don't want to risk Orpheus's anger, maybe Gaia can turn him into something that Lavinia wouldn't even bat an eyelid at."

Dad beamed. "So, do I finally get to meet the goddess?"

"I guess so, Dad."

The jars in the shop rattled.

The dragon lifted his head, fixing an intense gaze on the spot behind me.

Ezra grimaced. "Alisha, bringing in Gaia doesn't always calm things."

I shrugged. "What other choice do we have?"

The rattling grew more insistent. Light fittings swung.

I gripped Dad. "Pan's at it again. Take cover, everyone."

The dragon let out a roar so fierce I jumped out of my skin, but all eyes turned away from him and onto something or someone behind me.

My body quivered as I spun around.

"I thought you'd never call, druid." Gaia's eyes flashed with annoyance. "How rude of you not to introduce me to the dragon straight away. Worse still, you wanted to call a vampire ghoul to your aid instead of a goddess. If it were any other age, I'd put you across my knee and give you a spanking."

23

———

Gaia was a sight for my troubled heart. Not her beauty—although I had often known her to be beautiful—but her soothing presence. Ezra was sceptical about the gods, but in the time I'd known Gaia, I'd come to realise she didn't just make plants grow. She had the same impact on creatures, human or not. That was why it had seemed like a betrayal when she'd not intervened to save Mum. I hoped she'd make a different decision about Tielbu. The Goddess of the Earth was all about life, after all. If she couldn't provide camouflage for Tielbu, at the very least, then she wasn't fit to be a goddess.

Tonight, her hair hung in limp strands down her back as if it had been oiled. Her skin was free of makeup, and she wore a simple, short-sleeved nightdress that fell to her calves. Like any woman past middle age, she'd taken the time to put on a bra before leaving her house. The toenails on her bare feet had been painted fire-engine red.

I bowed my head in greeting and then met her shining eyes. "Goddess, I hadn't yet uttered a prayer to call you or made an offering. How did you know to come?"

A benevolent smile deepened the creases on her face. "Oh, I've been tuning in and out now that we're friends, druid."

She turned her eyes to those gathered, beaming at the sight of Tielbu.

Fei Yen and Faeza executed perfect bows with their hands pressed together.

"Goddess, welcome. Can we bring you some tea?" said Fei Yen.

Gaia beamed. "No, thank you, foxes. I had my chai tonight. Otherwise, I'd never sleep."

Marina curtsied. Ezra gave a wry smile.

Dad came forward and knelt at Gaia's feet. "Goddess, we meet at last."

She nodded at him. "Hello, Joshi, son of Rajika Verma, pitied by the leopard, broken by Pan's earthquake."

I frowned. "You knew? You knew Pan caused the tremors?"

She snorted. "Of course I did. There are not many things on God's green earth I don't know. But I also told you I try not to get involved in these things. The backlash is sometimes not worth the reward. Besides, I quite like Pan. He's not all bad, although sometimes he does bad things."

A ripple of annoyance ran through me. "You often point me towards danger when you are infinitely more powerful. Like sending an ant into a bullfight."

"You forget, druid. When the heavens crumbled, the power of the gods was rendered finite. So it's more like sending an ant to fight a monkey. Maybe you should listen more carefully. Like other humans, you only hear what you want to. What I said was danger is sometimes best avoided. A mind can do more damage than a sword 99.9% of the time. Why else do you think old women so often have the last laugh?" Her eyes sparkled. "Isn't this just a wonderful pyjama party? Now move aside so I can make the acquaintance of this wonder." She strode forward to meet Tielbu, showing not an ounce of fear.

He purred as she inspected him.

"Just marvellous." She opened his mouth and knocked on his teeth, unafraid that he might burn her with the fire that surely lurked within him. Next, she trailed her fingers down the length of his scaly body, like a trainer inspecting a racehorse. Then she picked up a translucent, bat-like wing to examine the bone structure underneath. When she had finished, she returned to his horned head with a nod of satisfaction. "Seeing him reminds me of the days when the Earth was young and teemed with creatures long forgotten. You wouldn't have received this gift from the universe unless you'd shown great selflessness, druid. It seems we have chosen well."

"Forgive me, goddess. What do you mean by *we*?" said Dad.

Gaia's eyes twinkled with mischief. "You misheard, Joshi, son of Rajika. Your human ears are no doubt full of residue. An affliction left over from when Adam was made of clay."

I clasped my hands together. "Goddess, is it possible for you to transform the dragon into another creature? I know it's a big ask, and I know you have to be careful about how much power you expend. But I wouldn't ask if it wasn't important. Without your help, the dragon risks being used in a war against the elves."

All eyes turned to Gaia.

She paced across the debris-ridden shop floor as if it were a stage, enjoying the attention. "I could do what you ask. I suppose I could transform him into a Komodo dragon. They are lizards, of course, but close enough in biology for it not to be too much of a stretch. Or maybe a dragonfly would be preferable? Petaltail dragonflies were around in the Jurassic age and are quite spectacular at aerial acrobatics. Or perhaps a black dragonfish. The males of the species are nothing special, but the females have long black bodies and fang-like teeth, plus light-emitting organs dotted about their heads and bodies. We could release him into the Thames. It could be a good fit if we changed his sex."

"Much as I love Tielbu in his current form, all three options would be much easier to transport and nourish than a dragon," said Marina.

"So, will you help us?" I said.

Gaia smiled. "No."

Behind me, Ezra groaned. "Bloody typical."

Gaia threw him a look of disdain. "Watch your tongue, werewolf, or the heavens will smite you."

Dad nodded at Gaia. "Well said, goddess. The men she brings home do make me wonder."

I gave a nervous laugh. We were running out of options. "Why won't you help us?"

"Because, my dear druid, why should the dragon—or you, for that matter—hide your light under a bushel? Your enemies should respect you. Not because you wish to cause bloodshed. Because without respect, there is no progress. You are no longer the druid woman with power over the wind. You are the mother of a dragon. The rider of a dragon. At least for today. My advice to you is to keep the dragon just as he is and hide him in plain sight. Take it from a goddess who hides amongst humans. It is far easier to hide in plain sight than one would think. A walking stick, a few grey hairs, a basket of grubby laundry… There are so many ways to convince someone that the dragon is harmless." Her eyes twinkled. "He could be a movie prop, say, or a statue or part of a grand festival. No one is going to think he is real. And if they do…" She shrugged. "Everyone else will think they are crazy. The average mortal mind just can't keep up."

I slumped down against a wall, defeated. "Forgive me, goddess, but that is shockingly unhelpful."

"Is it? The path is yours, Alisha, not mine. You must decide how to proceed. As they say, the date of your birth and death are written. Everything in between is your choice." She smiled. "Your choice to borrow those items from the Celestial Library was an interesting one. I can sense the power in the rucksack from here. Are you hiding a holy item in there?"

I chewed my lip. "Perhaps."

Gaia's eyes shone. "Is it from one of the prophets?"

I nodded. "One of them."

"Abraham's staff?" she said, approaching it.

My heart thudded. I wanted to trust her, but she was so wily. "Nope."

A look of frustration passed over her face. "Moses's basket?"

"No."

She giggled as Tielbu blew rings of smoke into the air, making the rest of us splutter. "Very well, druid. You may keep your secrets." A distant look entered her eyes. "My other work calls. One of my rascals is knocking on my front door as we speak. It may be the middle of the night, but my home is always a safe haven. I never liked the concept of latch-key kids. I'm the neighbourhood grandmother who feeds anyone who comes to my door and offers them a listening ear. I dare not keep him waiting. When youth crime goes up in London, I always feel a pang of guilt that I didn't bake enough cookies." She touched my back, and healing warmth pulsed into it, where I had cracked it against the floor of the Celestial Library during my test with Nightfall. "I wish you and the dragon well, Alisha Verma."

FEI YEN and Faeza dragged boxes from their storeroom and carefully unpacked them on the shop floor. Out came two colourful, lightweight dragon heads and two long serpent-shaped bodies on poles made from bamboo hoops and rich fabric. The yellow, gold, red and silver costumes shimmered in the twilight.

"Londoners are used to diversity on the streets of their city. This may not be China Town, but the people of Balham are kind. And often drunk. Dragons bring good fortune and prosperity. This will work," said Faeza.

Fei Yen nodded. "We will do a dragon dance across the city to your woods, werewolf. Faeza will wear the head of the first dragon, with Alisha and Ezra manoeuvring its rear. Tielbu will be sandwiched in the middle. I will lead the final dragon, with Marina and Joshi making up the body. We've just got to hope any passers-by think he is an exquisite costume. The goddess is wise for guiding us in this direction."

Ezra rolled his eyes. "The goddess is out of her mind."

"Who are we to doubt her?" said Dad.

I sighed. "Well, I guess we'll have to give it a go because the dragon is not the only problem on my list."

Melancholy amber eyes stared at me like he understood every word.

I'd have to be more careful about how I talked in his presence.

Faeza picked up a red dragon head. "Our aim is for the spectacle of the two outer dragons to mask Tielbu. It takes years to learn how to do a dragon dance with skill. For today, we will be a roaming dragon with wave-like movements. Just make sure the body keeps in time with the head."

Marina tied up her hair and sniggered. "This is going to be a car crash."

"Yep," said Ezra, grey eyes brooding. "I'm more a stand-at-the-bar-and-drink kind of guy."

"If we make it to the woods, my roadkill supplier is going to land us with a feast fit for a dragon," said Marina.

"This is the most fun I've had since Rosalie died," said Dad, picking up the green dragon's body. "I don't care if I have to be a dragon tail. I don't ever want this night to end."

I picked up the body of the red dragon. "At this time, the streets aren't going to be heaving. But we will be bumping into cleaners, nightclub revellers, transport workers, bouncers and bar staff." I approached Tielbu. He made space for me between his front limbs, but I had too much of a healthy respect for his sharp talons to get too close. "If you can understand me, please just copy our movements. We don't want anyone to notice you. There are rats and people and witches and fairies and worse in this city who would do you harm. Stay close. Stay on the ground. And under no circumstances breathe fire."

Ezra raised an eyebrow. "Like that's going to help, hellfire. Come on, let's get this over with."

I fetched my rucksack—ignoring Ezra's inquisitive glance—and we sorted ourselves into our teams. Faeza, Ezra and I headed up the procession in the red dragon. I coaxed Tielbu to follow me. Fei Yen, Marina and Dad brought up the rear in the green dragon.

There could be no comparison between the real and the fabric dragons. Tielbu was much larger, even when we held the fabric dragons aloft. His sunken eyes, protruding horns and scaly, turquoise skin made a mockery of our costumes. No artist or designer could have emulated the horror of his bone-crunching teeth. But still, we continued with our plan in the hope that both humdrum and peculiar eyes would be fooled by the mundane exterior of our world to give the possibility of a dragon credence.

Out, out into the cool early morning air, where the night was lifting, and the streetlights still shone. Out, out into the grimy South London streets with a magnificent dragon in tow, into a world where men still hunted animals for their skins. Out, with the dragon unfurling his cramped limbs and standing tall between us. Out, with my heart pounding and Ezra stiff with nerves in front of me, to spirit a dragon across London to deep dark woods at the edge of the M25.

24

———————

We crossed the city from Balham, heading northeast towards the woods. The streets should have been empty, but we came across pockets of people praying, their eyes shut in fervour. I spotted placards resting at their sides, blood red on white.

The end is nigh. Make your peace.

God dooms the unfaithful.

The tremors are God's anger brought to life.

I frowned. "What's going on?"

"It's the tremors," said Ezra. "The folk here think it's a sign of the end of the world. There are reports of atheists asking to be baptised overnight. Of priests having to turn strangers away from confession. Prayer houses are full to the brim with all-night mass. It will only make Pan stronger."

Still, our dragon dance didn't have a dedicated audience. We jolted and bumped and dragged the costumes through the streets, led heroically by Fei Yen and Faeza. Ours wasn't a fluid dance or imaginative one, but there was something special about it all the same. About the ripples in the red dragon, aided by my wind powers. About the feeling in the green dragon, aided by Marina's empathy.

The six of us had come together to sneak Tielbu to safety, even though the dragon dance was out of our comfort zones. If we'd been part of a parade in China Town, we would have drawn ridicule for our lack of skill, but at the early hour, we delighted passers-by too tired, preoccupied or stoned to look too closely. We danced down endless streets until the red and the green dragons achieved a rhythm of their own. Tielbu ambled along, snorting and sniffing overflowing bins. He followed me, less obedient duckling than distracted teenager on a school trip.

"Keep up," I urged, my arms aching from holding the prop aloft.

There was a sense of freedom about attempting something so brazen. Like riding the tube without a ticket or skinny-dipping in a public lake.

In a way, it made me feel alive.

Which was weird, given how close we were to discovery. How one false step could blow our plans to kingdom come and endanger us all for our duplicitous plan.

A four-year-old with a mop of ginger hair drew up alongside us at a zebra crossing. "Look, Mama. It's a dragon."

"Uh-huh," said his bleary-eyed mother. "Give the nice dragon a wave."

Next came a homeless man sheltering in the doorway of a charity shop, whose eyes followed us the length of the road.

"All right, mate?" said Marina.

He gave her a stained-tooth smile. "I'm still dreaming, love."

In Peckham, stoned students joined our parade for a few blocks, congratulating us on our lifelike blue dragon.

Gaia had been right. It was difficult to upend a prevailing reality, even when the evidence was in front of humdrum noses. They were much more likely to assign mundane explanations to extraordinary events.

Ezra was so close I could touch him, with his tight arse in his tux trousers and his grey-streaked hair curling over the white of his collar. I didn't touch, though. I wasn't a creepy old git in a pub. I gave his tapered hips and strong arms the odd admiring glance as we worked together to keep the accordion movement of the green dragon in motion. Our dragon dance took place without a drumbeat, which meant we could converse. I let my guard down and stopped focusing on Tielbu. I forgot he had understood my words and that I should be careful about what he heard.

"This is the most surreal mission I've ever been on," said Ezra. "You continue to turn my life upside down, hellfire."

I poked the small of his back. "Is that a good thing?"

He grinned. "Well, it isn't boring. Who knew middle-aged women would be such a handful?"

"In more ways than one." I teased.

Faeza tossed us a look over her shoulder. "Stop talking. Keep moving, you two. You have as much rhythm in your bodies as a pair of snails."

Ezra waggled his eyebrows at me as he manoeuvred the midsection of the green dragon in a wave movement.

I giggled. "If only there weren't a god meddling in this city again, a maniacal senate and a morbid vampire, I might just be prepared for a certain werewolf-wizard to swoop me off my feet."

Ezra's tone sobered. "I didn't peg you as an MC Hammer fan. What is it you have in that rucksack, Alisha?"

I sighed. "Odysseus's bag of winds and a piece of cypress wood from the bow of Noah's Ark."

He froze, disrupting the dance. "Bloody hell. You're going to take on Pan."

I bumped into his back. "I am."

"Keep moving!" said Faeza. We hadn't even reached the banks of the Thames yet.

"What's going on?" called Marina from under the green dragon.

Ezra ignored her. His eyes narrowed. "What if he kills you?"

Behind me, the dragon growled.

I shushed him and turned back to Ezra. "I don't think it'll come to that. And I'm so tired of people underestimating me."

Our eyes locked. "We are trying to protect you."

"Then stand by my side."

"Dammit, hellfire," said Ezra. "You're stubborn as hell."

"I'd rather die fighting than standby while innocents are in danger.

I'll take on the god. And if he turns his fire on me, I'll think of something. Or you will."

The dragon roared, and this time no chugging trains or spluttering buses could obscure the sound.

Nor could the costumes we carried mask the fact that he was real. Not when I'd lost control of him in the middle of the waking city. One minute, he was safely sandwiched between the red and green dragon. The next, he raised his head and stretched his translucent wings. We watched, gobsmacked, as he left our ranks and flew across London.

I wasn't sure how it happened or what spooked him. Whether it was the sense that I was in danger or that I wasn't in control. Animals did that. They took control if you lost it, and I was no alpha. I wasn't even a mother. I was just a druid woman out of my depth.

I prayed Lavinia's rats had their eyes downcast. I prayed nobody would look up. That if they did, they would see the dragon and think him to be an aeroplane. Or that they were in the middle of a mental health crisis. Anything but the truth. Because, dammit, I was days away from my magical trial, and it was a really bad time to be singlehandedly responsible for outing the existence of peculiars to all of humankind. There could be no punishment large enough for such a screaming faux pas. I would die of shame, even if they let me live. Unless a city-wide *Men in Black*-type neuralyzer was actually a thing.

I'd have to ask Orpheus, after all. Not that he'd help me once he found out I didn't fetch him the stake from the cross like a good little doggy.

We dropped the costumes and tracked the dragon's progress across the sky. Only when he disappeared from sight did we turn to each other in horror.

"I'll teleport after him," said Ezra. "Except we don't know where he went."

Dad was downcast. "Don't worry, Alisha. We'll get him back. The goddess was wrong."

"I told you religion always messes things up. Science is much more reliable. I'll get my tranquilliser," said Marina, ashen-faced.

"We need to get back to the shop," said the foxes. "It's almost opening time, and the dragon caused much damage."

Marina's mobile phone buzzed. "Robert? It's not a good time."

His voice came through loud and clear. "Mi5 chatter is going into overdrive. Apparently, there's a dragon sitting on Big Ben. You lost him, didn't you?"

Tielbu was in Westminster, atop arguably the most famous landmark in the country. Perhaps it was the chimes of Big Ben that drew him as the clock struck six in the morning. He was cleverer than I'd given him credit for—less mewling babe at my breast than a toothy, flame-throwing alien that was probably ravenously hungry. I had no idea how malleable or deadly he could be in the wrong hands. Instead of worrying about where we'd hide him, I should have taken the time to understand him better.

It couldn't have been any worse. Or so I thought.

I took a deep breath as Lavinia pinged me a text message.

You animated the dragon. You have until 4 p.m. to turn him over to me. I'll have the rats prepare a carrot cake and coffee to celebrate. L.

"What we need is damage control from Orpheus," I said. "But first, you're taking me home, Ezra. Transcender is in my knicker drawer. If I'm going to face a dragon, a vampire and a god, I need to be at my most powerful."

25

By the time Ezra had teleported me home, I'd looked like Hagrid from *Harry Potter*, in my too-small pyjamas and flip-flops loaned from the foxes, with my hair frizzy from the night's ordeals and my ridiculous rucksack on my back. I changed into joggers, a T-shirt and trainers in five minutes and dragged a brush through my errant hair. Then I opened my knicker drawer and pulled out the baldric Fei Yen had fashioned for me, together with Transcender. I stashed them in the rucksack, along with the items from the Custodian.

For too long, the sword had been hidden in either my knicker drawer or under my jacket. But it was about time to stop hiding who I was in Otherworld company. They wore their wings, fangs and claws openly, so why couldn't I bring Death's sword? I was counting on the fact that the mere sight of the sword would make people think twice before messing with me.

We stood outside Orpheus's gentleman's club in Charing Cross. Even here, the impact of the tremors was evident in the number of shows cancelled in the theatre district. The sets of *The Lion King* had been damaged, and the lead from *The Mousetrap* was still in the hospital after being crushed by a rocking chair.

We stopped at a newsagent so that Marina could string some bulbs of garlic around her neck, and I could neck a can of Red Bull. If I couldn't get my beauty sleep, then caffeine would have to do. I'd sent Dad home to rest with the promise that I'd call him if he could help. In actual fact, it helped more to have him out of harm's way being clucked over by Alma next door. I didn't want him to end up in the hospital again. That left Marina, Ezra, me and Echo, who sprang out of Marina's bedroom window into a chestnut tree to escape when Robert was on the phone to Marina.

"You abandoned me to a humdrum. I will never forgive you." The leopard honked with laughter. "It is for this reason the universe has ridiculed you. You are the only peculiar to have achieved the most magnificent feat and most absurd feat of your life within hours of one another. You both created and lost a dragon. This would not have happened had I been by your side. Instead, you turned me over to a babysitter. I suggest, given my good relationship with the vampire, you leave this part to me." He turned his nose up in the air. "And you, Marina Ambrose. I thought you were my friend. You high-tailed it out of there with the werewolf without a second thought for me. Next time you need me to consult at your practice, I won't be so willing to give up a night's hunt to help you."

"I'm sorry. Truly. You are part of the team, and we were stupid to leave you behind." Marina stroked him, her finger tracing the rosettes on Echo's coat.

He purred deep in his throat. "Keep doing that, and maybe you will be forgiven after all."

Ezra muttered. "A dragon on the loose in London, and the leopard is making it all about himself."

Emerald eyes gleamed. "I heard that, dog."

"Come on, you lot." I climbed the Edwardian-tiled steps to Orpheus's club. "We have no time to lose. It's time to face the vampire and beg for his help. Who knows what to expect in there? If this is a gentleman's club in the sordid sense of the world, we'll need to be extra careful. Between morbid, angry and hungry vampires, it's going to be fraught in there."

"Gunnolf's been here a few times at Orpheus's invitation," said

Ezra. "My red-blooded alpha was quite disappointed there weren't any strippers."

Echo purred. "Be on your guard. A vampire's lair is dangerous even to their friends."

I nodded. "Marina, you're our litmus paper. Any early warnings would be welcome."

She was still in her PVC skirt and bustier from the night before, but somewhere along the way, she'd lost her spiked collar. Her goth-girl makeup had softened through the night, and her space buns had unravelled to leave her turquoise, pink and purple hair free-flowing.

"You can count on me." She crossed her fingers and rubbed the four-leaf clover tattoo on her wrist.

"Marina, you do realise the garlic isn't going to help to ward off the vampires?" said Ezra.

She scowled. "Leave a girl her myths."

The building was a three-storey Georgian affair, made of a white stone with pleasing symmetry, multi-pane windows and pilasters at the entrance. Heavy curtains and nets marred the view of the inside. The business card Orpheus had given me held only a single line of the address in a stark font on a white card. On the back of the card was a request to knock seven times in quick succession on arrival.

"Here goes nothing." I rapped on the door seven times.

A window slot opened. Black eyes regarded us.

"Name," said a brusque voice.

Echo stepped forward, but he was too short to be seen by the man. "Chanakya Gunbir Hredhaan of Maharashtra, at your service. We wish to meet with Orpheus Might, Minister for History and the Today."

"Show yourself."

Echo leapt into the air.

The black eyes blinked. "Again."

Echo growled and leapt again.

"We don't let animals into this club."

"I'm not an ordinary animal, you imbecile," said Echo.

A pale hand shoved the man unceremoniously to one side.

The door clicked open, and a woman with tumbling red hair

appeared. Her black silk negligée emphasised her pale skin. "Apologies for Vorigan's bad manners. Welcome. I'm Oana. Orpheus told me to expect a druid and her friends. I didn't know it would be so soon."

I nodded. "Thank you, Oana. We need to see him straight away."

She gave a quick nod. "Follow me."

We followed her into the club, where green Chesterfield sofas and mahogany coffee tables filled a dimly lit room. Cigar smoke curled through the air, despite the early hour, and a record player played jazz in the corner. Laddered bookshelves and paintings took my breath away, and my eyes lingered on what could only be a Renoir and a Constable. Vampires lounged in various states of undress. One sipped a tumbler of thick, viscous red. I tore my eyes away from him to focus on Oana.

"There are eight of us who live here. Vorigan, who you met earlier, Orpheus, Quillan, Seskel, Aurel, Xanthe, Bianca and me. Bianca was the last to join our clan, but even she is over seventy years old, although she looked closer to her thirties when Orpheus turned her. Normally, women wouldn't be welcome in a gentlemen's club without an invitation, but Orpheus changed the rules back in the 1970s."

I gulped at the intense gaze of the scrawny, strawberry-blond vampire, who had set aside his tumbler and stood to join the tour. Nothing worse than an unknown vampire at our backs in a dark mansion.

Oana led us down a corridor with lanterns on the walls. "The bedrooms are in the basement. The rest of the building is comprised of three floor-to-ceiling libraries, a billiards room, a boxing ring, two bars, a chef's kitchen, a day room, formal dining room and a casino. We currently have three hundred people on the membership roll, with a waiting list triple that. A mix of the literati, politicians and old money. There's a strict dress code during club hours, of course, which are from two in the afternoon until two in the morning." Her lip curled. "We also have rules about not snacking on the patrons during those hours."

The scrawny vampire approached us from behind with a suddenness that made Marina squeak in terror.

"Piss off." She swung around as he sniffed her neck.

Blue soulless eyes like chips of ice.

Without thinking, I raised a hand. A gust of wind flung him back against a painting.

He snarled and came at both of us, fangs bared.

Echo growled and leapt at him, but the vampire was quick, quicker than my hands could react.

"He's hungry," said Marina, trembling with fear.

Oana's voice was a hard rebuke. "Enough, Seskel. Orpheus will be displeased."

Seskel ignored her, his body a blur as he advanced.

My hands tingled as I raised them, unleashing a column of wind that surprised me with its velocity and strength. It swept the vampire along the hallway, taking lamps, side tables and pictures with it. The wind rang in my ears.

Beside me, Ezra cursed.

I didn't stop to check what came next. I slipped off my rucksack and pulled out Death's sword, prepared to cut him down like a tree. To hell with politeness when a deadly vampire had my best friend in his sights. But a mould of dust lay where the vampire had fallen.

The lights failed, not one by one, but rather all at once, sucked into a void.

This time, I didn't need Ezra to tell me that he'd used his moon charm.

Ezra whispered in my ear. "The female vampire will not let that go unanswered. Orpheus's scent is not much further. I will teleport the women to him."

Echo roared, sending a shiver up my spine. "Go ahead. I will deal with this one and be right behind you."

Ezra cupped our elbows none too gently.

The ground disappeared from beneath our feet. I opened my eyes to a cavernous study with a marble slab for a desk and austere black shelving. Marina coughed up phlegm next to me.

"Are you okay?" I said.

She grimaced. "Just another man who can't take no for an answer. Is he alive?"

Ezra kissed his moon charm. "Deader than he was before. Thanks to you."

"Oh god, that's terrible. I didn't mean to." My heartbeat raced.

I caught the now-familiar whiff of beard oil before I noticed Orpheus. Dark chocolate and sweet cherry. He was nestled in an armchair reading a book of Siegfried Sassoon's poetry. And he only had eyes for me, despite the fact the three of us had teleported into his study without warning.

"I take it you had some trouble on the way?" said Orpheus.

His hair was damp from the shower. His attire—bare feet, an Oxford university sweatshirt and joggers—took me by surprise, but it shouldn't have. Most Londoners were still asleep at this hour, after all. I could hardly expect him to wear Wildwoods robes in his own club.

Ezra snorted. "Your man almost had us for breakfast."

We jumped as a body thudded against the door, and a dragging sound ensued along the corridor.

I gulped. "Orpheus, I think I...the vampire, Seskel. He's a pile of ash in your hallway. And Oana and Echo are battling it out by the sounds of it. She was quite cross that I staked her friend."

"He was a lech, though," said Marina helpfully.

"It took us under three minutes to work out who the wildcard is in your clan." I grimaced. "Was."

Orpheus held my gaze. "Why do you think I asked you to come here? I was hoping something like this would happen. He's been a thorn in my side for a while." Then he put down his book and sped to the door so fast he blurred. He opened it and grasped both Echo and Oana by the scruffs of their necks like they were puppies and not formidable in their own right. He barked a command. "Leave us, Oana. And tell Vorigan to clean up what remains of Seskel. The druid did us a favour. He'd become a liability."

Echo shook off Orpheus' grip and prowled into the room, spitting and clawing at his own tongue. "An untasty opponent is the worst kind of enemy." Emerald eyes settled on Orpheus. "A wonderful abode you have here, but your roommates leave a lot to be desired."

I snorted. "I bet those vampires don't wee in corners."

Echo inclined his magnificent head. "Touché, druid. Not every creature is so generous. I didn't need rescuing, Orpheus. I could have put her out cold. Well, colder. But I need someone to scrape the vampire off my tongue."

Orpheus's thin lips lifted in a hint of a smile. "It is not you I was worried about, Chanakya. You are a skilled warrior, and vampires tend only to feed on animals when there are no other options nearby. In case you haven't noticed, we are in the heart of London."

"I knew I was right to like you," said Echo. "Now that I have arrived, we may proceed."

I sighed. "I really am sorry, Orpheus. My strength surprised me. I'm still learning."

"Well then, it was good training for you, Alisha, because the Wildwoods trials are always dangerous," said Orpheus. "Truth be told, you've probably done me a favour. Seskel should have known new peculiars are off-limits. At least until the trial has passed. There are plenty of humdrums who are hooked on vampire venom and allow feeding in exchange for the high. All vampires are unpredictable, but I've never met one with such an insatiable hunger. He was a liability and would have long been called to justice by Gunnolf, had I not foolishly intervened on his behalf. Even a month or two in his coffin failed to persuade him to be more law-abiding." He frowned. "But I see now that is not the only thing you are here to apologise about. What disappointment do you have in store for me, druid?"

My chest tightened. "I could not do as you asked. The stake from the cross remains in the Celestial Library."

Black eyes narrowed. "Would not or could not? You reached the Celestial Library, somewhere I am unable to reach. I, a historian. I, a book lover. I, who crave new experiences and meaning. And you deny me."

"It's not her fault." Ezra stepped forward, his voice laced with a growl. "You expect too much from an initiate."

Orpheus stood up. He was taller and slimmer than Ezra. Not as muscly. But at that moment, he was stronger and fiercer. "Quiet, werewolf. You are here as an escort, nothing more."

"I am here as her mentor, Orpheus. And I tell you, she did the right thing."

"There is no such thing as the right thing, wolf. There is only the question of who benefits," said Orpheus.

Echo snaked between the two men, breaking their dance of cocks. "Focus, children. There are other pressing matters at hand."

Orpheus stared from one to the other, a nerve in his jaw twitching. "Yes, I see now."

I bit my lip and blurted it out before he could read more of our unfiltered thoughts. Better coming from my mouth, so I could frame the news advantageously. "We need your help, Orpheus."

He snapped. "Speak plainly, Alisha. To gain my trust, your words and thoughts must match. Embellishments are for lesser men than me."

"I am in trouble. I have broken the Founder's Law. My dragon has settled on Big Ben, and without you, the Otherworld will be exposed. Will you help me?"

The vampire grew still. "That is both an impressive and a stupid predicament."

Echo nodded. "Indeed. Who knows what havoc the dragon is wreaking as we speak."

"Actually," said Marina. "Robert is texting me a running commentary. No news organisations are involved yet, and sleepy Londoners are too busy looking at their phones to look up. But he reckons we'll be in trouble as soon as the tourists enter the equation or the dragon roars or eats someone."

Ezra's voice dripped with sarcasm. "No pressure then."

Orpheus's eyes darkened. "Nothing in the world is for free, Alisha. You did not help me. Perhaps your mentor has forgotten to teach you the value of reciprocity. It oils the wheels of the Otherworld and the humdrum one too."

Marina stepped forward. "Or perhaps the reason you want to die, Orpheus, is because you have forgotten that friendship doesn't come with conditions. That help doesn't always require a favour in return."

Orpheus turned on her. "You dare spout the secrets I keep hidden from the world, empath?"

He clenched his fists and flew towards us, then past us, sweeping his arm across his desk. A stack of textbooks, an inkwell and a carafe of red wine flew across the room, ending in a sorry mess on the floor.

A cracking of bones and a small, gut-wrenching moan that matched the horror of his morphing into a different creature. A stretching, a clawing, a writhing, and suddenly Ezra wasn't Ezra anymore. No more calm, clear eyes, soft lips and stubble. No more broad shoulders and chiselled jaw. No more tousled, grey-brown hair or a roll-up hanging from his lips. Instead, a copper-brown wolf, with a silver chain suspended from his neck, bared his teeth at Orpheus.

"Oh. My. God," said Marina.

"The wolf is smaller than me," said Echo. "I like this."

Ezra growled and came to stand sentinel between Marina and me.

"Relax, wolf," said Orpheus. "My anger is rooted in frustration, not in vengeance. Do you know how difficult it is to end an immortal vampire's life, especially one as strong as me? I have been buried in a coffin at the bottom of the Atlantic. I have travelled to the North Pole to be frozen in ice. I have been entombed in brick walls and welcomed being staked more times than I can count. And still, I am here. Still, I exist."

"I won't be responsible for ending your life, Orpheus. Like Marina, I believe in saving them. Unless I'm backed into a corner and am defending myself or my loved ones."

Echo sighed. "She even defends the lives of poodles. It's very inconvenient."

I chewed my lip. "Maybe you need more reasons to live, Orpheus. You are a man of learning. A man who craves new experiences. What historians would choose to die when a dragon has been birthed for the first time in an age?"

Orpheus hesitated. "I have never seen a dragon before."

I smiled. "There are plenty of new things in the world to see. And it turns out I can create them off the page."

"Are you promising me a lifetime of new experiences, Alisha?"

I shook my head. "No, I'm promising you that, even without my involvement, the world offers more to an immortal vampire than you have realised. No one experience is ever the same."

He raised his eyebrows. "You are an insufferable optimist, druid."

"I'm starting to find out that vampires are insufferable pessimists."

Orpheus rolled his eyes. "You have yet to tell me what is in the rucksack."

I grinned. "Just another few marvels for you to experience, Orpheus. Now, are you ready to help hide a dragon from the world?"

"I will come, druid, but I will not publicly act against the senate." He shuddered. "Now, if the wolf will stop posturing and change into his true self, we might be able to salvage the situation."

Echo honked with laughter. "We will also be able to judge the size of his nether regions."

26

____

We stood in a circle: Ezra, Orpheus, me, Echo and Marina.

Ezra, back on two feet, was in a grumpy mood. "I'm not holding the vampire's hand."

I skewered him and Orpheus with my most disdainful teacherly look. "You know, you both wanted to mentor me. Would it be impossible for you to get along for the purposes of saving this city and its people and creatures?"

Echo purred. "They tolerate each other. You cannot expect them to like each other."

"The leopard is wise," said Orpheus. "I must look at whether there is a Wildwoods vacancy for him."

"Actually," said Marina, "he already has a job consulting at my surgery."

"Who needs to mark territory when I have already made a lasting impression on the humans around me?" purred Echo. "I have not shamed my ancestral line."

I sighed. "I'll swap places with Orpheus. Make sure you're holding Echo as we travel."

"Take a breath," said Ezra. "Now."

We teleported. This time I kept my eyes open. Ezra was pale and

456

thin-lipped with concentration. Charing Cross to Westminster might have only been a few tube stops away, but I could tell taking so many of us through the void cost him. We clung onto each other, me between Ezra and Orpheus, travelling in this unnatural way, our bodies squeezed and stretched through space and time, flung to our destination. I didn't dare think what would happen if we let go. Who Ezra would save or where the untethered amongst us might end up.

Being in the Otherworld was an act of faith.

We emerged out of the monochrome world into the light, where the Houses of Parliament sat on the north bank of the Thames. Westminster Bridge had been closed to traffic and pedestrians after the damage sustained in the tremors. The Palace of Westminster stretched before us in the early morning dew, honey-coloured limestone carved in an intricate gothic style with the clock tower at one end. A homeless man gawped at us as we caught our breath and slicked off Echo's drool from our clothes.

"Oh broken world. Can you still surprise me?" Orpheus dashed over to the homeless man and mouthed a few words. The man picked up his carrier bag and blanket and walked as if hypnotised in the opposite direction.

The statues of Winston Churchill and Nelson Mandela stood vigil, and for a moment, I thought I saw them move.

My heartbeat was erratic, and I shielded my eyes and looked up at Big Ben. There, Tielbu perched, blue on blue against the London sky. It was an incongruous sight. From this distance, he looked like a gargoyle balanced on top of the world's most famous clock. The city had already sustained so much damage. My dragon couldn't cause more.

"We have to get him down," I said.

Robert ran over and joined our motley crew. Dark circles ringed his eyes. He gave Marina a kiss. "Thank God you're here. The Met just called in Special Forces to investigate that bloody thing. The Palace of Westminster is a UNESCO World Heritage Site. You've got mere minutes before the area is flooded. Good thing the Westminster bobby was sleeping on the job, or else that dragon would be wrapped like a joint of seared beef already."

I winced. "Here's what I want you to do. Orpheus is on mind control. Lavinia's are rats for Echo to deal with."

"What do you expect me to do? Lock them in the sewers or make them my breakfast?" said Echo.

"It's your call, but they need silencing. I can't have them reporting every move to the coven."

"I thought you were a healer," said Echo. "A lover not a fighter. A good girl, not a bad one. A soufflé, not a rotten egg."

"Name-call all you want, Echo, but there are times a woman just has to do what it takes."

He growled. "Very well, Alisha. The hunt begins."

Orpheus nodded. "I will meet the dragon?"

"I promise."

"Then make yourselves scarce. I have work to do."

"Marina, Robert, you clean up the chatter online as best you can."

She kissed my cheek. "Be careful, Alisha."

I looked at Ezra. "I need to get up there."

Grey eyes on mine. "Step into my arms, hellfire."

I secured my rucksack. Then I leaned against his chest, tuning into the thud of his heartbeat, and let myself be swept upwards and away.

My dragon perched on the clock tower of the Palace of Westminster. He balanced on the uppermost spire of the clock popularly known as Big Ben, although most Londoners would have told you that it was the bell in the clock tower rather than the clock itself that was named as such. That bell weighed 13.8 tonnes. Almost as much as two Tyrannosaurus rex, twenty-eight grand pianos or fourteen Asian wild water buffalos. Which was why it hadn't collapsed under the weight of Tielbu.

Thank everything that was holy and good.

Because on top of everything else, I couldn't be responsible for the destruction of part of a building that had survived World War II mostly intact and only toppled when it came into contact with me.

When I next saw Gaia, we were going to have serious words.

There wasn't enough space for the dragon and us to balance on the spire, so Ezra deposited us on the level below.

"You're going to have to do this last bit alone," said Ezra.

My throat was a desert. "I know."

His voice was urgent. "I'll be listening. Call if you need me, and I can be there in a flash. Your best bet is to use the air current and your abilities to hover next to him until you can decide if he is friend or foe."

"He won't hurt me."

A sigh. "You can't be sure of that."

"I have to be, or else the courage I have left would be in shreds. Take me up again, Ezra, and leave me there. I won't fall."

His eyes said no, but he opened his arms again.

The bottom dropped out of my stomach as he left me scrambling for footing in the empty air, a hair's breadth from the dragon. It wasn't my brain but my instincts that kicked into gear as wind tunnelled from my palms, making me feel like Iron Man. Only, Iron Man wore armour, and I was skin and bones and cells and blood, and the tower was a hundred metres tall. I didn't know how long I could keep up this hovering move. It was harder than anything I'd done before, with the exception of animating the dragon.

A moment of lapsed concentration and I would go splat.

The dragon's eyes were already on me, molten fury in those amber pools. As if he had no friend in the world. As if only lashing out would make it better. Even now, his beauty stunned me. Ivory horns, both elegant and fierce. Black talons held fast to the golden spire of the clock tower. Turquoise scales that shimmered in the early morning mist, where the clouds seemed within touching distance. I was the size of his forelimb, and he could crack me open like an egg. He hissed.

I flinched. I was invading his space. This wasn't even just about the city. It was about what would happen to him. His next choices would determine everything. Maybe he didn't want to be part of this world I'd dragged him into. Or maybe he fancied a bucket of Kentucky Fried Chicken. Either way, I was about to find out.

"Tielbu," I said, floundering in the air, unable to keep a stable level. "It's me. Alisha."

He blew rings of smoke out of his nostrils.

"I know you can understand me. I'm sorry for frightening you before."

A sound rumbled from his throat, or perhaps it was the sound of my own blood rushing to my head.

My position was getting more and more haphazard. With every word, I feared a failure in focus that would send me plummeting to the ground. "You can't stay here. It's too dangerous. It's dangerous for the people of the city, and it's dangerous for you. If they find you here, they will come with their helicopters and nets, and it will be out of my hands. You have to trust me."

I wanted to touch him, but I couldn't. My hands were my propellers. It was going to be all or nothing. Either I gathered the shreds of my courage and clambered onto his back, or I stayed in limbo in the air.

Beads of sweat broke out on my upper lip.

He opened his mouth, and what came out wasn't the mewling of a newborn. His voice was gravelly, slow and precise. "You gave me life, druid, but you assumed I was a simpleton. It has taken me mere hours to find my voice. Dragons are ancient creatures. There are worlds hidden inside us. And I find I don't like this world at all."

My movements jerked, and my jaw dropped in surprise. My instinct was to flee and call Marina for help, but this was my mess. Had he learned language so fast because his character had been rooted in Dad's stories? Or because of my affinity with teaching language? Or had this been growth all of his own? Like the time he had fallen through the sky, ambled through the streets or surveyed the city from above had given him words and wisdom. Like he was a sponge that had soaked up our language or that it had always been inside him, and I'd been too stupid or distracted to see it.

I locked my eyes on his, willing him to see my pure intentions. "We were taking you somewhere safe."

The vibrations of his voice resonated in my body. "How can I enjoy safety when you are in danger? You gave me no purpose. We are tethered to each other until you free me. So my purpose here can only be to protect you. Why do you think I am up here surveying the city from this vantage point? I will find this god you will die fighting."

My own words to Ezra came flooding back to me. *I'd rather die fighting than stand by while innocents are in danger. I'll take on the god.*

If I'd kept my mouth shut, we would still be threading our way across the city.

The dragon was taking control of our fate because I hadn't determined his with a purpose. But it was too late to assign him a purpose, as my grandmother had done when I'd forgotten it at the moment of his birth. What I couldn't work out was whether Tielbu and I were equals or whether he needed an alpha. Could dragons be led like a dog, wolf or donkey? I would have given anything to have Marina on a hotline, but all I had was my wits and instincts.

"Tielbu," I said. "You and I are going on a trip. In a moment, you're going to scoop me out of the air, and we're going to fly southwest to Richmond Park. My friends will wipe away the memory of any sightings of us, and we will use that window of opportunity to make sure the god does not pose a risk to any person or creature living in this city. Are you with me?"

He sighed and then stretched his wings, revealing the bony structure underneath, and swooped towards me.

I clung on, exhausted from my efforts to stay afloat, although it could only have been mere minutes. My stomach lurched. This wasn't a falling like into Shanghai Moon.

It was flying. His wings beat the air, and it was glorious.

And as he sped towards the south bank of the Thames, he roared. I had no time to think of Ezra or Orpheus, Marina or Echo. It was just me and my dragon and our common purpose to thwart Pan, just as I had thwarted Ra.

27

I preferred flying to teleporting. Flying in a plane was nothing like riding a dragon. It might have been the wind druid in me. The way I had always loved the wind in my hair and face when using the tube. How mountains and bridges were some of my most favourite places in the country—Snowdon, Ben Nevis, Tower Bridge and Pulteney Bridge—for the clarity of mind it brought me to be buffeted by wind there. I opened my eyes as we soared across the city, knowing I was the first.

Knowing that at forty years old, I was doing something children dreamed of. That I had dreamed of as a child.

Except it wasn't all bliss. This wasn't a joy ride. It was flying into the jaws of danger, and I didn't have the faintest clue how to solve a problem like Pan. When we faced Ra, I wasn't alone. Our plan had been concocted by many brains working together, by those who had experience of the Otherworld. We had rehearsed in Baba Yaga's and worked as a team.

I didn't know if my dragon and I could win this alone.

I didn't know the dragon, not really.

I only had meagre intel from Gaia, Robert and Echo on the sort of god Pan was, plus my own vague recollections from myths and legends.

And yet, my confidence had grown since the night in the Celestial Library, when I had managed feats I had never thought I, of all people, could bring about. I had spent so long doubting myself as my marriage crumbled and in the wake of Mum's death. But I had managed to change. I had leapt over barriers placed in front of me and grown. I mean, I had killed a ravenous, lawless vamp with as much effort as blowing out a candle. I felt bad about it, but it was pretty damn cool.

The senate had all advised me to focus on my upcoming magical trial. Even Ezra had wanted me to play it safe.

But I hadn't abandoned my principles to hone my skills in a padded room. Instead, I had walked through the world, ready to make mistakes. Ready to fight for what I believed in. To take on the bullies other people wouldn't.

I was proud of myself.

We landed in Richmond Park, amongst a thousand hectares of green space. Woodland, gardens and residences, which Pan had now claimed for his own. Herds of deer scattered like flies on Tielbu's approach, and I held my head up high, reminding myself of what I had achieved and determining to fake it until I made it, even if my courage and confidence failed. After all, wasn't that what men had done for centuries? I was capable of taking on Pan by the very virtue of being the only one willing to do it.

I slid off Tielbu's back and slipped on my baldric. Transcender's obsidian blade gleamed within its sheath.

I might have been in joggers, a T-shirt and trainers that stunk of Echo's urine and needed a wash, but when I put my sword on, I was a dragon-riding warrior woman.

The seed of an idea took root in my head. I turned to Tielbu. "We don't want to pick a fight with a god unless we can help it. We win this fight not by testing our might against an immortal but by persuading him not to use the herds to cause tremors. By taking away the Prime Sorcerer's reason to target the elves."

A rumbling growl came from the dragon. "I will heed your words, druid. Unless the god seeks to harm you."

I turned in alarm at vibrations under my feet. The herd of deer, which had fled on our arrival, parted like the Red Sea for Moses. Six hundred animals doing the bidding of the half man, half goat that came towards us in his stately Englishman's attire. Tweed, cord, a top hat to hide the horns that lurked underneath. In his hands, he held a flute.

"I am Pan, god of the wild, shepherds and flocks, companion of nymphs and lover of musical instruments. Formerly a porn site owner. In recent centuries, for my sins, also a royal gamekeeper and a board member at Battersea Dogs Home." His pale green eyes took in the dragon, and a smile lifted his lips. "That beast does not belong amongst my herds, druid. You would do well to move him before I do him harm."

I stilled my racing heart and clenched my damp palms. "And yet, you are harming innocents in this city."

Pan looked me up and down, lust filling his eyes. "Would you rather I had a different pastime? You might not look like a nymph, but perhaps you can blow some things as well as I can blow the flute."

Legend said he was lecherous and debauched. That he had taken the honour of defenceless maidens.

But I wasn't a maiden. Neither was I defenceless.

I stood in the shelter of Tielbu's body and took out my sword. Its double-edged blade made it hard to miss, and Tielbu's tombstone teeth and knife-edge talons stood ready to defend me.

Pan might be an immortal god, but he wasn't laying a hand on me.

I wrinkled my nose. "Your pick-up lines need work."

I would have said his missing thumb would have been a disadvantage between the sheets, but judging by his demeanour, it was his own pleasure that mattered most. What a tool.

"You're no fun. Taken a leaf out of the book of modern-day nymphs, have you?" He sniffed. "I prefer my maidens young and fertile. I want to ravish them around a fire while men beat drums and blow horns nearby. Ideally, I would have my wicked way in a threesome while the maidens are high on field mushrooms, performing sensual dances, giggling to themselves. Waifs with voices as sonorous as my flute."

"Well, I've got love handles, a barren womb, and I can't sing for shit."

He frowned. "How sad."

I snorted. "How lucky."

Tielbu's breath ruffled the top of my hair. He was becoming impatient.

Pan's pale green eyes narrowed. "You are here to stop me, but I am having fun. Too often, the people of this city have eaten up the green spaces. They have sullied fields with plastic waste and trampled wildflower meadows. They have forgotten how to marvel at the flocks and herds. They cast out the dogs they bring into their homes as pets. They fornicate as routine rather than for pleasure. And they have forgotten to pray to the gods. Their bleak, prayerless hearts weakened me." He smiled, and the dry skin of his cheeks cracked like the desiccation of a clay pot. "But I am stronger now. They fear the tremors. All I need to do is to move my herds. I cause panic, and panic leads to strength. At least for the one who causes it. Death. Destruction. Prayer. Ra was right. It's a good formula."

Tielbu roared, and the sound made the deer timid but not the god. He stood firm.

I saw it now. I saw how the stories had pegged him right. How he was both playful and terrifying. How he liked the order of the herds but the wilds of the landscape. How his animal nature intertwined with his divine one.

"I will stop you," I said.

Pan laughed with the abandon of a merry drunk. "How pitiful to see a mortal have no sense of their mortality."

I had to give him a show of strength.

I lifted my hands, and my body tensed as I drew from the vastness of nature to send a tornado towards him. When I looked up, I found that his lips rested on his flute, and he had darted to another spot and then another, so my tornado could never reach him, although I myself was utterly exhausted.

Even his hat stayed on his head. He was completely unharmed.

Pan grinned. "Not so easy trapping a trickster god, is it? Especially one so in tune with the land."

I felt the coming heat before I saw it. A warming of my dragon's chest at my back before a column of fire erupted from his mouth, narrowly missing me where I stood between his legs. "No, Tielbu."

The god lifted the flute to his lips, and the flames danced around him. They were even unable to harm a hair on his head or scorch what must have been cloven feet underneath his oddly shaped shoes. He extinguished them with a glint in his eyes, and the sound was so sweet that I was tempted to sit down and listen.

Like this was a game, not life and death.

He stopped playing and licked his lips. "You see, druid? I am not easy to subdue. Even by a dragon-rider."

Tielbu's gravelly voice boomed in my ear. "We must leave."

"No. We must stay." I lifted my sword, willing myself to hear the voices of my ancestors as Gaia had once promised.

My hands grew clammy. I heard nothing. I was fast running out of options, but I didn't want to use the sword. I wasn't stupid enough to think it would kill an immortal, but I did want the voices to return to give a clue about how to beat him.

"That is Death's sword," said Pan.

I shook my head. "Perhaps once. Then it was Gaia's. Now it is mine."

His mouth twisted. "You know her."

"I do. She told me you're not all bad, although sometimes you do bad things."

He gave a sad smile. "And what do you think, druid? Do you think I'm all bad?"

"It's not for me to say. I'm not a judge. I, too, have hurt people. We're all just trying to do our best."

Pan smirked. "It's good you don't judge me. Because a judge also wields an axe. And you have no authority over me or power to assert it. That sword might as well be a baguette in your hand. I'm enjoying myself for the first time in centuries. I'm not going to stop."

Fake it until you make it, I told myself. This was like chess. I didn't need to be physically stronger. I just needed to move the queen into the check position, and then the checkmate would follow.

I gave him a slow smile. "Do you know what my favourite feeling is?"

"An orgasm?" said Pan, looking me up and down.

"When an arrogant man has to eat his hat."

He was built to prance and saunter with his chest stuck out. A strutting peacock as much as a god. "I bought this hat for Queen Victoria's coronation, druid. I am certainly not eating it."

I didn't press the point. Instead, I steeled my nerves and replaced Transcender in my baldric. Gaia had told me not every battle was solved by escalating into war.

In that instant, my friends materialised next to me—Ezra, Marina, Orpheus and Echo—in a horseshoe shape that had probably been Marina's idea.

"What are you playing at, hellfire?" said Ezra, his eyes on the god. "And how on earth did you get the god to run from you?"

"Hello, dragon. You are safe from me. My nose tells me your meat is too tough," said Echo.

Orpheus turned his unblinking gaze on Tielbu. "The honour is mine, dragon. Alisha, this is your fight. Vampires and gods don't mix. I will bear witness to the fact that it is the god and his herds that caused the tremors, not the elves."

My mind whirred as Pan came towards us in his funny, forward-leaning gait. He sneered. "You have brought friends, druid. They will not improve your odds."

Echo roared. "I will chase you off and hunt a deer on my way. Just say the word."

"Will you all just shut up and let me deal with this?" I unzipped the rucksack with my items from the Celestial Library.

Pan's expression froze. "What's in there, druid?"

"Gaia sensed its power and almost figured it out. Can't you?" I pulled out the bag of Odysseus's winds and the remnant of Noah's Ark.

The god's eyes drifted from the wood to my face and back again.

Then, he lifted his flute to his lips. A sleepy melody akin to a lullaby filled the air, and Pan vanished.

My stomach dropped. That had been our chance to save the city and put an end to the ridiculous war against the elves, but I had blown it.

"He is gone." Tielbu gave a fearsome roar that scattered the herd.

An idea formed in my mind. I placed the artefacts back in the MC Hammer rucksack for safekeeping. "He's the royal gamekeeper. And there's no way he is abandoning his herd with multiple predators threatening them. A dragon, a leopard, a vampire and a werewolf."

"Hey," said Marina. "What about me? I can threaten the deer."

"Can you, though?" I said. "Pan's still here somewhere. I know it in my bones. Tielbu, this is our chance. Don't harm the deer but fence in the herd with your fire."

Tielbu rose into the sky. His neck arched up and down until he reached a height from which he unleashed hot, orange flames of spite. I wished Dad had been there to see it. And that it was less life and death. That my friends could ooh and aah like it was a particularly dazzling display at fireworks night rather than a gamble of wits.

But I had to focus.

The herd panicked. They darted this way and that, but Tielbu's ring of fire left them with no route of escape.

I steeled my own soft heart against their shrieks. My hands tingled in readiness.

"Stop," said Marina. "You're frightening them."

"Seared meat isn't as tasty as fresh cuts," said Echo.

Pan's voice thundered across the park. "Leave the herds alone, druid. Leave the herds alone, and we will talk."

"You heard the god," said Marina. "Stop it."

"Kill them all," said Orpheus. "And we will have a feast for the ages."

"I trust you," said Ezra. "But that dragon is a virgin. He can't go rogue here."

"I won't let them die," I hissed. "Keep up the bluff. Let me concentrate. I will coax the flames into submission myself. But I'm banking on the god's love for them to bring him to me."

"I'm warning you, druid," said Pan's voice.

Beads of perspiration gathered on my brow from the heat of Tielbu's flames, but I didn't call him off. I couldn't.

Pan had to reveal himself.

Just when I thought those poor deer wouldn't survive the shock, Pan re-materialised a few metres from where he had disappeared. His expression writhed in horror as he determined what to do. Crashing buildings and urgent sirens excited him, but it was another matter for his panicking herds of red and fallow deer in all their elegance and gentle beauty.

He came towards us with the puffed-up chest of vengeance, his flute ready to be used as a weapon. His eyes sparked malice.

My friends stood their ground. A buffer around me that I didn't need, but appreciated.

I let the flames burn until we were inches apart, and I could smell the smoke on his skin, the sweat from his pores. He made me retch, but I had my answer.

Pan's divinity still warred with his beast. He'd not baulked at the bag of Odysseus's winds. It hadn't scared him. So to use them against him would have been the wrong ploy. Instead, Pan had been scared of the holy cedar wood from Noah's Ark. He had proven to me he still loved the father of the gods. Like Gaia, the remnant had awed him. Maybe it had shamed him for his choices too.

He spat on the floor in disgust. "Call the dragon off."

My heart thudded, but I kept my voice cool. "Oh, you need my help?"

I beckoned Tielbu.

The dragon responded immediately. The ground thudded as he came to rest between me and the god.

I raised my hands and coaxed the flames away from the deer before quelling them with an effort that made me quiver and grunt, leaving a scorched ring in the grass. "It is done, Pan."

His voice whipped through the morning air. "You put my herds at risk. Now you will pay."

Ezra and Echo came to either side of me, their hackles raised.

I smiled to set them at ease and to show Pan who had the upper hand. "My dad once said that a man can lose his way if he drifts from his faith. In this bag, I have a reminder of faith. It can be yours for a short while if you wish."

"Open the bag, druid," said Pan.

I brought it out with care.

"Alisha—" said Ezra.

"I know what I'm doing."

Pan's eyes widened. "A piece of cypress wood."

I nodded. "From the bow of Noah's Ark. Found amidst the plains of Mount Ararat. It carried mating animals to repopulate the earth."

"I know what Noah's Ark is, druid. I knew the prophet. I lived through those times." He edged closer, trembling. "Let me hold it."

"First, a promise from you. No more mischief that harms innocents."

He smirked. "I can't promise that."

I couldn't trust him. Of course, I couldn't. A trickster god would always, always betray me in the end.

But this wasn't about me. It was about his longing for a godly item. A millennia-old god would remember all his victims or even all his wins.

He probably didn't even feel anymore.

But touching this disintegrating piece of wood would remind him of his godliness. Wasn't inspiration the basis of all change? I had to believe that holding this piece of lost treasure, knowing its place in God's plan, would remind him of his own godliness. That feeling would be something that was all the more precious for its rarity. It would be something he wouldn't forget.

And that was why I had him where I wanted him.

Checkmate.

I cradled the wood between my hands.

Pan looked at it like an addict at a crack pipe.

The dragon huffed behind us, and Ezra bristled. They trusted Pan as little as I did.

"It can be yours, Pan. I will give it to you," I said. "But if you feel an ounce of connection to this earth or to a greater power when you hold this, you must promise not to cause any more tremors. Or my dragon and I will come back." I swallowed hard, hoping my bluff worked. I couldn't, and I wouldn't hurt an animal. "And we will hurt your herds. We will burn everything to the ground."

His thin lips twisted. Then he sighed. "It is as you wish. Hand me the wood, druid."

A shiver ran up my spine.

I gave it to him, and when it left my hands, I was bereft.

His eyes gleamed, and he snatched it from me. For a moment, I thought I'd made a terrible mistake, but Pan sank into the grass. He put down his flute. A gentleness came over him as he studied its silver-grey colour, every grain, nail mark and dent on it. He held it to his chest.

"I'd forgotten what it felt like to hold something so holy." A tear threaded down his face. "It still echoes with the mark of the heavens. For that, I thank you, druid. I will keep to our bargain."

"Make sure you do." I looked at my friends and motioned to Tielbu. "Our work is done here. Anyone fancy a ride?"

Marina clapped in glee.

As we walked away, leaving the goat god in the grasses of Richmond Park, Ezra grabbed my hand and squeezed.

Echo purred. "You have a hunter's instincts, Alisha. I am proud of you, but I will make my own way to the woods the wolf has found. It is not normal for a leopard to be up amongst the clouds."

Orpheus frowned. "I must beg your pardon for being wrong about the dark elves, Alisha. I have much to discuss with the senate. But a dragon ride is a new experience, so I will join you."

"Tielbu," I said. "Will you do us the honour?"

The dragon inclined his head and sank onto the meadow for us to clamber onto the sheltered skin on his back. Marina crawled up first, eager as a child on Christmas morning. Next came Ezra, then Orpheus, refusing any help.

"Druid," called Pan.

I swivelled. "Yes?"

"Your womb is barren." Green eyes smouldered under his mop of curly brown hair. "It is within my gift to bestow fertility on domesticated animals."

I shook my head. "No, thank you. It is dangerous to be beholden to a god, especially one such as you."

A goat-like bleat of laughter erupted from him. "I heard your kin is not so discerning."

I frowned, unsure of what he meant.

Pan tipped his top hat to me. "What a strange human you are. You are not like other ones."

I shrugged. "All humans are not alike. And middle-aged women are a world apart. But we are all better off when we look out for each other."

I climbed onto the dragon and nestled close to Ezra. The wind rushed against us as Tielbu took flight, and I thought how far I had come and how the Wildwoods trial would be a piece of cake if I could convince a trickster god to lay down for me.

28

E zra's woodland lay situated between the A127 and the M25. Its position near noisy roads and landscape—comprised of a group of fields around a steep hill and tens of thousands of native trees—made it a perfect hideout. Yet it belonged to the city of London, with panoramic views from the hilltop of the River Thames to the North Downs and west across Docklands and Canary Wharf. It was a place of rest and respite and perfect for hiding Tielbu. Lavinia's rats preferred the sewers and rubbish bins of built-up areas for their natural habitat, and we would see the coven umbrellas approaching a mile off from the woods.

Little did I know, Tielbu wasn't the only secret Ezra had been keeping.

With Marina preoccupied with tending to Tielbu's needs and hooking him up with roadkill, Orpheus, Ezra and I walked into a wooded area when a rustling met our ears. Orpheus reacted first, his speed giving him a natural advantage. He pulled back branches of thick foliage to reveal the slim bodies in torn clothes and dirty, smiling faces.

I blinked hard, clutching Ezra. "Are those—?"

A small, muscular body barrelled towards me and hugged my legs.

Flinar smiled and looked up at me. The cut above his eyebrow had healed, and his milky eyes held joy. "Alisha the druid. I have been waiting for you."

His Roman tunic and knickerbockers had been replaced by an oversized Wham T-shirt and denim cut-offs.

I grinned and couldn't resist giving his billowing ears a tug. "You look well."

Flinar swatted me away good-naturedly. "The werewolf found me after I left Shanghai Moon. I had no place to go. Now, the Defence Minister and her rats can't find us. We sleep under the stars, and I have friends."

"I'm happy for you."

He jumped from one knobbly leg to another in excitement. "I have been eager to see you. You have been fighting for us. The wolf has told us everything. You gave us hope." He brightened. "But now that you are here, I can tend to your every need. What would you like me to do? We have cheese that is turning green, curdled milk and some pickled roots. Perhaps you would like a plate?"

My stomach heaved. "Actually, just a glass of water, a blanket and a place to lie down. I could sleep for ten years."

Orpheus rolled his eyes. "You have a day until the trial, druid."

"If Alisha wants to sleep for ten years, then that is what Alisha will do," said Flinar.

The vampire sighed, a storm cloud on a sunny day. "There are many reasons to dislike elves. Do not add to them."

Flinar frowned. "I have not forgotten that Alisha saved me. I will save her. Even if today that means creating a nest of leaves for her to rest in."

He scurried off. I burst out laughing, and joy danced in my heart.

Ezra leaned down to murmur in my ear. "I take it you approve?"

Butterflies darted in my stomach. "Of course, I approve."

He gave me a wolfish smile. "You didn't think I could stand by while my aunt mobilised against the elves, did you? Especially once we realised they were innocent?"

Orpheus rolled his eyes. "You two are gluttons for punishment. The coven is best kept onside."

Ezra protecting the vulnerable meant the world to me. It made him more of a man than the gung-ho senate.

I reached up to grab his face and planted a kiss smack on his lips. The scent of him—spice and smoke and musty man—intoxicated me. "Ezra, you're brilliant. I love you." I coloured and backtracked. "I don't mean 'I love you,' of course. I mean, I appreciate what you did here. How you put yourself out."

He grinned. "It's okay, hellfire. I don't think you want to marry me. It's nice to be appreciated."

I blushed. "How many are hidden here?"

"Eighty-odd, give or take. Not the ones who can afford to pay for protection in the city or whose money means they are exempt from the worst inclinations of the senate. I brought only the defenceless ones here. The ones too weak or guileless to ride out the storm of the senate's anger. I can only hope they can go back to their lives once this is all over."

I sighed. "It's definitely not all over. Lavinia wants me to bring Tielbu to her by 4 p.m. today."

Ezra frowned. "If you thwart her, your chances of passing the trial plummet. Remember, it's your actions in the maze of London's Underground tomorrow. It's about winning a majority vote of the senate that already has misgivings about you."

"If I hand Tielbu over, her power grows, and any gains we made against Pan tonight will be for nought. If I fail the trial, I won't be around to stop her from controlling him. But that's not going to happen because I'm going to pass the trial, and she can keep her grubby mitts off him."

"And what if my dear aunt decides to kidnap you to prevent you from showing up to the trial?" said Ezra.

I chewed my lip. "I might be wrong, but even though Lavinia is underhanded and difficult, I don't think she'd stoop that low. She has some kind of moral code."

"I hope you're right." His voice dipped into a growl. "But she'll have to come through me, a bunch of elves and a dragon if she wants to stop you from attending. And she'd risk the wrath of the rest of the senate if it came out."

His protectiveness of me sent shivers up my spine.

And then I realised. It was always the same with bullies. Lavinia probably wasn't used to people standing up to her.

Well, that was about to change. I pulled out my phone and began texting.

"What are you doing?" said Ezra.

Orpheus's eyes gleamed. "She's about to tell your aunt where to go. I'd tone down that language if I were you. Velvet gloves are preferable in internal wars."

I pursed my lips. "Okay, Orpheus, but just a smidgen. I've just about had enough of bowing down to people who don't deserve it. In fact, I've never been that good at deferential behaviour."

I typed. *Thanks for the offer of coffee and cake. Maybe another time. The dragon is staying right where he is. I'd think twice about launching an offensive to take him. I'm no longer the woman you tricked into drinking a green smoothie truth serum. I'm far better as an ally than an enemy, A.* I pressed send.

Ezra groaned. "Well, that's going to set the cat amongst the pigeons."

Orpheus nodded. "Your aunt is not a woman to be trifled with. Plenty have tried and lived to regret it."

"She can't fight a battle on two fronts." My phone pinged.

Lavinia's name flashed up.

How interesting you pick a fight on the eve of your Wildwoods trial. Rayna planned it so carefully, but two heads are better than one. I'm sure you'll appreciate my last-minute tweaks, L.

Ezra grimaced. "That sounds like a threat."

I set my shoulders back, pleased to find that exchanging blows with Lavinia didn't floor me like it once would have. My belief in myself had grown, and it felt good. "I wouldn't expect anything less."

Orpheus raised an eyebrow. "The druid is like a star athlete blowing their advantage by running onto the field, having poked themselves in their own eye. As her mentor, you failed to teach her the art of subtlety."

I shrugged. "Hide in the shadows all you want, Orpheus. I am ready to shine."

"Let's hope you all are, hellfire," said Ezra. "Marina and your brother have to face the same thing."

"To be honest, that's not my main worry right now. How can we be sure that the senate won't plough on with their path of malice against the elves?"

"You talk as if the senate speaks as one," said Orpheus. "Not all of us would have made the stark choice to target the elves had we known the allegations were false. The Prime Sorcerer, too, would be appalled that he himself has not acted justly."

I shook my head. "You were at the coven dinner, Orpheus. Phinnaeous Shine took the tremors as an opportunity to crush the elves without a thought for justice."

Orpheus glowered. "That man has done more for the Otherworld than you can possibly know. He is innately good and just."

I massaged my temples, tired of explaining the obvious. "Even good men can be unjust. If I gave you a penny for every time a person thought they were in the right but were mistaken, you'd be a rich man."

"I am already filthy rich, druid." Orpheus's coal-black eyes narrowed. "I will see to it that the Prime Sorcerer hears of the elves' innocence and that they may return to their homes." He paused. "Your trial is mere hours away. Be on alert. It would be a shame for an initiate of your calibre to throw it all away. As much as I desire you to pass, you and your fellow initiates must weather it alone."

My voice cooled. "It turns out we can handle quite a bit on our own. Maybe the keys to the Otherworld should be ours."

He stared me out. "Be careful what you wish for, Alisha. The burden of power is always heavy."

I sighed. "If you two gentlemen don't mind, it's been a long day. I'm in severe need of my beauty sleep, or else I'll never get back the glowing skin of my twenties."

I WOKE up as evening had fallen to Echo licking my face with a tongue that felt like sandpaper.

"Wake up, Alisha," the leopard said. "Your brother is here. We have much to discuss. Sky News is reporting that the scorched ring in Richmond Park is the work of a group of feral child flautists, who left an incriminating flute nearby."

I groaned, checked that my MC Hammer rucksack was safe beside me and wiped away spittle from the corner of my mouth. Thankfully, the bag was so uncool that no one had bothered to steal it. Maybe that was what clever Calypso had intended. "Let them dream up all the stories they wish. It's better than reporting what really happened. Seriously though, I'm aching all over, and my forty winks on this compact ground didn't help my back issue. What I wouldn't give for the firm touch of my osteopath and blow dry right now."

"There'll be time for that later," said Echo. "I miss evenings on the rooftop of our flat filled with cubed salmon steak and pussy harems. The world does not leave enough time for frivolity, but the Siberian minx around the corner will be mine soon. I will regain her with tales of our exploits, and she will be mine."

I sat up and pulled my dishevelled hair into a neat bun. "I missed you. How did you find us?"

He purred. "I know how to read a map, as you well know, but in this case, it was Ezra who came to find me. He thought you might appreciate a familiar tongue to wake up to. And it was his idea to bring Sahil and your father here too. A last supper, if you like, before your Wildwoods trial. Come. The fire is burning. Our friends and family await."

Echo led me to a grove where elves broke bread. Their children, in the absence of toys, foraged for golden leaves, smooth rocks and berries to trade. They kept a wary distance from the dragon but giggled nervously when he blew rings of smoke into the air or turned his amber eyes on them. Marina sat at Tielbu's side, but when we approached, she ran to welcome me.

She hugged me, and the words tumbled out of her mouth. "You slept for an age. The men brought the firewood, and Tielbu lit it. He really is very clever. He seared some steak for some of the elves, too, although it was too crispy to eat. Joshi refused to sit down until he saw you sleeping soundly, and Ezra has been checking up on you too.

But Flinar turned them all away until Echo scared the living daylights out of him and insisted on waking you." She leaned into me with an air of conspiracy. "Your brother is behaving very strangely. Orpheus was right about his jealousy of you. He almost turned green when he saw the dragon. I'm not sure what's going on underneath the surface, but I'd say he's not the most reliable of our trio going into tomorrow's trial."

"The story of my life." We approached the fire, where forked flames of orange and red hissed and crackled.

Dad rose to greet me. "Let me kiss my daughter, Marina. I can't get a word in edgeways with you two." He grabbed my face between his calloused palms, and the paint smudges on his fingers told me he'd been working at his art again. "Let me look at you. One day, I hope you will let a day pass without this old man having to worry about you."

I squeezed him tight. "How are you feeling, Dad?"

"Oh, much better for seeing you."

"You've been painting."

His brown eyes filled with warmth. "I have. I got home after our dragon dance, and I was inspired. I made a little chapbook of watercolours for you. It's nothing special. But with the trial coming and you being an animator, I thought you should have something in your back pocket. What's an animator without paintings to create from?"

I accepted a small notebook from him with eight drawings and flicked through the drawings: a gecko, a stork, a wasp, a giraffe, a penguin, a rooster, a panda and a crane. "It's beautiful, Dad. Thank you."

All my favourites smiled up at me. Dad, Ezra, Marina, Echo, Tielbu. Okay, Sahil wasn't a favourite, and he was sitting in a weird, pigeon-toed position. But it was about time I checked in on him.

I sat down next to him. "How are you doing?"

"I'm okay. It's been quite a week. My business is suffering from a lack of attention. I have squatters to deal with." He shuddered. "Plus, an invasion of pigeons in one of my North London buildings that the tenants are insisting I call in the exterminators for. And my secretary has left me because I inadvertently turned into a pigeon and then back again and was left standing butt naked with my clothes at my feet. After she screamed, she snapped a pic. It was cold in there. And now she's suing me for sexual harassment in the workplace. I couldn't exactly tell her the truth."

Next to me, Marina turned blue with corked laughter.

"How awful." I patted Sahil's leg.

"Well, it's all right for you. You've taken to this all like a duck to water. I feel like every atom of me has changed. You see the state of what my bowels produce. It's very disconcerting to see the colour change in the toilet bowl. From brown to white." He shook his head. "It's not even like I can see the doctor about it."

I hesitated. "Listen, there was something I meant to ask you. It was something Orpheus said at the coven dinner. He said you'd done something. That you'd made a poor decision that bodes ill for the future."

Sahil grunted. I felt for him. His pigeon nature made him weird, and for a man who had always prided himself on being cool, it was a cruel blow. "Nothing's wrong. My sister is an animator, and I am a werepigeon. What could be wrong? Are you going to listen to that stiff more than your brother?"

I winced. "All right, all right. I was only asking. You know how much is riding on tomorrow, don't you? If we fail, we won't even remember the Otherworld exists. It's so important we work as a team."

"Why are you directing this at me rather than Marina? It's as if you think I'm the weak link."

I frowned. "You're being sensitive."

He snapped. "No, I'm not. I know who you think the weak link is. Every single person around this fire thinks I'm just a laughingstock. Well, what if I did something about it?"

"What did you do, Sahil?" The low warning note in Dad's voice took me back to when we were children.

"Even my own father expects the worst of me."

"Do you see? The Otherworld always tears families apart," said Dad.

I shook my head. "Maybe it's just families that do that to themselves. I want to trust you, Sahil. Do you have our backs tomorrow? I don't want the memories of all we have learned these past few months to warp into something humdrum. For all the truths to be hidden. For Mum's death to be just a car crash. For Dad to be a painter who settles for postcard prints rather than the creator of real-life dragons. For me to be a teacher, not a druid. For Echo to be my missing Bengal cat. For Ezra to have just been a stranger on the street and Tielbu to have been a story. For you…"

A vein throbbed in his jaw. "I was happy being a property magnate until I found out there was more."

"Then we'll do this together. We'll pass the Wildwoods trial as a trio. All of us or none of us."

He sighed. "Yes. Okay. What else do you want me to say?"

Ezra's grey eyes found mine. "That's settled then. Come on, you three. We have some drills to do. A last push at preparation and then an early night. Alone."

"That's a shame." I winked. "Let's get to it then."

29

We stood outside Morden tube station, at the most southerly end of the Northern Line, underneath a crescent moon and cloudy sky. The underground had long closed, and the streets were deserted, with the exception of empty night buses rattling past and a takeaway owner pulling down the shutters on his chicken shop.

The three of us undergoing the trial had dressed in black, like robbers in the night, and shook with nerves. That was where our similarities ended. Marina's pockets bulged, clattering with acorns, crystals, horseshoes and rabbit feet. An unholy assortment of good luck symbols that would make no difference at all to how we fared tonight. Sahil had inexplicably decided to paint his face with stripes like he was on some army drill or a paint-balling jaunt with the lads. I had freed Transcender from my knicker drawer. The inch-thick shoulder straps of the baldric Fei Yen had made nestled against me like a second skin. The sword sat in a short scabbard on my back.

A shiver ran through me. I felt powerful.

But scared. Like knees-knocking-together scared.

I wouldn't give voice to what could happen if I failed. It was too painful. I had to hope I could see this through because if I lost the Otherworld, I would also lose Echo, Ezra, Tielbu and Flinar. I would think the foxes were two crazy Chinese ladies who ran an occult shop and forget they were *hu hsien*. I would return to being plain old me and forget how strong and brave I had been. I would never feel the wind from my palms or create new life from a page. It would have been for nothing.

"I have no idea what to expect," I said, although my heart ached with unsaid goodbyes.

Echo rubbed up against my legs. "It's the tube, Alisha. A labyrinth. What else could be in there except monsters?"

"Remember," said Ezra, "you have all the tools you need in your arsenal. You just need to keep your heads clear. Come morning, with any luck, you'll be fully-fledged members of the Otherworld, and you'll never have to think about this again until your own children have to go through it."

Dad wailed. "I'm so scared for you. My own trial was a disaster."

"Forget Morden." Marina glanced around uneasily. "More like Mordor."

"I've always hated the tube." Sahil looked like he wanted to run as fast as he could in the other direction.

I didn't blame him.

Echo's emerald eyes flashed. "Not helpful, Joshi. It is times like this I miss Rosalie. Her steadfast nature puts your lily-livered moaning to shame. Alisha, Marina, pigeon—"

Sahil butted in. "I'm a werepigeon, actually. Not a bog-standard pigeon."

"A pigeon is a pigeon. In any case, fight like a leopard. Be courageous. Be bold. Mark your territory to find your way out."

Sahil brightened. "I can help with that."

Echo purred. "Indeed you can, pigeon. We may laugh at your walk and feathery hair, but every pigeon plays his part on this green earth. Mostly, by leaving it splattered with waste."

"Druid. Empath. Pigeon." Rayna Willowsun said, her long, grey hair flowed behind her, intertwined with vines. Her wrinkle-free skin glowed in the moonlight, and the potions on her belt clanked, but she had wisely removed the dagger she usually carried. Old ladies with daggers might have drawn attention after all. Not that I could speak when Transcender sat snugly against my back.

"Werepigeon," said Sahil.

Rayna frowned. "I trust you have prepared well for this day and focussed your full attention on it?"

I plastered on a smile, although my ribcage tightened with anxiety. "Of course, headmistress. It has been the top of our priorities."

"You have no need to lie to me, Alisha. As Minister for Education and Headmistress of Wildwoods School of the Wondrous, I am well used to my students getting by on a wing and a prayer. Talent is no excuse for a lack of preparation. We will see how you all overcome the obstacles in your path tonight," said Rayna. "Lavinia and I have outdone ourselves imaginatively."

My palms were sweaty. I just wanted it to be over. "How do we know that the trial has ended?"

"It's simple, really. You just have to find your way out of the labyrinth. You may not go backwards, only forwards. You may only use force proportionate to the danger you face, and you must abide by the rules of the Magical Constitution. Ignore the orbs. They will be in flight behind you as witness to your choices." She clapped in excitement as if exams weren't anxiety-inducing at any time of life. "The hour is nigh. Mr Neuhoff will teleport you inside, and then we must leave you. He, too, has been preoccupied of late. This is as much a test of his performance as a mentor as it is of yours."

Ezra clenched his jaw. "Who could forget that?"

"I stand ready to come to your aid if you suffer any injuries," said Rayna. "It has been a long time since the senate and school community have taken such an interest in the outcome of a trial. There are bets afoot, and the Defence Minister herself has arranged a viewing party at Baba Yaga's Gym."

No doubt Lavinia wanted us to fall flat and for our shame to be witnessed by as many people as possible.

"One more thing, druid. Some amongst us feel we are indebted to you for preventing harm to innocents in this city. But you have shown a disdain for the rules and traditions of the Otherworld. You have cast away your training wheels and taken it upon yourself to make decisions that your betters avoid. You would have been wiser not to make enemies so quickly. From one druid to another, it is in our nature to be peaceable. Yet you are a whirlwind."

My gaze darted to the dark confines of the underground. "Plants are peaceable. The wind is not."

She gave me a slow smile. "Well, good luck to the three of you. Joshi, leopard, you may view the proceedings with me."

Ezra stepped forward, and his voice trembled. "Ready?"

Both of us knew how much we had to lose.

I gave him a shaky smile. Then I took a deep breath and joined hands with my brother and best friend. "As we'll ever be."

The damp, moist air filled our lungs. The lights had been switched off, but the orbs flickered above us, giving the station the air of an abandoned lunatic asylum. For all Lavinia's love of bubble gum pink, I had to give it to her—she had a flair for horror as well as Barbie chic.

I stood between Sahil and Marina, panting hard, not from exhaustion but from terror. Viewing rooms at Wildwoods and Baba Yaga's and who knew where broadcast our every word. Rayna had admitted there were bets on how we would fare. I wouldn't have been surprised if there was popcorn, too, as if we were actors on a stage, not real-life people trying to survive an ordeal.

Marina turned around and grimaced at the orbs that shadowed our every move. "This is horrendous. It's hard enough not knowing what's in that tunnel without every word and decision being watched."

"Just block it out." I gritted my teeth. I wanted to smack them out of the sky too.

A dark tunnel loomed in front of us. The Northern Line didn't run after 1 a.m., but that didn't make this a hospitable environment. Rats lurked down here, and creepy crawlies, and that were just humdrum creatures. There were other peculiar things that went bump in the night. Who knew what traps Lavinia had laid in store for us?

"Can pigeons see in the dark?" I said.

"Nope," said Marina.

Sahil frowned. "You could let the pigeon speak for himself."

"Sorry," said Marina. "Once a vet, always an answerer of animal Trivial Pursuit."

I pointed to the tunnel. "Shall we?"

"Must we?" said Marina. "I really miss Robert right now."

"You don't need a strapping man to make you feel safe, Marina. You have me." I tugged them with me.

At the platform edge, I jumped down onto the tracks. I was hedging my bets about them not being live. The senate might not like me, but I was pretty sure they'd choose humiliating us over killing us. It would kill the mood of the viewing parties for the night to end in our gruesome deaths.

Marina jumped down next. "So, all we have to do is find a way out. How hard can that be?"

Goosebumps trailed up my arms as the wind whistled down the tunnel. I pulled out my sword.

Sahil huffed as he joined us on the track. "What are you going to do? Quarter the rats?"

I grimaced. "Only if I have to. Shh. Do you hear that?" I looked down in horror as roots emerged from the ground, grasping at our feet. "Run!"

We ran, as only scared forty-year-olds do, with an ungainly, toppling forward motion.

Marina might have been a dancer, but she was no runner. She held her breasts as she ran, her legs akimbo. "I forgot to wear a sports bra."

"Let your boobs bounce, dammit," I panted. "Just move faster."

Sahil's longer legs took him further than us. "Look, a manhole."

He clambered up a ladder, but the roots crept up the wall, developing stems and leaves that covered the manhole in thick foliage in a matter of seconds. He gasped and leapt away as it sucked his arm into the mass.

"That's Rayna's doing." I climbed up and slashed at the vines with Transcender. Voices of the spirits overwhelmed me as I freed Sahil.

I fell to my knees.

"Get up." Sahil grabbed my hand.

We ran farther down the dark tunnels on Marina's tail. The vines reached the manholes before we did.

Panic set in. I didn't know if the rumbling of the ground was our feet or phantom trains or a creature from the unknown. My head filled with scenes from horror movies: Pennywise, the clown, hidden around a corner. Chucky, the doll, waiting in a dormant, abandoned tube carriage. Candyman and his bees behind me, always behind me, waiting for me to slip up. Waiting to devour me.

I had been so arrogant and stupid to think I'd been ready for this. That I could take on a witch of Lavinia's talent, a druid of Rayna's wisdom.

The truth was, I lagged far behind my grandmother. I couldn't even hope to come close. My ego had inflated when we had beaten Ra. It had inflated when I had left Pan unscathed and when I had animated Tielbu.

But any successes so far had been pure luck. They hadn't stemmed from talent. They had come about from stumbling in the dark.

Ezra hadn't trained me because of his faith in my abilities. He'd been strong-armed into it by Rayna. Dad had been right to wrap us in cotton wool. To tell us to stay safe. Even Fei Yen and Faeza had warned us not to trust the senate.

We could have lived as magical outsiders.

Instead, we had stepped into Wildwoods and made a pledge with the devil. All or nothing. Belonging or oblivion.

Why had I thought it would be any different for us?

I ran down those dingy tunnels with no escape and only the pounding of my weak, human heart. We were no longer running in tight formation. Sahil was ahead, Marina in the middle, and I lagged behind. The vines no longer grasped our feet, but they loomed overhead. A reminder that there would be no escape.

I pulled up short to catch my breath, leaning on Transcender. "Anyone else picturing horror movies?"

"Why would we need to picture horror movies when we can picture Jack the Ripper, the Moors Murderers or Fred and Rose West?" said Marina.

Sahil froze. "Will you two shut up?"

A putrid smell filled my nostrils. I gagged.

A man strode from one side of the tunnel to the other, disappeared through the wall and reappeared on the other side, only to repeat his motion, shaking his head and muttering all the while. He wore a threadbare tunic and stockings of coarse, undyed wool as if he'd stepped out of medieval England.

"I knew it," said Marina. "I knew ghosts were real."

"I'm not ready to meet Mum down here," said Sahil. "I can't tell her I'm a werepigeon."

"I hate to break it to you, Sahil, but I expect she already knows." I sighed and sheathed my sword. "I bet they put this in to tickle Orpheus's fancy. He loves a bit of history. No point bothering him. Let's wait until he disappears through one wall and run past. He won't harm us."

"Like hell, he won't," said Sahil. "The man's had to wear stockings for centuries. He must be livid."

"I like Alisha's plan," said Marina.

Sahil shrugged. "Don't say I didn't warn you."

We waited, and the man passed through again. He had hair like Friar Tuck and eyes that were only hollows, with claw marks underneath as if someone had taken them or he had himself torn them out.

I shuddered. "Now."

We stepped forward, but the ghost man came wheeling at us, bigger and wilder than he'd been in his calmer muttering state as if we'd angered him. Although in spirit form, he shoved us back with a monumental force that sent us sprawling.

I raised my hands and tried to return the favour, gathering a wind so wild that my hands stung.

The man sighed and continued his muttering and roaming like he'd not felt a thing, and yet when I stepped forward, he threw me again, the energy surge sending me farther than Marina and Sahil in punishment.

I stood in my signature kickboxing stance, legs braced, fists ready, in case he came at me again, but he continued his route, unseeing, deliberate, like he could continue for another century or seven.

"We can't keep this up, or we'll end up at the beginning," said Sahil.

Marina glanced around furtively. "Every second we stay in here is making me more anxious."

The orbs made it worse.

"Me too. We can't go backwards, Rayna said, but forwards isn't an option. Unless he lets us pass. So there has to be a way. It's not wind. It's not shapeshifting because he'll do the same. So it has to be empathy, Marina."

She bit her lip. "We need to get him to move on. But how?"

"Sahil, can you get close enough to hear his muttering?" I said.

He indicated the orbs. "You want me to shapeshift in front of all the people watching?"

"Please. What other choice do we have? We said we'd have each other's backs, didn't we?"

He held my gaze, and a second later, my brother's brown eyes shrank and repositioned themselves on the sides of his head. It was gross. They morphed into small, fiery, beady stones with none of Sahil's own handsomeness. Then he dropped to the size of a Wellington boot as we watched, his clothes falling away to reveal his weird, muscly, grey werepigeon chest with his pink, clawed toes, green-tinged head and orange beak. He grunted and took flight, trailing the hollow man, with his personal orb bobbing behind him.

"He's no robin redbreast, is he?" said Marina.

"Bless his heart. I really wish the universe had made him an eagle, at least. He would have dealt with that better."

Sahil fluttered back to us, landing heavily on the floor. "I know why he's here."

"Why?" I wrinkled my nose, desperate for some clean air.

"Because, my dear sister, that putrid smell isn't just the Northern Line. It's the smell of a mass grave underneath our very feet. Three thousand bodies were laid to rest here during the Black Death, and that man's wife and child are amongst them."

Marina's cornflower blue eyes welled up. "I know just what to do."

I grabbed her hand. "Be careful."

She walked with trepidation to the spot where the hollow man had repeatedly passed through and knelt there amongst the rail line with its gravel, soil, scuttling mice and the mass grave below. Then she dug in her pockets for the lucky crystals she had collected over the years from Shanghai Moon and other shops in Brighton, Norfolk and Stonehenge and all those places where free spirits dwelt. She piled her green jade, citrine, smoky quartz, malachite and rose quartz in a little pile, like an altar.

Then she stood up.

The hollow man made his rotation through the tunnel walls, but this time, he hovered over her.

Marina raised trembling hands to touch him but pulled them back like she'd been burned. Her grief-stricken face turned to look at me, and my heart hurt for her. "He's livid with rage. I can't help him."

I wanted to shield her from him, but this was her task. I was as certain of that as the sky was blue. "You can do it. Remember what you did for Elvira. And for Faeza. Remember how you calmed Sahil in the Wildwoods arena? Remember what you do for the creatures in your care every single day. This is no different. Counter his emotions with your positive ones, just like Ezra said."

She shook with fear and rolled up her sleeves like she meant business. Then she reached up with her glorious, tattooed arms and sank her hands gently into the hollow man. This time, she didn't pull away.

I held my breath, straining to listen.

Marina spoke of daisies and sunrises and the wings of hummingbirds, of technology and vaccines and children who lived to a hundred years old. The hollow man hovered over her and, this time, waited for her to finish. He crouched at the altar of crystals Marina had made.

Then the mass of his bulking shape broke into a thousand segments and rained down on the altar as if his very spirit had blessed it.

And he was no more.

She grinned. "I did it."

Relief washed over me as we joined her. "What did you say to him?"

Maria looked down at the crystals. "That the spirits of his loved ones live on in the beauty of the world and that medicine and technology mean that children born today stand a greater chance of living long lives. He seemed to like that."

"A good thing you didn't tell him about how Lavinia's rats bring death. I'm not sure he would have moved on so quickly," cooed my werepigeon brother.

By now, my trainers were wet with the damp ground. "We can pass now. Come on, before something else stands in our way."

Sahil flew over to his pile of discarded clothes. "Can someone carry these?"

I shook my head. "Best to keep our hands free, just in case."

He swooped past and fired a watery shit on my shoulder.

"Mature. Real mature, Sahil."

"You wanted me to have your back, didn't you?"

Marina sighed and gave her altar of crystals one last look, and we took off at a jog, with Sahil flying close behind. There was a deathly silence to the tunnels that drove fear into my heart. I preferred the bustling of the city to the sound of our feet against the ground, the heaving of our breath.

About two miles in, we came to a junction where the single tunnel split into two.

Sahil flapped his wings. "We should take the right one."

"The left one looks like a better bet," said Marina. "See the flickers of light?"

"Left it is," I said. We ran, and the air became cooler, as if the atmosphere had changed like there had been an airlock. The hair on my nape stood on end.

"This doesn't feel right," said Marina.

A shiver ran up my spine. "No, it doesn't."

A hiss met my ears.

I drew out Transcender, and this time when the sword whispered to me, I deciphered its call.

Basilisk. Basilisk. Basilisk.

30

———————

"**B**asilisk," I said.

Marina stopped dead in her tracks. "What do you mean?"

I frowned. "The sword said basilisk."

Sahil came to rest on my clean shoulder, his claws digging into me, his toothy beak millimetres from my face. His breath smelt like the mints he liked to chew. "Don't be stupid. They're not real."

"Neither are dragons," I said. "But they exist."

"Whatever you do, if you hear the sound, don't look at it," said Marina. "A basilisk causes death from a single glance. I read up on them after Ezra told us they were real. They are born from an egg laid by an old cock just before his death. A basilisk is born exactly at midnight on a clear night with a full moon."

I gulped as the hissing grew closer. "Thank goodness for your encyclopaedic, knowledge-searching mind because we sure as hell can't Google anything down here. We have two choices. We can run, or we can kill it."

"The other tunnel. Run," said Sahil.

"No! We'll fail the trial. Rayna said we can't go backwards, remember? Only forwards."

He flew ahead. "Well, run forwards then, Einstein."

The hissing grew louder and more pronounced, above and around us.

"Shit." I pulled Marina back to back with me. "Sahil, land on my shoulder. I can channel my powers to shield us. A column to keep us safe as we edge out of here. Keep your eyes shut."

"To hell with this," said Sahil. "I have my own shield."

"You what?" I opened my eyes, although I myself had warned against it.

My werepigeon brother flew before us. And it was true. He had a shield. A fluorescent yellow shield that presented as a cube around him. He tilted his feathery head at me pigeon-style as if riling me to challenge him.

I frowned, ignoring the hissing that drilled into my brain. "I don't understand."

Marina prodded me. "Alisha, now's not the time."

"Since when can you do that, Sahil?"

"You think you're the only one with friends? The only one with bargaining ability?" my brother cooed. "What is money when you've seen power like this? Why should I give it up? Passing this trial is as much my birthright as yours, Alisha." The fluorescent light from his shield revealed an air vent at the top of the tunnel. "I hope you make it out of here, but I'm not sticking around this hellhole to help. See you on the other side."

He looked at it, and the next thing I knew, my werepigeon brother shifted into something small and bulbous, with many more legs than a pigeon. His shield contracted with him, and he scuttled away through the grate.

His orb disappeared with him.

I clutched Marina. He really had left us in the damp tunnel with the basilisk hissing in surround sound.

"Aren't we supposed to stick together?" said Marina.

"It wasn't one of the rules, but I can't believe the wanker left us here and saved his own skin." I sighed. "There's no way we fit through that grate, Marina. Did he just change into a frikkin' bulbous spider to get through it?"

She shuddered. "And I thought a werepigeon was scraping the

bottom of the barrel. I'm *never* sleeping with him now. Even if my boobs reach my toes, and he's the only one left on Earth offering some nookie."

The hissing reached a fever pitch, making me break out in a sweat. Sahil was gone.

So much for teamwork. So much for us all being in it together.

I wasn't sure if I hated him or if I was just disappointed. But for now, we had to focus on making it out ourselves, and we still had no idea if this was one basilisk or many. Or how big and bad our foe was. For all I knew, it could have been a hologram conjured by Lavinia–including sound effects. There was no way Helio would have let one of his beasties loose in London's Underground.

"Er, Alisha?" said Marina. "Something just slithered over my foot."

I jerked her three feet away, flat against a wall. A creature wriggled past, and I thought I might pass out. Two orbs were left floating overhead. I held Transcender aloft in the light of one of the orbs, and my blood chilled.

Reflected there in the obsidian blade was a serpent with a crown-shaped crest. The serpent slid forward. It must have been at least thirty feet long with a girth wide enough to fit Marina and me side by side. And we weren't skinny chicks. We were curvy ladies with a lifetime of chocolate consumption on our hips.

King of the serpents, indeed.

Its venomous tongue flickered, and its eyes loomed larger than any snake I'd ever seen. Eyes that could kill us with one stare.

It looked like he belonged in the Congo or the Amazon, not at sorry old Morden tube station, which, let's face it, didn't even feel like central London—just some sort of junction between the big smoke and suburbia.

"He's behind us," I whispered. "Don't look at it. At least not directly."

"Is it bad?"

I shuddered.

"Oh shit," said Marina. "Why are we playing musical statues? Shouldn't we run? Bloody thing is probably sentient as well. It will probably quote *Paradise Lost* at us as it devours us."

I winced. "It's really long. Who knows if it can do that winding, suffocating trick I've seen on the Discovery Channel. We'd have to get past with our eyes shut."

She sighed. "Well, mate. It's been a thrill and a pleasure knowing you."

The hissing perforated my mind, making it difficult to think. "We can't give up."

A head emerged out of the wall next to us.

"Alisha doesn't have to give up," said a small voice.

I jumped three feet. "Flinar?"

"You gave me hope. I am going to save you."

I could only see half of his face. His milky eyes glowed. Two cold, four-fingered hands reached out and pulled us into a black hole before sealing it shut, leaving the two orbs and the basilisk in the tube tunnel.

The clamp around my chest eased. We seemed to be on a ledge with a vast expanse of blackness underneath us.

"But Flinar, I thought you could only hide small objects?" I said.

He broke into a smile. "I have been practising, Alisha. Our people were hunted, and the woods were quiet enough to practice. It is good to be useful."

Marina breathed a sigh of relief. "This is nice. Not cosy but much better than being in a confined space with a serpent king."

Flinar shook his head mournfully. "We can't stay here long. I told the leopard that Alisha needed more sleep. That she should stay safe in the nest I made her. But this will give you a few moments to decide how to defeat the basilisk. But where is the werepigeon? I hope he is not languishing in the serpent's belly."

"Don't ask," I said.

"I am sorry. We will arrange him a funeral befitting a warrior."

"Let's focus on defeating the basilisk. Thank you for this moment of peace, Flinar." I sighed. "What would my grandmother do? Or Echo or Ezra?"

Flinar leapt up and down on the ledge, the only one of us brave enough to do it. "You made a god believe in god, Alisha. Why can't you believe in yourself?"

Marina nodded. "He's right. All your successes, and you still don't get how badass you are. You've had so much on your plate, Alisha—the divorce, your mum's death, coming to terms with all this. Take a breath. We can still win this. But…call it my vet's disposition, but however horrific the basilisk is, I don't want to kill it. You know how animals are. It might be a sweetheart in a serpent's body. Maybe we can sing it kumbaya and lull it to sleep. An a cappella version with harmonies might do the trick."

I rolled my eyes. "That thing is not a sweetheart. But you're right. I don't think killing it will win us any favour. It's probably one of Helio's pets."

"It's pretty much impossible to kill anyway," said Marina. "You can try stabbing it with your sword, I suppose, but that's going to be hard if you're fencing blind. And according to legend, the only way to kill a basilisk is by the crowing of a rooster."

My heartbeat sped up. I hoisted up my arse on the wafer-thin ledge and reached carefully into my back pocket, where I'd stashed the chapbook Dad had made me.

I squinted at it.

There he was: a fat bird standing proud on the page, crumpled by my butt. Bold red and brown, he had a striking plumage on his tail and neck, a tell-tale crest on his head and red flaps of skin hanging on either side of his yellow beak.

I shoved the chapbook under Marina's nose. "Is this a rooster?"

Her blue eyes widened, and she punched the air. "Hell, yes! We are back in business!"

A weight lifted off my chest. I knew exactly what I was going to do. "Flinar. It's time to go back. It might be dangerous. Can you take us?"

Marina frowned. "Maybe you should animate that thing here. You know, in case it takes a while."

I gave a slow smile. "No, I'll animate him in there. Wildwoods wants a performance, and that's exactly what we're going to give them. Are you ready? Just follow my lead."

Flinar stood up. "Take my hands, friends. We will go to the basilisk. But if it's okay with you, I prefer to live."

He spun his back hole magic, and the ledge disappeared from under us.

The three of us stepped out of the wall. The serpent lurked for its prey in the dark. Patient. Vicious. Ready.

I didn't know if time had continued at the same pace or if hours had passed. Ezra had said the trial would take as long as was required to determine the outcome. I had to believe we hadn't already failed. That we had bent the rules enough to give ourselves a chance but not enough to turn the senate against us. Because I realised my advantages in the Otherworld had come from being an outsider. And I was about to do it again.

The orbs bobbed up and down, eager to find their targets again.

Flinar cowered behind Marina.

I flattened myself against the wall, working quickly. My fingers called out the rooster from the page. Warmth and cells and feathers and rubber-like wattles that weren't my favourite texture. But also shrewdness, daring and gregariousness.

This time, I didn't forget.

"Your purpose is to keep the basilisk at bay for as long as I require it. Don't look him in the eye, and don't crow unless I ask you to." I pulled the rooster out of the page. He was a warm bundle in my hands that I showed the orb, like Rafiki showing Simba to the kingdom. "Nice to meet you, Mr Rooster. Let's call you Roger, shall we?"

Roger clucked and wriggled out of my hands.

The basilisk hissed. It knew what was coming.

Roger was determined. He barrelled around, more sheepdog than rooster. The basilisk might have been long, but it was slow, and Roger's tiny wings propelled him up and over its body.

"Druid," said the basilisk. His voice sounded like the lowest notes of a cello, and it suited this dark, dank place. "You are playing a dangerous game. My venom will immobilise you before the rooster crows."

Marina shuddered. "If it makes no difference to you, can you drag us to the Jubilee Line before you strike? I prefer that one."

I held my finger to my lips to quiet her. Marina had suggested the basilisk might be sentient. I'd been counting on it. "The rooster has no other purpose but to crow for me, basilisk. You will let us pass, or you won't make it to dawn."

"Are you so sure of your talent? The witch told me you are not cut from the same mould as Rajika Verma," said the basilisk.

I closed my eyes and called my dragon. "The witch is right. I might walk in my grandmother's footsteps, but my mould is my own. You see, she played by the rules, and it got her killed. I don't play by the rules." I turned to the orbs. "I think we've done enough to prove ourselves tonight, but I'll give you one last spectacle."

I could feel Tielbu nearing. My hands tingled as I called forth a cushioning wind to surround Marina, Flinar and me. It didn't matter that I couldn't hold it for long. That I was exhausted and needed my adrenalin to subside because Tielbu wouldn't let me down. The threads of the universe held us together, like mother and child.

He broke through the city street to the walls of the chamber where we stood. My beautiful dragon, with his translucent wings and horned head, roared with passion. My wind protected us from the falling rubble that trapped the basilisk, and the three of us leapt onto Tielbu's back before I held out my hands to the rooster, calling him to me.

"Don't look at him, Tielbu. Seal the tunnel with your fire but leave him alive," I said. "The senate put him there. They can remove him."

Tielbu's roar deafened me, and his fiery breath raged down onto the tunnel, shattering the orbs at last, leaving a pool of molten concrete no person or creature could escape from.

"Thank you," I said as his strong wings took us over London's rooftops.

Marina clung on for dear life, with Flinar clamped between her legs like a misshapen yoga block.

I whooped, enjoying the thrill of the ride, although Roger most certainly wasn't, given how furiously he was pecking my arm.

"Do you think it will be enough to pass?" called Marina over the whooshing of the air.

"Not with all the chaos we left behind. But I don't care anymore. I was fed up with playing by their rules. Weren't you?"

31

———————

As per tradition, the Prime Sorcerer summoned both mentor and initiates to the vaulted cabin at Wildwoods as a new dawn rose. Ezra, Sahil, Marina and I waited in stilted silence outside the great tombstone door to be invited in. It was funny to end my Otherworld life in the vaulted cabin, where I had first understood how much this world had to offer and been introduced to the senate that first magical night when Ezra had led me into Wildwoods.

My heart ached with the loss I was about to face, but I was proud of myself. I couldn't have tried any harder to succeed in this new life. All I could do was be true to myself. I only wished I hadn't shamed Ezra.

He stood, handsome and stoic, at my side. "Maybe Orpheus would have been the better mentor after all."

I swallowed hard. Even now, he was trying to make it easy for me. I didn't want to ask whether he'd still search me out once my memory of the Otherworld had been wiped. How could he be himself around me if he couldn't even share his history and talents with me? If he had to lie about what he did every day? I knew then that he'd walk away. He would have to. But I didn't have to lay any blame at his door. The decisions had been mine alone.

"It wasn't your fault," I said. "And for the record, even with a fail tonight, you were the best mentor I could have hoped for. I didn't want a big dick swinging his opinions around. I wanted a supportive mentor who trusted me to take the lead."

Sahil gave a sly smile. "Well, this big dick is about to walk this trail. I showed my wares, got out of there, and didn't make a mess. Not one splatter of pigeon poo either."

I rolled my eyes. "You arsehole. It was supposed to be about teamwork. Wait until Dad hears you abandoned me there."

"It's not my fault that arachnids can see nearly 360 degrees around them and can't shut their eyes. Forget immobilisation. That triffid or whatever it was would have killed me if I had stayed." He paused. "I didn't want to leave you behind, though, Marina. I was worried about you."

Marina glared at him. "Talk to the hand, werepigeon spider hybrid. How do we even know you're Alisha's brother?"

He frowned. "Because you've known me practically all my life."

She was in full flow now, and watching her go was a thing of beauty—my best friend, scrapping like a cage fighter until the very end. "Yeah, well, maybe you're wearing face skin too. Like in that Nicholas Cage/John Travolta film. Either way, you're a slippery eel."

I studied the emotions flitting across Sahil's face. We'd all struggled to help him reveal his peculiar talents. It had been like coaxing a lotus to grow in the desert. Bloody impossible. But what he was good at was making deals. It was why he had such killer instincts as a property magnate. What was more, he was avoiding our eyes like he'd done as a kid and didn't want to be found out.

I turned on him, still sore that he'd just upped and left us. "How did you get that magic anyway?"

Ezra sighed, his voice rasped like he'd spent every minute of the trial smoking his cigarette roll-ups. By the looks of it, his nerves were as frazzled as ours. "Stop fighting, children. Now's not the time. Just remember the rules. Don't speak unless you are spoken to. Your chance to convince the senate has passed. This deliberation is not another chance for you to make an impact. It is a chance for you to listen."

The door creaked open to reveal the soaring ceilings and stained-glass windows of the inner sanctum. The thousand burning pillar candles burned again, and the meeting was already in full progress around the split stone table. Nine faces turned to face us, their expressions inscrutable, although by now, they were familiar to me. Hadn't we all just dined together at the coven flat? Yet, without batting an eyelid, they would go from breaking bread with me to walking past me on the street like strangers.

My stomach was rock hard with bundled nerves.

The Prime Sorcerer stood. His midnight skin glowed in the candlelight, and his straggly beard was streaked with silver, just as the cloud of hair around his head. A pen and lined paper hovered in the air beside him, recording his every word. "Another day, another group of initiates. Welcome to tonight's warriors. You may sit."

Four high-backed chairs faced the stone table. Sahil and I chose the outer seats, with Ezra and Marina in the middle. So much for sibling love.

"I would like it noted for the record that both the Minister for Education and the Minister for Defence did an excellent job planning this trial. The combination of grasping vines, Black Death spectre and basilisk, is one that was well appreciated by the spectators at our various viewing parties."

Lavinia, resplendent in a full-sleeved, glittering pink gown and a bouffant helmet of hair, inclined her head in acknowledgement and silently applauded Rayna next to her.

Phinnaeous Shine continued, his eyes glinting with glee. "Now, it is time to put the spectacle aside. I do love this part of the evening. It's almost reminiscent of the white smoke that emerges from the chimney of the Vatican's Sistine Chapel when the cardinals decide the next pope."

Orpheus rolled his eyes, but he didn't look at me.

I had no idea if we could count on his support. But it was clear how many would stand against us from their dispassionate faces. This was simply business for them—another vote.

Whereas for us, it would determine the rest of our lives. Perhaps

I'd never discover again who I really was. Like dementia, a cruel uncoupling of who I truly was and how my life unfolded.

"First, we will decide in the case of Sahil Verma and Marina Ambrose," said the Prime Sorcerer. "These two initiates fought with honour during the trial. They displayed their skills openly and with vigour and showed the courage and discerning natures required of peculiars. While Sahil Verma should be censured for escaping the tunnels without his sister and friend, his prowess as a shapeshifter cannot be denied. Marina Ambrose was able to bring peace to a ghost that had disrupted many a commuter train. They both pass the trial. The senate's vote is unanimous. Can I hear an aye?"

"Aye," said the senate.

"It is done," said the Prime Sorcerer. "You may leave the hearing."

Sahil grinned broadly and gave me a wave before prancing out of the hall.

Like I said. Arsehole.

Marina looked at me in awe. "Alisha, I want the same for you. I'll wait in the park with all my fingers and toes crossed."

"It's okay. I'm happy for you. Go." I willed my heartbeat to stop thundering. "I'll be fine."

She kissed my cheek and Ezra's. "Take care of her."

I watched her as she bounded out of the room, lighter than someone who had offloaded a giant poo.

Then I turned back to the senate.

Shadows cast by the candlelight cloaked the Prime Sorcerer's expression. "Granddaughter of Rajika Verma, you involved yourselves in matters that did not concern you."

"I did."

"Why?"

"Because innocent lives were at stake, and facts matter."

He shrugged. "You are young for your forty years. When you grow up, you will realise that sometimes the end is more important than the means. There are always winners and losers. It is our job as the senate to choose only those to enter our fold who will help us win."

"That sounds a teeny bit unhinged to me."

Orpheus shook his head in a pantomime fashion.

Ezra gave me a sharp elbow in the ribs.

"I see. It seems it is hard to teach old women manners," said the Prime Sorcerer. "There remains only one question to answer before we vote. Will you surrender the dragon to us?"

I frowned. "Does the answer to this have an impact on my vote?"

Phinnaeous nodded. "It may well do. Think of it as a way of showing us how hospitable you are to the desires of ministers."

Lavinia's eyes gleamed.

I sighed. They wouldn't let Tielbu be free. I knew it as surely as I knew the lines on my palm. "Then the answer is no."

His brow furrowed. "Then we vote."

They voted, one by one—my fate in the Otherworld in their hands.

The formidable shapeshifting wizard Prime Sorcerer, Phinnaeous Shine, as wealthy as the Queen and with connections deep into humdrum government, cast the first vote. He, whose plans for the elves I had derailed, whose motivations were entirely unknowable. "The druid raised a dragon, but her ego knows no bounds. She is incapable of collaborating with the senate and follows only her own mind. That bodes ill for the future. For that reason, I vote no."

Brooding vampire Orpheus, Minister for History and the Today, with his Roman nose and heavy brows, who could read my hopes and fears, even now, from across the room. Whose vampire I had haplessly killed without really meaning to. His hooded eyes turned on me. "She wasn't distracted by the fiction of an unjust war. I appreciate her uncovering who really caused the tremors. She has achieved things other peculiars could only dream of. Tonight, you sealed the tube line like a tomb, but still, she got out. I vote yes."

Ezra's witch aunt Lavinia, the Minister for Defence, with her love of bubble gum pink interiors, deadly weapons and rat spies, who I'd made to look stupid with my meddling. Her eyes twinkled with mischief. "It may come as a surprise to you, given the druid is sleeping with my nephew, that I am voting the way I am."

I scowled and opened my mouth, but Ezra squeezed my thigh. The wily witch meant to sway Gunnolf's vote against me, no doubt, by saying Ezra and I had slept together. Hadn't Ezra said he preferred werewolves to be with their own kind? And to add insult to injury, it was partly Lavinia's fault that Ezra and I had been so embroiled in work rather than play.

Lavinia adopted a sombre tone. "I have tried to welcome this druid into the Otherworld. I have helped her save humdrum lives, although it led to the loss of one of my own, led her in an aerobics class, although she quite frankly has no rhythm, and invited her to dine with the coven. But she is a disappointment. What good is a peculiar of her quite remarkable talent if they refuse to be a team player? The druid could have shared her elvish intel with me. Worse still"—she clutched her chest as if it personally pained her—"she escaped our orbs tonight and cheated. I vote no."

I rolled my eyes. No word about knocking me out with a truth serum, then.

Her rats had plenty of intel. She hadn't needed mine.

The druid headmistress of Wildwoods School of the Wondrous and Minister for Magical Education, gifted healer and mentor, whose gleaming hip dagger never left her side, played with the vine trailing her shoulder. "Alisha helped during the crisis at Wildwoods. The students look up to her. She didn't strictly play by the rules by involving the elf and the dragon, but she is inventive and brave. There is no doubt that she is too wild, but we can tame her still. She is a valuable member of this community. I vote yes."

I sighed with relief. The vote was even stevens with five more votes to come.

The fairy Bestiary Minister Helio, whose beasts included the octopus Kraglek and surely the basilisk we probably maimed that night in our escape, propped his elbows onto the stone table in a pensive mood. "I am torn. The basilisk lives, although she animated a rooster who could have killed him. She commands a dragon. But she refuses to share him with us. How I would have loved to study him. To command him myself. I vote no."

Shit. It wasn't looking good.

The leprechaun Minister for Finance, Cillian O'Meara, whose job was to move money for magical needs from rainbow to rainbow, to deal in good luck and to keep the armoury stocked, was up next. Wouldn't he, too, lust after my dragon and be on Lavinia's side?

Shrewd eyes darted to my face as I held my breath. "She takes on foes that would make others tremble. I'm a money man, but we need fighters with balls of steel amidst us. Luck is on her side. I vote yes."

It was down to the wire. Two more votes to go.

Ezra tensed next to me.

Gunnolf, Ezra's brawny, denim-loving werewolf alpha, the Minister for Justice who was a stickler for the rules and who, even now, curled his lip at me. Presumably, because he knew of the sparks flying between Ezra and me. "She is disobedient and insolent. She doesn't know her place and has no respect for the Magical Constitution that governs us. She is a distraction for our best seeker, and her choices tonight show she is willing to break the natural order to further her own goals. With absolute certainty that we would regret admitting the druid into our fold, I vote no."

Margola Silver, the selkie Minister for Information, with her flame-coloured hair, cat-like glasses and perfectly pointy bosoms, dabbled in divination. Ezra had told me her allegiances shifted depending on the story of the day. Her voice tinkled like a bell, high and thin. "There are dark times coming. We need all the help we can get. Besides, you saw her tonight. She's more skilled than even her grandmother. And the magical community loves her. Heroic stories sell. I vote yes."

Erelim the angel, Minister for Diplomacy, with his dirty wings, stringy blond hair, washboard stomach and a bottom that could crack a nut. As a conflict mediator, wouldn't he be on my side, given that I had helped solve the problem of Pan and the elves? "She damaged humdrum property. That causes difficulties for me. What is more, she conducted diplomacy with the elves without consulting me. I vote no."

The candelabras flickered.

The floating pen stopped writing.

Lavinia broke out into a wide smile.

My ribcage contracted, and the senate blurred. I felt like I'd been punched in the stomach. It was over. I was about to lose part of me. I didn't even know what life would look like on the other side. Whether this would somehow drive a wedge between Marina and me, whether

I would see Echo or my creatures again. What would happen to Tielbu?

Ezra took my palm in his hand. "Take a deep breath, hellfire."

The blood rushed to my ears. "You can't teleport us out of here. You'd lose everything."

"Like hell, I can't. They're not taking away your identity. Damn the consequences."

"The yew tree rune won't tolerate you teleporting."

He rolled the binary code charm on his necklace between his thumb and forefinger. "I have a little trick to bypass that."

Orpheus stood up, a tall shadow looming over the stone table, as if he knew what we were thinking.

The arched door to the vaulted cabin opened, and in strode Calypso, with her blade runners and dreadlocks and a kickass pocketed trouser suit, like she meant business. She smiled at me, and it was like the warmth of the sun on an icy winter's day.

My consciousness came back into the room, tethered by a thread of hope.

Phinnaeous Shine stood up, grimacing. He waved his hand, and the floating pen began once again to scribble on its page. "This is very unorthodox to leave the Celestial Library at such a dark hour."

"The threat has passed, has it not? In large part thanks to the druid."

"The vote is over," said Phinnaeous to murmurs of assent from the rest of the senate.

The Custodian set her shoulders back and spoke in clear, soaring tones. "The vote is not over until the initiate leaves this room as a fully-fledged peculiar or a humdrum revert. You know this as well as I do, Prime Sorcerer."

He inclined his head. "Still bookish, I see, Calypso? Very well. In that case, let it be said, it is not your place to meddle here."

Calypso's amicable tone cooled to ice pole levels. "My place is anywhere I choose it to be. I'm an equal. As much a member of this senate as you, Phinnaeous."

His eyes flashed with anger. He wasn't used to being challenged. "Yes, in theory. But why would you choose to intervene in this particular matter, Calypso, when you are usually far happier with your nose buried in books amongst the stars?"

"My role in the Otherworld is all about learning. The Celestial Library is perhaps the greatest source of learning in the known universe. And what is this sitting if not about learning?"

"You don't know what you are doing. Our laws cite—"

"I know what our laws cite. And I know why it is worth raising my head above the parapet to invoke this one. How often do we have initiates where the vote is so close? Alisha Verma is not just anyone. She is the granddaughter of the most celebrated Custodian in the Otherworld. She performed feats tonight that are exceptional for an initiate. She did something not one of you has done in years. She faced a god without fear and with candour. And she gained access to the library. It deemed her worthy. My vote is yes, making it a tie." She drew a deep breath. "Our laws state that in the case of a vote tie following the trial of a new peculiar, the balance must be tipped towards acceptance based on the principle that everyone deserves a chance." The Custodian turned to smile at me. "Alisha Verma passes her trial."

Sparks of happiness dispersed my mountainous anxiety. I jumped up from my chair and pranced around like a kid at a school disco.

Damn Lavinia and her assessment of my sense of rhythm. Dancing was joy.

Ezra picked me up and spun me around as the senate stared. "It's over."

"You are one of us now, Alisha," said Rayna.

The Prime Sorcerer's face shuttered. "Let's hope we don't live to regret it."

32

____

For once, my bedroom didn't smell of Echo marking his territory. Pink rose petals trailed across my bedroom floor and onto my bed. My silken bedsheets wafted of summer rain fabric conditioner. A breeze drifted in from the open window. A bottle of Prosecco and two glasses waited on my side table. Ezra lay on my bed—not naked and wrapped in a bow—but in bare feet and jeans, with his hands behind his head. Like he'd stepped out of a Levi's advert.

Yum, yum, said my brain.

"Hey, you," said my mouth. "What are you doing here?"

His soft lips curved into a smile. "I thought we could celebrate together."

I kicked off my shoes. "What, the rooftop karaoke with a drunk detective, two foxes, my empath bestie and a crooning leopard hogging the microphone isn't your idea of a celebration?"

He winced. "Those tracks from the *Glee* soundtrack that he keeps choosing are really starting to grate. Maybe we should sneak him into a real gig. Something with a mosh pit at the Hammersmith Apollo. What do you say?"

I neared the bed, my senses tingling in the low lamplight. "I'd say you're out of your mind."

His grey eyes held mine. "Out of my mind for you."

He caught my hand and pulled me on top of him.

My chest crushed his. I wasn't a double D cup for nothing. "Would you really have whisked me out of there in front of the senate just so I could keep this side of my identity? They would have thrown the book at you."

Ezra pushed my loose hair back over my shoulder and played with the front fastening of my bodycon dress. "I was following my instincts. It's hard to think straight around you. And besides, Gunnolf wouldn't have thrown me to the wolves. And if he had, he would have given me a cushy suite."

I caught his finger and nibbled it. "You have that much faith in his love for you?"

"He brought me up after my parents died, didn't he?" He rolled me over onto the velvet layer of rose petals, and I had never been as turned on.

"We really pulled it off," I said.

He caught my lip between his teeth and murmured against me. "We did."

Ezra kissed me, and I breathed in the mossy, earthy scent of him. The pressure of his lips was firm against mine as if he'd grown impatient of waiting, as if he couldn't get enough of me. Everything else—all our efforts and striving and exhaustion—receded into the background as it became only him and me on a bed of rose petals.

I could have spent a lifetime within that moment, feeling wanted and loved and the centre of his universe.

He propped himself onto his elbow as his hand toyed with the zipper of my dress and looked deep into my eyes. My nails dug into his back, and my vision blurred with passion. I didn't need the alcohol on the bedside table. Being in Ezra's arms was heady enough.

Ezra unzipped my dress, trailing featherlight fingers down my exposed ribcage.

I hadn't felt like this in so long. To hell with my divorce. I was ready to claim my flirty forties. I pushed impatiently against him, kissing his jawline, hooking one leg around his legs to bring us closer, his hard chest against my soft one.

He dipped his head to my lacy bra and kissed me on each breast through the material.

I wanted this so much.

A head of silver curly hair popped up next to the bed like a nightmare clown.

I almost lost control of my bladder there and then. The words burst out of me like machine gun fire. "Oh, my god. Lavinia?"

Ezra stiffened like a corpse before swinging around with a growl.

I shoved him off me and scrambled to pull down my dress, feeling like a teenager caught by their parents.

She shimmied over to sit between us in her yoga leggings and sports bra, swinging her umbrella, ruining the romance in a lightning blink. "Hello, darlings."

A vein throbbed in Ezra's clenched jaw. "Auntie, what the hell are you doing here?"

She pouted. "Can't an aunt come to see her beloved nephew?"

"Cut the crap, Lavinia." He quivered with anger. Or sexual frustration.

She shrugged. "Very well. I came to warn you about her. She might have passed the trial, but you might want to think twice about how easily she is driving a wedge between us."

Ezra sighed. "Leave Alisha out of this. When will you and Gunnolf realise I'm not yours to influence? I have independent thought. I know you, auntie. You came specifically to ruin our celebration out of pique. Like a dog urinating on a picnic because they aren't allowed to eat from it."

Lavinia clutched her hand to her chest. "How you wound me. Never mind. I do love you, you know." She scowled at me. "Alisha, on the other hand, I'm not so fond of. He'll find out soon enough that you're not worthy of him. Oh, and I'll find the dragon. It's only a matter of time before he's under my control." She stood up and dusted herself off. Then she glanced around my room, pinched his cheek and winked. "It's not going to be so easy to get it up now, is it, Ezra dear?"

Her laughter hung in the room as she slipped out the window in a fine display of the granny acrobatics that had impressed me the first time I had met her.

Ezra stood up, sighing heavily. "God, she can be awful."

"Families, eh?"

He took my hand and pulled me into his arms, then turned me around, pulling my back against his bare torso. His hair brushed against me as his lips found my neck.

I nestled into him, butterflies darting in my stomach.

A dreadlocked head loomed through the window as a woman— who lived amongst the stars and books with a horse named Nightfall —leapfrogged into the room.

"You've got to be kidding me. What is this, a train station?" said Ezra.

Calypso pointed to the wall. "Sorry about that. Nothing a lick of paint won't fix."

Gratitude bubbled up in me. "Calypso."

I'd not seen her since the senate vote when she'd intervened on my behalf. I disentangled myself from Ezra and ran to hug her.

Ezra groaned and grabbed his shirt.

She patted my shoulder awkwardly. "Apologies for the intrusion. I figured it couldn't get much worse after the witch parachuted in here with that brass-handled deathly umbrella of hers."

The sounds of a raucous rendition of "Don't Stop Believing" drifted down from the rooftop.

Ezra sighed. "The mighty leopard has really failed at his protection duties tonight."

"I suspect Lavinia Drach has been waiting outside your window to pounce during the least opportune moment," said Calypso. "That woman always was too spiteful for her own good. She really should take more sugar in her tea. It might make her less bitter."

"You were brilliant the other night, Calypso," I said. "Thank you. Why didn't you say you were a senate member?"

She patted my shoulder awkwardly. "There are lots of things you don't know. And I rarely leave the library to take up my seat there. There are far more efficient ways to change the world. In any case, congratulations, Alisha. You deserve to be one of us."

My heart sang. "That means a lot."

"Actually, I didn't come to say that. I came to collect what you borrowed from the library. At least, what you still have in your possession."

I nodded and delved into the bottom of my wardrobe to retrieve the bag of Odysseus's wind and *The Rose of Jericho* book Mum had loaned.

She winced as I tripped. "Careful, careful. I'll take the bag."

My legs were still jelly after those stolen minutes with Ezra. Imagine what he could do with an hour.

Calypso looked inside the bag. A stormy wind erupted from its folds, lifting her off her feet and swelling her hair like she'd stood in front of a megawatt fan, sending the rose petals swirling through the air. She shut the bag with deft fingers and nodded.

"All present and accounted for. But you should keep the book. You and your friends might yet need it. That reminds me." Her hand delved deep into her pocket to retrieve a velvet pouch no bigger than her palm. "Now you've passed the trial, it's time to give you this. Your mother only gave it to me for safekeeping."

I accepted the pouch and tipped the contents onto my hand. A necklace fell out: an oval amber stone on a choker-type gold chain. Chokers had fallen out of fashion in the early nineties, but my eyes filled with tears all the same.

"It's beautiful," I said. "I wonder why Mum wanted me to have it."

She frowned. "For you and the empath to finish the work she started, of course. Why else do you think she needed the book on the Rose of Jericho?" She glanced at her wristwatch. "I must go. I have a Battersea Dogs Home board member to see about another borrowed item."

"I'm not sure whether you'll get a hospitable welcome. Do you need my help?"

Calypso shook her head. "My dear Alisha, I can handle myself. I have the power of the Celestial Library behind me. Besides, the god has had a reminder of the heavens. In my experience, that softens the heart." She headed for the window. "This isn't goodbye, though. More like an *au revoir*. We still have our swap day to look forward to. And you can always come and find me, can't you?"

"Do I have to pass the test again?"

Her eyes lit up with mirth. "Of course. But everything's easier the second time."

LAVINIA WAS RIGHT ABOUT one thing. All the interruptions ruined the frisson of desire between Ezra and me. Not entirely, of course. All it took was a lingering, heat-filled glance from him to make my heart leap again. They said twenty-year-olds had all the fun, but seriously, my lady parts smouldered in his presence.

That fire didn't need to blaze today. I could wait a bit longer. It would make the experience all the sweeter.

If all else failed, at least I could purge the image of Lavinia out of my head beforehand.

So, a whispered word from me, and we teleported across London. A velvet black sky dotted with stars blanketed the woods as we arrived. The wind rustled through the firs and oaks and sycamore trees, making me feel right at home. Quiet reigned, disturbed only by the gentle lull of the distant motorway.

I stepped out of the circle of Ezra's arms.

Ezra was still a little peeved at his thwarted efforts earlier. "Are we here to say goodnight to the dragon?"

"Something like that."

"Going to read him a bedtime story?"

I grinned. "Stop sulking."

He shrugged. "It feels weird here without the little guys, that's all."

The elves were home at last after Erelim had led diplomatic talks between injured parties. Rumours had spread across the Otherworld that the elves had received a tongue-lashing from the senate. That played well to those who wanted the persecution to continue. But Flinar didn't mind. He was just happy to return to his hovel and had invited me over for elvish flatbread when the dust had settled.

"You were so brave to help them. Now there's one last soul to take care of." I cupped my hands around my mouth and called out, although the magical trial proved that the dragon didn't need to hear my voice to respond. "Tielbu."

Our thoughts were connected. Maybe it was my fear that called to him, or maybe because I was his mother in a strange sense. I could work all that out later.

He came, his wings beating in time to my heart. The ground shook as he landed in the clearing, dwarfing us. "Druid."

"I'm here too," said Ezra.

Tielbu snorted like he didn't care a jot. His ivory horns glowed in the moonlight. He turned his gentle amber eyes on me, and it was as though he could see to my very core. "I knew you would come, but I can't do as you wish."

My chest tightened. "I listened when you perched on top of Big Ben, just as I listened when Dad told me stories about you. About your courage and heroism. How you always saved people in need. And then I realised you were happiest in those stories when you were soaring free."

His slow, precise voice sent a shiver down my spine. "Those stories are like a dream to me. Vague memories. They tell me who I am. But I can't tell whether the voice I hear is yours, your father's or my own."

I nodded. "It doesn't matter which parts of you are us. It just matters that you are a force for good."

"Perhaps. But I still have no place in the world. These woods are little more than a jail now the elves have gone."

I gave a small smile. "That's why we must take you somewhere safe. You don't belong to me. Just as you don't belong to the senate. You are free, Tielbu."

His roar made my bones rattle. "What about my purpose?"

"If I need you, you will come if you are able." I walked towards him so I could feel his hot breath rippling through my hair one last time. "But I'll let you in on a little secret. I think I am different to my grandmother. I think I don't have to assign a purpose at the moment of animation. I think you can find your own purpose, and purposes change."

"There's a settlement of peculiars in Eastern Europe," said Ezra.

"On the surface, it's like any old ski resort. With brochures about the snowy landscape, spas, picturesque chalets and restaurants serving fondue. But when you get there, it's something else altogether—a haven for peculiars. I went there a long time ago with my parents. I go there sometimes to be close to them. I think the dragon could be safe there too. There are deep forests and caves where he wouldn't be seen and witches from other covens who could help with a glamour."

I nodded. "Then that's where I'll ask the goddess to take him."

"That sounds like quite the plan, druid. It's nothing less than I have come to expect from you and your merry group of friends," said a familiar voice.

I swung round to see Gaia in the shadows, dressed in a simple green chiffon sari with a blue border and her hair in a neat chignon at her neck.

Tielbu gave a roar of deep pleasure. It rumbled through me, making me feel alive.

"I've just come from a lovely dinner with Pan. What a wonderful artefact you brought him, Alisha," said Gaia.

"Hello, goddess," I said. "I was hoping to see you tonight. I thought maybe you could help Tielbu to a safe haven far from here in exchange for leaving it up to me to deal with Pan."

Gaia beamed. "Of course, Alisha. I am happy to help a druid and her dragon." She planted a kiss on my forehead. "Bravo. You did very well against that mischievous beast of a god. I'll have you know my absence during your shenanigans with him was entirely intentional. You didn't need a new mother. You needed to find out what you could do on your own. I gave you just enough counsel to show you that a war can be won with gentler means. Besides, a god is more beloved when they make themselves scarce. Nothing worse than a meddler. We are much better when we pull the strings from behind the curtains."

"I don't much like riddles, goddess."

"More fool you. They are very good at keeping the brain synapses firing. Forget all this New Age nonsense about multi-vitamins. Dig up some greens from the earth and add a few mind games. I credit Sudoku and *The Times* crossword for lubricating the wheels of my old head. They haven't let me down yet." She dug around in her sari blouse and pulled out an old Nokia with a cracked screen. The screen cast her wrinkled cherubic face in a glow as she peered at it, sticking out the tip of her tongue in concentration. "Such a sturdy little thing. Let me just find the browser. Google Earth is a godsend, even for me. It jogs my memory about all the changes on the planet." She offered it to Ezra. "Just type in where this ski resort is, werewolf, and we'll be on our way."

Ezra did as he was told and handed it back to her.

Gaia's sari fluttered in the wind behind her as she approached Tielbu, who lay down at her feet, much like the effect Gaia had on Echo. She murmured a few inaudible words to him before climbing onto his back with a hop, a skip and a jump that belied the centuries of her age.

We gawped at the sight of the goddess sitting atop a dragon in her green chiffon sari.

"Well, this is going to cause a bit of bother with the flight plans from City Airport," said Gaia. "What fun."

"He will be safe?" My voice quivered, and Ezra's fingers found mine.

"You have my word, Alisha." Gaia paused. "Although the night is still young, and more mischief awaits, and I haven't yet had my nightly cup of masala chai. Do you remember the place I mentioned?"

I nodded. "A café opposite Tooting Broadway tube station, squeezed between a fast food restaurant and a betting shop."

She clapped her hands in glee. "That's the one. Perhaps you lovebirds would like to join me there in an hour? Your treat."

I burst out laughing. "How about it, Ezra?"

He grinned. "It would be wise to say yes. And I quite like masala chai."

"A man of hidden depth," said Gaia. "Say your goodbyes, dragon."

I swallowed the lump in my throat and walked closer to the dragon. "Go now, Tielbu. Go now under the cover of darkness, and don't let the senate catch you. We will come to visit."

The dragon's amber eyes didn't move from my face, as if he

wanted to remember every detail. Then he dipped his great head to draw level with my face. He could have torn the flesh off my face with his tombstone teeth. But he didn't.

It hurt to let him go, but he wasn't mine to keep.

"Goodbye, druid," the dragon said.

I breathed in the charred scent of him. "Goodbye, Tielbu."

Tielbu lumbered across the lawn and launched himself skywards, reptilian scales glimmering in the moonlight, and we watched as he disappeared from sight with the goddess on his back.

I thought of all we had accomplished, all the stories I had to tell and the secrets I had to keep. For the first time in years, I was excited about what came next and damn sure I could handle any curveballs life threw at me.

ACKNOWLEDGMENTS

To my husband Jan, who played Monopoly with the children and took them to the park during the brief windows of clear skies during this washout British summer. *Midlife Tremors* literally would not have been completed without you holding the fort while I locked myself in our garden office for weeks. Take my heart and hold it in your hands like a bird because there is no one I trust more.

Thanks again to the Fab13, who founded this genre and who allowed me to host a takeover in their gorgeous Facebook group for fans of Paranormal Women's Fiction. I'm so grateful for your support of new authors. Books about wise women over forty kicking arse have been so fun to read and write this past year, and I have you to thank for that.

My deep thanks, as always, to my book team. To my editors Jeni and Toni, your skills take my stories to the next level and, in doing so, give me more confidence. To my cover artist Maria, your patience and skill astound me. Debbie and Sherry, my beta readers, I am grateful for your book instincts, kindness and support. I'm lucky to have you in my corner.

To my children, seeing the world through your eyes makes me a better writer. Never lose those sparks of pure joy. Sorry-not-sorry for how often I've told you to keep the noise down.

Thank you, readers, for following Alisha's story. My feisty, caring, control-pants-wearing, dragon-raising druid has so much more to come.

DRUID HEIR
BOOK 3
MIDLIFE NEWS
N. Z. NASSER

THE PLAYERS

Alisha Verma - Druid Heir
Ezra Neuhoff - Alisha's half-werewolf, half-wizard mentor
Echo - Alisha's leopard sidekick
Marina Ambrose - Alisha's best friend
Joshi Verma - Alisha's father
Sahil Verma - Alisha's brother
Alma - Joshi's neighbour
Orpheus Might - Vampire, Minister for History and the Today
Margola Silver - Selkie, Minister for Information
Gaia - Goddess of the Earth
Joe Dumfrey - Alisha's boss at the community centre
Fei Yen and Faeza - hu hsien, shapeshifting foxes
Alisha's night class students: Pert, Mirabel, Nagma, Santiago, Marek and Farzad
Robert Jameson - Detective, Shadow Squad
Phinnaeous Shine - Shapeshifter, Prime Sorcerer
Gunnolf Zev - Werewolf, Minister for Justice
Gunnolf's pack - Maximillian, Dominic, Deirdra, Ruud, Rashida
Rayna Willowsun - Druid, Minister for Education, Headmistress of Wildwoods School of the Wondrous

Lavinia Drach - Witch, Minister for Defence
Helio Woodwink - Fairy, Bestiary Minister
Erelim - Angel, Minister for Diplomacy
Cillian O'Meara - Leprechaun, Minister for Finance
Calypso Archer - The Custodian of the Celestial Library
Tielbu - a dragon
Flinar - a dark elf
The Ravenmaster

1

———————

I trembled on the main rope bridge at Wildwoods in my silk gown. Goosebumps raced up my skin, not from the cool London night but from terror. I didn't want to leave the comfort of the towering oaks and fir trees. Not when the movers and shakers of the Otherworld waited for me inside the vaulted cabin.

Ezra tipped my chin up and scanned my glum face. He wore a tuxedo and looked like he'd walked off the pages of a romance novel. "It's a medal ceremony, not a funeral. Try and enjoy this. Your friends and family will be in there—"

"Yeah, and about a million other peculiars. Some with claws and fangs."

"Come now." He pulled me against his hard chest. "It's not that bad."

I liked being the centre of his world. Being the centre of attention in the Otherworld made me sick with nerves.

Echo nudged his head in between us. Leopards didn't like playing second fiddle to wolves. He'd been hunting in the rain, and his fur left a damp patch in the crotch area of my dress. "Alisha is right to be nervous. They will look at her like vultures eyeing up a piece of meat. Still, your grandmother learned how to enjoy fame, and you will learn too. Fame is a route to accomplishing great things. Indeed, the lyrics of the song by the same are so apt that I have decided to adopt it as my personal anthem."

"Maybe you're right." I took a ragged breath and raised my hand to dry the damp patch. Being a druid with wind powers had its perks.

"You are lucky to have an adviser such as me," purred Echo. "Is it a good time to remind you to stock up on our freezer supply of sirloin steaks?"

"Don't push it. On paper, you're a Bengal cat. Shall we?" I hooked my hand through Ezra's arm, feeling like a jittery bride. The rope bridge was a physical impossibility in heels. Any woman worth her salt knew slippers were infinitely preferable.

We stepped towards the vaulted cabin, Echo padding at my side. The heavy arched door creaked open, though no hand touched it. Inside, a thousand lit pillar candles floated in the air, and a throng of peculiars—vampires, werewolves, druids, fairies, angels and elves— draped in finery stared at us before erupting into cheers.

The crowd parted as Phinnaeous Shine approached, resplendent in his flowing Wildwoods robes. His lips curved into a smile, but his eyes were cold. He still considered me an outsider, even after I'd passed my magical trial. Even after I'd animated a dragon and thwarted the will of rogue gods. Maybe he liked to keep women small. I'd heard the rumours about the succubi who worked in his home. My intuition told me he was one of those men who constantly worried about the size of his dangly bits or his wand. His posturing didn't bother me. I'd long since given up begging anyone to like me.

I kept my voice cool as the cheers subsided. "Good evening, Prime Sorcerer."

His silver-streaked afro gave him a distinguished look, together with pearly white teeth too perfect to be his. "Alisha Verma, granddaughter of Rajika, when we met mere months ago, who knew you would be honoured in this way by the magical community?"

"She is of good stock," Echo purred as if I was in a breeding programme. His golden coat glimmered in the candlelight, and his chest puffed up with pride. Little wonder. He had pledged himself to my family line, and it wasn't every day a Verma received a medal of honour from Wildwoods School of the Wondrous. I wouldn't put it past him to burst into song in the middle of the ceremony. Maybe some Lionel Richie or Kool & The Gang.

"A rare talent," said Ezra, turning hooded grey eyes on me—bedroom eyes.

A shiver ran down my spine. "When the Information Minister rang to tell me, I had to ask her to repeat herself. I haven't won anything since coming third in the egg-and-spoon race at primary school. An evening in my honour really wasn't necessary."

"But it really was," said the Prime Sorcerer, dark eyes gleaming. "Nights like these hold many secrets. Your exploits have captured the imagination of humdrums across this city. A medal ceremony is as good a place as any for friends and foes to find common ground."

The crowd was growing impatient for a closer look at me. I could feel the hairs standing on end at my nape and in the shifting and pressing of the masses. Which foes was he talking about? Lavinia, who blamed me for derailing her attempt to crush the dark elves? Helio, the bestiary minister, who had longed for control over my dragon Tielbu? Or Gunnolf, Ezra's alpha, who complained I didn't know my place and I was a bad influence on Ezra?

"Follow me. It is time to lay the gold around your neck." Phinnaeous Shine's lips pressed together. He swivelled on his block heel, heading for the stage where the senate awaited: nine peculiars of immense power and privilege, each with their own agendas.

Ezra gently uncurled my fingers from his hand. "You look beautiful. Go ahead. You have to do this bit alone."

"Everyone's watching," I hissed.

"It is better to be in the spotlight than in the gutter," said Echo.

Ezra put a hand on the small of my back and urged me forward. "Now go on."

I climbed the steps to the stage, quivering with nerves, and willed myself to see the audience naked as a distraction but found myself unnerved by the anatomy of magical beings. A spluttering sound came from the on-stage senate members. Judging by his mottled face, Orpheus the vampire had done his pesky mindreading trick again.

I frowned at him. *Stay out of my head.*

At the podium, Prime Sorcerer leaned into the microphone. His velvety voice boomed through the vaulted cabin. "We are here today to honour Alisha Verma, druid, dragon-raiser, god-challenger. There are those of you who argue that Alisha Verma broke one of the cardinal rules of the Otherworld by meddling with the gods. You would be right."

My legs turned to jelly.

Would I be arrested instead of honoured?

Would Justice Minister Gunnolf's pack drag me to the Court of Wolves in my dress?

The Prime Sorcerer milked the moment, relishing the murmurs from the crowd. My best friend Marina caught my eye and signalled to the fire exit. As if we could hightail it like Thelma and Louise. Dad's brow furrowed in worry. Echo tail swished back and forth, suddenly on the alert. Only Ezra stood relaxed, hands in his pocket, his expression not betraying any anxiety. He knew well how the Prime Sorcerer, true to his shapeshifting nature, liked us all to be putty in his hands.

Phinnaeous Shine rocked on his heels at the podium like a pastor finding his rhythm. "You could say that Alisha Verma is a maverick. You could say that she is a thorn in our sides. You could say that disobeying the rules of the Magical Constitution is a way to get yourself killed. But there is another reason why the senate decided to award the Wildwoods medal of honour to her." He paused. "She is an example to us all that an old dog can learn new tricks."

Charming.

At the rear of the stage, Orpheus rolled his eyes like he knew how tempted I was to send an *accidental* burst of wind to knock the Prime Sorcerer off his feet.

"Let Alisha Verma be the reason that ostracised peculiars submit themselves to the Wildwoods trial," said the Prime Sorcerer. "Let her be a reason why peculiars attempt ambitious feats." His eyes twinkled. "Although, please do yourself a favour and seek out the guidance of the appropriate senator."

The crowd laughed, clearly enjoying this public slap and tickle.

The most powerful peculiar in the Otherworld waved his hand with a flourish. "Alisha, please step forward."

I approached the podium, every nerve in my body tingling. Fireflies danced in an arch around us, a glittery cheerleading squad all their own, utterly at odds with my instinct to fight or flee. I forced the corners of my mouth to turn upwards like a constipated Cinderella.

The Prime Sorcerer plucked a firefly from the arch and smothered it in his fist. He opened his hand with a glint in his eye, revealing a medal threaded with a navy blue ribbon and stamped with the Wildwoods crest before placing it around my neck. "Alisha Verma, I award you the Wildwoods medal of honour. May you walk in the footsteps of the greatest peculiars through the ages."

The medal was heavy around my neck. I shook his hand, not keen on the thought of harking back to the past. If my divorce had taught me one thing, it was to look forward. And to always beware of a man who refused to use a washing machine.

Deafening cheers filled the vaulted cabin up to the rafters, a surge of sound that made the flames from the floating candles dance above our heads. Dad, Marina, Ezra and Echo glowed with pride. I wished we'd made it far enough to embrace our identity as a magical family while Mum had been alive. Of course, my werepigeon brother wouldn't have been seen dead at an event to celebrate me.

The Prime Sorcerer murmured in my ear as cameras flashed. "Your grandmother, too, was sometimes too big for her boots. Maybe you'll learn now to fall in line. You are truly one of us now."

Sweet. He still thought of me as a little fish. I might have landed in a pool of sharks, but I was a badass in my own right. I could rescue myself from any situation, couldn't I? "Oh, I don't know, Prime Sorcerer. I think I was a humdrum for too long to fall in line completely. I enjoy my freedom of spirit too much. In fact, my favourite people are cut from the same mould."

He flushed at the intended insult.

The ability to deliver a polite burn was satisfying and so very British.

Orpheus stepped forward, his eyes lingering on the neckline of my dress where the medal had found a home. "I'll escort the wayward child down from the stage, Prime Sorcerer."

Pale, piano-player's hands cupped my elbow.

Gratitude flared in my belly. Orpheus and I weren't exactly friends, but he'd come through for me before. I also was pretty sure his adventure with my dragon had inspired him after a blip with depression. A dragon adventure was bound to give anyone a bounce in their step, even a vampire who had become bored with life.

"Congratulations, Alisha. From your internal monologue, I can tell that—like me—you don't enjoy the limelight." Orpheus's stern lips twitched. "Although, never fear. It's quite remarkable how quickly you are able to alienate people. You must teach me that trick."

I grinned. The cameras flashed as we walked down the steps in sync with one another. At the bottom of the stairs, Ezra bristled, although I had no idea why. Orpheus floated off into the crowd, too introverted to stay by my side as well-wishers swarmed me. I made a beeline for Dad and Marina, but I didn't manage to reach them. Grasping hands, shouts of congratulations, mobile phones held aloft in film mode, kisses pressed to my cheek, snatched conversations. Only Ezra and Echo managed to remain beside me, creating space for me with their bodies.

"Alisha, Alisha," called a sultry voice. "Just a few words for *The Otherworld News*?"

Ezra, in full bodyguard mode, groaned.

I looked over my shoulder and spotted Margola Silver, Minister for Information, clutching a dictaphone with a camera assistant in tow. A channel opened amongst the throng for them to catch up with me. I pushed on, anxious for air.

"Alisha! Our readers would love to get under your skin."

Well, that wasn't creepy. I swatted away a hairy hand from my medal. Ezra couldn't teleport in Wildwoods, but what I wouldn't have given to have my elf friend Flinar conjure up some of his black hole magic right now.

"As your adviser, I must tell you that it would be wise to give an interview. Control the narrative, as it were," Echo purred.

I gave an exasperated sigh. "You're not my adviser, Echo."

He growled. "Be like that."

"Okay, okay." I plastered a benign smile on my face and swivelled around to face her. Ezra had told me during a drinking game that Margola Silver was a selkie—a being capable of changing from a seal to a human by shedding their skin—but I wouldn't have known it to look at her. "Of course, Minister. I'm happy to answer a few questions."

Margola Silver had pale skin, flame-coloured hair and brown eyes framed with cat-eye glasses. She was perhaps thirty-five, but age was nothing but a number in the Otherworld. Her hourglass figure and pointy bosoms poured into an unforgiving satin dress the colour of the ocean reminded me of the golden age of Hollywood. The sort of woman that made both genders stare. Hell, you would have had to have been a lamppost not to fancy her. We hadn't had dealings before, but she had cast a yes vote for me after the trial. The Minister for Information was known for publishing the Otherworld newspaper, but as her formal title suggested, she had a murkier side. She was a whizz with computers and coding, and her role included surveillance of social media and private messages.

I would rather have told Vladimir Putin my secrets than her.

Margola's brown eyes danced with excitement. She held a manicured finger to her lips. "Shh. That's it. Quieten down everybody, or we'll not hear what the woman of the hour has to say."

Just like that, the writhing mass of bodies around us stopped being quite so grasping and stilled in anticipation. The cameraman with her, who on closer inspection appeared to be a fallen angel, shone a blinding light in our faces.

"She's tired. Five questions only," Ezra growled.

Margola flashed him a sultry smile. "I think the lady is perfectly capable of speaking for herself."

Ezra stiffened, Echo preened like a peacock, and I clenched my arse cheeks together in case I let off a rogue anxiety fart at the worst possible moment.

"Tell our readership, Alisha. Who are you?" said Margola.

"I'm just a new peculiar finding my way," I said. "Pretty unexceptional apart from that."

Margola cocked her head. "To the contrary, in your recent past, your marriage combusted, your mother was murdered, and you animated a dragon. Not to mention befriending the dark elves, drinking tea with the goddess Gaia, visiting the Celestial Library, and somehow escaping with your life after you tussled with two gods." Her scathing laughter tinkled through the air. "I think we all want to be as unexceptional as you."

Ezra raised an eyebrow. "Are you going to ask a question?"

Margola swung to face the camera. *The Otherworld News* video segments had proven to be very popular in the past. "The wolf is very protective of the druid, although they have only known each other for a hot minute. But, dear viewers, I wasn't the only one to witness the chemistry between Alisha Verma and Orpheus Might tonight. The wolf could be in for a cold shower yet."

"What the hell?" said Ezra angrily.

Echo purred. "She is baiting you."

He wasn't wrong. The thought of Orpheus and Ezra fighting over me was quite frankly ridiculous. I reached for Ezra's hand to assure him who I wanted.

Margola thrust the dictaphone under my nose again. "Why did your marriage fail?"

I drew in a deep breath. There was no way I was airing my dirty linen in public. "No comment."

"Can you tell us about the circumstances surrounding your mother's death?"

"It's all in the police report."

Margola gave a disappointed sigh. "In the history of the Otherworld, it has only happened once before that the senate vote following the magical trial of an initiate has split down the middle. Why do you think you inspired such division?"

The crowd buzzed with curiosity.

I would've liked to have known the answer myself. I could only guess that my late admission to the Otherworld meant I wasn't made in the same mould as others. I'd raised my head above the parapet once too often when I should have fallen in line. "You'd have to ask them. I guess I'm not everyone's cup of tea."

"That's very diplomatic of you," said Margola. "But you're not always a peace-lover, are you, Alisha? I'm sure many of us are wondering why you sided with the dark elves, even though infamous prisoner Meriel Naehorn killed your grandmother?"

That smarted. "I think you are confusing being peace-loving with standing up for what's right, Minister. How can one elf's crimes lead us to tarnish a whole community? Do I hate bees because one once stung me? Do I hate all men because my ex-husband was an arsehole?"

Margola looked into the camera and raised a sceptical eyebrow, and the murmurs of the crowd suggested she wasn't the only one. "If you say so." Her eyes sparked with mischief. "What do you say, Alisha Verma, to those who think you have been hyped up? That you are no better than the rest of us? That the medal of honour you received is more to do with who your grandmother was than who you are?"

Ezra scowled, his fingers clenching mine. "Time to wrap it up."

My stomach churned. "I can't influence what others think of me. I can only be myself."

She tossed her mane of red hair, shimmying closer. "I suspect you barely understand your powers. In fact, many would say that what you have achieved so far has been sheer blind luck."

My mouth went dry as the camera zoomed in on my face.

Echo let out a growl. "Blind luck? This is a Verma you are talking about. Let it be on record that you are all invited to a performance of Alisha's animation powers. She will animate the creature of your choice, picked by any peculiar in attendance. You will see. She is one of the most talented peculiars of the era."

Margola's pink-coated lips curved into a smile. "Perfect. There's nothing quite like a magic show. That will set to rest whether what we witnessed during your magical trial was a one-off or something more." She turned to the camera. "You heard it here first. Margola Silver, reporting for *The Otherworld News*."

The camera stopped recording, and the crowd around us dispersed, like Margola had singlehandedly pierced the bubble of illusion that I was anything special. I didn't know whether to be cheesed off or relieved.

I turned to the leopard. "What did you do?"

"A showboating druid isn't going to solve anything," said Ezra.

Echo's emerald eyes narrowed. "You have to give the crowd what they want, Alisha, or they will eat you alive."

2

Ezra teleported us to the pack farmhouse in a swirl of monochrome and stolen breath. "Listen, hellfire. The pack are a solid bunch, but they're not always welcoming to strangers. Introducing you to them might not be plain sailing."

I shrugged, looking around in awe. "What families are easy? I think I can handle a bit of aggro."

The farmhouse stood on the outskirts of Windsor, surrounded by woods. It suited the wolves to live away from the city. Here, they responded to the call of the moon without provoking the suspicions of neighbours in packed London streets. The house itself was a sprawling building with white cladding, bordered by bright orange dahlias in the summer sun.

I tucked my arm into Ezra's. "It's beautiful. It's a shame your parents aren't buried here."

His Adam's apple bobbed in his throat. Even after all this time, it was hard for him to talk about them. "I begged for them to be here. Lavinia bartered for their bodies to lie in the witch cemetery. It was part of her deal with Gunnolf. That way, he got to raise me with the wolves. Lavinia got to keep my parents' bodies. In the end, all that matters is that they are together."

I chewed my lip. "Do you think Lavinia wanted your dad's body to find out the secret to teleporting?"

He frowned. "It's crossed my mind, but she's better than that. And he was family. She wouldn't desecrate his body. Power and family have always meant the world to her. But family a little bit more."

I wasn't so sure, but it wasn't my place to shatter his illusions about his aunt. I didn't trust Lavinia anymore—no doubt, she'd finish me off, given half the chance—but Ezra had to make up his own mind. Lavinia wasn't all bad, either. She had introduced me to the Wildwoods reading nook after all, and I'd never seen an older woman perform such incredible aerial acrobatics.

"Are you ready to meet the pack?" A vein throbbed in his neck like he was nervous too. "There are about fifteen minutes to show you around before the pack meeting."

Gunnolf had summoned Ezra back to the farmhouse to deal with pack business. I hadn't wanted to intrude, but Ezra figured bringing me along was perfect. I'd get to meet the pack, but I wouldn't be subjected to a lengthy grilling with a pack meeting scheduled. We'd keep it short and sweet. It had sounded like a decent plan, but now I wasn't so sure. For the second time that week, I wished I wasn't being paraded around. It would have been easier if I had Marina's extroverted nature or Echo's self-confidence, but I could only be myself.

My stomach fizzed with nerves. "Ready as I'll ever be."

He gripped my hand as we walked across the lawn and over the creaking deck. Judging by the state of it, the wolves weren't into DIY. The front door swung open.

Creatures with terrifying teeth and hulking strength didn't need locks.

A roomy kitchen was situated at the front of the house, with a large picture window over the sink with a view of the woods. The kitchen was hardly a chef's dream. It smelt of overripe onions and sweat. Muddy pawprints marred the stone floor. Empty beer bottles stood on a wooden counter crying out for a coat of varnish. An old Aga burned in the corner, stacked next to a grubby fridge.

But it was the wolves that made my breath catch in my throat.

They sat around a long table in their human form and assessed us for a long moment as if nothing happened in this place without the alpha's say-so.

"At last, the errant wolf brings his girlfriend home to meet the pack," said Gunnolf, Ezra's paternal uncle and Minister for Justice.

"Who are you calling errant? My mission tally matches yours. There's a reason I'm your beta." Ezra smiled and pulled me forward with a flourish. "I want you to meet my girlfriend, Alisha Verma."

Gunnolf, a grizzled bear of a man with worker's hands and a smattering of white hair peppering his hairline, glowered. Many peculiars disapproved of relationships outside their own kind, and Gunnolf was a case in point.

He pinned Ezra down with a stare. His broad chest and coiled energy signalled he'd be a formidable wolf. "A beta should know better than to dip his wand in outside waters."

Ezra dipped his head to break eye contact while the rest of the pack shifted uncomfortably. "We've had this conversation."

Black eyes like flint. "So you know where I stand."

Ezra ignored him and pushed on regardless. "Alisha, you know the minister. Let me introduce you to the rest of the pack. Ruud's over there in the green T-shirt, Dominic's the bruiser next to him and Maximillian's the youngest of us all."

"We saw the latest broadcast from *The Otherworld News.*" Maximillian's lip curled. "What did you do to get underneath Margola's skin? We were expecting a puff piece after your medal. Not a grilling. Time of the month, maybe."

The brunette next to him elbowed him in the ribs.

I shrugged. "I didn't take it personally. Drama sells, I guess."

Ezra continued. "Deirdra's the one with the sharp elbows. She and Max are together. And Rashida, well…"

"Hello, my love." A copper-haired, flat-arsed werewolf sashayed over to us, taking her sweet time, and held out a delicate hand for me to shake. Then she pressed a kiss against Ezra's cheek, leaving a smudge of coral lipstick there. She tossed her fiery hair. "Have you been taking the druid to our old haunts?"

"I'm pretty sure a teleporting wolf has the pick from the globe," said Gunnolf.

I raised an eyebrow. Ezra could have warned me about her. She might as well have lifted a leg to mark her territory.

I'd only been inside for two minutes, and my female intuition told me the farmhouse was like a bed-hopping university dormitory. If I'd taken a match to the sexual chemistry between the wolves, the place would have gone up in flames.

Ezra ushered me over to the table and pulled out a seat for me next to Ruud. "Can I get anyone a coffee?"

Ruud gave me a sheepish smile.

I flashed him a smile in return. A silent welcome was better than a frosty one.

"Actually, now we're all here, we should press on," said Gunnolf.

Ezra glanced at him in surprise. "If you insist. Alisha can wait in my bedroom while we deal with the pack business."

Gunnolf pushed back his chair and prowled the room. "Sit down, nephew. Let the girl stay. I'd tell her to leave, but this will be common knowledge in the Otherworld by evening anyway."

Ezra took a seat sandwiched between Rashida and me. "Why are we here?"

In a heartbeat, Rashida draped herself all over him.

My side-eye left her in no doubt that her behaviour was unsisterly. She was welcome to make a tit of herself, though. I knew who Ezra was coming home with. He'd made it clear in bed last night.

"We're no closer to knowing the identity of the two dead wolves on pack land," said Gunnolf. "This morning, I found a third body less than a few hundred metres from where we're sitting. Killed the same way."

"Dammit." Ezra pushed the fawning Rashida away.

I gave her a winner's smile to rattle her.

"Three's a pattern, Gunnolf. What are we going to do about it?" said Ezra.

No one else had the balls to speak up. I understood why he was the beta of the pack.

"Until we find the culprit, no wolf in this pack runs alone," said Gunnolf.

The pack exchanged glum looks, but the alpha laid down the law. This family wasn't like my own, flawed as we were. Here, they just obeyed.

I cared about Ezra and wanted to understand his family. What had led to Gunnolf becoming alpha? Was it age, strength, alliances, wisdom or fate? Was Gunnolf a patriarch or a mini dictator? Ezra trusted him, so they had to be more to him than a grumpy old wolf.

"Dominic, will you do the honours?" said Gunnolf.

According to Ezra, Dominic was the strongest of the pack in both human and wolf form, a possible rival for beta. He stood up from the table in a display of bulging muscles and thumped Ezra's shoulder as he passed. A moment later, he returned with a wolf carcass slung over his shoulder. He flung it onto the kitchen table without ceremony, an unholy foul-smelling mess of blood, flesh and guts that somebody had once loved.

The pack didn't flinch.

I ignored Ezra's worried glance. Pathos sent a lump of tears to my throat, but I refused to show weakness. Not here, amongst seasoned predators. I'd killed before, of course, but a vampire didn't really count, given they were technically not alive. At least, that's what I told myself.

Ezra stood to take a closer look. "These were clean killings. Executions. We can send a team out to follow the scent, but we all know what happened last time. The best noses here failed to find the scent of a perpetrator."

I turned my eyes away from the poor wolf's limp body, raised my hand like a schoolgirl then dropped it. "Maybe Echo can help follow the scent. My friend Marina is a vet. She could do an autopsy."

Gunnolf's voice rumbled like distant thunder. "It's bad enough that you're here, druid. I don't need your silly suggestions. Leave your leopard protector and empath weirdo out of this. This isn't amateur hour."

He had called me *girl* and *silly* and had voted against me at my magical trial. I was tempted to launch a tornado at his arse. When someone showed their true colours, I'd learned to believe them the first time. Still, I wasn't a fool. Ezra was on my side, but I was surrounded by predators. I kept very quiet, channelling a silent assassin with her finger on the trigger.

Ezra kept his tone even. "She's my guest, Gunnolf."

The alpha scowled.

Ruud broke the awkward silence. He was the friendliest of the pack, the one who played mediator when there was a fight. "Let's stay on task. What if this is a real threat to us? We are only seven. It feels like there's a fight coming. Maybe it's a good time to swell the pack. There's plenty of options knocking at our door."

Gunnolf glared at me. "That's the druid's fault. Her exploits have brought more peculiars than ever out into the open. Old ones, who have been hiding for decades. Unskilled ones, who wouldn't know their tail from their snout. Young upstarts, with more brawn than brains, who have no sense of order and rules. We can do without them."

At the far end of the table, Deirdra, a brunette dressed head to toe in denim, shook her head. "I don't know, Gunnolf. More numbers might not be a bad idea. This is looking pretty hairy."

I could see her point. It wasn't every day that a family had a dead wolf on the kitchen table. I gagged. Hopefully, someone would give it a scrub with some anti-bacterial spray before serving their Sunday roast.

Gunnolf growled, moving behind her in a flash, intent sizzling in his predator's eyes. "Are you questioning my authority?"

Deirdra cowered. "I'm with you a hundred per cent. You know that."

"We shouldn't accept any riffraff into our pack, but we should keep an open mind if the right wolves come along," said Ezra.

"That's not your call. It's mine." Gunnolf pointed a thick finger at the dead wolf. "And right now, we should concentrate on the fight someone has brought to our doorstep. Make the change, wolves. Use your god-given noses to find the culprit of this heinous crime."

The pack reacted to his invitation like Pavlov's Dogs. Chairs fell against the stone floor, and they stripped out of their clothes, some discarding the clothing with abandon, others like Ruud choosing to neatly fold theirs in piles.

Only Ezra stopped to glance at me, yearning in the depths of his grey eyes.

I gave a small nick of my head. No way I was standing in between a wolf and his needs.

He discarded his clothes like the others, and then the bone breaking began, an eerie, inhuman sound that made me shudder. They turned into their wolves, panting and groaning as they did, but Ezra was silent as he endured the change, even as his bones stretched and his claws emerged. When he was his other self, he padded over to me, his charm necklace still around his neck, and put his wet nose in my palm. Then he turned, raised his copper-grey head and gave a mournful howl, and the pack responded, mimicking his cry.

I pressed myself up against the fridge, out of harm's way, and matched each person to their wolf. Burly Dominic had become an enormous tawny wolf. Maximillian was medium size, silver-white in colour, with piercing blue eyes. Deirdra's copper brown fur was the same shade as Ezra's, but she was smaller, with less lustrous fur. She was perhaps the runt of the litter, judging by her skittish eyes. Ruud was the smallest, a grey beast with rough fur and a white muzzle. It was Rashida who was the beauty, a red wolf with a snow-tipped tail. Not that I was going to be complimenting her anytime soon.

The pack sniffed the body of the dead wolf laid out on the table, pawing at him. Then Ezra raced out of the front door towards the woods with Dominic on his heels so fast they were a blur. The rest of the pack followed close behind—Maximillian followed by Rashida, Ruud, then Deirdra—howling with joy.

"Well, I hope you find the murderer."

Gunnolf smiled. "Clean up while you wait, will you?"

What a jerk. He didn't deserve an answer. As a teacher, I had plenty of practice doling out scathing looks.

I met his gaze and held it, gasping as he, too, transformed before my eyes.

He wanted me to be scared, but if things turned nasty, if all else failed and even Ezra turned against me, I could still save myself. I had my wits, I had the winds, I had a dragon and I even had a rooster. I would be fine.

His transformation wasn't painless. I could tell by how his arrogance dimmed, and he entered survival mode, rocked by the churning and breaking of his own body. The twisting of limbs and growing of thick silken black fur. Until all that was left was a beast who smelled of fire and earth, and the man had entirely gone.

Gunnolf leapt towards me, six-foot long and the stuff of nightmares: teeth and claws and so very strong.

I raised my hands in fright but also power. My hands tingled. *Just you try it*, I thought.

He spun around, seeming younger as a wolf than as a man, and bounded across the creaking deck to join his pack in the woods.

3

———————

My job as an English night class teacher at the local community centre wasn't glamorous, but I loved it. Especially as a counterweight to the unpredictability of the Otherworld. Teaching was all about routine and building blocks. I knew my students' strengths and fears. Often, I even knew their personal lives. We were a close-knit family, which was why it surprised me when my manager Joe Dumfrey popped his bald head around the classroom door with some news.

"Joe, I didn't expect to see you here tonight," I said. He was a creature of habit. Usually, he would have been down the road devouring a dinner of cod, chips and mushy peas at the local café.

He bustled in, beaming from ear to ear. "Marilyn's pottery class is usually the centre's most popular class. That flyer of hers featuring Patrick Swayze and Demi Moore is savvy marketing. But you've managed to outdo her. You did get my email?"

I frowned. "I must have missed it. How many am I expecting tonight?"

Joe flashed me a nicotine-stained smile. If cholesterol didn't kill him, his dental bills would. "Twenty-seven."

"Jesus, Joe. That's short notice."

Worry lines marred his forehead. "You know our funding is tied to uptake."

I glanced at the wall clock. I didn't even have enough time to make a mad dash to the photocopier to prepare more materials. I sighed. I'd have to wing it. "Of course. I'll make it work."

He relaxed. "Oh, that's marvellous. Thanks for being such a good sport."

Five minutes later, my regular students filed in, jostled amongst faces I knew but couldn't place. The new students rushed to occupy the seats in the front rows, muscling out my regular students with sharp elbows, all politeness forgotten.

"There are plenty of seats, everyone. No need to fight over them."

My pleas fell on deaf ears. The family resemblance in the front row could not be denied: four slight bodies in heavy coats, with button noses and blond hair. In the second row, a group of raucous boys in their late teens clearly had no interest in learning. Behind them sat three men in dark clothes who would look more at home in midnight gambling dens than in my fluorescent classroom, judging by the pallor of their skin.

A buck-toothed boy of about sixteen years old wove through the desks and pushed a notebook under my nose. "Can I have an autograph?"

I frowned. "No, you can't. What's your name?"

His voice was like the tides, quiet and strong, with brown eyes as wide as saucers. "Pert Pailach."

"Take a seat, Pert." I turned my attention to the class. "Good evening, class. Welcome to English 101."

"Good evening, Ms Verma," chanted the class in eerie unison.

"We have lots of new students tonight. I assume you all came prepared with pen and paper?" I held up a blank sheet of paper. "Please tear out a sheet from your writing pads and fold it in half lengthways like this." I demonstrated. "Write your name in large lettering and prop it up on your desk so we can learn each other's names."

There was a flurry of activity as some newer students shared their equipment. I wrote my own name on the blackboard in capital letters, and as I turned back to face my students, a blonde girl in the front row whipped her hand back from my unzipped handbag. I always kept my handbag shut. A blush crept up her face as I stared at her, the gold tip of my lipstick clear to see in her palm.

I let it slide for a moment, not wanting to call her out in front of everyone. Humiliating her wouldn't help. I could deal with her thievery at the end of the lesson.

I gave a welcoming smile. "This isn't a normal class. We're here for learning, fun and support. We don't follow a strict curriculum, but you will find your English skills grow week by week. Here, you can expect to learn conversational and written skills in the English language, a smattering of culture and literature, and a few kickboxing skills if time allows. My night class is a special place, full of special people…" I grimaced, raising my voice a notch. "What are you doing? Put those away."

The raucous boys in the second row turned their backs on me. Phones aloft in selfie mode, they photographed themselves in the foreground doing the sign of the horns with me in the background.

"That is very rude," said Faeza, a long-term student and now friend. Not so long ago, I discovered she and her wife, Fei Yen, were shapeshifting foxes called *hu hsien*. They had facilitated my passage to the Celestial Library through their tarot deck and had saved my life at least twice.

"Sorry," said one of the boys, though he didn't sound sorry at all.

I gave a brisk nod of acknowledgement. At least there wasn't any chance of them posting to social media right now. "No phone use in the classroom. That includes you over there. Are you secretly filming this lesson?"

My senses were spinning like a weathervane in a storm. I didn't feel in control of my own classroom. I cursed Joe under my breath.

The door flew open, and in tumbled Mirabel. Mirabel, the fairy I had once rescued from a group of bullying werewolves at Wildwoods. Who had been in a tank with Kraglek, the octopus.

"Hi, Ms Verma." She gave me a cheery wave and bounded over to a spare seat.

My mouth fell open. "Mirabel? What are you doing here?"

"I applied online for a place in your night class," she said. "Sorry, I'm late."

The room spun, and I swept my eyes across the bodies crammed into it. There was no way my new influx of students could be from the Otherworld. That made no sense. Why would they even bother?

Pert put up his hand.

I forced myself to focus. "Yes, Pert."

"What's your favourite animal, Miss? My dad said it was a rooster, but I said it must be a leopard. But my gran said it must be a drago—"

The truth dawned on me.

My stomach heaved as I rushed to interrupt him. "A dragonfly? Yes, that's an option."

He opened his mouth again.

I raised my hand to stop him. My eyes darted to the three pale men, whose stillness set my teeth on edge. They couldn't be vampires, could they? Could the ephemeral family be hiding fairy wings underneath the jackets they had kept on in the summer heat? One of the raucous boys launched himself across his friend's desk, giving me a glimpse of a hairy expanse of back. My heart hammered in my throat—definitely a werewolf.

A shiver crawled up my spine.

This was a recipe for disaster. This class was supposed to be for humdrums learning English as a second language. Not for interlopers from the Otherworld. What the hell did they think they were doing there? I'd already fallen foul of the Magical Constitution once too often. How on earth was I supposed to get through the next hour without my humdrum students stumbling across the existence of peculiars?

I waggled my eyebrows at Fei Yen and Faeza. As long-term students of my class and members of the Otherworld, I'd need their help to get through the night.

They waggled their eyebrows back as if it was some kind of greeting.

I tried again, and Fei Yen added a thumbs-up to the eyebrow wagging. Clearly, they still deserved their place in the class.

I'd have to think of something else. The new students gawped at me like I was an exotic zoo animal. I was going to give Joe an earful about springing last-minute surprises on me.

I kept a close eye on the vampires, knowing full well that not all of them were as reliable in a room full of fresh meat as Orpheus. "With so many new students, the first thing we are going to do is a baseline assessment."

Nagma, a Bangladeshi woman in her mid-sixties, raised her hand. "Baseball is bad. It is not easy to play in a Punjabi suit."

I shook my head. "We're not playing baseball, Nagma. We're going to do a test to make sure our new students are in the right place."

"But we always play a game to start the new term," said Santiago, one of my Portuguese students.

"Not today," I said in a singsong voice, turning to the blackboard. "All you need is a pen and a piece of paper. That's it. Nothing to worry about. I'll write them up on the blackboard." I wrote five questions: *Write a sentence introducing yourself to a stranger. What are your favourite hobbies? Give directions from here to the bus station. Describe your ideal holiday. Tell me about your family.* I finished scribbling on the board and dusted the chalk off my hands before sitting at my desk. "You have ten minutes. Try for two sentences per question. Each question is worth two marks. One mark for vocabulary and one mark for grammar." I looked at my watch. "Write your name and desk number on your test. Then you may begin."

The vampires didn't even pick up a pen. The arseholes.

I gave a bright smile. "No test. No class."

They relented, scribbling so fast my eyes couldn't keep up with the progress of their pens across the pages before putting down their biros with an air of insolence.

The clock ticked on, and my sense of peril grew. Waves of nausea rose in my stomach.

"Okay. Pens down," I said when ten minutes had passed.

Students groaned. Papers rustled. A werewolf opened a copy of *The Otherworld News* with my face on the front.

I strode over to him and snatched it away with a glare before stuffing it in my handbag for Dad, who was sure to get a thrill out of seeing me in print. I had to get the Otherworld interlopers out of my class.

Fei Yen and Faeza gawped, finally wise to what was going on.

I collected the papers, hoping they had walked into the trap I had set. "I have to be honest. I wasn't expecting such a full class tonight. And I'm not sure all of you are here for the right reasons."

"I am," said Marek.

"I am," said Santiago.

"I am also," said Farzad.

"Well, of course, *you* are. I'm talking about the three of you there taking selfies. And you there, who secretly filmed me under the desk. And you, who stole my Lancôme lipstick from my bag. That's a cardinal offence, by the way. Fei Yen and Faeza, will you do the honours, delete the footage and retrieve my belongings?"

Faeza nodded. "With pleasure, Ms Verma."

Chinese culture valued respect, and my fox friends were very good at calling me Ms Verma in a classroom situation.

"Even though some of you have come here without the intention to learn, I am willing to give you the benefit of the doubt." I dug in my handbag for a packet of Hobnobs. "You can share these and talk quietly amongst yourselves while I mark these tests."

Suitably chastised, the students helped themselves to the biscuits. Even the vampires nibbled sheepishly while awaiting their fate. I rushed through the tests, not expecting perfection from my own students. After all, that was why there were in my class.

I handed the tests back with a circled number in the top right-hand corner. "If you scored six out of ten or under, please line up to the left of my desk. If you scored seven and above, please stand to the right of my desk."

One by one, the students separated into two lines. To the left stood my regular students, looking glum at their low scores. On the right-hand side, with the highest scores in the class, the peculiars queued up. I wondered how I had missed their true natures when they first walked in. The more I looked, the more obvious it seemed they were of the Otherworld.

But what I didn't know was why they had infiltrated my class.

To be honest, it didn't matter. I just needed them out of there.

I took a deep breath. "Those of you on my left, well done on your scores. They are an excellent start to the term. Let's get the blood pumping through our bodies by doing a kickboxing sequence in the car park before returning for the second half of the lesson. You've earned it. Off you go. I'll be out in a second."

My regular students whooped and congratulated each other before filing out of the class. Only Fei Yen and Faeza hovered, knowing what dangers lurked in that classroom. Knowing I might need them.

I stood up, planting my feet in an A-frame, not so much an instinctive power move as understanding that Otherworld grievances often ended in a physical altercation. I wanted to be ready just in case. "Those of you on the right, pack up your things and go home. You have no need for these classes. Teaching you would be a waste of my time and yours."

"Ah, that's not fair," said Pert, clenching his fists. "You can't turn us away."

Mirabel teared up. "I'm sorry. We shouldn't have come. I was so excited about spending time with you."

"Orpheus will hear of this," said the tallest vampire.

I rolled my eyes. "Orpheus has no say in this place."

The petite blonde fairy's hands fluttered in distress. "But we've paid good money for this."

"You'll get your money back." Refunds wouldn't be good for Joe's blood pressure. He was going to be livid.

The wolves surged forward, their pack mentality turning them into bullies.

"Yeah, well, Margola Silver thinks you're a fraud anyway. You're just worried you're going to cock up the demonstration of your powers. We were going to put money on you pulling it off, but not now," said one.

"Yeah, I bet you couldn't even defend yourself against us if we tried one on you," said the delightful one with the hairy back, even in human form.

Quick as a flash, Fei Yen and Faeza darted to my side and unbuttoned their blouses at the neck in case they had to shift. They might have looked like old women but were as fierce as they came. I wouldn't have bet against two wily old foxes. They were all the stronger for how often people underestimated them.

Just like they underestimated me.

"Leave before I make you regret it." My voice was like the quiet before a storm.

My hands tingled with energy. I could unleash a wind and sweep unsavoury types out of the community centre without breaking a sweat. I raised my hands and directed a strong wind at the fire exit. I could challenge my powers with more precision now. Just my peripheral vision was enough to accomplish a feat that only a month ago would have taken immense concentration.

The fire exit swung open.

The Otherworld interlopers gawped at me.

"It was a poor choice coming here tonight. My humdrum life is my own, and you put the Otherworld at risk by presenting yourselves so openly. Go home."

They left, fury in the straight backs of the vampires and the laced growls of the wolves. The fairies, Pert and Mirabel, were more sanguine.

I grabbed Mirabel as she left. "I'll make time for you whenever you want at Wildwoods, Mirabel."

She perked up. "Can you teach a class there?"

I sighed. "Maybe one day when I know enough."

I shut the fire exit behind them and turned to Fei Yen and Faeza. "Well, that was hairy. Who knew that fame would have such unexpected consequences? Thanks for having my back, ladies. If Shanghai Moon"— they ran a tea and occult shop around the corner from my flat— "ever fails to bring in the money, you could have a lucrative bodyguard business instead."

Fei Yen nodded. Her silken black hair shone under the fluorescent lighting and caught the shadows under her eyes. "Well played, Alisha. You are right to keep your two worlds separate. That could have gone very wrong. But I fear the danger has not passed. Our tarot reading this morning gave us great cause for worry."

Faeza gulped. "It told of mixed messages and the crossing of thresholds."

"And it gets worse. We saw another bad omen." Fei Yen shuddered. "A raven in the tea leaves."

"A raven?" I frowned. "Whatever does that mean?"

The foxes spoke as one, as if they were heralding a great misfortune. "A terror is headed our way."

4

A downside to living with a magical leopard was Echo's skills in gaining access to my bedroom even when I'd shut the door. After years of parading as a Bengal cat, all pretences had fallen away. Once, he had scratched my door for attention in the early hours or miaowed plaintively at my door until he pierced through the curtain of my sleep. Now, he had no qualms about launching eighty kilos of kitty bulk against my door. He'd destroyed the lock and hinges, obviously. The door might as well have been a swing door, which was why I woke to his upper body crushing my chest and his fishy breath in my face.

A growl rumbled down my ear canal. "Wake up, sleepyhead."

I pushed him off the bed and was rewarded with some goop on my hands. Who knew what he'd been hunting. "Bad kitty, you've ruined my sheets again."

Echo sighed. "Imagine focusing on laundry when your alarm clock is a majestic creature such as me. I have an odd tale to tell you, Alisha. There is no one else I share my life with. I thought you might be interested. Especially after all my years of imposed silence when I had to pretend to be a Bengal cat. It was torture, I tell you."

I propped myself up against my pillow and pushed the strands of hair out of my face. "You have Marina."

"The empath already senses how I feel. She doesn't need me to tell her. Her skill is growing. It's very frustrating."

Living with Echo was like having a toddler, except with sharper teeth. He demanded food, burst into random songs, urinated with abandon and needed a lot of hugs. Plus, he had the odd hissy fit. I patted the bed next to me. The sheets needed a wash so he could do his worst on them, and he obviously needed some attention. "Go on then. Fill me in. What could have upset you so early in the morning?"

He jumped up next to me and nuzzled close. "I was hunting down a kill early this morning. I'd tasted the flesh once, but the little lost French bulldog had more spirit than I thought. I let him think he could get away, just to add a little fun into the game, and was about to pounce when I got distracted."

I tried not to notice the mud and blood on the duvet and traced the rosettes on his golden coat, a trick that instantly relaxed him. "Well, what distracted you?"

"Early morning is a very good time to hunt. At that hour, people in this country are usually glued to the television, gulping down chocolate cereal or staring at their teeny tiny phone screens. But, on this sleepy street in the middle of Clapham, in the middle of my hunt, neighbours began spilling onto the streets in twos and threes, shouting at one another like they'd lost all sense of decorum. And in the midst of that, the bulldog escaped, leaving me with only a tantalising taste of his meat on my tongue."

I rolled out of bed and sipped water from the glass on my bedside table. "Maybe you were in a rough part of town. Neighbours war all the time. They'd fight over spilt milk if they could, or a bin left out a day too long."

Echo stretched out. His eyes were the shade of a misty forest. "Perhaps. But then, why did I see that same scene on countless streets on my way back here? People at cross purposes, raising their voices, more discord than after the pubs shut on a Saturday night?"

Prey didn't usually escape Echo. It had obviously knocked his confidence, and he was weaving tall tales to explain why the little bulldog had gotten the better of him. I didn't rub his nose in it by spelling it out.

"Well, I'm sure they'll all be back to being friends in no time, whatever's at the bottom of it." I pinged Dad a text to give him a heads-up that I was coming over. Now the mourning period for Mum was over, Dad had been trying to keep busy and kept getting into scrapes. "I'm popping over to Dad's this morning. Would you like to come? He was very upset about what happened at the half pipe the other day."

A few weeks ago, he decided the best way to keep the local youth out of trouble was some intergenerational bonding. So, he joined them for a skateboarding session. Despite turning up with all the gear—a new skateboard, a helmet, and knee and elbow pads—he still managed to get a concussion. On top of that, some kid had pulled a knife on him and called him an old man, which he was very upset about.

Echo's tail swished. "That's South London for you. Although happily, it has plenty of pussies and poodles to make up for it."

"So, are you coming?"

"If you don't mind, I'd rather not be crammed into a cat carrier and ride the bus with you. I've done my fair share of babysitting you and Sahil when you were young. Babysitting magic grandpa is your duty, not mine." He raised his head from the duvet. "Unless Joshi wants me to put on a concert for him? I've been learning 'California Dreamin'' by The Mamas and Papas. I do all the parts myself."

I put on my best poker face. "Maybe next time."

Nobody needed to hear Echo decimating that classic.

AN HOUR LATER, I rode the bus to Tooting Bec Common, ignoring an angry spat on the top deck. I felt safer travelling nowadays, even with my headphones in. My druid skills meant I was a match for most assailants. I hopped off the bus at my destination, my head swimming with worries about Dad. When once it had been Mum letting herself into my flat to stack my fridge with batch-cooking, the tables had turned. With Mum gone, Dad needed me to check in on him.

At first, the shock of losing the love of his life stopped him from painting. Next, he had only painted Mum. Then, he'd gone into helicopter parent mode, forbidding me from claiming my place in the Otherworld because he was scared of losing me. All understandable emotions, of course. I'd been rudely awakened to the fact that grief is a rollercoaster. Psychologists warned of five stages–denial, anger, bargaining, depression and acceptance—but Dad's grieving didn't seem to be following any pattern. His stages didn't match mine, either. My periods of longing and loneliness. My need for duvet days and mountains of chocolate. The physical ache to hear her voice and touch her face. Dad's grief was as unpredictable as a hand grenade.

He hadn't answered my text message, but I was always welcome here. My parents had an open-door policy, and I loved them for it. I walked up the drive, mentally checking off my to-do list, and rang the bell. When there was no answer, I checked for twitchy curtains and went around the side. A pop of wind from my hands sent me soaring over the side gate like a javelin. I grinned, enjoying the surge of power, then grabbed the key from under the geranium planter and let myself into the house.

"Dad?"

Giggles came from inside the belly of the house. The sort of uninhibited giggle that reminded me of smoking pot with Marina.

Definitely not the sort of giggle that came from my grieving dad.

I followed the sound, cocking my ears, my curiosity piqued. The garlanded photograph of Mum at the shrine looked on, her expression sanguine.

Dad didn't court company. Mum had been the social one. Without her, he would have lived as a hermit with just us and his paintings for company. How I had begged him to leave the isolation of their empty house. To find some mates and go to the pub or make the weekly bingo a thing or get a cat. A real one, this time. Not a pretender. It sounded like he may have taken my advice and found a friend.

I popped my head around the door of his studio, and my mouth fell open.

Dad held a palette of paints in his hands. He stood at his easel, dressed in a Superman outfit, complete with tights and a cape. His brown eyes twinkled, and his cheeks glowed with happiness. At the other side of the easel, his semi-naked neighbour Alma posed, wrapped only in a cotton sheet, shoulders and cleavage bare, with her mouse-brown hair newly curled and one foot pointed like a ballerina's.

I flushed. "Oh, oh. I'm so sorry. I'll come back later."

Alma had seen me grow up. I knew her as someone scrupulous about taking her bins in and a dedicated member of Neighbourhood Watch. After Mum died, she'd been a shoulder for Dad to lean on.

It seemed she'd taken a leap forward in my dad's estimations.

Dad looked around in surprise, like a teenager caught in the act. "Alisha!"

"Hello." Alma giggled and adjusted the fall of the bedsheet. Dear god. From bringer of lasagne to occasional caregiver to Botticelli's Venus in just a few weeks.

I stifled my laughter. "You didn't reply to my text. I thought it was still okay to come around."

"I thought your text was very rude, so I decided not to answer it." Dad swished his cape. "We've been at this since the early hours to catch the dawn light falling across Alma's skin. I found this get-up in a charity shop. Alma was nervous, and wearing something silly put her at ease. She's doing very well, aren't you, Alma?"

Alma, worried she would compromise her portrait, barely moved her lips. "I hope so, dear."

Dad gave her a fond smile. He turned to me in a flash of Lycra, his eyes wary. "Want to see the painting?"

A quick glimpse at the canvas showed a study in curves, curls and an arched foot. I cringed. An erotic painting if I'd ever seen one. "Maybe when you're finished."

Perhaps it was a professional painting commission, but my gut told me it was the start of something new. Luckily, Echo wasn't with me, or he would have started crooning Barry White. I averted my glance from the canvas, and my heartbeat sped up.

Ravens. Ravens everywhere. Black paint on canvas. Dark slashes of black feathers, thick throats and beady eyes.

My brow furrowed. Hadn't the foxes mentioned ravens too? "What's with all the gloomy birds? There are ravens everywhere. I should bake them in a pie like in the nursery rhyme."

"I think you'll find it was blackbirds in the nursery rhyme, not ravens," said Alma helpfully.

Dad shrugged. "They just came to me. You know what I'm like, love. An obsessive. I get something in my head, and I have to work it out on the canvas like a kink."

Fair enough. It was just a coincidence. A moment of fascination for a painter in love with the living form. Human or otherwise.

Alma's face creased with worry. "Your dad does have a lot of kinks."

Dad gave a sheepish grin, but when he turned to me, his expression cooled again. "Shall we have a word outside?"

I nodded, wondering what I'd done wrong. "It was lovely to…see you, Alma."

"I'll see you out." Somehow Dad's cape got tangled with the legs of his easel, and he lurched forward.

Alma put her hands out to steady him. Her sheet dropped, giving him—and me—an eyeful of her in all her glory.

"Ay, caramba." Dad righted himself and rewrapped Alma in the sheet, burrito style.

A red flush, hot with embarrassment, swept across her face.

I scurried out of the room faster than you could say *chimichanga*, pretending I'd not seen a thing. Although I was definitely going to share a blow-by-blow account with Marina and Sahil.

Dad chased after me, his superhero cape flapping behind him. "Sorry about that, love. I miss your mother, I do, but Alma's giving me a new lease on life. It's nice to have company my own age. So I was surprised at the contents of your message. I thought you'd understand."

I frowned. "What are you talking about? What message?"

He sniffed. "The one at nine a.m. this morning when you told me that I was focused on myself and didn't care about you."

"Dad, I didn't send you that." My eyes darted around the hallway for his phone. "There must be some misunderstanding. Show me your phone."

"Don't get impatient with me or try to wriggle out of it. I suppose I should be glad you shared your feelings with me."

I missed Mum too. I didn't want another woman taking her place, but tragedies happened. "I swear I didn't text you. You've done nothing wrong, Dad. You deserve every happiness. And I *much* prefer this to you trying your hand at skateboarding."

The loves of our lives were knitted together like patchwork quilts. Mum might have had the greatest share, but if Alma could bring Dad happiness, I was grateful to her.

Tears ran down his face and mingled with his wiry white moustache. He hugged me in a burst of affection. "It's such a relief to hear you say that. Let's move on, shall we?"

I clung to his Lycra-clad body.

He dropped his voice to a whisper. Alma didn't have the foggiest about the Otherworld. "There was such a throng of people at Wildwoods that I didn't get a chance to tell you how proud I was to see you receive the medal. You're just like your grandmother. If only she and your mother had been here to see it."

I smiled. "Thanks, Dad. Although I'm not sure how I feel about all the extra attention."

He beamed. "It just gives you more of a chance to shine."

"I don't know about that. Did you see the Margola Silver interview online? She seems to have it in for me."

He scowled. "Underestimate that selkie at your peril. Selkies are slippery beasts. She may not be the most powerful minister, but she is the most resourceful one. Her information technology skills are legendary, but I've seen her work with much less. A rumour. A chain letter. A leaflet bomb. All with a smile that would melt butter."

"She sounds delightful. Well, I'd better impress her at the performance of my animation skills."

He nodded thoughtfully. "In that case, it's time to give you something." He scampered over to the sideboard in the hallway to open a drawer. "Here you go, darling. You'll need this for the performance of your animation powers. It was your grandmother's once."

I accepted the book, a thick artist's block in a soft leather cover with hand-stitched binding. "You kept it all this time?"

"Of course I did. Your grandmother was here one minute and gone the next. But the things I'd created for her, I couldn't throw them away. Just remember, once you animate them, the page disintegrates. But there can be no giving of life without responsibility. My mother took that duty very seriously. The creature's purpose is tied to your wishes. You must find a way for them to be useful, happy, or free. Oh, and I've included as many creatures as I could think of, given that stupid cat of yours decided the crowd could choose which one you animate."

I opened it with care, marvelling at the artistry. There were beavers, swordfish, giant squid and soaring vultures.

He smoothed down his costume, paying particular attention to the Superman emblem. His swirly chest hair poked out of the top. "Anyway, love, I'll see you at the performance. I should really get back to Alma. I wouldn't want her to get cold feet about finishing the portrait." He hesitated. "Are you sure you're okay about it?"

"I'm happy for you."

Dad beamed. "Send your brother a message, will you? Just so he knows you're thinking of him. I know you don't believe it, but he really does long for your approval."

5
______

Marina and I arranged to go underwear shopping. I would've loved to have taken after Mum's French nature, who revelled in her sexuality even though she was almost a pensioner. But instead, my Indian side won out. I was a prude. The sort of woman who disliked getting undressed in open changing rooms and would much rather change in a smelly loo.

That was why I needed Marina. This was a woman who could wear PVC leather out with aplomb, turn heads and revel in the attention. She was the perfect person to coax me out of the rut I had been in during my marriage to Alex. Adjusting to being Ezra's girlfriend after years of being a wife meant I wanted to spice things up. I was just too afraid to do it without Marina holding my hand. She was my sister in all but name: my sounding board, my cheerleader, my therapist and my favourite person to try new things with. Her free spirit was the perfect foil for my more reserved nature.

We walked into town, perplexed by the pockets of discord we stumbled across but too busy nattering to give it much thought.

"So let me get this right. Robert Jameson is ignoring your messages? But that man is crazy about you."

Marina toyed with the end of her rainbow-coloured plait. "I

know. It's weird, right? I mean, it's usually me who does the dumping. But it's not just that. The last time we were together was good. Like really good. All night long good. Tingling sensations in my toes good. And now radio silence. I can't believe he's ghosting me."

The high street was a hive of activity, as if shoppers were on edge. There was more hooting of car horns on the streets, more rows at the supermarket checkout till, and an increase of police and ambulance sirens. Two grown men came to fisticuffs in the street—men who should have known better. Upstanding men, in corduroy trousers and polo shirts, throwing punches that were slow and clumsy but which stemmed from real anger. They were stone-cold sober yet vexed enough to end up brawling in the gutter.

People could be shits sometimes. Nothing anyone could do about it. Cities like London, especially, could be hotpots of anxiety and stress.

But it was happening elsewhere too. At least, that was what the rumours said. My postman was always a reliable source of juicy rumours. He'd reported all sorts from up north, the Midlands and even as far as the Scottish Highlands. The BBC reported it too. Discord in streets up and down the country. Misunderstandings between politicians who had once backed the same causes. As if the country was gearing up for a civil war. As if we'd turned into a Jerry Springer show overnight.

We ducked into Marks and Spencer's.

"We're not spending all our time talking about Robert. We're here for you." Marina launched herself into the underwear section with the gusto of a kid eating ice cream. "I can't believe you're getting hung up on the fact your control pants could be a turn-off for Ezra. Bridget Jones would weep."

I bit my lip. "I've forgotten what it's like to date. To be in a new relationship. You and Robert were together for five minutes before you were swinging from the chandeliers."

"Stop bringing up that jerk. Seriously though, Alisha, Ezra isn't going to care what you wear in bed as long as he has his hands on you."

I gave a shy smile. "But some nice underwear will help. Maybe even a thong."

Marina winced. "Only girls in their twenties wear thongs. Grown women know that a thong creeping up your crack is a health hazard. Big knickers can be sexy. Marilyn Monroe wore big knickers. Even *Vogue* thinks big knickers are in. I hate to break it to you, but you could have worn nipple tassels, and Alex would have carried on staring at his gaming screen. But those wolf eyes of Ezra's tell me he doesn't need the bells and whistles. He's already hooked."

"I guess so." I headed for the muted colours, casting a sceptical look over the very small underwear, and showed her a black balcony bra with good coverage. "How about this one?"

She put down a set of frilly knickers in the style of a 1950s pin-up and rolled her eyes. "You have a dozen bras like that. Live a little." She grinned. "If I'm here helping you seduce Ezra, the least you can do is spill the beans. Or are you going to make me beg for all the glorious details? Does he live up to the promise? All that tousled hair, hard muscle, and pent-up energy have to translate to something special under the sheets."

I gave her a teasing look. "It does, actually."

Marina punched the air. "I knew the wolf man would deliver. Hell, after all of Alex's robotic foreplay, you deserved a win in the bedroom." She rummaged through a rack of racy bras and thrust one at me, all pink lace and stiff under-wiring.

"Urrgh, no." I handed it back. "We've not exactly sealed the deal, if you know what I mean. We keep getting disturbed. Then Ezra decided we should find somewhere special to pop that cherry."

"Sounds like excuses to me. You need twenty minutes, not a lifetime." She shook her head ruefully. "The man can literally teleport to the perfect place for you to have a rumble in the jungle. What's holding you back?"

I sighed. "My own head. Starting over at midlife isn't the same as dating when you're a fresh young thing."

"Alisha, it's better. So much better. All the time you were married to Alex, how many relationships did you see me start and end? There was Susie and Abdul and Elsie. She was a hottie. And now Robert.

And each time, I get closer to my dream companion." She picked a tangerine cotton bra with zip detail and matching knickers from a rail. "How about this? I saw something similar on Instagram. It's all the rage."

A group of girls had come in off the street, raucous and looking for trouble. I gave them a wide berth and refused Marina's choice of undies. Ideally, I was after something bigger than a handkerchief but smaller than a bodystocking. "How much time do you spend aimlessly scrolling on that app? All those perfect posey pics and the filters that give women a complex."

She grinned and put the hanger back. "Speak for yourself. Instagram is life. How am I going to feed my addiction to tattoo art and home interiors? Although I've been getting images of dog meat festivals in China, which have been really upsetting. The algorithms must be up the duff." She grabbed a lacy cream teddy and held it up to the light. "What do you think?"

I gave her a thumbs-up. It was beautiful, offsetting her rainbow hair and buxom curves. Jessica Rabbit, eat your heart out. "Is that how you're going to get Robert's attention."

Her blue eyes sparkled. "As if. More like a treat for myself. Rob knows where I am. I'm not going to chase after him. But this teddy will bring me joy one way or another. I thought we said we wouldn't talk about Rob. Stop changing the subject from Ezra. Honestly, darling, you just need to get your confidence back. Alex is in the past. You know what you want now. You've had some detours, and you've learned the lessons. This relationship with Ezra doesn't have to be a huge, life-changing romance. You can just have some fun."

By now, I had an armful of underwear to try on too. "Changing room?"

I ignored the raucous group of girls, who were ogling our haul and giggling as if middle-aged women couldn't possibly want nice underwear.

Marina nodded. "Lead the way."

We made our way across the shop floor to the unstaffed changing rooms. I stepped over hangers strewn across the floor, ducked behind the curtain of an empty cubicle and stripped off, leaving my own underwear on. I sighed at the sight of myself in the mirror. My posture was good. I liked my curves and the thick waterfall of my dark, curly hair. But being here made me want to grab Marina and run screaming into the nearest cocktail bar. The claustrophobic space, enormous mirrors and harsh lighting of changing rooms didn't do anyone any favours. Unless you were Cindy Crawford.

I slid the first set of underwear off its hanger. A teal blue bra, with plenty of support and coverage, with a barely there thong I could have flossed my teeth with. It was a more adventurous choice than my usual fare, but sometimes a girl had to throw caution to the wind.

"How's it going?" called Marina from her cubicle opposite.

I grimaced as I fastened the back of the bra and shimmied into the thong over the top of my knickers. "Yeah, okay. You?"

"Not going to lie. I look like a sausage stuffed into a meringue."

I giggled, but my smile slid off my face as the curtain of my cubicle opened. I squealed like a pig. One hand flew up to cover my breasts, and the other flew to cover my nether region while my legs folded into a weird twist. "Oh, my god."

Marina's worried voice met my ears. "Alisha?"

The girls' eyes widened in glee as they gawped at me. Their translucent skin shimmered in the light.

"It's her. It's the granddaughter of Rajika Verma."

Fairies. A red blush of humiliation flooded my cheeks. "This changing room is being used. Bugger off."

One picked up her phone to snap a picture.

With a flick of my hand, I sent the gadget skidding across the floor. I would have given them an earful, but my arse was plain to see in the mirror reflection, and my exposed bikini line looked like an English sheepdog. So instead, I channelled my powers and sent the curtain shooting across the rail again, sending pretty underwear raining through the changing room like confetti.

"That's so cool," said an awestruck fairy.

Anger, red and hot, surged through me. "Get the hell out of here."

"You should chill out, or you'll lose your fans," said the fairy. "People are so uptight these days."

I poked my head around the curtain, quivering with rage. "I take it you're Wildwoods students? Rayna will hear about this."

They ran off laughing, having utterly humiliated me. Mission accomplished.

Marina tumbled into my cubicle, still buttoning up her jeans. "What was that all about?"

I tugged on my clothes with trembling hands. "Fairies, I think. They saw me starkers. I'm mortified. I blame Margola Silver. She's the one who's whipped up all this attention."

I looked at the state of myself in the mirror and almost cried. I had a right mind to ask Lavinia for a glamour until the interest had died down, but she'd probably land me with a turnip nose out of spite.

Marina laid a hand on my arm, and I felt immediately calmer, as if her very touch was medicine. "What knob heads. We should tell the security guards. Get them turfed out."

A rush of noise met my ears. A scuffling that I couldn't decode. "Do you hear that?"

I pulled Marina onto the shop floor, hoping the security guards had cottoned on and booted out the fairies. That would teach them.

A ginger-haired shop assistant froze in her act of restocking socks, mouth aghast. "Oh, my god."

I followed her gaze. Cameras filmed three well-heeled officials, but the officials had dropped any semblance of respectability or professionalism. As the cameras rolled, the trio had a very public spat. A stick-thin man with a mop of carefully combed hair shouted down at a petite woman, waving a phone in her face. To the glee of the cameraman, the woman snapped. She tugged the tall man's tie, hard. The third person bodily lifted her and dumped her in the homeware section like a discarded pillow.

I gawped. Marks and Spencer, the epitome of middle-class restraint, had turned into a hen house.

The shop assistant motioned to us from behind a display of tights. "They're Lambeth councillors on a filmed walk-about to boost the high street. All this argy-bargy. Aren't politicians supposed to be the grown-ups? We were all told to be on our best behaviour."

She gasped as the shorter man delivered a knockout punch to his colleague.

The cameraman looked thrilled to have footage that would inevitably be shown on prime-time television.

Marina nudged me. "Aren't you going to do something?"

I shook my head. "They're lawmakers. I'm not going to get involved. You could do that hand thing and calm them all down."

She shuddered. "No thanks. Maybe they'll feel better after they've worked out what's bothering them."

I kept one set of undies, tossed the rest and gave the shop assistant twenty quid before grabbing Marina's hand. "Come on. We're not hanging about here."

We strode through Marks and Spencer's with the attitude of two assassins walking through a hail of bullets.

6

The following afternoon, Echo, Marina and I scoffed down sushi in the staff room at Marina's veterinary surgery: avocado and cucumber rolls for vegetarian me and a mix of tuna and salmon rolls for Echo and Marina. She didn't usually open on the weekend, but ever since her patch-up job on Faeza, an influx of peculiar creatures had been turning up on Marina's doorstep.

"I always found English men and women a puzzle," said Echo. "Their emotions are laced up so tightly. In India, emotions are much closer to the surface. Indians say what they think. They wrap their unpalatable truths in charm and poetry. They don't hide them. But now, the people of this country are wearing their emotions on their sleeves. It makes me wonder…"

"If they are all on drugs?" Marina dipped a roll into soy sauce.

Echo gulped down a chunk of salmon. "Something has changed, has it not?"

Marina waved her chopsticks in the air. "Well, yes. I mean, the Prime Minister just reshuffled his cabinet. There was only a reshuffle last week. He's ousted some of his closest allies. There's definitely something funky in the air."

"It's the wind of change." Echo farted.

Marina didn't even blink. She carried on sucking out the shell of her edamame beans.

I gave a heavy sigh, accustomed by now to Echo's noxious gases and fluids. At least he didn't leave the toilet seat up.

"We've definitely had more clues recently about who would cannibalise their neighbours if society really were to break down." Marina waited, chopsticks poised in the air, while another flurry of sirens sped by. "So the pack didn't find any leads that could point to why wolves are turning up dead?"

"Afraid not. I suggested you could take a look at the body, but Gunnolf almost bit my head off."

"Wolves have a tight ranking. You probably overstepped the line," said Marina. "You need to tread more carefully if you're going to win Gunnolf's trust. Otherwise, it could make things hard for Ezra."

I grimaced. "I thought I was on my best behaviour. At least they're not blaming the dark elves this time. Ezra says Gunnolf will get to the bottom of it."

Marina raised an eyebrow. "That look on your face tells me you think otherwise."

I squeezed out some more wasabi from a sachet and popped in a mouthful of sushi. "My intuition tells me not to trust him. But Ezra trusts him completely. Gunnolf is not only his alpha. He's his uncle, his dead father's brother. Ezra is loyal to him. He doesn't want to see Gunnolf's faults, especially so soon after being disillusioned by Lavinia and her phoney war against the elves."

"If you're worried, you could pick up an object of Gunnolf's from the farmhouse. Something that's been close to his body, like a jumper or a watch. I can use it to get a reading about him." She used her powers generously in her veterinary surgery and out in the world without thought for the toll it took on her.

Echo gave a low growl. "The answer is quite simple, Alisha. If Gunnolf and Lavinia can't be trusted, you just have to open Ezra's eyes to it, or you risk being the one left out in the cold. Failing that, just say the word, and I will urinate all over that farmhouse. It will drive those territorial wolves crazy, and they won't be able to blame it on you."

I wrinkled my nose. "Please don't. Urination is not my choice of tactic."

Marina pulled her rainbow-coloured hair over one shoulder. "I think a much better approach would be not to jump the gun. Gunnolf is Ezra's uncle, after all. Give him the space to show you who he is without all the bluff and bluster that goes with being the alpha of a wolfpack. Just focus on Ezra. Forget about anything else."

"I would love to just focus on him. There's just a little performance of my animation powers in front of *the whole Wildwoods community* to get through first, thanks to you, Echo."

A string of tuna hung from Echo's teeth. "Stop exaggerating, druid. It doesn't become you. And don't blame me for your lack of libido."

I gave him a withering look.

"Don't look at me like that. There's a distinct lack of sex hormones emanating from your bedroom. And you're hardly going to do the dirty at a farmhouse full of wolves. Their hearing is as good as mine, and they would tease you far more."

I changed the subject with the subtlety of a ten-tonne truck. "Did I tell you? Dad seems to be doing better. I caught him in a Superman outfit painting a portrait of semi-nude Alma. My eyes were burning, I tell you."

Marina blinked. "He did *what*?"

Echo honked with laughter. "It is a long time since Joshi Verma has impressed me."

I grinned. "It's so good to see him painting again. Ravens are his new obsession."

Marina picked up her last roll with a deft pincer-like movement of her chopsticks. "Did you say ravens?"

I nodded. A familiar swirling started up in my belly. I pushed it down.

"That's funny," said Marina. "I saw on the news this morning that all six ravens, plus the spares, left the Tower of London."

"They're flying birds, aren't they? They must leave all the time," I said.

My best friend shook her head. "Sometimes they are dismissed for performing their duties poorly, but they can't leave of their own accord. Their flight feathers are clipped on one wing."

Echo swallowed down a chunk of salmon and tossed his head dramatically. "I would die if anyone took my freedom."

Marina's blue eyes grew troubled. "Legend says that if the ravens are lost or fly away, the Crown will fall and Britain with it."

My eyes watered as a dollop of wasabi hit my taste buds. "Oh, for crying out loud. I love you, but not even you can believe that nonsense, Marina. It's as bad as taking Fei Yen and Faeza's tarot reading and raven in the tea leaves seriously. Crystals, tarot and tea leaves are just a bit of fun. It's like horoscopes. They're comforting when they sound good, but when they sound bad, you just ignore them."

"You are foolish to doubt omens after all you have seen, Alisha," said Echo.

My stomach churned. I didn't believe in omens, but if I kept stumbling across the same image, did it mean the universe was trying to tell me something? Did true sight mean I had to listen to things I'd once ignored?

"We should be wary," said Marina. "In mythology, ravens are associated with Apollo, the god of prophecy and war. They symbolise death or bad luck."

Echo cleaned his paws with slow, deliberate licks of his enormous tongue. "The empath is right. Ravens are born of primordial darkness, and their jet black colour represents the night, the great void."

I shook my head. "Let's keep some perspective. Mythology is varied. I can point to as many myths that say ravens are a sign of good fortune. That they symbolise wisdom, longevity and healing powers. That they are symbols of metamorphosis, change and transformation."

Echo rolled over with the lethargy that came from a full belly. "All the more reason to tell the senate. There are those practised in divination amongst them. Let them discern the meaning of these omens."

"Can you imagine the raised eyebrows if I went to the senate with something as nebulous as this? They'd laugh me out of Wildwoods," I said. "Like you said, they have their prophets. Let them decipher their own omens."

Marina collected the rubbish from our takeout and swept it into the bin. "There's no time for a nap, Echo. We have an injured shifter to see at three-thirty p.m., and I'm nothing without the help of my consultant leopard."

Echo purred with pleasure. We'd learned that compliments, steak and salmon were key to keeping magical leopards happy. Well, that and the opportunity to maul prey.

I caught Marina's eye. "You are coming to the performance tonight?"

Marina looked at Echo. "We wouldn't miss it for the world."

I'D NOT SEEN Ezra since leaving the farmhouse. He and the pack had been preoccupied with wolf sleuthing, and Gunnolf demanded pack business come first. So we made a date to meet in Crystal Palace Park on the day of my performance.

I waited in a meadow of long grasses, knowing he'd find me. He told me once that as a boy, he'd been unpractised and had teleported into precarious situations, landing on people as if he'd fallen out of the sky. His father had schooled him then how to choose his locations more wisely. How to seek out quieter places to appear or to return to scents he recognised. To stay in the folds before emerging completely. Like a magician behind a curtain.

He said I smelt of wildflowers and cocoa, and I decided there and then to carry on using my Tom Ford perfume.

A whisper of noise, like the dissembling and reassembling of particles in the universe.

Ezra materialised next to me. He kissed me, his stubble grazing my cheek, and then he looped his arms around me, exerting gentle pressure until we stood chest to chest. His head dipped, eyes on my lips, and when he pulled away, I ached for him.

Grey eyes, flecked with copper, met mine. "I've missed this. I considered turning up unannounced at your flat last night to surprise you."

I gave him a shy smile. "Unannounced sounds just fine. I mean, so long as Echo doesn't mistake you for an intruder."

His hands rested on my waist. "So I don't need an invitation?"

I held his gaze for a moment. "I think we've passed that stage, don't you?"

"And I don't need to worry about what Margola Silver has been writing about you and Orpheus Might?"

I shook my head. "There's nothing there. He's just a weird old vampire."

Ezra murmured in my ear. "Good. One step closer to our happy ever after."

My heartbeat leapt, and I locked his words away to savour.

A young couple argued nearby. We grimaced and walked away to give them some space.

I entwined my fingers with his. "Everyone's a bit fractious at the moment. Have you noticed?"

The smile dropped from his chiselled face, highlighting the shadows there. "It's been pretty hellish running the investigation."

"Is the pack any closer to finding who killed the wolves?"

"Not really. We took a good look at the bodies. The wounds were jagged, not clean. That tells me they were killed by an animal. But then, vital organs were targeted. The neck, the heart, the eyes." He frowned. "So that points to a sentient creature. A peculiar, perhaps. A shifter. I was thinking of paying Robert a visit. The Shadow Squad might have some intel."

"He and Marina have drifted apart. He keeps ignoring her messages."

Ezra's brow furrowed. "I could have sworn he'd have bitten off his own hand to marry her." He paused. "Do you know what gets me? There was a rage in these killings. I could smell the lingering stench of fury still on the bodies. Like it was personal."

I shuddered. "That's awful. I bet Marina could get a sense of the emotional residue."

Ezra gave an exasperated sigh. "The alpha has spoken. Besides, there aren't any bodies to look at. We burned them on a pyre last night. Can't risk a humdrum uncovering a werewolf corpse. It raises too many questions."

Marina had counselled me to be supportive, but I couldn't help myself. "Isn't it a bit premature, cremating the bodies before the investigation has concluded?"

He stiffened. "We had to weigh the risks. But Gunnolf has it under control. He isn't the Justice Minister for nothing. He always finds the perpetrator."

I bit my lip. "If you say so. I mean, you do sound a bit like a propaganda bureau. Not even *CSI: Miami* has a one-hundred per cent success rate. And Horatio is good."

He folded his arms across his chest, and his biceps strained against his T-shirt. "Stop that."

I gave him my wide-eyed innocent look. "Stop what?"

A vein throbbed in his jaw. "You know exactly what. Gunnolf's not only my alpha—he's family. Promise me you'll try to be friends."

I sighed. "I'm sorry. I was just trying to help."

"I realised." He softened. "Shall we do what we came here for?"

Slipping into the rhythm of mentor and mentee came more naturally than creating a new musical score.

We flicked through Dad's catalogue of creatures, but I worried that expending my energy now would weaken me later, and I didn't want to be a laughingstock. I wanted to prove to all the naysayers that I could animate as easily as breathing when the truth was I'd only done it a few times.

"You're not a battery, Alisha. You don't need to worry about running out of energy," said Ezra. "Druids draw their energy from the Earth. And Earth's resources are infinite. I think it might be why Gaia has had a natural affinity with druids across the ages. Why she helped you. The trick is to relax and believe."

"You make it sound so easy. I can't see you going on stage and shifting in front of strangers to prove a point."

He laughed, and I enjoyed how his good humour rubbed off on

me. He allowed me to blow off steam and didn't belittle how I felt but made me feel better just by being there.

"It won't be that bad. Come on, choose one of these and animate it. Just for me. To get your juices flowing. How about the beaver? Or the squirrel? Then you could let it go in the park."

How could I stay crotchety when a sexy werewolf-wizard was cajoling me into using my newfound magical powers? A million women would have bitten off my arm to exchange places with me.

I shook my head. "Just something small." I flicked to a page where Dad had painted butterflies in a myriad of styles and shades. My finger landed on a bronze-and-black one with elegant tiger markings. "I'll try with this one."

He nodded encouragingly.

I took a deep breath and closed my eyes. Motes of light played in the air, infiltrating the nebulous pink of my eyelids. I opened my eyes. The world slowed as I drowned out all the noise of passers-by lamenting the tech blackout, children playing frisbee and the chirping of crickets in long grasses. I focussed only on the tiger butterfly, blocking out even Ezra and the scent of cigarette roll-ups on his fingers and the taste of his tongue.

The threads of the universe loomed in my mind. I was no longer myself. I was a conduit. A harpist. A surgeon. A seamstress who crafted marvels worthy of royalty.

My fingers traced the painting, and the dimensions deepened into velvet softness and quivering fragility. An intake of breath, marvelling as I sensed rather than saw the veiny wings, antennae and fine legs of the butterfly, and the wings fluttered within the page, a secret only I knew. Instinct told me when to pull the threads, and the tiger butterfly emerged, small and perfectly formed. He came clean off the page and rested on my palm as if he were catching his breath.

And then he was gone, camouflaged amongst the flower borders at Crystal Palace Park.

I laughed because, as much as I sometimes feared and doubted myself, when my talents shone, it empowered me. At that moment, I believed there had never been anyone like me.

Ezra's smile mirrored mine. "You're ready."

I reached for the catalogue of creatures and hooked my arm through his. We meandered towards Wildwoods, which beckoned to me like the sea calls to a mermaid.

7

The sphinxes stood vigil over Wildwoods in the summer sun. As we neared, I noted how their great, stone bodies shivered with intrigue. Only Mammatas brightened at our approach. His mood had improved considerably since a restoration funded by friends of the park.

"It is good you are here," he said. "Usually, the most exciting part of our day is when a child trips and swallows their teeth, but today we are witnesses to a true drama."

"It's the end of days," said Rhokon, the second sphinx, whose grumpiness stemmed from the fact that one of his legs was in a state of severe disrepair. "The ravens have fled the tower. Soon, the sun will fall out of the sky, and you will be turned to stone like us."

"Settle down, boys," said Ezra with a briskness that made me wonder if he'd ever been in the military. "Or you'll give yourself cracks."

I patted Rhokon soothingly and sensed the rumble of appreciation in his unyielding body. "I'm sure it's not as bad as that. Everything will be up and running soon enough. In the meantime, we can all enjoy some peace and quiet."

Rhokon's voice was as dry and gritty as sandpaper. "Have you looked at the sky this morning?"

I hadn't, actually. I'd had my head down on the bus and en route to the park. Once, I had relied on my wits, kickboxing skills and keys clutched in my hand to see me home safe at night. As a druid, I could stuff in my earphones with abandon, listen to podcasts or rock out to music, safe in the knowledge that I could triumph over most foes. And having headphones in meant I could pretend any peculiars stalking me didn't exist.

Rhokon sniffed. "Sorry to say, Mr Neuhoff, but werewolves always have their noses to the ground. But I thought better of you, granddaughter of Rajika Verma."

We looked up.

A message loomed against the sky, flamboyant and stark, carved into the vast blueness in a deep mauve ink.

RESCHEDULED OTEROR JIGOT TRANSPORT FEDORAN

My eyebrows disappeared into my hairline. I turned to the sphinxes. "Well, that's weird. Who's behind it?"

Ezra frowned. "Was that part of a Red Arrow display? Is it supposed to mean something?"

Mammatas's unblinking eyes regarded us. "The humdrums contemplate whether the fall anticipated by Nostradamus has finally arrived. The more obvious question is: when will we get our clear view back?"

"We are unsure where or when it originated," said Rhokon. "I can't tell you how hard it was for us to swivel our heads to take in the full effect. It was very frustrating not to be able to decipher it. It would have been much easier, of course, if they were hieroglyphics."

For two beings tasked with the job, the sphinxes had utterly failed at standing vigil.

Rhokon continued. "I know what you are thinking. Our stone necks cope quite well with a 360-degree rotation, but angling our heads upwards risks cracks. We could discard these stone bodies, of course, but the humans have enough problems right now without a pair of sphinxes scaring the bejeezus out of them."

"So you see now, Ms Verma, why we've been feeling a frisson of excitement this morning," said Mammatas.

I cupped my hand over my eyes to squint at the message. Crosswords were my jam, but this was different. It could have been French or Latin or a made-up language. Maybe in all the chaos, someone really had stolen a Red Arrow plane and would spend the rest of their life regaling the geezers in the pub about the nutty message he had written in the sky over South London. But unlike the vapour in Red Arrow displays, this didn't dissipate.

I dropped to my knees in the grass and rummaged in my bag for a pen and a scrap of paper, then scrawled out the words.

"What are you doing?" said Ezra.

"Hang on a sec." I chewed the end of the pen, staring at the words, and then the old magic happened. The one that made me brilliant at crosswords, word searches and *Countdown*. The letters unscrambled, and I scribbled the options down, crossing out dead ends until I finally had the answer. I held the page aloft in jubilation. "I solved it."

Ezra grimaced. "I can't read that thing. Spell it out for me."

"It's an anagram." Excitement made the words spill into each other.

He nodded. "Okay. What does it say?"

Pinpricks of anxiety blurred my vision. "It says, 'Rejoice and prostrate. For the old gods return.'"

Ezra cursed. His grey eyes met mine. "Not again."

Mamatas turned his pharaoh head towards me like he'd done dozens of times before. It still made me jump out of my skin. "Isn't she clever?"

Rhokon's deep voice rumbled through his body. "You should tell the senate."

I ignored them and focussed on Ezra. "I've probably got it wrong."

In fact, the sinking feeling in the pit of my stomach told me I was right. My teacher's brain was already breaking down the language. The words *rejoice* and *prostrate* were strangely biblical, and the *for the* construction was archaic. We were clearly dealing with a fruit loop.

And a god.

The swirling in the pit of my stomach grew stronger. *Rejoice and prostrate. For the old gods return.* But what did it mean?

I drew in a shaky breath. *It's not my problem.*

We'd tell the senate and then wash our hands of it.

In fact, if anyone suggested I get involved, I'd take a handful of crystals and shove them where the sun didn't shine. My priorities were clear. Survive the display of my magical prowess. Teach uneventful night classes. Enjoy long, lazy days in bed with Ezra. As wish lists went, it wasn't asking a lot.

I turned to the sphinxes. "The senate must be preoccupied with these developments. I'm sure a magical display is the last thing anyone needs."

Mammatas shifted on his platform with a grinding and shuddering I feared could be heard across the park. "To the contrary, I heard the Information Minister say that a bit of light entertainment is just what everyone needs."

I sighed. He made me sound like a kids' party entertainer. I leaned towards Rhokon. "You're my favourite."

His stone lips curved up in a smile. "Knock them dead, granddaughter of Rajika Verma. Blow them all away."

I gave him a jaunty salute. That was the intention. I would dazzle Wildwoods with my skills and then take cover with my lover boy until the dust had settled.

AT THE GNARLED YEW TREE, Ezra stood back and waited as I pressed my palm to the rune. The cool bark reacted to my touch as the rune activated, recognising me and sending heat pulsing through my arm. Beneath us, the ground trembled, and the trees shifted. A blink and Wildwoods School of the Wondrous materialised, complete with its grand arena and myriad of cabins and rope bridges nestled amongst the trees.

Our hands entwined as we walked into the grounds. The circular motion of Ezra's thumb against the back of my hand sent a shiver up my spine. Our relationship was so fresh and new that this public declaration of togetherness felt big.

"You know, we could pay the detective a visit and find out what he knows about all this," said Ezra. "If a god is behind all this, we can't just sit on our hands."

I laughed. "You can't be serious. Weren't you the one that was a stickler for the Pragmatist's Law?"

We chanted together. "Never meddle in the affairs of the gods."

Ezra gave me a rueful smile. "Yeah, well. You're the one who taught me that rules are all well and good until they collide with reality. I think you'll find I've broken the rules a number of times for you."

"What happened to Ezra Neuhoff, Mr Black and White, he of the Justice Minister's wolf pack?"

The copper flecks in his eyes danced. "I met a wayward druid."

My heart expanded in my chest. A flash of colour caught my eye. "Will you look at that?"

The cabins at Wildwoods changed with the seasons and, on a whim, an evolving, blooming and shifting that took my breath away. Today, they had been painted with the bright stripes of beach huts and patchwork bunting fluttered in the wind, at odds with the sinister message in the sky.

It's not my problem. I said the words in my head like a mantra.

Margola Silver had outdone herself in organising the event. Together with Rayna, she had arranged for stalls in the arena for students who showcased their magic and learning. My heartbeat raced at the sight of a grand stage at one side, backed by the obelisk.

Ezra followed my gaze. "It'll be okay. You animated a dragon, Alisha. You can do this magic show."

I gulped. "I just can't wait until it's over, that's all."

A quick scan of the crowd told us that Dad, Echo and Marina had yet to arrive, so we set off to explore. I spotted alchemists brewing murky potions in tiny cauldrons and turning matter into tiny jewels. Vampires practised mind control on brave volunteers. Druids coaxed sunflowers and camellias to grow from seed to full bloom in seconds. Shifters—a bear and a bull—faced off against each other in a show of strength, speed and wits. Fairies instructed visitors to their stall on the wonders of a glowing, chattering caterpillar and an inky blue kingfisher with the power of invisibility.

How I wished at times to be invisible. How had I gone from a woman craving attention to an object of curiosity?

I sighed as whispers reached my ears.

"It's her. The druid."

"Rajika Verma's granddaughter. She's the main attraction today."

"Margola Silver splashed her all over the front page of *The Otherworld News*. Did you see?"

"You're quite the talk of the town. And you have Margola to thank for it." Disapproval coloured Ezra's voice. "She never was one to ask the stars of her stories if they want to be taken along for the ride. How about we head up to the library and find a quiet nook to catch our breath before your performance?"

I nodded, and he led the way to the cable cars. I loved him for not needing to spell out how uncomfortable the attention made me. There was a softness to Ezra that my ex had lacked. Losing his parents at such a young age had honed his intuition, allowing him to pick up on others feeling overwhelmed.

Ezra stole a kiss as we rode the cable car towards the heart of Wildwoods. When the doors opened, we stepped out onto a rope bridge, which swayed with our weight, and made for the library, tumbling through the cobalt blue arched door into the cherrywood interior with its endless rows of books. The boughs, vines and stone that entwined to form the skeleton for the room had sprouted foliage, and the carpet of desiccated autumn leaves had vanished. In its place was a floor of soft rose petals in peach and sunshine yellow.

He pulled me towards the travel section.

I trailed my fingers along the shelf, breathing in the heavenly scent of old books and flowers. "So, how do you decide which one to read?"

"I tend to choose the ones that are more damaged on the outside. A well-thumbed book means that what's inside is special."

God, he was sexy. I dropped my bag and melted into him amongst Lonely Planets, Rough Guides and Bill Brysons. When the door to the cabin opened, and voices came our way, it took us a second to come up for air. I giggled and put my finger to my lips. It was one thing coming in here to soothe my frazzled nerves but quite another to be discovered like horny teenagers creeping away for a bit of nookie when we were in our forties.

The voice that filled the library sent a frisson of fear up my spine, and I knew we'd made a terrible mistake.

8

———————

I'd have recognised the Prime Sorcerer's voice anywhere. This wasn't the sort of conversation we should be a party to. Wildwoods safeguards meant Ezra couldn't teleport us out of there. We could have sauntered out of there clutching an armful of books as cover, but something about his tone rooted me to the spot. I clenched my butt cheeks together in fear.

"It is a shame so few of us are here for this discussion. The others are tending to pressing matters and will meet us in the arena," said Phinnaeous Shine. "We have full authority to proceed in this matter. You deciphered the code with typical speed, Orpheus."

"Indeed, Prime Sorcerer," said Orpheus. "Anagrams were a favourite pastime of mine back in the 1940s."

Phinnaeous harrumphed. "Well, thanks to you, we know the gods are stepping out of the shadows again."

I sucked in my breath and exchanged glances with Ezra. So it was true.

My first instinct was to call for Gaia, but I didn't always need to be in the cavalry. I repeated my mantra. *Stick to your goals. It's not your problem.*

"How easily the humdrums fall apart," said Phinnaeous. "It was pathetic yesterday. I skin-walked into the Prime Minister's office yesterday pretending to be the Home Secretary. He was lamenting about the Queen's private secretary coming to fisticuffs with the head of the Royal Guard. The Prime Minister himself had only just dealt with conflict within his own cabinet and was spitting with rage about the conduct of the Environment Minister on WhatsApp."

Lavinia piped up. "Any trouble between the humdrums means peculiars are stronger in comparison. My rats tell me it seems centred around mobile phones, and even peculiars have seemed more ruffled than usual. I have advised our kind to refrain from using their mobile phones for important communication. I say we ride out the storm. It wouldn't be difficult to improve the magical post. My rats and Helio's birds could be trained to carry messages. We have a whole ecosystem that is not dependent on the human one."

Echo had told me about the cloud master and magical post. There was still so much I had to learn.

Orpheus sounded gruff. "We don't live apart from the humdrums. We live amongst them. Anything that troubles them is our problem too. Our oracle warns that Crown and country may fall. I say that if the message is true, if the gods are interfering in everyday lives, then we should take action. The Magical Constitution was written in a different time. The gods were stronger then. Now we stand a chance of winning if we stand united against them. What is power unless we use it well?"

Lavinia's laugh tinkled. "Underneath that fatigued, tragic exterior, you have a poet's heart, Orpheus. But you forget, there's an opportunity in every crisis. It would be advantageous to see how the situation plays out. Aren't you tired of living in the shadows? This could be our chance to swing the system our way. To come out on top."

"Hush, Lavinia," said the Prime Sorcerer. "Wasn't it you who saved the humdrums along with the druid when the scientists were being targeted?"

My ears burned. I turned imploring eyes on Ezra. We should have left when we had the chance.

Lavinia's voice had the tartness of a lemon. She didn't like being challenged. "Indeed, Phinnaeous, but it wasn't a gesture of magnanimity. I weighed up what I would get out of it. And in this situation, the chaos suits us. Weakened humdrums mean that, in comparison, we are stronger."

The Prime Sorcerer struck out like a whip. "You have made many mistakes of late, witch. Without your cock-ups, we might have had a dragon. But as it happens, this time, I agree with you. Perhaps we should listen to what Margola has to say."

He must have been very secure in his ability to defend himself because Lavinia wasn't the type to let an insult slide off her back. She was made for revenge. I peeked through the bookcase. Margola's flame-coloured hair shone through green foliage.

"Of course, Phinnaeous, we would be in a different place right now if you had agreed to my proposal to launch a social media app, but the senate deemed it a low priority," said Margola archly.

My eye roll almost gave me a neck injury. Yeah, right. Or maybe it would just be another way for the senate to keep tabs on everyone.

"I thrive on discord. My readers love it. Conflict means friends turn on each other. They become loose-lipped about secrets they once would have died to protect." Margola's sultry voice belied her dark heart. "I care little for humdrums. It doesn't matter which god is behind this or how he is achieving this. I say let the world burn as long as peculiars survive."

Like I said, she was like Vladimir Putin in a Christina Hendricks body.

Anger coursed through my veins at her casual disregard for humdrums. I'd lived most of my life as a humdrum. I couldn't believe anyone could be so callous as not to lift a finger to help those more vulnerable. Wasn't she even curious as to what was going on? What kind of Information Minister was she anyway?

My rage propelled me into the open.

I gave Ezra an apologetic glance and slipped out of his reach, only to find myself pushed unceremoniously back onto his lap.

Orpheus stood glowering above me. "Just fetching a book, Prime Sorcerer." He hissed in my ear. "Your mind is as loud as a Mahler's

Symphony no. 8. When *will* you learn to be quiet? If you know what's good for you, you'll stay here."

I clambered up and pushed past them both.

Their groans echoed in my ear, but sometimes you needed to stand up and be counted. Even if it meant you landed in hot water. And from the look on Lavinia's face, her cauldron was boiling. Her helmet of silver curls only just hid the steam coming out of her ears.

I didn't hold back. "You know the gods are up to no good, and you won't even investigate? Why would you hold all your power and not even try to help?"

Phinnaeous Shine's righteous anger was a sight to behold. "Of course, it would be you skulking in the shadows. How dare you eavesdrop on senate business?"

Ezra walked out from behind the shelving, his cheeks flushed. He avoided my gaze.

"What, Neuhoff, you too?" said Phinnaeous. "This is very unusual. It seems Gunnolf doesn't have his pack under control."

Ezra's head dipped. "My deepest apologies, Prime Sorcerer. It won't happen again. We were…reading when the senate contingent entered the library and were loathe to interrupt."

"Yes, well, Neuhoff. The druid has shown poor judgement, but I expected better of you."

I smarted. Was it just me, or had Phinnaeous Shine belittled the women in the room? Those succubi forced to be his house servants probably hated him. A question plagued me. "What would the Wildwoods community think if they knew you refused to help the humdrums we live side by side with?"

Phinnaeous Shine dusted off the shoulder of his robe like I was a mere gnat bothering him. "What makes you think Wildwoods is a democracy? The peculiars out there couldn't care less what happens to humdrums. They don't want us to waste time following a thread that could lead nowhere. So what if a god is up to mischief? We live a double life. It means if one combusts, we always have the other."

Orpheus stepped out. "Phinnaeous, you can't believe that."

"But I do, dear friend. We have survived all this time because we have chosen our battles carefully. But if the humans err, we could discard our double lives. Aren't you ever dissatisfied with only having a small part of the world? I agree with Lavinia. We do nothing."

"You are cowards." I turned to Margola. Her hourglass figure had been squeezed into a pencil skirt and silk blouse. "And you, Minister, have made my life hell by reporting on me. I mean, a small feature is one thing, but you have whipped up your readers with intrigue about my grandmother, my mother, the dragon, even my marriage and relationship."

Ezra shifted uncomfortably. Orpheus, at least, had the grace to look away. He couldn't have been happy that Margola had been gossiping about our supposed chemistry.

"Alisha, you are a funny old fish. Who told you news is fair? Or that it is about the truth? Of course, sometimes it educates. But it also titillates. It distracts. It muddies the waters. Depending on who it's in service to," said Margola. "And that's even more true of humdrums than of peculiars. A decade of immersion in the new technology has changed the way their minds and systems work. More fool them for growing used to the constant stream of communication and distraction. Whatever is going on with the mobile phones, let's take a step back and enjoy the show."

I flexed my hands. She was so smug and so utterly morally bankrupt that I itched to send her flying onto her arse. Just a little push. It wasn't like a selkie had powers that could retaliate. Not in this environment, anyway. But we weren't alone, and as much as I disliked her, Margola Silver had the power of the pen and microphone. She could shape opinions while filing her pretty nails. I couldn't declare all-out war.

I smiled. "Well, I can see I'm not going to convince you with rhetoric. So once I perform in front of the Wildwoods community tonight, I'm going to get to the bottom of this myself. It's not like I needed your help for Ra or Pan. And if you want to bring me up on charges for falling foul of the Pragmatist's Law again, I'll just tell the truth at trial—That you yourselves considered intervening in this matter. That you considered rewriting the law now that the gods are less powerful. And the reason you didn't was pure selfishness. And that little old truth tonic you knocked me out with, Lavinia, is used at trials, right? So you can't lie."

They looked at me in horror—all of them.

"Oh, shit," said Ezra.

Orpheus rolled his eyes. "Wow. Just wow."

Lavinia folded her arms. "I can't believe you gave her a medal of honour, Phinnaeous."

So much for my mantra.

ANY SECOND NOW, I'd step out onto the stage. The obelisk had been wrapped in fairy lights. There was a hush in the arena. The stalls had been cleared away, replaced by theatre-style seating. The semi-circles of green velvet chairs under the starry night and crescent moon took my breath away. My nerves, at least, had subsided. The run-in with the senate had been a good distraction, and now I couldn't wait to go out and show everyone what I was made of.

"I can't believe you did that," Ezra said. He usually couldn't keep his hands off me. Even with other people around, there'd be a frisson in the centimetres between us. A promise of what might happen if we were alone. But no. I had well and truly made his hackles rise.

Oops. "I didn't mean to put you in it. I mean, they would have discovered us eventually, right? Orpheus could read our minds."

"Correction. Orpheus could read your mind. I learned a long time ago to block out the voodoo powers of vampires." Ezra shook his head. "Orpheus is a lot of things, but he isn't a snitch. And for whatever reason, he seems to have a soft spot for you. I mean, didn't he use his faster-than-light speed to ask you to stay put? At risk to his own neck, I might add. His role as a history scholar means he is more aware than most about what disasters can befall the world when good men don't act."

I bit my lip. "You're right. He was the only one there who didn't sound like a psycho. I had to go with my gut, Ezra. We've seen it before. Bored gods are trouble. We can't just turn a blind eye."

"The investigation into the dead wolves is taking up all my time. I don't know if it's wise for you to get involved in this."

I perked up. "We could just give Robert a ring. Maybe have a word with Gaia. Ruffle a few feathers. Follow our noses."

"Stop. Just stop it. Put all that out of your head, go onto that stage and get through the next few minutes."

Goosebumps raced up my arms at the sight of the audience. "Can we talk about it later?"

He sighed. "Of course. Go thrill them."

I turned to the stage, where Wildwoods headmistress Rayna Willowsun, a silver plait trailing down her back, prepared to take the microphone. The audience twitched with anticipation: pupils and their parents, impassive senate members, lone wolves, raucous leprechauns, timid elves, sulking vampires and fairies whose wings glistened in the night. Margola's cameraman, the fallen angel from the medal ceremony, filmed the proceedings. Margola herself waited alongside him, twirling her microphone like a weapon.

Rayna stepped up to the microphone. "Ladies and gentlemen, welcome to the Wildwoods arena. First, an enormous thank you to Information Minister Margola Silver for arranging such an inspiring event for our pupils and their families. Now, without further ado, the woman you have all been waiting for. Put your hands together for the granddaughter of Rajika, fellow druid, animator, and winner of the Wildwoods Medal of Honour, Alisha Verma!"

I stumbled out under the bright lights in my slim black jeans and a button-up shirt, with the catalogue of creatures tucked under my arm. When I gave the crowd a wave, the applause ratcheted up a notch, and I wondered what magic prevented the late-night dog walkers in Crystal Palace Park from hearing us.

Marina and Dad gave me a thumbs-up. Echo quivered with excitement. He liked a display of pomp more than anyone, especially as he could bask in the glory of my achievements by virtue of being in my inner circle.

I shook Rayna's cold hand and stepped up to the microphone. A high-pitched squeal of feedback made me wince. I adopted a game show host persona to mask the sudden resurgence of my nerves.

"Hellooooo, Wildwoods. For those who don't know me, I'm Alisha. I've only been a peculiar for a few months."

"Show off," shouted a stranger.

I braced myself and ploughed on. "I'm here to demonstrate what it means to be an animator. Like my grandmother before me, I am able to lift animals off the page and bring them to life. I have raised a dragon, a rooster and a butterfly."

"She's going downhill," said a voice from the back of the arena.

The audience tittered.

I located Orpheus in the audience. His granite face betrayed no emotion. "Orpheus Might told me once there haven't been many animators in history. They are scattered between continents and sometimes come only once in a generation. If they do not find an illustrator, an animator's powers lay dormant. Unused. There is no animator without an illustrator. We come in pairs. I just get to steal the limelight."

The crowd laughed. I didn't have them in the palm of my hands, but they were warming to me. The encouragement in Dad's eyes strengthened my resolve.

"Just as each illustrator has their own personal style and their own subject matter, each animator has different quirks. For example, my grandmother assigned her creatures a purpose as they were born. I am able to reassign a purpose after birth. Like those of you learning new skills, it has been a case of trial and error. Many errors." Teacher 101. Show that making mistakes is a path to learning.

I picked up the leather-bound catalogue of creatures, turned it outwards and flicked through some pages for the audience to see. There was a unicorn with a purple mane, a jellyfish with intricate veining and a stern eagle with ruffled feathers. "This catalogue of creatures was painted by my dad. It was once my grandmother's, and now it's mine. There is one cardinal rule of animating. We may not bring to life a creature unless it can be useful, happy or free." A bead of sweat rolled down the side of my face under the hot lights. I gave a shaky smile. "So now it's over to you, Wildwoods. I will now animate a creature from the catalogue for you. One creature only. Chosen by you, as agreed by my very naughty magical leopard, Echo."

Echo gave a roar of approval.

Another titter of appreciation.

I held a hand up. "Just remember the cardinal rule. I ask you, Wildwoods, would it be wise for me to animate a jellyfish here?"

"No," came the united response from the arena.

"That's right. Because we are not close to the ocean." I was enjoying myself now. I was a teacher, after all. I just had to remember how to handle the performance like a lesson. "How about a giraffe?"

Mirabel's voice met my ears. "A giraffe is not native to this country. Unless you wanted to gift it to London Zoo."

I nodded. "Excellent analysis, Mirabel. You're getting the picture. Now, over to you, Wildwoods. I'll flick through the catalogue so you can see your options."

Lavinia stood up and raised her umbrella, which I knew now to be her broomstick, her wand and her weapon. "And I will project the choices into the sky."

I nodded my thanks, but the smile didn't reach my eyes.

Neither did hers.

I flicked through the options as the catalogue of creatures became a projection in the night sky, sitting amongst the constellations. "How about a snail?"

The arena groaned. "No."

"Too boring," said a voice.

I held up a page full of insects. "Or a beetle."

"Too small."

On and on the list went as if it were a cinema reel or a gallery of Dad's works, the exhibition he craved. The crowd booed or applauded based on their preferences: a bear, an owl, a kraken, a vulture, an otter, a fox, a nightingale, a zebra, a phoenix, a hippo, a pegasus, a bee, a monkey. Judging by the peaks and troughs of the applause, the owl seemed a favourite. Dad had painted one that filled the page, its feathers an inky blue, with large amber eyes set in a flat, grey face and a small, sharp, orange beak. Who didn't like owls and their night-time calls, reputation for wisdom and entanglement with tales of old? It was the perfect choice for pupil demonstration.

I could sense the threads of the owl, its talons and its tufty plumes, leaping under the pads of my fingers. I took a deep breath. "An owl. I will animate an owl."

Suddenly phones started pinging all over the audience. Little rectangles of light appeared in the arena as they checked their messages.

Margola, too, checked her phone, then abruptly turned to address the audience, her sultry voice drifted over the audience. She lifted her phone into the air like a call to arms. "A fox. It has to be a fox."

"Fox. Fox. Fox." The chanting started slowly but quickly gathered pace, like the demented crowd at a gladiator fight.

If I could animate a dragon, why should I be afraid of a fox? It was much better than being asked to animate a pegasus or a phoenix because what the hell would I do with those even if I managed it? Surrender them to the Bestiary Master for captivity? Foxes—not my *hu hsien* fox friends Fei Yen and Faeza, of course—were ordinary. I could manage that. A fox could be freed after the performance and would blend in. The London streets were full of them.

I ignored the churning nerves in my belly. "Agreed."

A small smile toyed at the corner of Margola's painted lips.

Lavinia sat down, her job done, with a quizzical look at Margola and me.

My heart hammered in my throat as I returned to the page featuring a skulk of foxes. Dad had drawn four variations. A rusty vixen with a snowy white tip to her tail. A few cubs with slanted eyes and too-big ears. In the centre of the page, a rangy male with a bristly unkempt coat and whiskers was ready to leap off the page. I chose him, knowing my animation powers did not allow me to assign sex. The fox's sex would be the luck of the draw, just like in nature.

I sat cross-legged on the stage, with the catalogue in my lap, and blocked out all those present until they were in my peripheral vision but blurred out. No longer important. I heard the sway of the trees in the wind and sensed the presence of the stars above. My breath became one with nature, with the heartbeat of the Earth. Only then did I allow my fingers to drift over the page, to call the fox forth, to imagine who he was and who he could be. Like a mother envisaging her child.

But the pull and tug of the threads were strangely absent.

I doubled down, determined, trusting that my skill would not let me down. My fingers searched the page. Where were his blood and veins, his wily, resourceful nature, teeth like tiny knives, and eyes that knew all the secrets of the universe?

I grew desperate. I couldn't fail. I had talked myself up. Hell, Margola had talked me up.

My fox would appear like magic any second.

The audience leaned forward, eager to see the marvel. Believing and not believing.

But my fingers couldn't coax the fox into being.

Orpheus's voice filled my head. *Focus, druid.*

My eyes flashed to him. *Get out of my head.*

He came at me again. *The stakes are too high for you to fail now.*

I chewed the inside of my cheek, willing my fingers to do their thing. To be the harpist. The midwife. The giver of life. The page remained dimensionless, however much I sought its depth.

Closing the catalogue, I looked up, tears blurring my vision.

The audience gawped at me.

My toes curled. I tried to brazen it out and stop the flush creeping up my neck.

One unkindness could make the difference between holding your head high and being crushed.

"She's bottled it," called a gleeful voice.

I died inside.

I let the whispers wash over me as I stumbled to my feet.

Orpheus rose from his seat and bellowed at the audience. "I think that's quite enough for one evening. The children should be in bed."

I caught Margola's smile of triumph as I fled the stage into the shadows.

9

The audience dispersed at Orpheus's command. My ears burned as fragments of whispers floated my way. Pupils and their families, some enjoying the schadenfreude, many angry I hadn't delivered as promised, and others crowing they'd known I was a fraud. It didn't seem fair to have been put on a pedestal only for it to come crashing down so publicly. I hadn't asked for the extra attention. I was only trying to live my life.

It needled the part of me that still doubted myself. Were my wins down to luck or talent?

Ezra put his arms around me. "This will pass. It'll be okay."

"Will it?" I wished he could whisk me out of there, away from prying eyes—the sort of eyes that ghoulishly turned to look at car crashes as they pass—but the defences of the yew tree blocked teleporting. "Can we get out of here?"

He nodded. Heat spread through me as he threaded his fingers through mine, and the meaty part of his palm pressed against mine. We waded our way out of Wildwoods, my thoughts like treacle.

But my humiliation wasn't yet over.

A senate contingent floated towards us as if a rogue god hadn't written a message in the sky. As if they didn't have a care in the world except for me and my misdemeanours.

Ezra murmured into my ear. "Let them say their worst. I believe in you." He put a protective arm around me as they closed in. "Ministers, whatever needs to be said doesn't have to be tonight."

Cillian O'Meara, Minister for Finance, patted me awkwardly on my arm. He was a short, stocky sort, with a peach fuzz of beard growing in scraps across his face. "Your charge could have done with the luck of the leprechauns tonight, Neuhoff."

Phinnaeous Shine's lips twisted in the moonlight. "All those threats she made have come to nothing. How can she expect to challenge a god if she can't even perform a few tricks to dazzle Wildwoods pupils?"

Rayna put a hand on the Prime Sorcerer's arm. "Leave her be, Phinnaeous. At her age, our mouths also ran away with us. That must have been a hard lesson out there, Alisha. I was sorry to witness it. Take heart; you are still learning."

I gulped. "I appreciate that, Minister."

"Now, if you'll excuse us, we have business to attend to." Rayna ushered the Prime Sorcerer and Finance Minister towards the cable cars.

That left Gunnolf and Lavinia.

Oh, goodie, my favourites.

Plus Orpheus, whose brooding eyes searched mine.

I shuddered, wondering if he viewed me as prey after my humiliation.

He pushed his voice into my head. *You've always been prey to me, druid. I just choose not to take advantage of you.*

I balled my fists. *Seriously? You're sticking the boot in too?*

Orpheus gave a sardonic smile.

Ezra looked between the two of us, instinctively sensing that he was missing something. A tiny part of me enjoyed his hackles rising when Orpheus showed an interest in me.

Lavinia distracted Ezra by throwing her arms around him, sending a cloud of berry-scented hairspray over us. "You should be more careful where you stick your tent pole, Ezra. Even I thought the druid was something. But she is nothing."

A growl. "You are wrong, auntie."

"Take this as motherly advice, given my dear sister is no longer with us. Who you spend your time with has a direct impact on who you become. So be careful where you lay your head to rest each night." She stood between Orpheus and Gunnolf, a pint-sized pocket rocket in pink between two dark, brooding men. She twirled her umbrella and gave Gunnolf a dazzling smile. "You have told Ezra the news, haven't you? You'll be very excited to hear this too, Orpheus, given your oversight of genealogy for the senate."

Gunnolf searched Ezra's face. "This is best discussed back at the farmhouse, Lavinia."

My toes curled. I could sense this display was for my benefit. I guess she still blamed me for Elvira's death. Or simply thought I wasn't good enough for her nephew. Lavinia might look pretty in pink, but she was as much a strutting cock as the rest of them.

"Spit it out, auntie. You obviously have something on your mind." A growl laced Ezra's words. His thumb drew comforting circles on the inside of my hand as though he was trying to tell me to hold on just a little longer.

"Very well, if you insist. Your aunt Isadora has been doing some work. You know what a talented matchmaker she is. She's practically the godmother of a dozen peculiar children. And it so happens that the sexy red wolf Rashida you once dated has been meeting with Isadora. Their bloodline work has shown that the two of you are wonderfully compatible. Not only that, but Rashida is fertile. Almost unheard of for a female werewolf. Isadora's dark arts show your children would survive the birthing process." She gave me a triumphant glance. "The first wolf born—not made—in a generation in this city. It's quite magnificent."

My humiliation was complete. My posture slumped, and my vision blurred. I didn't often dwell on not being able to have children. My life was full, after all. But to be completely cast aside while Lavinia discussed Ezra's ex-girlfriend's fertility was too much to bear.

"This is ludicrous." Ezra looked from Lavinia to Gunnolf and back again. His grip tightened on my hand, but all I could think of was how he'd choose Rashida over me.

Gunnolf addressed Ezra as if I didn't exist. As though this conversation had nothing to do with me at all and I was simply an object to be discarded. "It pains me to break it to you this way, Ezra, but the witch is right. Have your fun if you must, but in the end, you must choose duty to the pack. You loved Rashida once. It is obvious to all that your mate bond is strong. You will love her again. And we will have pups running around the woods once more."

The black night seemed even blacker to me now. Ezra and the red wolf already had chemistry, or they would never have been together in the first place. She could give him children. I couldn't. His alpha wanted them to be together. The senate was excited about the union. I didn't stand a chance. It was case closed.

Breathe, druid. Orpheus sighed. "This is welcome news, Lavinia, but quite odd for you to share it this way and not in a formal meeting."

I waited, stunned into silence, hoping Ezra would come through for me.

Lavinia pouted. "Always such a killjoy, Orpheus. You should be pleased. You know as well as I do that the senate might turn a blind eye to rumbles between the sheets but magical unions are only blessed between peculiars of the same sort. It's too much of a risk to bring a mixed-race mewling into the world when they might have uncontrollable or demonic powers."

Was I just a rumble between the sheets? What I wouldn't have given for the chance to have a mixed-race mewling with someone I loved. My emotions stretched taut, almost at breaking point.

Ezra bristled. "Sometimes it works out just fine. Or are you wishing me away too, auntie, as well as Alisha?"

"Why so prickly, nephew? Of course, I'm not wishing you away. You're all that's left of my sister," said Lavinia. "I'm only trying to help. I truly want you to succeed."

"I'm not sure you could have handled this any worse." The vampire's look would have made a lesser women wither.

Ezra ignored him. "When have you ever helped me, auntie,

without wanting something in return? Your love, too, Gunnolf, has never been without conditions. So can you speak to me of love?"

The alpha released a growl of warning. "This is not a discussion. You will do your duty."

Ezra's posture changed. His grip on my hand loosened, and grey eyes no longer challenged. The alpha had spoken, after all. His biology compelled him to be obedient.

I couldn't stand it anymore. Something in me broke.

I wrenched my hand from Ezra's, and it slid away like butter, no friction, no attempt to hold me back.

I ran, tears trickling down my face. I pounded through the empty woods and past the yew tree, past the sphinxes whose stone heads didn't bother to turn my way, through the park and towards the double-decker buses hurtling down the main road. I wanted to be in my flat, with Marina's arms around me. I wanted to nuzzle against Echo and pretend he was still just my Bengal cat—just my friend. I wanted to leave all the magic behind me. All the pressure to succeed and battle, the relentless quest to improve.

Wasn't that what I wanted?

No children. No magic. No lover.

My fight drained out of me like water down a plughole.

When I heard footsteps behind me, my heart ricocheted inside its cage.

My fragility scared me. I didn't want to be found. I didn't want to be strong.

A hand caught mine, and I jerked to a stop, a cry on my lips as I spun against a man's chest, and his arms closed around me.

Ezra's heart raced against mine. "Why did you run?"

I looked up at him. The wind rustled his brown hair, and the shadows played in the crevices of his face. We could have been something. I knew it in the deepest parts of me. I'd known it from when we'd first saved Melissa. I wanted so much for him to be mine. For him to stand at my side and look at me like I was his world. To protect me.

Not that red-haired hussy.

I drew in a shaky breath. "You have to choose her. It's the only thing that makes sense."

"It doesn't make sense to me."

"Don't you ever think about children, Ezra?" A deep, shuddering breath. "I can't have them."

His eyes on mine. "I haven't thought about children. But I do think about you. All the time."

A catch in my voice. "I don't want my heart to break. I won't recover again."

Serious grey eyes compelled me to believe him. "Your heart is safe with me."

"Prove it." I knew how strong the alpha bond was. I didn't want to be hurt again.

He inched forward, less man than wolf, his eyes full of raw intent, until there was no one else, no noise in the world except his breath and mine. He kissed me, teasingly at first, not giving me enough, until I wrapped my arms around his head and pulled him closer, deeper. My salty tears ran into his mouth.

Then he pulled away. "I know you're scared, but I need you to know I'm more my father's son than my uncle's nephew. Your heart is as important to me as my own. I would disobey pack law and the Magical Constitution to put you first. Does that make me weak?"

I searched his eyes for the truth. My heart fluttered. I knew I'd pushed him, but he'd not pushed me away. Not yet.

The copper flecks danced in his grey eyes. "It's not up to Gunnolf and Lavinia to decide who I love. It makes me proud to follow my heart, just like my parents did. Their love burned so brightly that it was worth the fallout. I would take risk after risk for you, Alisha, because I love you. I love your passion, your belief, and your sense of humanity. I love your stubbornness and the way you shoot off your mouth." He swept back the tangled mess of my hair and pressed a kiss to my forehead. "It makes you real. I feel more alive than I've felt in a decade, and it's all down to you."

My heart expanded in my chest until I thought it would explode. How long had it been since a romantic partner had told me they loved me without prompting? I trusted that he meant every little syllable. I wrapped my arms around his neck and jumped up, entwining my legs around his waist. My joy bubbled.

I took his face in my hands, raining featherlight kisses over his stubbly cheeks. "You love me."

His hands splayed across my bum, holding me in position. He nodded solemnly. "I do."

I looked at him from under my eyelashes. "Can you take me to bed now?"

His eyes darkened. "Soon, hellfire. If that's our first lover's quarrel, I want to settle it properly. You wanted proof of my intentions, didn't you? Well, I have just the thing in mind. And aren't you going to tell me you love me back?"

I gave him a teasing look. "Soon, Ezra. Soon."

10

____

Marina and Echo waited at the flat for us. We piled into the living room, undone by the events of the night. I put on the kettle as we picked over the bones of what had transpired: the message from the god in the sky over Wildwoods, eavesdropping on the senate, my grand-scale humiliation and finally, Gunnolf and Lavinia's declaration that Rashida was the one for Ezra.

Not even a never-ending cup of tea, a foot massage from Ezra, or a tin of shortbread could lighten my mood. Okay, I lied. The foot rub was pretty amazing. I had to stop myself from moaning in pleasure. There was a promise in how Ezra's hands kneaded the arch of my foot and in the light in his eyes.

I hugged the three little words he had uttered close to me.

Marina wasn't fooled. She grinned as she soaked up the chemistry between the two of us. "The senators were out of line, of course, but it doesn't seem to have pierced your little love bubble."

Echo pored over a copy of *The Otherworld News* fresh off the press that had magically appeared in my living room. As if out of spite. The front page featured a picture of me on my knees at the moment my skills had failed me, and the headline sent colour rushing to my face.

Washout at Wildwoods. Can This Really Be Rajika Verma's Granddaughter?

"I just want to crawl into a hole and never come out." I chomped on another biscuit. "You know those dreams people have about being naked on stage? Well, it was worse than that. Do you know what really gets me? Dad was just getting back on his feet. He was happy and excited, and now I've crushed him."

Marina reached over to squeeze my hand, and calm washed over me. She didn't even need to focus anymore to do her empath thing. It came so naturally to her. "You're not responsible for Joshi's feelings. He'd be the last one to want you to pressure yourself that way. So what if you messed up? Nothing worthwhile comes without a struggle."

"Look on the bright side. It should put an end to all the fans." Echo began whistling. "Do you know the Monty Python tune? Whistle with me. It will cheer you up. Or we could go and hunt poodles."

Marina sighed. "Not the time, Echo."

He looked up hopefully. "Is it time for steak?"

I shook my head. "Not yet. I can say one thing for sure. All that self-confidence I had about taking on the god has drained out quicker than air leaves a balloon. I thought I was Wonder Woman there for a moment, but the universe taught me a lesson."

Ezra tugged my feet in reproach. "I'm not having you doubting yourself. It was a blip, that's all." He pushed my feet off his lap and motioned to the three of us. "Come on, Alisha's not going to sit around here feeling sorry for herself. I made her a promise. I'm due at the farmhouse at dawn, but there are still a few hours until then."

I exhaled in a huff of air. "To do what?"

He held out a hand. "To visit your most brilliant creation."

I met his eyes as my black feelings dispersed, letting in a little light.

Marina grinned. "Atta wolf boy. Can we swing by the surgery first to pick up some roadkill and my gear?"

Ezra nodded. "Your wish is my command, Ambrose."

EZRA'S olive skin was pale and clammy when we emerged on the green bank of a river in Bulgaria. He'd confided in me how teleporting was easy enough for him if he was alone or going short distances. Teleporting groups of people, however, took a toll on his body. Teleporting three people, plus a leopard, across Europe was a mean feat.

But my heart sang with joy. We were here to visit the dragon in his safe haven. It was exactly what I needed to buoy me after the evening's disaster. It had been weeks since Gaia had brought Tielbu here for safekeeping. The senate still hadn't forgiven me for not turning Tielbu over to them, and I didn't put it past them to attempt to capture him themselves. Secrecy was of paramount importance. It was risky coming here. I could tell Ezra knew it, too, by the set of his jaw.

He was taking the risk for me.

Though a blanket of night masked much of the view of the village, I spotted chalets, quaint hotels and a church with a bell tower in the shadows. The evening was warm and made lovelier by snow-capped mountains in the distance and the sound of the gushing water.

Echo's jaw dripped with drool as he surveyed the landscape with the demeanour of a creature about to evacuate its stomach contents. Luckily, we hadn't fed him the steak. "What fresh hell is this?"

"It's beautiful," I said. "No wonder your parents holidayed here, Ezra."

Ezra's grey eyes grew melancholy. "They loved the summer trekking and hot springs here as much as the winter skiing with its crystal white ski trails lined with trees."

Bulgaria was a special place. It had both mountains and plains. It had the Black Sea coastline and the Danube and was a melting pot of diversity, with Greek, Slavic, Ottoman and Persian influences. Bansko was the perfect hiding place for a peculiar community.

"Come on," said Ezra. "We have a dragon to find."

"Tielbu's going to love the roadkill I've stashed away in this cool bag for him," said Marina.

"It'll mean we are off the menu, at least." The sheen had returned to Echo's lustrous coat. He bounded ahead through a lane of pine trees. "Follow me. I have caught the dragon's scent."

We trudged through an eerie forest, not a soul in sight, with glee in our hearts and pine needles crunching underfoot. At the mouth of a cave, Echo unleashed a roar and forged ahead into the even deeper darkness within.

"These mountainous regions with their plentiful forests and water supplies are renowned brown bear habitats." Ezra raised a wry eyebrow. "Let's hope it's the dragon and not a bear that the leopard is tracking."

I scanned our environment, alert to every footfall. "Now you tell us."

Her expression grim, Marina zipped open her vet bag and loaded a tranquilliser gun. "We have plenty of weapon options between us, what with wolf man, leopard teeth, dragon-fire and whirlwinds. But it makes me feel better to have this in my hand. Just as a last resort."

"Let me carry this." Ezra picked up the cool bag of roadkill. "Stay behind me, ladies."

I lassoed him to me with a draught of wind. "Forget that. You stay behind me."

I didn't wait for an answer. My dragon and leopard needed me.

The temperature cooled as we entered the cave. We stepped over stalagmites emerging from the floor. Icicle-like stalactites grew from the cave ceiling, too, although some of the rock formations had crumbled onto the cave floor as if something large and clumsy had come this way. A layer of smoke lingered at our feet.

Tielbu. I ran through one cave hall into another, deeper and deeper, my heartbeat pounding in my ears. I blinked as my eyes struggled to adjust to the change in light. Goosebumps ran up my bare arms when I spied three bodies around a small fire.

A smiling old woman.

A snorting dragon.

A purring leopard.

"Hold on!" called Ezra.

Deep-set amber eyes glowed in the darkness. The dragon lifted his head in recognition and snorted rings of smoke towards me in greeting. "I have missed you, druid."

I laughed and ran towards Tielbu to press my cheek against the iridescent turquoise scales of his cold reptilian skin, drinking in the scent of smoke and meat.

Not so long ago, he had been mere lines and paint on paper. I might have failed at animating the fox, but I couldn't be a complete failure. I had managed this. His bulky frame told me that he had been well nourished. His teeth and horns had retained their menace, and his wings hadn't withered away.

I drew away from him. "Are you well?"

"I am," the dragon said.

A bubble of tension I hadn't known I was holding evaporated.

I turned to Gaia and bowed my head, joined by Ezra and Marina as they caught up behind me. "Goddess. I am glad to see you. I thought of you just today."

She smelt of hair oil and curry spices. Her plump midriff spilt out of her sari blouse, and shadows cast by the fire swept across her lined face. "The universe told me you were on your way, and I thought it would be a nice evening for a reunion. I visit the dragon often for a cup of chai. He is accomplished at reheating a lukewarm brew that would otherwise be ruined."

Echo had rolled over at her feet like the hussy he was.

"Yes, Chanakya, I have missed you too." The goddess tickled his exposed belly, and he unleashed a purr of ecstasy.

The cave was alive with warmth and friendship, although I had been shivering only a few minutes before. We gathered around the fire in the cave that Tielbu had made his own. Marina checked him over with her stethoscope and various gauges, cooing all the while. When she had decided all was well, she tore open the bag of roadkill and encouraged the dragon to eat to his heart's content. The dragon used teeth and talons to devour the deer carcass, leaving scraps for Echo.

"Are you happy here?" I asked the dragon.

Tielbu lifted his rounded skull. His table manners left a lot to be desired. Lumps of flesh landed in the hissing fire and inches from the goddess's luscious peach-coloured sari.

Gaia didn't flinch as if she was accustomed to the grime of living.

"I am." The dragon's voice was an ancient rumble in my ears, like the moving of mountains.

"And have you found your purpose?" I didn't mean the question to sound weighted, but as soon as the words spilt out of his mouth, I knew I was talking about me as much as him.

Tielbu snorted twin rings of smoke. "The goddess tells me that sometimes it takes a lifetime to find one's purpose. A dragon can live for centuries. I have food, freedom and friends. The Bulgarian witches here have conjured a glamour for me. I am told humdrums see me as a black vulture. I am judicious about how often I prune the herds in neighbouring villages, and I have found a way to be useful in heating the hot springs for the tourists to enjoy. I have only one worry."

I frowned. "What is that?"

"That I will be too far away to protect you when you need me." He bent his head to his meal. The bone-crunching sent shivers up my spine. So did his use of the word *when*, as if he knew with certainty that my peace wouldn't last.

Echo licked the blood off his jaw with relish. "There is no need for you to worry, dragon. Alisha has many allies. I have been at her side since the very beginning."

"The leopard is right," said Ezra. "It is far more important that you stay here, out of the clutches of the senate. There is little you can do from a continent away, but rest assured that I can be at her side in a flash."

I glanced at Marina and rolled my eyes. What was it about the protective urge of the men around me? I appreciated their care, but it was like they had completely forgotten that, even before I had magical talents, I had been slinging right hooks and putting my shoe in sorry behinds. Hell, the first time I had met Ezra, I'd flipped him on his back. "It's okay. I'm not planning on getting embroiled in any more Otherworld fights."

Gaia's dark eyes hid the secrets to endless worlds. "And what, pray tell, makes you think you have a choice?"

My voice was small and hollow. "There's always a choice. My run of luck is over. I completely failed in front of the Wildwoods community tonight."

The goddess's eyes gleamed. "That's what you're worried about? Progress is never a straight line. It comes in fits and starts. That's the way the world has always been. It's the way it has been programmed since the dawn of time."

"Be that as it may, I almost went into warrior mode again, but my failure reminded me to focus on my personal needs. The world doesn't need me to save it. There are plenty more qualified people." I shrugged. "I thought growing older would make life simpler, but somehow I've ended up in a soup of competing needs. I have an ageing dad to care for, a wayward brother, a classroom of students and a hot boyfriend." I smiled shyly at Ezra. "Tonight sealed it. I'm going to put a huge sign in my lady garden to tell everyone to go and knock at someone else's door. I prefer a quiet life."

Gaia's eyes twinkled. "Good luck with that."

Tielbu snorted. Not a snort of disdain or mirth, more like an anxiety hiccup. "When we journeyed to Bulgaria together, you told me who the druid is. She should know the truth."

Marina looked at the goddess in alarm. "If there is something we should know, a heads-up would be brilliant. As the empath in the group, I end up a little exposed. Like a snail without a shell. There have been bad omens in the tea leaves, and I saw on the news the ravens have left the Tower of London."

Gaia's back had been curved as a question mark, but she suddenly sat as straight as an arrow. In her eyes was a warrior of the ages, all trace of the cherubic old woman gone. "No need to plead with me. Is it not obvious to you all by now? If the ravens have fled the tower, then that thieving old bastard Hermes is up to his old tricks."

My brow furrowed. Hermes. The messenger god?

Marina clapped, pleased to have her superstitions confirmed, even though I had pooh-poohed them. "I told you the ravens leaving the Tower of London was bad news."

"That's who wrote the message in the sky tonight?" I asked.

"That old codger. He always did like grand gestures. Less than a day old, and he stole Apollo's herds then turned a witness to stone." Gaia fixed me with a stare. "Whatever shapes you twist yourself into, Alisha, whatever doubts plague you or humiliations you suffer, you must know by now that you are the eternal girl. You may resist your calling, but you cannot escape it."

Ezra cursed under his breath.

Echo shivered with pleasure. He would have given the spots on his golden coat for this to be true, particularly if the goddess had taken an interest in the proceedings.

Marina looked from me to Gaia, a stupefied expression on her face. "Err…what on earth is the eternal girl?"

I grimaced. "A saviour fable that has the senate dumping little girls into a tank with an octopus."

I knew it to be bollocks. How could I be the eternal girl? I was hardly fresh as a daisy. My arse ached if I sat on the floor, my eyesight had deteriorated something rotten, and my skin was starting to head south. Anger coursed through my veins like molten lava. "That's the most ridiculous thing I have ever heard. There's not even a cat's chance in hell I'm the eternal girl. I'd know if I was. I'm in control of my own fate. You're not going to make me a central character in some fairy tale handed down through the ages."

"*What?*" Marina pinched her arm hard and twisted. "Just checking I'm actually awake."

Gaia ignored her, adjusted her sari and wrapped the train around her waist. Evidently, even a goddess could have dirt under her fingernails. "Some things are written and always have been. You are an accomplished woman, Alisha, but even you cannot withstand a current that has been churning for centuries. You must understand two things."

The fire no longer warmed me. A coldness seeped into my very bones. "And what are they?"

"You're only as powerful as the weakest link in your circle. And that weak link is a pigeon."

I frowned. I still hadn't sent Sahil that text. "A werepigeon?"

Gaia blew out a huff of breath in exasperation. "Am I speaking Aramaic again? There is only so much I can tell you, druid, or the Fates will scold me for intervening."

I chewed my lip. All this intrigue was enough to make me want to head out on an expedition to the artic where no one could find me. Possibly with my wolf in tow. And I was a beach lover. "And the second thing?"

"We are all cogs in a grand scheme, and only one path is blessed. You see, human lives aren't just reliant on talent, sheer willpower or choices. More often than not, it is a thought, a prayer, an alignment of the stars or the sneeze of a god that means the difference between jubilation or devastation." Gaia's brown eyes blazed. "Your ego, your exhaustion and your preferences have nothing to do with it."

My chest tightened. "You don't believe in choice?"

The goddess gave a sad smile. "To the contrary. But choices are only available within the parameters we set ourselves. And you're a heroine, are you not?"

I resented her for asking me to give more of myself than I was willing to. "I'm just a middle-aged woman."

Gaia's voice reverberated around the cave as her body faded into nothingness. "And the possibilities are endless."

11

The air in the cave suffocated me. The thought of being tied to an inescapable fate made me shrivel with terror. I was finally the mistress of my own life, and I didn't want anyone else, not even a goddess, manipulating me. Had I made the choice to involve myself in this Hermes business, or was I only walking a path that had been marked out for me? If I didn't have agency, what was the point of anything at all? I laid my head against Tielbu's dry turquoise scales.

"Fly with me," I whispered against his sternum.

"You are upset, druid," said Tielbu. "We will fly."

Ezra stood, his forehead creased with worry lines. "I'm coming with you."

I nodded. We had a mutual love of heights. Usually, a werewolf would have preferred being grounded, but Ezra's ability to teleport had changed his nature. We followed the dragon out through the cave chambers, over the smoke-filled floors, past the stalagmites and stalactites out into the clear air that tingled on my skin, a far cry from the smog of London.

Hermes is up to his old tricks.

You must know by now that you are the eternal girl.

She is nothing.

A sharp intake of breath. It wasn't my problem.

Tielbu waited in the clearing outside the cave, and when we reached him, he bowed and flattened himself to the ground so we could clamber onto the space between his fragile wings. My wind powers gave me the ability to propel myself up and lower myself down, but it was safer to climb. I had to focus to keep my trajectory clean and not end up on the floor like a pancake. Besides, I savoured the feel of Tielbu's skin against my palms. The scent of musty dragon smoke mingled with Ezra's cigarette roll-ups as I nestled against him. No sooner had I steadied myself than Tielbu made a running leap, launching into the air.

I lurched. Ezra's arms clamped around my waist. A lifeline.

You must know by now that you are the eternal girl went through in my head like a merry-go-round.

We soared above a rippling lake and circled the snow-capped mountains. The cave in which Marina and Echo waited was a distant speck. Tielbu dipped and curved through the starry sky. The wind rushed in our faces. He swooped, his wings beating to the time of my heart, and before I knew it, my anxiety fell away and bubbled out of me like a fountain.

After the first rush of energy, the dragon snorted and stilled, catching the slightest current of air, like a paper plane floating on a breeze under the watchful eye of the moon.

I turned to Ezra. "I don't believe it, do you?"

He gave me a grim look. "I should have known that whenever the goddess appears, there is more trouble coming our way. She speaks in riddles and then disappears. I know from experience that when a god speaks, the rest of us just fall into line. We keep this under wrap for now. No need to rock any more boats than necessary."

We glided through the sky, and when the cave came into sight, Tielbu angled his wings and dove towards the earth.

Ezra clutched me tight. "It doesn't matter what I believe. Whatever my reservations, if you need me, Alisha, I'll be there."

MIDNIGHT NEARED as we returned to my living room, grimy from our journey into the Bulgarian cave. I longed for a scalding shower to cleanse my body and mind. I sighed at seeing Echo's discarded copy of *The Otherworld News*.

Ezra's deep voice was a growl. "So we're agreed? Not a word of the eternal girl to anyone. Alisha doesn't need any more heat from the senate or the Otherworld press."

It made sense to keep quiet. "There's no way she's right. We're all taking an oath of silence here and now. I mean it. Promise me."

Ezra had reacted with incredulity to Gaia's revelation, just as I had, but Marina and Echo seemed to be having a whale of a time imagining the what-ifs.

Marina blinked in awe. "How awesome would it be if the Chameleon Tale was real? An eternal girl who blends in even though her talents are brighter than the sun. Who, once she has a disintegrating tome in her possession, can stop the coming dusk when Death opens the door. You'd be part of a myth, Alisha."

Echo fizzed with glee. "I have long mourned my choice to follow Rajika Verma across the globe merely to pretend to be a cat. This revelation would validate my life's path. I wouldn't have merely been a babysitter to snotty Verma children. I would have had the eternal girl as my charge. Somebody put on the Supremes so we can celebrate."

My nerves were frazzled. "I'm so tempted to stuff a sock in your mouth. Not a word to anyone. I mean it, you two. Promise me."

Empath and leopard both gave a solemn nod.

"Thank you for taking me to see our friend tonight. I hope the dawn meeting at the farmhouse is fruitful." I pressed a kiss to Ezra's lips and Marina's cheek. "Now, scoot. This tired body is crying out for sleep. And stay off mobile phones. We can't trust that our messages are private or free from tampering."

When Ezra had melted into the hidden realms, I escorted Marina to her van and waited until she drove off before returning to the flat. I showered, slipped into a nightie and went into the hallway to check my answerphone machine. There were a handful of messages from Dad.

Echo padded past. "I thought you were tired. Do you need a lullaby? I can offer you 'Moon River' or perhaps 'Somewhere Over the Rainbow.'"

I scratched his ear. "Go to sleep, Echo. I'm just checking the answerphone."

He sighed. "Humans and their gadgets. If it's not mobile phones, it's blenders or vibrators. I despair."

"Actually, would you mind taking a letter to the postbox? I should stick to old-school means. I thought I'd drop Sahil a note. You heard what the goddess said tonight. It made me worry again why he's gone off the radar. Mum would expect me to check up on him."

"You and he are not so dissimilar. The werepigeon is just spreading his wings, that's all." Echo's lips pulled back into a gurn, his version of a grin. With his crooked teeth, he didn't exactly have an American smile, but at least his gums were pink.

"Maybe you're right. Can you do me a favour?" I pulled out a postcard, my address book and a stamp from the sideboard and scrawled a few lines. I blew on the ink and set it down. "The postman comes at six a.m., I think. Can you send it off by then?"

He snorted. "This task is beneath me, but I will do it for you."

I kissed his head. "Scrubbing your urine off the wall is beneath me, but I do it for you."

"Goodnight, Alisha."

"Goodnight, Echo."

He wandered down the corridor and, within seconds, snored on the sofa, grunting like an orc worthy of Tolkien.

I listened to my answerphone messages from Dad. He had always preferred calling my landline. I suspected it harked back to wanting to check I was home and safe and not boozing in some bar.

10:05 p.m. "Alisha, this is your dad. Call me when you get this."

10:38 p.m. "Wake up. Are you asleep already?" A pause. "Is the werewolf with you? Make sure you use protection."

11:42 p.m. "Darling, call me whatever time you receive this. It's your dad, by the way."

My hands turned clammy as I dialled. Maybe something had happened. Maybe he'd needed me. The dialling tone went on for an age, and just as I was about to give up, Alma answered the phone. Had she stayed over? Alma, hanging about my dad like his wife hadn't just died. I wanted him to be happy, but slower steps would have been nice.

She sounded sleepy. I pictured her picking up the telephone in the bedroom. "Hi, Alisha. I hope you're eating your greens."

I did a poor job of masking my grouchiness. "Can I speak to Dad?"

"Of course. I'll fetch him. He's been in a tizzy in his studio all evening." Rustling and heavy breathing came down the line as she made her way to the studio. "Here you go, love. It's Alisha on the phone."

Dad grappled with the line. "Alisha. Finally. Wait a second." The line grew muffled as he spoke to Alma. "You go on baking your pie, Alma. I'll be right in there to taste it." He came back on the line. "Alma's been working very hard making apple pie for the neighbour's party. She's very good at bringing people together."

I sent a silent apology to Alma for jumping to conclusions. "I got your answerphone messages, Dad. Did you need me?"

The sound of a door closing came down the line. He dropped his voice. "Yes, love. It came to me in a flash after the performance. Once I'd had my dinner. It really was awful to see you so upset on the stage. You know how I think better on a full stomach."

"Dad, what came to you in a flash?"

"Darling, what if the reason you failed to animate was because you can only animate winged creatures?"

My heart pounded as a moment of silence stretched between us.

His worried voice came down the line. "You're not offended, are you? I should have thought of it straight away. It makes sense, doesn't it? You said it yourself. Not every animator is the same. Just because your grandmother could animate all creatures doesn't mean you can."

I thought back. I'd managed a dragon, a rooster and a butterfly. I had failed at a fox, but before that too, when Dad had attempted to teach me to animate. There'd be a frog in his attic I'd not managed either.

"Wait a second. I have to try something." I ran to my bedroom for the catalogue. I'd hidden it in my knicker drawer alongside Death's sword, the choker necklace Mum had left me and my Wildwoods medal. I really did have to find a better hiding space for them.

I bounded back to the hallway and opened the catalogue, Echo's snores filling my ears. I searched for the unicorn, my pulse a hummingbird in my throat. There it was, in all its purple-maned glory. It would be very, very reckless to try to animate a unicorn in my bedroom, but what girl wouldn't love to see a unicorn? And after the day I'd had, the universe couldn't hold it against me if I threw caution to the wind.

I breathed deeply, shut my eyes and pictured the unicorn in my mind's eye. Then I focussed on the page, stroking my fingers across the unicorn's rump, its elegant back, and the horn that protruded from its forehead.

Nothing. Nada.

No ripple in the page. No warmth of a beast's skin. No neighing that precluded a mystical creature coming to life.

More fool me.

"Alisha, are you still there?"

"Just one more minute, Dad."

I turned a few more pages until I came to a swarm of bees. I'd always been afraid of that end scene in *My Girl*. But bees were inherently good. They were central to our ecosystem. Without pollination, wildflowers and food sources decreased. Not to mention honey production. And I liked honey in my tea. The universe would thank me for animating a bee.

I picked a little fellow and focussed on his mustard yellow-and-black-striped jacket, his antennae and tiny legs. He flew off the page before I could blink. I attempted it again and again until the bees buzzed around the hallway, and Echo stirred. The bees flew out to the open living room window in formation. I picked up the handset, full of wonder.

"You're right, Dad. You're right. I just animated a family of bees. I don't know how, but you did it."

He whooped like a man decades younger. "It's entirely logical that you should only be able to animate winged creatures, now I think about it. Life and colour always found you. Before the witch bound your powers, you went through a spell of winged creatures following you. Ladybirds, crickets, house flies, you name it. In the end, your mother took you to the doctor like you had a common cold. She was always looking for a scientific reason for anything." He giggled. "Anyway, the doctor thought your mother was barking mad. He was quite perplexed. He'd never seen anything like it. At first, he put you on a regime of daily baths, like uncleanliness might be the reason insects were following you."

"Charming."

"Eventually, he suggested you wear insect spray year-round. In the end, we just used mosquito nets to keep them out of the house at least." He gave a contented sigh. "It's funny how comforting those memories of your mother are now. Sahil was different, of course. He hated flying creatures with a passion, even as a boy. His fear made him wheeze. When he was really scared, he'd pinch his eyes shut and hold his breath until someone tapped him on the back, and he popped like a cork. It must be so hard for him to accept his werepigeon nature now."

I sighed. "Yes, poor Sahil."

Dad's smile came through his voice down the line. "Anyway, darling, it's simple, really. You are a mix of your mother and me. The vampire told you your mother's line traces back to virgin priestesses in Brittany, the Gallizenae. They could calm the winds, predict the future and take the form of different animals. Your mother didn't know this, of course. That culture had been lost long before she was born, but it remained in her blood. You have your wind powers through her. And your animator powers come from my mother."

My head spun. I had thought it was my fault for failing to pull off the performance, but it hadn't been in my capabilities all along. The knowledge empowered me. It gave me a starting place. Maybe my powers would grow to match my grandmother's. Maybe they wouldn't. But somewhere in my cells, I had something from my grandmother and my mother, and that made me more powerful, not less.

"Dad, I don't know how to thank you," I said.

"You don't have to thank me, love. That's what fathers are for. A little bit of support, a little bit of elbow grease and belief in your brilliance. I knew that you had been short-changed at Wildwoods tonight, and I wasn't going to let it stand."

"I love you, Dad. Listen, I need you to avoid mobile phones for now. Can you do that?"

"I love you too, Alisha. And you know I rarely touch my mobile phone. Frustrating thing."

"Do you think you can paint some of your ravens into my catalogue of creatures?"

"Of course. Now I must go and eat some pie. Otherwise, Alma will never let me go to bed." He paused. "And Alisha?"

"Yes, Dad?"

"Beware of Margola Silver. I think she's sabotaging you on purpose."

12

———————

I rolled out of bed at the crack of dawn before my alarm sounded. A few minutes later, I had thrown on a hoodie and trainers and headed out to the high street in my PJs. With any luck, my misfire at Wildwoods meant that my fickle fans had found another target. The last thing I needed was to be caught in public without a bra on. I was pretty certain Mum tutted down at me from the heavens for my impropriety.

I eased into a red telephone box and fed it some change. It paid to be cautious. The god wouldn't control me. I dialled the detective's landline number. His role in the Shadow Squad meant he worked ungodly hours. My words flew out, garbled and anxious. "Robert. I know you and Marina have fizzled out, but I hoped you wouldn't mind me ringing."

"Alisha? You don't usually call me on this line. Slow down, will you?"

I sighed. "Did I disturb you?"

He sounded exasperated. "If you're asking me if you pulled me out of bed, then no. I've not had a wink of sleep. I've been working on a case. Now, what was this you said about Marina? Are you saying she dumped me? That cuts deep. We're not teenagers. She could have told me herself."

I frowned. "That's funny. She said you'd ignored her messages, that she was the dumpee, not the dumped."

"What nonsense. The thought of that woman has been getting me through the day. It's only been just over a week since we saw each other. I've been trying to chisel out time to go and steal a kiss." He paused. "Although what you said chimes with what we're uncovering in the course of the investigation. There's been a severe unravelling of trust in this country in the past few days. And I think normal people like us are just as impacted as those in the upper classes."

"What's good for the goose is good for the gander."

"Huh? Anyway, the Prime Minister is on his third reshuffle in as many days. The Lords were uncharacteristically venomous during a debate in the Upper House yesterday. And a fight broke out between the Royals in their private box at Ascot. Camilla lunged for Charles, but Princess Anne caught the brunt of it and gave as good as she got. There were hats flying everywhere. You wouldn't believe how many everyday people are in lock-ups at the moment. Local police stations are packed to the brim. The courts can't process cases quickly enough. At first, the Health Minister wondered if it was perhaps an airborne virus that triggered hostility. It wasn't farfetched. There's a lot of chaos in the natural world. But then, the message in the sky appeared, and my eyes opened."

"Oh, so you're good at anagrams too?"

He grunted. "So you deciphered it?"

"Well, yeah. On the hoof. With a scrap of paper and two scary sphinxes and a werewolf-wizard eyeballing me," I said breezily.

"Fair play to you," said Robert. "I might have got there sooner if we weren't so short-staffed. Once it was clear gods were involved, it was a case of tracing which one. I had a hunch, but I couldn't interrogate the Prime Minister and his cabinet. Or the Lords or the Royals. There's strict etiquette to these things. The higher up they are, the more difficult it is to question them. Plus, there's the issue of the veil. The hidden world must stay hidden. It was only when I picked out some low-level delinquents out of lock-up that I realised mobile phones, specifically messaging apps, were at the root of all the disharmony. Distorted messages, fabricated ones, and messages that fell into a black hole. And then it all came to me. It's related to tech."

I butted in. "It's Hermes. The trickster god. The messenger god."

There was a moment of disbelief. "Dammit, Alisha, will you just once—*just once*—not steal my thunder? I was just about to tell you that. I should bloody well recruit you to the Shadow Squad. At least then you'd be on the inside of the tent pissing out."

I grinned. The situation was serious, but I could still take a moment to revel in being right. "That's what I was ringing to tell you. Gaia confirmed it last night, but the truth is there have been signs everywhere. I just hadn't put the puzzle together. However, we shouldn't say his name. Gaia told me once that the gods have an inkling when we name them."

"I should have realised when the ravens left the Tower of London. He's the Ravenmaster there. All those birds have buggered off because he's busy causing chaos, and they won't listen to anyone else." A slow exhale of breath. "I wonder if the goddess could be convinced to be a source. So you're calling to offer your help, Alisha? Because we sure as hell need it. There are very few people at Number 10, the PM included, who are in the know. He's very worried that any number of countries—China, Russia, Saudi Arabia—will be champing at the bit to destabilise this country, and Hermes has given them the perfect opportunity."

"You've been in this game longer than me. You must have a plan, Robert."

"Very clever of you to use a landline, by the way. I'll suggest that at once. We can't just confiscate mobile phones or shut down apps. I raised it with the PM, of course, but the general public won't stand for it. For now, I'm going to treat the symptoms. Arrange for mediators and therapists to calm matters down. I was hoping Marina could help with her empath talents. Maybe Fei Yen and Faeza can concoct some tea from Shanghai Moon for me. But cauterising the wound has to be down to you. I'll do what I can to help, but I don't have your skills. And this is a powerful enemy. We need you in this, or we don't stand a chance."

I sighed. "Has the Prime Minister been to Phinnaeous?"

The detective groaned. "Why would he, after what happened with the earthquakes palaver? Phinnaeous Shine didn't exactly cover himself in glory when he pretended the elves were behind the tremors. That relationship isn't getting back on track any time soon."

"Probably for the best. The senate are well and truly up their own arses."

Robert blew out his breath. "Fighting a tech war isn't like arm-to-arm combat. If all enemies could be dispatched with a Walther PPK and silencer—"

"—or Death's sword." I'd been practising with Ezra and was keen to use it.

"Then the world wouldn't be as dangerous. But tech is an invisible enemy. We are fighting in the dark, and the enemy is in each citizen's hands. From ten-year-olds to pensioners."

"I didn't think the Queen would have a mobile. I pictured her as a landline-only type of gal."

Robert gave a sardonic chuckle. "Her handbag holds a handkerchief, a pistol, a powder puff and a mobile phone. Word is, shortly after Tony Blair won the 1997 general election, he convinced the Queen to get a Nokia 6110. Soon afterwards, palace officials started complaining about how much time she spent in the loo. They almost called the royal physician, but it turned out she was addicted to playing Snake."

"Better than shooting grouse, I guess."

"Whichever way we play it, Alisha, this is going to be a tough ride. I don't see how we're going to come out on top."

What was that saying? The only thing necessary for the triumph of evil was for good men—or women—to do nothing. It didn't matter if I was being manipulated or pulled along by fate. It would be wrong to sit this one out when I knew I had the power to help.

"That's easy, Robert. I'm going to visit Hermes." I sounded braver than I felt, but it was clear we didn't have any other options. What kind of woman was I if I sat pretty while my country suffered?

Robert hesitated. "Marina will hate me for sending you into danger." A rustling of pages came down the line as if the detective had opened a file. "Our intel tells us he's still living at the tower. His previous professions were calligrapher, forger, head honcho at Royal Mail and Senior Manager of the Nokia text message team. He's not to be trifled with. He's clever, resourceful, and gifted in translation and interpretation, trading and thievery. Some say he escorts the souls of the deceased to the afterlife. Roads and boundaries are his bread and butter. Perhaps that's why he excelled at Royal Mail. His winged cap and boots give him flight, and his staff has the power to make people fall asleep or wake."

I gritted my teeth. "Sounds delightful."

Robert paused. "Alisha? Over the centuries, he's been known as a god of the winds, but I don't believe he has power over them."

I sighed. "That's something, at least."

"I hate to do this to you. But it's for Crown and country, you know?"

I ignored the knots in the pit of my belly. "Well, you know me. I like a challenge. I just need you to do one thing for me in exchange."

A note of determination. "Name it."

"Go and see Marina, will you?"

13

With its moats, two concentric walls and protection towers, the Tower of London remained the most heavily fortified place in the city. It had a formidable reputation. Henry VIII had sent two wives and dissenting clergymen to be imprisoned and executed there. I had visited as a tourist to see the crown jewels and armour displays, view the poppy installation and ice skate in its moat under twinkling Christmas lights.

Once, I would have worried about what to wear to face a god. I knew now that all we had been told about respect and rituals should be labelled myth and dogma. Some of these gods were as flawed as the rest of us. It didn't matter that I hadn't washed my feet or prepared an offering. It didn't matter that I wasn't wearing virgin white or flowers in my hair.

All that mattered were my intentions and those of the gods.

As a precaution, we arrived under the moonlight when Ezra would be his strongest. I carried my catalogue of creatures in a satchel and wore my baldric and sword on my back. Echo had been tempted to wear the armour Rajika had commissioned for him, but we didn't want to give the impression of war, not when the Ravenmaster might be amenable to peace. I hadn't even told the goddess we were coming here. It was a scoping mission only.

We gathered by the Starbucks across from the Tower of London. That hadn't been there in the thirteenth century.

Like me, Ezra had dressed all in black. His chin-length hair, usually loose, had been tied in a man-bun. He obviously meant business. "I can't believe you talked me into this."

"You're coming because you know me well enough to know I'd go through with it without you."

Ezra grimaced. "If you're getting into trouble anyway, I'm going to be there to protect you. Think of it as penance for setting you up to fail at the performance. I should have realised your animation powers might differ from your grandmother's."

"How could you have known? I don't blame you."

A vein throbbed in his neck as if his perceived failure pained him, but he tried to lighten the mood. "We get in. We find the Ravenmaster and figure out if he's a friendly. We fix this, if only because I can't take another one of the PM's reshuffles. I'd rather Mr Bean ran the country than him at the moment. In fact, I might go and find Rowan Atkinson after this."

"If we get out alive, young wolf." Echo's emerald eyes scanned the coffee shop as if Hermes might be picking up a latte.

I bit my lip. "At least the ravens should be gone. They have some of the biggest bird brains in the animal kingdom. If that wasn't scary enough, even the English language calls them a murder of crows or unkindness of ravens."

Ezra raised an eyebrow. "I'm pretty sure they brought it on themselves by eating the flesh of the dead. It probably began with them feasting on human flesh after bloody executions in the tower."

"All carnivores eat the flesh of the dead. In their eagerness for carrion, the ravens have no airs and graces about it. They are simply opportunistic survivors. It's quite commendable, really."

A coffee-slurping customer emerged from the shop and did a double-take at my sword and the cat.

"We're off to a fancy dress party. The cat wanted to come," I said.

"Looks like you're in for a wild night. Have fun, lass," said the man.

I waited for him to disappear around the corner and gave a grim smile. "Come on. Let's get this over with."

The keys to the Tower of London were kept on an enormous iron ring, guarded by Beefeaters in their dark blue-and-red tunics, topped by a round-brimmed hat. Once inside, the building was a maze with endless stairwells and arrow-slit windows. But with Ezra at our side, we didn't have to worry about walls, security or even floor plans. As a creature of the night, Ezra knew the scent of ravens, which was our key to entry and placement. The ravens may have fled the tower, but their night enclosures remained in situ, together with their fallen midnight feathers. Ezra only needed to orient himself to their stench, and with a sense of smell a hundred times greater than a human nose, this would be a home run. He could smell prey over a mile away.

We teleported and materialised within the inner walls. The room was vast and dull, with the night enclosures taking centre stage. Travel-sick Echo heaved onto the stone floor, leaving his dinner spattered there. Meanwhile, Ezra checked the room. His body moved differently in here, alert to potential threats, and revealed his predator nature, however gentle he was with me.

Ezra's tense whisper reached me. "Not a raven in sight."

"Then that feast is mine." Echo devoured some chick and quail carcasses with a side of bird biscuits soaked in blood.

I shuddered at the sound of odd knocks and bangs that grew ever closer. The Ravenmaster came for us. I could feel it in my bones. "Quiet, Echo. We're not here for a luncheon. It's spooky enough in here without you chomping on those bones."

A knock sounded inches away.

A chill ran up my spine.

We spun, standing back to back to cover all angles of the room: the wolf, the leopard and I. The knocking echoed in my brain. I focussed on keeping my breath calm. I wanted to exude power, not fear.

There had been no reasoning with Ra, but Pan had been different. I hoped Hermes, too, would be open to conversation. Our plan was to establish a rapport and trick him into revealing his motive and end game. Everyone wanted someone to listen to them. It had been one of my most important life lessons.

The Ravenmaster walked straight through the door, like a ghostly apparition, and then hardened in form. A round-brimmed hat perched on a head of strawberry blond curls and a clean-shaven face. His blue eyes had the brilliance of glaciers.

I almost wet myself.

"Why the surprise? Boundaries are no barrier to me." His voice was throaty and thick, like he'd spent an eternity walking through the halls of the tower. The shadows deconstructed and remoulded themselves around him. "Did you not come here, to my home, with the intent to see me?"

I trembled. "We did, Ravenmaster."

The Ravenmaster stepped closer. He wore the distinctive Yeoman Warder's Tudor-style tunic in dark blue with scarlet trim. A scarlet crown and the Queen's initials EIIR embellished the chest area, and a belt accentuated his slim build and broad shoulders. In his manicured hands he held a short staff entwined with two snakes and topped by a pair of ornate wings. Knock, knock went his staff on the stone floor.

He towered over me. "Why did you break into my home, druid?"

Echo and Ezra bristled next to me, but we had a plan: keep the peace and make him talk.

I held my ground, although there was a hair's breadth between us, and I could see tiny golden wings fluttering from his hat and boots. My heartbeat drummed in my ears. My mum had taught me to be polite. "We wondered if you could tell us what happened to the ravens."

"Pah," said the Ravenmaster. "The ravens. I have lived through centuries, known countless kings and queens and the All-Father himself, yet all anyone wants to know about is the ravens. How I tire of this world."

"You don't seem to like ravens very much," said Ezra.

"So you might surmise, wolf. I feed those creatures, tend to them when they are poorly and counsel them when stressed. I bury their bodies in our raven cemetery and utter a prayer. Ungrateful swine. Did you know how mischievous those creatures are? Raven George was dismissed for eating television aerials, and Raven Grog was last seen at an East End pub called the Rose and Punchbowl. He had a penchant for a pint of Fosters."

I frowned. "Are you saying that your ravens went for a drink?"

His eyes flashed. "Of course not. Ravens can't just disappear. I clipped their secondary flight feathers myself to limit flight. They're only capable of short flights. It's not like they can go for a jaunt across the countryside. Pesky little creatures."

"Ungrateful too," Echo purred. "Having snacked on some of their food, I feel you treated them very well."

The Ravenmaster glowered. "Mice, rats, quail, even an egg a week and they still act like strutting deviants. I didn't serve twenty-two years in the military and achieve an exemplary record for those fools to make it look like I can't do my job. Last week, Raven Merlin attacked Yeoman Warden Harold's lip just for looking at him the wrong way. I had to pull him off and hope Harold would still have some lip left."

Echo growled. "The ravens do seem like scoundrels of the lowest order. At least in this job, you get to eat beef every day."

The Ravenmaster gave a heavy sigh. "Leopard, the origin of the Beefeater nickname does indeed stem from beef-eating. The king wanted to ensure the Yeoman Wardens were a muscular type. But sadly, nowadays, with veganism running rampant through the palace officials, we now only eat it twice a week."

I'd been hyper-alert since he'd entered the room, but I started to relax. Whatever was going on, the Ravenmaster seemed like a grumpy old man. "You still haven't told us what happened to the ravens."

Blue eyes narrowed at my tone. "I broke their necks."

I sucked in my breath. Maybe this god was a killer, after all.

"Or maybe I didn't." He smiled, and his large, pearlescent teeth glimmered in the moonlight. "All that matters is that, with their absence, I gave fair warning of the coming calamities, just like I did during my years of service on the battlefield. It would be ungentlemanly to attack Crown and country without warning."

"And the message in the sky?" I said.

"Just a little fun. I invented the alphabet, after all. I knew it would tickle your fancy. You are a linguist, after all, as am I. You, too, have an affinity with the winds. In another universe, we could have been friends. It was I who escorted your mother's soul to the afterlife."

A knife twisted in my gut. I found no depth in the Ravenmaster's glacier eyes. The longer we spent in his company, the less I trusted him. "You're lying."

He leaned so close I could smell the sweat from his pores. "Not this time."

Echo snarled in warning, but the Ravenmaster didn't flinch.

Ezra reached for my hand as the air left my lungs.

His bulky form, clad in navy and red, added to the oppressiveness of the raven's quarters. "It was she who told me what your weak point is."

The wound in me, caused by Mum's death, stung. "I don't believe you."

He shrugged. "Suit yourself."

Stick to the mission. Don't get distracted, I told myself. "Why have you been disrupting our communication?"

His blue eyes were overly bright. "Because I am a nostalgic old man who misses the old ways."

"You make it sound like you're harmless, but you're not, are you? You gave Pandora the gift of curiosity, which is why she unleashed the sorrows into the world…greed, envy, hate, pain, disease, hunger, poverty, war."

He was peeved. "When will humans understand that it was a jar, not a box? It wasn't all bad. Pandora unleashed hope into the world after all." The shadows shifted, and I wondered whether his role as an escort of dead souls made shadows dance around him as fire danced around wood. "It is true—I'm not harmless. All gods have the power for creation and destruction in them. For millennia, we have been lambs, but I am enjoying this new era. It alleviates the boredom."

"Boredom?" said Ezra. "Boredom is your reason for wreaking havoc on a country you have served?"

"There speaks a wolf who understands duty. But do you understand desire? Let me spell it out for you. There was a time when I would carry letters sealed by Zeus himself. What a golden age it was.

I was revered and trusted with great tasks. I knew things that no one did." The Ravenmaster sighed. "Once, humans communicated over distances by smoke signals or drumbeats. I trained whole flocks of birds to carry messages. Then came telegraphs and fax machines. How I hated their sound. The headaches they gave me. But they were still slow and ponderous. So I adapted. Telephones rendered me somewhat obsolete, but I am an inventor. I appreciate progress, within reason. I championed postmen. I was the Head of Royal Mail. But then came the internet." His thick voice brimmed with disgust. "Does anyone ever thank me for paving the way? Men have forgotten what they owe the gods." He shook his head. "All these messaging apps. Hundreds of millions of messages sent globally per minute. Meaningless messages. Memes. Emojis. Gifs. I took a job at Nokia, but the other companies accelerated past us. I couldn't keep up. I want to go back to the old ways. How better to do that than to destroy trust in the new technology?" He glanced at the night enclosures and jerked his staff into the air.

I instinctively recoiled, my hands aloft, ready to go on the offensive.

He widened his posture and raised his staff again. "Now get into the cages."

A vice tightened around my chest. "Excuse me?"

The Ravenmaster smoothed out his tunic. "Did you think I'd tell you all that and let you walk away? I've very much enjoyed getting to know you, druid, but your time is up. Meeting the enemy is key to understanding them, and I understand now why you defeated Ra and Pan. You might be a woman, but you have gumption. This is my chance to prove I am stronger than those who have rolled over before me. I will not underestimate you." His voice hardened, and he waved his staff. "Now get in the cages. A little nap until this is all over. I promise you'll be safe."

Echo growled and whipped around. Captivity was a death knell for him. "We cannot trust this god's promises. He has as much integrity as the raven faeces lining the cages."

The Ravenmaster struck a fist against his heart cavity. "It wounds me to hear you say that, leopard. I promise I will provide you with all the chick and quail meat you desire. Your safety is guaranteed. Once you are in there, no one can tamper with you. No mortal nor immortal will find you unless they have this key." He showed us a large key on an iron ring. "No soul can escape. These enchanted enclosures are one of my cleverest inventions."

Ezra gripped my hand tighter. His other hand flew to his charm necklace. He was ready.

"There's no way we're going to sleep in this creepy little haunted tower." I raised my hands. We hadn't come for war. It didn't mean we were going to leave peaceably, but I didn't want to make the first move.

The Ravenmaster nodded. "I respect those who choose death over captivity."

A trickle of wee definitely escaped me. This god was a heathen.

His thick voiced boomed, and I crumbled inside. "I will not kill you here. There has been enough blood shed in this palace through the centuries. The old laws state that to skin a visitor to one's home is the foulest sin. So I will give you a chance." His sensual lips parted, and his words were a whisper. "Run, little mortals, run!"

I blasted the god with wind, hoping to force *him* into the cage.

His tunic fluttered, but he held his ground easily.

"Run." This time his voice was a foghorn.

Ezra's hand became a vice around my wrist. Echo leapt against his chest, and we fell, fell between the seams of the world, out of the tower, that dark place of blood and torture, bright jewels and black feathers. The breath left my body as we tumbled through the mists and the stones, and I didn't know if the grasping hands were Ezra's or mine or the Ravenmaster's.

We emerged by the coffee shop, spluttering and sprawling on the floor, with Ezra's chest slashed red by Echo's leap.

I looked at him aghast and pulled off my scarf so I could wrap his torso.

He winced. "There's no time. I'll live. My thistle charm will heal me."

Echo swayed with motion sickness. "I am sorry, wolf."

And then the Ravenmaster was there, in his Beefeater tunic and hat, his face contorted with malice. He lunged for us, and we scattered under flickering lamplight in the now deserted courtyard.

I gasped, unleashing a whirlwind that tore branches off nearby trees. "We have to split up. It's the only way."

The god kept coming, murder written on his face.

"Don't go home, Alisha." Ezra had already torn off his clothes, a grim look in his grey eyes. A sad smile. He looked up at the moon, and already his body contorted, hair sprouting and bones cracking as he took on his wolf form.

My heart twisted. He could have teleported somewhere safe. To the Parisian café we had dined at or the top of the Eiffel Tower. The Ravenmaster had flight, but he couldn't have followed him there so quickly. Except he was protecting me. As I watched, my brave, silver-copper wolf launched himself at the Ravenmaster with a growl that shook me to my core.

I pushed Echo's rump in the opposite direction. "You heard what he said. Go. We're safer if his attention is divided."

Echo bounded off, gathering speed. I winced as the sounds of the fight behind me grew more intense.

A tearing of flesh. Could a god bleed?

Intent laced through every sinew of Ezra's silver-and-copper wolf. He sprang at the Ravenmaster, knocking off his hat. Then he rounded back, attempting to disarm the god of his staff. When that failed, the wolf twisted, clamping his jaw on the Ravenmaster's forearm, where the birds had found a home over the years.

The god struggled to control the beast, frustration chiselled into his features. He might have lost his wide-brimmed hat, but the wings on his boots gave him an edge. He was spritely for an ageing god—and cunning. The Beefeater's uniform hung in shreds, but its wearer remained determined. He shook off the beast time and again as a bullfighter taunts a bull.

The god raised his staff.

Claws and teeth and the wolf's eyes implored me to make use of his sacrifice, and then he went limp.

Grief wailed inside me as I ran, the image of Ezra's limp body in my mind. I wanted to turn back, but I pressed on, my mind whirling.

The catalogue of creatures bumping against my thigh as I ran was useless in the heat of battle. I needed calm to animate. Doing it while running was next to impossible. My wind powers had little effect. I pulled my sword. I could run with my sword and poke the Ravenmaster in the eye before he waved his staff.

I didn't stop to look behind me.

The shadows twisted. My heartbeat thundered like hooves.

I ran through cobbled alleys and past closed pubs until my chest heaved, and I didn't know where I was. I was a forty-year-old woman whose legs were already jelly from my sprint. My eyes blurred with tears as I tripped over a homeless woman. I didn't apologise but raced on, my lungs burning.

I'd been stupid to attempt this. I'd been stupid to put my friends in danger. I couldn't do this without them.

Just when my legs were about to give out, a hand reached for me in the darkness.

I unleashed a blood-curdling scream.

14

───────

The hand, consisting of four knobbly grey fingers, pulled me onto a ledge in the darkness.

I cried out as a triangular head with large, milky eyes loomed into focus.

"Flinar!" I threw my arms around him, forgetting for an instant our precarious position in the black hole he'd created.

The elf smiled with delight. "I like helping my druid friend. The elves remember what you did for us when we were blamed for the tremors. Thanks to you and the wolf, we have a community now. I was drinking mead when one told me you were running through the streets like a madwoman." He hiccupped.

I put the sword back in my baldric and peered at him in the darkness, my pulse still heightened. "Are you drunk, Flinar?"

He hiccupped again. "Just a little. The elven community is a very merry sort, especially now we have you as a friend. We feel understood." He leaned his wispy head against my shoulder. "I feel loved."

I clutched his tiny muscular body. "A god was chasing me, Flinar."

Flinar's sail-like ears, situated high up on his skull, twitched. "Many elves, including me, have had run-ins with Hermes. It started when he was at Royal Mail. He hated mischievous elves who spun road signs or created dead ends and lost pathways with their black hole magic. He takes roads and boundaries very seriously. He never gave us credit for how we clean the streets of cigarette butts, splatters of pigeon poo and gloopy chewing gum."

I shook my head. "I can't get my head around the fact they've been walking amongst us for so long."

His ashen face creased into a smile. "We all have, Alisha. You just weren't alive to it before."

My chest remained tight with fear. "Can the Ravenmaster find us here?"

"I was a naughty elf. I created a black hole for him too." A throaty chuckle bubbled out of him. "It was deeper than this with no ledge, so he must have fallen like a stone in a well unless his boots and hat stayed on. My magic can't hold him for long, though. I think he's escaped already. We can stay here for as long as you like, but we would get hungry." He patted the ledge from which our feet dangled. "And uncomfortable."

I stood up on the ledge, a sense of urgency in every fibre of my body. "I have to get back to Ezra. I have to help him."

Flinar's milky eyes widened. "The wolf is in trouble?"

"I think so. He shifted to fight the Ravenmaster. He was bleeding. He went limp."

His nostrils flared, and he set back his knobbly shoulders. His knickerbockers had been updated. He wore leggings with his tunic instead. "I will take you to him. Where did you leave him, Alisha?"

"The Starbucks. Outside the Starbucks by the Tower of London."

His four fingers wove through mine.

We vanished, and a popping sound filled my ears as we emerged on the forecourt where Ezra had bled.

Flinar's eyes swept the area, his billowing ears alert to every sound. "No wolf. And no blood. Are you sure it was here?"

Sorrow and panic swept through me. My eyes blurred with tears. "He must be here. Or in the Tower. Maybe the Ravenmaster took him back there."

He reached for my hand. "Or maybe he went home. You need to tell the alpha."

ECHO HAD BEEN TOLD NOT to go home. I needed to make sure he was okay. I had a hunch that he'd head for Marina's surgery. It was nearing the dead of the night, but we found a phone box and telephoned Marina anyway. It wouldn't have been the first time. Flinar pointed out which women were his friends from the postcards from sex-workers in the telephone booth while we waited for Marina to pick up.

"What do you mean Ezra has disappeared?" Worry clouded her usually sunny voice. "Yes, yes, Echo's here. He disrupted my reunion with Robert. I'd only just slipped into that lacy teddy. Thanks for egging him on, by the way. What a swine the Ravenmaster is. What can we do to help?"

"Stay put for now. Don't let Echo out. I'm not sure it's safe. I'm heading to the farmhouse to tell Gunnolf what's happened. Maybe Ezra's there."

A rush of words. "You're going to walk into a den of wolves without Ezra at your side? No way, José. Over my dead body. I'm calling Orpheus at his club to give you some backup."

I grimaced. "Why would you do that? I don't need Orpheus to daddy me."

"Talk sense, Alisha. Orpheus is one of your few allies in the senate. He cares about you. You don't need to be an empath to feel that. And he has real clout. You need him in your corner when you face the alpha."

I swept back the escaped tendrils of my hair with a shaky hand. "Okay, okay. You win."

"Head to his club. I'll ring ahead and let him know you're coming. And Alisha?" Her voice came down the line, a caress that made me long for a hug. She gave the best hugs. "Echo said Ezra might need stitching up. I'm only a phone call away."

I hung up. "Flinar, will you take me to Orpheus Might's

gentleman's club in Charing Cross, please?"

He reached out his hands. "It would be my honour."

We appeared with a pop in front of Orpheus's three-storey Georgian building.

Flinar bowed. "I wish you luck, Alisha. I must leave you here. The senate are no friends to elves."

I crouched down to his height. "I understand."

The elf pursed his lips. "It might be nothing, but tonight, as the elves indulged in mead and merriment, a redhead arrived to speak to one of them. I heard snatched conversation. I think she means you harm."

"The wolf, Rashida, perhaps? She's in love with Ezra," I said. Ezra wouldn't tolerate open warfare, but I wouldn't put it past Rashida to be underhanded. "Pale skin, big brown eyes, flame-red hair."

He nodded. "That's her. I'll find out what I can. Be careful."

"Thank you, Flinar. You saved me tonight."

"As you have saved me many times before." He hiccupped, stepped into a slice of night and was gone.

I dusted off my trousers and scanned the house. A single candle burned on an upper floor, visible through the netted multi-pane windows. The last time I'd been here, I'd had my friends in tow, and now they were scattered god-knew-where across the city. I recalled the business card Orpheus had once given me and rapped on the door seven times in quick succession.

Silence reigned, and I raised my fist to knock again when the door opened with a click.

Orpheus opened the door with a tumbler of whiskey in his hand. He wore a slick tuxedo. His bowtie lay undone around his nape, and his unbuttoned collar revealed the pale skin beneath. "What brings you to my door at this hour, druid? I was relaxing with Charlotte Brontë's *Jane Eyre* after hosting a rather fractious casino night here. Of course, I first read it almost two centuries ago. On my copy, the author is known as Currer Bell."

"Didn't Marina call ahead?"

"The landline rang, but the lackey who answers it was already in his coffin."

"Sorry, do you mind?" I took the whiskey from his hand and downed it in one fell swoop, wincing as I handed the empty glass back to him.

"Whatever is the matter, Alisha? It can't be that witch Lavinia's meddling." His brow furrowed as he read my thoughts.

I allowed him to delve into the horrors of my night without a word of censure. If I asked him to come with me. I owed him that much, at least.

Orpheus swore under his breath. "Wait here. I'll get my keys."

He was gone and back in a flash and pulled the door closed behind him before ushering me into a panther-like vehicle at the kerb.

I wasn't good at cars. After all, I didn't even own one. It was only when I climbed into the swanky, dark leather interior and peered at the badge on the steering wheel that I realised it was a Lotus.

Orpheus threw me a glance. "Extravagant, I know, but I only own the one. I like my cars to go as fast as me."

He reached across to fasten my seatbelt, and I caught the scent of his dark chocolate-and-sweet cherry beard oil from his goatee.

Goosebumps raced up my arms. Ezra smelled of mountain air and cigarette roll-ups. Or maybe he didn't anymore. Maybe he was just ashes scattered in a raven cemetery by now. I shuddered.

Orpheus turned on the engine and put his foot on the accelerator. "The wolf knows how to take care of himself. You did the right thing coming to me. The motorway will be clear. We'll be at the farmhouse in no time." He threw me a sideways glance. "Lavinia went out of her way to hurt you at Wildwoods. I don't agree with the purity decrees regarding mating, even if genealogy is my responsibility. Diversity in nature is of great merit. And I understand carnal desires more than most men."

I gulped. It probably wasn't my best idea to be locked alone in a car with a vamp at night.

He sighed. "I learned long ago to control my desires, druid."

We sped down city roads until we reached the motorway. The Lotus purred like a cat, lulling me into a daze, with my thoughts fracturing into tiny horrors of what could be.

Orpheus's piano-player hands rested lightly on the steering wheel, although the speed gauge showed we were well over the speed limit. His profile, with his Roman nose, stern lips and longish black hair, fell alternately into shadow and amber light. "I want to chastise you, Alisha, but you're more courageous than those with thrice your power. This city has been my home for centuries. How can I admonish you for standing against those who wish to harm it?" He sighed. "It pained me to see you fail at the Wildwoods performance."

"It doesn't matter. It pushed me to realise I can only animate winged creatures. That's why I failed, Orpheus. An owl would have worked, but a fox…a fox set me up to fail."

His heavy brows pulled together. "Margola's manoeuvring forced your hand. It is not like her to be so obsessed with undermining someone. She usually has a better relationship with the truth. Senate members are too advanced for me to read their thoughts. Perhaps there is female jealousy at play."

I laughed. "She has no reason to be jealous of me."

He shrugged. "When does jealousy ever need a reason? Isn't it more about the jealous person's insecurities than it is about the recipient of the ire? Although, Margola is well within her rights, of course, to suggest you are terrible at being told what to do. I will try to smooth things over with Gunnolf, but I need you to follow my lead. Can you do that?"

I nodded. I couldn't get the image of Ezra's limp body out of my mind.

"I need you to say it, Alisha."

"I can do that. Thank you, Orpheus."

Orpheus grunted. "We only tell the alpha as much as he needs to know. If you need to pass something by me, you do it telepathically. I can read your thoughts and push my own thoughts into your head. Do it casually. It's a trick the alpha dislikes. It reminds him of how basic his own talents are."

He turned onto a slip road, manoeuvred a roundabout, past a set of traffic lights, and soon we pummelled down a dirt track towards some woods. A few minutes more and the pack farmhouse appeared.

Orpheus parked the Lotus next to a pick-up truck and let the engine idle for a moment longer as if collecting his thoughts. Then we climbed out. As the car doors thumped shut, the wolves howled in response.

The sound made me tremble.

"Here. The night is chill." Orpheus draped his jacket around my shoulders.

We trudged across the lawn where I'd been only days before when Ezra introduced me to the pack. The sprawling, white farmhouse lay ahead, bordered by the orange dahlias, and already, wolves waited on the dilapidated deck. Gunnolf stood in the centre, dressed in head-to-toe denim. On his left, Dominic, the huge, tawny wolf, bristled. On his right stood Rashida's beautiful red wolf and Maximillian's silver-white wolf, their eyes never leaving our faces.

"We could smell you a mile away." Gunnolf turned his nose up at us. "You know I don't like unannounced visits, Orpheus."

Orpheus raised an eyebrow. "Who does?"

"I could have made an exception for a game of cards, but you brought the druid." His lip curled at Orpheus's attire. "A little overdressed for a trek in the woods, aren't you? And you dare to bring a sword to my house, druid?"

Deirdra, in human form, waved from the kitchen window.

I didn't dare wave back.

"There is no time for our usual games, Gunnolf," said the vampire. "Is Mr Neuhoff here?"

The red wolf showed her teeth and emitted a low growl.

Gunnolf frowned. "I am not my nephew's keeper, as you well know. He is less obedient than the other wolves."

I clenched my fists. Anxiety made half-moon imprints of my nails in the soft flesh of my palm. "So he isn't here?"

The alpha's gravelly voice pulsed with irritation. "No, druid. My nephew is not here."

I cried out in anguish. The Ravenmaster had taken Ezra—perhaps worse—and without his teleporting skills, there was no way to return to the tower. To check if he was okay. In my hurry to solve this crisis, I had assumed my lucky innings against Ra and Pan meant I would always succeed.

And now Ezra had paid the price for my hubris.

Next to me, Orpheus stiffened. *If you want to save your boyfriend, stop drowning in pity. We have no choice but to tell him. And by that, I mean me because the alpha's disdain for you is obvious.*

I flinched. *You really need to work on your sensitive side.*

Orpheus stepped forward. "We should go inside."

Gunnolf's hackles rose. "Just spit it out, old man."

"As you wish. Mr Neuhoff was on an unsanctioned mission tonight with Ms Verma here. They got into trouble and scattered. The Ravenmaster captured the wolf."

A growl ripped from Rashida's red wolf. She lunged forward, flying through the air.

Gunnolf sprang forward off the deck, plucked her mid-leap and held her to the ground. His hand lingered on her panting body, both a scold and a caress.

She whimpered and quietened.

He straightened up, his dark eyes brimming with hatred. He pointed a finger at my chest. "You convinced my nephew to go after a god? We told him you were bad news. We told him to walk away. Are the two of you incapable of listening? We should cast you out." He swung around to Orpheus. "She is consumed by her desires and has no thought for duty. I stood against her at her trial vote, did I not? And yet the fools amongst us decided to give her a cloak of respectability. Well, look where it has led us."

The timbre of Orpheus's voice was a sharp prick of warning. He flicked Gunnolf's finger away from my chest. "Careful who you call a fool, alpha."

Their eyes met, and neither backed down.

Gunnolf glowered. "There will be consequences for this lack of discipline. First, I will need to interview the druid to find out what she knows. You may leave, Orpheus."

"On the contrary," said Orpheus. "The druid need not stay. I have read her thoughts and can tell you what has occurred."

"I will not let the druid leave unless she makes an oath on her father's life not to go after Ezra."

I won't abandon him, I thought.

Then you will never leave here. And what good will that do your wolf?

Orpheus nodded at Gunnolf without a step change. He'd been practising this trick for centuries. "You mean to find the wolf?"

The alpha's lips twisted. "How do you expect us to track a teleporting werewolf? It is suicide challenging a god. How are we supposed to get inside the tower undetected without my nephew's skills? It's not like the wolves can storm it. No, Orpheus. We won't seek Ezra." He cast me a glance. "As much as I love my nephew, he made his own bed. I will not sacrifice the pack in a hunt we are sure to lose."

He would leave his own nephew to rot, I thought.

Don't do anything stupid. Orpheus inclined his head. "Then I am sorry, Gunnolf. Your nephew is a good man."

"My nephew should have known better who to trust. Like his father before him, he let his desire for a woman stand in the way of his duty."

Orpheus searched the alpha's face for a fraction longer than comfortable. "I heard about the murder investigation. You are no closer to finding the culprit."

Gunnolf gave a bitter laugh. "You are right. I have my own troubles here, but even with a closed case, my answer would have been the same."

One thought rolled through my head. *What an arsehole. He's known Ezra all his life.*

A nerve twitched in Orpheus's neck. *The alpha is merely putting his own skin above his nephew's.*

I tried hard to swallow my emotions, but they broke the dam of my control. It didn't matter that the alpha and the god scared me or that I ignored Orpheus's counsel.

Druid, don't—

I squared my shoulders to hide my fear. "I won't leave Ezra's survival to fate, even if you are willing to."

Orpheus dropped all undercover communication and spun towards me. "Don't be ridiculous, druid." *I can't help you now.*

Gunnolf's eyes lit up with unconcealed malice. "Then welcome to your new home, Alisha Verma. I hope you don't live to regret your decision."

15

Gunnolf flung me into Ezra's room. "You'll be staying here. I've confiscated your sword until this is all over. You can keep your little book of creatures. Fat lot of good it does you. We'll make sure you're fed and watered. I promised Orpheus I wouldn't harm you, but if you try any funny business, I won't be responsible for what follows. Rashida is on first watch outside your door, and she doesn't need an excuse to rip your throat out."

I ached for Ezra.

Would I even know if he had died?

I sorely regretted not keeping my mouth shut. I could have grabbed a cat nap in Orpheus's Lotus on the way back to London and gone after Ezra without Gunnolf being any wiser. I had to find out what happened to him and make the Ravenmaster pay. "How can a Justice Minister think it's okay to lock away a person without due process? What kind of archaic system is this?"

Gunnolf smirked. "I can do whatever I want, Alisha. Who's going to stop me?"

He strode out of the room, giving me a glimpse of Rashida still in wolf form.

The door clicked shut, and a key turned in the lock.

This wasn't how I had imagined alone time in Ezra's room. I'd only been here once before on my whistle-stop tour, but this time, I surveyed my surroundings properly. It was a spacious room, furnished simply, the stripped floorboards topped with a threadbare rug. A king-sized bed with charcoal bedding took centre stage. A small chest of drawers had been placed on one side of the bed, a lamp and framed picture of Ezra's parents balanced on top. There was a slim wardrobe, a sink, and a cracked mirror in the corner. The window had been left open just a sliver—the whole house reeked of damp wolf— but I had no hope of escape with the pack lurking on the decking below. Not when there were so many of them. Not when I was alone and didn't trust my own powers.

I sighed and dumped my satchel on the bed before pulling out my mobile phone to check my battery life. Thirty-eight per cent. Enough to get me through the night. Then I'd be well and truly cut off from help. Orpheus was long gone. He'd been pissy about me ignoring his instructions and roared off into the night in his Lotus like a bat out of hell. My instinct was to ping a text to Marina, but I held back. The Ravenmaster could alter the intent of my message, block its sending or track me here, where I was a sitting duck. Even a phone call would be risky. Not to mention that Rashida's wolf hearing meant nothing would be secret.

Ezra's limp wolf body flooded back into my mind.

A sense of urgency came over me. I had to get out of there.

I could try to blast myself out of the room, like a twisted Dorothy from Oz creating the tornado that ripped through Kansas. But I was pretty sure Ezra loved this place. Targeting my wind powers could work against the pack if they were one-on-one, but they worked as a team, and I was all alone.

I screwed up my face, trying to ignore the *rat-tat-tat* of my heart, willing me to be quicker, cleverer, and braver so I could save Ezra. I could feel the silent tug of my connection to Tielbu, but his journey here could last through the night and every second counted. It stung my pride that the wolves hadn't even bothered to confiscate my catalogue of creatures in case I tried to animate a giant getaway goose or something. However, when I opened up the catalogue to instil life into a winged creature, my fingers couldn't find the dimensions I needed, and I felt like a screw-up all over again.

But when I barely had time to go to the loo in peace, how on earth was I supposed to find time to train?

Love had been a good emotion to ground me when I tried to animate, but how could I feel love when separated from and fearful for my loved ones?

No, my escape would have to be more humdrum.

I sped around the room, checking for anything that might give me an advantage. In Ezra's chest drawers, I found rolls of boxer shorts, like he was some sort of Marie Kondo folding genius. I uncovered a plentiful supply of grey socks, a man-bag of toiletries, a packet of flavoured condoms that made me blush and a stash of Stephen King books at the bottom of his wardrobe.

Nothing to help me escape. No knives, no whips, no handcuffs. Nada. What was that man thinking?

A cooing at the window caught my ears. I swivelled and noticed a set of enormous teeth and fiery eyes. The creature squeezed in through the open window and perched on a small chest of drawers beside the bed, its pink claws scratching the surface. It looked rabid, with unkempt feathers, a muscly chest and an orange beak that barely contained its huge gnashers. Then it transformed before my eyes, stretching upwards and outwards, his beak, teeth and feathers morphing into his human self in a mind-boggling feat I would rather not have seen.

I sprang forward just in time to prevent a framed picture of Ezra's parents from clattering to the floor. "Sahil."

My brother cupped his hand over his bits and darted across the floorboards to grab a pair of jeans from Ezra's closet. "Hello, sis. I don't suppose the werewolf would mind me borrowing these? A little birdie told me you needed my help."

I averted my eyes. "Orpheus?"

Sahil pulled on Ezra's trousers. "The vampire? Of course not. Marina called me."

"I'm surprised you answered. I wrote you a postcard this week.

You used to love them when we were kids. I figured you'd respond to that."

He shrugged. We had the same mouth and slim nose, but his eyes were more almond than round. "It's probably buried under a pile of junk mail at the penthouse." He might not have been my favourite person, but it was a relief to see his face. "So they put you in Ezra's room, eh?"

"I think they want me to drown in guilt. Trapped in a nest of vipers, and I only have myself to blame. Keep your voice down. I don't suppose you're here to break me out."

Sahil dropped his voice to a whisper. "I'm afraid I'm not the Tarzan type. I can't carry a fully grown woman on my werepigeon back, either. I'm here to make up for abandoning you during our Wildwoods trial. I did feel a bit of guilt about that, you know."

I hugged him. "I should have been there for you more after Mum died. I've been distracted. You know I love you, though?"

He regarded me quietly for a moment, and then his face broke into a smile. "It's not easy when your little sister suddenly becomes a star in a world neither of you knew existed."

I grimaced. "I think you'll find my star is falling fast."

"My powers are developing too, you know," he said. "We seem to be a family of secrets and surprises."

"I saw. So you're a shapeshifter with shield skills. That's pretty damn cool. How did you get them anyway? They don't seem...you know...in line with the family genetics." Even Ezra, with his experience of mentoring initiates, and Orpheus, with his knowledge of genealogy, had been surprised at the unnatural medley of skills Sahil possessed. I had my suspicions Lavinia was the one who had supercharged Sahil's powers. It was the only thing that made sense.

He grinned. "If you must know, I had a little nudge in the right direction after the dinner at Baba Yaga's. The night you animated the dragon. Funny, isn't it? How we were pimping our powers at the same time."

Fingers of apprehension crawled over my skin. I knew we shouldn't have left him alone at Lavinia's, but if he were here to help, I wouldn't be a sourpuss.

"Listen, when Marina told me your predicament, I had an idea. I'm going sneak into the Tower of London and check whether Ezra is there."

A chink of hope opened up in me. "You'd do that for me?"

"It'll be a cinch. I can go wherever I want to these days. I don't need tickets or invitations for anything. You just need to tell me how you hid from the Ravenmaster. In case he comes for me too."

"Flinar the elf helped me."

Sahil nodded slowly. "Of course he did. Black hole magic?"

"Yes. He trapped the Ravenmaster and created an alternate pocket for me."

"Right, I'll be off then and will report back."

I gripped his arm. "Just be careful, will you? I can't lose anyone else. And I *really* want to fill you in on Dad's shenanigans with Alma."

He dropped his trousers.

"Jesus, Sahil. Keep it clean, will you?"

"Sorry, sis. Shifters get used to the nudity pretty quickly. We don't have much choice."

Even as he spoke, his voice transformed from intelligible and manly to a pigeon coo. He sprouted feathers in his nether regions first, his nose flattened, and his mouth became a beak.

Then pop. He was the size of a Wellington boot.

We were, without a doubt, the weirdest family ever.

He looped around the room to show off and then soared out of the window. I watched his progression over the sleeping wolves and into the woods, feeling both proud and envious. He'd just disappeared from sight when my phone buzzed in my pocket.

"Alisha?" came Marina's voice through the line. "Orpheus told me you're a fool who asked to be imprisoned."

"You shouldn't be calling me on this."

"What choice did I have?" she said.

I cupped my hand over my mouth. "They've got me holed up in Ezra's room."

"Listen, I made a mistake. I was worried about you. I called Sahil and told him what happened, but I shouldn't have, Alisha. I really shouldn't have. I sensed something down the line—a blackness. Don't trust him. And don't tell him anything."

Oh, shit. I listened, my ears burning.

She hurtled on. "Echo's out trying to get Ezra's scent, so we'll get to the bottom of this. You hear me?"

"Yeah, I hear you." I cast my mind back through my conversation with Sahil. What had I told him? Had I willed him to be on my side when he really wasn't?

"I'm going to hang up now. Just stay safe. Tell me you're safe."

"I'm safe." I'd mentioned Flinar, but his black hole magic had grown stronger and he knew this city better than anyone. He could look after himself.

"Stay that way." Marina ended the call.

I had to get our lives back on track. I couldn't sit around waiting to be rescued. What was I missing? I had to be cleverer than I had been with Pan, and my allies were scattered everywhere. I had no idea anymore who was foe and who was friend.

The Ravenmaster's whole reason for messing with humdrum lives —and ours—was because he felt out of control in this new world. He'd been at Nokia, but that meant the world was progressing too fast for even him to keep up. Which meant his skillset fell short. It suddenly seemed so obvious. To intercept messages in a city the size of London, he needed expert help. But who could be helping him?

The seeds of a plan took root in my mind.

If my brother was playing both sides, I needed to find another way to help Ezra as well as flush out our enemies. As far as I could tell, there were three of us who loved Ezra and would move mountains to help him.

A few hours later, when the moon revealed the wolves asleep on the decking and the house was quiet, I slung my satchel on, splashed water on my face at the sink to chase away my drowsiness and knocked on the bedroom door.

Rashida's sleepy voice filtered through the hard wood. "I have my orders. I'm not opening up, druid."

"Do you always obey orders when the life of someone you love is at stake?"

A pause, and then the lock clicked open.

I stood back just before Rashida shoved the door open.

She stood barefoot, in light joggers and a T-shirt, her red hair cascading across her shoulders. Her lips formed a snarl. "I should tear you apart for what you've done to him."

I nodded. I'd feel the same way. Ezra had followed me into battle. We'd been unprepared. I wouldn't make that mistake again. "How about we work together to save him instead?"

Her brown eyes narrowed. "Why should I trust you?"

"We both love him, don't we? And as far as I can see, Gunnolf is doing zilch to rescue him."

"Gunnolf hasn't been himself recently. He's under a lot of pressure." She hesitated. "But that doesn't mean we leave Ezra in the lurch. Pack is family. All right, druid. Let's hear your plan."

"You have a better relationship with Lavinia. I'd like you to ask her rats to report on Ezra's whereabouts. Or she can get one of the witches to scry for him. We need to know where he is and if he's moving."

Rashida nodded. "Say I agree. What next?"

It was true. In a way, we were on the same team, but that hadn't been the main reason for me to reach out to her.

She'd unlocked the door just as I wanted her to.

I channelled calm and stepped back slowly towards the window. The wolves were still sound asleep on the deck. Rashida was on the rug, just where I needed her. My hands tingled as I raised them. Before Rashida could react, a gust of wind knocked her off her feet, and another one rolled her into the rug, wrapping her tight, with her hands pinned against her sides. Not so much sexy lady as sausage lady.

Her muffled cry followed me out of the room. I locked it behind me, pocketing the key. Even in her human form, Rashida would be a formidable adversary. I didn't know how long it would take her to unravel herself or rouse the sleeping wolves, but she wasn't getting out of that room until someone helped her.

My heart hammered out of my chest. I crept down the stairwell, cringing with every creak lest I rouse the pack. My back lay flat against the wall as I rounded corners, and I chose the back door to give the sleeping wolves a wide berth. A triple padlocked door caught my attention in the downstairs hallway, given the wolves were so lax with security, but I didn't have time to linger. I swept my sword out of an umbrella stand and swiped the pick-up keys from a hook on the wall by the back door.

Easing the door open a fraction, I slipped through it and fixed my eyes on the pick-up in the distance. When I reached the lawn, I ran like the devil was after me, hoping the long grass would muffle my footsteps. The pick-up was parked at the top of the estate, not more than a few minutes away at a run.

I had to make it.

I thought I was going to until a crash sounded behind me. I risked a glance and almost collapsed there and then.

Rashida had jumped through Ezra's window in wolf form. Clean through it, as if her anger at me had made her invincible. There was resolve in her eyes and every leap. She howled as she ran, stirring the other wolves to action.

I was an English teacher, not a bloody warrior. Fear made my knees wobble. My satchel bounced against my thigh, and the sword in its baldric poked my back. I desperately began pressing the automatic door button for the pick-up, hoping I had the right one. Hoping I'd make it to the car and remember which peddle was the accelerator and which was the brake. Hoping the damn wolf wasn't going to bite my arse off.

Up clicked the locks.

Copper eyes in the woods beyond caught my attention, but there was no time to think.

I dove for the door, my feet sliding in the dirt, and wrenched the handle. The door flew open, but just behind me, something in the air changed. I turned, my sense of dread surging.

The red wolf launched herself at me, teeth bared, drool frothing at her mouth.

I lifted my hand, instinctively sending her spiralling into the dirt with a furious wind.

The red wolf bounced off the earth, her bloodlust for me driving her on, the other wolves almost at the pick-up.

I had no choice. I drew my sword, just as Ezra had trained me to do. In the heat of the moment, it felt heavier than ever before. I swung it clumsily as the red wolf charged at me, slicing her front leg.

She howled in pain as she collapsed in a heap on the cold earth under the starry sky.

I tossed the sword into the open pick-up, clambered into the driving seat and stuffed the key into the ignition.

Let there be fuel. My fingers fumbled to find the headlights. I released the handbrake and slammed my foot on the accelerator, pulling away in a whir of wheels as a tawny wolf leapt for the back of the pick-up.

He missed, landing in the dirt next to Rashida.

I sped towards the motorway, jerking and cursing as I got to grips with the truck.

The wolves didn't let up, muscles pounding, gaze fixed on their prize: Gunnolf's big black wolf, Maximillian's tawny one and Ruud, the small grey wolf with the white muzzle. Each of them wanted a piece of me. I ran a red light ahead of a roundabout and prayed the road would be clear. It would have been insane to stop with those beasts in my rear-view mirror. Ezra's wolf had the capacity for gentleness, but I couldn't be sure with these ones. The pick-up swerved as I tried to maintain my speed on the roundabout, and the wolves parted ways to corner me, ruining borders in their wake.

Gunnolf leapt at the side of the truck and clung on, hitting the window with his muzzle, his wolf eyes red in the darkness.

I couldn't have him hanging on like a leech until London. The car swerved as I used one hand to manually roll down the window a third of the way.

The black wolf lunged for me. There was no mercy in his eyes.

Power pulsed through my palm as I sent a tornado to take him to the ground. Just like I'd wanted to do ever since he told me to clean the pack kitchen. His body turned through the air like a ping pong ball, and I returned my focus to the road, pressing hard on the gas, a scream building in my throat. Only when I reached the motorway did Maximillian and Ruud lose ground, slipping away amongst the grasping trees that lined the road.

Exhausted from the impact of the adrenalin, I kept one hand on the steering wheel while I called Sahil for an update on Ezra. It went straight to answerphone, and I had the sinking feeling again that Marina was right.

And Gaia.

And Orpheus.

Hadn't they all told me my brother couldn't be trusted?

Had I been wrong to pooh-pooh all the warnings about him? The cogs of my brain blipped, and not even Smooth Radio could settle my fraught nerves.

Think, Alisha. What are your priorities?

Ezra. Hermes. Sahil.

The empty expanse of the motorway, in noir colours and lighting, acted as a balm for my soul. I reached London as dawn broke over the city, my sword—sticky with Rashida's blood—on the passenger seat.

16

My foggy, sleep-deprived brain fought to stay awake as I wound through the streets of Balham towards my flat. I'd been surprised on my drive through the city to discover how many more homeless people lined the streets, as if overnight. Where once there had been the odd person in a doorway with a sleeping bag and collection bucket, now there were tenfold more. The same was true of every town I drove through. Sad, cold, lonely faces poked out of charity shop doorways, railway bridges and bus stops. Had I become so used to being whisked between destinations in Ezra's arms that I'd not noticed the change in the city?

At a red light, a bus driver peered into the car and baulked at the bloody sword lying on the passenger seat. I gave him a wave—hoping that nonchalance would stop him from reporting me to the police—and pushed the sword onto the floor, letting him pull ahead of me as the lights turned green.

A surge of light filled the cab, and I shut my eyes for a moment against the bright dawn. I opened them and jumped out of my skin.

"Sorry it took me so long to get here." Gaia plugged her seatbelt in, despite her immortality. "I was slightly irked that you went to the undead for help. I did hear your prayer while you were being chased into the pick-up truck, but I decided you could handle it alone. I find succeeding during the heat of battle does marvellous things for one's confidence and aptitude. I didn't want to take that learning opportunity away from you. And I hadn't finished my cup of chai. It is such a shame to let that beautifully stewed concoction with all its spices go to waste. I would never have forgiven myself."

I stared at her. "I could have died."

Her cherubic face broke into a knowing smile. "Oh, I doubt it. They might have given you a spanking, but they wouldn't have stooped much lower than that. You're not any old peculiar, after all. You're the granddaughter of Rajika Verma."

"I have to say my grandmother's legacy is more of a burden than a gift."

"But you have so much in common. She, too, fought injustice. Isn't it terrible how many more homeless people have appeared on the streets from London to Leeds, Bath to Belfast, Southampton to Swansea?" Gaia shook her fist. "I have a right mind to cut Hermes apart and bury the pieces of him in pits so far apart that it takes him millennia to reform. But that would blacken my own heart, which I fight so hard to keep clean."

"Why has there been a surge in homeless people? I don't understand it."

"People nowadays never talk to each other. Even in tea shops, where you are supposed to sit face-to-face. All they want to do is stare at their devices. To interact electronically. With strangers. With their mothers, even. I've never seen human nature change. Humans need touch. Now they get most of their touch from screens and tablets. Can only blame themselves, really. Little addicts. Don't they know that a hug is much more satisfying than a game of Candy Crush? Add Hermes to the mix, and of course, these people are on the streets. A few crude texts exchanged for real messages, and he's engendered a family fallout. Or an irate, trigger-happy boss. It's not like warring people pick the phone up to each other anymore. They block away. Wipe the offending person clean out of their life. Et voilà. Relationships fractured overnight."

"The Ravenmaster's doing all of this?"

"Well, of course, he is, child. He's a devious god, after all. Did you expect him to be sitting around twiddling his thumbs, waiting for you to get around to standing up to him?"

I gawped at her. I'd been expecting a shoulder to cry on, and here she was, just prodding me onto a quest that surely should have been hers. The cheek of it.

Gaia rearranged her sandalled feet in the footwell to avoid the blood-stained sword. "I see you've not yet unlocked the full potential of Transcender, but you will. It is forged by a god after all and blessed by another."

I indicated left to turn into my street and swallowed my frustration. I'd seen some of Gaia's faces—the mother, the crone, the warrior—and I knew how quickly she could swing between her personalities. I decided to ask nicely for her support. "Are you here to offer your help? I'm in quite a quandary. Ezra is missing. Hermes is after me. My brother might be a wanker."

Gaia tutted. There was something about her matter-of-fact persona that brought me comfort, even on a night like this. "Language, Alisha. A talented linguist like you should be able to come up with other ways to express yourself."

"Yes, but swearing is good for stress release. And I like the way it emphasises a point."

The goddess nodded. "In all my years, I have only sworn once when Death refused to change the burning pyres of hell into a more environmentally friendly option. It really was very stubborn of her."

Despite my sluggish brain, I logged away the information that Death was female.

Gaia continued. "I did tell you to beware of the pigeon. A trifling but vexatious little creature. But no, druid, I'm just here as a cheerleader. A little bit of motherly support. You're the eternal girl. This is all playing out exactly as I hoped it would. Although I have one piece of advice: don't believe anything Hermes told you unless you see it with your own eyes."

"I think he killed the ravens." A painful lump in my throat. I couldn't let myself imagine it. "Does that mean he'll kill Ezra too?"

"Pah," said Gaia. "That god is a gifted liar. He loves those birds. He loved that job."

I sighed. "Who knows what he's done with them. Or if Crown and country will fall without them."

"I see the superstitious empath is rubbing off on you, druid. It's like seed dispersal in nature. Ideas spread based on who we spend our time with. They catch on like wildfire. Just remember, stories are not all as true as the Bible or Torah or Qur'an. But you must stop the miscommunication, Alisha. Without reliable communication, whole empires can crumble. I have seen it time and again through the ages. I have seen how one cross word tears apart a family. How misreported facts turn communities against one another. How even a king can be manipulated by a carefully planted lie in his mind. He who controls communication controls the world."

A shudder ran through me as I pulled up to the kerb outside the flat. A light shone from inside. I knew my friends awaited me there. "Goddess, I need to know what drives him."

"To Hermes, this is just a game. Do you think he cares for mortals? We all miss the heavens, but some of us learned to care for life. Not Hermes. Mortals are just pawn pieces to him. He is a master of chaos. He won't kill unless he has to. If he has taken the wolf, it is merely to distract you. He saw how easily you dealt with Ra and Pan. His ego drives him to be the one to beat you, and he will want to see your pain and humiliation."

"And the ravens?"

"They are a symbol, that's all. But they are important to him." Her eyes darkened, and she looked down at her fingers, still caked with mud. "If they were dead, he'd have buried them in the raven cemetery, but they are not there."

I gawped at her, imagining her in her sari, knee-deep in bones and feathers and soil-slick with gore.

She frowned. "Don't gawp at me, druid. I've been seeding a meadow of sunflowers. I'm not a grave robber. The soil spoke to me. I am the Earth goddess, after all."

"Of course, goddess." I turned off the ignition.

"Do you know what I find, druid? Often, with mysteries, if you pull one string, the whole ball unravels." She unplugged her seatbelt. "Now, aren't you going to help me out?"

I clambered out of the pick-up, opened the door for her and held out my hand. Her outward appearance gave the impression she was in her seventies after all.

She leaned heavily on my hand as she climbed out and smiled at the tweeting of the early morning birds. The winds quieted at her smile as if to allow her to hear the chorus of the birds better. Gaia stepped onto the pavement, rearranged the folds of her sari and stretched her back.

I reached into the footwell for Transcender, and when I turned, she was gone. There wasn't any point looking for her. The goddess only appeared when she willed it. I sent her silent thanks and staggered up the path to my building, dragging myself through the hallway towards my flat.

Marina, Robert and Echo rushed at me as I tumbled through the door. I sank onto the chair in my hallway as my legs turned to jelly. I didn't have to be strong with my friends here to hold me up.

Marina's hug squeezed the air out of my lungs. "We've been keeping vigil all night. I thought the worry would kill me."

Echo licked me, his dry tongue seeking out any bare skin he could find. My arms, my ankles, my neck. Less ferocious leopard than pussy cat right now. "Let us never split up again, Alisha. In the heat of battle, it was my duty to obey your command, but I have lost a decade of life not knowing how you were faring and not being there to help."

"You look like you've been in the wars," said Robert.

"Yeah, well, we're here to take care of her now." Marina took off my satchel and shoes. Then she unpeeled my fingers from the hilt of Transcender, her mouth a grim line at the sight of the blood, and left the sword in the bathtub.

My whole body trembled.

"Make her a hot cup of tea with lots of sugar," said Marina to Robert. She led me into my en suite bathroom, helped me undress, and then pushed me under the hot jets of the shower while she and Echo paced my bedroom.

I scrubbed myself until my skin was red and sore, gave my hair a cursory wash and grabbed a towel before my legs gave out. In the bedroom, I slipped on knickers and a sports bra over my damp skin with some help from Marina. The clock on my bedside table said it was nearly six a.m. "I have to fill you in."

She bundled me into my bathrobe, fussing to make sure I was wrapped up warm. "We know everything. *The Otherworld News* arrived an hour ago." Marina popped her head out of the bedroom door. "That tea ready, Rob? Bring the newspaper, will you?"

I sank down on the bed. "Already? She keeps making every situation worse."

Echo padded over to sit by me and nuzzled against me. "Deliberately, I fear. My gut tells me she is mixed up in this. Although, my gut is not very reliable when it is empty."

"You know that old saying? I'm not sure if it stems from Socrates or Buddism, the Bhagavad Gita or whether it's just perennial wisdom —before you speak, consider: is it true, is it kind, is it necessary?" Marina sighed. "Well, I'm pretty sure, for someone whose words are currency, Margola Silver has never considered those questions in her life."

Robert came in with the steaming cup of tea and pressed it into my hands. He chucked a newspaper onto my bed.

The hot, sweet tea soothed my aching body as I read the headline.

Trouble at Dawn: Druid Heir Deals Deathly Blow to Wolf Lovers

I sighed. Hadn't Flinar said a redhead had it in for me? I'd assumed he meant Isadora, who'd meddled with matchmaking Ezra. But could he have meant Margola? "Is it too much to ask her to get my version of events? And how did she get that hideous picture?"

She'd chosen one of me running through the woods after Gunnolf and Lavinia's revelation of who Ezra's mate should be. Had she been eavesdropping?

Echo nodded. "You are quite right, Alisha. That is not your best look. Pity it's gone out to the whole of the UK like that. Less Donna Summer's 'Hot Stuff' than Celine Dion's 'All by Myself.'"

I grimaced while skimming the paper. "No need to hammer it

home, Echo. Well, she got the basic facts right. I did abandon Ezra, steal the pick-up and wound Rashida. Looks like she's going to be all right, though."

I wasn't sure how I felt about that.

Echo inclined his head. "Wolves heal quickly, even those who aren't in possession of a healing charm like Ezra."

I flicked through the rest of the newspaper. The inside pages devoted coverage to seven girls who would be facing the Kraglek trial at Wildwoods after the summer holidays. The back page summarised the peculiar sports fixtures, and tucked into a small space next to a crossword was the briefest mention of the communications fall out impacting the humdrum world.

Robert shook his head. "We're coming up to eight cabinet reshuffles, the PM's been caught with his trousers round his ankles after he texted his wife, not his mistress, and there's been a tenfold increase in the number of houses going on the market and petitions for divorce submitted. With the number of petty arguments, I'm worried the birth rate will be impacted. And we can't even tell the population there is a god behind all this, or they'd either label the PM insane or go insane themselves." He reached for Marina's hand. "Marina's been helping out with her empath skills, of course— without her, I'm pretty certain the PM would have thrown in the towel and called a general election by now—but he's exhausted, and we can't afford an election right now. It takes months for a new PM to recover from the shock of hearing about the Otherworld."

Marina's wan face softened into a smile. "I am tired, but you introducing me to all these powerful people is quite an aphrodisiac, darling."

The detective flushed. "Oh, stop it."

She kissed his cheek. "No, you stop it."

"Urgh," said Echo. "Both of you, stop it."

I took a slurp of my tea, my insides warmed by more than the hot brew. Marina glowed at being reunited with the detective, and her happiness meant the world to me. I made myself concentrate on the matter at hand. "When I was trapped at the farmhouse, I was trying to work out who could be helping the Ravenmaster. We know that he's not tech-savvy. At least, not tech-savvy enough to disrupt modern comms all by himself." I hesitated, gathering my thoughts. "What if Margola Silver has taken this dislike to me because she is the Ravenmaster's secret helper? We know how adept she is with tech. We know she operates in the shadows just like him. And we know she has thrown curveball after curveball at me."

The detective nodded slowly. "It makes sense that Margola's knee-deep in this. We used to take a spin class together at Baba Yaga's, and she always struck me as a neutral force. Neither benign nor evil. Just someone who could be manipulated either way. Her coming after you is out of character unless it serves some unknown purpose."

Echo growled. "Then you need to isolate the selkie and speak to her when she is vulnerable, Alisha. And I know just the place to do it. A selkie needs access to the water, and it so happens that I know, from my hunting of the deer at Richmond, where Margola Silver lives. She has a place there that backs out onto the river, and she swims there each morning."

I screwed up the newspaper and arced it into the bin with a display of wind precision that surprised even me.

"I am coming with you," said Echo. "I will not take no for an answer."

"Then the answer is yes." I buried my head in his neck, but even as I did, my head whirred like a computer running different programmes. I remembered Durga, the multi-armed Hindu goddess that Dad had once read me stories about. This must have been what it felt like to be a mother: the competing priorities and the striving to do my best by everyone. "But first, we must move the wolves' pick-up truck. It's a dead giveaway out there. And I must call Lavinia to find out if she has been able to track Ezra. She does have a landline, doesn't she?"

17

Richmond, which sat on the south bank of the Thames, was one of the most affluent boroughs in London, with breath-taking open spaces, a royal palace, riverside views, boating, bridle and cycling paths, independent shops and a weekly farmer's market.

Of course, Margola lived there. She was hardly the sort to be slumming it in the poorer parts of London, with her push-up bra and perfectly coiffed hair. I bet her handbag drawer was full of Louis Vuitton, and I'd definitely seen her carrying a Hermes Birkin, which now seemed like an indisputable link between the two.

I would have liked to have napped at home, as Marina had implored me to do. There was a reason sleep deprivation was delineated as a torture method in international law. But it was only a matter of time before Gunnolf's wrath caught up with me, so I had to make every minute count.

We rode up the tube escalator with Echo in his cat carrier.

"So the witch sent her rats into the tower?" His miaows attracted the stares of a cleaner. "They must have been in good company there."

I kept my voice low and melodic as if I was comforting my stressed Bengal. "She said countless rats had searched for his whereabouts, and not one had made it out alive. The witches' scrying yielded no results either. Maybe the tower has its own magical defences. Or maybe Ezra is…"

Echo growled. "Don't think like that. The wolf might not have a cat's nine lives, but he is an impressive warrior, with wit as well as great natural strengths and the charms given to him by his aunts. We must hope he has survived. As for the Defence Minister, at least she tried. It's more than we can say for his uncle."

"Lavinia said Rashida called her, you know. Even after I sliced her leg. She called the witches before she'd even been patched up. She loves him too. I was right about that."

"I can hear your doubt, Alisha. You love him, but you don't believe yet you are worthy of him."

"Well, I put him in danger, didn't I?"

Echo pawed at the zipper of the cat carrier. "No. He put himself in danger for you. There's a difference. Now, will you please let me out of this wretched thing?"

I unzipped him as we exited the station.

He sprang out and stretched luxuriously like we had all the time in the world.

"Come on," I said. "We have to get going. You know, cat prams are now all the rage in the USA. I could get you one if you like."

Echo's lip curled in disgust. "Why not get me a bonnet and a dummy too? Need I remind you that I come from a regal family? A pram. A pram! What has my life become?"

"I was only asking, Echo." I rested a soothing hand on his head. "Tell me what you know about the apartment."

He tossed his head, a little touchy still, but rumbled on. "It's in an Edwardian mansion block on the banks of the river. Four bedrooms, fireplaces in every room, beautiful stained-glass windows in the entrance hallway, ceilings not out of place in a maharaja's palace, hardwood flooring, three floors including the basement and gated parking to boot."

I stared at him. "How do you know so much about it?"

Emerald eyes glinted. "She leaves the sash window in the kitchen open a fair bit, and sometimes I come by after hunting deer in Richmond Park for a nap in her back bedroom when my belly is full.

She doesn't use it for anything other than airing the laundry. Since I served your grandmother, it's been part of my job to keep an eye on senate members. The Otherworld is a cutthroat place. Every piece of information might contribute to our survival."

My voice was a high-pitched squeak. "When were you going to tell me that? And how many other senate members do you snoop on?"

"The leprechaun. He has no sense of smell, so I can rub myself all over his bedding, and he is none the wiser. The druid headmistress. Her abode is as fragrant as they come, and I like how she is not materialistic. Most people are hoarders, but somehow, she has retained an admirable simplicity. Oh, and the fallen angel. He's a slob. He stays up all night playing video games and is addicted to wasabi crisps. It's harder to spy on the ones who live in a community, like the witches, wolves and vampires. I have a healthy fear of the Bestiary Master. He's wily and has too many tricks up his sleeve to be easily fooled. Phinnaeous Shine's house is in Marylebone but teeming with succubi, and Calypso resides in the Celestial Library with better security than Alcatraz."

I whistled in awe. "We really need to talk more."

"I dislike verbal incontinence, Alisha, but if you book a karaoke booth and marinate a steak to Michelin standard for me when this is all over, I may well be convinced to prise open my clam heart and share some secrets."

I shook his paw. "Deal."

"We're almost there," said Echo. "For a dwelling in the heart of London, Margola's flat has ample privacy. She swims most days just after the sun has come up to avoid detection. Although the local papers have a running joke about local loonies reporting seal sightings."

"She turns into a seal?"

Echo sighed with the heavy burden of someone explaining a matter which should be common knowledge. "You grew up on these isles, didn't you? A selkie always longs for the sea. Though she may choose to live in her human form, the sea calls to her. Usually, selkies can only remain in their human bodies when the conditions of the tides are correct, but she is more gifted than most." Echo's teeth clamped around the edge of my T-shirt and pulled me behind a bush. "There she is."

The Thames, a quiet river that was neither deep nor wide, glistened under a sky peppered with candy floss clouds. A few canal boats bobbed on the water. Margola Silver stood at the edge of the river in a silk kimono with her back towards us. She had twisted her flame-coloured hair into a topknot. She let the kimono fall from her shoulders, revealing her alabaster skin. Then she stepped into the water without a scrap of clothing on, shoulders back, pointy breasts leading the way, without any shame for her state of undress or any hurry. She didn't flinch at the cold and soon was submerged, swimming in a dolphin stroke.

"That's funny," said Echo. "Why isn't she in her seal form?"

I frowned. I had always found Margola's confidence off-putting. It bordered on arrogance, with no chink of vulnerability in her personality. But when she came up for air, her puffy eyes, drooping shoulders and empty stare were a far cry from the armour she presented to the world. I thought I hated her for highlighting my mistakes and weaknesses in her newspaper for all to see, but seeing her mask slip made me wonder what I had missed.

Echo's whiskers drooped. "I rather fancy a swim in the river."

"Maybe later." I hid the cat carrier behind the bush.

We edged towards Margola's apartment, taking care not to be discovered.

Echo nudged me towards an open sash window. "She swims for twenty-five minutes on average, so we have twenty minutes tops to find any clues."

I pushed it down and hoisted myself up on the ledge and into a kitchen of sleek grey lines, hanging pendant lights over an island and copper accessories. I moved aside a lonely cactus from the windowsill as Echo squeezed himself through the opening. The most recent edition of *The Otherworld News*, with my face plastered on it, lay abandoned on the worktop next to a lukewarm cup of coffee.

He landed on the marble floor and extended his claws to scratch a kitchen cabinet. "I have the *Mission Impossible* theme tune in my head. Do you?"

I swatted him. "Focus. No marking. We leave everything as we found it."

"Spoilsport." No sooner had he retracted his claws than his ears twitched. He leaned his head against the floor, his rear end still pointing in the air. "Do you hear that? From the basement."

I shook my head and held my fingers to my lips. Echo's hearing was remarkable, but he wasn't the only creature in the Otherworld to possess acute hearing. We crept through the house towards the basement stairs at the other end of the corridor.

The rooms were sterile. There were no pictures of family or friends, no vases filled with flowers, and the only artwork was of the sea, slashes of blue and black on mammoth canvases. A meagre bookshelf in the dining room had been filled with back copies of magazines— such as *Private Eye*, *The Spectator* and *National Geographic*—and current editions of newspapers. But no fiction.

As beautiful as the bones of the apartment were, the overwhelming impression was of lovelessness.

I didn't know what I expected to find here. It wasn't like Hermes would be lounging in Margola's roll-top bath with a single malt by his side or that I could somehow disrupt her next edition from here. Gaia had told me to pull a string, and the whole ball would unravel. And so I was here on a wing, a prayer and pure instinct.

Echo searched the bedrooms while I sank onto my knees to leaf through past editions of *The Otherworld News*. Margola's coverage seemed to have only recently taken an overtly gossipy and vitriolic turn. Her coverage of the tremors, too, had been even-handed.

So what had caused the change?

I looked at my watch. Eight minutes before we had to scarper. The furtiveness of our act wasn't good for my heart rate. I wasn't even good at sneaking snacks into the cinema.

Echo urged me towards the basement, his wet nose in the small of my back. We crept down the stairs, side by side. I'd always hated basements. They brought back suppressed memories of horror films I should never have watched as a child. A tapping reached my ears the nearer we got to the door at the bottom.

Echo's nose twitched, and his tail swished, making my own anxiety peak.

Six minutes before Margola returned.

A concert of sounds reached me as we grew closer. The tapping noise. A humming of machines. A cooing. I crouched at the door and leaned my ear against it. My mouth grew dry.

Echo hissed. "We have to go. She'll skin us alive if she discovers us here."

I shook my head. We were so close. A small square window provided a view into the dimly lit basement. There was no time to dilly-dally. I had to peek inside the room if we wanted answers, even if we risked discovery.

I inched upwards on the right side of the window. Echo stood on his hind legs to view the left side.

My eyes widened.

The basement ran the length of the apartment. Computers and servers lined endless rows of tables. Cables ran like snakes from computer to server, server to computer. In front of each computer, basking in the glow of the screen, sat an elf, grey fingers flying over the keyboard.

The elves didn't talk to one another. Their pallor was dull, and their eyes glazed over with focus. Their screens showed familiar typography and branding colours. On the back wall, seven ravens perched in seven cramped cages, doors ajar, their beady eyes watching the progression of the elf workforce.

I scanned the elves for Flinar, but he wouldn't be caught doing something like this.

I dropped down to the floor. "Holy cow."

Echo followed suit, growling. "Not cows. Dark elves."

"The Ravenmaster has employed them as bots. That's how he is disrupting communication."

"The birds live." Echo grinned. "Who would have thought it? They are not victims of a massacre. They are cunning, bloodthirsty taskmasters, much like the Ravenmaster himself."

"We need to get in there, destroy those servers and free the elves."

The three-inch scar from the corner of Echo's eye reminded me of how ferocious he was in battle. "You—or those feathery balls of murder—will be the death of us. But I will follow a Verma where she leads."

I turned the door handle. To my surprise, it wasn't locked.

Then why hadn't the elves already escaped? It wasn't like Margola had guards upstairs.

The elves looked up, ghostly grey faces zapped of energy by the screens. God knew how many hours they had been sitting there. The poor things looked dazed.

The ravens did not look dazed. They looked and sounded furious, judging by the cacophony coming from their midnight bodies.

I raised my hands, and a gust of wind surged from them, slamming shut six cages just in time but missing the last one.

Echo roared as he leapt against the last cage, slamming an emerging bird back into its enclosure and nudging the door shut, but not before he received a gory peck on the nose that made him howl.

"Are you okay?" I asked.

"No thanks to you," he said.

I crouched down next to an elf. The screens flashed with branding from different social media sites and telephone companies. There was code and text and icons that didn't match the elvish faces. But with the ravens taken care of, why were the elves still staring at the screens, still typing away?

"Pull out the server cables," I said to Echo.

He leapt over to the humming machines, tearing out cables with his teeth.

I prayed he wouldn't be electrocuted but didn't utter it to completion.

The elves—there must have been twenty of them—emerged from their trance, fury written into their usually benign faces.

"What are you doing?" the one nearest me asked.

I didn't expect a thank you, but this was a little odd. "Rescuing you."

The ravens' clamour continued.

Echo's tail swished as he reached my side. His emerald eyes caught mine. "I think we may have misjudged this."

I frowned. "No kidding."

Shit, they were doing that winding thing Flinar did when he produced a black hole. What happened when they did it together?

"Oh no," said Echo. "Where is the wolf when you need him? Run!"

We scampered down the corridor and knocked over the cactus in our hurry to escape through the kitchen window. I shoved Echo's rump onto the driveway and used my wind powers to vault over the ledge myself.

"What are we running from anyway?" I bent over, panting, my hands on my knees.

He hissed at an eerie sound like the stars had been sucked out of the universe. "That."

I turned around. The ledge I had just jumped from no longer existed. Neither did the three floors of Margola's flat. They had clean been sucked away. "What the hell?"

"Now do you realise why elves give many peculiars of other races the heebie-jeebies?" said Echo.

I gawped. "I mean, how cool would it be if they could suck the world's litter into a black hole and then just inferno it?" I hiccupped, still struggling to calm my breathing. "Did we actually beat the Ravenmaster at his own game? You did quite a number on the cables, *and* there's no internet in a black hole. Even if they pop up again, they are screwed. Pretty weird, though, that they didn't thank us for the rescue. It's almost like they wanted to be there. I'm feeling kind of shitty that we pretty much destroyed Margola's home."

Echo spat out the plastic coating of some cabling. "I know you're excited, but you should probably stop talking."

I frowned. "Why?"

A scream of rage pierced my eardrum. The selkie had returned.

Fear snaked up my spine. I was in for it now.

Echo bounded away and then launched himself into the river with the gusto of a toddler at a waterpark. So much for backup.

"What on earth has happened to my apartment?" Margola tied her damp kimono, her voice a screech. Brown eyes flashed with horror. "This is *your* fault, druid. What were you thinking coming here?

Where is my home?" She balled up her fists like she was going to explode.

I hadn't seen a selkie fight, but seals could be vicious. I'd seen a brutal battle on a nature documentary once. I winced and put up my hands in defence. "About that. The elves in your basement went nuclear."

A look of doubt darted across her face. She frothed with rage. "They wouldn't. They *couldn't*. This is you. You're a tsunami of trouble." She grabbed my shoulders and shook me. "Wait until Phinnaeous and Gunnolf hear of this. The whole Otherworld will give you a whipping by the time I've finished with you."

I accepted her mauling for a moment. I had been partially responsible for her home disappearing, after all. Then I looped two currents of wind around her wrists and pinned them to her side. "I expect your apartment will pop back eventually. I have it on good authority that the elves never stay in their black holes for long. There's no food or water in there, and they're not cannibals. At least, I don't think so. I mean, they did have ravens with them. And ravens are opportunistic survivors, I'm told, so that doesn't bode well for the elves..." I took a deep breath to stop my rambling.

Margola stared at the remnants of her home, words failing her. Not only that, a shadow of guilt crept across her face.

I leapt on it. What was she wrapped up in? "Minister, why were you harbouring a room full of elf bots? Are you working with the Ravenmaster?"

She baulked. "You don't know what you are talking about."

I sighed. "I saw the evidence with my own eyes. I saw the ravens. Sooner or later, your home will return like a pop-up shop, complete with its basement of evidence. You might as well own up to it. You know as well as I do that getting ahead of the news is your best bet right now."

She shuddered. "The Ravenmaster and I have always had a natural affinity. We both deal in information. His rumours have powered my news. He is a maverick, a lover of language and an inventor with a flair for the dramatic. If someone like that asks me for a favour, I'm not going to say no. All I had to do was provide him with my unused basement." She hardened. "Not that you deserve an explanation. Why are you here, druid? I can't decide if you are foolish or brave."

Behind her, Echo frolicked in the waves.

I pursed my lips. "I came to find out what you were hiding and why you've spent the past few weeks destroying my privacy. I guess I know the answer to one of those questions."

Her brown eyes narrowed. "I'm just doing my job."

"No. It's more than that. It's personal. I've seen your work. You're not a common hack; just writing for paymasters.

"We do what we have to do to survive." Her voice cut through the morning quiet, defiant. "Isn't that why you stabbed the wolf last night? Unless you enjoyed it." She turned to track the whereabouts of the leopard in the water, and a fleeting expression of melancholy slipped across her face.

My thoughts whirled. She had emerged from the river in her human form. "You're trying to rile me. Why would a selkie who longs for the water swim in her human form?"

Margola's eyes grew dull. "Leave it alone, druid. You'll only make matters worse. You know nothing of my culture, my way of life. You know nothing about the call of the sea, the compulsion that haunts me every second of the day or what it costs me to stay in my human skin."

I didn't expect the swell of sympathy that washed over me. "Tell me what I am missing."

"Why? You and I are nothing alike. How many men have stolen your skin to make you do their bidding?"

"Who would do that to you?"

"Selkie folk have always suffered. I am no different. My skin has been taken by sailors, by men who profess to love me, and by my own child to stop me from returning to the sea. It is always men. Always men seeking control. Humdrum, peculiar, it doesn't matter. They are all the same. This time, too, you know nothing about what levers are being pulled behind the curtain."

"I am sorry you lost your home. How are you going to explain this away to the humdrums in this community?"

"I'm a newsmaker, aren't I? I suppose I'll have to say it's a gas explosion. The truth is, there is only one of my possessions that is worth saving, and it wasn't in my house."

I sucked in my breath as the penny dropped.

That was why she hadn't transformed into a seal in the water. That was why her behaviour had changed. "Who stole your skin, Minister?"

The particles shifted behind me, a moving of molecules to make space for something else.

Goosebumps ran up my bare arms as I recognised the sensation. The scent of the wilds came with him, but I didn't dare turn around just in case disappointment crushed me. I thought I'd never hear his voice again.

"It was Gunnolf, wasn't it, Minister?" said Ezra. "He stole your seal skin, and that isn't even the worst of it. And when we steal it back for you, you're going to tell us everything."

18

———————

I held it together until Margola left our sightline, picking over the foundations of her lost home. Then euphoria crashed over me like a wave, and I threw my arms around Ezra.

I kissed him. "You."

His smile chased away the darkness in me. He wore the same dark clothes from the night we sneaked into the Tower of London. His T-shirt was ripped. My fingers pushed it aside. Underneath, his torso had healed, leaving no scars.

Echo raced from the river. The wet leopard launched into the air and knocked Ezra onto his arse amongst a smattering of daisies, then proceeded to nuzzle him in rapture. "We feared you were dead, dog. I am sorry for maiming you. I see you have healed."

"I'm okay, Echo." Ezra pushed him off, his grey eyes focussed on me. "I need to speak to Alisha, though."

His tone made me wary. "Where've you been? I thought the Ravenmaster had captured you. The worry almost killed me. I went to see Gunnolf and even called Lavinia."

"I know, hellfire." He reached out to me. "I'll tell you, but you have to promise to stay calm."

I nodded but kept my distance.

"It goes back to the investigation with the dead wolves. It's when you said that we shouldn't have burned the bodies that it clicked. The reason we couldn't sniff out a perpetrator for the murders. The reason Gunnolf didn't want Marina involved. The way how from the very beginning, he's been all talk and no action to get to the bottom of it. I mean, the Gunnolf I know is *all* action and no talk, and that's a change in behaviour, right? But any time I wanted to speak to other packs about which wolves were missing, to put names to those bodies, he shut me down."

I frowned. "But what has this got to do with the Ravenmaster? With him capturing you?"

He sighed. "Nothing and everything."

"Spit it out, dog," growled Echo.

He bowed his head as if he was ashamed. "The Ravenmaster didn't capture me. I just needed everyone to think he did. Even you."

I saw red. The wanker. Endless hours of guilt and fear that he'd met a sorry end, that I'd never hear his voice again or experience the exquisite pleasure of disappearing into the folds of the universe with just his arms to hold me. He'd been just fine and dandy all along and not even bothered to let me know. I flew at him like a banshee, raised my fists and pummelled him, not caring if I hurt him, wanting to hurt him like he'd hurt me.

"You show him, Alisha. The wolf is an imbecile. I always suspected it," said Echo.

When my energy was spent, he caught my wrists and placed a kiss on each palm. "Don't be angry."

I pulled back to search his face, panting hard. "Why, Ezra?"

He chewed his lip. "Because I knew you'd go to *him* for help, and he would read your mind, and that would give you the alibi to keep you safe while I solved the case."

I frowned. "Orpheus? You knew Orpheus would read my mind?"

Ezra nodded. "You can't deny that he is your closest Wildwoods ally after me."

I swallowed hard. "There's nothing between us."

"Can't you see? It's not about what you feel for him. It's about what he feels for you. I knew he would protect you when I couldn't and that he is powerful enough to make a stand against Gunnolf and vouch for you. It bought me time to investigate the murders without Gunnolf breathing down my neck."

I clenched my fists. "You didn't have to go through this ruse. We could have found a way to figure it out together."

He shook his head. "No, Alisha, you have your path, and I have mine. The alpha was *my* problem to fix." He softened and reached out for me. "But even then, you threw in a curveball when you refused to give up on me. You distracted Gunnolf with your tenacity just when I needed him to be distracted. Almost as if we were working in tandem without even realising it."

I had a lightbulb moment. "That was you in the woods? I felt watched just as I made it to the pick-up."

"I heard the call of the pack. I had to make sure you were okay."

Echo inclined his head. "I spoke in haste. It was a good plan."

Relief that Ezra was safe vied with bitter disappointment for his choices. He could have involved me. We could have found a way to figure out what was going on together. His instinct to protect me had belittled my power. Even Orpheus hadn't tried to be my saviour when I had decided to shoot myself in the foot.

"Was it worth lying to me?" My voice was the cut of a cold knife on warm flesh. "Did you have to put me through an emotional wringer to achieve your goals?"

Ezra scraped a hand through his hair. "That's not fair, Alisha."

"It is fair, wolf. Her pain was clear for all to see," said Echo. "However, let it be said, I am not a monogamous creature. In fact, my happiest coupling was with three sisters. But despite his machinations, the wolf has eyes only for you, Alisha, and you would be foolish to let this relationship swirl down the toilet pan like human faeces."

"I solved the case. But if this is the end of us, then no, it wasn't worth it," said Ezra.

My heart did a black flip in spite of myself, but he wouldn't win me over so easily, even if I were a gooey puddle. "And what did you find out?"

His expression tightened, and his words slowed as if it pained him to say them. "That Gunnolf is the murderer. Those poor wolves wanted to join our pack, but Gunnolf was worried he wouldn't be able to control the… His strength isn't what it was. He was worried he wouldn't survive an alpha challenge, so he killed them. They didn't even see it coming."

Echo growled. "If what you say it true, this will have wide-ranging consequences, dog. An indiscriminate murderer cannot be allowed to remain on the senate. We must do everything in our power to bring him down. But it will be difficult. It is Gunnolf, after all, who presides over justice in our world."

A vein pulsed in Ezra's neck. "A beta wolf can call the Court of the Wolves. I need the backing of the Prime Sorcerer, but I think I have enough evidence for him to be tried." He hesitated. "And that's not all. Gunnolf was always possessive of me. He fought tooth and nail to make sure I grew up with the pack and dissuaded me from claiming my witch heritage. He hated the closeness between Alisha and me. He's right. I have grown more distant from the pack."

"At this precise moment, you would be wise to focus solely on Alisha rather than your family sagas."

"That's just it. Tell me, leopard, what is the Jailor's Law?"

Echo lifted his magnificent head and recited with ease. "It is forbidden to interfere with the compos mentis of another peculiar."

A vein throbbed in Ezra's jaw. "And what would happen to a peculiar if you took away the very thing that makes them magical?"

I frowned. "You have no evidence that Gunnolf has taken Margola's skin."

"Did you not see the look of fear on Margola's face when I suggested it?" Ezra implored me to believe him. "Gunnolf made no pretence of the fact he didn't want us to date. He sees you as a threat. He voted against you at your magical trial. When all else failed, he and Lavinia used fertility as a wedge between us. Just before Margola egged you on to attempt to animate a fox at the Wildwoods trial, she and Gunnolf exchanged glances. I think Gunnolf stole Margola's skin so she'd agree to discredit you."

My heart raced as I recalled the padlocked room in the pack farmhouse.

Echo hissed. "That is unconscionable. I would die if I were stuck as a Bengal cat forever."

A small, sad smile on Ezra's lips. "So you see, I might have lied to you, but I did it for us."

I wanted so much to believe him. He was so focused on the pack that he'd lost sight of anything beyond the end of his own nose. "Echo and I found out today that Margola is hiding something in her basement."

"Unfortunately, we don't know precisely what. But whatever was in there hummed and throbbed."

I grimaced. "For all we know, it could be a room full of sex toys à la Christian Grey. But she's in there now. We'll have to find out another day."

"Just tell me what you need from me." Ezra's face tightened with resolve. "But I need to face Gunnolf first."

I let out my breath in a whoosh. "Then I'm coming with you. I know where the selkie skin is."

We must have been stupid to go back to the pack farmhouse. As if we were invincible. As if we didn't bleed. As if our enemies couldn't wound us. Yet, standing beside Ezra, I didn't think anyone could. We were so powerful together. If we couldn't fight, then we could flee. He could teleport us anywhere in the world, couldn't he?

But he'd tangled me up in his ploy to get the bottom of the wolf murders, and I didn't know if I could accept it. It was a bitter pill to swallow. I'd wanted Ezra to choose love over everything. Even though his eyes—and his mouth—told me he loved me, I couldn't help but think he had put his duty to the pack above me. That his love and desire for me had come a distant second to his responsibilities to his wolf family and that I could never compete.

We walked across the lawn to the farmhouse. Ezra's broken window had been boarded over. This time the border of orange dahlias didn't seem romantic, despite the noon sun that lent warmth to the building. The flowers turned and twisted like they had agency of their own accord. Like they could leap from the earth, as treacherous as the wolves inside. I held Ezra's hand, but our fingers hung limp. They didn't mesh together. Distance had set between us, even though we walked side by side.

My voice quaked. "I stole the pick-up and wounded Rashida."

A vein throbbed in his neck. "I know. The pick-up was a pile of junk, and Rashida will heal. You did what you had to."

I stopped to dig in my pockets. "The pick-up keys. And your room key."

He accepted the car key but handed me back the rusty old silver key to his bedroom door. "Keep it."

I gulped and slipped it back into his pocket. How could his timing be so off? "Ezra, why did you and Rashida break up?"

A weighted sigh. "She didn't trust me. I couldn't breathe in that relationship with her."

My brain told me to back off. My heart wanted me to dig deeper. "How long were you together?"

I could cope with two or three years. It took that long sometimes to work out if something was worth fighting for. Hell, it had taken me twice as long as that to work up the courage to leave Alex.

"Six years."

Oh shit. They were serious then. I shrank into silence.

Mere yards from the farmhouse, his hand tightened around mine. "You've got to stop this. Gunnolf will take advantage of any split between us."

I bit my cheek as the pack came pelting out in their human forms: Gunnolf at the apex, with the two strongest males, Dominic and Maximillian, in formation behind him, and finally, mousy Deirdra, her boyfriend Ruud and a wan Rashida. Not even Deirdra raised a smile for Ezra.

Gunnolf spoke first, glowering with anger. "The prodigal son returns."

Ezra nodded but kept his distance, every nerve in his body alert and ready to defend us if he needed to. He didn't give Rashida a sideways glance. Yes, he was focussed on Gunnolf, but his heart was with me.

Gunnolf sneered. "That slut turned you against me, just like I knew she would."

That was a bit rich, given Ezra and I hadn't even gone the whole way.

Ezra didn't flinch. "You drove a wedge between us yourself. I wanted us to stay family."

The alpha let out a mirthless laugh. "I wanted you alive. I've known you since you were a babe in arms, nephew. I raised you as my own, but there you stand, not rushing to me. Returning with the druid, as if to rub salt in our wounds. Do you know what she did?"

"I know what you did." Ezra's voice was a statement of fact, not recrimination, and all the stronger for it.

Maximillian frowned, suddenly unsure. "What's he talking about?"

"Tell them." Ezra stared at the alpha and didn't back down. "Or I will."

Suddenly I realised what this encounter would do to their relationship. How there would never be a going back, however it played out. How Ezra wasn't acting like the beta of the pack anymore. He'd made the decision to be something more.

I fancied the pants off him, but lust had to wait. Obviously.

"He's out of his mind," said Gunnolf. "The Ravenmaster has broken him."

Ezra shook his head. "I found the traps you set. It took me a pretty minute to work out it was you, but once I had, the evidence was hard to ignore. Even if you had rushed into burning the bodies. You taught us those skills yourself. Your knots. Your ambush places. Your prints in the mud. We couldn't smell the perpetrator because we were looking for an outsider. It was you all along."

The deck creaked as the pack backed slowly away from Gunnolf. They, too, could sense the tide turning.

"You're not going to listen to him, are you? It's ludicrous. Why would I kill my own kind? I taught you how to be wolves. I protected you. And now you believe this halfling?"

Sadness tinged Ruud's quiet voice. "He's not a halfling. He's our family. And we can smell the fear on you."

Rashida looked from Ezra to Gunnolf. "Ezra is many things, but he is not a liar."

A roar ripped from Gunnolf's throat. "You turn my own family against me? You ungrateful swine."

"I have to fight him," Ezra murmured to me. The pack will wait to see who is crowned alpha. Get the selkie skin."

A primal scream built in me as Gunnolf leapt from the decking and transformed into his black wolf.

Ezra's clothes ripped, and his bones cracked as he, too, transformed into his wolf. His grey eyes met mine as they changed shape, and then he turned to meet his match.

I backed away, shuddering to see how the black wolf was bulkier and aimed to maim or kill, whereas the copper-grey one was loathed to strike a deathly blow. They circled each other and flew through the air in a tangle of limbs and teeth and claws.

Grunts and growls filled the air. A battle of rage, resolve and skill.

It was impossible to tell from the horrified expressions of the pack who they wanted to succeed.

I prayed to Gaia that Ezra would come out on top.

Bodies slammed against each other as I ran around the back to the door I knew was open and the padlocked one I'd have to break into. The selkie skin had to be behind that door. Why else would it be padlocked? There was no time to look for bolt-cutters, and I had the strength of a gnat. The monkey bars at school had been my nemesis.

But Gaia had taught me that I didn't always have to win with brute strength.

I had another idea. My hands quivered as I took the catalogue of creatures from my satchel and chose a pair of woodpeckers on the central spread. I closed my eyes to ground myself, pushing away the images I knew played out on the lawn.

Dad's painting on the page fluttered in my mind's eye, telling me I was ready. I waved my hands over the page. The threads waited for me there and leapt into my fingers as if they longed to be made real. To be born into this world of pain and power. I sensed the chisel-like beaks, the tiny bodies, the tail feathers and their tongues. Two palm-sized woodpeckers with black-and-white markings—one with a crimson head—came to life beneath my fingers. A sense of elation came over me. I whispered their purpose to them and pulled them out of the page.

They greeted me with a churring sound and then flew to the padlocked door in a fierce beating of their wings. The woodpeckers worked in tandem, laser-focussed, drilling with their beaks in a semi-circle each. I stashed away the catalogue of creatures in my satchel as they toiled. My anxiety rose with every second. How long until the drumming sound of the beaks against the wood roused the pack's suspicion? How long before I would be discovered red-handed and alone while Ezra fought for his life?

The woodpeckers had no thought except to break through the door. The tempo of their drilling reached a crescendo as they neared the finish line, and the circle they had excavated, complete with the three padlocks, fell to the floor with a thud.

"Thank you." I held out my hand, and they flew to me, tiny feet on my palm, purring with pride next to one another. I took them to the back door, released them to the woods, and then returned to my task.

I pushed the door open and stepped over the obsolete padlocks.

The scent in the room made my stomach turn. It stank of old boots or something worse, and there were no windows to let in fresh air. The room itself was no bigger than a box room in an old Victorian house. Shelves lined the walls, stacked with dusty accountancy notebooks—squared paper filled with sums and household calculations. I frowned. There were much better apps for that sort of thing nowadays. A humming came from the far end of the room. An industrial-type freezer had been squeezed into the space at the end, the sort of one that was more horizontal than vertical.

Dread stirred in the pit of my stomach.

I made a beeline for it and reached out to hoist up the lid when a voice behind me gave me pause.

"Haven't you done enough?"

I swivelled to find Deirdra there.

At least it wasn't Rashida. I wasn't sure how I would have managed that rabid redhead in such a small space. I'd already pissed her off enough without burying her in accountancy notebooks. Death by maths wasn't a way anyone wanted to go.

I raised my hands in surrender. I could talk Deirdra around. She'd been the friendliest pack member right from the get-go. She hadn't been wary of me just because I didn't belong.

"You have to let me open this," I said.

Deirdra's growl of warning echoed in the small space and made me wish I'd worn a pantyliner. "You've split apart my family and didn't even wait around to see who walked away."

"That's not true. I wrenched myself away. I don't want anyone to get hurt." It was a small lie, and I sold it well. There wasn't even an inflexion in my voice.

Deirdra launched herself forward, suddenly more Danger Mouse than field mouse. She grabbed my arm and twisted it behind me as her were-teeth came out to play.

I had no intention of being imprisoned or a dog chew, but I didn't want to hurt her either. With my spare hand, I fashioned a channel of wind between us, holding her at bay long enough to break free and throw open the freezer.

I recoiled from its contents and spun away to vomit on the floor. I wiped the back of my hand across my mouth as Deirdra looked at me in horror.

Then we both peered into the freezer together.

"Holy mother of—" said Deirdra.

"Uh-huh."

The freezer was jammed full. Not of frozen bags of vegetables, casserole portions, Yorkshire puddings or turkey left over from Christmas. It held three dead male wolves, packed tightly like a game of Tetris. Their glazed eyes stared up at us, their fur gouged and iced white. At one edge, underneath a leg protruding at an unthinkable angle, I spotted a blubbery seal skin.

My stomach heaved.

Deirdra closed the freezer. "This room is Gunnolf's. The padlocks went on a few months ago. We never questioned why. No one ever questions the alpha."

"Ezra did. I don't suppose you have a carrier bag?"

She stepped over the splash of vomit and disappeared in the direction of the kitchen, returning with a Tesco's bag.

I opened the freezer again, carefully plucked out the selkie skin, silently grossed out by its weight and slick texture, and put it in the bag. "My job here is done."

Deirdra turned her head in the direction of the warring wolves. "Ezra's job isn't."

We took one look at each other and rushed outside. The selkie skin slopped in the carrier bag at my side. My stomach went rock hard with fear, and my knees locked as I took in the carnage outside.

The lawn had been shredded by their claws, and the pack watched on, grim-faced, jerking with every blow. They loved both of these men.

They must have been fighting for a quarter of an hour already, and still, they hadn't eased their pace. Gunnolf's black wolf lunged time and again, tearing strips off Ezra. Ezra had taken a deep cut to his snout. It oozed blood. His tail hung limp, but there was a resolve to his body. He stood tall as he rounded on Gunnolf, sinking his teeth into the black wolf's flank before circling again.

Gunnolf reeled around, powering off his muscly legs and pinned Ezra to the floor. He sank his yellow teeth into Ezra's neck, just above his charm necklace. Ezra yelped, and the sound drove a stake into my heart.

I clapped my hand to my mouth to stop myself from crying out. Ezra couldn't afford for me to disturb his focus.

Why didn't he teleport? Why didn't he fight dirty? He was holding back; I knew it.

Then it happened. His head flopped in my direction.

I flinched, thinking it was all over. A wail ripped itself from me, an avalanche of sorrow.

Ezra's beautiful copper-grey eyes focussed on my face, and suddenly he rolled over, his ears upright and no longer flat against his head. He flipped the position so that he was the dominant force, pressing down on the black wolf.

The black wolf frothed at the mouth, raging at Ezra.

Ezra lunged, clamped his jaw around the black wolf's foreleg and twisted. The bone snapped, clear for all to see, its ivory-white fragment poking through the black wolf's flesh wound.

The copper-grey wolf leapt aside and sat, watching with narrowed eyes, waiting for the black wolf to make another move.

The black wolf righted himself and bared his teeth. But his body could no longer match the attack in his eyes. He fell into the dirt, curled up into a ball and licked his foreleg, growling a warning at Rashida when she ran to help him.

"It's over," said Deirdra. "We have a new alpha."

As Ezra's wolf surveyed the farmhouse, the land and the peculiars on it, I realised she was right.

19

Marina tended to Ezra in her surgery, supervised by Echo. Fae Yen and Faeza were there, too, applying healing ointments from Chinese herbology they insisted would complement Marina's traditional methods. Although, from what I could tell, it was Ezra's thistle charm that had done the most work, supercharging his innate werewolf healing powers. His wounds had already started to knit together.

Marina tutted. "This really would be much easier if you had stayed in wolf form, Ezra. I'm not sure how I'm supposed to sanitise all your wounds and keep you free of infection, with you presenting yourself here in another form."

Ezra was pale and shivering in his boxers on the stainless-steel examination table. "Teleporting as a wolf is tricky, especially in this state. I have to make sure my mind is wholly centred to emerge in the right place."

I brought him a blanket. "Why didn't you teleport when you fought Gunnolf? You could have finished him off easily before he'd even left a mark on you."

"I wanted to give you enough time to get inside the house and get what you needed. I held on until I saw you get back." His voice was monotone, his eyes empty. He didn't take any joy in displaying his power over his uncle. "And it wouldn't have been fair to fight him with an advantage. This way, the pack knows I won a fair fight, and they'll accept me as their alpha."

I bit my lip. It was hard to see him like this. "You knew that if we returned to the farmhouse, it would result in an alpha challenge, didn't you?"

Ezra scrubbed a hand over his face, his eyes dull. "I owed it to my uncle to give him a chance to explain."

"I have caught the whiffs of your scent-marking, wolf." Echo curled his lip. "You do not seem like an alpha to me. More a beta or omega. But not an alpha."

"You're right. The pack system sometimes suffocates me. I prefer to roam, much like you, leopard." Ezra's eyes found mine. "But sometimes life forces us to be things we might not have chosen. I have to trust that it will all work out okay in the end."

"We did your tarot card reading, wolf. Your path is not easy." Fei Yen closed one pungent bottle of ointment and gave me another. "Put this on this pillow when he sleeps. It will help him recover his strength."

Faeza winked. "In more ways than one."

"I'm proud of you both. Let's celebrate this weekend. I have to get on now. My next patient is in twenty minutes." Marina gave Ezra a stern look. "I know you heal quickly, but alpha or no alpha, I'm prescribing rest and relaxation."

He gave her a weak smile. "Aye, aye, captain."

"We can drop them at Alisha's flat," said Fei Yen. "It wouldn't be any trouble."

"We can check our grammar homework with you on the way there," said Faeza.

Ezra sat up with help from me. He shook his head. "I can take Alisha home."

My brow furrowed. "Are you sure?"

"You don't need to worry. I'm fine." His voice rasped, and I couldn't help my mothering instinct respond, despite his protestations.

I turned to the foxes. "In that case, I have another favour to ask. I've been worried about Flinar and wondered if you might track him down for me. If anyone can find him on the streets, it's you two."

They nodded, entirely in sync with one another. "It would be our pleasure."

"We will call you as soon as we know more," said Fei Yen.

"Marina, can you keep this Tesco's bag in your freezer for now?"

She wrinkled her nose. "To be honest, I'm not that keen."

I grinned. "The time will come when we'll need it as a bargaining chip. I'll be back for it as soon as I can."

I tucked away the ointment in my satchel. Ezra stood shakily and wrapped his arms around me, and we melted between the worlds.

Echo's growl rang in our ears. "Clearly, there's no space for a leopard between those lovebirds."

Moments later, I stepped out of the circle of Ezra's arms and surveyed my surroundings in awe. We stood in a beautiful, landscaped garden with hedged enclosures and a sunken lawn. At the end of a pathway was a small thatched cottage. Wisteria climbed up its walls and draped over the front door.

"Will you excuse me for just one moment?" said Ezra. "I need to call the Prime Sorcerer."

I nodded, and he stepped away, whispering furiously. But when he returned, all his angst fell away, and his expression became open and happy.

"Where are we?" I asked. "I thought you were taking me home."

"This is home, Alisha. It was my parents' once. You're the only woman I've ever brought here."

I swallowed hard and allowed him to tug me down the winding path.

At the front door, Ezra crouched down in his bare feet and boxers and reached under the mat for a key. Mottled bruises covered his body. "I rarely come here but used it as a base the night the Ravenmaster attacked us. I have a few clothes here and bought a few supplies to keep going."

I pursed my lips. "Why didn't Gunnolf look for you here?"

"He might well have if you'd not distracted him. But the truth is

Gunnolf is singular-minded. The pack house is everything to him, and he never understood why I kept this place." His grey eyes lit up. "Come. I have a surprise for you."

"What surprise?"

He led me through the cottage, looking back now and then to gauge my expression. Though the sun shone outside, the cottage itself was dark, with heavy curtains drawn across its windows and dust sheets covering the furniture. The house smelled abandoned, as if no soul had lived there for a hundred years. As if a coldness had crept into the walls that could never be clawed out. There were no books, family pictures, or children's drawings. The floorboards creaked as we reached the back bedroom.

His grey eyes darkened. "There are two bedrooms upstairs. My parents' bedroom and my childhood one. But I prepared a room downstairs for us."

Lights flickered from under the door. My heart rate spiked as he pushed the door open.

This room took my breath away, from the textures to the ambience and scent. Fairy lights lined a four-poster bed that had been made up with white linen. A vase of burnt orange roses, a bowl of Maltesers and a tray of essential oils sat on a side table alongside a burning amber-and-vanilla blossom candle.

I soaked up every detail and then turned to him. "This is beautiful."

He stood in his boxers and charm necklace, his hands gently clasped around mine. "I promised to make our first time special. I want to feel close to you before the coming storm. You can feel it, too, can't you? I don't know if we'll be the same."

My breath hitched in my chest. It meant so much that he'd brought me here, to the place of his family's happiness before it was all torn apart. But the sense of dread in me was all-encompassing.

I didn't understand it. We had come out on top, hadn't we? But I could feel it too. We were being pulled apart, despite our attempts to edge closer together.

The past few days had shown me that we weren't perfect, but give me a relationship that was, and I'd show you a lie.

I loved him. I could feel the truth of it beating in my chest. My reaction to him being in danger proved it. We had earned this moment of peace together, and I was going to take it.

A fluttering in my chest. "Are you well enough?"

"Oh, I'm well enough."

I traced my finger over the scar on his neck, where Gunnolf's teeth had met his soft flesh. "You need to heal."

The alpha's eyes on mine. A low growl in his throat. "I need you."

My breath quickened, and my tongue tied as he edged towards me.

There was an inch between us, and still, he didn't touch me. "I'm at a disadvantage here, hellfire. Take off your clothes."

I held his gaze as I shrugged off my bag and kicked off my shoes. My fingers fumbled with the button of my jeans. I sucked my tummy in, suddenly conscious of how I wasn't perfect. How I hadn't done enough sit-ups or had time for running and had eaten too many spoonfuls of Nutella when I should have eaten a carrot. Without hummus.

His fingers brushed mine, featherlight, as if he was holding back.

I quivered as he unfastened the button and slid my jeans over my hips. I stood, vulnerable and aching, as he pulled my rose-coloured T-shirt over my head.

He stepped back, his eyes roaming over me.

I stood there in my huge tummy-sucking knickers and a bra that had been designed for scaffolding rather than sexiness, and he hadn't run in the other direction. In fact, the fire in his eyes told a different story. I stuttered, my words a whisper of uncertainty. "I bought new underwear to make it special, but I don't have it here."

"I can't wait to see it, but you couldn't be any more perfect than right now."

With infinite gentleness, he traced his fingers over the scar on my arm, the circle of raised dots that the birds had drilled into my skin as a child. He leaned in to kiss me, the pressure of his lips gentle on mine.

I needed more, but he had other ideas. I giggled as he scooped me up as if I weighed nothing, forgetting his wounds for a second. He buried his face in my hair as I lay against his chest. I wanted him to dump me onto the bed so we could lose ourselves in each other. So we could forget about the world, and everything would slow to just us in this little cottage, a pinpoint on the map that he had brought no one to but me.

Disappointment swelled in me as he used his back to open a door I hadn't noticed. Inside was a small en suite bathroom with a simple shower, fresh towels and a bar of soap. He let me down on my feet wordlessly as I held my breath, my lips parting with my need for him.

A moment later, he'd turned on the shower and spun to me with an invitation in his smouldering eyes. I swallowed hard and stepped out of the remainder of my clothing, just as he did, then followed him into the shower. Hot jets of water ran in rivulets down our bodies, and finally—mercifully—the distance closed between us as he pulled me to him, and our bodies merged. Every nerve ending in my body tingled as his hands found my hips and his mouth met mine. The hot water, his touch, and the desire that pulsed between us made me lightheaded. I arched against him, urging him on.

He shook his head. "Slower."

I trembled as he picked up the bar of soap and washed every inch of me. Then I returned the favour, taking care to avoid the parts of him that were still red and raw.

He took the soap from my hand and turned off the water before wrapping me in a towel and carrying me back to the fairy-lit four-poster bed.

My inhibitions had long fled. My nails clawed his back as he explored me with his hands and tongue. I shivered with pleasure, my head empty of all cogent thoughts. There were only Ezra and me, and our bodies damp from the shower and lust. We forgot the world and its machinations, forgot his enemies and mine, and forgot everything except the tender sparks between us. The way our hearts raced in proximity to each other and our pupils dilated.

He pulled me so that I straddled him. I didn't feel self-conscious about being on top, the extra inches I carried on my stomach, or the fact my breasts weren't as pert as they once had been. I bit my lip as he cupped them, turned on by his arousal, and lost myself in the feeling of being desired just as I was. I bent my head to trail featherlight kisses down from his collarbone to his pecs and lower still to where he was hard. He moaned and pulled me up for a kiss that left me dizzy with need. I rocked against him, begging him with the motion of my body to give me what I wanted, but he wasn't in a hurry.

He wanted me to beg.

All it took was one word. "Please."

Ezra smiled and flipped me over onto my back, and entered me. I gasped and clung onto the bed post as we found a sweet dance all our own. His hands clasped mine, but I needed him to go faster. I freed my hands to clutch his tight buttocks and urge him on. His eyes darkened, and my name was on his lips. When we reached our apex, we collapsed against each other, spent.

After a while, Ezra pulled the duvet over us and kissed my forehead, a satisfied growl in his throat. "Don't sleep too long, Alisha. I bought those essential oils knowing *exactly* what I am going to do to you."

I flushed and raised my head from the crook of his arm. "I love you, Ezra."

His smile made my heart do a backflip. "And I love you, hellfire."

I didn't ever want to leave this cocoon.

20

As the moon rose in the night sky, I received a cryptic message from Fei Yen and Faeza about my ginger tea being ready for pick up. Given that they knew I hated ginger tea, I took it as a klaxon to rush to their shop, despite the post-coital delight of sleeping entwined with my wolf.

I set aside my glowing mobile phone and kissed Ezra awake—the alpha.

"Just one more minute of this bliss," he grumbled and pulled me closer. I melted into him, revelling in the feel of my skin against his, but not fully relaxing. He opened one eye. "I can hear your brain churning from here. You are a naughty druid."

I nipped his lip with my teeth. "Will you take me to Shanghai Moon?"

He sighed. "I guess the party is over."

The cloud of dread, which I had pushed aside, bubbled to the surface. "For now."

"What time is it?"

I checked my phone. "Ten p.m.. We've been asleep for hours."

He sat bolt upright. "Shit. That only leaves me two hours."

"For what?"

"To get to the Court of the Wolves."

We dressed quickly, with a shyness that belied what had gone on the night before. Ezra's body had almost completely healed, and I said a silent word of thanks to his aunts, whose charms had saved him—and me—from sticky situations more than once. However, there could be no friendship between us if they had supercharged Sahil's powers, as I suspected.

We switched off the fairy lights and left the cosy ambience of the bedroom with regret in our hearts, then teleported to the tea shop. Two houses down, a couple screamed at each other, their argument playing out in silhouettes across their beige curtains while the cries of their baby drifted out of the open window.

"We closed down the bot basement. Shouldn't there be peace and harmony on these isles?" I said.

Ezra shrugged. "It's just a one-off lovers tiff. They happen without meddling gods."

In Shanghai Moon, a night light shone, and an incense stick burned on the counter. The foxes, wearing matching kimonos, huddled together with the intimacy only lovers shared. Echo was in there, too, with his nose buried in a pile of dried mushrooms.

I knocked on the window, where a display of teapots took precedence.

A worried expression marred Fei Yen's smooth visage as she detangled herself from Faeza's embrace to open the door. "Come in, come in. After you told us about the bot room full of dark elves, we were worried our message would not arrive without interference. But then I remembered how much you dislike ginger tea, and I knew you'd understand to come here."

She closed the door and locked it behind us.

Echo bounded over, purring with delight. "I have been trying to advise the foxes about how to achieve more custom."

I kissed his head. "I am sure they are very grateful for your advice."

He sniffed the air. "This shop smells of herbs. Herbs are a curse on all of mankind, ruining the pure taste of meat. If the foxes wish to appeal to leopards, it is imperative they rid themselves of half of these jars."

"It is a shame that you dislike herbs, Chanakya Gunbir Hredhaan of Maharashtra," said Fei Yen. "Since the land of your ancestors is rich with them. We will not change the shop since leopards aren't the clientele we wish to appeal to."

"How rude," said Echo. "But you are only foxes. What could you know of business?"

Faeza rolled her eyes at him and embraced us. "You look better, wolf. Our tonic has worked wonders."

I shot Ezra a teasing glance. We both knew it wasn't the tonic that had cured him.

The look between us didn't go unnoticed.

Fei Yen and Faeza exchanged glances and then giggled.

Echo's emerald eyes narrowed, and then he, too, grinned. "Has somebody been up to hanky panky?"

I spluttered. "We're not in kindergarten."

Dark shadows lurked under Faeza's eyes. She took pity on me. "Quite right. Let's get on, shall we? We looked for Flinar in all his usual haunts. At his home, on Streatham Common, under Blackfriars Bridge, in the alley behind the Vicarage and even as far as the woods where he hid with Tielbu and the runaway dark elves. We followed graffiti tags and dust trails and couldn't find him anywhere. We checked the elves' new drinking spot in the secret garden in Regent's Park. At first, we thought that, too, had been a wasted trip, but just as we were in the pergola tunnel leading to the cast-iron exit, one of Flinar's friends appeared out of nowhere. Fei Yen let out a squeal because he was a particularly ugly specimen of dark elf—"

"To cut a long story short, we found him," said Fei Yen. "Or at least, we know where he is."

Faeza trembled. "The rumour is that the Ravenmaster took him as revenge for him helping you. The elf should have known better than to meddle with the gods, but I suppose his love for you overrode all common sense."

Ezra cursed. "So he's in the Tower?"

Faeza nodded. "We think so."

Tremors coursed through my body. I thought we'd beaten Hermes. I couldn't bear the thought of my friend all alone in that cold place and the fact that my big mouth might have led the Ravenmaster straight to him.

"Do you think my brother was behind his capture?" How else would the god have known to target Flinar? It was his friendship with me that had put him in danger.

"It could be," said Echo. "Stinky werepigeon."

My eyes filled with tears. "We have to rescue Flinar. Right now."

A weighted look passed between the foxes, and then Faeza spoke for them. "We will come too. We love the elf."

Ezra's gaze ping-ponged between me and the rest of the group, and his lips pressed together in a slight grimace. "Dammit. What am I being roped into again?"

I glared at him. "I know. But I have to go, with or without you."

"Always so stubborn." He brushed his calloused thumb across my cheek and sighed. "Okay, for you as much as the elf. But I have to make it to Wildwoods by midnight, come what may."

Echo growled. "I go where the druid goes. And I like that weird little fellow. Is there time for a snack before we go?"

"No," we said in unison.

Echo grinned. "It is good we are on the same page. I did that."

"Ezra teleports us in. We get Flinar, and we get out. We watch each other's backs. No chit-chat. No heroics." I gulped. "If Sahil is there, we'll have to be careful. He's not trustworthy."

"The stinky werepigeon will pay," said Echo.

I bit my lip. I couldn't hurt my brother. I put a hand on my satchel. Feeling the edges of the catalogue of creatures in there comforted me. "Ezra, I need my sword. It's in my knicker drawer at home. Would you mind?"

The corners of his mouth lifted in a wry smile. "Not the kind of invitation I expected, but I'll take it."

He disappeared and came back in twenty seconds and handed me my weapon.

I wriggled into the baldric, and we stood in a circle.

"Ready?" said Ezra.

I didn't feel ready, but I nodded all the same. The five of us spiralled between the worlds through the monochrome layer beneath all colour and logic. We emerged in the vast, damp, moonlit room where the raven enclosures loomed. We scanned the room, alert to a small whimpering sound, but the cages were empty.

I frowned. "I don't understand. Where is Flinar? The Ravenmaster has him here. He can't bear to leave behind all the remnants of prestige, even though the ravens have flown. He has no intention of leaving. Which means Flinar is here too."

Worry painted frown lines on Fei Yen's face. "I have caught the elf's scent, but that doesn't mean he is in this room. There are endless miles of secret tunnels in and under this city, and many of them are in this very building."

Another muffled sound met my ears, a shaking and a scratching.

Echo prowled beside the central raven enclosure. "I can smell the werepigeon and the elf. They are here. Hidden by magic.

"The leopard is right. I can smell them too." Ezra touched the moon charm on his necklace, and the lights in the room blazed to life.

I gave a startled gasp as the light revealed my brother skulking in the corner.

He grinned. "Well, isn't this a party? How clever you are, my little sister."

In his hand, he swung the same key on an iron ring I had seen in the Ravenmaster's manicured hands.

A chill ran up my spine.

Echo hissed. "You're not a werepigeon. You're a weasel."

"I'm many things." Sahil shrugged. "But carry on underestimating me. It seems that is all anyone has done since this new life of ours unfolded."

"So it's true," I said. To think, all this time I had thought Lavinia to be the one who had led him astray after the coven dinner. "You're working for the Ravenmaster."

"I like to think I'm working *with* him, sis. But don't get your knickers in a twist. We each make our choices, isn't that right? Speaking of choices, why did you bring two old Chinese women with you?"

"He means it as an insult," said Fei Yen to Faeza. "But ageing is the greatest privilege in life."

"Is that from a fortune cookie? Never mind. I'll show you your little friend if it makes you happier, Alisha." He strode to the raven enclosures, whistling a merry tune, then waved the key over the lock of the middle one.

A growl laced Ezra's voice. "Stay together."

My breath caught in my throat. It was as if a curtain had lifted. Flinar slumped on his knees in the central enclosure. His parched lips hung open, and a handful of his wispy hair lay at his feet like he had twisted it out in anguish or someone had torn it from his scalp. His milky eyes were slow to register our arrival. They grew large and fearful.

"I knew you would come, Alisha. The Ravenmaster said his birds would peck my eyes out. That he wouldn't even give me the coins for my passage to the afterlife. That I deserved it for creating the black holes." He lifted his chin, and there was a ligature mark around his neck, a red rim of pain on his dull grey skin. His voice quivered. "For helping you."

"You're my brother," I said to Sahil. "We're a family. Give me the key. Let him out. You wouldn't have shown me he was here unless you wanted to help."

"Nah, Alisha, I just wanted to show you I won," said Sahil. "He's staying right where he is. It's more than my life is worth to defy the Ravenmaster, but at least I got to brag a little. He will be back any minute, and you can speak to him yourself."

Flinar gripped the bars of the enclosure. His eyes darted to the shadows behind us. "Save yourself, Alisha. Please leave. If I die here, you should know that the red-haired woman in the elf drinking hole wasn't Rashida."

"Quiet, elf," hissed Sahil.

Flinar cowered and stuttered on his words. "It was Margola. I got them confused. I'm not good at non-elvish features. When I found out, I was bundled into a postbag and brought here. There's a roomful of elves intercepting messages in her basement."

"It's okay," I said. "We found it. We just need to get you out of here."

Then Ezra would do his thing at the Court of the Wolves, and we could get back to enjoying each other. I drew my sword and eyeballed my brother as only a little sister knew how. "What would Mum and Dad think? One way or another, I will take those keys off you."

A sly smile lifted his lips. "They'd tell us to sort it out between ourselves like grown-ups. But I know you, Alisha. You don't have the killer instinct. You would never cross that line. You wouldn't hurt a fly."

Wasn't I supposed to get into adulthood supporting and supported by my sibling? Now wasn't the time to tell him about the vampire I had turned to dust or the wolf I had slashed.

"I would cross that line," said Echo. "And sing a song while I mauled you."

Faeza held Fei Yen's. "My wife and I feel the same way. We strongly believe in karma."

"Sorry, mate, if I weren't technically your mentor, I would too." Every cell in Ezra's body looked active. He didn't seem ready to attack my brother, but he'd defend us to his dying breath.

My sword whispered to me. I replaced it in its sheath like I'd been burned, ignoring Ezra's look of concern.

"He's right about one thing. A sword's not the way to deal with my brother." I adopted a kickboxing stance, widening my feet, bending my knees and raising my fists. "I don't need metal to kick your arse. Now give me that key."

Sahil's lips twisted into a sneer. He put the key in his pocket. "Come and get it."

"Keep an eye out for any sign of the Ravenmaster. And hands off. He's mine." I ran at my brother and landed two punches to his jaw, an uppercut and a hook.

He clutched his face, shocked that I'd actually had the guts to do it.

I didn't give him time to recover. I delivered a right hook kick to his legs. I was smaller, but he hadn't taken the self-defence classes I had. His legs buckled, and his self-assured swagger disappeared quicker than water down a drain. He curled into a ball on the stone floor, and I almost felt sorry for him. He'd always gotten by on his good looks and deviousness. But I knew he had a soft side too. I didn't want to hurt him. I just wanted that bloody key.

"Would it be bullying if we all jumped on him?" Ezra drawled.

Faeza sounded eager. "I have seen WWE. We could try."

I could not believe how undignified this was getting. I took a deep breath, ready to pin my brother down and stick my hands down his jeans to fight for Flinar's freedom.

"Oh. My. God," said Fei Yen.

Sahil shrivelled before our eyes, warping, shrinking and cooing, and out popped a jubilant werepigeon with the key gripped in its orange beak. I leapt on him, but he evaded me, flying up. The beginnings of a blue glow emanated from him.

"He's engaging his shield," I cried.

Echo had a hunter's instincts. He sprang up on his powerful hind legs and caught the grunting werepigeon in his mouth. If Sahil's mouth had been free, maybe he would have chomped down on Echo in a bid to escape, but his beady eyes swivelled in his head in terror, his shield fizzled out, and the iron key clattered to the floor.

I tossed it to the foxes, my gut wrenching at seeing the hope flooding Flinar's face.

Then I returned my attention to Echo and Sahil, terrified that Echo's powerful jaw would maim Sahil forever.

Not that he didn't deserve it.

I needn't have worried. The werepigeon shrank in size again, transforming into the bulbous spider that was my brother's other form. He slipped from Echo's grasp and fell to our feet, scuttling away.

Ezra's urgent voice. "I hear the knocking of a staff. We have to leave."

Echo surged into the shadows and dipped his head, sucking my brother off the floor and into his mouth.

I squealed. The knocking grew louder. "Echo, spit my brother out."

His emerald eyes begged me to change my mind, his words hard to decipher, given the creepy crawly in his mouth.

"Spit him out!"

Echo spat. "He tasted disgusting anyway."

Out came my brother in all his spidery glory, wet with Echo's gloopy saliva.

The foxes scooped up a weak Flinar between them just as a flash of red and navy of the Beefeater's uniform came into my peripheral vision.

Blood rushed to my head as Ezra grabbed us all and teleported us to safety.

Glee bubbled up inside me as we escaped. Take that, heathen god. He deserved neither respect nor fear. I would refer to him forever more as Herpes, not Hermes.

The Ravenmaster's bellow of fury chased us into the unknown.

21

F linar was dehydrated and could not walk unsupported. His thin legs buckled repeatedly on the way up the stairs to Fei Yen and Faeza's flat. In the end, Ezra cradled him against his chest and laid him in the foxes' bedroom, a room of sumptuous red and brown velvets and silks. The elf closed his eyes against the plump pillows with a painful grimace, and we tiptoed out. He seemed to have survived his ordeal intact, but his psychological state scared me. He must have felt so alone.

My stomach clenched, thinking of my brother being in cahoots with the Ravenmaster.

"We will let him sleep and patch him up and feed him broth to build up his strength," said Faeza. "And he can sleep in our bed, even if he smells like a rotting corpse. I suppose there is truth to the rumours about elf hygiene."

Fei Yen scolded her. "Darling, this is one of those moments we were talking about. The poor elf has been held captive amongst raven mess. You mustn't always believe what you read."

Ezra looked at his watch. "I need a quick change of clothes. Then we must go. The Court of the Wolves awaits."

"What kind of justice happens this quickly anyway?" I said.

"Justice in the Otherworld is always swift, Alisha," said Echo. "Or else it doesn't happen at all. Tonight, the whole senate will be in attendance to see what happens to one of their own."

"We will stay and look after the elf," said Fei Yen. "Wildwoods is no place for us."

I nodded and hugged them before placing a kiss on Flinar's grizzled cheek. "Then we will see you on the other side."

TRADITIONALLY, the Court of the Wolves took place under the moonlight. It needed neither a building nor an audience. In fact, justice in the Otherworld happened so quickly that it was down and dirty. A few hastily gathered facts, a drink of truth tonic, a witness or two, a majority verdict of peers, an assembled pack of the ruling wolves, a sentence decided and carried out by the Justice Minister. A draining of magic, imprisonment for the ages, the wiping of fortunes or rehabilitation under the tutelage of gentle giants.

Except, rules had to be hastily rewritten when the peculiar in charge of proceedings happened to be in the dock himself. It was unconscionable and unprecedented that the Justice Minister himself could be on trial.

But there we were.

For the purpose of Gunnolf's trial, it fell to Phinnaeous Shine—as the Prime Sorcerer and the most senior member of the senate—to step into the role of presiding judge. It was a task he was born to perform —a man who loved the drama, flourishes and oratory that came with a grand stage.

We met Marina at the Yew Tree, and she handed me a cool bag.

I hugged her. "This is it?"

"As you asked. You know, Robert says there hasn't been a change in civic relations since you destroyed the bot room, but it takes time for human relationships to heal after they have fractured." She turned to Ezra. "Neuhoff, you look hot."

Echo purred plaintively. "Why does no one ever say things like that about me?"

I ignored him. "What will happen to Gunnolf if the senate decides against him?"

"Who knows? Gunnolf called the shots, with Senate approval. There was always a grey area. I wasn't comfortable with the Prime Sorcerer as the presiding judge. His instincts are more sadistic than some." There was a tightness in Ezra's face. Seeing his uncle like this, his role in putting Gunnolf in the dock wasn't easy for him. He cleared his throat. "When we're in there, I'll be presenting the case. I may have to call one or all of you as witnesses. Even in small doses, the truth tonic is potent. Just remember, only answer the questions I ask."

Marina grimaced. "I didn't much like it the first time when the witches spiked our drinks. Green juice is awful enough without taking it up another notch."

"There are many people who are outed as fools when they take truth tonic. I look forward to evaluating the inner monologues of my enemies. It gives me a wonderful sense of superiority," said Echo. "But since we are on the same side and most peculiars are too unintelligent to pay attention to the subtle body language of a leopard, I will swish my tail like a flag as a signal for you to stop talking."

"Much appreciated." I hoisted the cool bag onto my shoulder.

Ezra's voice made my skin tingle. "It's nearly midnight. Ready?"

I squeezed his hand. "You'll be fine."

The corners of his lips lifted in a sad smile.

We followed him through the trees. Goosebumps ran up my bare arms as we arrived in the arena, where quiet reigned. The senate, with Phinnaeous Shine at their centre, sat on a long bench, whispering amongst themselves. Globes of light floated above them, untethered to any electricity. Only Gunnolf sat apart, alone on a stark, straight-backed chair, as if all the vestiges of comfort afforded the senate and the support of his pack had already been stripped from him. His beard had grown unkempt, and his eyes stared straight ahead as if he refused to acknowledge or partake in the grave proceedings. Ezra's pack had gathered on the right of the senate. Five wolves waited, anxious and alert to every movement, and incomplete without their alpha and beta to lead them.

Ezra wore a white, open-collared shirt and black trousers, with his hair slicked back in a more formal style. He strode towards the Prime Sorcerer with more confidence than he felt. They exchanged brief words as Marina, Echo and I filed into wooden pews that seemed to have dropped from the sky into the sawdust.

Orpheus's dark eyes smouldered as we took our seats. *Trust you to escape from the pack farmhouse and not take your punishment like a good girl. Although perhaps congratulations are in order? Robert Jameson told me what a busy girl you've been.*

I grinned at him and didn't fight his voice in my head. It was no longer an intrusion. Somewhere along the way, we had become friends.

Not so much with Gunnolf, however, whose eyes seared with hatred at the sight of me, even though it had been his own decisions that had led him to this point, not mine. Calypso, whose blade runners shimmered dangerously in the moonlight, was deep in conversation with Lavinia. The witch's pink-tipped fingers curled around a decanter of truth tonic.

But it was Margola's reaction that stood out to me. She stood up, her eyes fixed on the cool bag as if her skin called to her like a beacon.

We were no longer enemies. At least, I didn't think so.

Sometimes the way of the world pitted women against each other. I understood now that her hand had been forced, and there were many things that would cause me to act in a way others might judge harshly. Hadn't I struck my own brother?

I met Margola's eyes and softened my gaze, willing her to understand that the selkie skin was hers and always had been and that I wouldn't keep it from her, whatever came next.

She stared at me, and only when Orpheus laid a hand on her arm and whispered in her ear did she sit down, her eyes never moving from the cool bag.

I gave the minister your message. You continue to surprise me, druid. Most other peculiars would have used the skin you hold as a weapon against their enemy. Or at least strung out the pain as revenge for the thoughtlessness with which she has treated you, said Orpheus. *Although I would do well not to run to your rescue so often, given what happened last time.*

I'd started to like our private moments. *Yeah, sorry about that. My instincts are always more important than rules or traditions. I hope I didn't leave you in a bad spot when you vouched for me.*

Orpheus rolled his eyes, but the rest of his body remained still. *Given how things have worked out for the werewolf, I dare say it doesn't matter—this time. But if we are to remain friends, I'd like to think that sometimes you could follow my advice.*

Marina nudged me and broke our connection. "Are you making eyes at Orpheus Might?"

I flushed. "Err, no. Of course not."

"Shh," said a fallen angel in the pew behind us. "It's about to start."

The Prime Sorcerer rose to his feet. His robes swept the floor, and the shape of his silver-tinged afro mirrored the moon above, giving him a celestial aura. By now, I was pretty sure he'd carefully dressed to create that impact. His keen eyes scanned the arena and lingered on my face.

A piece of paper and quill shot up in the air from the presiding bench and documented the proceedings.

"We have convened here tonight at the Court of the Wolves to address a most grave matter." The Prime Sorcerer cast Gunnolf a haughty glance. "Those who serve on the senate do not do so for their own advancement. We are here to serve the Wildwoods community. To shape it in a way that benefits peculiars for generations to come. To betray this duty is almost as grievous a sin as the murder charges. We are here to decide whether Gunnolf Zev is guilty of the charges of murder and if he has betrayed the post of Justice Minister by behaving in a manner unbefitting his post. Stand, werewolf."

Gunnolf stood, keeping his eyes lowered.

"Do you understand why you are here and the charges which have been filed against you?" said the Prime Sorcerer coldly.

The response rang out across the arena, amplified by magic. "I do."

"You understand that the decision we reach tonight will reflect our mutual wisdom and is non-reversible. It will be binding."

This time Gunnolf lifted his head, and his eyes blazed with barely restrained anger. "I do."

"Then let us proceed." Phinnaeous Shine paused to gather his breath, and a pin drop could have been heard. "Who is presenting this case?"

Ezra, who had waited silently amongst the wolfpack, stepped forward. "I am, Prime Sorcerer."

There were no defence or prosecution lawyers at the Court of the Wolves. Those functions had been rendered obsolete by the truth tonic. There was only the truth, the testimonies, the evidence and the verdict.

"It is very unusual to be presenting at your own alpha's trial," said Phinnaeous Shine. "Do you promise before the court that you will drink the truth tonic so that neither pack nor familial bonds will compromise your presentation?"

"Forgive me, Prime Sorcerer, but my uncle is no longer the alpha. I am," said Ezra. "I'll take the tonic."

"Then let us drink the tonic brewed by the naked witch Ravynne," said the Prime Sorcerer.

Marina giggled. "She's sitting behind us, sheathed only in a pashmina. The sort of woman who gives you an eyeful in the sauna when you're least expecting it."

"Shh," I said. "Gunnolf will only get what's coming to him if Ezra doesn't lose his nerve, but he's got to drink that stuff too."

The Prime Sorcerer waved his hand, and the crystal decanter in front of Lavinia uncorked itself and bobbed along to the end of the bench, stopping before each senator to pour a shot's worth of viscous amber liquid into the glasses before them. Each senator drank their portion in turn, grimacing as they gulped down the noxious fluid. When all had finished, the decanter poured out another two glasses.

Ezra picked them up and offered one to Gunnolf, who clenched the glass so hard I thought it would break. The two men exchanged a long glance, and it was Gunnolf who dropped his eyes first. They chinked glasses and poured the liquid down their throats.

"Begin, Mr. Neuhoff," commanded Phinnaeous Shine.

Ezra grimaced, put the glass down and addressed his uncle. "Gunnolf Zev, you have been an upstanding member of this community for many years. That is not in question. Yet you stand before us accused of murder. Let us establish first, are you a killer?"

Gunnolf's lips curved into a hard smile. "We all are here. You. The pack. The senate members pretending to be holier than thou."

Ezra nodded. "How many have you killed unjustly?"

The older wolf gulped, but it was impossible to lie with the truth tonic coursing through his veins. He spat the words out. "Six wolves that did not belong to our pack. I did what was necessary in the name of harmony."

"Whose harmony, Gunnolf?" said Ezra.

Gunnolf made a jittery movement with his fingers. "The harmony of our pack."

"It is time, Prime Sorcerer, for the vault of evidence," said Ezra.

Phinnaeous Shine lifted his arms and brought them down with force.

I gasped as the freezer from Gunnolf's padlocked storeroom landed in the arena. The senate remained stoic, neither moved nor surprised by the theatrics or the horror that lay within.

"I see the meat has landed," said Echo.

Ezra walked over to the freezer and opened it. "Here lie the remains of three wolves. What did you do to the other bodies?"

"I instructed the pack to build pyres to burn them," said Gunnolf.

"Why did the wolves come to our land?"

The words flew out of his mouth, but his clenched fists showed how he fought to resist. "Because there are forces gathering that no one understands. The wolves wanted to join a stronger pack."

Ezra suppressed a shudder. "How did you kill them?"

"I know the woods like the back of my hand. They didn't expect me to strike. Even if they had, a black wolf seems like a shadow in your peripheral vision until it is upon you. I bit them cleanly."

"You could have just turned them away," said Ezra.

He glowered. "I turned away many more. After taking you in, many made the mistake of thinking the pack would take in stray wolves. But had I accepted them, I could not be certain I had the strength to rule over a larger pack with unknown parts within it. I am old. I thought I would not survive an alpha challenge. Indeed, I was right. I just didn't think it would be my own nephew who usurped me."

A shadow passed over Ezra's face. "An alpha's job is to protect the pack. Not to endanger it. If times are darkening, then a larger pack would have been in our best interests."

"I had already investigated another way to save us, boy, but you refused to see sense. We would have grown our pack with pups who were loyal to us." A bitter laugh erupted from him. "Even our own kin can be a disappointment. Isn't that right, nephew?"

Ezra bit the inside of his cheek. For a private man, playing out this family drama in public must cost him. He swivelled to face the Prime Sorcerer. "I ask permission to call a witness before the court."

"Who is this witness?" Phinnaeous Shine leaned forward.

Ezra took a deep breath. "The druid Alisha Verma."

Phinnaeous Shine sighed. "Why is it that the druid is always at the centre of all our troubles?"

Ezra's expression shuttered. "I cannot say, Prime Sorcerer."

"Then you are not very candid, Mr Neuhoff," said the Prime Sorcerer. "Step forward, druid."

I left the cool bag with Marina and tripped over my feet in my hurry to reach the bench.

The Prime Sorcerer glowered. "You dare come armed to the Court of Wolves?"

Orpheus rolled his eyes. *You need to come back to my classroom, druid, so I can teach you some manners.*

I mumbled an apology, ripped off Transcender and my satchel and handed them to Calypso for safekeeping. The decanter of truth tonic poured a fresh glass under Lavinia's watchful eye.

"Drink it," said the Prime Sorcerer.

I swallowed it in one go and wiped a hand across my mouth.

Nice work, said Orpheus. *Talk slowly so you don't say more than you intend. The tonic is a tricky thing, even for me.*

Ezra rubbed the back of his neck. "Alisha Verma, can you tell the court what else you discovered in the freezer at the farmhouse?"

I nodded. "A slimy selkie skin."

"Who did the skin belong to?"

Margola Silver leaned forward, her expression pained.

"To the very beautiful, very manipulative Information Minister Margola Silver, who has absolutely no qualms about frolicking naked in the Thames. At like six o'clock in the morning when most people are grouching over their cup of coffee."

You have as much restraint as a leaky faucet. Orpheus's face was red with suppressed laughter.

I frowned at him.

"A one-word answer will suffice." Ezra blinked. "And where is that selkie skin now?"

"Wrapped in a Tesco's bag, stashed in a cool bag, on my friend Marina Ambrose's lap, here in the arena. We'll be glad to return it to its owner, actually. A bit odd having that next to a packet of fish fingers in the freezer. Worse than those weirdos who freeze their placentas and then chop them up into little bits to eat. What goes out should stay out. You know?" I clapped my hand over my mouth.

Echo's tail swished furiously.

Ezra sighed. "You may return to your seat."

I clasped my hands together in apology, retrieved my belongings from Calypso and gave wolf Deirdra a thumbs-up before returning to my seat.

"You are an embarrassment," said Echo. "But you are our embarrassment."

"Gunnolf, did you steal Margola Silver's selkie skin?" said Ezra.

The ex-alpha spoke in a flat voice. "I did."

Ezra neared him, hackles rising. "Can you enlighten the court as to why?"

Half-lidded eyes regarded Ezra. "I needed her to distract you and the druid. I knew my only chance of getting away with the murders was if your mind was otherwise occupied. And I hoped bad publicity for her would drive you into Rashida's arms, and my plan for the pups would come to fruition."

Ezra's posture went rigid. Chords twanged in his neck. For a moment, I thought he would give in to the urge and become his wolf. His desire to hurt Gunnolf warred with his duty to complete the proceedings as per convention. He wasn't the executioner here. He was merely the person who brought the facts to light.

He closed his eyes and exhaled, and when he opened them, his veneer of control was back, although I could only imagine what raged underneath. "Margola Silver, do you corroborate this information?"

Margola held her chin up, though her eyes filled with tears. "I do. Gunnolf stole my skin and threatened to set it alight. We were friends and colleagues for years, but he thought nothing of taking the most precious part of me, even though every shifter at this court knows how callous a crime it is to steal the very thing that allows us to be our true selves."

That was it—the turning point.

The moment when every person in the arena turned against Gunnolf Zev.

It didn't matter that Gunnolf was a murderer. Nobody knew those dead wolves. But they recognised the truth in Margola's words. That Gunnolf had betrayed the very people he should have understood the most. That even as Justice Minister, he had shown no sense of fairness and justice to even those he knew.

The wolves howled. And Ezra, too, threw back his head and howled.

A mournful howl that sent shivers up my spine.

The Prime Sorcerer stood and smoothed out his robes. "The wolves have spoken. They have deemed this the point at which we decide. What say you, senate?"

They each spoke in turn, the ones who had been Gunnolf's allies and others who didn't care a jot about his fate, such as Erelim, the fallen angel, looking bored but oh so hot.

Will you concentrate? said Orpheus.

The verdict was unanimous.

"Guilty," boomed the Prime Sorcerer.

Lavinia smiled.

I couldn't help but think that, without Gunnolf there, her witchy manicure would sink deeper into Ezra.

"As presiding judge," boomed the Prime Sorcerer, "it falls to me to pass the sentence. We live in a world where shadows vie with the light. Where those in power, in the halls of Westminster and the palaces of this country, too often have feet of clay. It falls upon this senate to be exemplary in discharging our powers. Gunnolf Zev has sadly fallen short of this expectation. He has murdered in cold blood and stolen from one of our own to protect his power. I ,therefore, sentence him to fifty years in confinement in the dungeons under the Ritz Hotel and for him to be indefinitely stripped of his powers by a witches' binding potion."

Gunnolf's body sagged. "Phinnaeous, please—"

The Prime Sorcerer raised a hand. "Count yourself lucky not to have been sentenced to death."

Gunnolf jumped up and glanced about in frantic desperation, then looked up at the moon.

"Uh oh," said Marina. "That's a cornered animal if I ever saw one."

My mouth fell open as Gunnolf transformed into his wolf, his back arching and limbs cracking, clothes tearing and teeth growing.

But Ezra was there too, and he didn't hesitate. His shirt ripped and his trousers too as muscles bulged and his wolf emerged, snapping and snarling at his uncle, tossing him to the ground with skill and ease.

We fled the pews, and the senate scattered as the rest of the pack joined Ezra, circling the black wolf who had once been their alpha. A disgraced wolf who soon wouldn't even be a wolf anymore. They showed no mercy in subduing him, tearing flesh and fur from his graceful frame until he was a pitiful, cowering wreck.

Lavinia took her chance. She whipped out her dull but remarkable umbrella. I knew better than to underestimate her. A spike emerged from its end. The wolves parted to allow her access, and she stabbed the black one quickly, then tore a strip from Gunnolf's clothing that lay in scraps in the sawdust. Her eyes gleamed.

"This will do. Sorry, brother-in-law." Then she ejected the blood onto the clothing from the point of her umbrella, chanting all the while. With a swish of her umbrella wand, the blood-soaked ribbon burst into flames. The witch blew out the flames with a satisfied smile and dusted the ashes off her hands.

When I looked to Gunnolf, the black wolf had gone, and instead, his human body lay curled and panting between the paws of the pack. They circled him, howling. He wept at their centre.

I didn't care. I'd save my sympathy for his victims.

As we watched, Ezra accompanied Lavinia to the ranks of the senate.

"Do you know what this means?" said Marina.

"I do," said Echo.

I had no idea what it meant. But I had a feeling I was about to find out.

22

The wolf pack left first, ushering a broken Gunnolf through the trees, presumably to his fate in the basement of the Ritz. Next, the freezer of wolf bodies sank into the sawdust, but the metaphysics of magic meant I couldn't be sure whether the bodies had been buried beneath the arena, whisked to another place to be studied and prodded or returned to the families for funeral ceremonies.

Then, the Prime Sorcerer plucked the notes and quill from the air and shook the page. It multiplied into two, and he offered Margola a copy.

She folded it and slid it into her handbag, then hurried over to me to collect the cool bag. "All I could think of while sitting up there was ripping this from your hands. I am grateful for you retrieving it but furious that my home is missing. Still, I didn't earn your friendship."

"Lady, we're not friends," I wrinkled my nose. "And if I'm honest, I couldn't wait to get rid of this thing."

Margola's eyebrows snapped together.

I realised the truth serum was still doing the talking. I wasn't the only one still impacted, either. Marina tugged me over to Orpheus and Ezra, still in wolf form. My ears burned red.

Orpheus's eyes were hard as flint as he stared down at Ezra. "I played poker with that wolf for years. You're no replacement for him. You don't deserve the druid either."

My eyebrows shot up. *Now who's letting the truth serum do the talking?*

Hardly. Those were intentional insults now that Mr Neuhoff has gone up in rank, just so both of us realise who the superior is.

I gave him a death stare, then crouched down next to Ezra and buried my face in his soft neck. "Shall we go home?"

Every sinew in Ezra's body tensed as he let out a warning growl.

Echo bounded over to my other side with a hiss.

I looked up. The trees shifted, and a nightmarish vision approached. I blinked to check my sight didn't deceive me. Anxiety curled its fingers into my vision and swirled in my stomach.

The Ravenmaster stalked towards us in his red-and-navy tunic. The red of blood and the black of the ravens and night, just as Marina had warned me. His strawberry blond curls and clean-shaven face reminded me of heavenly cherubs, but I knew by now that his heart was charred black. As we gawped, he walked clean through us with the slow gait and supreme confidence of a ceremonial procession. His staff swung in the air, and golden wings fluttered on his hat and boots. When he reached the bench, he occupied the central seat that had only just been vacated by the Prime Sorcerer.

As if he owned the world.

This could never end well.

My breath hitched in my chest as my eyes darted to the Prime Sorcerer. He was the leader here. Surely he'd do something? But all I saw was his retreating back, taking half the senate with him. What on earth was he playing at?

Calypso sighed. "And so the faithful remain, and the lily-livered leave. It was always so."

Rayna grimaced at her departing colleagues, then addressed the Ravenmaster, putting on her best headmistress voice. "Leave this place. You are not welcome here."

The Ravenmaster jerked his head towards her. "Are all druids this tiresome?"

"Keep Marina safe," I said to Echo. Ezra's throat reverberated with a growl as I stood and faced the Ravenmaster. "You lost, Hermes. Everything is going back to normal. It's only a matter of time."

The Ravenmaster smirked at me as if no one else in the arena existed. "No, druid, you might think you have won, but look around and see how divided you are. The leader of the Otherworld has fled, leaving just a handful of you to defend this great emblem of peculiars."

Orpheus stepped forward. His voice betrayed no hint of fear, even though vampires tended to have a healthy fear of gods, what with stakes and crosses and holy water. I worried for a moment that he might take this chance to die at the hands of a god if he still willed it.

In the name of literature, forget about my emotional health and concentrate on the immortal being in our midst, druid. Aloud, he said to Hermes, "You stand on protected ground. Why did the yew tree allow you entry?"

"Such tepid barriers can't keep me out, vampire. The gods have walked this earth for millennia. And look at your compatriots. Not even a truth serum helped you find common ground. That's the thing about communications. I didn't need to take a jackhammer to cause divisions between you. A little spark, and you are perfectly capable of it yourselves."

I frowned. "We destroyed your room of elf bots, Hermes. It's over."

"You think I have one bot room? How small you think. I have any number of rooms dotted across this measly island. With every keystroke, a seed of harm is sewn. Take your Wildwoods performance, for example. A flurry of messages to those in this arena and you were pressured into an attempt to animate a fox. Imagine that—a wind druid thinking that her animation powers would stretch to foxes. You mortals are very stupid sometimes. Anyway, a little prompt from my hackers and you ended up with egg on your face and didn't even connect it back to me."

Lavinia smirked. "Wonderfully devious when you think about it. Perhaps we could learn a thing or two from him."

"I learned long ago not to fall for sycophancy, witch. Save your compliments for someone else. I am well aware of my brilliance. And soon, my reputation will spread. When I'm finished here, wait and see what havoc I'll wreak in Silicon Valley." His glacial eyes nullified his jaunty tone. "Elves are wonderful little fellows. What they lack in digits, they make up for in nimbleness and perseverance. Very hard working and quite wasted as street cleaners. They remind me of myself in some ways. All I have to do is offer them a few trivial powers, a tiny Faustian contract in exchange for what I want."

So that was why the elves hadn't escaped of their own accord from Margola's basement.

"Extraordinary how many are tempted by the offer of flight," said the Ravenmaster. "It tends to be a top five superpower wish list. It was only a matter of time before you found out. You are so meddlesome that I decided to pip you to the post. I didn't want you coming to my home again. So you and the wolf aren't going to make it out of here tonight."

Ezra lunged forward. I held him back with the slightest touch. He bared his teeth at the god, every sinew in his body alert.

Leave, said Orpheus. *Take the wolf and go. It is too dangerous for you here.*

You leave, I said, although my knees were so wobbly I needed a lie down. *I started this. I'm going to finish it.*

We couldn't run this time. How could we run from Wildwoods when it was the emblem of our country's Otherworld? Abandoning it would mean the god had won. And I wouldn't let him win, not without putting up a fight.

I addressed Hermes, "Wildwoods will adapt to destroy you. Or we will."

I looked at the motley crew left in the arena. Seven remained, who lined up with me against our foe, our backs to the cabins in the trees that made up Wildwoods: Ezra, Marina, Echo, Orpheus, Rayna, Calypso and inexplicably, Lavinia, wielding her umbrella like a cricket bat. Calypso removed her suit jacket like she meant business. Would eight against a god be enough? I closed my eyes and said a silent prayer for Gaia to hear us. Although, hadn't she said she was a cheerleader only?

"You won't turf me out of this place so easily. You came to my home uninvited. The Tower of London has been my sanctuary for decades. It has kept me safe, even while others were mutilated there. It is where I lay my head to rest at night. Where I weathered crises of faith. Where I have met dignitaries and tended to souls entrusted to me. And yet, you violated my home by breaking into it. Even then, I respected the rules of hospitality. I gave you a chance to run. But then you destroyed the temporary home of my ravens. You returned to my sanctuary when I was not there." He toyed with his staff. "So I came to yours."

"I dislike the druid as much as anyone. But the fact remains, you are not welcome here, Hermes." Lavinia pointed her umbrella at him with her right hand and raised her left arm in an *en-garde* position. "And you will not harm a hair on the wolf's body."

"Settle down, witch. I remember Salem," retorted the god.

Orpheus was as still as a cobra about to strike. I had yet to see him in action as a warrior. I had no idea if he was a biter, a strongman or a martial artist. Did he fight open-handed or with closed fists? Did he hold a weapon or ride a stallion? Was he a damsel who would need rescuing or a scrappy fighter who could hold his own?

For the love of life, druid, stop distracting me. "This is your last chance," said Orpheus. "You heard the druid. Leave."

The Ravenmaster stood up. "I am a god. You would do well to remember that. Not all of you have to die." He raised his hat, and a spider scuttled down his face and onto the bench. "In fact, our brother would prefer you lived, but mortal lives don't always play out according to plan."

With a pop, Sahil transformed from the bulbous spider into his werepigeon form.

A bitter taste filled my mouth. Just when I thought this couldn't get any worse.

Marina groaned. "I'm starting to think I should have stayed in to play doctors and nurses with Robert."

"The werepigeon does it again. He is incapable of making an entrance to cheers," said Echo.

Hermes chuckled. "The beef-obsessed leopard is amusing. He may remain at my side once this is all over."

I turned my eyes away from my brother, whose beady yellow eyes were fixated on me, and focused on the god. "All this to alleviate your boredom. All this because you wish to return to the old ways of pigeon carriers. All this because you can't bear not to be the one with your hand on the tiller. The one in control."

"A bored mind is an idle mind. How can a god not see the possibilities of this world?" said Calypso.

"So what if the world is a little chaotic and disjointed?" I said. "When did you lose faith in beauty?"

"The day we fell from the heavens," said the Ravenmaster. "How can there be beauty when He is dead? How can our Father expect us to continue acting in God's image when he is not here to provide an example? The world is not what it was. Humans no longer pray to us in gratitude. They pray only in fear and need."

"Yes, I know. And those diminished prayers are why the strength of the gods has diminished over the centuries. Gaia told me."

His blue eyes narrowed. "But she didn't tell you everything, druid, did she? Gaia is a master at chess. She only reveals one piece at a time. Haven't you wondered why, after years of living beneath the radar, the gods are coming out to play?"

Lavinia cleared her throat. "I am the Defence Minister. You should be having this conversation with me, Ravenmaster."

"I have never seen a Defence Minister dressed head to toe in pink." The Ravenmaster gave a bark of laughter. "I will continue to speak to the person in the room with power." He turned to me.

If Lavinia didn't hate you before, she does now, said Orpheus.

The winds around us rose. I didn't know if it was nature or if my emotions were bringing about the change.

"She told me as much as I need to know." I believed it to be true. Gaia was infuriating, but she had never let me down when I needed her. She had always told me enough to survive. "I know the gods are toying with humankind just for fun. That you have lost your faith to such an extent that you have become a nihilist when once you were an inventor. A creator."

Marina spoke up in a small voice. "And I know that you are raging against your slide into irrelevance. I know that the reason you wear that uniform is that you like pomp and pageantry. But the fact is that change happens to everyone, even gods. And you take yourself too seriously. Lighten up, dude. In the olden days, I heard you fashioned an instrument from a tortoise shell. But have you ever been in a mosh pit? Go to a gig and tell me there's no joy left in the world."

Echo nodded. "I can share the Beatles back catalogue with you."

"You dare speak to me like I am your equal?" He punctuated his words with the slamming of his staff on the bench. "I no longer hear my Father's voice in my head nor sense his divine presence. It has been centuries. And you think this can be solved with a little revelry in a mosh pit?"

I nodded. "Yes, Herpes. I think it can."

Oops, that was the truth serum speaking.

Orpheus guffawed. *Did you just liken the god to a sexually transmitted disease? I thank you, Alisha, for giving me cause for laughter before we meet our ends.*

The Ravenmaster glared at me, and his cherubic face turned red. As if the moon above wasn't a shimmering yellow orb but a blood moon that tinged his skin. The wings on his round-brimmed Beefeater's hat and his boots quivered to life and soon became a golden blur mortal eyes could not discern. His slim blue-and-red-booted body shot into the air, and I knew the talk was over. My werepigeon brother fluttered into the air next to him and pooed a big white splotch on the judge's bench as if he were making a promise to defecate on us all.

Fear seared through me, and I drew my sword. My back twinged, a sure sign I was in severe need of yoga. We had to stop Herpes. "Leave my brother out of this."

"Why?" said the Ravenmaster. "I wasn't lying when I said I escorted your mother to the afterlife. She asked Gaia to look after you. And she asked me to look after your brother."

Whispers rushed into my ears as the hilt of my sword grew hot in my hand. I held on and raised it aloft, convinced we were on the side of right, even if we stood no chance. I cast a look at those standing beside me, left and right. "Without prayer, his power is not an infinite well. We can weaken him. Avoid his staff. He has the power to send people to sleep."

Battle cries sounded around me. Ezra's growl, Echo's roar, Lavinia's cackle of glee, a scraping of blades as badass Calypso whipped out two knives from leg holders. Orpheus flung off his long, dark coat and limbered up like a boxer. Rayna set aside her potions belt, but not before retrieving the knife from it.

Only Marina looked like she was about to wet her pants.

"Get to that treeline and stay away from the action," I said.

She hugged me and headed for the treeline. Sahil's beady eyes watched her go, but I knew him well enough to know he'd not harm her. Whether he'd harm me was another matter entirely.

Then there were seven of us left. Seven left to take on a winged god and a werepigeon.

"There is no time to call the coven. He is a formidable enemy, despite those boyish curls. We will need to make every blow count," said Lavinia.

The Ravenmaster didn't wait another second hovering in the air. He flew at us, cherubic face mottled with fury. His staff transformed. The entwined snakes around the staff woke and turned a searing red, with tongues that darted in and out, their eyes hypnotic. He set me in his sights, weaving with ease to avoid pellets shooting from Lavinia's umbrella.

"It is Alisha he wants." Echo roared and leapt into the air to disturb the god's trajectory as he tore towards me.

The god didn't slow. A casual flick of his staff sent Echo sprawling.

The leopard cried out, his hind leg burned by the staff, and Sahil fell upon him, werepigeon teeth sinking into Echo's exquisite fur. Ezra was my brother's next victim, and feathers flew, Ezra's experience in battle giving him an advantage over Sahil's untrained attempts to cause havoc. A spell from Lavinia stuck Sahil headfirst in the sawdust, with his pigeon toes wiggling in vain above ground.

The god kept coming for me.

I raised my sword, slashing.

Ezra arced into the air with radar-like precision, matched by Calypso on the other side, whose strong thighs and blade runners gave her soaring height. They grabbed the god's heels and brought him down hard to the ground, winding him. In came Orpheus and Rayna in a dance of knives and fangs. Orpheus's speed and boxing gave him the grace of Muhammad Ali, except with the additional advantage of his fangs. Rayna's vines grew from the arena to bind the god, roping around his limbs. He broke free easily as if the vines were paper chains.

It wasn't enough. An immortal couldn't be killed.

He flung them off as if they were flies and reared up into the air again, clearly locating me despite the chaos, his gaze confirming he wanted Ezra too.

I sent a whirlwind to destabilise him, but he evaded the current and the trees that grasped him at Rayna's behest. He rushed at the headmistress first, touching her with his staff, and she slumped to the ground in a deep sleep.

He'd keep coming for us. How long could I expect this motley crew of peculiars to protect us? I knew the ones who had stayed were partly driven by the audacity of the Ravenmaster in desecrating Wildwoods, but they couldn't be expected to lay down their lives to protect us.

You underestimate how much the witch loves her nephew. And how you have moved me to act in ways I haven't for centuries, said Orpheus.

Echo and Ezra bounded over to my side as the Ravenmaster came flying towards us, slowed by Calypso, whose whizz of knives threatened to separate the wings from his hat and boots. Orpheus, too, had the grim look of a man careless about his own safety. A man willing to sacrifice himself in pursuit of his enemy. Fists and fangs and jumps took him as high as the god, and he didn't flinch from the burning staff, didn't hesitate to touch a being that had once been so holy.

I remembered Gaia's words. *I have a right mind to cut Hermes apart and bury the pieces of him in pits so far apart that it takes him millennia to reform.*

I had to bring this to an end.

I dragged in a breath and reached for my catalogue of creatures. "Echo, take Marina to the sphinxes. They are touchy fellows, but the two of you may be able to convince them to help. They are guardians of Wildwoods, after all, and this place is in danger. We need more people. He is too strong."

No sooner had I spoken than he raced away, legs pounding hard against the earth.

Lavinia came towards Ezra and me in a tumble of umbrella and Lycra.

"I have a plan," I said, "but I will be vulnerable for a few minutes, so you'll all need to keep him busy."

What do you think we're doing, druid? said Orpheus.

Lavinia jutted out her hip like she was on a catwalk and not in a battle. "Who died and put you in charge?"

Ezra nudged his auntie, warning her with bared teeth and a low grumble that rolled through his throat.

She relented. "Very well. Being an alpha suits you, nephew."

Orpheus and Calypso fought on. The Custodian's eyes narrowed in conversation, dreadlocks flying as she danced with her knives. But she tired, and Orpheus noticed. He tried to use his speed to wear down the god, running circles around him and throwing jabs and hooks, but Hermes was just as fast. The staff blocked each punch, and though the vampire didn't fall asleep, his skin sizzled.

Ezra and his aunt ran into the fray together as I sank to my knees in the sawdust, ignoring Sahil's wriggling legs nearby.

The imbecile.

I knew the catalogue back to front by now. I had studied it during waking hours and in my dreams. When one creature was animated and the page disintegrated, the catalogue rearranged itself in my consciousness as if it were a secret language that would always be mine. As if fate had determined, my hands would hold it.

The ravens. Dad's ravens.

I found them in an instant and ran my hand over the page, getting a sense of their dimensions, width and depth.

The page spoke to me. These weren't happy creatures. They were always craving, always unsatisfied, a black hole of nothing where their soul was, waiting to be filled by the purpose I assigned them.

My command would have to be foolproof, my concentration unwavering.

Calypso, Orpheus, Ezra and Lavinia advanced on the Ravenmaster time and again, in a relay, as a team, the witch riding her umbrella, the others from the ground. They grew weary, bloody and bruised, welts appearing on their skin as the god barely took a hit. When Calypso collapsed into a dead slumber, the arena itself finally came to life to protect its own. It threw sand in the god's eyes, sending arrows of glass at his head and body, trapping him in a cube he shattered with one touch of his poker-hot staff.

In rushed the two sphinxes, Mammatas and Rhokon, with their lion bodies and human heads, bellowing with the joy of movement in their stone bodies, permitted only when Wildwoods came under threat.

Marina rode Rhokon with the gusto of a cowgirl. She slid off and ran back to her position of safety, leaving Echo to follow the sphinxes into the fray.

Orpheus, I said. *Tell the sphinxes to hold Hermes down. They should take his arms. He can't harm their stone bodies to put them to sleep, given their very purpose is to be vigilant. Echo and Ezra should take his feet, the safer end. Stretch him taut as if he were on a rack in the Tower of London torture chamber. The rest of you should strip him of his boots, hat and staff.*

I hope you know what you are doing, said Orpheus.

I blocked out the sounds of the battle and found the breath of the universe. The winds swirled around me as my fingers found the threads of the ravens. Sweat broke out on my upper lip, and my hands grew clammy. The ravens' cells and veins and feathers crept towards the surface, and they broke through, pecking at my hands, ten black, mischievous, clever birds. I told them their purpose, and they made gurgling croaks that would always haunt me.

They were my creations—and Dad's—but I feared them.

I turned, lightheaded, and staggered to the god, who lay writhing and stretched between the sphinxes, their stone mouths clamped around his limp wrists. Stripped of his wares, without his staff, with orange-peel feet and a bald spot, he looked pathetic.

But even pathetic gods inspire fear in mere mortals.

Fear was writ large on the faces of my allies. Only the impenetrable sphinxes knew no fear. They needed me to lead them.

I stood astride the god.

No amount of face cream was going to make up for the stress lines I gained at that moment.

"You shrew." The Ravenmaster's glacial eyes bulged, and he lobbed great globules of spit at me.

"You know what to do," I said to the ravens.

The Ravenmaster looked confused. He clicked his tongue, trying to find a common language and rapport with the birds he had trained for decades.

But these weren't any ravens. They weren't his ravens.

They were mine.

And I had told them to dismember him. I had told them to bury the pieces of his body in every corner of the British Isles.

And they listened to their purpose.

I stood above Hermes as he was pulled taut by my friends. I stood and directed the black ravens like a conductor at a symphony. I clenched my jaw as I worked, flinging out my arms this way and that to indicate which pieces the birds should assail first.

The sphinxes roared, Ezra howled, and Echo clutched the foot for which he was responsible until it became dislodged from the whole. The raven's sharp beaks broke Hermes apart with such voracious hunger that even Lavinia looked away. Orpheus stood vigilant over the fallen staff, unblinking in the face of the horrors.

Blood and flesh fell like nightmarish confetti over me as the ravens did my bidding.

I left the god's heart and head for the very last moments.

His head, separated from the rest of him, rolled on the ground. It didn't lose its venom. "Those who attack immortals never survive long, druid. You may win tonight, but I have an infinite life to exact my revenge on you."

There was no way I was picking up his head, so I asked two ravens to pick it up by the curly blond hair and dangle it in front of me. I looked the Ravenmaster in the eye, and the teacher in me came out. "One day," I said, "you will re-form and rise again, and when you do, maybe you'll have learned to be a better person. A lack of faith is one thing, but you don't have to be an utter arsehole."

His hovering head opened its mouth. "I am a—"

I lifted my hands, and the ravens flew at his head and heart. Hermes looked surprised, like no one had ever interrupted one of his rants before. The ravens carried off chunks of meat, their battle cry punctuating the tearing of flesh. I closed my eyes to the slaughter.

One day, he would live again. Just not today.

When the sounds stopped, and the cries and cursing of the god fell to nothing, the beating of wings filled the air around me. I kept my eyes squeezed shut, lifted my hands and sent a burst of wind 360 degrees to speed the ravens on to their destinations with the flesh bundles. Then I sank to the ground and rolled onto my side as a black cloud crept into my vision. I tried to slow my heartbeat, but I couldn't. My whole body quivered, and even though I told myself to get up, my brain wouldn't respond.

"Get Alisha to the infirmary," said Orpheus. "Who knows what damage she has done to herself by animating nearly a dozen of those hideous things at once. Did anyone know she could do that?"

Marina's voice, panting and full of worry, "Let me help."

"What are you waiting for?" Orpheus snapped. "Sphinxes, back to your position. A stretcher for Rayna and Calypso. And where the hell did the Prime Sorcerer go?"

Someone scooped me up into their arms—someone naked, who smelt familiar, like mountain air and roll-up cigarettes. I laid my head against his chest as voices muttered around me, my body ragdoll limp.

"There's something rotten at the heart of this place. She won't survive another encounter like this," said that someone.

"Our new Minister for Justice is right. The ground has shifted. We can dilly dally no longer. We have to find the eternal girl," said Lavinia.

"Yes. Yes, we do," said Orpheus. "I am afraid a dark age is upon us. Without her and the disintegrating tome in the prophecy, we don't stand a chance if Death does open the door between the worlds."

My last thought was of my brother, upside down still in the sawdust. Then I drifted into unconsciousness.

23

Alma woke at the crack of dawn to cook us a feast in my mother's kitchen. She was of Spanish origin. Given Mum had been French, I had the sneaking suspicion that Dad had a penchant for European babes. Despite her obvious disapproval of our—Echo notwithstanding—meat-free household, Alma had cooked up a mouth-watering array of dishes befitting her heritage. It was an obvious but much-appreciated attempt to woo us for our first meal together since the romantic development between her and Dad. There was vegetarian paella, fig tapas, Catalan grilled vegetables, croquetas, white herb and bean salad and churros with salted chocolate sauce.

Mum had been a feeder too. The thought drifted through my mind, and for the first time, the memory of what she had been brought comfort rather than pain.

Animating the ravens had drained me, and I still hadn't recovered my entire strength. But at least there were no wounds for Dad to worry about. It did me good to see him happy at last, and I wasn't going to spoil that.

In their excitement, Dad and Alma had laid the table in the dining room with a frilly tablecloth and an extraordinary number of doilies handmade by Alma herself, an award-winning hobbyist. I couldn't think of why anyone would award prizes for doilies, but Dad was quite adamant about that point.

Alma fussed over the table while Dad and I nattered over a cup of tea in the living room.

He checked the coast was clear, then lifted a sofa cushion to slide out a copy of *The Otherworld News*. "Alma's very tidy. An absolute dab hand with the duster, but she'd never think to look under here. Have you seen it yet?"

Druid Heir Does It Again in Wildwoods Showdown

"Damn it. I quite liked the attention dropping away from me when everyone thought I was a failure. I wish Margola would move on to a new subject of interest," I said. "I don't know where she gets her information. Half of it is wrong, and the other half is embellished, so it bears no relation to the truth. Not to mention all the omissions."

Dad grinned. "But your legend lives on, eh, Alisha? Quite a recovery after what happened at your animation performance. You make me so proud."

Alma popped her head around the door. "Lunch is ready."

Dad froze like a rabbit in the headlights.

"What's wrong, Joshi? Keep that paper for me, will you?" said Alma. "I quite fancy a crossword later."

"Yes, love," said Dad.

Alma scurried away.

Dad pushed the paper at me. "Bin it. Burn it. Feed it to the leopard."

I laughed. "He's too busy traumatising the koi in your pond. Come on. Everyone's waiting."

We went arm in arm into the dining room.

Dad and Alma sat opposite each other at the heads of the table. They smiled at us.

"I'm so glad you could join us, Gaia," said Alma. "It's a wonder we haven't met before. Joshi has been telling me all about what an upstanding member of the community you are."

Gaia beamed. She wore a turquoise-and-green Punjabi suit with a sequinned border. Her black hair cascaded down her back. It had been freshly died with henna, giving it an orange tinge. "That's so kind of Joshi to say."

Alma offered the white bean and herb salad around the table. "How long have you been living in South London?"

"About two hundred years, give or take," said Gaia.

Alma gave Dad a sympathetic frown, assuming that Gaia had Alzheimer's.

He shrugged and turned to Sahil. "You're quiet today, son. Something on your mind?"

A nerve twitched in Sahil's jaw, and he hitched his neck back and forth like the pigeon he was. I suspected Sahil was traumatised enough by the sawdust he kept coughing up after all that time with his head buried in the arena. It served him right.

I scowled at him. It was killing me not to vault over the table and slap him silly. I had decided not to be open with Dad about the fact his son was a villainous prick. A further fracturing of our family unit would steal any last remnant of joy he had, and I couldn't do that to him. Playing the happy family sucked, but I had to trust that karma wouldn't let Sahil get off scot-free. And who knew, maybe I'd get to give it a little nudge.

Sahil spluttered into a tissue and balled it up for the umpteenth time.

Alma frowned. "You really should see a doctor about that cough."

"He's quite all right, dear. Another two hacks, and he'll have cleared it all. Then there'll be space for your churros." Gaia smiled at Dad. "Has he always been a problem child?"

Sahil glared at her, but when he opened his mouth, an unintelligible series of coos burst forth that scared the bejeezus out of Alma.

Gaia winked at me and gave me a self-satisfied smile.

Dad frowned. "All children have their ups and downs."

"Pigeons have a more wayward trajectory than most. They seem to defecate from spite rather than need," said Gaia.

Alma looked at her like she was a lunatic. "Please, everyone, eat. I want us to be one big happy family."

I sighed and shovelled food onto my plate.

After lunch, Gaia and I walked in my parents' garden under tangerine ribbons of sun threading the sky.

The goddess picked her way across the lawn in her sandals, like a ballerina crossing a minefield. "I like to give the worms a fighting chance. Poor things always end up squashed before they even get to live. Their ability to regenerate was one of my better ideas." Her lips curved in amusement as she watched Echo play in the koi pond. "Only a few minutes more, Chanakya, or those poor fish will leave this earthly realm."

Echo landed on the lawn in a spray of water before launching himself back in. "Of course, goddess. I would not dare to defy you."

Gaia slipped her arm through mine. "Your heart is heavy. Speak your mind."

I grimaced. "I prayed to you on the night the Ravenmaster attacked Wildwoods, but you didn't come to our aid."

"I am sorry, druid." She pouted. "I didn't abandon you, although it might feel that way. I was there in spirit. I put that idea in your head about dismembering him."

My eyebrows shot up. "That was you?"

"Of course it was." She sighed. "It really is very unfortunate. His wasn't a dignified end. Not an end at all, really. He'll probably be furious by the time he is resurrected, but with any luck, you'll be dead by then, so you won't have to deal with it."

I stared at her before sinking onto a bench. Sometimes I couldn't wrap my head around how much my life had changed.

"Do you forgive me?" said the goddess.

"Of course I do." I smiled at her turn of phrase. As if a goddess would need to ask me for forgiveness. "I think you made quite an impression on Alma."

Gaia sat. "It is not my job to consider what impression I make on others. I can only be myself. I like Alma. Her croquetas were some of the finest I have tasted, and she has one of the qualities I admire most in mortals."

"What is that?"

"The ability to make a home. Not many can do it well, but to have the ability to create a space that others can feel at ease in takes a special kind of person," said Gaia. "Many people underestimate how important that feeling of belonging is. The dragon has a home, but he misses you. You have a home, but you have found many more these past weeks. Hermes had a home, but now he is in the dirt. The disgraced alpha was ripped from the home he loved and now resides in a dungeon. The pigeon has many homes, and still, he defecates in the wrong place." She looked into the distance, entranced. Her pupils expanded, and in them, I saw mountains rise, and cities burn. "Then there is duty and desire. You set aside your desires to do your duty. Hermes set aside his duty to fulfil his desires. The new alpha is torn between his desires and his duty. The pigeon knows only desire. One day, he may choose duty. Or better yet, his duties will align with his desires."

She sounded like a garbled tape.

I frowned. "Are you okay?"

"Oh yes, dear. I'm just a little tired. Nothing that a hot water bottle and my desire for a cup of chai won't fix. I am afraid the offering here falls beneath my expectations, so I give you my thanks, druid, and my praise, and now I must go." She pressed a kiss to my forehead.

It healed the aching parts of me, body and spirit.

I bit my lip. "Gaia, when I held Transcender, I thought I heard Mum's voice."

"Of course, you did, Alisha. Why did you think your sword is called Transcender? I did say that you'd be able to channel your ancestors if you mastered it."

"It was just a whisper. I couldn't catch it all."

The Earth turned in her eyes. "Well, it's not a walkie-talkie. It's just a spark of essence."

I looked away in case I couldn't process the truths there. "I think she wanted me to go easy on Sahil."

"Well, mothers know best. How lovely of her to reach out to you with something positive rather than the usual haunting malarkey." Melancholy filled her voice. "You must gather your strength, for this is not yet over."

I gulped. "Will you always be in the shadows rather than at my side?"

She blew out her soft velvet cheeks with their sprinkling of rouge. "This game the gods are playing is one I refused. For that, I pay a heavy price. But I have plotted a path for us, and it is still possible we might win, Alisha, if you just hold on."

"Do you know what might happen next?"

"Might is such a powerful word, don't you think? Such potential. I think it's just perfect leaving the future open. I'm not being deliberately tiresome. I am bound by an ancient oath to neither reveal nor thwart my Father's children." She grinned. "At least, not directly. You do understand, don't you?"

I nodded, but how could a mere mortal possibly understand the choices of a goddess? Instead, I remembered the MC Hammer rucksack I'd stashed for her in the wardrobe of my childhood bedroom. "I have something for you. Wait here."

I brought it downstairs, frightened Alma would catch me on the stairs with it glowing in my arms. As an afterthought, I popped Dad's copy of *The Otherworld News* into it, too, to save Dad a spate of tricky questions from Alma. She was an Otherworld virgin, after all.

Then I returned to Gaia. "These are yours for safekeeping. Calypso thought them too dangerous to keep in the Celestial Library."

Shrewd eyes fell upon the rucksack, and Gaia took it from me. "The Custodian is wise not to keep items that would imperil her." She stood. "Before you go home, talk to the pigeon. Even anger can be wrapped in love."

I chewed my lip. "I can't forgive him."

"Then you hurt only yourself, Alisha." She gave a little hiccup of recognition. "Speak of the devil. Thank your father and Alma for me, will you?" She put on the MC Hammer rucksack as if she were a school child and not a centuries-old goddess, walked a few steps and went to say her goodbyes to Echo, who by now was sunning himself on the grass.

Sahil skulked over, his mouth in a frown. "You can tell me to bugger off if you like."

"Why would I do that? This is your home as much as mine." I scowled at him. "I don't have to like you, though."

"Touché," he said. "Have you ever liked me?"

"Of course," I said. "But you are a prize wanker far too often. I mean, what were you thinking? Why did you let me think you had those powers from Lavinia?"

He shrugged. "I've always played a good hand at poker."

I punched his arm. "Hermes could have killed me. Would you have let that happen?"

His brown eyes met mine. "You're speaking like it's an option to say no when a god wants something."

My frustration was nuclear. "It is," I said through gritted teeth. "Wouldn't you have tried? For me? It's like you don't care one iota about who you hurt. Even if it's your own sister."

He puffed out his chest, and it showed the pigeon in him. "I know my limits, Alisha. I'm not the one who stands up to playground bullies. I *am* the bully. It's who I am. It's how I've been so successful at work. You can't expect me to change my colours."

"How did you even meet him?"

Sahil frowned. "The Ravenmaster? He made Mum a promise to look out for me. Then he found me. Turns out Mum leaving her car to me in her will wasn't so bad after all. It's been touched by the gods. It's like a beacon from them."

My head jerked up in surprise. "Bloody hell, Sahil. Where is it now?"

"Keep your knickers on," he said. "It's hardly roadworthy. It's in my garage."

I eyeballed him. "You should destroy it."

His face tightened. "What is it with you always trying to tell me what to do? You should stay out of my business, little sis."

I let out a huff of breath. "Grow up, Sahil, or I'll…"

He smirked. "What? You'll run to Dad? We're in our forties, Alisha."

I rolled my eyes. "No, I was going to say you don't get kid gloves from me just because you're my big brother."

"Do your worst, little sis." He crossed his arms, making his biceps bulge. "I'm not scared of you."

I wanted to scream. I didn't want him to be scared of me. I wanted us to be on the same page. To be close.

A hand on each of our shoulders made us jump.

"It's so good to see you two spending time together." Dad shimmied around to the front of the bench, squeezed into the middle of us and put his arms around us. "That's right, make space for your old man. How long has it been since we enjoyed a day like this?"

24

I lay back against the fluffy silk pillows with a contented sigh. On the bedside table, a cup of English breakfast tea—just the right colour—and a good book waited for my attention. Not that I had spent the morning reading.

I'd been otherwise occupied.

The receiver pressed to my ear as I stretched my toes. "I can't believe that while I was resting up, you took my cat to a karaoke booth."

Marina's warm laugh reverberated down the line. "Robert literally couldn't believe his ears. He was a very reluctant ally. I had to make him mouth the words every time someone popped their head into the room to cover up the fact Echo was my duet partner. And the foxes were wild. They have lungs on them. You should have heard their rendition of 'I Wanna Dance with Somebody.' Whitney Houston, eat your heart out."

It was so good to be able to use our mobile phones again without fear of manipulation. "So, is Robert happy with how everything is panning out? Ezra and I thought Flinar could be in charge of the rehabilitation of the errant elves."

Ezra had refused to let me get involved, but in the past three days, he, Robert and Lavinia had teleported to locations across the United Kingdom to dismantle all of the Ravenmaster's bot rooms. Without the Ravenmaster, the assorted powers he had given his elf bots no longer worked, stripping the errant elves of their fear of and motivation to help him.

"That's a brilliant idea," said Marina. "Robert's ecstatic. The bot rooms fell like a house of cards. He said he's not been part of such a satisfying operation since the time he headed up a team in the drugs squad."

The current front bench in Her Majesty's Government had lasted a week. The Prime Minister was very pleased his personal life was running smoothly again after he bribed his wife to forget the affair with the promise of posh new wallpaper at Number 10. The Royal family turned up en masse at the Chelsea Flower Show without a cross word between them. There was a reported drop in divorce petitions and domestic incidents. Not to mention an incremental decrease over the last few days in rough sleepers. And my programmed ravens were doing a stellar job at the Tower of London. The new Ravenmaster was very impressed. He even had more spares than usual.

Still, a frisson of apprehension tempered the lightness in my chest. "Wonderful. It was all worth it then."

Marina immediately caught my mood. "Alisha, I don't want to go through that again. I thought you were a goner when you went limp like that. Whatever wins we have from being part of the Otherworld, it's not worth losing you over. I would rather be ordinary with you than extraordinary without you."

She made me feel safe even through a phone line. My throat scratched with tears, and I swallowed the lump there. "Marina, you are always extraordinary. Even when you're hungover with your rainbow head over a toilet bowl."

"Oh, you say the nicest things. But I've decided. I always feel like you're the one doing the protecting when I want to protect you." A note of uncertainty flooded her voice, the crack before she asked me something big. "Do you remember when Calypso told us about the necklace your Mum left with her for safekeeping and that Rose of Jericho book she loaned from the Celestial Library?"

I braced myself. "Uh-huh."

"I've been looking into it, and it turns out that flower has healing properties. I think that's what your Mum was doing in the lab. That's why she didn't share her work with Melissa, even though they shared everything. Because that project was about you and keeping you safe. And I want to finish what she started if you'll let me."

"What did I do to deserve you?"

"I'm glad it's a yes. I had a whole speech planned."

I smiled. The buzz of the electric toothbrush in the other room stopped. I said to Marina, "See you tomorrow?"

"Why, are you busy?" she teased.

"Bye. Love you." I put the phone down.

Ezra came in from the en suite, his teeth tingly fresh. We'd started to fill his parents' cottage with our things and opening up all the rooms that had been unlived in for so long.

He sprang onto the bed, bent his head to nuzzle my neck, and peered at the bedroom floor, where my new underwear lay in a heap. "Where were we again?"

I giggled. "Round one was a stellar performance."

The copper specks in his eyes danced. "I aim to please."

I kissed him, breathing in his scent, revelling in the feel of his stubble against my skin, his strong hand threaded through the hair at my nape.

"Ezra?" I murmured against his lips.

He raised his head. "Uh oh. That tone tells me you're thinking. My job is to chase all the thoughts out of your head."

I pressed a lingering kiss to his cheek and then pulled away. "I thought you'd be all serious now you're a senator."

With Gunnolf gone, Ezra had become not only alpha but Minister for Justice. It had been stupid of me not to realise it the night at the Court of Wolves when his ascendancy onto the senate had been clear as day to Marina and Echo.

I knew he could do it, but I had always thought of him as a warrior rather than a paper pusher—a renegade rather than a committee member. I couldn't help it, but a part of me didn't want him to have conflicting interests in his life. I always wanted to be the one at the centre of his universe.

"Do the rest of the senate know Gaia told me I'm the eternal girl?" I asked.

Ezra sighed and lay back against the pillow.

My skin immediately craved his touch, so I reached for his hand.

He traced a slow pattern on my palm and shook his head. "I didn't tell them. I made a promise to you. But, Alisha, if I doubted it before, I don't doubt it now. And my aunt suspects. The vampire too."

"Orpheus isn't the problem." I bit my lip. "And maybe Lavinia isn't either. I respect her for fighting alongside us."

Ezra nodded. "I do too. But we have to be wary of her. She is unpredictable. I think, however, that between me, her and the vampire, we have enough votes to force the rewriting of the Pragmatist's Law."

"Never meddle in the affairs of the gods."

He grimaced. "Quite. Because if the gods meddle with us, how can we stay neutral? There are more links between the gods and the senate than we realised. If nothing else, the past few weeks have proved that."

"They proved that I love you too."

A sad smile tugged at the corners of his mouth. "Things have changed now that I'm a senator. I'll need to keep things from you even when I don't want to. I can't always be on your side. I need to show impartiality."

I frowned. How could you be impartial about love? How could we be so close one moment and on different paths the next?

Ezra pulled me into a bear hug with a tenderness that made me ache. "I don't want to lose what we have. I'll fight to keep it."

I had the distinct impression that the ground was falling beneath me. I clung to him, and his lips chased away all my worries, like the sun chases the clouds.

ACKNOWLEDGMENTS

To my readers, thank you for taking a chance on this story. Your enthusiasm spurs me on. I'm so grateful for every message and review, and yes, I always want to know if you are #TeamEzra or #TeamOrpheus.

A big thank you to my book team, particularly my editors Jeni and Toni, whose skill and instincts I have come to rely on. To my cover artist Maria, your work brings me so much joy. To Debbie and Sherry, my beta readers, what would I do without your encouragement and steers? A thousand thanks and an extra hot bedroom scene are yours.

To Nafu Aunty, who loves words and crafts her own. Thank you for always understanding the joy of creativity and encouraging mine. I wish I could bring to life a protective, teleporting werewolf-wizard just for you.

To our three beautiful children, each one of you is a gift. I hope you know that even if sometimes I stick my headphones in and tell you I'm busy. I promise once this book has been submitted, we'll bake, kitchen dance, and take the dog for long walks in the woods where you can find the Rabbit Kingdom again.

To my husband Jan, my first reader. Sometimes life is such a whirlwind that I forget to tell you, so here it is in black and white: I am the luckiest woman alive to have you at my side. Thank you for being you. For being constant, funny and kind and for being a magnet for my cold feet at night.

A SNEAK PREVIEW OF MIDLIFE DRIFT

DRUID HEIR BOOK 4

DRUID HEIR
BOOK 4
MIDLIFE DRIFT
N. Z. NASSER

MIDLIFE DRIFT: DRUID HEIR BOOK 4

By now, my hopes of a quiet life in the Otherworld are dead and buried. I've accepted that I'm the prophesied eternal girl, but Ezra wants me to keep it under wraps. We can't be certain unless I step into a tank with the magical octopus, and I've had quite enough of batty Wildwoods rituals, thank you very much.

When I receive an offer to turbo charge my druid training, I jump into the deep end and don't flinch. A new threat is rising. I can feel it in my waters, even before Dad is kidnapped and I'm forced into working with my wayward brother. To make matters worse, a rogue goddess emerges to take Londoners to their watery grave.

With Ezra now a senator and Marina knee-deep in researching how to keep me safe, my allies are few and far between, but I still have my trusty leopard. A visit to an otherworldly chiropractor to fend off the midlife aches and I'm ready to live up to my true potential. I'll be damned if Dad and countless others succumb to dark undercurrents on my watch.

If you're a fan of Paranormal Women's Fiction and magic-wielding heroines over forty, continue this journey with Druid Heir Book 4.

THE PLAYERS

Alisha Verma - Druid Heir
Echo - Alisha's leopard sidekick
Marina Ambrose - Alisha's best friend
Ezra Neuhoff - half-werewolf, half-wizard Minister for Justice
Orpheus Might - Vampire, Minister for History and the Today
Joshi Verma - Alisha's father
Sahil Verma - Alisha's brother
Alma Bluejay - Joshi's new love
Fei Yen and Faeza - hu hsien, shapeshifting foxes
Rajiv Chawla - Rajika Verma's brother
Gaia - Goddess of the Earth
Calypso Archer - The Custodian of the Celestial Library
Robert Jameson - Detective, Shadow Squad
Mirabel, Janey, Angelus, Xavier, Ayshah, Sage, Violet, Benny and Drew -
Alisha's Wildwoods class
Phinnaeous Shine - Shapeshifter, Prime Sorcerer
Lavinia Drach - Witch, Minister for Defence
Isadora, Chandra, Ravynne and Agatha - Lavinia's coven
Rayna Willowsun - Druid, Minister for Education, Headmistress of
Wildwoods School of the Wondrous

Margola Silver - Selkie, Minister for Information
Helio Woodwink - Fairy, Bestiary Minister
Gunnolf Zev - Werewolf, former alpha
Annie - a little girl
Gordon Stevens, Henry Radcliffe and Ali Sheikh - victims
Manfred - a chiropractor
Kraglek - an octopus
Mami - a tattoo artist

1

———

The streetlamp on the dark London corner flickered, and a light drizzle fell as I pressed my phone to my ear, clear in the knowledge that I had upset my wolf.

That morning, we'd woken in a tangle of sheets in the cottage he'd inherited from his parents, the one at the end of the world, where no soul thought to disturb us. Where his pack or senate duties couldn't creep between us. Thankfully, his teleporting skills meant he wasn't tied to the pack farmhouse or to Wildwoods.

We ate our breakfast in the overgrown garden, warmed by the autumn sun. Ezra had bought sticky buns from the French bakery at Charing Cross. A sudden gust of wind whipped my hair into my face as I took a bite. Ezra leaned forward to hold my hair back, and I thought maybe we could make it work.

Then his phone buzzed, and he gave me an apologetic smile. Again.

Here we were again, in separate places and opposing mind-sets. Still, I listened to his worried voice, wanting to make it work. Wanting us to succeed.

Ezra drew in a ragged breath that rattled down the phone line. "With Ra, you were under my mentorship, so the buck stopped with me. With

Pan, there was no real harm done. Sure, you hid a dragon, but you had also awed the senate by *animating* a dragon. With the Ravenmaster, you had no choice. Half of us made the same decision when he attacked Wildwoods." A growl. "But you can't keep jumping into the messes the gods make. I can't see you behind bars. And I can't see you hurt."

"You won't." Before he became Justice Minister, Ezra was a seeker. He had this uncanny knack of always knowing where I was. I really hoped he didn't teleport to my location.

"I mean it, Alisha. I can't be seen to bend the rules for you, even if I want to," said Ezra. "The Prime Sorcerer has warned you that he won't have it."

I heard him. That didn't mean I agreed with him.

I didn't have the smallest regret about my choices. Yes, I had fallen foul of the Magical Constitution and squeaked by without sanction, but because of me, good things had happened. Mum's killer had been punished. The elves had been proven innocent after being blamed for the tremors. And most recently, I had given the Ravenmaster his comeuppance for disrupting tech to sew discord and for corrupting my brother.

It was always the same with this topic. Ezra and I talked at cross purposes but didn't shift our standpoints.

He wanted me to be safe. I wanted my nightmares to stop.

Nightmares in which I instructed the ravens to tear the Ravenmaster into tiny, bloody pieces. But instead of overcoming the god, I stood paralysed as my friends were ripped to pieces instead.

Until no one was left but me.

The only way to move forward was to arm myself with the knowledge, skills and tools to ensure I came out on top if trouble found me. Since I'd joined the Otherworld, trouble found me quicker than flies find honey. What was more, with Ezra and Orpheus knee-deep in senate business, our vulnerability was heightened.

I had to help myself.

Prickles of frustration crept into my voice. "Phinnaeous Shine is a coward."

"Just please stay out of trouble. One mistake and it can all go wrong. And these days I can't always just parachute in to help." Ezra sighed. "It's going to be a while before this senate meeting ends. I might be late back to yours."

"How about we catch up tomorrow? I'm seeing Fei Yen and Faeza for a cuppa tonight." Technically it wasn't a lie. They served tea whenever I visited.

"Okay. I miss you."

"I miss you too." A pang of guilt ran through my stomach. Ezra Neuhoff was the man of my dreams. I'd tell him everything as soon as we were back.

I ended the call. My trainers squelched on the pavement as I crossed the street and walked into Shanghai Moon, the local tea and occult shop run by my fox friends. Inside, curls of incense wafted through the air, and three bodies gathered at a sumptuous, candlelit tarot table, draped with a velvet tablecloth.

"Everything okay?" Echo purred. He perched on the chair intended for my best friend Marina. In the bright light of the shop, his golden leopard coat with its rosettes was a kaleidoscope of different shades.

I sat down next to him. "Ezra wants me to stay out of trouble. But sometimes a little trouble in midlife is just what the doctor ordered. He'll be proud of us when this is done."

Fei Yen and Faeza sat across from us in solemn repose, card deck ready and waiting.

"We better get started then," said Faeza, ever the blunt one of the two. "But please, try not to make a mess. It's been a long day, and I could do without having to get the hoover out."

Fei Yen nodded. "A little consideration goes a long way. Even on adventures."

The journey to and from the Celestial Library was a little rough and tumble. The last time we'd attempted this feat, I'd ended up somersaulting through the galaxy and crash landed a dragon in their shop. They hadn't forgotten.

A second later, Marina tumbled through the door in a black leather catsuit and a flash of rainbow hair. A swirl of autumn leaves followed her into the shop. For once, her plentiful tattoos had been covered, but the catsuit left nothing to the imagination.

Jessica Rabbit, eat your heart out.

Echo's lips split into a grin, revealing tombstone teeth in need of flossing. "Marina Ambrose, the queen of grand entrances."

Marina grinned and pulled up an extra chair. "Sorry I'm late. I have the Rose of Jericho book. Do you have your mum's necklace, Alisha?"

"It's right here." The necklace nestled at my collarbone, an oval amber stone on a choker-type gold chain, just hidden from view under my hoodie. For a hefty piece, it was surprisingly light.

Faeza leaned forward conspiratorially. "Now you're all here, we wanted to double-check. It's not been a moment since we put the whole Ravenmaster thing behind us. Are you sure you want to go through with this? Maybe it would be sensible to take things easy for a while. A new Chinese takeaway just opened around the corner. We could have a quiet meal instead."

My body sagged. My intuition and my hips told me now wasn't the time to rest on my laurels and indulge in a Chinese takeaway. Why did everyone want to put the brakes on and pretend life would potter along without hiccups?

It was only a matter of time before another god came knocking.

Gaia had told me as much.

"That's a wonderful idea," said Fei Yen. "There is nothing wrong with a quiet life. No jumping through portals, no shifty senators, no battle-training, no ripping an immortal god limb from limb. How about some chicken in oyster sauce, a tofu noodle dish, maybe a spring roll or two and a fortune cookie?"

A dollop of drool trickled down Echo's jaw. "I am always in the mood for food. And singing. How about chow mein and karaoke?"

She edged forward to look past Echo at me. We had discussed the risks. The Celestial Library didn't stay at a fixed point and the journey was perilous. There was a chance we wouldn't make it past the entry hall or that we'd be unable to find our way back home.

Echo's head dropped. "Anyone would think I'm invisible. You

know it's an emotional wound of mine after years of being seen as a Bengal cat."

I scratched his ears. "Without you, I wouldn't know who I am."

Marina hugged him. "You know how much we rely on you, but we have to make this trip. We witnessed the Ravenmaster's attack. We've comforted Alisha after a nightmare. The only way to protect her is to complete Rosalie's work on the Rose of Jericho project. For that, we need more information than is available to us in this world." She drew in a deep breath. "Forget the spring rolls, Fei Yen and Faeza. We're off to see a library amongst the stars, guarded by a dreadlocked woman in blade runners. Doesn't get much better than that."

Faeza sighed. "Very well."

A heavy, midnight blue curtain hung from a circular ceiling rail. She pulled it around us, enveloping us in silver sequins reminiscent of stars.

She picked up the deck of cards and shuffled them with the fluidity of water. "This is your journey, Marina Ambrose. Tap the cards and spread your energy through them."

It wasn't the same deck we had used for my last journey to the Celestial Library. The foxes couldn't work with an incomplete deck, and I had burned the last gateway card. This one was hand-drawn cards with blood-red edges.

Marina's blue eyes widened. Unlike me, she truly believed in the power of the cards. She took a deep breath and gave the cards a wallop.

Faeza continued. "Now concentrate, Marina. To get to the Celestial Library, you must ask a question of it. An open, undemanding one. Learning takes humility, after all. Approaching any library, let alone this one, with a selfish heart is a fool's errand."

Marina considered her options for a moment. "How can a library amongst the stars help me keep my best friend safe?"

Fei Yen beamed. "Well done." She spread the shuffled cards across the table with a flourish. "Now clear your mind and choose two cards that draw you."

Marina tapped two cards in quick succession on opposite sides of the spread.

Faeza flipped the cards. On one, a handheld a wand sprouting with shoots, with rolling hills in the distance. "The Ace of Wands speaks of family and inheritance, of invention and creation. It is telling you to follow your heart and make a plan. This plan might take great effort, but you should surrender yourself to it."

"I'm not scared of hard work," said Marina.

The other card lay upside down. It showed a semi-clad woman stepping forward, a laurel wreath on her head.

"The World reversed signifies extended travel," said Faeza. "You stand at the precipice of a large project. It warns against shortcuts and tells of the cyclical nature of life's seasons." She tidied the remaining deck and pushed the two cards from the reading into the middle of the table under the flickering light of the candelabra.

I'd hoped for a clearer sense of an upcoming victory, but that wasn't the point of tarot cards. They provided guidance, not answers.

Fei Yen cleared her throat. "One of these cards is a gateway to the Celestial Library, and although Alisha has taken this journey before, it is you, Marina, who must take the first step and pull her after you. The journey is yours. Choose the door. Once you step through it, we will guard the card until your return."

Marina stared at the cards, her bright blue eyes drawn time and again to the Ace of Wands.

The candles danced and twitched, and then with a fizz, one went out.

The foxes looked at one another in alarm.

"Quick. The chance of passage is shrinking," said Fei Yen, as the second candle fizzled out.

"Hurry!" Faeza's eyes widened as the final candle began to spit.

"Echo, stay here and guard the portal until we return," I said.

Marina dove for the Ace of Wands with her right hand and reached for me with her left hand.

Echo's roar met my ears as we slipped into the card with its blood-red edges. Marina's body jerked away from me, her eyes prised unnaturally wide, but I clung on. My eyes were also open, and yet I couldn't decipher the shapes before me. I couldn't see further than our bodies being sucked upwards and sidewards, jolted like riders on the world's worst buckaroo.

Hadn't the Custodian told me that no journey to the Celestial Library would be the same?

I winced as heat hit my skin. Unbearable heat. Heat from the unyielding sun. Heat from a dragon's breath. Heat from the Earth's core.

"Trust in the journey. Don't feed the universe your fear," came Faeza's voice from worlds away.

Marina, too, shrivelled in the intense heat. Her body curled into a ball, but her rainbow head jerked backwards, strands of bright hair spooling as if she were a supernova shooting across space and time and not a mere woman, a fragile cargo of all the things I loved best in one person.

I ached to protect, her but I was as vulnerable as she was. A ping pong in a machine. My mouth gelled shut, but I willed her to hear my thoughts.

Just hold on.

I clutched her tighter, intertwining our fingers like a Ziplock as we zigzagged across the universe.

2

———————

I needn't have feared she'd give up. The universe might knead us like dough and whack us over the head with a rolling pin, but women in midlife were tough. We responded to anything that hurtled our way. We had learned to be malleable, resilient and strong. And we weren't scared of being soft.

Marina's eyes locked on mine as the stars flew by, as the dark became blacker and deeper than I ever imagined it could be. We allowed the universe to pummel us. Just when my breath had become a mere wisp and my fingers ached from clinging on, the universe spat us out.

I landed on my hands and knees on a concrete floor. Without a blanket or yoga mat to pad them, it bloody hurt, but the cooled temperature was a relief. Marina, with a dancer's instincts, rolled a turn then emerged in a standing position beside me. I almost expected her to perform a finishing pose, but instead, she offered me a hand and tugged me up.

"That was wild, but we'll need therapy," she said, only the hint of a quiver in her voice.

In the Otherworld, trauma came as frequently as a London bus.

Our hair looked like we'd been through a wind turbine. We patted it down as best we could and looked around. The great hall with its marble pillars no longer held an armchair and fireplace.

Instead, two striped deckchairs and a cocktail bar awaited us on a bank of sand.

Awe filled Marina's face. She took off her rucksack and her Dr Martens. "After the scorching heat out there and the boob sweat underneath this catsuit, this is exactly what I need. Come on."

I started after her then lurched to a halt at the clip-clop of hooves across the floor and a whinny. Joy bubbled in me.

"Nightfall." I rushed to the black stallion, whose trust I'd gained to win access to the inner halls of the library.

He whinnied again, nuzzling his silken head against me.

I smiled up at his rider. "Hello, Calypso."

Calypso slid down from the horse, taking care her blade runners didn't strike him. "Hello, druid. I had a feeling I might see you both today." Not a scrap of makeup covered her skin. Crescent shadows pooled under her eyes, and her braids were untidy, as if her mind had been too busy to care about mere appearance. Tonight, she wore a tracksuit rather than a trouser suit. "I've been preparing for your arrival."

Marina gave the deckchairs one last longing look and inched over.

"You have come to help your friend, empath," said Calypso. "Rosalie Verma couldn't have hoped for a better ally for her daughter than you. Perhaps that is why she laid down her life without regrets. And yet your path within these hallowed walls won't be easy, Marina Ambrose. I hope you can draw on your inner strength when the night seems dark. First, your trial. Because no soul may enter these hallowed halls unless the library deems you worthy."

I shuddered. Blind courage when it came to myself was one thing, but I wouldn't survive if anything happened to Marina. She was my found family, as important to me as my biological family. "Let me do this for her."

Calypso shook her head. "This is the empath's burden to carry. Each of us have a part to play for good to prevail."

Marina gave me a bright smile. She pulled out a four-leaf clover from her bra to match the newly tattooed one on her wrist. It peeled away from her clammy skin. "See? I came prepared. I have luck on my side."

Nerves churned in the pit of my stomach. I'd move heaven and hell to help her if she needed me. I didn't give a damn about the rules.

"That's the spirit, empath," said Calypso.

Marina frowned, suddenly uncertain. Then great lumps of marble rained down on us as the ceiling crumbled.

"Marina!" I surged forward.

Dust and stone fell around us, and yet Calypso, Nightfall and I were unharmed as if the library had carved out an island of safety for us amidst the carnage. As if it intended only to attack Marina.

Calypso's hand clamped around my arm like a vice. "Breathe, druid. It will soon be over."

I fought to calm myself. "Libraries are places of safety and comfort. They aren't capable of doing real harm."

"Actually, this one can." Calypso's cheerful voice contrasted with the horror painted on my best friend's face. "But Marina Ambrose isn't on its hit list. She might lose the tip of a finger or two, maybe a toe, but no need to fear any real damage."

My insides twisted as Marina executed a roly-poly to escape plummeting concrete. Her fitness regimen of dance classes, swinging on bedroom poles and the odd walk to buy wine didn't make her especially strong, but it did make her agile. Although, the catsuit impeded her full range of movement.

"You can do it." I gave her a thumbs up, resisting every sinew in my body that strained to help her.

"I have seen hundreds of trials staged by the Celestial Library during my time as the Custodian, and one thing is always the same," said Calypso. "The library is fixated on what we do when we are isolated and whether we choose to protect strangers. I think it's symbolic of the library's own loneliness. It holds the stories of countless beings. It sees what happens across galaxies. And yet its halls are almost always quiet."

Nightfall whinnied and tossed his mane.

Calypso eyeballed him. "Apart from your racket, Nightfall."

By now, Marina looked green around the gills. My own feet might have been steady, but the floor beneath Marina rocked like the deck of a ship on high seas. The striped deckchairs lay in wretched pieces amongst the rubble. Slithers of night crept into the great hall through cracks in the floor and ceiling.

Marina leapt over them in survival mode, but her exertion had taken a toll. Her leaps were smaller, her breath came faster and the fierce determination on her face slipped into hopelessness with every passing second.

How could she bring this to an end?

I scanned the room, my pulse thundering. When I had faced my trial to gain entry to the Celestial Library, I'd protected Nightfall with a cushion of wind ahead of myself, gaining the horse's and library's trust in the process.

But Marina was an empath, not a warrior. Her skills were based on intuition and emotions, not on the elements or raw physicality. She couldn't piece this broken hall together. She didn't have a shield like my werepigeon brother, Ezra's teleporting skills or speed like Orpheus the vampire. What could the library possibly expect of her?

Then I remembered Faeza's advice. *Approaching the library with a selfish heart is a fool's errand.*

I blinked as a fine layer of dust covered my head and hoodie. We weren't protected anymore. We were sitting ducks. I swallowed hard and spun to face Calypso. "You knew this was coming. That's why you didn't wear your posh clothes."

Calypso's brown eyes gleamed. "The library and I can read each other's thoughts. It's not always detailed. More a vague understanding of our mental trajectories. A bit like having a sibling. I know its patterns, but it can still surprise me." A blanket of dust had turned her black dreadlocks grey and dulled her smooth skin, like a premonition of who she would become four decades into the future. A badass granny with blade runner prosthetics who awed neighbourhood children. "I had an inkling it would get messy. Expensive dry-cleaning bills make me grumpy, but this tracksuit can be tossed into a forty-degree wash and spin cycle, no problem."

Her talk of laundry was so casual I wanted to shake her. She didn't even attempt to dodge the falling debris. Neither did she bat an eyelid at the crumbling of the ceiling, hand-painted with images of angels and cherubs.

I whirled around to track Marina's progress, more concerned about her fate than my own. We stood ten metres apart, maybe more. The ground had become a patchwork of broken, uneven slabs and nothingness. A crack sounded as the pink-veined pillars gave out at last, like the spilling of sugared candy as they disintegrated, bringing the ceiling down above our head.

Marina's blue eyes widened as our gaze met, revealing her worry not for herself, but for me. Resolve sparked in her. She kissed the cross that she wore at her neck.

Then she took a leap of faith.

My best friend, who always managed to find her courage—sprang across the floor, where the void had opened up and darkness waited. She propelled herself onto the patch of dwindling ground I occupied, pressing Calypso and me down as her body shielded us from further debris.

Sweat lined her face. "Get on the horse, both of you."

I shook my head. "He'll never make it."

Calypso watched us, an enigmatic smile on her lips.

My heart slammed against my ribcage. Soon there would be no ground left.

"I have a hunch." Marina stood and coaxed Nightfall over, deadly focus in her eyes. "Hurry."

Calypso sprang onto Nightfall, though he didn't wear a saddle, and pulled me up behind her. I wrapped my arms around her waist and clenched the horse with my thighs, but they were like jelly. I should have done more lunges and squats when I'd had the chance. I shuffled forward to make space for Marina.

She shook her head. "He can't carry the weight of three."

"What about you?" I cried out. A jagged piece of concrete came from nowhere. I raised a hand to send my winds to flick it away from her, but my powers fizzled, blocked by the cunning library. The stone scraped her cheek, and a cut bloomed like a rose in its wake. My fear amplified. Was I really unable to help her?

"Trust me." She stepped through the cloud of dust to Nightfall's head. Her lips formed a word I strained to hear. "Fly."

Beneath my dangling leg, the horse's flank shuddered. Where it had been a sleek satin to touch, it rippled. Plumes of black feathers emerged from his sides.

I gasped, rearranging my legs to accommodate the wings. They began to beat, a caress of feathers at odds with the scream wrenched from my throat. I shook Calypso. "Do something. We're not leaving her behind."

The Custodian remained stoic, in cahoots with the library.

Nightfall soared into the air, leaving my best friend amidst the collapsing hall.

Marina smiled and clasped her hands to her heart as we rose higher in the air. Her face shone with pure love. She took solace from our escape, even if it meant her own doom.

A wail wrenched from my throat.

"Keep your knickers on, druid," said Calypso.

At that very moment, a strange sound met our ears, cutting through the beating of Nightfall's wings—it was like the shuffling of poker chips at a casino. Nightfall hovered in the air as the great hall rebuilt itself around us, piecemeal.

I held back tears of relief as the floor around Marina repaired itself. The pillars re-emerged from pools of candy pink dust. The painted cherubs and angels danced on the ceiling once more, and the deckchairs returned to their splendid form. The cracks knitted together, as if their creation had been merely a temporary blip of the imagination. Dust from the great hall and our bodies faded away, leaving us squeaky clean.

Beneath us, Marina clapped in glee. "I did it."

Nightfall landed, retracting his wings.

I ran to Marina, enveloping her in a hug, the kind of never-ending hug that rocked back and forth. "You stubborn, brilliant woman. How did you know Nightfall could fly?"

Marina's eyes twinkled. Only her catsuit showed evidence of her toils, with a rip on her right knee and at her hip. "I thought he looked a little chubby around the middle when we said hello. I figured there was more to him than met the eye."

"Of course there is. That horse was animated by Rajika Verma," said Calypso.

Nightfall's hooves danced with glee.

"We're practically family, Nightfall," I muttered.

Marina hopped from one foot to the other in elation, still high on adrenalin. Either that or she needed a wee. "So, did I pass?"

The Custodian nodded. "Yes, Marina Ambrose, you proved you have an unselfish heart. The inner sanctum awaits."

3

Marina had a handful of healthy fetishes, and libraries were one of them. Her jaw hit the ground at the sight of endless rows of cherrywood shelving holding first editions and lost tomes. She browsed without hurry, knowing that neither Calypso nor I would scold her for her excitement. Only a pitiful soul could walk in the Celestial Library without awe, and there was nothing pitiful about Marina. She burst with colour from the roots of her rainbow hair to the purple goth nail varnish on her toes. Her love for life and learning seeped out of every pore.

The sound of Nightfall cantering through the library faded into the background as I turned my attention to the bookshelves myself. One particular volume sprang forward as if it had been pushed under my nose by invisible fingers, startling me. As thick as an encyclopaedia, it had a chestnut-brown leather cover and gold embossed lettering on its spine. I tilted my head to read the lettering.

A GENEOLOGY OF THE EUROPEAN OTHERWORLD

My heart pounded as the book shuffled towards me of its own accord and then tipped into my hand. It was held together by a crimson ribbon and blanketed in a thin layer of dust. I blew gently to dislodge the dust and tugged on the ribbon. Brittle parchment pages opened to reveal a hand-inked family tree, with clouds of annotations filling all any white space.

One word leapt out at me.

Verma.

How strange for a record of our family to be tucked away in this place amongst the stars for all of perpetuity. The spiky cursive lettering made reading painstaking. I sucked in my breath and traced my finger down the lines of ink that wove up and down the page, wishing I hadn't pooh-poohed the optometrist when she had suggested reading glasses on my last visit. My entire family was represented here—Mum, Dad, Sahil and me—together with Mum's French family from Brittany, names I recalled from Mum's patchy retellings of her past. There was my grandmother, Rajika, and my grandfather, Sohail Verma, after whom Sahil had been named. Each name was followed by a bracket denoting date of birth and date of demise, where that had already happened.

Tears filled my eyes at Mum's date of death, but I read on, anxious to soak up all the knowledge.

My parents had hidden the Otherworld from me until I reached middle-age.

There was so much still for me to learn.

I attempted to take a picture with my mobile phone, but however hard I tried, the image blurred into an undecipherable mess. Instead, I doubled down to absorb all the information, frowning. My great-grandparents had two children: their daughter Rajika and a son called Rajiv. The bracket that followed his name noted his birthdate to be 1933.

But there was no date of passing.

I squinted at family tree, light-headed from the discovery. My legendary grandmother had a brother I hadn't known about. And he lived. I screwed up my face as the creaky cogs in my maths brain churned. That would make him eighty-eight years old.

A voice at my shoulder made me slam the book shut. I spun around.

The Custodian's eyes lingered on it. She blew out her breath in a puff of irritation, then stuck out her hand. "Oh, hell. Hand it over."

There the senate went again, pretending to protect us by hiding the truth. Didn't they realise by now that knowledge armed us to take better decisions in the future?

I jerked the book out of her reach, my heart beating out of my chest. "Not a chance."

Hiding dirty laundry meant it piled up all the same. I was living proof of the fact. Dirty laundry was the bane of my life since joining the Otherworld. I'd had enough of family secrets. She could spill the beans or prise it out of my cold, dead hands.

Calypso's eyes narrowed, and she shook a balled fist but not at me. She shook it at the building like a crazy woman.

"Are you okay?" I soothed, but I took a step back just in case she was on mushrooms. Who knew what the diet consisted of in the Celestial Library? Come to think of it, I hadn't once seen the Custodian eat. It was possible she existed on fumes and it had messed with her mind.

She rolled her eyes. "No, I'm not okay. There it goes again, sticking its nose in where it's not wanted."

I followed her gaze to the bookshelf that shuffled the book towards me. "The library?"

"Yes, of course the library. What else would I be talking about? There is a time for knowledge and a time for patience, but this mischievous beast of a library likes to alleviate its boredom by skipping forward a few steps." She glared at the bookshelf. "It really is an awful habit."

The bookshelf behind her launched a stealth attack, sending a steady stream of book missiles directly at her.

I leapt out of the way. "Look out."

She batted them away with a haughty flick without a care for broken spines or torn pages. "It'll have to do better than that."

The books flapped in what looked remarkably like an F-you dance then returned to their positions with a hop, skip and a jump.

I locked my eyes on Calypso. "Did my grandmother have a brother called Rajiv?"

She sighed. "I see Pandora's Box is open. You already got to the good part, huh?"

"But why have I heard nothing of him?"

Dad had never mentioned a peep about his uncle, and neither had Echo. I would have liked to have travelled to India to meet him. We could have wired him money or sent him a haul of Cadbury's chocolate and invited him to come and stay with us for holidays. Families were supposed to stick together, weren't they? What possible reason could Dad have had for keeping this from me?

The Custodian shrugged. "Rajiv was a black sheep. He wasn't easy to work with, but he was brilliant. Who did you think your grandmother's illustrator was all those years before your father took up the role? It was he who drew Nightfall. But Rajiv had many flaws. He didn't like how your grandmother received all the praise. Being an animator is an ostentatious role. An illustrator is altogether different. They work all cooped up, forever at the whim of the animator. Rajiv didn't like being in the supporting role. He wanted the reins."

"So my grandmother just abandoned him?"

That didn't fit with what I knew of Rajika. She was a badass. She fought for her family and her community. Why would she have walked away from her own brother?

I'd been tempted to walk away from Sahil, but I couldn't imagine forsaking him entirely. Sometimes my eyes watered from biting my tongue around him, but he was still my brother. Every werepigeon feather of him and every ambitious bone. He was my kin.

Calypso's brow creased. "It was before my time, druid. My knowledge is gleaned from stories passed down through the ages and the odd snippet in the dusty books held in the library. By all accounts, it was a relief for your grandmother when your father's illustrator skills emerged."

"All the same, I would have liked to have known Rajiv. To have made up my own mind about him." An idea sprang to mind. There were many perks to dating a teleporting werewolf-wizard. "Maybe Ezra can whisk me to India to find him."

"Actually, he's not in India. Once an illustrator has seen his creations come to life, seeing stagnant art on the page is a little difficult. Whatever his criticisms of your grandmother, Rajiv could never bear to be apart from her. When she came to South London, he did too. But I don't think it's a good idea for you to seek him out, Alisha. He's notoriously volatile." Calypso's gleaming, almond eyes met mine, and she held out her hand for the book again.

This time, I relinquished the book to her. After all, I had my answers. Some of them at least.

"For what it's worth, my advice would be to steer clear of Rajiv. After all, the eternal girl has bigger fish to fry."

My mouth dropped open, and the words fell out, tiny rocks of denial. "I'm not the eternal girl."

Only those in my dragon's cave had heard Gaia's revelation.

Marina, Echo and Ezra would never have betrayed my trust. The Earth goddess had let me grow at my own pace. She guarded the secrets of the universe. She wouldn't have outed mine. Tielbu the dragon hid in Bulgaria still, far from the grasping fingers of the senate.

Besides, there could be no certainty I was the eternal girl. It's not that I was calling the goddess a liar. It's just that we wouldn't really know unless I stepped into a tank with the magical octopus, and I'd had quite enough of batty Wildwoods rituals, thank you very much. I'd never forget the barbaric ceremony, when Mirabel and other Wildwoods girls had been forced into a tank with Kraglek the octopus.

The truth was, I wasn't ready to be the eternal girl. I'd never be content to sit on the sidelines, but leading the whole charge was another matter entirely. I'd only succeeded so far because of my allies. The thought of having to lead the charge made me want to hide in the corner with a bottle of gin. Or at least a huge bar of Cadburys.

The Custodian smiled. "I see the shine of truth in your eyes, druid. Thank goodness you know. For a moment there, I thought I was going to have to explain the Chameleon Tale to you."

Lavinia's words had been branded into my head the first time I had heard them in the Wildwoods reading nook. *There will come the eternal girl, who blends in even though her talents are brighter than the sun. When Death opens the door, only the eternal girl may stop the coming Dusk, together with a disintegrating tome lost to the world.*

Calypso tossed the genealogy book across the aisle, where it slotted into place. "It took me a while to piece it together, but now it all makes sense. You passed the Celestial Library's trial with flying colours with barely a lick of magical experience. You have repeatedly outwitted, if not outgunned, immortal beings. You're the culmination of both a Hindu and a French druid line. And for all the waiting across the centuries for the eternal girl, you come in the shape of a middle-aged woman, with all the compassion and life experience that entails. It couldn't be more perfect."

Yeah, because what the world needed was a saggy-boobed, rapidly ageing woman like me—who'd rather be flat on her back on the sofa eating biscuits—to save the world. The major thing I had going for me was that I actually gave a damn about the world. Too often, those with power seemed content to focus on filling their own pockets and peacocking about, rather than making the world a better place.

"There is no proof I am the eternal girl," I said.

The Custodian grabbed my shoulders and squeezed. "Proof is overrated. It's self-belief and courage that will see us through. You've seen them come thick and fast: Ra, Pan, Hermes. It's only a matter of time before another god comes your way. Do you see now why you can't be distracted by Rajiv?"

A pang of regret permeated my stomach. As much as I hated to admit it, maybe the family black sheep had to wait. I already had Sahil to wrestle back from the dark side. With the Ravenmaster torn to shreds and buried in pieces, we had a window of opportunity to get my brother on side.

What was more, Calypso was right: a new threat was rising. I could feel it in my waters.

FREE SHORT STORY

If you enjoyed this book, please leave a review online to help other readers find this story.

The Druid Heir novels are written in Alisha's perspective, a 40-year-old teacher living in London. The short stories explore the world from an alternate character's viewpoint.

You can get the Druid Heir short stories for free by signing up for my fantasy newsletter at www.nillunasser.com.

ALSO BY N. Z. NASSER

DRUID HEIR

Midlife Dawn, Book 1

Midlife Tremors, Book 2

Midlife News, Book 3

Midlife Drift, Book 4

Midlife Portals, Book 5

Midlife Eclipse, Book 6

Midlife Battle, Book 7

Druid Heir Collections

MAJESTIC MIDLIFE WITCH

To Save a Sister, Book 1

To Curse a Rival, Book 2

To Trick a Raja, Book 3

To Hunt a Foe, Book 4

NEWSLETTER EXCLUSIVES

The Magical Grandmother, Druid Heir Short Story 0.5

A First Date in Paris, Druid Heir Short Story 1.5

Midlife Battle, Druid Heir 7 Bonus Epilogue

To Become a Witch, Majestic Midlife Short Story 0.5

Biryani Junction, a Majestic Midlife Witch Cookbook

ABOUT THE AUTHOR

N. Z. Nasser is a writer of paranormal women's fiction. Her stories are about women who change the world, filled with magic and rooted in friendship.

A lover of barefoot walks along the beach, she is glad to have left behind her career in the civil service and to never wear heels again. Whether she is writing in her garden office or wrangling laundry, she is happiest with a cup of tea at her side.

She lives in London with her husband, three children, two cats and a fox-mad dog.

For new release alerts, you can follow her at Bookbub or Goodreads. For a more personal touch, join her Facebook reader group Nasser's Book Nymphs, say hi on social media, or visit her online store at www.nillunasser.com.

facebook.com/nillunasser
instagram.com/nillunasser

9 781915 151155